Metaphorosis

2017

Also from Metaphorosis

Score – an SFF symphony

Reading 5X5: Readers' Edition
Reading 5X5: Writers' Edition

Best Vegan Science Fiction & Fantasy
Best Vegan SFF 2018
Best Vegan SFF 2017
Best Vegan SFF 2016

Metaphorosis Magazine
Metaphorosis: Best of 2018
Metaphorosis: Best of 2017
Metaphorosis: Best of 2016

Metaphorosis 2018: The Complete Stories
Metaphorosis 2017: The Complete Stories
Metaphorosis 2016: Nearly Complete Stories

Monthly issues

by B. Morris Allen
Susurrus
Allenthology: Volume I
Tocsin: and other stories
Start with Stones: collected stories
Metaphorosis: a collection of stories

Metaphorosis

The Complete Stories 2017

edited by
B. Morris Allen

ISSN: 2573-136X (online)
ISBN: 978-1-64076-094-3 (e-book)
ISBN: 978-1-64076-095-0 (paperback)
ISBN: 978-1-64076-096-7 (hardcover)

Metaphorosis
a magazine of speculative fiction

from
Metaphorosis Publishing

Neskowin

Contents

From the Editor

Metaphorosis finished its first year – 2016 – having more than met my expectations. We got plenty of stories, and they were good. There were a few logistical stumbles here and there, but largely things worked as they should. So, we were well positioned going into 2017. I'm happy to say that 2017 worked out just as well.

One of my worries on starting the magazine was whether we'd get enough stories to meet my ambitious story per week target. Mostly, we did, but in mid-2016, there was a brief risk we'd run short. I'd planned for this, and my makeshift was to run one of my own stories. I'd always planned to run one a year – on the September anniversary of the pre-launch story, "Metaphorosis". But with this near-crisis, I decided to shift that to two per year, roughly six months apart – which happened to roughly match the magazine's birthday and my own. I continued that tradition in 2017, though the story stock was more stable by then. Frankly, though, it feels odd to run that many of my own stories. In 2018, I'll cut back to one in September – unless, of course, there's another supply crisis.

A more substantial challenge in 2017 was time. I'd started *Metaphorosis* during a welcome and extended hiatus in long-term employment. Short-term consulting brought in enough money to cover expenses (including the magazine), but the lower income put a burden on my spouse (who never said a word about it, and encouraged me in what I was doing). So in 2017, I moved across the country and went back to work full-time, with lots of travel and a long-commute. Something had to give. It couldn't be work, because I'd just started the job. It was either the magazine or my own writing. I'd also just started the magazine. So, the writing got cut – which also meant I had less material available for magazine crises. I enjoy writing, editing, and having money. I can only have two, and at some point the balance may shift again. Not for a while, though. *Metaphorosis* 2018 is on a sound footing.

One of my goals for the magazine was to give rapid feedback to all who want it, and I'm happy to say that, so far, we've managed to meet that goal. It's a little less regular now – those long flights get in the way – but it's still usually within 24 hours for rejections. We also initially offered overview feedback – for those who had submitted over five stories without an acceptance, I provided reasonably thorough feedback on overall writing quality, with an eye to suggesting recurring issues. I very much enjoyed giving it, and a number of people took advantage. In 2017, though, I made the overview feedback a perk of Patreon support, and I'm sorry to say that the requests nearly vanished. I like to think it was useful, and it's fun to do, but it takes considerable time, so I'm still considering whether to leave it as Patron-only perq.

Some elements of the overall *Metaphorosis* plan have changed. My plan was always to start at semi-pro rates, and move to pro eventually – because those are the prestigious magazines, and that's where I wanted to be. But as time goes on, my thinking has changed. Sure, I'd like to be one of the top-line magazines. But I've learned a few things over time. First, I'm still terrible at promotion and fundraising. Pro rates would cost 6-7 times as much, and if that were to come out of my pocket, I'd have to retire later, which would mean putting off raising the rates, etc. The other reasons are less mercenary. Much to my delight, I learned you don't need to pay pro rates to get great stories. The stories in this volume prove as much, and I continue to be grateful to all the authors who appear here, and to all who've submitted stories to us. While I still sometimes consider shifting to pro rates, I think it's much less likely now. It would mean more submissions, and therefore a likely cutback on feedback. More importantly, though, I like the stories we get now. Paying more money wouldn't gain as much as I initially anticipated. We'd get bigger names, perhaps, but I'm not so certain we'd get better stories.

There have been surprises too – we don't get as many repeat submitters as I'd thought. That is, we get repeat submissions from those we haven't yet published, but not so many from those we have. Of course, repeat authors don't get any special preferences – our submissions are fairly anonymous – and we do turn them down. But it's possible we'll develop into a stepping stone market, from which people go on to bigger and better things. That's fine with me; it's always exciting to find that someone brand new to me has submitted a fantastic story.

I continue to be a very hands-on editor – virtually every story we publish starts with a 'Rejection – rewrite' label and a letter that offers a revision opportunity and points out flaws. Those that accept the opportunity (about half) can expect several rounds of rewriting. That's a fun part for me, and a hard part for the writers. All I have to do is understand what the writer is trying to do, and point them in the right direction. They have to do the actual rewriting. And, to be clear, those that work hardest at it do best. The first thing I do on receiving any revision is to run an automated comparison to see how much has changed, and compare that with what I requested. The stories that show a lot of revision tend to be those that work best. In my experience, the authors who only tweak a word here and there are those who are likely to resist suggestions. Happily, some of those stories go on to sell to other venues, so who's to say they're wrong? I can only say that I think one of our strengths is that we don't just weigh up stories as they are – I'm willing to work with the author to make it better. Extensive surveys during year 1 suggest that most (though not all) authors feel it pays off. Of course, it takes time and work – maybe that contributes to the dearth of repeat submissions.

One of the great things about running the magazine is that I've automatically developed a list of authors whose writing I like. I took advantage of that in 2017 to invite authors to contribute to a charity anthology (*Reading 5X5*) that came out in early 2018. I got a great response, and a bunch of great stories. The anthology (which explores how different authors react to the same material) worked out very well, and I look forward to a series of other projects with *Metaphorosis* authors.

All told, despite some challenges, 2017 was another great year for the magazine, and we published another great set of stories. I'm tremendously proud of the work these authors have done, and I envy you if you're encountering these stories for the first time. Curl up with your favorite animal, a glass of something hot or cold, and read on!

B. Morris Allen
Editor
1 July 2018

January

Snow Queen

T.R. North

"Do you remember the first time we met?" she asked, her voice thick and opium-drowsy, the slight thaw of early spring making her as lazy as the white-hot sun of high summer makes the old cows in their pastures.

I did, but she didn't, and I stopped my teeth with an embroidery thread instead of telling her. She watched me with those ice-pale eyes as I clipped the thread, a gold-scarlet against my lips, hardly an accidental choice after all this time, and put my needlework away to come crouch by her divan.

She'd been in her sleigh, her half-dozen white reindeer snorting and stamping proudly in their traces, and everyone in town had turned out to see her. I'd been all of fourteen, barely noticeable in the throng with my secondhand coat and my dishwater hair and my cheeks that refused to pink no matter how hard I pinched them. I could hardly be offended that she didn't remember.

"You were walking through the paddocks, stunning songbirds," I lied. "You looked so lovely against the green."

I took her hand, and she pressed my wrist gently against her cold throat so she could feel my pulse beat against her skin like a bird's heart.

She smiled at the memory, her lips sliding up over her sharp icicle teeth, and I turned my hand so my fingertips rested just below her ear. She sighed like ice cracking on a pond.

She'd stopped the sleigh in the town square with the barest wave of her hand, the driver as awake to her whims as a flock of starlings are to a predator's gaze. She'd leaned forward, gossamer cape shifting over the blue-tinted silk of her bodice. She'd summoned a boy I loved hopelessly and from afar, and he'd gotten into the sleigh with her like one mesmerized. He had been, of course. The weight of her regard is terrible, if a person isn't prepared for it.

"I didn't think you'd be out so late in the afternoon," I continued, resting my cheek against her gown and tracing the hen-tracks of silver shot through the cloth with my free hand. "I didn't think you'd see me."

I'd been heartbroken when she started the sleigh again, taking him away from me, away from the village. I'd been unstrung and stupid with grief when I went to the wisewoman, the old woman who napped by the fireside at the inn, the woman I asked how to win him back, that boy who'd never been more than passing kind to me, that boy who couldn't recall my name quite right. She'd patted my cheek and smiled kindly and said, "You don't."

"I had my brushes," I said, "and I was painting your peacock's feathers, because I felt sorry for him."

I'd felt sorry for myself, too, when I'd walked all that way for nothing. The wisewoman had warned me, when she finally gave in and told me how to get to the ice palace, that I would not finish the journey the same as I'd started. "And, succeed or fail, if you come home again, you'll be a different person even from that."

It had been difficult to get here, and dangerous. It had taken five years and a day, and a great deal of cleverness. And when I found the boy, he didn't want to leave, and he didn't know me, and he wasn't handsome anymore, with all the fire drained out of his cheeks and all the strength gone from his limbs. He'd been like a fish, pale and cold and listless, and about as eager to escape the palace as a fish was to leave its lake.

I couldn't even blame him, not entirely, for not recognizing me. I caught a glimpse of myself in a looking glass as I crept out through the servants' entrance, and I wouldn't have known my reflection except for the gray hood, my gray hood, pulled low over my much-changed face.

My hair had been burned black when I stood in a fallow field and asked the sun which way to go, when I'd come to a place with no signposts or shadows. My face was hollow as the moon I'd followed up a mountain made of glass, her waning light the only road. My eyes were gold as the hairs I'd plucked from the devil's own beard, while he slept and I whispered riddles in his ear. More damningly, the girl who'd spoken to the sun and chased the moon and tricked the devil hadn't been able to remember the boy's name, not quite. Hadn't cared, either.

I wondered sometimes if it was even that the boy's beauty had truly been dulled by his time with her, or if the flaw was in my perception. Had some mote lodged itself in my eye when I watched those naked princes, so lately swans, dance for joy in a meadow? Had I been dazzled by the dragon's golden cloak? Had I looked too long on the flower-queen's daughter and blunted my appetite for any other sight?

One thing I was certain of was that the girl in the mirror had startled me out of care. I hadn't seen the peacock in the moon-blanched courtyard until it was too late to hide, too late to go back, too late to pretend I was anything but what I was, for all that I was leaving the palace empty-handed. He'd been weeping, that part was true, and I had felt sorry for him, but mostly I'd wanted him to be quiet instead of raising the alarm, close as we were to the queen's chambers. If the bird had cried out then and there, neither cleverness nor quickness would have saved me. His desires had blinded him to duty, though, and her faithless guard had been only too ready to meet me at the edge of her estates the next day, when the sun blazed brightest and his mistress often slumbered.

"He shed diamond tears, because the hens wouldn't love him," I told her, stroking her milk-white neck. Her flesh shifted under the fabric, the first rumblings of an avalanche, and I did it again to tease her. "Who wouldn't have taken pity on him?"

"If you hold your tongue now, I'll come back when your mistress sleeps and gild your tail, and they'll follow you and sigh after you and eat their hearts over you," I'd promised. I had known what to do for him, poor bone-white thing that he'd been, for the same reasons I'd turned away from my handsome young man gone wan and bloodless. She could bleed the color from their coats more easily than their wants; the hens wouldn't have him as she'd made him.

"I strung his tears on a golden thread, and I braided them into my hair for safe-keeping, and then I took out my pigments and my combs and set about making him as beautiful as a blooming rose." Her eyes glittered like those diamonds when she turned to look at me, kissing my hand now, her tongue cold and burning against my skin. I let myself smile to look upon her, so beautiful and so ruthless. "And then you came, so softly I didn't hear you, over the meadow. What did you think when you spotted me?"

"That I wanted to speak to you more than anything," she purred, her breath coming in soft pale gusts. "That no one had ever fled from me before."

I'd run, doe-swift and barefoot, the moment I'd realized she was there.

"I was afraid," I said, smiling. "I was trespassing. I thought you'd be unhappy."

I hadn't been afraid at all, which was strange and even more foolish than tears shed over a boy who'd smiled and held a door once or twice and met my eyes from across the hall when he was trying to find one of my companions. I'd been caught out, though, discovered, where I'd slipped so many snares before, and I'd wondered if the earth could swallow me up and spare me the humiliation of being taken for a thief. To have done so much and come so close only to make such a mistake had seemed unbearable to me, and my pride had rebelled at faltering so close to the end.

"But you came back," she reminded me. "The next day, and the day after that."

"I hadn't finished," I said. "The next day I found him weeping agates because the hens looked on him but still didn't love him. I strung them on a copper thread and hung them from my neck, and I painted his tail to rival a sunset. I was almost done, when you found us again."

"I had hoped you would be there." Her eyes shimmered like the aurora when she looked at me.

"I was in agonies at the thought of coming back, but I'd promised." I had, at that: promised to make him beautiful if only he remained silent that night. He'd kept his part of the bargain, and so I'd been bound to keep mine, no matter how dear the trade became or how I cursed myself for making it. "The last time, he wept sapphires, because of what he would be but wasn't yet, and I strung them on a silver thread and hung them from my belt. I painted his tail with the glitter of sunlight on waves."

The last time, when I'd run, the grass had turned slick and icy under my feet, and I'd fallen, and I'd finally been afraid. She'd offered her hand, and helped me up, and taken me inside. I had pretended not to see when she lifted her long pale fingers to her lips and sucked the blood of my scraped palms from them, staining those lips red as a ruby. She had pulled the diamonds from my hair, and the agates from my throat, and the sapphires from my waist, and I had kissed her ruby lips and seared my tongue on her pale skin and followed her to her cold bed.

"I was so pleased when you stayed with me," she said, curling toward me, melting. "I dreamed all that night of you running, so quick even the north wind couldn't catch you, and not slowing no matter how I called to you."

I'd thought all that night of running. I'd told myself to be wise, to go home, to be changed but still a girl. Instead I'd watched the moonlight trace paths over her skin and followed them up her mountains and down her valleys and found purchase on the glass, and I'd made my eyes silver with her hair and turned my lips white and chattering with her mouth. In the morning, when I might have asked the sun which way to go, I saw the frost-rime on her coverlet turn to green fern coils, and her cheeks pink as a primrose, and her hair burnished like live coals, and I stayed.

But I was not so foolish as to tell the truth, when she would sometimes ask, later, now, "Do you remember the first time we met?"

A question for the author

Q: How do you generate story ideas, and how soon do you act on them?

A: I take inspiration wherever I can find it—a great live performance, an inspired piece of installation art, something unusual that happened while running an errand. I've gotten some of my favorite ideas for stories at the least expected and least likely of times. As for how soon I act on them, I have to confess that I'm not always the world's most patient writer. I usually start fleshing out what I want to do with an idea and where I want the story to go as soon as the idea is fully formed, even if I know I won't have time to write a proper first draft for weeks or months.

About the author

T.R. North was born and raised in Florida and has never been featured in a "News of the Weird" column run in another state.

northonthegulf.wordpress.com, @northonthegulf

T.R. North's story "Snow Queen" was published in *Metaphorosis* on Friday, 6 January 2017.

Business As Usual

N.R. Lambert

"Thank you for registering with NamMo.com, America's #1 personalized munitions retailer..."

The message arrived at 8:46 a.m. Andy was fixing his coffee for the drive to work when the alert dinged. He finished stirring and sat at the counter before flipping open his hybrid and tapping the tablet's screen.

"Thank you for registering with NamMo.com, America's #1 personalized munitions retailer. As required by Section 80166 of the Violent Crime Control and Law Enforcement Act of 2026 (18 U.S.C. 1214 (d)), "Vicki's Law," we are informing you that a .45 ACP bullet was recently purchased, personalized with your name, on Tuesday, April 20th at 8:45 a.m.

"As a reminder, we are only required to notify you of the date and time of the purchase. Federal privacy laws prohibit the release of any additional information, including the name of the purchaser or the state in which it was purchased. Please bear in mind that while our custom products are live ammunition, the purchase of a personalized item does not constitute a threat and should not be perceived as one. NamMo Corporation and its employees are not responsible for the use, misuse, or transmission of personalized products after the purchase.

"This is an automated message, please do not reply. For questions, please contact customer service."

The site forced Andy to navigate a gauntlet of FAQs before the customer service page would direct him to any actual useful information.

We cannot release information...despite rare anomalous events... no reason for alarm...multiple U.S. residents with similar or the same name...not liable...NamMo Corp. does not endorse or promote the use of NamMo personalized products for the purpose of intimidation, threat, or harassment.

Did you find the answer to your question?

No.

Would you like to chat with a customer service representative?

Yes.

Finally, the site revealed an 800 number. An automated voice, warm and a little husky, answered after the first ring and reminded Andy that most questions could be answered by visiting the FAQ page of NamMo.com. Then the voice, which he dubbed "Mama NamMo," launched into a list of available automated options.

When he'd registered for the Vicki's Law notifications, Andy had never thought about actually getting one. At the time, it felt like a responsible thing to do and forget about, like signing up for one of those credit protection programs. It was weird to actually get an alert, but it would be a funny story and—Andy was sure—fertile soil for a lot of wise-ass comments at the office later.

"If you'd like to speak to a NamMo representative, please say, 'I'd like to talk to a representative.'"

Andy rolled his eyes and over-enunciated, "I'd like to talk to a representative."

"Okay, I'll connect you to a representative. One moment please."

Heavily muzacked Nirvana kicked in.

Why did his chest feel so tight? There were probably hundreds of Andy Wrights in America, even more globally. Statistically speaking, it was improbable that this had anything to do with him. Like NamMo said in their FAQ—was he really quoting the FAQ now?—there were "a myriad of reasons and occasions" for which someone might buy personalized bullets. NamMo.com even sold "handsome, hand-carved display cases" in a "stunning array of sizes and finishes," and offered "boundless custom options" that would allow the "simultaneous display of a photo, certificate, or trophy with the personalized bullet." Maybe some other Andy Wright had just finished boot camp, or made sharpshooter on his high school rifle team...

The music stumbled as Mama NamMo cut in to inform Andy that due to an unusually high call volume, his wait time would be approximately fifteen minutes. He glanced at the clock and popped open a chat channel with his cube-mate at Viance, an integrated telephonics tech company that specialized in "customer service solutions," including AI personalities like Mama.

hey, running late

everything okay?

yeah on hold with nammo.com

uh-oh, placing an order? should we be worried? lol!

ha. no, got a VL alert, I'm pretty sure it's just a glitch

there are probably a million of you getting the same msg right now

yeah, definitely

but I'll make sure we stick an intern up at reception just in case lol!

Andy cringed and started to reply, but his email chimed again. A new message from NamMo.com, probably to tell him that the whole thing was a big mistake.

"Thank you for registering with NamMo.com, America's #1 personalized munitions retailer. As required by Section 80166 of the Violent Crime Control and Law Enforcement Act of 2026 (18 U.S.C. 1214 (d)), "Vicki's Law," we are informing you that a .45 ACP bullet was recently purchased, personalized with your name, on Tuesday, April 20th at 9:03 a.m."

If it weren't for the new time stamp in the alert, Andy would have thought it was a duplicate message, a bug in the automated notification system, which sent the messages out within a few seconds of purchase. He'd ask the rep about this one too, if he ever escaped hold purgatory, which now featured a string quartet deconstructing "Paranoid Android." Andy drummed his fingers along with the staccato bass line for a moment, then swiped open a browser and Googled his name.

Sure enough, dozens of Andy Wrights popped up in the results. He scrolled through, looking for a military dude or a high school kid. It was somewhat comforting to see all these other Andys. He assumed they'd all received the same alerts; at least the ones who'd registered for them after Vicki's Law passed.

Mama NamMo pierced the cello solo.

"NamMo Corporation's high quality personalized products make perfect keepsakes and souvenirs that will be treasured by your family for generations. Ask about our same-day delivery to make sure your gifts *always* arrive on time. NamMo Corporation is not responsible for the use, misuse, or transfer of NamMo products."

Andy recalled when NamMo first launched. Actually no, to be more precise, what he recalled was the moment he'd become aware that NamMo existed—that office massacre in Ohio. Not the Layton one, the Sumnerville one. That guy who bought ammo bearing each of his coworkers' names—every coffee-sharing, email-forwarding, birthday cake-cutting, cubicle-dwelling colleague, arranged together in a velvet-lined, handcrafted, custom cherry wood box.

Then, after, arranged together again in the parking lot, in plastic-lined, mass-produced body bags that the Sumnerville EMTs had to borrow from neighboring counties because their piecemeal volunteer station just didn't have enough on hand.

you still on hold?
yeah, just got a second alert, definitely a glitch or something must be
anyone else there get an alert?
not that I know of, why?

Mama NamMo punctured Lite Inch Nails to remind Andy that NamMo's personalized products also made great holiday gifts.

"Are you kidding me?" Andy couldn't help it, even though he knew no one was listening. Hadn't anyone vetted the hold scripts? Did they just not care?

you're not going to believe this, one of the hold msgs: "nammo makes great holiday gifts"

the fuck? srsly, that's messed up.

right?

There was no way NamMo had forgotten, but obviously they'd hoped (or expected) that everyone else would. Vicki's Law wouldn't exist if it hadn't been for a "holiday gift," the so-called "Santa Slaughter."

After Sumnerville—or maybe it *was* Layton—NamMo bullets became *the* trendy gift for edgy celebrities, a punchline for late-night talk show hosts, and occasionally, a prank for teens with too much expendable cash. But then, around the holidays that same year, a guy in Newton, not *that* Newton—different guy, different Newton—bought pairs of customized bullets bearing the names of his ex-wife, his two estranged sons, his ex's new husband, and their infant daughter, Vicki.

He sent one of each pair, carefully wrapped, to his ex's house on Christmas Eve. Then, he showed up early on Christmas Day to deliver the matching bullets personally. He posted images of the slaughter on his feed, then shot himself with a single, impersonal bullet. The rabid, practically gleeful, media coverage reinvigorated public outrage toward NamMo Corp.

Mama interjected again; Andy's expected wait time was now less than four minutes.

less than 4!

lucky you! listen Naomi wants to go over the deck for tomorrow

shit, yeah, I'll follow up when I get in

k, good luck

thx

After the vigils, the thinkpieces, the thoughts and prayers, there was finally, *finally,* some action. "Vicki's Law." Originally, it was set up so that NamMo Corp. would be required to notify everyone who registered, and their local police precinct, that a bullet purchase in their name had been made, when and where it was made, and by whom. There was even a built-in wait period for delivery. Millions of Americans signed up for the service. But before it rolled out, the NRA got to work. Leaning heavily on privacy acts, they got Vicki's Law sanded down until it was as small and useless as a child's wooden toy coin.

The email chimed again. A new purchase alert, this one for 9:30 a.m.

Three?

A slow, cold panic pushed up from his gut and into Andy's chest. According to Mama NamMo, there was only one caller ahead of him. His coffee, forgotten, was a cold still life, caught in a weak sunbeam on the counter.

His email issued another gleeful chime. A new bullet. 9:31 a.m.

It had to be intentional. Why else would anyone buy one bullet at a time, when the site obviously allowed bulk purchases? If it was for a magazine's worth, the buyer could have bought them all in a single order. But to do it this way, one by one? Someone, somewhere was definitely trying to send a message to one of the Andy Wrights...

Andy didn't think he had any enemies. Then again, had any of the Sumnerville 33 expected their quiet, Rush-loving comptroller to—

A car door slammed outside.

Another ding.

"...We are informing you that a .45 ACP bullet..."

There was that one guy from Viance sales. Michael? Matthew? Always got way too aggressive during the inter-company softball games. One time, he and Andy had shared some heated words at the bar after a game, during which a tiny cup of ketchup might or might not have been dumped on Mike/Matt's head. But that certainly wouldn't justify something like this, would it? Besides that bar thing was years ago, no way Mike/Matt would still—

"Thank you for calling NamMo.com. This is Casey, how can I assist you?"

Andy was so used to Mama NamMo's smooth, but not-quite-sultry voice, that the perky, pipsqueak drawl of the rep made him jump a little.

"Hi, um, so I keep getting these notifications and I think maybe there's a glitch or something."

Casey waited a beat. A tactic Viance also taught its customers' fleets of reps, but usually one reserved for hostile callers. Her power pause was punctuated by the ding of another notification arriving.

"Okay sir, I can look into that for you, can you give me your name and account number please."

"Sure. It's Andy Wright. I don't have an account."

"Okay, Mr. Wright, I'm happy to assist you. What's the problem?"

"I keep getting these notifications about bullets personalized with my name, like I've gotten five or six now, and I think there might be a glitch." He didn't recognize his voice, taut and sharp as piano wire.

"Okay, Mr. Wright. Let me take a look." She tapped some keys and for a few moments, there was only the faint, steady sound of her breathing. Andy took a deep breath. His chest felt even tighter.

"Hmmm. Let's see." More tapping. "Okay sir, nothing to worry about."

Andy exhaled hard. He knew it had to be an error. But then Casey continued.

"There's no glitch, the notification system is working just fine. Those messages all correspond to actual purchases of NamMo personalized products."

"But, I've received," Andy quickly counted the emails, "six notifications in the last hour."

"Yep, that's correct Mr. Wright. I'm showing here that those correspond to six separate product purchases. Can I help you with anything else today or will that be all?"

"I mean...just...who would want this many bullets with one person's name?" Andy's thoughts touched on that guy down the hall who was always leaving enraged notes on neighbors' cars about their "shitty" parking jobs or hyperarticulate missives tacked to the cork board about the "increasingly pressing issue of sustained dog barking in our building." Was he the kind of guy wh—

"Sir, privacy laws restrict us from releasing information about the identity of our customers." Andy's head started to throb.

Another chime.

"But isn't there a limit? Like when do you start investigating? There has to be a level where it triggers some sort of 'suspicious activity' alert, right?"

Even before she replied, Andy sensed Casey's chipper attitude turning into something far steelier.

"Sir, NamMo Corp. is not responsible for the use, misuse, or transfer of our products."

"Wait. Are you serious?" Andy shouted, knowing immediately that it was a tactical error. At Viance, they would have trained Casey to end the call at that point. But he could still hear her breathing.

"Sir, I have to ask you to calm down. There are many reasons and occasions for which people purchase NamMo's personalized products. There is no cause for alarm."

A new message. New purchase. 9:43 a.m.

"That's eight!" Andy knew he sounded hysterical and a small part of him marveled that Casey hadn't yet terminated the call. "I mean, shouldn't you at least tell the police?"

"Sir, we encourage you to do what makes you feel comfortable. But we're not legally responsible for notifying law enforcement agencies about the purchase of our personalized products, nor can we release additional information to the authorities without a federal warrant..."

Andy barely heard her. His thoughts were scattered and skipping in all directions, like a handful of dried beans spilled on a hard tile floor. He closed his eyes and pinched the bridge of his nose.

His mind spun through the zoetrope of possible candidates: That one IT guy who glared at everyone and never spoke. The boyfriend of that assistant he'd flirted with at the company party last year. That random internet dude who'd filled Andy's feed with streams of threats and gory images for weeks after Andy posted a mildly political opinion about an upcoming election. The possibilities blurred, a bright orange streak of panic running through his entire life.

"Sir? Did you have any other questions today?"

Andy opened his eyes. Several floors down he heard his building's front door slam shut. Probably just the mailman...or an equally late neighbor. But he stood to check the locks on his apartment door anyway. Then he sat again, though slightly further from the door than before.

"Sir?"

"Yes. Okay, but isn't there some kind of protocol, just in case?" Andy tried to keep his voice calm, but he could barely squeeze out the words. "I mean...should I go to work today? Or is that the last place I should go?"

Unless someone was planning on coming to his apartment? Maybe it would be safer to drive around for a while. But then, what if someone was waiting for him in the garage? Was anyone actually watching the security camera footage?

"Sir, if safety is a concern for you," Casey tapped a few more keys as she spoke, "I've just been authorized to offer you a special discount on a NamMo custom personal security package."

"No. No. I don't want that. I just want to know who's doing this. I want to know why!" Andy's shirt was heavy with sweat.

"Mr. Wright, as I mentioned earlier, I am legally restricted from violating our customer's privacy." Casey let the silence hang between them. Andy's breathing felt forced.

"But what am I supposed to do now?"

"Well sir," she was bright again, her allotted time with him was winding down; Andy could practically see the countdown clock on her monitor, "we suggest you go about business as usual. If you find that the notifications are disruptive, you can unsubscribe at any time by simply clicking on the 'unsubscribe' link at the bottom of the message."

Andy imagined Casey sitting in a white, brightly lit room— sterile, secure, safe. Just like the faceless "craftsmen" who right now were etching his name into metal over and over again, the shipping team who would soon pack boxes with personalized dread and send them to a stranger. He imagined the sharpened smiles of NamMo sales reps as they flaunted their hollow samples at gun shows and shooting ranges; the practiced grimaces of puppet politicians blanketing the country with their thoughts and prayers like junk mail. He thought about all the fingers that would touch those bullets, his bullets. The same ones that had held Vicki's bullet, before, and hadn't faltered—not even for a moment—after.

"Sir, have I answered all your questions today?"

Another chime. Andy tapped the mute toggle on his screen.

"Sir?"

"No. Not at all."

"I'm sorry to hear that. After this call, you're invited to complete the NamMo Corp. customer satisfact—"

Andy disconnected. A new email notification drifted down from the toolbar, somehow more ominous in its silent descent. 10:05 a.m. Andy stared at the screen for a long moment before reopening the chat channel.

hey, not going to make it in today

they can't keep you on hold forever dude LOL!

heh. let Naomi know too?

sure. no prob! see you tomorrow

thanks

Andy flipped the hybrid shut just as another alert ghosted across his screen. He stood, poured his coffee into the sink, and lingered there a moment before leaning forward to lower the blinds.

About the story

I started writing "Business As Usual" in 2015. I wish I could remember exactly which of the many horrific gun-related incidents that year first planted the seed of this story in my mind. It would mean that these events occurred rarely enough to stand out from each other. Unfortunately, each day in America, an average of 93 people are killed with guns; and, last year alone, we had 384 mass shootings—more than one per day.

In the wake of all this violence...nothing changed. Many people have discussed this issue far more thoroughly and expertly than I can here. But in short, "Business As Usual," was born from a blazing infuriation with my country's preposterous pattern of being surprised! shocked! outraged! saddened! sending thoughts and prayers! after these events. And then, refusing to even *consider* changing our laws.

With "Business As Usual," I wanted to depict an American future with even more normalized gun lust. I wanted it to point a spotlight on our current lack of legislature, imagine where the continued apathy from our politicians might lead, and reflect how hopeless and powerless many Americans feel in regard to the ongoing and escalating violence. I also tried to touch on all the people who benefit financially from gun violence—the manufacturers for sure, but also the politicians, the lobbyists, and the media—to show how greed perpetuates the cycle.

If we don't change something, the scope and quantity of incidents of gun violence in America will only continue to increase. I'm not so naive as to think there is an easy solution and I don't have an answer myself. Just endless questions, deep frustration, and a lot of anxiety, which is what I hoped to convey with "Business As Usual." Thank you for reading.

A question for the author

Q: What's a genre you'd like to write, but don't or can't?

A: I love reading biographies, but (to date) it is one of the few genres that doesn't appeal to me as a writer. As someone who often falls down deep wikiholes chasing answers to even the most innocuous questions, I think I'd become utterly lost in the sheer volume of research required to write a biography (and do it well). As with Scotch, Key lime pie, and graphic design, this is a case where I'd much rather sit back and enjoy the fruits of someone else's labor.

About the author

N.R. Lambert grew up in the most frequently disparaged borough of New York City before escaping to Queens, which she now proudly calls home with her family and two saucy cats. After a brief stint in the hotel industry, she found her people in Booktown and hasn't left since.

www.nancyrlambert.com, @nanbits

N.R. Lambert's story "Business as Usual" was published in *Metaphorosis* on Friday, 13 January 2017.

Be Prepared to Shoot the Nanny

Rachel Kolar

By the time her husband came downstairs, Miranda was nearly frantic trying to find a kill switch for the nanny.

"Katie got herself eaten over the weekend," she said without looking up, her fingers dancing across the surface of her smartphone. "Some drunk driver hit her car, and her boyfriend reanimated before she could get to the gun in her glove compartment. Honestly, what idiot keeps her gun that far out of reach?"

Her husband grimaced. "That's too bad. She was so good with Henry."

Miranda snorted. "If she couldn't even pay enough attention to notice all those 'armed is prepared' ads, how could she have paid enough attention to notice what Henry needed?" The zombie safety awareness campaign had been inescapable—it seemed like every time she'd clicked a YouTube video or watched something on Hulu, she'd gotten an ad where that smirking guy from Saturday Night Live reminded everyone to keep a loaded gun within arm's reach; you never knew when someone might die, reanimate as a zombie, and try to eat you. How had Katie missed the message?

"Anyway." Miranda found another nanny agency's website—and another wait list. "The funeral's Thursday, and we'll go, of course, but for now, we need a second nanny."

A pause. She brought up the next dead-end website, silently willing Stephen not to say what she knew was coming next.

He did anyway. "But... He cleared his throat. "Petra is still coming today, isn't she?"

"Yes. She is. But one isn't enough. You know that."

"We never had trouble with one. Nobody ever had trouble with one. That au pair who fell down the stairs in Houston was a freakish one-in-a-billion—"

"That's easy for you to say. You weren't following the news." Another dead end. When everyone had two nannies, the agencies ran out fast. "The only reason those kids survived after she reanimated was because the oldest girl paid attention in firearms class. Henry won't even be old enough for Mommy and Me marksmanship for another three months."

"What are the odds that Petra will fall down the stairs and break her neck? And even if she does, our HOA has the best snipers in the county, maybe the state."

"That'll only help if she reanimates outside. The odds are slim, sure, but I'm not gambling with Henry's life. We need someone else here who can handle a gun. And anyway, she's not the only one who might die. What if today's the day Mr. Shaw decides to kick it? Do you want Petra to be here alone if he's shambling around the neighborhood trying to eat people?" She tapped the phone. Were there any nannies in the entire DC metro area? She was going to have to look in Baltimore at this rate.

"If you're only looking for someone to be a kill switch, you don't need a nanny. Hire
a security guard."

"Security's even harder to find than nannies." Something in her inbox, thank God. She skimmed the email and let out her breath in a whoosh of relief. "Graziela can come back tomorrow."

"He'll be fine with just Petra today."

"No, he won't. I'm telecommuting." She was already pulling up the number for the office.

"Miri, for God's sake—"

"I don't want to hear it. I have plenty of personal days saved up." *And unlike Katie, I always keep a loaded pistol at my hip,* she added silently.

Stephen probably would have argued further, but at that point, Henry's voice started babbling over the monitor, and Miranda ran upstairs to retrieve him. She cradled the phone against her ear while reaching into his crib, which still had its reinforced steel rails back from when he'd been young enough for them to worry about SIDS. By the time she came back downstairs, she'd already snagged the day off. No room for Stephen to argue, and while his goodbye kiss felt more cursory than usual, she knew she was doing the right thing for her son.

Petra arrived a few minutes after Stephen left, as usual, wearing layers of clothing around her skinny frame despite the April warmth— she'd once explained to Miranda that it was an old Eastern European habit to give them extra protection from teeth. Well, actually, she'd explained it to Henry in a big, overdramatic baby voice that was clearly directed at Miranda. "We always wore our clothes like this back home, didn't we?" she'd said, eyes as wide as her smile. "We didn't have snipers like some lucky little boys, did we?" Miranda didn't know whether she did that because she was too diffident to address her employer directly or if it was just something they did in Slovakia or Slovenia or wherever, but it was one of the reasons she preferred to let

Stephen handle Petra. Having someone talk to her indirectly in a baby voice made her want to tear out her hair.

When Petra came inside, Henry whimpered and clung to Miranda more tightly, his thumb creeping into the corner of his mouth. The separation anxiety was usually an odd mixture of annoyance and relief, but since he wasn't keeping her from getting out the door this time, she could just enjoy cuddling him closer.

"Things are going to be a little different today," Miranda said, and briefly outlined the situation. Petra made some sympathetic noises about Katie, but not many—apparently she also wasn't sure what kind of idiot drove without a gun in arm's reach. Either that or she couldn't summon much grief for a girl who had only been there to shoot her in the head.

"At any rate, I don't want to be in your way, and I can't get anything done if I have to keep one eye on Henry the whole time," Miranda concluded. "I'll just be in the office upstairs. Keep the monitor with you, and I'll be able to hear if you need me."

If Petra was bothered by what lurked under "if you need me"—*keep the monitor with you, and if you die I'll be able to blow your brains out before you eat my baby*—she didn't show it. She was a professional, after all, and she probably understood Miranda's concerns, having children and grandchildren of her own in Slovakivenia-wherever. She just nodded with an expression of almost exaggerated solicitousness, eyebrows furrowed and lower lip pooching out. "Sure, sure! Mommy won't even know we're here, will she, Henry?" Her voice was a coo, and Henry stopped squirming and batted tentatively at her face.

Miranda felt the usual pang as she passed him over. Still, no time for angst; she was telecommuting, not calling in sick, and her cost-benefit analysis on installing landmines around nursing homes wasn't going to write itself, so she headed for the office.

She tried at first to keep the monitor's volume cranked up so she could listen avidly for any disturbance, but it was hard to get any work done when every calculation had an undercurrent of Henry pounding away on Mozart's Magic Piano or Take-Aim Teddy or of Petra reading him *Runaway Bunny*. She lowered the volume grumpily, unable to stop herself from mentally nitpicking the way Petra did the bunnies' voices. It wouldn't matter, probably—if Petra died, it would be an accident loud enough for her to hear even without a monitor—but dialing down her vigilance was an irritating reminder that Stephen had probably been right. Really, what were the odds that Petra would fall down the stairs today?

A siren whooped, intruding on her thoughts. Miranda's head snapped up as she saw the ambulance swooping around the corner, Kevlar-armored EMTs leaning out the windows with machine guns ready. *Mr. Shaw*. Her hand went to the pistol at her hip as she pushed out of her chair and hurried down the stairs. "Petra? Are you—"

She trailed off. Petra was helping Henry into his shoes. The nanny flashed her a nervous little smile, turning back to Henry so quickly that Miranda barely saw her face. "Yes?"

"You're—you're not taking him outside, are you? There's a zombie out there."

"The EMTs are taking care of it, aren't they, Henry? We'll be fine. And even if something happens, the playground is fenced in, so you'll be safe, won't you?" Petra shot her a sidelong glance, clearly trying to gauge her reaction without actually making eye contact.

Miranda ground her teeth. It was true—their playground had keyed entry and sniper nests, everything that a parent could want. Still, the thought of her son playing outside while the paramedics gunned down a rampaging Mr. Shaw, even if it was in his house...

"It just seems like a shame to stay inside on such a beautiful day," Petra said as Henry clambered out of her lap, still looking at him and using that stupid baby voice. "Did you know, Henry, that it's supposed to rain for the rest of the week?"

"It doesn't seem safe."

Petra's brow furrowed and the corner of her mouth pulled down into a frown that she almost immediately turned into another tiny smile. Her eyes darted from Henry to Miranda to somewhere just over Miranda's shoulder. "Well, we've—we've done it before."

"You've *what?*"

"Last month when someone had a heart attack. I told your husband, and—" A burst of machine gun fire interrupted her, followed by the low, musical whoop of the all-clear. Petra's shoulders dropped with relief—whether because Mr. Shaw was taken care of or because she was now free from the conversation, Miranda couldn't say—and gave Henry another one of those goopy smiles. "See? Nothing to worry about, is there, Henry?"

"Wait. You told—" She made herself stop, briefly entertaining a vision of throttling Stephen and then sending his reanimated corpse after Petra. "Fine. Take him out. It's fine."

Miranda retreated to her office, cheeks burning. She tried to type a few more notes, but it was no good; her mind was a hot, twisted knot of irritation, and she found herself peering out the window instead.

Petra was right, as much as she hated to admit it. The playground was probably the safest place in the entire neighborhood. It always made Miranda a little sad, going there; she'd never had to worry about keyed entry or snipers when she'd been a little girl. She and her playmates knew how to handle a pistol, the neighborhood watch had their ears open, and that was all anyone needed. But that had been before the massacre in Portland, of course, and now every outdoor public area had turrets and digital keypads.

If Petra felt any of that sadness, she didn't show it. She tipped a wave to one of the snipers—Ted? Todd?—and he waved back, calling down something that made her laugh and point at her handbag. She didn't seem to have any trouble talking directly to *him*. Henry had already started toddling over to the swings.

It was almost suffocating, watching them outside while she was stuck at her desk. She found herself almost hoping Petra would keel over so Miranda could shoot her and play with Henry. At the very least, she could open the office window. As she did, the breeze carried her son's giggling voice into the room, and the air conditioner kicked in with a low thrum.

Miranda snorted. She couldn't help it. The air conditioner? On a day like today? No, Petra wasn't going to waste money on utilities in her house. She made her way through each floor, opening every window she could find to let that sweet spring breeze carry in the laughter of her boy, the drone of the bees, the distant *thwack* of Mr. Harrington practicing with the crossbow he'd bought from the Amish market.

She went back to work in good spirits, plugging away on the cost-effectiveness of various perimeter defenses. Over the monitor, she heard Petra bring Henry back inside, put her handbag in the closet, and start making lunch. It was all background noise until she heard the thud of windows closing.

Oh, come on. "Petra, it's a beautiful day, can you just—"

Petra screamed. It was a short sound, barely more than an "oh dear, I just saw a cockroach" squawk, but there was a bloody edge of raw panic underneath.

Miranda shot to her feet, sending the wheeled office chair rolling across the room. "Petra?"

"Fine, fine! It's fine!"

Her voice was too high-pitched, too quick. Miranda did not sit down. "Are you sure you don't want me to come down?"

"No, no, no! It's fine, we're fine, we're fine."

Six "fines" directed at her instead of Henry. Right. Miranda was out the office door and in the hallway. She could hear a series of heavy, rustling thumps near the front door—not the windows, something else. What was Petra doing?

"I'm just going to poke my head down for a minute, OK?" Miranda hurried down the stairs, moving as quickly as she could while trying not to be too obvious about it. An umbrella skittered past the foot of the stairs—Petra was throwing things out of the hall closet. Miranda reached the ground floor, turned the corner, and froze.

Petra was on her tiptoes, her arms reaching up to the closet's top shelf. She was making thin, rapid little squeaking noises, like air escaping a balloon a second at a time. Her face was pale and blotchy, its flesh beginning to bloat and swell, and her eyes had a vacant, glazed look.

She was wheezing instead of moaning, but otherwise it was a textbook reanimation, and Miranda didn't hesitate. She yanked her pistol out of the holster, fumbled her shaking thumb over the safety, and fired three times in rapid succession. She thought she'd aimed too low—her hands were trembling, and there was a big difference between a practice dummy and her reanimated nanny—but she must not have, because Petra immediately went down, spraying blood across the closet. *At least it'll be easier to clean off than the time Henry got into the Sharpies,* Miranda thought crazily. The handbag clattered off the shelf, sending spare change and makeup and something that looked like a glue stick rolling across the floor.

Miranda's ears were ringing badly, but she could still hear Henry crying—it had been louder than she'd ever guessed, firing without earplugs. She glanced around and saw him toddling into the foyer, big cartoon tears rolling down his chubby face.

Miranda took the last step down to the foyer, slipping a little in the blood as she did, her foot almost kicking Petra's chipmunk-cheeked face. Why had no one ever talked about the swelling? She hadn't heard of that aspect of reanimation before. "Henry, baby, it's OK—"

Henry looked down, and his tears immediately stopped. He bent over with a curious little coo and reached into the puddle of blood, grabbing a roll of quarters in one hand and the glue stick in the other. "I play?" he said, looking up at her.

"*No!* Bad, Henry, bad!" Miranda scooped him up, forcing his arms down by his sides despite his shrieks so he couldn't get his bloody hands into his mouth. If any of that blood made it into his mouth, or his eye, or if he had a little cut somewhere she didn't know about...

Bleach wipes. Right, the bleach wipes were in the upstairs bathroom. Henry squirmed against her chest as she lugged him up the stairs, and she managed to bump the bathroom door open with her hip so she could keep her hands firmly clenched around his.

She sat on the floor with Henry pinioned between her knees and pried his fingers from the quarters and the glue stick, ignoring his screams of protest at being parted from these fabulous treasures. "I know, baby, I know," she cooed, wiping his hands down with the bleach wipes before releasing him with a kiss. He hurled himself at her, reaching for the quarters and the glue stick as though they were the greatest toys ever invented. She pulled them up out of reach—they were still covered in blood—and as the glue stick crossed her field of vision, she saw the text on it for the first time.

It wasn't a glue stick. It was an EpiPen.

Miranda stared at it, feeling her stomach go hard and heavy, the breeze from the windows that Petra refused to open ruffling through her hair. Her ears were still ringing, but if they hadn't been, she imagined she'd have been able to hear the bees buzzing.

Petra's face hadn't bloated up because of some little-known aspect of the reanimation process. Petra hadn't been dead yet.

You need to call your lawyer, that same crazy part of her brain yammered. *Maryland just passed Defend the Living laws, you'll be fine if you can just show you honestly and reasonably believed she had reanimated ...*

A thump sounded from the foyer. Another thump, and a moan.

Miranda's breath stopped. She *had* aimed too low.

Her hand went to her cell phone, and she had started to punch in 911 before she stopped herself. No. No, she couldn't call the police before she had the chance to talk to her lawyer. They'd see a zombie with a gunshot wound to the chest, and what would they do? They'd arrest her, that was what. And it wouldn't be quiet, either; this was the sort of thing that would draw a media circus. They'd have to move just to avoid looking the neighbors in the face. And if (God forbid) she was found guilty and thrown in prison, what then? They wouldn't be able to move anywhere with a decent school district, not on Stephen's salary alone, and private schools would drop Henry's application in the paper shredder the moment they saw her name. What kind of life would that be?

No. She wasn't going to let Henry's future be ruined because Katie had been too stupid to keep a handgun in reach. If Petra had a headshot to go along with her chest wound, the "I thought she was a zombie" defense would be a lot more plausible, and she could deflect at least some of the scrutiny.

She closed her eyes and forced herself to breathe. She could do this. She'd put in plenty of hours at the shooting range—it was time to make those hours pay off by protecting her boy.

She scooped Henry up and carried him to the nursery. "Mama will be right back, baby," she crooned before stepping out and locking the steel reinforced door behind her. She took another deep breath and removed the gun from its holster; then she scurried along the hall and partway down the stairs, trying to keep her footfalls as quiet as possible on the hardwood floor, and craned her head over the banister to look.

Petra was hobbling back and forth in the doorway to the dining room. One of her shuffling feet bumped against Take-Aim Teddy, and he lit up bright green. "*A* is for *ammo!*" he chirped. "Always keep your *ammo* nearby!"

Petra lurched downward, grabbed the bear with one hand, and ripped his head off with her teeth, spilling hypoallergenic stuffing across her chin. Miranda winced. Take-Aim Teddy had been a gift from her mother.

No time to worry about that, though. Petra was distracted. Miranda darted the rest of the way down the stairs and took aim. Her hands were shaking again. *Breathe, breathe ...*

She pulled the trigger. A puff of plaster exploded from the wall about a foot from Petra's head. Petra turned toward her, the teddy bear dangling from her mouth like a mouse from a cat's.

Dammit. Hold the gun still. She pulled the trigger again, but holding the gun perfectly still was a lot easier when a bloody-chested zombie wasn't glowering at her, and the shot went wild again. Petra growled and started shuffling closer.

Miranda screamed and fired again. Again. Her heart was pounding so hard that she was sure it was making her entire body shake to its rhythm. A bullet zinged past Petra's cheek, but didn't embed itself in her skull. Petra was getting closer. Closer...

Miranda's nerve broke, and she turned and fled for the stairs. She was almost there when her feet skidded in the blood and sent her to the floor. The gun went flying from her fingers.

She crawled toward it, and as she did, she pictured Katie scrambling toward the gun in her glove compartment. It wasn't *fair.* Katie had been stupid, but Miranda had been so careful, she'd done everything right, she didn't deserve this ...

Petra's fingers closed on Miranda's ankle.

Miranda closed her eyes. *I* knew *Petra would reanimate today. I just knew it.*

And then, as the nanny's teeth sank into her leg, *I hope Stephen remembers to hire a kill switch for Graziela tomorrow.*

About the story

I'm fascinated by stories that take place long after the zombie apocalypse, from *World War Z* to *Fido* to the last five minutes of *Shaun of the Dead.*

Horror fans and academics have spilled gallons of ink analyzing the popularity of zombies in a post-9/11 world—the zombie apocalypse helps us process that apocalyptic day, the breakdown of order helps us work through the way order has collapsed in our own society, and so on. For me, though, these "after the credits roll" stories are the ones that really describe life in the 2010s. The initial shockwave is over, and everything has returned to normal ... except that it hasn't, not really, because nothing will ever be normal again.

I regularly go back to the idea of what a post-zombie world might look like, but it wasn't until I became a mom that I thought of how it would prey on parental anxiety. With all the ads and articles that convince parents their child will die—or, worse, go to a bad college!— without the help of the latest expensive gadget or exhausting strategy, the idea of a "kill switch" pretty much wrote itself.

Of course, if your only purpose is to watch for the moment when you're supposed to shoot another person, you're going to read that moment into every interaction. That, combined with the fact that the only way to survive a post-zombie world is to fill it with good guys with guns, bad guys with guns, and normal, fallible, easily-frightened guys with guns, gave the story much sharper satirical teeth than I'd originally planned.

A question for the author

Q: What are you reading now?

A: I'm currently reading *The Martian* by Andy Weir. I'd been reading a lot of depressing cyberpunk like *Neuromancer* and *Feed*, so *The Martian* is a breath of fresh air. I love the humor and the way it makes the science relatively comprehensible for an English major, and as an epistolary junkie I'm a fan of the log format. As a fun side effect, it also makes me feel like MacGyver every time I jury-rig something during a simple household chore. I put up the Halloween tombstones in a creative way? Oh, yeah, I'm **totally** ready for Mars.

I'm also listening to the audiobook of *Revival* by Stephen King. Based on the title, I was wary of reading it at first—I like King a lot, but his Christian characters tend to be a thousand and one variations on Carrie's mom. When I learned more about the premise, I gave it a try and am thankful that I did. Here's hoping that the second half is as good as the first.

About the author

A graduate of Kenyon College, Rachel Kolar lives with her husband, two children, and lunchmeat-addicted cat in the Baltimore/Washington area. When not writing stories or changing diapers, she enjoys playing overly complicated board games, hiking, and getting far too excited about Halloween.

www.rachelkolar.com, @KolarRachel

Rachel Kolar's story "Be Prepared to Shoot the Nanny" was published in *Metaphorosis* on Friday, 20 January 2017.

The Snow Queen's Daughter

Sean R. Robinson

I extended my hand out the window, reaching as my mother had taught me since I was old enough to understand her words. Palm up, an invitation to the distant skies.

The steppe ended in the distance, the horizon shattered by snow-choked mountains. From my window, I could see the clouds roiling white, the azurite sky behind it a challenge.

Not a challenge, I reminded myself. I could hear my mother's voice in my ears. *Never a challenge. A welcome. Welcome the cold. Welcome the snow, Daughter.*

I waited, palm up in invitation until my arm grew sore. Until even my cold-hardened face was uncomfortable. And when my attention drifted to the desk beside me, I gave up, cursing. I didn't want to welcome the cold, didn't want to turn the weather.

I wasn't a magician, and no matter how much my mother wished otherwise. I wanted to be a scientist.

My mother's house was, of necessity, a place of cold wars. I carried the newest declaration in my hand as I went to find her, ignoring my ever-disappointing lessons in magic. I had read the paper a hundred times, trying to gather my wits for my mother's frigid regard.

Her palace was a wonder of ice, wrought into walls and doorways, galleries, and apartments. Each morning, she would sit in her apiary, a tray beside her, cups of white bone china ready for her morning tea. My mother had always preferred Jasmine tea as her snow-bees danced around her. I preferred Gunpowder Black.

Today, she sat in her snow-wicker chair, a leopard curled around her feet. She wore white damask, a bear fur shrug across her shoulders. Mother sipped her tea and listened as the snow-bees told her of the sights they'd seen in their travels. They danced for her, and she understood—she was their queen.

There was a looking glass behind her, hairline cracks breaking the reflection into a thousand pieces. I watched as Mother sent a snow-bee into the distance. There would be a blizzard somewhere in the world.

I knew she was disappointed that her only child did not have wings like snowflakes and eyes like dark winter. I had never been small enough to dance on her fingertips and proclaim the wonders I'd seen. I had settled for essays and letters and books of dark leather.

She was magic and I—no matter how much I tried—was not.

I unfolded the paper that had arrived by post that morning. I read it again. Mother did not look at me as the bee-swarm grew thicker. One or two landed on my hands, but I brushed them away. I had learned to hate my snow-winged siblings.

"I've been accepted to University," I said. There could be no preliminaries for that conversation; no warnings or advisories.

She did not speak.

"In Copenhagen," I added. "I'm to take a degree in Boreal Alpinology."

It was my concession to her. If I could not be magic, I could be snow. She loved the snow.

My mother did not speak for a while longer. She sipped her pale tea and watched her bees. I was the dark-haired daughter she had borne and that was the latest in a long line of disappointments. I did not care for her gentle teas, her precious insects, or the bluster of winter through the fjords.

We were too different, and we were both tired of pretending we were not.

"Why?"

I sighed. "I will study the movement of snowstorms. The growing and shrinking of glaciers. I will learn why the Aurora glows."

There were only so many words to make her understand.

A single pale brow rose on her face. "Why not simply ask them?"

Because that was magic.

She had tried to teach me to love the blizzards that hunted the palace grounds, and the squalls that danced through her many galleries. I could not love her snow-choked rose gardens any more than she could understand why I read the diaries of Meta Brevoort and Lucy Walker.

"Because," I said. There was no answer my perfect, icy, mother would understand. "Because it will be a place where I am not a pale copy of you. I have failed miserably at frost-craft, so perhaps I will learn something worth knowing."

"No," my mother said. "You will learn here. You have not been a diligent daughter."

I knocked her teacup from where it sat. It shattered on the floor

"When will you let me live my life, Mother? How long will you keep me trapped behind the drifts? I am not you. I will not have a Storyteller come over the hills, break my heart, and leave me with child. Perhaps in Copenhagen I might be free."

And perhaps I was as much like my father as I was unlike my mother. That, I left unspoken.

The Snow Queen stood and her ice swarm erupted out into the air. She did not look back as she left the apiary. The wind that blew off her skin carried her voice back to me. It held a bitter edge.

"You think that I am a queen from a Fairy Tale. Fairy Tales are never true, Daughter."

The silence that followed was bitter cold.

"You will take a sledge south before the spring, then," the wind said. "And when you have learned to be warm, perhaps you will come home to learn that there is more to winter than the cold."

I nodded, heart in my throat. She would spend the rest of her day maintaining her frozen kingdom, attended by her bitter-wind courtiers.

"I hope you are happy, Ylsa. I hope you find what you seek," the wind said in a quiet, final breath.

"I'm sorry," I said, but my mother had always been too far away. I could name what I sought: my place.

My leave-taking was quiet. Mother's snow-bees whirled around the sledge as I hitched up the bears. They were restless; the air had begun to smell of spring. Mother did not wish me good luck or good speed. The gentle kiss of the bees was all the farewell I received as we went south. I had packed everything I thought a young student would need: quill pens and dark ink, sensible shoes, and a wool sweater to keep out the chill.

I was not prepared for Copenhagen. It perched beside the Baltic beneath a coal-fire cloud. The bears liked it not at all, but they deposited me in the midst of the yellow-painted buildings outside the University. When they left, my trunks piled in the dirty snow, their white fur had been painted an ugly shade of grey by the sooty air.

By then, a crowd had formed and I was reminded of my earliest childhood lesson: it is not easy to be the Snow Queen's daughter. Too many people had read the stories and confused fairy tales with real life, me included.

It took most of the afternoon to find a room to rent. The University bursar kept a list of homes that would rent to lady students. The proprietor of each boarding house was polite, offered me tea, and said that they did not have accommodations that would be appropriate for me. Then they sent me on my way.

Mrs. Lang did not. Her house was on the edge of the harbor. The room she offered was a tiny place under the eaves.

"If you're lucky, you can see the sea on a good day," she said, pointing to the windows. "I'll expect payment first of every month. I'll treat you the same as all the other girls, princess or not. We English women have had our fair share of White Queens. I am not so easily intimidated."

I was intimidated, even with her wink, but I took the room. The fur blanket that I laid over the end of my tiny bed seemed out of place next to the checkered flannel sheets. That night though, as I breathed in the raw city air, I coughed and wondered if it were not the most beautiful feeling in the world.

My classes were challenging. I hadn't expected to be the only woman with the half-dozen men. Each of them hoped for postings from the Danish Crown, and royal patronage to line their pockets. They were, in their own estimation, the next generation of adventurers, prepared to capture fame and glory on the frozen expanses of the world.

I was as quick-witted as any of them. Better read, by far. We studied more places than I could admit were within my mother's lands. But they had no use for me. I had been to the glaciers they dreamed about in their blue-smoked parlors. But as the holidays came and went, as faces changed and the seasons moved, I was not one of them.

I had left my mother's frozen halls and found the University just as chill. I was unwelcome, a scientist among strangers.

They said that royalty was not fit for their taverns, or to socialize with their ladies. I had no interest in sipping vodka from shared bottles. They told me to find trees to whisper to, or cast spells, to stop pretending and go back to where I belonged. I was lonely.

A man spent three days outside my library carrel. At first, he pretended to search the stacks just outside my line of sight. It was unlikely that anyone in Copenhagen would be so interested in the library's collection of Tropical Gardening instructions. He wore a blue frock coat and had dark hair. His fingers were long and thin and he traced the spines of the books with delicate touches.

"The books don't change," I said as he glanced at me for the fifth time in an hour. I was preparing for an exam and had books piled on the desk, marking them with slips of paper to go back to research. I did not appreciate men staring at me. I was not a white-furred bear to dance for anyone.

"Nor do *I* much change. So you'll be as welcome to stare at me from between the books next week as today. I have exams, and your staring is more than a bit of distraction."

He jumped away from the shelf as though it has frozen over. "I'm sorry. I—"

"You're leaving," I offered and then turned back to my studies.

"I'm actually Jonas," he said, "But I'll follow your orders, your Highness. In case you decide to turn me into a snowman or some such. It's true what they say about you, Snow Princess."

He tipped his head toward me, tapping his fingers against his head as though he were a respectable man wearing a hat, and then turned to leave.

"What?" I said, slamming shut the book on S. A. Andrées' Arctic balloon expedition. The words echoed in the silence of the library. There were more than a few young men who shot disapproving glances toward me. I did not care.

"Your Highness?" the man—Jonas—said.

"What is it that they say about me?"

"That the Princess Ylsa has skin of the most delicate frost, and she is too smart, too sure, more like a story than a real person. Good day, your Highness."

"You think it's so simple?" I raised my voice to follow him, like the echoing of a scream down the crevasse of bookshelves. "When everyone who doesn't hate you because a woman does not belong in this University is terrified that every snow flake might be the Queen's harbinger, come to freeze them in their sleep?"

"I would never imagine what it would be like to walk through a winter palace, waited on hand-and-foot by polar bears, and want for nothing in the world. I am merely a student of business and a servant of the King." He turned back away from me. "I have heard stories of your mother for a long time. I'd come to see if they were true."

I followed him, stung, but determined to show this strange man the truth of me. I left my studies in their book-drift piles. And when Jonas Collin asked me to accompany him to a tavern for rye bread and smoked herring, I did not think about balloons over the arctic or the stunted trees that grew up from the snow. I thought about the way he called me Snow Princess as though I wasn't the queen's dark-haired, misfit, child.

When we kissed the first time, his breath came away white, like winter, blue like crag-ice.

I took him as a lover. Perhaps it was not the way things were done in the civilized age, but I learned the shape of him in the darkness and the lines of his smile lit only by moonlight through the open window of my rented room. If Mrs. Lang had an opinion, she kept it to herself.

When morning broke from that first night, I opened my eyes to find him warm beside me, the paleness of his skin looking beautiful beneath the bear fur. There was a strange weight at the end of my small bed, though. As I looked away from him, I saw that the window was open and that the winter wind gusted through my garret room.

Jonas smiled when he woke beside me. I was still, unmoving. I would not be bent, or bribed, or intimidated. He grew quiet when he saw my mother's leopard at the foot of the bed, staring at him— judging him. He laughed when the cat crawled up the bed, pressed its cold muzzle against my face and left the way it had come in.

He pulled me close and kissed me again as I tried to apologize, to explain.

"One must expect strange things from the Snow Princess," he said. He tasted like the warmth beneath the blanket, when the storm clouds feel very far away. "But I am glad to find no mirror-glass in my eye this morning."

They liked to say that my mother had stolen her sweetheart by piercing his eye with a shard from her broken mirror. I wanted to tell him it was a lie, a Fairy Tale like so many others, but his lips on mine were enough. The kisses were what I wanted, something that was just for me. It was more than enough.

Students wrapped thick scarves around their faces and did their best to stay warm as the wind pulled at their skin. I walked bareheaded and smiled to myself as I left the lecture hall.

Jonas wore a dark frock coat. He saw me in the snow—I know he did—but he walked past me as though he hadn't. He'd looked at me and kept walking. I turned, called out his name, but he was gone, as though he had never been. Only his footprints in the snow proved he'd passed.

Some days he lurked by me in the library, stealing kisses when I should have been studying. He had classes and seminars of his own, but he always seemed a little sad when I asked him to accompany me to the theatre, or to see a musical performance.

My mother's kingdom did not have engagements or betrothals. I did not understand the ways of mortal men. The winds took lovers when they wished, left them when the time was right. I had meant to do the same and let Jonas choose when and where we met. It had been my mother's way—the only way I knew to love. Though I tried to be like the snow-storm zephyrs, to let the fickleness leave me unmoved, it did not work.

The Storyteller had come north out of Copenhagen. My mother had loved him with all her cold heart as she'd never loved me. He'd taken her story and left the Queen a daughter with his dark hair.

The Storyteller had sold stories of my mother in Copenhagen, stories that her bees carried to her and her broken mirror. They had been lies, stories and untrue. All untrue. I wondered if all men were liars and for the first time since coming to Copenhagen, I felt myself grow cold to the fickleness of Jonas Collin.

He liked to ask questions of her, of me, after we made love. Were there really snow-bees in her castle? Did she have a mirror that looked out onto the world? Did I have magic? Had she stolen a boy away and made him love her? Yes, and yes, and no, and no.

Things came to a head one day as the winter grew deep and long and the students at Copenhagen were off to visit family in the country. Mrs. Lang's boarding house was warm, despite the weather. It was too cold for snow, and the sky was the clear blue of forever.

Jonas lingered beneath the bear skin blanket. I had begun to think of him as two separate men: the one who was at home in the private warmth we shared, the second a colder man who only lurked and lingered at the edges of my life. No one should have stood for it.

But he was warm, and I looked into his brown eyes as I wrapped myself closer around him.

"What is she like? My uncle tells me so many stories about her. Everyone does," he asked me. His voice was still thick from sleep. He buried his face in my hair.

"The stories are lies," I said. I felt hot all through. I hated the Storyteller for the way people thought of her. Hated what they thought of me as her daughter.

"Does she really have a broken mirror? Does she make the snow fall?"

He was quiet when I didn't answer immediately, running his fingers through the ends of my hair. Waiting.

"She's a bit like you," I said.

"How?"

"On some days, she's the winter every child dreams of. She's gentle and soft and when I was little, dancing with her through her palace was like being wrapped up in a cloud of gentle snow. It's like when you kiss me, Jonas. Or when we come up the stairs and you lay back against the blankets."

He smiled.

"Other times," I said, "she is like you when you see me passing from class to class. She is cold and uncaring. The winter does not love many, and even those the Snow Queen loves can feel the chill of her regard."

"Ylsa—" The man pulled away from me. "It's not like that."

"There are days where you say that I'm all you think about, Jonas. There are nights where we watch the Aurora Borealis from the window and laugh and sip tea. There are days where you don't even act like I exist. And always there are questions. Are the stories true? And I tell you again and again that they are lies."

Jonas was quiet as I dressed. I did not put on a thick cloak or braid my hair. Instead, I opened the window and welcomed the cold against my skin. The coal-dusted air did not taste as sweet as it had. I suddenly longed for the silence of my mother's house and the cold embrace of winter.

"There are times, Ylsa, where you are bright and wonderful and smart. You are going to be a scientist and the world will know your name. And other times you are a squall coming off the harbor and everything in me screams to brace myself for the impact of you. They say so many things about you."

I wondered if the Storyteller had told my mother such lies, before he left her. Was that all I was? A story?

"What do they say, Jonas?" I asked.

"That when your classmates fare better on exams, you send snow-bees to their rooms and threaten to freeze them. That the winter wind howls through their garret rooms. That you've taken lovers and left them cold in the snow."

I turned to him and laughed. It was an ugly noise, like the cracking of ice or the harsh sound of frozen snow underfoot on a starless night.

"This is not a fairy tale, Jonas. My mother did not spirit you away or break a mirror into your eye, any more than she did the Storyteller who made her so infamous. I have no magic and whatever they say of me is lies even more."

"Ylsa," he said, standing. He left the fur on the bed as he came to me, all naked and beautiful. "I have been as honest as I can be. There is no one else and sometimes I fear that beneath your smile, your temper, your ferocity—the things that I love so much about you— is something cold and I will be another story they tell to children. Sometimes I worry that there is a magic in you that has bespelled me. When I am not near you, I want to be. And sometimes I want it so badly that the only thing I can do is be aware from you, so make sure that it is still a choice I have."

"I am no magic, Jonas. I am a scientist. I have never been magic. I thought you understood."

He tried to kiss my neck, but I pulled away.

"I am going home," I said.

"Please don't."

I ignored him and went to take my trunks from beneath the bed. Jonas followed and took my hands in his. His hair was still disheveled and he'd kept his face shaved because I had hated his moustache.

"Come and meet my parents," he said. "Come to dinner and meet them. Meet my uncle, who was so enamored by the stories of your mother. Let them see you. I am sorry that I have not been certain about my feelings for you, Ylsa. It has taken me time to learn how to love you, and I am still a novice."

I forgave him, because I was a novice in love as well, and Jonas was so warm, even when I missed the simplicity of the cold. I agreed to visit his parents, in their house at 9 Amaliegade.

My hired carriage slowed before the Collins' house, built back from its siblings along Amaliegade Street. I had dressed in white linen and scalloped lace. I had pulled my dark hair up into a complicated braid and did my best not to be nervous. I wanted his parents to like me. I wanted the man I saw as I entered the house to be the warm Jonas that I loved, not the cold man that seemed to face me too often. I wanted him to forget the stories that he'd heard and live in the moments we had made together. Not someone who thought I'd bespelled him. I had a secret to tell him, and I was worried that he would not like it.

The footman bowed deeply as I entered the house. The foyer was lit by gas lamps and it was warm. I had never been to a party before. Not one where the women wore sparkling jewels and bright feathers. No, I knew only the parties of storms, and as quickly as I entered the Collins' house, I was adrift in the flow of people.

It was some time before I found Jonas. He wore a dark suit coat with a pale blue cravat. My lover spoke to a tall man who had his back to me. I smiled when Jonas looked up and he smiled back.

"I'm so glad you came," he said as I approached. "I was just talking to Uncle about you. I wanted you to meet him."

The man turned and the world slowed.

Jonas' uncle was tall and gawkish. His clothing was well made, but fit poorly. His hair was dark and his eyes were two black coals over the beak of a nose. Jonas moved him forward, still smiling.

"Ylsa, I would like you to meet my uncle Christian. Christian, this is Ylsa."

Jonas' uncle did not extend his hand.

"Hello, Ylsa," he said. His voice was thin, like mountain clouds. "Jonas has told me so much about you."

I felt like I'd been slapped.

The air went cold inside the house. The glasses with their fancy champagne became rimed with frost.

"Hello, Storyteller," I said.

Jonas' smile was frozen to his face, he looked back and forth between us.

"You should not trust her, Nephew," The Storyteller said, holding his iced-over glass. "As I've told you and you've chosen to ignore. I *know*. She will freeze your heart as her mother did mine."

"Ylsa?" Jonas said, looking at me, then back at the glass.

"I am not magic," I said, shaking my head. Why now? Not now, please not now. "I am a scientist. I came to Copenhagen to learn and it seems that what I have learned is that there are lies here just like everywhere else."

There were a thousand other things I could have said, answers I could have demanded, but I turned around, wrapping my hands around my stomach.

"Ylsa!" Jonas yelled. I looked back to see the Storyteller—my father—holding his arm.

"She is just like her mother. Using you, Jonas."

I walked back through the Collin house and then out onto the street. It had begun to snow, and there were carriages still arriving, turning the white to muddy water.

Jonas followed behind me.

"I don't understand. Ylsa, what's happened?" he said. He reached for my hand. I was tired. "You haven't met Mother or Father. You know Uncle Christian? I don't understand."

"Your Uncle is Hans Christian Andersen," I said. "The Storyteller."

"Yes," he said.

"He told you I was bespelling you," I said. "Told you I was..."

The words ran out and the look on Jonas' face did not draw them out.

Someone called out Jonas' name from an arriving carriage. I felt the cold mud as it hit me, leaving brown tracks against my dress. The carriage wood was carefully polished, the wheels high enough not to notice when the street-muck was disturbed.

"Jonas!" the Storyteller was at the doorway, calling him. "Jonas! Magic! Do you still doubt me? Let her go, she doesn't love you."

I laughed and turned away from them both. A cold wind raced down from the North, freezing the mud and snapping at my face. My mother's story repeated itself. When Jonas reached for me again, he pulled his fingers back, frost-burned.

"You said you weren't magic," he said, eyes wide.

The tear that slid down my face froze as it fell.

"Uncle Christian, stop talking. Ylsa—" Jonas called out to me as I stepped toward the street. My dress was ruined. It didn't matter what impression I made on his mother and father. It didn't matter what impression I made on his uncle, it only mattered that my feet follow their way north.

I had stayed too long in Copenhagen. It was time to go home.

Mother sent the bears for me on my second day of walking. The city had given way to snow-clogged fields. My pretty dress had gone to tatters, my embroidered shoes lost somewhere along the city canal. I didn't recognize the bears at first as they crossed the field. Their paws were quiet in the stillness of the gentle snowfall.

I was cold, but it was my heart that ached, not my body.

It was another full day before we reached my mother's house. It was still a place of cold wars and frozen secrets, perched between a nameless fjord and an ancient glacier. In the afternoon sun, the ice-walls were green, and the storms that cavorted around its towers caroled our homecoming. It was only then that I looked behind me and my broken heart froze a little bit more. He was not there. I had not actually expected Jonas to follow. The Storyteller spun his lies. And Jonas had believed. The days where he was cold and distant. The times where I did not exist.

Mother sat in her apiary. The snow-bees were quiet as she sipped her tea. Mother's leopard sat at her feet and looked at me with sorrow in his eyes. I sat in my chair beside the frozen fireplace and was quiet. The Snow Queen and I were quiet for a long time.

"Did you love the Storyteller?" I asked at last.

She sipped her tea.

"Yes," my mother said. "I loved him more than evergreens love the first snowfall."

The mirror behind her reflected the smoke-clogged rooftops of Copenhagen. I could see the window of my garret room.

"Did you know his nephew would break my heart?"

"We must all live our lives, Daughter."

I pulled my legs up beneath me, as I had when I was a child. "I did not want magic. I wanted to be a scientist."

I wanted Jonas to love me.

I touched the place where the mud from the party had stained my dress.

Mother stood slowly and waved the snow-bees away. She stood close enough to me for me to scent the jasmine tea on her breath. Where she touched the linen, it changed, until it was white again. As I looked, it was white like fallen snow, the ripped lace pulled back into place as though it had never been rent.

"I loved the Storyteller and he loved another. He fled to the North because the man he loved could not love him in return. I knew all of it and chose him anyway."

The Snow Queen, in all her years as my mother, had never held me. She did then, pulling me to her as I cried. She was not warm as Jonas had been. But she was the thick fall of snow that covers the world. She was my mother and she would never leave me to the dirty world.

"I'm sorry I left," I said. "I should never have gone. I'll never leave again. I have magic now."

"Silly girl. How can you say you'll never leave again? You have a degree to finish. Trees to question, snow to study. All of the world to explore."

I could not look at her. Not when I saw the look on Jonas' face. Not when I knew that I had followed my mother's story, right until the end.

"I hope my daughter does not look like him," I said softly.

The Snow Queen said nothing, only smiled still.

"You will choose whether you will follow my story or not, Ylsa. You can choose to let your love freeze, because your Jonas listened to words that were lies. You can let your daughter grow up cold and lonely."

A snow-bee landed on her shoulder. She looked at it with pale eyes as it danced, nodding as it flew off.

"Or, you can go out to your Jonas Collin, who is half-dead in the snow, calling your name. He is out on the Steppes, even now, Copenhagen far behind him. He made good time for a man who does not know the first thing about winter or the cold. But perhaps he's learned to love the Snow Queen's daughter, no?"

Mother smiled at me. I felt a strange tightness low in my stomach, not what grew there, but fear and a needling of hope.

"He followed me?" I asked. I looked at the Snow Queen's broken mirror. Jonas was there, wrapped in a coat that was too thin, in a squall that he fought with each step.

"Foolish," I said, standing and crossing to the mirror as Mother had since I was a child. I stepped through the mirror and out into the white, to see if the man who came was the cold creature, or the warm. Mother's snow-bees guided my way out into the drifts.

He standing in the snow.

"I'm sorry," he said. His eyes did not leave my face. "I listened to someone I thought I could trust, instead of my heart. I love you, Ylsa. Snow and frost and everything besides."

He was shivering. And in one moment I had my choice. I could leave him in the cold, to find his way. To freeze. I could gather my anger around myself, my rage that he had believed the Storyteller and not told me. Or I could go to him.

I crossed the distance between us, pulling him into my arms.

About the story

I have a crush on Hans Christian Andersen. More than that, I have a love of Fairy Tales. In my graduate program, I completed a thesis on the relationship between Hans Christian Andersen and a man named Edvard Collin. HCA's unrequited love for Edvard Collin was the impetus for the fairy tale "The Little Mermaid". I wanted to build off the story, reimagine history. Edvard Collin's son, Jonas, factors into the story here. It's mixing and matching and playing fast and loose with history. And when I started writing about Ylsa, I wanted to know her story, her Gunpowder black tea, and her love of all things North that were not her mother. So the story was written.

A question for the author

Q: Do you write with a particular audience in mind?

A: I don't, really. I think I ascribe to Stephen King's idea that the "perfect reader" exists in the head of every writer. I hope folks are willing to believe in the story that they're reading. I hope that it can provide them entertainment, or escape, or whatever else brought them to the story. My hope is that, by coming to my work, someone finds something for them unexpected that resonates inside of them.

About the author

Sean Robinson works as a social worker in the White Mountains of New Hampshire. He also teaches at the small liberal arts university he graduated from. In his free time he breathes fire, plays with his cat, and can be found (infrequently) on Twitter @Kesterian.

www.SeanRyanRobinson.com, @Kesterian

Sean R. Robinson's story "The Snow Queen's Daughter" was published in *Metaphorosis* on Friday, 27 January 2017.

February

Halfsies

Eric Del Carlo

The new word seemed somehow old-fashioned. *Halfsies.* Like how Tariq's sun-shrunken, onetime surfer grandfather would say "rad" when he deemed some event or circumstance especially good. Halfsies, as a term, sounded funny and harmless. But it wasn't meant to be funny, Tariq had learned. And it sure as hell wasn't harmless, not according to Tariq's friend from the liberated camp, Kayleigh, who explained to him, "It's a prejudice word."

The human soldiers who had come to the camp after the Blues fled had been helpful, but not what could be called friendly. Everyone in camp was hungry because the food had run out. Tariq remembered the gnawing from his gut, the hollow brightness ringing in his skull. The soldiers had brought supplies and provided medical attention. They were combat troops, battle-strapped and war weary. Tariq wandered amongst the looming, battered, dirty figures. They were the first adult humans he'd seen in a very long time.

How different they were from the Blues. Their manner was blunt, assertive. They assumed roles of authority and expected—demanded—all the children to acknowledge their supremacy in this chaotic situation. Whenever Tariq or any of the kids failed to obey an order immediately, it was barked a second time. The armed women and men watched their every movement.

The soldiers certainly weren't cruel, but they treated the newly freed prisoners the way one might a pack of stray dogs, administering field treatment in preparation for a trip to a shelter. It took Tariq a little while to understand how this made him feel. He was *affronted,* which was an adult kind of anger. He and the other kids should be wholeheartedly welcomed by these troops, he felt.

But no soldier had called him a halfsy during the liberation. The word came later. It was something civilians said, and also some people in the media, and a few politicians, now that the world was adjusting to its postwar phase.

"They think we're half one thing and half the other," Kayleigh said over the phone.

The young prisoners at that camp had originally been collected by the invading Blues from all over the world. Now they'd been processed by the Earth military and returned to their homes; but he and Kayleigh were staying in touch.

"Half human and half Blue?" Tariq asked unnecessarily.

"What else?" Kayleigh said, rolling her eyes. For a twelve-year-old, she could be sarcastic like a grownup.

Tariq, also twelve, didn't feel he came off quite as sophisticated. But he had kept his head in the camp when others got scared, which had made him proud. He studied the image projected by his phone into the middle of his bedroom. Kayleigh was blond, where his hair was dark. Not that it mattered much since they both only had stubble on their heads.

Her Caucasian skin still had more of a turquoise sheen to it than his own naturally duskier flesh. But the blue color was fading from both of them.

"What're you looking at?" she asked.

He had stared too long. If they had been on a playground somewhere, by now somebody would have said teasingly, *Oooh, Tariq likes Kayleigh!* But all that seemed idiotically childish after life in the camp. The experience had changed him, obviously. But he was also aware of awakenings in himself, new urges that came from the body.

"Just looking at you." He said it in a straightforward way, as if those schoolyard embarrassments meant nothing now. Even so, he felt a flushing heat.

"It's okay. I like looking at you too." She spoke just as frankly, then tilted her head. "My mom's calling me. I got to go. Let's talk again soon!" With that she winked out.

Tariq gazed around his room. It looked surreal, even though absolutely nothing had changed. After the Blues had taken him, his parents had preserved everything, every detail. He had been gone for fifteen months.

He had missed home every day, had missed his dad and mom. But after a long while at the camp he had stopped imagining what it would be like when he got back here. Then, after an even longer time, he'd quit wondering *if* he would ever get home.

Now that he really was back, he wanted all that pure simple happiness he had promised himself. But being home was more complicated than he had expected. That sparked anger in him, a directionless sort of fury. Really, though, he could only be mad at himself for not responding the way he thought he should.

When the aliens had first appeared but before the war started, Tariq had been fascinated by them. He had put up posters of their ships and images of the aliens from the broadcasts they had sent to Earth. Now, in the grotesque familiarity of his bedroom, he had Blues and Blue spacecraft looking back at him from his walls.

He knew he should take all that stuff down. But he couldn't. He knew he should hate the Blues...but he didn't.

"We're here for you, sweetheart. Whenever and whatever you need."

"It's just so good to have you back, kiddo."

Tariq preferred *kiddo* to *sweetheart,* so that gave his dad the edge. But Dad also looked like he might start crying again, so Mom got points for keeping her cool. It was a little game he had played when he was younger, tallying up his parents' daily "score" and awarding one or the other a gold star from his 3D printer.

Now he was using that same system to see which parent was reacting better to his return. Silly, really. They were both patently overjoyed that he was home. But some part of him remained wary, recalling the soldiers' benevolent leeriness toward the camp children.

He said, "I missed you too." And that did get his dad crying. Both parents held him. It had been like this since the army flew him here, after a quarantine period when officers had debriefed him about his time in the camp. He had answered many, many questions. In some ways the experience had been more unnerving than being a prisoner of the Blues. Or the Bhlooverrrtsii as they formally called themselves, a name no human could pronounce.

Tariq's home looked the same, clean and comfortable with plenty of space. But he hadn't been outside in the two days since his return. He almost felt trapped in here.

Dad wiped his eyes and made an embarrassed laugh. "They're happy tears, Tariq."

"I know, Dad."

Mom took Tariq's hand, squeezing. Something unsettling flickered across her face. Tears flashed in her eyes too. "Yes," she said. "Happy tears only."

Tariq looked at his own hand as she released it. The blue tinge was visible. The chemicals the Blues had given him and the other prisoners, the ones that had changed his skin color and made all his hair fall out, were leaving his system now that he was no longer receiving doses. The last effects would soon dissipate, the military doctors had promised.

Was his mom uncomfortable at his appearance? Did she think of him as...a halfsy?

Before the thought could even settle, he was rebelling fiercely against it. *No.* He wouldn't believe that.

At dinner that evening, his parents brought up school. Tariq had been dreading this.

Dad said, "While you were at that terrible camp, the schools were closed. The war put a lot of things on hold." He shook his head. "It was a mess."

"A mess?" Mom tried to laugh, but it sounded off-key, jarring. "That's your word for spaceships landing, alien soldiers ravaging the land, cities being bombed—"

"Gert..." Dad said.

Mom stopped, took a breath, and said, "Sorry, Majed."

Tariq's dad smiled, then went on with what he'd been starting to say. "They're reopening the schools. Of course, trying to get every kid back into the right grade is going to be a m— Is going to be difficult. It'll be especially tough for you, kiddo, having missed so much time."

"But I've been learning!" Tariq blurted, the words bypassing any instinct of caution. Instantly he knew how big a mistake he'd made. His parents looked across the table at him, wide-eyed. He was home, yes; his mom and dad were joyful about it, yes. But he wasn't the eleven-year-old they'd known. More than mere time—more than those fifteen months—had elapsed. The clock of Tariq's soul had continued ticking onward. It was a new hour.

"What," Mom asked softly, "do you mean, honey?"

They knew about the prison camp, about life inside, because the army had shown them the reports. But they didn't really know. It was strange for Tariq, at twelve, to have had an experience that was so unusual. His parents couldn't give him advice. They couldn't share their wisdom on the subject. Simply: they couldn't understand what he had been through.

What he was *still* going through. Some part of him, he realized, remained back at the camp, attuned to the old daily schedule, expecting the art and history lessons. That part of him missed the routine, as well as absorbing the fascinating details of the culture of the Blues. Guilt tried to seize him, but he resisted it, even though he knew he was supposed to reject everything about the aliens.

"Answer your mother, Tariq." Dad was staring at him. "What do you mean you've been learning?"

Tariq had barely touched his dinner. He was used to the camp food as well, to Blue food. He pushed aside his plate. Finally he said, "The Blues taught us. It was like school. We had lessons. We learned math and art, history and reading."

Now his parents gaped at him. Mom even looked angry. She said, "How can you say `like school'? Tariq, you were in a prison!"

"I know that, Mom." He tried to stay calm. His nerve endings crackled. Anger mixed with fear. In his old fantasies of returning home, he had always imagined his parents being totally understanding about what he'd been through. But that wasn't how they were behaving. The anger edged out the fear in him, and expressed itself as impatience. It was strange to be impatient with his parents. "But the Blues did teach us," he said firmly.

His dad shook his head, looking confused. "Art? History? You mean *their* art, *their* history..."

"And reading?" Now his mom sounded really mad. "They made you learn their crazy language? Those monsters!"

"They weren't all monsters, Mom. They—"

"They were the enemies of Earth, Tariq," Dad said. "They killed many people during the war. They abducted children like you. If we hadn't defeated them, they would've conquered our world."

It was true, and Tariq knew it. The war with the aliens had been terrible and costly. The Blues had indeed wanted to colonize Earth. Now that they'd lost the war, they had reversed their whole strategy and were asking for diplomatic contact with humans.

His stomach felt tight. He looked at the unappetizing food. It was all his formerly favorite stuff. Now he just wanted the Blue meats and vegetables he had been eating for the past fifteen months. He wanted that forbidden familiarity.

Quietly he asked, "Can I be excused?"

Mom was about to say something sharp, but Dad reached over and touched her arm, and said, "Yes, Tariq." As Tariq got up and left the dining room, he heard Dad add to Mom, "He just needs time to readjust, Gert. He'll be fine."

Tariq went up to his bedroom and stared at his posters. Maybe he really would readjust. But the Blues, and their technology and their culture, felt right to him on a level he had never experienced before the war.

A deep uncertainty gripped him. It had been a whirlwind since the camp was liberated. How could he know what he really felt? One thing he was sure about, though: he didn't like how his parents had just badmouthed everything about the Blues.

The next afternoon Dad, dressed to go out, knocked on his door. "Want to come shopping?"

Tariq longed to go outside, but he still hesitated. "You think it'll be okay?" He held up his blue-tinted hands. The war was over, but it was still blisteringly fresh in everybody's mind. He had seen the news, the cultural and political commentary streams. The pervasive disposition was to be gracious in victory over the aliens. But a cottage industry of resentment and distrust had sprung up across the national landscape.

His dad looked serious. "I can't promise nobody will say anything, or point, or whatever. But I will keep you safe, son." He patted his open-carry in its holster.

Tariq tried a smile. "Let's go."

They drove to the mall. Mom was at her job, and Dad had done his work today online. The mall was different than Tariq remembered. Half the stores were closed, and people seemed to be walking around in a kind of daze. There was no water in the indoor fountain.

"Things are still bouncing back from the war," Dad said, seeing Tariq's wandering gaze. "It'll be a while before everything's normal again."

Tariq caught himself before he laughed one of Mom's weird bitter laughs. Normal? He didn't think anything would ever be normal again; or even if every institution and public service and piece of the culture was perfectly restored, it would all still feel peculiar to him. It was good to be out of the house, but he felt like a stranger here.

And people *were* looking at him. They would break out of their private stupors and stare as he passed. Most weren't trying to be rude, he thought. They were just curious. Everyone knew human children had been abducted and altered by the aliens. But few people had ever actually seen one.

Tariq withstood the scrutiny. Some part of him was afraid. But another, perhaps stronger, part seethed with defiance. He followed Dad from store to store, waiting for someone to call him "halfsy" and unsure how he would respond to it. But nobody did.

Out in the parking lot a woman wearing a shabby Earth military jacket looked up as she was getting into her vehicle. She had a prosthetic leg. She fixed Tariq with eyes that danced with an disturbing energy. "You make up your mind yet, boy?"

Tariq stopped. He stared back. His spine tightened, and his fists started to ache where he held them at his sides. She was probably like the extreme politicians and commentators who reproached the Blues day and night on the streams. He couldn't talk back to those aggravating remote personalities, but he could challenge this woman's views, right here, right now. He started to take what he hoped was a menacing stride toward her.

But Dad stepped between him and the ex-soldier before he could really make a move. Dad's hand didn't go to his open-carry, but he made sure the woman saw it. "Don't harass my son."

The woman hobbled a step toward them, leaving her car door hanging open. She ignored Tariq's father. "You can't be both, kid! Pick one." Tariq understood what she meant.

Dad hustled him along to their vehicle and threw the purchases in the back. Tariq didn't break eye contact with the woman until Dad fairly shoved him into the car. He drove out of the mall's lot, saying, "Don't let her upset you. She might have mental health issues."

He said it like Tariq might be afraid of her. But in that moment of confrontation he hadn't felt any fear. Instead, he had wanted to stand up for himself. And for the Blues.

"I want to see you."

Kayleigh's image shrugged in Tariq's bedroom. "You're seeing me right now."

"No. I mean *see* you. In person." They had been assigned to the same barracks in the camp. During their internment he had seen her every day. Together they had helped the other children, the ones too frightened to function. At first, neither thought of it as cooperating with the Blues. The aliens had, after all, abducted them; they were at war with the Earth. But gradually he and Kayleigh had seen the sense of going along with the camp routines, absorbing the lessons, making the most of what they had.

Kayleigh was a girl of stony will. But she had seemed almost cheerful lately, as they kept up their friendship via phone. "What's wrong with you?" she asked.

He gazed at her image with the new longing he felt. He knew now that he should have said something to her when they were still together. Should have expressed his feelings. Should have done *some*thing.

"I just," he said slowly, "miss you." Then the frustration caught up to him, and he threw his hands up. They were still bluish and would remain so for another month.

She looked at him with sympathy. "Tariq, I live in another state."

He knew he was lucky she wasn't on the other side of the world. But he still wanted to see her. It arose from more than these new—sexual? yes, they must be *sexual*—feelings he had toward her. He wanted to tell her everything he was feeling, the confusion and vexation and fear, and ask her what he should do.

"We have to figure out a way to meet," he said.

"Isn't this enough?"

He stepped forward and swung his arm through her image—very poor phone etiquette, but it made the point. "I want to touch you," he said boldly.

She blinked, taking that in. Once, expressing anything like this so brazenly would have terrified him. But being brave in prison had proved he could be as brave as he liked in his bedroom. Eventually she said, "I...want that too."

Tariq understood that if his parents—or any adult in authority over him—were to hear this little exchange, they would freak out. But his connection to Kayleigh ran deeper than sex, deeper than any potential sex between them, deeper than whatever sex would ultimately turn out to be.

She said, "If you can figure out a way, Tariq, then I'm in."

With that she abruptly had to go. But it left him humming with hope, staring at the empty space she'd just occupied.

During the war, a lone Blue craft had swooped out of the sky over her city and snatched her right off the street, just as one had him. They'd both been taken to that camp, in territory the Blues had captured. The aliens didn't exactly mistreat the hundreds of children they had collected, but they *were* prisoners, all of them ripped away from their families and homes.

There had been the daily routines—mealtimes, bedtimes, times when they were free to play and times for lessons. Not all the guards at the camp were friendly, and if you tried to escape past the fences, you got punished. But the teachers weren't cruel. They seemed—to Tariq, anyway—helpful and earnest, very much wanting to impart knowledge to the human children.

The lessons at first had daunted Tariq. But they soon came to fascinate him. Blue math was complex, almost incomprehensible until he had grasped the fundamentals. Then he saw how the aliens arranged numbers and used geometry. It was an elegant system.

Their written language was also intimidating, but again he had seen how it was structured. None of the children could speak it, of course, but many had learned to draw the Blue letters. Tariq had helped some of the kids who were struggling, at first because it made him feel smarter and braver in comparison, but later because it just felt like the right thing to do.

And the art of the Blues! It was wild stuff—part sculpture, part light, part music. Tariq was enthralled by it.

But life at the camp had meant more than just schooling. They were fed Blue food. They were given the chemicals which changed their skin colors and made them lose their hair. Some of the children got very upset at this. They threw tantrums or tried repeatedly to escape. But Tariq remembered the pictures of the Blues on his bedroom walls and how mesmerized he'd been by their appearance. Secretly, before the war and the camp, he had sometimes imagined himself looking like one of them. Those silly daydreams somehow cushioned the shock of his own transformation.

Blues had blue flesh, and their strangely shaped heads were hairless. Though they didn't appear much like humans, it was obvious they were trying to make the prisoners look more like themselves.

Indoctrination. That was the big word the Earth army people had thrown at Tariq and the others when the war ended and the camps were liberated.

"They were trying to indoctrinate you." Tariq remembered the officer who had told him this at the quarantine site. He had been a big man, not very patient. "Do you understand?"

"Uh…yes, sir," Tariq said.

The officer went on like he hadn't answered. "It means they wanted to get inside your heads, change you, make you think like them and against your own people. We have to know if they succeeded. There's also something called the Stockholm Syndrome. We need to determine if you've succumbed to it."

Tariq had answered the questions how they wanted him to. The Blues hadn't changed him, he'd said.

But of course they had. He'd been in the camp over a year, learning the aliens' ways, exposed to their culture. He had hated the war and the awful loss of human life, but the Blues weren't just a warlike species. Like any powerful nation on Earth, they had politicians and military leaders who pushed for war, even when the common people didn't want it, even when war went against the principles of peace expressed through their art.

At the dinner table that evening Mom asked, "Sweetheart, what's that song you're humming?"

Tariq hadn't been aware until now that he was doing it. It was a Blue melody, very distinct, evidently so encoded in him that he'd hummed it aloud at the dinner table. Once more he was having trouble eating his food. "Um, nothing."

Both parents were looking at him in that way that said they knew he was hiding something. Suddenly, Mom's eyes shone with tears. They didn't look like happy tears this time. In a choked voice she said, "Is that a song you learned at the camp?"

He froze a moment, then unexpected anger surged in him. *"So what if it is?"*

Dad looked shocked for a second, then said, "Don't you talk to your mother that way!"

"It's okay, Majed." Mom wiped her eyes. "You don't like the casserole, Tariq? You don't have to eat it. You can go to your room if you like."

He rose, surprised, even astonished. He had stood up for himself. Proudly, he went up to his room. He wondered how Kayleigh was handling situations like this. He would find out when they got to see each other—somehow.

Tariq's skin would still be slightly blue when classes restarted at school, but after a week or two he would look normal. He knew he was expected to be pleased about this fact, but every morning when he saw that the turquoise sheen had faded further, he felt let down. His dark hair was growing back too. Now he just looked like he'd gotten a crewcut.

He was living as two people, it seemed: the perfectly normal eleven-year-old his parents had expected to return to them from the camp, and the sexually acute, irascible, independent twelve-year-old who had grown from his harrowing experiences. More often, it was the latter who made himself known, despite his efforts to suppress his own behavior and attitude.

The morning of orientation came, and Dad drove him to the reopened school. Mom came too, for the special occasion. She looked tired, unfocused. As they were all saying goodbye, Tariq tugged on Dad's sleeve and whispered, "What's wrong with Mom?"

Just as quietly, his dad said, "She's been online a lot, doing research."

Tariq entered his old school. He breathed in remembered smells, followed corridors according to the map in his head.

The day started with everyone assembling in the big auditorium. Tariq saw kids he knew and many he didn't. The school district's boundaries had been expanded. Not every learning institution was reopening. A few old acquaintances said hello to him, going out of their way, it seemed, *not* to comment on his skin. When the principal came out, he welcomed all the students, then gave a lecture about how everything had been disrupted for a while but now things would get back to normal. He managed to do all this without once actually mentioning the war.

It was the same at each class Tariq went to. The teachers explained what the year's courses would be like, but never said anything about the alien invasion. Some families at the school had lost someone in the fighting, but the faculty was acting like nothing had happened. Certainly no instructor remarked on the fact that children had been taken away to indoctrination camps.

That glaring omission ate at Tariq. He was, again, affronted, just like at the camp when the soldiers had treated the liberated children so warily. What had happened to him and the others deserved to be talked about. Not mentioning it only made his special condition worse, like he had a hideous disease everyone was too embarrassed to remark on.

Eventually, one kid he knew did say something about his skin color, but only to ask him if it hurt. Tariq, startled, actually laughed. That felt good, easing some of tension he'd carried all day.

When school let out, though, one girl caught up to him on the outside steps, glared, and said in a tight indignant voice, "My mom got killed by your kind."

The school had a zero tolerance policy for bullying, but Tariq wasn't interested in intervention by a teacher. He stepped right up to the sneering stringy girl, his heart beating fast, his fists again tightening at his sides, like in the mall parking lot with that ex-military woman.

"Most Blues weren't soldiers. Don't you know that?" He wanted to explain how the Blue diplomats were now offering the Earth technological advancements in exchange for trade relations. That was something of a hard sell to the war-stricken world, but the goods they were suggesting were, by most political estimates, too good to pass up.

But this girl with the dead mother wouldn't want to hear any of that, he could see. He saw too her intolerance, the lifelong grudge she would surely harbor against the Blues and anyone associated with them.

For a second she seemed ready to swing, but two of her friends stepped in and quickly led her away.

She had called him *your kind*. Was that just some random insult, or did she mean something specific by it? Regardless, the words stayed with him.

Only his mom came to pick him up. Tariq tried to look composed as he got in the vehicle.

"How did it go?" she asked as they drove off.

He said harmless things about his first official school day in more than a year. He could see the dark circles under her eyes.

Very deliberately, like it was something she had worked out word for word, she asked, "Do you think anything you learned at the camp will help you in school?"

The question startled him. She had been so upset when he first mentioned what he'd learned. "Maybe..." he said cautiously. Actually, he was sure the new knowledge would help. He felt like he was way ahead in mathematics, though it would take some reverse engineering to apply Blue principles to regular math.

She only nodded, but he stayed wary. They drove in silence awhile until she stopped a few blocks from their house, on an empty street. The car hummed as she sat with her hands on the steering wheel. Tariq saw how tightly she was gripping it.

"Tariq," she finally said, "how comfortable are you? With the Blues. With what you learned about them and from them."

His stomach fluttered violently, and for a second or two he thought he might actually throw up. "What do you mean?" But he understood, just like he'd understood the veteran with the prosthetic leg when she'd told him he had to choose between being human or Blue.

"I mean," his mother said, knuckles white as she clung to the wheel, "who do you like more? Humans or Blues?"

He couldn't believe she was asking so bluntly. It was such a loaded question. His answer, he sensed, would be momentous. It could decide his immediate future, maybe his entire fate.

"Um..." he started, cautiously. "What if I said Blues?" Then, hastily: "Just *what if!*"

She appeared to have her response already prepared. He wondered if this was a result of the online research Dad had mentioned. She said, "There are therapies. We could look into those.

There are facilities. They're new. You could go stay at one for a little while. Though that seems kind of awful, since we just got you back and have missed—"

Her words touched nerves gone excruciatingly raw. Suddenly he found himself lunging for the door handle, leaping out of the car and running.

It was stupid, of course. He had nowhere to go. He couldn't run all the way to Kayleigh. He couldn't even go anywhere on foot where he wouldn't eventually be found. After a few blocks he grew aware of the car following him. He saw his mom keeping pace, letting him run himself out. He put on extra speed, but it was useless. Soon he was staggering, sweat in his eyes. He sat down limply on a curb.

Mom pulled up and got out. Neighbors were looking on. "I'm so sorry, honey. I didn't mean to upset you." She sat next to him and tried to hug him.

But it was all trying to come spewing up out of him now, all the anger and fear and confusion he'd been feeling since the liberation. He wanted to yell, *I want to see Kayleigh!* But he bit the words, ground them down. He hadn't told his parents about Kayleigh, and even if they knew of her—say, via his phone log—they couldn't understand what she meant to him. They would just want to know if she too liked humans or Blues better.

So instead of talking about Kayleigh, he choked out, "I don't like the Blues better. I don't!" It was all he could manage.

Now it wasn't sweat stinging his eyes but hot tears. He could feel the neighbors looking at him, probably disturbed by the blue-skinned boy. With another surge of unpredictable emotion, he threw himself into his mother's embrace. He knew he was going to have to betray her. Betray both his parents. And he wept over that.

Mom held him for a long while. A week later he enacted his betrayal.

The train shot through the countryside, and Tariq saw all the rebuilding underway. He sat on the edge of his seat, counting down the minutes until arrival. He had never traveled alone before. Even when he'd been transported to the camp, he had been in the company of his Blue abductors.

The trip was exhilarating and daunting. He had been clever, using a school server to arrange for a train ticket from his own meager credit account. After that, everything was timing. He'd dressed for the journey, waiting for the window of opportunity he knew would come when Mom was still at work and Dad went out on a routine daily errand.

Tariq had used public transportation to reach the train depot. He'd studied the layout online and knew right where to go, as well as how to present his ticket and which train to board. Like at the mall that time, people still looked a bit dazed. He had just marched on through and taken his seat, ignoring the stares his blue skin garnered and waiting for the bullet train to take off.

The arrangements with Kayleigh had been just as circumspect. Hopefully his parents wouldn't figure any of it out too soon. He had left a note behind, promising he would come back. With luck his disappearance would be taken for a fit of preadolescent pique.

He would go back...wouldn't he?

As the scenery flashed past, he questioned that fundamental assumption of his plan for the first time. He felt an autonomy he'd never before experienced. The train hummed and shivered with cool mechanical efficiency. He sat alone. No one was directing his movements, setting his timetable.

A grim, very adult-feeling smile touched his mouth.

Finally they pulled into the big station, where repairs were going on. It had been near enough to a battle to take damage during the war. Tariq fairly flew out of the train car, looking up and down the platform eagerly.

He saw people waiting to board, waiting to meet other passengers. He saw a man in a military jacket, a policewoman, a blonde girl—

A girl? Blonde?

Tariq looked back. And stared. It was Kayleigh. But she had blonde hair down to her jaw. And her skin...it had no trace of blue whatsoever.

He started toward her on numb feet. She walked toward him, her strides confident. She smiled at him. She had come alone, as promised.

"*There's* my friend!" she crowed, and pulled him into a fierce hug.

He had never imagined he would be eager to end a hug with Kayleigh, but he stepped back hurriedly when it broke. "What happened to you?" he blurted. There was no way her hair could have grown out in so short a time.

Kayleigh shrugged broadly. She had agreed to meet him here, pledging secrecy. His emotions had throbbed in anticipation of seeing her again, in the flesh. Now confusion tore through him.

Again Tariq asked, "What did you do to yourself?"

She flicked the ends of her hair. "Don't you like it?"

"Kayleigh, please. Answer me."

She got serious. In the camp she had always known when to quit kidding around. "I got a fast-grow treatment. My folks sprang for it."

He had been so used to her hairless skull. He had even liked how it looked after a while. "What about your skin?"

It was a Caucasian hue, even up close. "Injections. Counteragent for what they gave us. It was expensive, but again, my parents were willing to pay. They could see how looking like a Blue was affecting me."

It stunned him. It was too much to absorb. The busy platform in this strange distant city seemed to echo hollowly all around him, isolating him, separating him even from Kayleigh, whom he'd traveled so far to see. Hoping for her understanding. Expecting it.

She was the girl he had known. She was attractive. On some bodily level he couldn't yet fully process, he wanted her...but when she moved toward him again, as if to take him in another embrace, he stiffened. She hesitated, then regarded him solemnly.

"Kayleigh..." He struggled to remember what he had rehearsed. "Kayleigh, do you ever feel like—like we lost something when we left the camp?"

"No," she said at once, then less certainly, "I mean..."

"Yeah?" he prompted.

"I do miss you, and the other kids from our barracks, the way we all stuck together."

He shook his head. "I don't mean the camaraderie. I mean, the Blues themselves. What they taught us, their art and culture. Do you miss any of that?"

His heart beat hard while she silently considered his words. The train's departure was announced, and a last flurry of movement swept around them.

At last she said, "Tariq, whatever we learned there won't do us any good in the lives we have now. We've got to let it go and get back to normal."

He'd felt stunned before, by her unexpected appearance. Now he was staggered, benumbed. Thoughts knifed sideways through his head. He wondered if her parents had influenced her, if they'd sent her to therapy. Maybe. But he could tell she meant it. Even if she did believe they'd gained something at the camp from the Blues, she rejected it now. Because she felt she had to. Felt they both had to.

He had come hundreds of miles to see her. He smiled softly. She would rejoin the human race. She'd already done so. She would grow up, maybe marry somebody, and have—he hoped—a very good long life.

This time he initiated the hug, and held onto her for a long moment. Then he said goodbye and walked away down the bustling train platform.

"Hey! Halfsy!"

He had been taking inventory. He had some actual physical money on him. There was a return ticket in his pocket, which could be cashed in. Pangs of dull hunger prodded him along toward food. He'd come to an open-air section of the station. Beyond was a view of the city, which was much bigger than his own home town. This was Kayleigh's city, though already her name failed to impart any special allure to it. He didn't hate her. He never would. But she didn't have any of the answers he needed.

Tariq halted sharply at the words called to him. He felt his hackles go up. He had almost been in a couple of fights since coming out of quarantine, at the mall and at school. Now might be the time to see one of these confrontations through to the end.

He turned, with bunched fists.

Atop a low wall a row of young people sat in various stages of postured insolence. Teenagers. City kids. They wore some peculiar fashion Tariq didn't recognize but which was nonetheless oddly familiar. One boy was staring at him. He was the one who'd just called Tariq *halfsy*.

"You got a problem?" Tariq said, because it was what tough characters in old movies said. Before the war, before the Blues had ever even made themselves known to Earth and become his early obsession, he had liked streaming old films, with their campy dialogue and outdated special effects.

The boy, unexpectedly, broke out laughing. But it wasn't mocking laughter. A few of his friends noticed the exchange.

"No problem." The boy, maybe as old as fourteen, hopped down from the short wall. "Your hue is flash, mano. Where you get it done?"

Tariq realized the boy's head was shaven. He was also wearing a strange pair of boots—more like booties, with a curious cut to them... again, familiar. Then Tariq understood. He saw how the others were costumed. They wore approximations of Blue attire. About half of them had hairless skulls, and at least two had gone so far as to shave their eyebrows off as well. Six or seven sported skin in shades of blue. Most appeared to have applied stage makeup, but a couple looked to have actually dyed their skin.

The color wasn't a proper Blue turquoise, though, Tariq noted. These weren't kids from any of the dozens of camps that had held abducted children during the war. These were street kids, off the grid, adopting the Blue look just for fun or out of a sense of rebellion. Or maybe because whatever they'd learned about the Blues appealed to them on some level.

Whatever they knew about the Blues, though, Tariq knew more.

He smiled at the toughs as the boy and several more approached. None were threatening him. All were gazing, fascinated, at the color of his skin.

Maybe he could stay with them, stay here in this exotic city. Live like they did. But as they got closer, he saw how underfed they looked, how unhygienic. Was it worth being homeless just to be among his "own kind"?

The fantasy collapsed even before it could stand fully upright. These kids hadn't been abducted by aliens, given chemicals to alter their appearances, been exposed to the depths of the culture of the Blues. They surely didn't genuinely appreciate all the subtleties and profundities of that civilization. They were pretenders, wannabes. They saw the Blues only as a tool for shocking other humans.

They certainly wouldn't understand how he himself was torn between two worlds.

He lingered with the group for half an hour, answering their questions, even enjoying their attention. They didn't seem to know much of anything about the camps. But when the next train heading back home was announced, he broke away and boarded.

He accepted his punishment without complaint. He had run away. His parents duly disciplined him. They tried to understand what had motivated him, and he attempted to explain it. But it was difficult to put voice to the complex fear, anger, and confusion. Those emotions stayed with him, and they only intensified.

The chemicals in his system dissipated, and he looked like he had before the aliens had come.

He tried getting back into his hobby of streaming old movies, but it bored him. Instead he found online pirate sites that featured Blue content—art, language, all the things he had studied at the camp. In school he got in trouble when he tried applying the alien knowledge. He finally did get into a fight with another student, who had actually used the word halfsy on him, even though he no longer had blue skin.

He felt miserable. His parents worried.

One evening they called him to the dinner table. When he got there, he found no plates set out.

"Sit down, honey," Mom said. Dad was beside her. They both looked very serious.

Uneasy, Tariq sat.

"Tariq, sweetheart, this is hard to say..." Dad took Mom's hand and held it, and she went on, "We want you to be happy. That's important to us. More important than anything. We know you're sad, and that just tears us up. We want to ask you something. Please answer us honestly."

"I don't want therapy," he said bluntly, interrupting. "I've already been in a prison camp, remember?" Once, it would have been unthinkable to him to speak to his parents this way. But he was only feeling more petulant and rebellious by the day.

Incredibly, they didn't respond to his insolent tone. Dad said, "That wasn't what we had in mind."

Mom squeezed Dad's hand tightly as she drew a breath. Here it was, whatever it was, thought Tariq, bracing himself.

"Tariq, would you be happier if...if you could live like a Blue?"

"Yes," he heard himself say immediately, decisively. It was the way his body might have reacted to an electrical jolt. His simple honest answer seemed to echo in the room.

It froze his parents for a moment, then Mom laughed, and it wasn't one of those strained laughs. She sounded relieved. Dad presented a smile, one that looked carefully constructed but nonetheless sincere.

"The government and the military," Mom said, "they're reaching out to families. Families with children who were in the camps. They contacted us. There is going to be formal, non-hostile communication between the Blues and Earth. Not just talks. The aliens are going to be allowed to establish bases on our world. Ambassadorial compounds. They'll be like...like *villages*. Separate communities. That's how it was explained to us. And the government is asking for volunteers to act as go-betweens. To live in these compounds. Humans, you understand? Humans who feel comfortable being around Blues. It's a serious responsibility. You wouldn't be doing any official negotiating, of course. You—and others like you—would just be there to try to integrate our two cultures. Or at least make a beginning at peacefully understanding each other."

It hung there, as powerful as his emphatic *Yes* of a moment ago.

After a minute Dad said, "Well, kiddo, what do you think?"

Tariq had already given his answer. Now he could only grin, as an unfamiliar but very welcome joy thrummed through him.

Relations had officially opened between Earth and the Blues. Some humans would never be able to put the war behind them, but most people now saw the advantage of trading with the aliens. The Blues were allowed to set up their compounds on Earth, staffed with ambassadors and scientists. Tariq went to live in one of these places. There were lessons again, in Blue culture; but the teachers just as often asked Tariq and the other students questions about Earth and its history. It was always dialogue, never lectures. Never indoctrination.

Though not all the young human emissaries did so, he willingly took doses of the chemicals which changed his pigmentation and left him hairless. He felt *right* this way. He excelled at his studies, showing a striking talent for mathematical theory. He had made several good friends here.

His parents visited often. The embassy compound wasn't far away. It wasn't like the camp. Tariq knew he could leave any time he wanted. He also knew he was contributing to the betterment of his own world, his own people. The technology that had already passed from the Blues to the humans was changing the Earth in a positive way. The aliens' science would make space travel more efficient. Climate change could be virtually halted using their methods.

No one used the word halfsy anymore, not even on the extreme political streams. It was a word reserved for usage by really awful people who were full of prejudice. Instead, the accepted dignified term for Tariq's particular state of being was "trans-species."

It wasn't a funny or harmless word. It wasn't a grave or cruel one. To Tariq, happy as he'd never been before, the word sounded true.

About the story

I don't usually draw a straight line from real world situations or social phenomena when conceiving a science fiction story, but the genesis of this piece is quite clear: I wanted to do an extrapolation/reimagining of the issues facing transgender youth. Having a child more comfortable in an alien skin than a human one was a way to go about exploring that.

A question for the author

Q: What's your favorite story?

A: It may be that, as I read recently, there really is only one story: Things are not as they seem. As for favorite ready-made plots, I honestly do not have one I favor over any other in the sense of plot mechanics or story movement. I am much more drawn to themes, which grow out of characterization. One of my personal maxims is that what happens in a story can never be more engaging than the people it happens to. Without characters who elicit emotion, a story is artless. It becomes a scholastic exercise. A writer will know this when her or his work is greeted with this soul-shriveling comment: 'Your story was really clever.' That indicates a tale that is a literary mousetrap, a ba-da-bum of words leading (rather than inviting) the reader toward a prefab conclusion. The reader has to care. I vastly prefer sympathetic characters to tell my stories, though some successful writers manage with sets of players who elicit no empathy whatsoever. (I don't care for this sort of work.)

As far as themes, my favorite is probably personal redemption. A Christmas Carol wasn't about three ghosts hounding an old man; it was about a miser's spiritual reclamation. I also like, in this mode of personal redemption, to tell the big story through a small lens. I often put relatively insignificant characters (as far as their place in my imagined society or future) in the foreground and have them fight their little battles, while commenting on something much bigger—i.e., a character resists some oppressive aspect of a futuristic society, making the struggle immediate and desperate, rather than broad and epic. In my stories an evil empire might crumble, but you'll find out about it through a guy trying to put together the money to cover next month's rent.

About the author

Eric Del Carlo lived in New Orleans up until one day before Hurricane Katrina made landfall in 2005. Since then, he has resided in his native California.

Eric Del Carlo's story "Halfsies" was published in *Metaphorosis* on Friday, 3 February 2017.

A Nightingale's Map of the City

Suzanne J. Willis

The white stone buildings of the city gleam like scattered pearls, their peaks and towers reaching for the vertiginous blue of the sky. Atop the spires and turrets and minarets, domes and curlicues of gold-leaf sparkle, making the city seem dusted with slow-burning embers. The ghost of the giant Gustav, the city's architect and creator, walks cobbled alleyways that are carpeted in moss, skimming past the tiny ferns growing from arched doorways. It is the city he built for his flame-haired Julietta. His place of torment since the day she left.

Everywhere – *everywhere* – are monuments to Julietta. Ivy-covered statues, beaten copper friezes, emerald-roofed cenotaphs carved with elegiac verses. As though all of them together might be woven into a spell under the splinter-moon to bring her back again. Julietta left the city long ago, much longer than Gustav cares to remember. So he holds the city close like a well-worn photograph, folded and re-folded and disintegrating with time. Without it, he's scared that he wouldn't remember her face, her voice, the touch of her skin.

Sometimes, he thinks he sees her as a silver shadow slipping through the streets, leaving an unearthly sheen on the darkening stone. In spring, he glimpses her running in her yellow velvet cape towards the opera house, flanked by the singing fae who bear the remnants of her voice.

Gustav tries to be content with the scraps time has left behind. But doubt frays his edges. Once, this was a city for two. But before she left, Julietta opened the city to mortals, left it behind for them like a discarded toy. He can't remember if, in doing so, she had been deliberately cruel or just thoughtless. The people now living there are tiny and insignificant and shiver just a little when they pass through Gustav's ghost as he sits by the glass butterfly house or, in petulant moments, sprawls across the palace steps.

In the city of giants, of grandeur and vast sorrow, jewels and alabaster, red-haired sylphs float, unseen by its inhabitants, who are busy in the business of being ordinary. They are wisps of women, a thousand images of Julietta woven and rewoven, painted and sung, sculpted and remembered and reshaped in the years since she left.

Red-haired sylphs float as twists of breeze or phrases of song the ear can't quite catch. They drift and glide, wrapped in tresses studded with tiny blue flowers, smiling lasciviously at Gustav, who can only watch as people overrun his city.

He stares at the sky. He wonders, yet again, if one day the sylphs will forget him, too.

They wrap themselves around him and whisper

We are echoes, too.

Gustav shakes them free. He does not feel like listening to them today, whispering in her voice about the roads she might have taken, the places she might be found. Reminding him that he no longer remembers exactly the colour of her eyes, or whether she smelled of rosewater or sandalwood. As though unfolding the old photograph, he traces his hands over the lines of the buildings and the streets, where each day the gold dulls a little, the cobbles wear just a bit more. Only the ghosts of giants and half-maidens who were never more than an imitation remember how it felt when the city had its soul. The warm pliability of compliant stone; the seasons that formed themselves around Julietta's moods.

The door to the palace, banded with iron curled into daemons and lovers and winged serpents that change with the light, resists his touch. Beyond are frescoed rooms, gas lamps and clockwork faeries to serve a princess's every need. But the door stands firm, the treasures beyond it shielded from sight.

The longer she is gone, the more your city slips away from you. Only the doors with gilded handles are open to you now, the sylphs sigh. Gustav can count those handles on one hand. They fade further every day. He sits heavily on the marble outside the butterfly house – to the mortals it feels like a squall of wind gusting by – and presses his ghostly nose to the glass. Butterflies – sapphire, citrine, fuchsia, amber – flit up to him as though he is a honeyed treat laid out by their keepers. Above the entrance, a clockwork butterfly, an imitation of the real ones inside, flutters its wings, takes flight on the quarter hour then lands again. The sylphs stroke Gustav's hands, trying to cheer him in their sweetly savage way.

Once upon a time, an emperor's courtiers built a nightingale from glass and rubies and gold and ribbons. The emperor loved the clockwork bird much more than he had ever loved the real one, with her plain brown feathers and unpredictable tune. Yet she continued to love him long after he had forgotten her in favour of the imitator.

The giant poked his finger moodily at the glass, scattering the butterflies.

Your Julietta, she waited for you as long as she could, dearest, while you were building her memorials. She had cities inside her, waiting for you. Vast and unpredictable and waiting to be explored. One day, all the doors here will be closed to you and you will just be thunder fading in the distance. That is the way of echoes, dear Gustav.

If they weren't so like her, he would wrap their flaming tresses around their throats. Swallows dart and swoop from the sky, skimming through his chest in a gust of air. He follows them as they make their way back to their nests in the city's walls, which were carved with stories written for Julietta, lit at different hours by the sun or moon. The swallows have burrowed through the words so the stories are now just nonsense phrases.

...creature of star-flecked night, chasing
a hollow moon and ever-ebbing tides...

...she reaches for the belly of winter, pushing against
diaphanous clouds...

...silver and green, its rhythm mirroring the ocean
crashing through her, speaking to the moon moths
and wind-ridden gulls...

Is there nothing left in the city that remains as it was in the beginning?

Gustav walks along the wall, reading its broken stories in the late afternoon light. He stops at the south-west corner, where he had long ago tethered a hot air balloon to the wall with creeping vines of purple roses and ruby-seeded pomegranates. He used to bring Julietta here, lift her up to sit in the basket to view the city, its architecture his ever-expanding love letter to her. Surely she had never doubted his heart, laid bare in the streets and passageways and grand buildings with their solid language of stone? But it is this corner to which she made her own way one day, climbing the tethers and scattering purple blooms and red, red seeds in her wake. It is the corner from which she made her escape.

The word jolts Gustav and he repeats it aloud, rolls it around on his tongue. "Escape. Escape..." Until today, he had always thought of her as running away, having left him and spurned his gift of her own city. But that word – *escape* – bubbled up from a forgotten city deep inside him.

Another broken story on the wall glows golden in the afternoon light; like the gilded handles, it admits him to somewhere that could easily have been lost.

...true, you are skin-hungry, your desire washed to
a faded wraith-story of missing her.
But it was not she who doubted....

With that quiet realisation, Gustav sees his city as Julietta must have seen it, in the end.

"My dearest Julietta, there is nothing of you here," he whispers to the swallows as they dive through air. The rose vine is just thorns now, tangled among the pomegranates that have run wild. As he speaks, one of the wispy wraiths, a distant echo of Julietta whose colour has faded to a rosy silver, snakes through the vine. She beckons to him, giggling, and curls herself at the base of one of the rose bushes.

He pushes his hands through the vines towards her. She fades until nothing is left but a beating light the colour of the sun. Reaching further, towards the buttery glow, Gustav wishes that he could feel the thorns scratching at his skin. Chunks from the wall are scattered among the gnarled roots of the bush, the carved words insensible as even sentences, let alone stories.

Curlew. Spice. Glimmer-deep. Longing.

Two of those clay-cast words glow in the aftermath of the sylph's touch, a lighthouse call across the years to Gustav.

Find me.

They gleam brighter as he stares at them. **Find me.**

He thinks about all the things that she loved: moonlight, early morning, stone bridges over fast-flowing rivers. He smiles as the memories rush through him pulse-quick. Bitter chocolate, wild storms, autumn frost, the light of deepest winter.

He stares at the sky. He wonders. Then he begins to run, along the wall, through the gates, up and down the streets until he finds the sylphs giggling and splashing in the city's central fountain.

What happened to the emperor? Gustav asks.

The clockwork bird ran down and the real nightingale came back, singing him songs from the cherry tree, singing him back from death.

The sun sets, the changeling light serpentine as it twists through hidden alleys and doorways collapsing on themselves. Gustav lies on the cold earth as the sylphs pull the darkness over themselves like a blanket. Sighing, crooning, slipping into sleep.

This city is a story no-one bothers to read, a clockwork nightingale whose gears have rusted silent. But as Gustav lies down next to his red-haired sylphs who smell of cinnamon and autumn, he no longer sees Julietta's pale flesh in the alabaster stone. Julietta's smile peeking from the ivy statues. Julietta's touch in the mist that rolls from the palace windows.

He stares at the indigo sky. He knows what he must do.

Tomorrow, the city may fade a little more, but it no longer matters, for he will not be here to witness it. Tomorrow, he will leave from the corner of roses and pomegranates, and follow the winds that took her away. With those two burning bright words – **find me** – he will search across lands and ocean, seasons and storms.

He will find her and they will build a new city together, one of bridges and clock towers without hands to stop the passage of time. A city not of stone, but of all the thoughts and longings unspoken that fill the spaces between the rooftops and hover above the streets. With sylphs and olive-plump moons and infinite brightness inked by their careful hands. A city that they will call home, with unchartered streets they will explore together. Be she old and faded, or bones and ghost, Julietta will write her own words on the walls and Gustav will beg her leave to map the cities running wild inside her.

About the story

In 2014, my partner and I travelled to Europe and visited Vienna. Aside from being an amazing city with incredible culture, I was blown away by how visually stunning the city is, especially the architecture. I remember making a comment as we wandered the streets that it was like a city made for giants; the buildings, the palaces, the statues are all so quietly imposing.

Vienna was also the home of my favourite artist, Gustav Klimt. Visiting the Belvedere Palace, the Secession Building and other wonderful museums left my mind full of the images of the beautiful women that Klimt painted with such love and reverence. Then I began to think about those women and how their lives might have been superseded by the images that the artist created of them. Such art must be underpinned by love, but is there a point that the artist loves the images, the art itself, more than the person who inspired them? When does what she represents to him as his muse overtake who she is as a person in her own right? And does the artist ever regret or rue what might have been, had the art, the beauty, the passion to create, taken a back seat to woman he loved?

A question for the author

Q: If your writing style were a bird, what type of bird would it be and why?

A: A bird uncaged, flying about a wonderfully strange garden. A bird who collects the beautiful shiny things that catch its eye, then weaves them into a story-nest, built of twigs and branches and Spanish moss. The garden is the framework, the rules of writing, but they're there to support the story, not to constrain it. Within the rules is an abundance of space to play and to map one's own path. The story-nest is pruned and plucked and woven over and over, with the bird discarding some of the bright, shiny objects so that the nest becomes something lovely in its own right, more than the sum of its parts. And sometimes, a bird that flies clear of the garden's boundaries to test what lies beyond, for that is where the best monsters live.

About the author

Suzanne is a Melbourne, Australia-based lawyer and writer. Her spare moments are spent with stories and music. There is a garden outside her little library that was built in the hope that the stories and the greenery might coax the faeries to make a home there. Her tales are inspired by fairytales, ghost stories and all things strange, but her favourite time is spent chilling out at home with her patient partner and pampered pooch.

Suzanne can be found online at suzannejwillis.webs.com

Suzanne J. Willis's story "A Nightingale's Map of the City" was published in *Metaphorosis* on Friday, 10 February 2017.

The Naked Me

N. Immanuel Velez

Jareth eased into a parking spot, turning off the rock 'n' roll screaming from the radio. The wind nipped at his skin, so he zipped up his jacket a little tighter. His silver necklace winked at him in the reflection off the convenience store windows. A month ago this place would have been teeming with evening rush hour customers, but not today, not anymore.

The bell dinged. Plastic sheeting and caution signs still covered the glass refrigerator doors. The mob had made a hell of a mess, so he was surprised to see such a quick restoration. And glad. He needed his cigarettes. For a bad couple of weeks when a lot of stores were still shut there had been hardly available at all, but he'd made a point of keeping his habit. It was a matter of pride, even with his wages cut to the bone. They'd opened the restaurant again, but on short hours, just another service business slowly adjusting to the new world.

He kept his gaze down when he approached the cashier, his visor blocking eye contact. You couldn't make eye contact.

"Hi, Miguel." Jareth said. "A pack a cigs, please. The usual."

"Sure."

Miguel also wore a visor; everyone did. If you couldn't buy one, you made one or wore a hat. Really dark shades also did the trick. You needed something, anything, to keep you from meeting another person's gaze.

"Still cleaning up?" Jareth asked.

"Almost done." He nodded at the plastic sheeting. "That's the last bit of broken glass. It'd be easier if they'd worked out insurance yet."

Jareth retrieved the cigarettes. He only saw the pack and Miguel's tanned, large hand.

"Man, it's been one hell of a month, huh?" Jareth focused on the change in the give-a-penny basin.

"Yeah. It's the cell phones I can't get used to. I hate texting."

"I hear you. Some people would rather talk. I'd rather text, but, hey, to each his own. There's always voicemail. At least the TV's okay."

"It'd be easier if I understood *why* it happens. I still don't get it."

"They say maybe it's psychological. Some kind of subconscious one-on-one connection." Which was about all Jareth had been able to follow; for all the long words and the attempts at quiet reassurance, he was pretty sure the government didn't know *why* the phones were affected any more than Miguel did. They'd said on the news the night before that they were testing—slowly, just like everything was slower now—some kind of micro-delay recording system, so you weren't actually talking to the other person, just recording a message that their phone would play to them a second or so after you left it. Not quite a conversation, but better than nothing.

"Whatever it is, I still hate texting."

"Someone'll figure something. See ya later. Thanks." Jareth almost raised his head, but checked himself. He paused before finding the courage to ask one more question. "When was the last time you looked someone in the eye?"

"Not since the whole thing started."

"Same here."

He walked back to his car and lifted the visor with a sense of relief. Not another person in sight. Time to go see Gina. He'd been putting it off, waiting for things to settle, telling himself he shouldn't message her, but should talk face to face, then telling himself to leave it another day, that maybe *she'd* message him. He'd heard nothing, and now he'd run out of excuses. The fear of what she'd say ate at him, but it was time, and he was as ready as he'd ever be. Assuming she'd even talk to him, and wouldn't just slam the door in his face after what she'd seen.

It had been a little over a month since everything changed.

Jareth had strolled through the restaurant's back entrance, and taken off his black leather jacket. Inside his cramped, rusty locker he had his cigarettes, a half-empty pack of gum, his waiter uniform, and a sweatshirt he'd left there weeks ago. He unclasped his necklace—against dress code, though for some reason they were okay with earrings—and removed his jeans, t-shirt, and sneakers, replacing them with the white Oxford shirt, black slacks, and black loafers.

"I'm surprised you made it today," Dave said as he barreled in behind Jareth. "You might wanna do something about your eyes."

"Red?" Jareth rubbed them, feeling a burn like grains of sand under his lids.

"Very."

Jareth pulled some drops out of his pocket and tilted his head back to apply them.

"You were really wasted," Dave said, grinning. "Gina get you home okay?"

She had; Jareth had woken on the couch, still fully clothed, with a vague memory of lurching arm-in-arm with her back to his place. Of her propping him against the wall while she fumbled with his keys, and shushing him so he wouldn't drunkenly wake the neighbors. He'd been disappointed, despite his pounding head, to find she hadn't stayed after he passed out. Having her there would've made the fight to straighten himself out and get ready for work much more pleasant.

"You'll have to make it up to her, hauling your sorry ass across town." Dave slapped him on the back.

"Weekend plans already," Jareth said. The sting in his eyes retreated. "I got us a room at this bed-and-breakfast near Winchester. Just the two of us out in the country for a few days."

"You sly dog."

It couldn't come fast enough, if he were honest with himself. He'd had a crush on Gina for a year before asking her out, but she'd been in a relationship with a broker named Saul. Jareth had flirted with her regardless, and thought he'd seen signs of a latent attraction for him. Her hand lingering on his arm, a simple look becoming a stare, a wink across the room. There was something remarkably seductive about her. When she split from Saul—"It wasn't working."— he pounced, and rebound be damned. It was still early days for them as an item, but that meant they were still in the sweet spot where just the thought of her touch on his skin, the feel of her lying beside him, her warmth or her scent, was enough to get his blood pumping. Where he wanted as much of her as he could get, like part of him was afraid it was all a dream and he might wake at any moment.

"You good to go?" Dave said.

"Yeah, it's only the lunch shift. Shouldn't be too bad."

"I asked Tom to give you section six."

"Awesome. Thanks, man."

Section six tended to have the fewest diners during lunch. Perfect for a waiter with a hangover. Black-and-white tiles checkered the floor, and aged photos of various cities in the Forties plastered the walls. A patron sat at a wooden booth and perused the menu.

"Hello!" Jareth said with a smile. "Welcome to—"

"Please. I'm not in the mood. Just get me a water and give me time to make up my mind," the man said. He tapped his index finger against the menu like a machine and never looked up.

Prick, Jareth thought. "Sure. Anything you say. I'll give you some time."

Jareth sauntered off toward the smoking area, and lit a cigarette. He would give this jackass all the time he needed. He took deep, deliberate draws of the smoke until it was down to the filter.

He returned to the table with a smile and water. "Did you figure out what you want?"

The man looked up at him. "Yes."

Damn, he looks cheap. Probably leaves change for a tip, Jareth thought. As he did, his head swam, as if something foreign, whose presence left him shuddering inwardly, had scattered his thoughts. Maybe the hangover was worse than he'd thought.

"What did you say?" the man said. "I bet this punk spat in my water."

"What?" Jareth pulled himself together. "I asked if you were ready to order."

"That's not what I heard. I'd like to speak with your manager."

"What?" he said again. *Why would he say that?* But he left before the man could respond, aiming for Tom's office. Across the room he heard a plate shatter, a commotion afterward.

Jareth knocked on his manager's door.

"Come in," Tom said.

"Some prick wants to talk to you. Not sure what his problem is." Jareth didn't care much for Tom, who bombarded him with double shifts even when he asked for singles and who he suspected gave the bartenders an unfair percentage of the pooled tips.

Tom didn't look at Jareth, but continued typing and staring at his screen. Heaps of paperwork riddled his desk. A minute crawled by before he raised his eyes and locked them with Jareth's. "What the hell did you do this time, you idiot?"

Again Jareth felt something cold and alien turn over his mind, thoughts running together. Just as suddenly, it pulled back. He shook himself in embarrassment. Tom's mouth hadn't moved. And yet he could have sworn he'd heard his boss right. *Did this weasel just call me an idiot?* Wonder if he'd like everyone to find out what he does with the tips.

Tom's eyes lit up and his eyebrows clenched. Once more Jareth shivered inwardly. "He knows about the money?" Again the man's mouth hadn't moved. Tom looked back at the screen and loosened his tie.

"Uh, did *you* just say something, Jareth?"

"The customer. Did you just say something? I thought I heard you—"

"Um, never mind. Let's go." Tom marched out of the room and motioned for Jareth to follow.

They reached section six, only to find the guy had left. Julie, one of the waitresses, rushed past and tugged Tom's arm. "I'm really not feeling well," she said, practically panting. "I've gotta go."

When Tom turned to her to speak, she let out a scream and ran.

"What the hell is going on?" Jareth said.

"I don't know. Something isn't right."

Jareth looked around. All of the customers had left. The front doors were just closing behind the last two. He saw the bartender heading out. "Hey, Simon, wait! Do you have any idea what the hell is going on?"

"No," Simon said. "But I have to go."

Another sickening sense of something invading him, violating his thoughts. This time Jareth saw a Rottweiler chewing a bone.

What the fuck is happening? Jareth darted toward the locker, changed his clothes, and threw himself into his car, his hangover a distant memory.

He flew down Route 28, heading for home. His hands pattered as they shook against the steering wheel. His mind was a garbled mess. Tom speaking without moving his lips, the customer reacting to an insult he couldn't have heard, Julie, Simon, everybody running.

He felt like he had that day when he was eight and thought his parents had left him behind at an amusement park. He'd been scared, so scared, waiting at the information desk while the staff tried to reach his folks. Except they'd never left, and within minutes they'd heard the announcement over the PA and come to find him. But it looked like this time there'd be no easy ending, no seemingly miraculous reversal where everything turned out okay and he could just go for ice cream afterward and forget all about it.

When he reached his apartment complex, he saw his neighbor lurching unsteadily away from the building. "Hey, Jake," Jareth said. "Have you noticed anything strange happening?"

The other man just shook his head, mumbling, "I don't know, I don't know."

Jareth fumbled his keys in the lock. Inside, the apartment was cramped and stuffy, the one bedroom lonely. He took a water bottle from the fridge and downed it in one swig. Sitting at the cheap stand that posed as a dining table, he pulled out his cell phone and called Gina. Calm. *Stay calm. You imagined it. It's just a passing thing. This will all be over tomorrow and you can take her to that cottage and spend the whole weekend in bed and we can spend hours just having*

—

"Oh my God, Jareth! Is it happening to you, too?!" she cried as soon as she answered. He had a yawning, vertigo-inducing sense of standing suddenly naked, cold and utterly powerless against a presence that slipped like ice water through every memory he had. Humiliation at his weakness and exposure flooded through him. Amongst that, an image of Gina and Saul holding each other on a yacht. She was smiling and laughing. "I—oh my God." She hung up.

The image, and the feeling of invasion, disappeared as soon as she killed the connection. He wanted to throw up.

Gina didn't answer when he tried again. He sent her a text message asking her what was going on, if she was okay, if he should come over. The reply was short, terse, and missing all those little markers that normally dotted their messages.

Just stay away for now. This isn't right.

When he messaged back, all he got were network errors. There were sirens wailing in the street, but the radio and TV news stations all seemed to be off air. He paced the apartment, torn between the lingering hope that maybe she'd call back or message him, get in touch somehow, explain what was wrong, and the desire to race off and talk to her face-to-face.

A couple of hours later he heard a knock at the front door and his heart jumped for a moment, until he opened it to find his sister Rachel standing there, head down. "Don't look at me," she said. "Let me in but don't look at me."

Jareth shuffled back into the room to allow her through. She removed her jacket, sat on his aged couch, and used her hands to cover her eyes. "Damn, it's a fucking shit show out there. You do know what I'm talking about, right? It's not just me?"

"Yes. What the hell is going on?!"

"I don't know. Nobody knows. People are flipping the fuck out. Every time I look at someone I hear voices or see things and I feel like… like someone's breathing in my ear or… or… like nothing's safe."

"When you look at someone?"

"You don't think it's that?"

"I dunno," he said, and as he did so she glanced up at him, red eyes hopeful.

He returned the look and again felt something slide through him, a foreign force oozing through his thoughts, turning them over while he flailed helplessly to keep hold of them. Dizziness and shame swam through him at how helpless he was against this *thing,* this presence, and as it did he saw Rachel's boyfriend Matt drinking a glass of water with a shaking hand.

"Oh Jesus," she said, turning her head, "it happened again. I heard Gina talking. Oh Jesus. I feel awful."

"I saw Matt drinking water."

"I was thinking about Matt. Right before I came over. He wanted to know if I'd be okay coming here by myself. I was thinking of calling him to tell him I was with you."

"Don't," Jareth said. "The networks are jammed, and the exact same shit happened to me when I called Gina. Don't use your phone." He paused, planting himself beside her, careful not to look in her direction. "What did you hear Gina say?"

"It was just her voice, saying 'Oh God,' like she was scared."

"That's what she said when I called her. She hung up on me. She told me to stay away, but I was thinking about going round to see if she's okay or what's going on."

"Matt and I are stocked, but you might want to stop off for food and water when you go; you know what people are like, and this is just crazy. Wait, you were thinking about what happened with Gina?"

"Yeah."

"And I was thinking about calling Matt."

"Holy shit," Jareth said. "You think we're seeing what we're thinking? We're actually reading minds? Why? How?"

"I don't know. I don't even know if it's real. I mean, how can it be?"

"We should test it," he said.

"Really? How?"

Jareth snatched a pad and pen from the coffee table. "Here, write down something ridiculous that I could never guess," he said, ripping off a sheet. "I'll do the same. Fold it and hide it behind your back. Then we'll look at each other and think of what we just wrote. If we can recite each other's sheet, word for word, then we know it's true."

"You sure you want to do this?"

"No," he said. "But we'll know for sure then. Just look away if you have to."

She lowered her hands, scribbled on the paper, then folded it and placed it under her leg. Jareth did the same.

"You ready?" he asked.

"Yes."

They counted down from three and then made eye contact.

"Enough!" Rachel screamed. She swiveled around. "Pink elephants flying through the rain."

"Sometimes I drink coffee at midnight," Jareth said as the feeling passed of being laid bare, utterly exposed and open. He was alone and safe in his own head again. "Do I even have to look?"

"You can if you want, but you know what it says." She sniffled and wiped tears from her eyes. "It's like I can feel you there in my mind. Like there's something inside me and there's nothing I can do to stop it. I want a shower."

"I know," he said. "It's horrible."

"And it's the same over the phone? What were you thinking when you spoke to Gina?"

"I was telling myself this was all going to work out, that we'd go to a bed-and-breakfast for the weekend and forget all about it." He stopped. He'd been thinking of all the things they'd do together, taking refuge in their escape, in the fantasy, most of it sex. Rough, dirty, filthy sex. If she'd seen that... "Oh shit. I need to go talk to her."

When Jareth turned the corner by the local convenience store he saw cars everywhere, some of them abandoned, gridlock in every direction. Horns filled the air, and a mob at the store's entrance was shouting and banging on the glass, turning on each other here and there as they made eye contact and saw each other's panic and need to survive at all costs reflected back.

Oh, hell no. No way. Screw this.

He jetted out and sped toward Gina's. He was so focused on cutting through the chaos on the streets and making it to her in time that he barely managed to stop the car before it hit her garage.

He bolted to the front door and rang the bell. Moments passed before he heard a familiar voice. "Who is it?"

"It's me, Jareth."

He heard the lock turning before the door cracked open an inch. "Don't look at me," she said.

"I know, I know. My head is down."

The door widened. He saw blue jeans and black suede boots over cream tiles.

"Gina!" a woman's voice shrieked from inside the house.

"Look, Jareth," Gina said, "this isn't a good time. My parents had a major fight. She just kicked Dad out. Their marriage wasn't all that great to begin with. I don't know what Mom saw or heard, but it wasn't pretty."

"I'm really sorry, really, but can we talk for a minute? On the phone—"

"Jareth, please. No need to explain."

"I wasn't... that's not what I—"

"No need to explain," she repeated.

"I saw you thinking of Saul. On his boat."

"So?" She sighed. "Random thoughts enter your head all the time, Jareth. You know how it is. You could be in a grocery line and something might remind you of a red notebook you once owned. Or you could be in an accident, bleeding, and the spinning tire might make you think of a bike you loved when you were thirteen, when you should be thinking about calling nine-one-one. Doesn't mean anything. I was freaking out before you called. I was probably just thinking of an escape. But the way it felt when we... I've got to think about things."

Jareth saw her feet shift. "Message me or email me?" he said. "So I know you're okay?"

"Gina!" her mom's voice bellowed.

"Sure, Jareth, I have to go. Bye."

She shut the door and he rested his head against it, his necklace clanging against the wood like a bell tolling. He closed his eyes, clenched his fists, and trudged back to the car with his head down, even though no one else was around.

Jareth headed home in silence.

In his peripheral vision he saw an SUV pacing him on his left. The blast of a horn shook him. The SUV barked three more times before he turned his head. He saw three young men staring at him and couldn't help but lock eyes for a moment with the smiling one in the passenger seat.

"I can see inside your mind, asshole!" Something jammed into the space behind his eyes, burrowing through his memories with a force and intent he couldn't resist. An image of the men in a room, laughing at the idea of raping minds, like their new-found ability was something they'd been waiting for all their lives.

He sped up, queasy now, but they followed.

They must have seen Gina in his head. Maybe they were hoping for an introduction. He'd almost passed the next exit when he mashed the brakes and swung hard right while the SUV shot past, the guy's grinning head lolling out the window like a dog.

At home, he flung himself on the couch and flipped on the television. News stations were back on the air. An aerial view from a helicopter over Washington, D.C. showed scores of people rioting and looting. Flames erupted from buildings. An anchorman, eyes kept carefully out of frame by the camera's tilt, described the carnage. He reported the same devastation in other American cities. The flush of the anchorman's cheeks distracted Jareth, and for some reason he wondered if the makeup crew had overdone it, or if they'd quit and it was just the man's own raw emotion showing through. Then he wondered if the effect even happened over TV, whether they were just playing it safe—after all, he could still *hear* the anchor and nothing was happening—and found he couldn't blame them if they were.

On another channel the President was addressing the nation in a prerecorded statement. He urged citizens to remain calm, and promised that the government would find a solution to the inexplicable situation. He told people to wear hats, visors, anything to keep from looking directly at each other and exacerbating the hysteria. To stay indoors if possible. To keep off the roads. To wait for further advice. He suggested texting instead of calling. He said that while the emergency services were overburdened, they were already working hard to find ways of doing their jobs despite the phenomenon. He pleaded for those who could, and those employed in critical industries supplying food, power, or other vital services, not to abandon work, to keep the economy from failing and the country from collapsing. He reiterated that America wasn't alone, that the event was worldwide, and that the country would stay in a state of emergency until the current mania diminished.

Jareth had enough food for a few days if he stretched it. Enough smokes for two if he didn't cut down. If it meant he could stay hunkered indoors until the world was sane again it'd have to do. He meandered toward his bedroom, lit one of his precious cigarettes, and pulled out his guitar. He half-heartedly strummed a few songs, let the nicotine buzz spread through him, and tried not to think about Gina or the shape of the future.

A month since he'd last seen her. Jareth sat in the car, flicking his necklace against the empty soda can in his hand while he stared at Gina's front door, willing himself to get out. It made a sound like pennies falling out of someone's pocket.

A month.

It had to be over by now—she would have been in touch otherwise, wouldn't she?—but he still didn't know why, and it didn't deserve to have been left the way it had, hanging loose in all the early panic. With what they'd seen in each other's heads left unexplored and unforgiven. Maybe they could still get past it. Maybe it wasn't all lost. It could be good between them again. Even though it had taken him weeks to build up the courage to go see her, the final step was still a hard one.

He knocked on her door. She wore a purple visor when she answered it this time. "Hi, Jareth."

"Hi."

"Come in."

He wondered whether he should have come, feeling like he was here to ask her for a loan he couldn't repay.

"I haven't seen anyone if that's what you're wondering," she said when she sat down.

"I was wondering about us. Is there an us?"

"I don't think there can be, not now."

He looked down at her feet. Brown suede boots on the fluffy carpet.

"How are your parents?" he said.

"They're done," she said. "So many couples didn't make it. Seeing what the other person truly thinks, their deepest secrets, I'm not surprised." She sighed.

"You remember Rob and Jenny?" he said. "They didn't break up. They wear visors now, of course, but they weathered the storm."

"Great for them." She moved her feet. "I hear it's all casual sex for most people now. No ties. No drama."

He laughed. "Yeah, I've heard the same. Like being at college."

"Makes sense," she said, "considering how hard it is to have a real relationship now when nothing's private."

"Julie from work set up an agency. 'TruDate.' They have these speed-dating sessions where sign-ups intentionally look each other in the eye so they can figure out if they're compatible, or if the other person's a liar or worse."

"Oh my God," she exclaimed. "I could never do that. That's dangerous. I'm not strong enough."

"She's run a couple evenings already. Apparently pretty popular with the right type of person once they get over the sensation of it. Keeps everyone honest."

She crossed one leg over the other. "You know, it's one thing for someone to see different shades of who I am. The happy me, or the sad me, or the angry me. But it's another thing for someone to see inside of me."

"I don't know," he said. "Maybe it's something you can manage in time. Hey, think how many arguments it could solve... "

She shook her head. "It's like my mind is completely bare. Now I have to worry that someone could see the real me. The naked me. And for that person to be someone who has the power to break my heart, it's the scariest thing in the world. That's why I can't be with you, or anyone else. Not now."

"I'm sorry—"

"I don't care what you were thinking or what I was thinking. But you've seen inside me, Jareth. Just the fact that you've been in my mind—it's more than I can bear."

"I understand," he said after a while. He couldn't, no matter how much he'd have liked to, come up with a counter argument, something to persuade her otherwise, that she could trust him and that it didn't have to be over. But it was. "I guess I should go."

"Take care of yourself, Jareth."

"Goodbye."

When Jareth reached Rachel's house she offered him a beer, and they both sat in her living room, not looking at one another. The habit came easily now.

"How's work?" he asked, breaking the quiet. "You went back, right?"

"Yeah, but it's so different. Everyone has visors now. It's all emails. It feels so empty. Lots of people haven't come back yet. They're recruiting, but that's something else."

"People who can hold eye contact?"

She leaned forward. "How did you know?"

"Customer at the restaurant I was talking to yesterday. One of the few we've got. He's a cop. They're trying to identify officers who can do the same thing, look at a suspect without giving away too many of their own thoughts and without freaking out at the mental contact. Could revolutionize investigation, he reckoned, once people get used to it."

"Huh. That's a mess of lawsuits waiting to happen."

He grinned, wondering as he did if she even saw him, and pulled out his phone to read the text on the photo he'd taken. "Funny you should say that. I saw my first billboard on the way over. 'Are your 4ᵗʰ Amendment rights being abused? Don't let a cop look you in the eye without contacting us first—Jeffrey & Dermichael.' There's nothing on Earth faster than a lawyer with a niche to exploit."

Rachel laughed. "They've got a point, though. The first time evidence derived from reading a suspect's mind comes to court it's going to be argued over for months. You can't go fishing in someone else's mind on a whim."

"Your company's trying the same."

"The opposite, and strictly voluntary. We're looking at the commercial side. Trying to train people to focus on business only, to allow clients to see the truth behind an offer and buy in confidence without giving away that you think they're a jerk or that you can't wait to go home and get laid."

"'Eye Contact Approved'?"

"Something like that. I'm not sure how they'll get past seeing the client's thoughts as well. They'll have to figure something out. The world's got to keep turning. We can't wall ourselves off from each other forever."

"Tell me about it. We've put screens across the tables at head height at work, but not many want to come and eat in public. We sell take-out now as well. That does a whole lot better. A lot of shut-ins out there now. Still, if half the staff weren't already gone, I don't know if I'd still have a job." He raised his bottle in toast. "At least Tom's gone. Died in one of the riots before the cops figured out how to keep order without having to eyeball everyone. Prick. How's Matt?"

"Okay. As okay as can be. We're getting by." She swallowed some beer. "So many families have fallen apart."

"I guess it's traumatic to find out what someone truly thinks about you. Even when you love someone there's always something in the background."

"Even the few seconds you and I had looking at each other was too much for me. Not that you had any terrible thoughts about me, but just you being there made me sick. I'm glad we didn't see anything neither of us wanted to."

"Me, too. It was like if you saw me naked, but worse." He took a healthy swig. The bubbles fizzed until the beer settled.

"Gina?" she said, voice softer.

"All over."

"There'll be someone else. Someday. Things will get better, right?"

He tried a smile. "The world's got to keep turning."

Later, as Jareth stood by his window and lit a cigarette to take the edge off what he knew would be another hangover come morning, he rolled Rachel's words around his head. The silver of his necklace reflected in the glass and winked at him. There were a couple of people waiting at the bus stop down the street, heads down, visors on. None them had turned on their fellow citizens or gone mad from the shock of it all. Life was returning to normal, sure, it was just that the rules had changed. You had to keep your guard up, protect your naked self, but it also kept you honest, for fear a stray glance would show you to be a liar. People would exploit it or block it or find ways around it because that's what people always did, but the world would never be what it had been before. They knew now, unequivocally, that they all shared the same fears and guarded the same secrets. What made them vulnerable also made them equal. And sooner or later he'd find someone able to handle the new nature of things. He'd put Gina behind him and move on, and he hoped she would too.

"Things will get better," he said, looking his own reflection straight in the eye.

About the story

A few years ago on July 4th a friend of mine was telling a story about a girl he'd just met. A group of us listened, and very quickly it became clear that he was embellishing much of the detail. We all gave each other sly glances, but no one called him out on it. I thought if only I could read his mind to see what really happened. Then, out of the blue, maybe it was the alcohol, the question hit me, "What if he could read my mind, too?" I would know what really happened between him and the girl, and he would know that I knew.

The idea stayed with me mostly because it wasn't the typical telepathy story where one person has the gift and no one else does. And it spawned a ton of questions. What would the world be like if everyone could read each other's minds? Would we go crazy and kill each other? I thought that would be too easy of an answer. Could we learn to live like that, and how would society adapt? Once I started coming up with my own answers to that question the idea eventually developed into, "The Naked Me."

A question for the author

Q: If you could have a meal with a character from any classic novel, whom would you choose?

A: One of my favorite classical characters has always been Victor Frankenstein. He dared to uncover the secret of life, a mystery humankind will forever wish to know, and actually succeeded. During the meal I'd ask him if he would do the experiment again, and what he might do differently considering the previous tragedy.

About the author

N. Immanuel Velez lives in Virginia, and when he isn't writing or crunching numbers he spends most of his time with his wife and two daughters.

N. Immanuel Velez's story "The Naked Me" was published in
Metaphorosis on Friday, 17 February 2017.

Chambers of the Heart

B. Morris Allen

Despair and Ecstasy are the simplest. Ecstasy is the small and cozy room of a cottage that looks out on a broad meadow in the forest. In the spring, elk come to posture and to mate, and the wildflowers bloom on every side. In the fall, mist dances in silver swirls framed by gold and bronze and copper trees. It is always spring or fall.

Despair is a vast, dark hall of low ceilings and small windows. In winter, snowdrifts sometimes cover the windows so that they are only squares of gray against black stone. In the summer, shafts of hot, bright light do nothing to warm the room, and only blind us to the room's darkness, so that we must carry candles to the Master's hard throne. It is always winter or summer.

Ecstasy and Despair are the simplest chambers, and the worst, and they are where the Master spends his time.

Today, though, I am pleased to find him in the low hall of Longing. He sits by the fire, a book spread open on one leg, his eyes on the soft river of cloud beyond the window, and the shining peaks in the distance.

"Sunset is beautiful," he says. "The way it paints the snow of distant mountains with ..."

"With crimson?" I suggest. It is always sunset in the hall of Longing, but our Master is no poet.

"With crimson." He sighs, and raises his book. "The poet Lanoy said that 'the sun's bright ardor brings a blush and a glow to the earth's shy breasts'. It sounds better in Clanetian, but I fear Lanoy was a man desperately in need of a lover. He should not have become a monk." He puts the book back down. I have never seen him read it.

"*Would* that I had a lover," the Master says. His latest has just left him. I can see one fist clenching, the fingers working deep furrows in his thigh. I go to stand beside him, as if my presence could deflect him from his course.

"Please, Master," I beg. "Don't go again into Despair." He has spent the past weeks in that dark hall, slumped in its hard stone chair, punishing himself and us. Better Ecstasy than that.

"No," he says, and his grip relaxes. I imagine the welts beneath his cotton trousers, the bruises they will leave. "I must distract myself," he says. "I will go to the theater. I will talk, I will laugh, I will smile." He gazes out again, across the blushing peaks. "And yet, I wish I had someone to laugh with. Someone to smile at. Ah, well. We cannot have all we want."

He is safe now, I think, and I go to prepare a meal. I will find him again in the hall of Longing, or in some byway near it, perhaps, in an alcove of Yearning, or a gallery of Ache.

As I climb the narrow backstairs, I pass other servants, all quiet and intent on their errands, as I am on mine. We seldom speak, and I do not know their names. As I pass behind the walls of Satisfaction, my foot slips, and a chambermaid reaches out to catch me. I draw my hand away, ashamed, but she is as old as I, and there is no pity in her gaze. Her hair is gray, like the clouds of Longing, and as I look upon it her eyes widen. I wonder what she sees. I open my mouth to speak, but then I turn away. I am an old man now. In my youth, I kept my passions in check, until they left me for other, wilder spirits. The maid and I go our ways in silence.

I eat my meal in silence, in the warm staff kitchen, at the little table that is always set. With the Master lost in the ways of Distraction, I have time. I watch the cooks as they do their quiet work. One stirs a pot of stew — a tasty concoction of roots and sharp spices. He jokes quietly with a flour-handed baker stoking her oven. It warms my soul to see them. The young so often waste their youth, and I have myself for an example. These two are wiser now than I ever was. They are shy to have an audience, but I see their looks, hear their soft laughter, and I rise to leave them be.

I make my leisurely way down toward Longing, but though I have gone slowly, the Master is not here. I wait for some time, and even make the long descent to Despair, but he is not there, though I search its darkness with careful steps, quartering back and forth with my dim candle across its obsidian floor.

I climb the steep stairs back from Despair, but Longing is bare, and I do not hear or feel him near. I know what this must mean, and I am tempted to stop, to rest, to wait. To fail. But I have served the Master all my life; it is my life. My duty will not cease because I am tired or selfish.

I climb the long, gentle ramp from Longing to Fulfillment, passing through and past rooms of Relaxation and Relief. I wonder idly, as I pass through Tranquility and Quietude, whether the old chamber maid cleans these rooms, whether some day we will pass again in one chamber or another. Perhaps we have often done so.

The Master is not in Fulfillment, but I knew that, and though it is the most beautiful of chambers, I pass through its moonlit wooden chairs, with barely a glance through the windows to its quiet dawn-flecked lake. No, the Master was in Longing, and he has gone out to company. If he has not returned to Longing or to Despair, there is only one place he can be, and I pass on.

The Master stands by the wood-framed window of Ecstasy, his narrow frame bathed in sweat, a smile across his face like the rictus of lockjaw.

"Oh, but the world is a beautiful place," he says to the wildflower bouquets of spring. "The colors, the rush of life, the flow of nature's grace." He shakes his head, but his smile is fixed, and no mere shake will dislodge it. "What have I done, I wonder, to deserve such happiness?"

That way lies Despair, and I know, with the certainty of experience, that this interlude of Ecstasy will be a brief one. "Do not say that, Master. You, as no other, deserve happiness." I try, but I know he will not listen, cannot listen to other than the voices in his head that tell him otherwise.

"He is so beautiful," he says. "A dancer, lithe as a willow, strong as an oak. He could pick me up with one strong hand. He did so!"

"You are a lucky man, Master. And strong in ways that he is not." I know he does not listen.

"What could he see in me, I wonder?" As he speaks, he wipes himself with a soft towel, leaves it to dry on the arm of a chair. The chambermaids will find it. "A frail reed with little to offer. A poor artist. A dreadful poet with the voice of a crow." He is already on his way to the door.

"A good man," I insist, though the tears have already started in my eyes. "A hard worker, and a kind master." Doomed to bounce endlessly from Despair to Ecstasy and back, and only because he is not strong or handsome or, in fact, very wise. But he is gentle and caring and honest, and someday, if he can only muster confidence, he will find a man who values that.

Now, though, I can hear him in the passage. "It is no wonder he has not come to call," he says, and then his voice fades, and I must rush to follow. The Master has his own ways, fast and sure and painful, but I can only scurry and stumble through the long halls and stairs and byways toward Despair.

In the narrow path of Desperation, I run headlong into the old chambermaid. She catches me again before we both fall. "You must not make this a habit," I say, and am shocked to find such wit in my dry mouth. But my courage fails as she drops my arm, and I realize that my tongue has failed me, that in so many dour and taciturn years, it has lost the knack for banter, has rendered my poor jest harsh and bitter.

My face settles back into its familiar, comfortable lines, all angles and ridges. I see the shine in her eyes vanish, but it lingers in the soft silver bird's nest of her hair, and I grasp for something to say. "I am Akro," I say. "The Master's Ear."

"I know," she says, and moonlight glimmers in the windowless passage. "I am Lucy." And she rushes away.

It is as well, for the Master needs me, and I must scamper on my way, but even in these dark lower stairs and alcoves, my heart is light. For once, Despair holds no dread for me, and I walk with a quick step toward the Master's cold throne.

"He has not called on me," he says at once. "And he has been seen at the Berry Wreath with Lord Consany — half my age, and broad as an ox. But no brighter." He turns his eyes toward the glare of a summer window, and the light shows the tracks of tears down his face.

"You are intelligent, Master," I say, because it is true. There is no sign that he has heard me. There is never a sign. "And gracious, and thoughtful."

He looks out the window to the burning sun beyond, and out of habit, I warn him not to look, to mind his eyes.

He wipes a hand over his eyes, smearing the shadows he painted there to make his pale eyes luminous and rich. "I will never be happy," he says, and begins to sob. It is my task to listen, not to speak. I have spent my life listening.

"Not if you act like a child," I say, and wonder how my tongue, earlier so cold and clumsy, has suddenly become so sharp. "You are a good man, Master, but you seek what you will never find. You eat rich foods and complain of belly pain. You contest at sports you cannot win. You love young men who want only to play." You talk with those who cannot hear.

"What is this?" The Master has a card in his hand. "He has come!" He throws himself from his chair, and I hear his laughter dwindling as he makes his rapid way to Ecstasy.

I set my foot on the stair from Despair, to follow, to listen, to be my Master's Ear, as I always have been, as I always will be. And yet, I wonder as I climb the dark steps, whether the Master might be better served by absence, whether, without a willing Ear, he might be forced to listen for himself, and whether, doing so, he might hear something.

As I pass through the low hall of Longing, I gaze across its sun-lit mountain peaks and remember youth. I turn away from the window's rosy lure, and climb the long, gentle ramp. I will wander the hallways above until I see the glint of bright eyes and silver hair. Then, if she is willing, we will enter my favorite chamber, and stand together in the gentle light of dawn.

About the story

I have a very minor heart condition. Confirming its nature required a day wearing a heart monitor, which naturally had me thinking about the heart and its chambers. I wondered what life in those chambers might be like if they were neither biological nor purely metaphorical, but actual physical places. The opening line came quickly after that, and with just a little tweaking to decide on seasons and views, the main elements were in place. Because the heart is an actual building, there are of course other, more minor passageways. The building, of course, reflects its master's mood – it's a hard climb to Ecstasy, and a quick slide down to Despair. I soon had the idea that the master inhabits the rooms, but that he never clearly interacts with his servants, and that his dialogue with his principal servant could just as well be a monologue.

It's a somewhat odd piece, but I had fun with it, and it emerged fairly quickly. I liked the ending's focus on fulfillment rather than the master's constant, fruitless chase of ecstasy.

www.BMorrisAllen.com, @BmorrisAllen

B. Morris Allen's story "Chambers of the Heart" was published in *Metaphorosis* on Friday, 24 February 2017.

March

Just Five Minutes

George Allen Miller

"Can I get five for fifteen?" an old man said.

Jerome looked up from the sidewalk and into the old man's eyes. Junior was a local; he'd grown up two houses down the street, though he didn't live there anymore. He usually slept in the alley behind Tenth Street, beside a dumpster. His wrinkled face, half covered with patches of gray beard, held a mix of sadness and pain, just like every other long time resident of the neighborhood.

"Five for twenty, man," Jerome said. He sat on concrete steps that led to his aunt's home, a hundred year old brick row house with a half-caved in roof and lead paint coating the windows and walls.

"I ain't got twenty," Junior said.

Jerome shrugged. "Not my problem."

Across the street, a young white couple, two of the gentrifiers boldly stealing the neighborhood, pushed a double-seat stroller down the sidewalk. Jerome could hear them talking about their renovated home with its new granite counters and designer appliances. Their house had belonged to a veteran of World War II. He'd been evicted when he couldn't afford the rising taxes.

Jerome wondered what living in air conditioning was like. Fixing up his aunt's home was a long time dream, but one that Jerome didn't think would ever happen.

"I'll be back, you gonna be here?" Junior said.

Jerome nodded.

The sound of metal slamming into metal filled the neighborhood with the regular beat of gentrification. Construction crews, already building the next condo building, had started slamming steel girders into the ground to hold up the walls of dirt they would soon create. Not long after the building was finished, another two hundred young professionals would flood the area and demand fancy restaurants and high priced gourmet super markets that neither Jerome, nor any of his family, could afford.

"Excuse me," a woman said.

Jerome turned and recognized the woman as a neighbor. She was maybe just over twenty-five and looked at him with contempt and anger, as if to say he was the one trespassing. Like Jerome didn't belong anywhere near her home. Had her grandmother been born in the house on Eighth Street? Had her brother been shot on the corner two blocks down? Had her family been living here for a hundred years?

"Yeah?" Jerome said.

"What are you doing?" she said.

Jerome shrugged. "Sittin'."

"Are you selling drugs here? This is where my children live," the woman said. She stomped her foot on the ground as if making her stand, as if saying she wouldn't tolerate bad behavior.

"No," Jerome said.

"Yes, you are. And you need to stop it or I'm calling the police."

Jerome looked into her eyes. White, young, on top of the world, making more money in a year then he'd see in his life, taking over the neighborhood he and his friends called home. And still, she was pretty stupid. People still got shot around here for less. Someone had gotten stabbed on a bus for stepping on a girl's foot just last month. And here was this neighbor thinking she was going to change the world, one black man at a time. Jerome tried his best not to laugh.

"Not sellin drugs, miss." Jerome held up a patch with the number five written on the back.

The woman stepped back, her eyes darting between Jerome and the patch. "Is that what you're selling? Some kind of patch laced with heroin?"

"Naw, nothin' like that."

"Then what is it?" the woman said.

Jerome shrugged. "Don't know. My cousin went to college, real smart. He made them."

"Well, whatever it is, you can't sell it here, it's illegal. I'm calling the police."

"Wait, miss. It's not a drug and it's not illegal." Jerome peeled off the back of the patch and held it up for her. "See, ain't no drugs on this. Can't get high from a patch, miss."

"You need to leave my neighborhood, ok?" She turned to walk back to her house.

Her neighborhood? Sudden and quick anger bubbled up inside Jerome. This was his neighborhood, and his father's, and all of his friends', long before she even knew the place existed. He stood and placed the patch on her exposed shoulder. The woman spun around, her face twisted in confusion and then rage, her hands rising in defense. After a moment, a smile grew on her face and she spun in a wide circle.

"What happened? Where's the trash? The sky is so blue," She said. She looked back down to Jerome and screamed. "What happened to you? You're white!"

Jerome half-laughed, nodded, and sat back down on his aunt's steps, his anger giving way to humor and contempt. "Like I said, my cousin's real smart. He made this so it would show you what you want to see, so the world doesn't look so bad, for five minutes' worth anyway. That's the trick, miss. People wouldn't do so much drugs, wouldn't be so sad, if they had a little hope. This just gives them a little hope."

She stared at him, even after the patch wore off, even after he had sat back down. Eventually, she turned and walked back to her house. She'd probably call the police anyway and tell them it was battery, or drug dealing, or whatever else she wanted to say. Cops would believe her. Besides, maybe it was all of those things.

Jerome peeled another patch and placed it on his arm, and let himself remember the neighborhood with his friends playing stickball in the street and running into the alleys to light firecrackers. He smiled and laughed, for just five minutes anyway.

About the story

This story started as a writing prompt in an online class run by The Brainery and taught by Jerome Stueart. The prompt was to write about your city. Gentrification is tearing through DC and changing the city in drastic ways. This story evolved from my experiences with gentrifiers and families that have lived in my neighborhood their entire lives.

A question for the author

Q: Aliens. Are they out there?

A: In short, yes. Scientifically speaking, we have proof that water and organic compounds exist in space. We have a growing body of evidence that planets are plentiful and that they do exist in the habitable zone of solar systems. Which means life is almost a certainty. If life exists, there's no reason to think technologically advanced life wouldn't also exist. I think the one dimension not spoken of in the Fermi Paracox is time. Life has existed on earth for four billion years and in all that time a technologically advanced species has only risen on the Earth once and only in the last 100 years. If we add a time dimension to the Fermi Paradox, I think it answers the question quite nicely of where is everyone. They either have already existed or have not yet evolved. If you add to the Fermi paradox the odds to have developed technology *and* managed to do so in the same 100-200 years that Humanity has, the millions of alien species that should exist are so spread out over time that their odds of crossing another species are likely pretty remote. We also have no idea of the longevity of a technologically advanced species.

About the author

George lives in Washington DC with his loving wife, mandarin-speaking kids, naked-foot-biting cat and elderly dog. When not writing he spends his time losing chess games, taking acting classes and working in the software industry.

www.georgeallenmiller.com, @G_Miller

George Allen Miller's story "Just Five Minutes" was published in *Metaphorosis* on Friday, 3 March 2017.

The Lost Heirs of Rose McAlder

Kate Lechler

When Rose McAlder died at eighty-five, it took us all of an hour to congregate on her property, rubbing our hands and stamping our feet against the October chill.

We hadn't known it was she who had lived in the big old house on the corner of Seventh and Price all those years. When the news broke that morning—not only was Norbury's local recluse dead, but she also happened to be a famous author—we poked camera lenses into brittle thickets of hydrangea to see inside basement windows, smeared our noses on the glass-paned double doors, and rooted around in the shed. What did we imagine we'd find: family photos? Handwritten journals? Uncashed royalty checks? We weren't sure ourselves, but we knew it had to be there. A scrap, a clue, some insight into the genius who had hidden, nameless, among us for decades.

See, Rose McAlder's seven bestsellers had been some of the most important works in the twentieth century. And—not that we Vermonters are the sort to be impressed by public opinion—they had changed the face of American literature. Critics compared *Miranda's War* to Tolstoy, a sweeping historical drama with a doomed romance at its heart. *Arthur Bradley Goes to the Moon,* an avant-garde science fiction novel, was Vonnegut's inspiration for *Slaughterhouse Five.* And *Je Suis Sharon* was domestic realism that, *The New York Times* stated, had set the standard for "introspection without indulgence." But McAlder hadn't published a word since *Maxwell Lives!,* a Newbery Honor-winner that came out when she was fifty-one. And we wanted to know why.

Why had she lived alone in our town for sixty years? What had inspired her books? And what stopped her writing over thirty years earlier?

But we found no unpublished manuscripts hidden in the hydrangeas or peeping from beneath the welcome mat. The only slightly titillating find was seventeen hoary copies of *Juggs* piled on the gardener's workbench.

Dolores Camp, the postmistress, checked windows to see if they were cracked, while Tom Steadman jiggled doorknobs. Missus DeLoitte, whose family had lived in the big old house for a time in her youth, looked hungrily at the second-floor balcony, reminiscing about being seventeen and spry enough to climb lattice-work in the dark.

"What had you been doing, that you needed to climb out your window at night?" Sylvia Chittenden, the church organist, muttered. She stared down the long slope of the tree-lined lawn to Seventh Street, where her husband, Jonas, loitered as the look-out.

"Oh, nothing," giggled Missus DeLoitte, shoving her hands deeper into the recesses of her tweed overcoat. "Nothing at all."

But everything was locked as tight as it had been when McAlder was alive. No one but her lawyer had a key to the house. When he arrived in his sleek black Lincoln, he marched to the front door, let himself in, and shut it behind him. Click went our cameras. Click went the door. And we collectively raised our eyebrows, pursed our lips, and went back to minding our own business.

"She may well have been a genius—I never read her books, myself—but she never made herself too friendly," remarked Barbara, Tom's wife, as we huffed back to the center of town to commiserate over coffee in the lobby of the Hartfield Hotel.

For a month after her death, the news was filled with McAlder's praise. The USPS issued a stamp. The literati quoted her constantly. Celebrities tweeted about how reading her works had inspired them to act, sing, play football, or become television chefs. Tourists began to flock to Norbury to pay homage to Rose McAlder.

Except for Lucy at the five-and-dime, who turned a pretty penny on homemade Christmas ornaments with McAlder's face on them, Norbury stolidly ignored the attention. "If she didn't want to be one of us," Jonas Chittenden said, "why should we act as though we have a special claim to her now?"

On the heels of honoring her legacy came the speculation. In the few phone interviews she granted in the mid-70s, McAlder had been charismatic, even charming about art, writing, the life of the mind. But she kept her anonymity close. Now that McAlder's identity was public, journalists found correlations between her early life and her book *Simone,* an erotic novella that told the story of a lesbian finding herself in Jazz Age Brooklyn.

Reporters hounded us, calling on our home phones during dinner time, asking questions to which we had no answers: Was McAlder herself a lesbian? Or did she see marriage, and indeed love itself, as a patriarchal trap, as depicted in her standout Broadway play, *What's the Deal with Dahlia?* Had she been abused as a child? Or was she, like most successful female novelists, secretly a man?

We did not justify impertinent queries with responses.

Three months after her death, the tell-alls erupted from old schoolmates and next-door-neighbors from McAlder's childhood in Connecticut. A second cousin wrote a misty-eyed book about what it was like growing up with "Rosie," painting her as a fun-loving imp with a penchant for the outdoors. But we dismissed this tender concoction wholesale, agreeing, in the words of her gardener, Gregory Totts, that whoever Rose McAlder had been, she was "*certainly* not one for making mudpies."

It was at this point that Alphronsia Gallagher-Burton came forward to a prominent tabloid with a new theory—and evidence. A native Norburian, she had moved away to Burlington when she was in her teens. But her father, Martin Gallagher, had been the town doctor for decades. On his deathbed, Alphronsia reported, he told his daughter that he had secretly helped the town recluse give birth. Not once, but seven times, and each out of wedlock, he was sure. The first six were all stillborn. The seventh and final child was born alive, but with a weak heart. "The last thing I saw as I left the house," he said, his voice quavering, "was her cooing to him, cradling that sweet baby in her arms."

At the time, Alphronsia had dismissed the story as the ranting of a man in the grip of senility. But once McAlder died, Alphronsia searched through her father's files and found records of the births, signed R.M. Furthermore, she realized that each of the births predated the publication of one of McAlder's books by about a year. "Could it be," she posited, eating up the media attention, "that her books were written out of post-partum depression and grief?"

We surreptitiously bought copies of the magazine, hiding them inside coats and bags.

No one in Norbury had known about the children. But then, we hadn't known anything about McAlder either. She lived in hermitical solitude: groceries delivered and all house-calls turned away at the door. Alphronsia's hypothesis about the one living child was that he'd eventually been given up for adoption. Her explanation to the press was simple and condescending: "In a town as provincial as Norbury, illegitimate children are a blight on a woman's character."

At which we sniffed and muttered to each other about the corrupting influence of the big city.

After Alphronsia's story was published, an Internet campaign was launched to find "the lost child of Rose McAlder." Several dozen people, adopted as toddlers and without clue to their parentage, took DNA tests but no relation was ever found (although two orphaned brothers, separated at birth, met, struck up a relationship, and realized that they disliked each other intensely). Soon, however, a controversy about leash laws in national parks began to dominate public discourse and the conspiracies around the lost heir of Rose

McAlder began to die down—we hoped for good. It was early spring and we didn't want anything to distract from maple syrup season.

The big house on the corner was eventually sold to Tom Steadman, who took out a large mortgage. He was Norbury's best contractor and reckoned he could make a mint turning it into an upscale resort catering to the fall-color tourists. He began renovations right away, starting with the peeling paint on the wooden siding. When he began the final phase, finishing the basement—which did not even have a poured cement floor—he found the secret we'd all been so eager for.

The digging had unearthed seven small coffins, most only a foot and a half long. Each was home to a carefully arranged collection of tiny bones covered in dried flower petals. Sylvia Jones had to look away from one skeleton, with a locket twined around its fingers. At another coffin, Rev. Robinson pulled a dusty velvet ribbon from a delicate wrist. The largest of the coffins, about three feet long, lay under the northeast basement window, looking out onto a bank of ferns. The crabbed fingers of the inhabitant clutched a stuffed bear, and its skull was missing all its teeth.

At the bottom of each coffin, peeking from beneath the skeletons, a handwritten manuscript was discovered. They were first drafts of McAlder's seven books, written in rusty ink on crumbling paper. Each book was bound in leather as fine as a newborn lamb, but badly tanned, as though it had been done by an amateur. Barbara stroked the smooth skin with a gentle finger, then recoiled, shuddering.

"What is that?" asked Tom, lifting a silky braided cord that formed the clasp of one of the books.

Missus DeLoitte peered close, then straightened, eyes wide behind her glasses.

"Hair."

Tom set the book down as quickly as he could without dropping it.

The book from the largest coffin was different. Instead of a featureless cover, its cover was studded with baby teeth, like twenty tiny irregular pearls, ornamenting out the title: *Maxwell Lives.*

Sylvia gasped, looking around the room. "Do you think ..." she started, then bit her lip, shaking her head. "Losing a child is a terrible thing. To lose seven, one after another, when you're all alone ..."

"People do powerful strange things in the grip of grief," Rev. Robinson nodded.

We could have written our own bestselling novel about that discovery, or sold photos to any national publication. But that wasn't our way. We covered those coffins up and, a week later, Tom had leveled the ground over them, poured a solid concrete floor, and installed several large screen TVs. He rented the space to the

Presbyterian film club on alternating Tuesday evenings. And we did our best to forget what had been found in the basement ... except for Dolores, who had the same comment every time a tourist mentioned the mystery of McAlder's missing child.

"Her books were her children," she said. "That's all there is to it."

About the story

The first was my own thoughts about having children. For now, I'm happy living the kid-free life, investing in the kids of my friends and in my own creative work. I once told my husband "my books will be my children." Once I said it out loud, though, I thought about all the grotesque meanings that phrase could have.

The second was a house in my town of Oxford, MS. The Ammadelle house, built in 1859, is a gorgeous, spooky old house at the end of a row of gorgeous, spooky old homes. When I first moved to Oxford, it was occupied by an elderly woman who soon passed away. The house sat empty for a year or two and I loved to walk by it at night, peering through the wrought iron fence that surrounds the property, imagining what was inside. I couldn't see it without thinking of "A Rose for Emily" (which Faulkner, an Oxford boy himself, wrote about another house in Oxford) and the genre of Southern Gothic in general.

But Southern Gothic, done right, needs to intentionally tangle with the ghosts of slavery and of the Confederacy. And for this story, I wanted to write about other things. The relation between motherhood and creativity. The sexual double-standard. The urge to canonize—and capitalize on—our literary heroes (an effort I'm familiar with in the figure of Faulkner, whose grave I can almost view from my front porch). So I set it in small-town Vermont, among a lot of stolid, insular New Englanders who have a very clear idea of what it means, and doesn't mean, to be part of their town.

A question for the author

Q: How has your writing evolved over time?

A: I didn't start out as a fiction writer; I was an academic writer first, but realized while I was writing my dissertation that I hated it. When I started writing fiction—bad fiction, like most baby writers!—it was still immensely easier and more pleasurable than writing literary criticism. Over time I've gained confidence, both in my ability as a fiction writer and in the process itself. When I don't have an answer to a problem a story poses, instead of panicking, I trust that it will reveal itself ... and that writing more, rather than getting stymied, will probably show me what I need to know. Drafting fast and ugly, tidying it up in round two, and then getting lots and lots of feedback has been the key (for me) to telling the story I mean to tell.

About the author

Kate Lechler is an outgoing introvert who teaches British literature at the University of Mississippi in Oxford, MS, where she lives with her husband, a dog, a cat, and seven fish. When she's not at school, you can find her haunting her favorite bookstore, Square Books, or sitting on a lawn chair in her carport, writing about genetically-engineered unicorns and dragons.

katelechler.com, @katelechler

Kate Lechler's story "The Lost Heirs of Rose McAlder" was published in *Metaphorosis* on Friday, 10 March 2017.

Bad News from the Future

Angus Cervantes

"If you're really my future self," I said, "convince me."

"Because stopping time isn't convincing."

"I believe you have a time machine. Prove you're *me*." I tried again to straighten my head. "If you're me, you know how."

He smiled, sort of, anxious lines softening around his mouth. Would I become this sour-faced man? "And I know you've thought this through. Three secrets nobody knows."

"Now, only things I'd never tell any—"

"In the treefort with D'Arcy. What you threw in the library window. And that red-haired girl from choir."

"Ouch," I said. I wasn't talking, not exactly, but he could hear me. "Okay, I wish I'd forgotten those."

"Never did." He rubbed the purple scar across his forehead. Since I couldn't look out the windscreen of the van, I kept looking at him. At myself. I should smile more, or my two happy twins would grow up to be worried children. Smile more...parents have strange responsibilities.

"So," he said, "do you believe me now, or should I mention the red sports bag you hid—"

"You're me," I said, too loud, and he stopped. "So—huh. So we did it. We invented time travel—well then, listen, about the friction battery..."

"You stop working on that today," he said. "Just time travel, from now on. And it takes you ten more years."

"Wait," I said. "Should you tell me details like that? What about paradox? If I stop trying because I can't fail—if I do that, would I fail?"

He reached to touch the scar again, then lowered his hand with a jerk. "You won't fail, and you won't stop trying. As long as you believe me, you will keep trying." He glanced into the back seat, where the twins were safely buckled into their little seats.

"Believe you what?"

"It's complicated," he said, and took a deep breath. "Look, this is very bad news—"

"Oh, no," I said. Something went cold inside my belly, and I tried to close my eyes. They didn't move; I kept staring at his ugly, sad face. "Bad news from the future. What could possibly...?"

"You're having a car accident," he said, "The girls both die."

"No," I said. I couldn't breathe. I didn't have to breathe, in a frozen, unmoving moment stuck out of time, but I still needed air. "You can't let—we have a *time machine.*"

"I know we do. That's why I built it. Will build it."

"Ok," I said. "Got it. I'll stop the van. Switch off the—let me move —"

"It's too late," he said, and leaned back. "That bus there, behind me, it doesn't stop."

"No, look—" The bus' turn light was on. The driver's eyes were wide open. Wide, wide open. He looked helpless. Like he had just realized what was going to happen and couldn't do anything about it. "It's signalling."

"But it's not *stopping.* The front of this van shears right off, and I survive." He looked into the back seat. "But the girls *don't.*"

"So pull them out—" I started, then stopped. "Time machine. You could have come ten minutes ago, in the driveway."

"No, I couldn't. I can't change what seems to happen. The girls don't survive in this time. They don't."

"I'm turning the wheel," I said, and my voice was high—or whatever was making my voice in this timeless helpless moment. My arms didn't move, of course.

"Listen," he said. "This is what happens: they won't really die, because I'm taking them with me to the future."

My heart was still working. I heard it in my ears. Everything else was quiet and faded. "No," I said. "That won't work. Will it work?"

"It does work," he said. "And yes, I can prove it." He reached into his jacket for a picture, printed on a silver polymer, and he held it in front of my face. Ruthie and Jessie, maybe eight years old, longer in the face but so easy to recognize, so easy to love. They were running across a new backyard, laughing. A blurred adult figure after them, a dog. And the twins were happy. Alive.

The feeling—once I tried old-fashioned bungee jumping, and it was the same feeling: free-fall terror, then a sudden jerk and twist and you're flying. Now I was still helpless, but flying free, not falling. All the the terror and the weight of the world, gone, and all I wanted— knowing my children will survive.

I could die now.

No—I couldn't die. I had to invent a time machine, so I could come back, to here and now, with a scar on my face, and save them.

I stared out at the street, the stop sign I'd rolled through, the double-length bus unmoving on Fairfield Road. My mind started working. "Wait. The girls are three years old right now. If you do save them, they're still three. But how old are they in this picture? How did you even get this?"

"In the picture," he said, "they're eight. It's from us. From five years in my future, fifteen years in yours. Of course I need to know that the rescue will work, or what's the point of building the machine? My future self came back to my lab, where I was, and he brought me this."

I looked at the silver family picture again, and his grimy, split-nail fingers, holding it in front of my face, obscuring the bus that was about to destroy everything in my life. "Just the one picture? Nothing else at all?"

"A message, I guess. Information, really—for me mostly but also for you." He shifted to look at me more directly, and I noticed the deep lines around his eyes. "We're gonna die of a stroke."

"That's awful," I said. "No. Wait. How could he know, if he's still alive—"

"He, and you, and I, have all known since just this second," said my future self. "Time travel causes brutal compression waves in the blood. Even one trip is dangerous. More trips are like Russian roulette, adding bullets every time."

"I don't—" I said. "I don't quite get it." The shape of the rest of my life was just there, in front of me, and I could nearly understand it.

Then I did, the whole cascade, just as future self explained it to me, just when he didn't need to. "Future-future self," he said, "dies—died—in the lab, on the day you become me. The moment I invent the time machine, he appears in the lab, with blood coming out his ear. Holding this picture, for me to bring back to you today. He knows he'll die and he comes anyway."

"God," I said. "There's no choice in all this. He comes anyway, and he dies?"

"He was still warm when I left," said the world's first time traveller, to the man who would become him.

My future self was bumping around in the back, spreading some metallic net over the matching purple carseats. I was alone in the front, unmoving as ever, staring helplessly at the frozen bus. My nose was running and I couldn't wipe it. "I want to talk to them."

"You will," he said from behind me. "In ten years. You'll get them back, self." A pause. "It's worth it." His voice cracked. "Ready?"

"Wait," I said. I sniffed to clear my nose. It didn't do a thing. "Okay."

A deep violet light flared in the mirror, and I pressed backward in my seat, straight through the stop sign, ahead of the bus, which wasn't stopping, coming into the side passenger door, tires really do screech, the driver's mouth wide open now, squeezing his eyes—"No," I said. I hadn't caught up with the process of what would happen—with the *implications*.

From the back seat, a tiny thunderclap. I started to turn my head.

The sound of the crash was deep and surprisingly hollow, like kicking a cardboard box.

Then I was spinning away, still strapped in, the front of the van ripped off. In flashes as I whirled: the fuel-cell ruptured and a cloud of gas ballooning like a toy into the air, then trees, then the bus again, then a broad *whumph* and flames and a spinning fragment of—

I woke up with a heavy fireman kneeling on me, silhouetted against a pyramid of flame and black billowing smoke. "No," he was saying. "Stay the hell down, mister."

"My girls," I said. My forehead was numb, and wet. "In the van. Two children. Let me go," I said. "Please. Children, two carseats—". Then I stopped, and thought carefully. "Did you get my children out of the van?"

The fireman blinked twice, and his jaw tightened. "I don't know," he lied. "But stay down."

Ten years, the man said.

About the story

This story's creation was surprisingly literal. First it nearly happened, and then I thought about it happening, and wrote it down. I took a corner cavalierly and barely missed a significant car accident. I was horrified by how close I'd come to the most terrible consequences. I knew I'd never be careless again while driving my children, and how lucky I was that I learned that lesson without actual harm. What if I wasn't lucky? I would have learned the same lesson, at a much higher cost. I would want desperately to teach the lesson to my earlier self. Maybe I'd even be motivated enough to build a time machine just to teach the lesson. Parents have some pretty extraordinary motivation sometimes. But if I did go back in time, I would expect my past self to follow every instruction exactly. Yet if my future self appeared to me today, I'd be highly suspicious. Who's this know-it-all from the future? How does he know what my best choices are? Are they even choices, if there's really one best one? (Thanks Jack "Pak" Brennan) And from that confusion came the basic structure of this story. A final note: in "Bad News from the Future", the main character doesn't "have any agency", as they say today. That's not just bad writing; it's a comment on the nature of time travel and information. Also because he's trapped physically, mentally, and chronologically. Also, it's sometimes what a parent feels like. Also, I should drive more carefully.

A question for the author

Q: Do you often include children in your stories? What role do they play?

A: Yes, I do, very often, include children in my writing. I have two small daughters and when they came into the world, everything changed entirely. That change was a vast surprise to me, and probably the biggest event of my life. I think children evoke a completely non-rational principle that most everyone agrees on: we protect children. By "non-rational" I mean that there might sometimes be logical arguments for allowing children to be harmed ... but in those cases, logic can go jump in front of a train: we protect children. Should we risk the lives of ten adults to save one drowning child? Yes. And count me in. So children can represent a universal truth, a shared humanity, an absolute. These days, with post-modern post-everything uncertain, I find that certainty very comforting. Of course, children, about whom we care so much, are also dreadfully vulnerable, and I find that unsettling. Children evoke strong feelings. That's a useful role in writing.

About the author

Angus Cervantes is a West Coast writer with a keen sense of nostalgia and a blurry vision of the future. He is working on designing new tenses for when time travel will have to be-en invent.

Angus Cervantes's story "Bad News from the Future" was published in *Metaphorosis* on Friday, 17 March 2017.

Lake Oreyd

Damien Krsteski

The lake's still surface was a golden quilt. The churches which amassed along the shore over the centuries now had their fossilized features balanced between day and night. A most sacred moment. The eyestalks, V-shaped like the chalice from which the Savior had drunk her poison, framed the setting sun, the tails like the scepters with which she'd been prodded to trial facing the rising moon.

One intake of breath, the sun dipped down, pulling the moon up, and the alignment was broken.

The podvodnya sank; my ears popped as we descended, and looking out the thick, round window it seemed as if the lake's waters darkened in hue with each blink of the eye. When we neared the bottom some hours later, all was pitch black. The vessel's searchlight turned on to sweep below us.

Corroded broken pipes lay in the sediment, barnacled and covered with algae. Our podvodnya crawled the lake's bottom, much like benthic creatures of the past must have when they sought the source of God, tentacles sifting through silt, clawing at mud, chasing away eels which sparkled in the dark.

We could see only within that circle of pale light: our window to His underwater Kingdom.

TAPE A/0; ARCHIVED

Q: [garbled]

A: Woolsbnick College. On the first, second, and fourth expedition. I was slated to join the last one, too, but certain *academic* obligations kept me from doing so. Fortunately, as it turned out.

Q: [garbled]

A: Ah, apologies. Professor Vyktor Claude.

Q: [garbled]

Prof. Claude: That's a very personal question.

Q: [garbled]

Prof. Claude: Yes, I suppose it is relevant. Well. Why couldn't one believe in both? I've spent my entire life—not just academic life, mind you—reconciling my faith with science. And while it hasn't always been straightforward, I believe I've managed quite well thus far. My work in academia is an extension of my beliefs, you see, a study of the color and shape of the individual tiles making up our Universe. Science is the details. But then I pull back, and admire the mosaic. And that's my faith. So, yes, both.

Q: [garbled]

Prof. Claude: No, I don't think that makes me biased. I'm an academic first and foremost.

Q: [garbled]

Prof. Claude: It was a tragedy. I lost brothers and sisters down there, and it's an insult to their memory to so casually dismiss the expeditions as unsuccessful. One must look beyond the official records, peel away the dry facts on the surface to realize we didn't altogether fail to find something. Perhaps we failed to *define* that something. But down there we knew, may the Savior bless the souls of those now gone, we knew we felt it. Certainly those of us unblinded by bitter skepticism did. I kept a journal of my research which I may someday publish, primarily as a counterweight to that bland report released by the College, and perhaps people will accept the truth then.

Q: [garbled]

Prof. Claude: It's difficult to describe to somebody so obviously skeptical.

Q: [garbled]

Prof. Claude: You're right. I'm not here to disabuse you of your notions. [sighing] A presence. That's the simplest way to describe the feeling, even though that particular word, loaded and full of connotation, a cliché, really, doesn't do it justice. And before you even bring it up, yes, I do take into account underwater pressure, dizziness, claustrophobia, low levels of oxygen, anxiety, the hypnotic effect of the drone of the podvodnya sonar exacerbated by the syncing of our breathing. All those figure into the equation, as it were, and I still end up with the conviction that the particular presence we—that *I* felt, was a physical manifestation, and not something imagined, conjured out of fantasy.

Q: [garbled]

Prof. Claude: Glad to, but first, may I have a glass of tap water?

TAPE B/0; ARCHIVED

Q: [garbled]

A: Helmsman Petr, sir. I piloted the podvodnya on two of the five dives.

Q: [garbled]

Petr: Only as a replacement for the Master Helmsman, may the Savior cradle his soul in Her arms.

Q: [garbled]

Petr: Descent number two and descent number three.

Q: [garbled]

Petr: No, sir, didn't pay them much mind, truth be told. They had their faces stuck to the windows, fogging 'em up with their breath, and they scratched notes in their little pads. My eyes were on the path ahead. Hands never leaving the control levers.

Q: [garbled]

Petr: Like I said, mainly quiet. As you'd expect from learned types, professors.

Q: [garbled]

Petr: Sheets of rusted metal from old sunken vessels, broken pipes of sewage, silt, mud, the occasional fish here and there. I've been to the bottom dozens of times when training with the Master, and these two descents with the scholars weren't any different, I can assure you.

Q: [garbled]

Petr: Why, of course, sir. I loved him like a father. [pause] More than an employer, he was my mentor. [pause] And to think how much I still had to learn from him...

Q: [garbled]

Petr: That's all right. Thank you.

Q: [garbled]

Petr: No, we never spoke of clients, that'd be unprofessional. They weren't more than cargo to us, if you see what I mean. We pilot our vessel, we take passengers down, bring them back up. All there is to it. The Master never spoke of what went on in the podvodnya, and neither did I. At the end of the day, we got paid, that's all that mattered to us, that we'd a hot meal on our table.

Q: [garbled]

Petr: Of course. Will try, sir.

Fish swam into view in our light cone. Each a miracle of life, a proof of the versatility of the Creator and His blessed agile hands, but also a gift from this world to our Savior, the holy daughter who sacrificed Herself so we can enjoy our lives here.

The tentacles of the podvodnya cleared away corroded debris from our path. The boy helmsman, wet behind the ears but utterly focused on the task at hand, started when I put my hand on his shoulder.

"Here," I said, my finger on the topographical map of the lake's bottom. "We should be in this section by now. We can pause here."

He shot me a sidelong glance, as if questioning the gall of my dishing out orders in his vessel, then he blinked, and his expression was that of a naïve child again. "Of course, sir."

The area was part of a bay around which many of those gigantic molluscs had gathered to slake their thirst. I gazed into the dark waters, enthralled. Innards grumbling, the podvodnya crawled to a stop. I recited a short prayer (my two colleagues indulging me with silence) and pulled the plunger set into the curved wall of the pod, slowly drawing out the one liter of water from the lake I needed for studies.

The boy watched us intently while my colleagues fiddled with their instruments, performing their own studies, and while I marveled at the murky view.

When we surfaced, we emerged from one darkness only to plunge into another: night had fallen, and starlight rippled around the buoyed vessel. The boy helmsman switched off the main engine, and popped the top-hatch; I climbed half-way out of it to help paddle to shore. As if sailing over the heavens themselves, I was rearranging constellations with each dip of my oar.

On the shingled beach, the boy started to service his podvodnya, and my colleagues broke into a livid discussion on the aquatic life— and incongruity thereof—we'd just witnessed. Quietly, I walked up to one of the churches, preserved forever perched with its beak dipped in the lake.

Its mother-of-pearl shell was coated with creamy starlight, the preserved ommatophores sticking out of it. I caressed the hollow shell with the tips of my fingers. I could sense the thrum of the wind inside it. The tremor spread into my hand, arm, torso, and legs, and my knees buckled. I crawled through the opening into the shell of the animal, into holy ground, and prayed in whispers.

TAPE C/0; ARCHIVED
    Q: [garbled]
    A: Professor Perevana, Woolsbnick College, Department of Natural Sciences.
    Q: [garbled]
    Prof. Perevana: I joined the rotating cast of researchers from Woolsbnick, once. Went down on the very first expedition. The helmsman was a burly, bearded man. Poor soul.
    Q: [garbled]

Prof. Perevana: I don't think I recall—oh, you refer to the helmsman's apprentice, perhaps? Now that you brought it up, I do remember a young boy milling around at the dock.

Q: [garbled]

Prof. Perevana: Once proved enough for me.

Q: [garbled]

Prof. Perevana: Because God is not to be found lurking in the depths of some lake. There's nothing there but mud and rusted iron.

Q: [garbled]

Prof. Perevana: My colleague's *theories*? No, I've heard no *theorizing* from him, I'm sorry to say, only posturing. He's a blowhard interested only in himself, his own fame and fortune.

Q: [garbled]

Prof. Perevana: Wasn't I clear enough? Of course I don't believe him. Neither him nor any of the other endemic-religiosity quote-unquote researchers. I've been opposing Oreyd creationist myths my entire career. That's why I signed up for this expedition, why I went down. To shut those nutters up once and for all, to have an ace up my sleeve: *Yes, I went down there, and saw nothing preternatural, and nothing was unearthed, and nothing ever will be.* The skeptics are always right, remember that. Professor Claude is a clown with an agenda.

Q: [garbled]

Prof. Perevana: Feel free to leaf through my section of the official Woolsbnick report.

TAPE A/1; ARCHIVED

Q: [garbled]

Prof. Claude: Yes, let's talk about the churches. [sipping water]

Q: [garbled]

Prof. Claude: I'm sorry but I see no contradiction. Like I said before, I am a scholar first, conciliator of faith and science second. I accept scientific findings, and see how they can be superimposed over my view of the world. Fit into the mosaic, to return to my earlier analogy. So, I say the fact these churches are of biological origin does not make them any less divine. Those creatures, whose anatomy resembles our most holy of symbols, were drawn to Lake Oreyd, miles away from the southern mangroves, despite an abundance of drinking water from lakes and rivers near their initial habitat. No one in their right mind can chalk that up to chance; it took me a while to understand, but it was a pilgrimage, pure and simple.

Q: [garbled]

Prof. Claude: Papers have been published claiming either way. But based on recent fossil dating techniques, these creatures lived around 255 S. E. The first symbols of our faith had already appeared —see the great archaeological work of Professors Swolia and Alynia, around Mynistiris—circa 100 S. E., so the chalices and the rulers' scepters appeared some 150 years prior, before our race had even set foot near any of these creatures' habitats.

Q: [garbled]

Prof. Claude: Absolutely. A simultaneous appearance of our Creator's symbols in our world, half a continent apart.

Q: [garbled]

Prof. Claude: There seems to be a certain connection between us, these creature-churches, and the lake. A symbiosis. It is my belief the link *itself* is of divine nature, yet another intricate puzzle our Creator has set up for us to attempt to solve. We always try these puzzles, and always end up with a small but crucial piece missing.

Q: [garbled]

Prof. Claude: No, I see that as the Creator's sense of humor. [laughter] A way to show us there still remains joy in this world.

TAPE C/1; ARCHIVED

Prof. Perevana: Humans have imitated nature since time immemorial, we derive symbols from natural occurrences, recognize patterns where there are none. The quote-unquote churches are the remains of an extinct species (*nautilus giganteus superior*) that used to feed in the lake, most probably on the endemic trout (*salmo letnica*), now also extinct. Our ancestors must have been drawn to these magnificent shells, and their fossilized eyestalks and tails, and fashioned religious symbols out of them.

Q: [garbled]

Prof. Perevana: Many species migrate for one reason or another. These creatures might have shared the fertile land around Mynistiris with the early human settlers before being driven away by hunters; or humans might have traveled south to explore warmer climates and encountered the beasts there. In my opinion there's a higher probability of beasts and humans coexisting long enough for early hominids to derive religious symbols from the animals' appearance, than this ridiculous story of spontaneous manifestation of the Creator.

Q: [garbled]

Prof. Perevana: Yes, probability, possibility, *may* be, *could* be. That's the key difference. Our camp avoids speaking in absolutes.

Laboratory examinations of the lake's water proved inconclusive. Apart from plankton already studied and cataloged by scholars fifty years before, no further microscopic life was found. Could there exist life even more minuscule than what our apparatus can see? Or should I discard biology altogether, and trust my instinct, my belief that this water itself is of divine provenance, regardless of what microbiota swirl within it?

No, my belief is my belief, but it won't silence the skeptics. Further experiments need to be performed.

Electrolysis, and spectroscopy, and its effect on physical materials, and administration to living tissue.

TAPE B/1; ARCHIVED

 Q: [garbled]

 Petr: Thank you. Good to see you too, sir.

 Q: [garbled]

 Petr: Yes, I suppose that's how these things happen. Out of grief, I'd just ... didn't want to think...

 Q: [garbled]

 Petr: Some water would be great.

 Q: [garbled]

 Petr: The other day I was at the cabin by the lake, you know, from where we ran our business. Went through the equipment, checking, re-checking ropes, pipes, pulleys and levers, the diving logs again—

 Q: [garbled]

 Petr: No, everything was in its place. It's just—holding the Master's tools again, his pencil, his yellow scratch-pad diving log, it made—it made me remember things that'd slipped my mind, sir. I mean, truth be told, I don't know whether it's important, or relevant to your investigation, but last time you said to let you know if anything came back. Anything whatsoever. Regardless of how unconnected it might seem. Well, holding my Master's tools like so, I remembered the night before the last dive. [pause] How he was up all night.

 Q: [garbled]

 Petr: The night prior to, yes. Which was unusual, he always slept soundly. I sleep in the room next to his, and on this night, I remember hearing his bed creaking as he'd get up and then lie back down, hearing him pace his room, open and close desk drawers, the clinking of tools, even. They woke me up throughout the night, those sounds coming from his room, but I'd cover my head with the pillow, each time, and go back to sleep.

 Q: [garbled]

 Petr: No, just in his room.

 Q: [garbled]

Petr: The vessel seemed to be in good condition. So far as I know. Normally, I help him check it myself before each dive. Another pair of eyes, he always said. But this morning he seemed uninterested in my assistance. I did a sort of cursory glance inspection, so to speak. Then he said everything was all right, I'd better get back to cleaning the storeroom.

Q: [garbled]

Petr: I know it's not much, but you said anything, and this came to mind...

Q: [garbled]

Petr: Well, who knows? I'm going to take a breather, first. Clear out my head. But then, I suppose, I'm going to keep running the shop. I owe it to the Master's memory, if nothing else.

I held the last drops of the lake sample in a vial in my hand. Pale blue water swirled in it, a piece of the depths, of the dark of the lake now brought to light in my laboratory. In my hand.

Into my pocket.

I hurried home.

Enough of this. The machines have declared no difference exists between holy water and what comes out the faucet, but that's to be expected, because machines don't have the eyes to see the Creator.

One more crucial test remains, a test whose results cannot be jotted down in numeric symbols. The test of subjectivity.

TAPE A/2; ARCHIVED

Q: [garbled]

Prof. Claude: Well, she can insult me as much as she wishes, but same goes for her, don't you think? Milla Perevana built a career out of trying to dismantle our arguments. She, too, has something at stake. She's not the impartial observer she portrays herself as.

Q: [garbled]

Prof. Claude: No, we avoid each other skillfully at Woolsbnick. Our paths cross only in scholarly journals, taking shots at one another from opposite thematic sections. [laughter]

Q: [garbled]

Prof. Claude: Yes, let's go back to that.

Q: [garbled]

Prof. Claude: Well, tell me, have you ever set foot in one?

Q: [garbled]

Prof. Claude: There's a hum that envelops you, and you sit down in the middle of the shell, breathe in, breathe out. You can hear your pulse. But gradually, as you calm down, the hum becomes a whisper, morphing into a speech consisting of your inner thoughts, and you breathe in, breathe out, and listen to what you're thinking. The Creator speaks to you, through you, then. It's a beautiful experience. You learn about yourself.

Q: [garbled]

Prof. Claude: That I feel... Look. Can I tell you a story? Tape won't run out? All right. When I first started going to church, one particular memory seemed to resonate in that shell. When I was a kid my mother would sometimes read to me at bedtime from this book, *Stories from the City in the Mirror*. Not often, but some nights. Nights when my grandfather was out and it was late and we wanted to keep each other company. We wouldn't speak of him: I never asked where he was, she pretended not to care. It was our ritual. She'd read, I'd listen, and we'd try not to think of what would happen when he returned. One particularly rainy night, she read to me, and I remember the drone of her voice—I could hear it in the hum of the church—and the rain lashing against my bedroom window as if in waves, at the mercy of the wind. From the hallway came the sound of key turning in lock, of our heavy oak door opening—being thrown open—before slamming shut. A tremor passed through the walls. My mother stopped reading to listen to her father's footsteps, mentally charting his stumble through the house. When the footsteps neared my bedroom, she shut the book, and got out. Throughout the clamor that ensued I had my eyes glued to my little bedroom window, at the pale starlight smeared onto the pane by blotches of rain. A while later, she returned. I tried not to look at her face. She placed the book in her lap again, and picked up the story where she'd left off. Growing up, I've been telling myself stories were her way of getting away from everything, keeping his looming presence and the crushing agony of our poverty out of her mind. Childishly protected, almost, in that fairytale bubble we shared. But the Creator's voice, distinct in the hum in His church, made me reconsider my interpretation of events, and memories returned to me of her focus, her verve, the cadence of her reading voice. No, it wasn't a perfunctory act. To say her reading was an escape would demean the act. She was there because she felt an obligation to the stories, an obligation magnified by those bursts of unkindness of which she'd been on the receiving end her whole life, and storytelling was *really* sacred to her, one of the last sacred things, a way to preserve some kind of balance. She must've believed what I myself believe now, that all stories are windows into one big, eternal Story, a Story that screams to be told, even to a frightened, bedwetting child who wouldn't remember a single word come morning.

Q: [garbled]

Prof. Claude: When you're told a story, you experience a created world, a world in which everything has purpose. Characters say words for a reason, sunbeams caress the faces of pretty women, kings rule over kingdoms, and peasants revolt; there exists a beginning, a middle, an end. A plot drives the actions of the protagonists of the tales; there is a reason for the telling, a moral to be derived at the end. When one believes in the Creator, one applies those same principles to this world we inhabit. Every individual moment happens because it's been slated to happen, every monad is placed where it ought to be. Our world has a beginning, a middle, an end. It has a plot, and a reason for being.

Q: [garbled]

Prof. Claude: Life means something, don't you agree?

I am sitting on the beach. I write this as it happens. Important details could be lost, and it's crucial I note down everything.

I drank the water less than an hour ago. When I did, I felt like vomiting, but I chalk that up to nerves. It tasted fresh, still cold. I felt as if drinking our Creator's essence.

The sky won't give up its darkness. The lake is calm, ready to accept us once again into its depths. Dawn is moments away. The city still sleeps behind the hill.

I sit, and wait.

TAPE C/2; ARCHIVED

Q: [garbled]

Prof. Perevana: One could easily whip oneself into a frenzy, especially if one has the predilection to believe in one's own mysticism.

Q: [garbled]

Prof. Perevana: Papers have been published by colleagues of mine, which you can read through, studying the so-called *self-delusion effect:* it appears in children who've suffered trauma, supplanting painful childhood memories with made-up stories; in dying patients who see visions of dead relatives; in sleep-deprived people hallucinating scenarios where they—

Q: [garbled]

Prof. Perevana: Point being, *seeing* things, *having visions,* is not medically mysterious. It's quite common. Keep in mind, the subject might be dead certain the hallucinated events had transpired—they might not necessarily be lying.

Q: [garbled]

Prof. Perevana: I'm not accusing anybody of anything. Citing research is all I'm doing.

Q: [garbled]

Prof. Perevana: Look. [pause] Understand, it's far from innocuous what they're doing, diverting precious College funds from vital research and into expeditions to prove their ... *fantasy.* There's nothing personal here.

Q: [garbled]

Prof. Perevana: Not necessarily *my* research, but more important, scholarly work. Lives could be saved if those funds are funneled into, say, medical studies.

Black gives way to violet gives way to blue. The lake's surface brightens, reminding me of that emergence from the depths, that coming back into the world. The lake is a womb, our each resurfacing a rebirth.

A light breeze picks up.

The churches around me glimmer with the light of a sun still unseen. Their nacreous shells catch color. Catch the first rays of sunshine, as the sun quietly rises.

I breathe slowly, contemplating my work. Tingling in my legs. Like spiders crawling all over my skin. Tingling becomes a burst of electricity that grips me. Excitement courses through me, and I begin to laugh, laughing hard and loud, because I realize—how stupid I'd been to think otherwise—I realize the machines were right all along.

Yes, there is no difference between faucet and lake water. Of course. They are both one and the same—holy water, touched by our Creator, drunk by our Savior, by all of us.

The world is starting to spin around me. Waves on the lake. Surf, nibbling on the shingled shore. The ground beneath me gives way, I feel unsteady, as if on a buoy.

These churches, creatures, their thirst for this lake's water was a pilgrimage, not for the contents of what they'd lapped up on these shores, but because every step is a pilgrimage and every movement a celebration of life. All of us, searching, we're nothing but pilgrims.

A noise. From further down the beach. The cabin.

Clanging of metal. Voices. The sky is radiant with light and I'm sprawled on my back.

I'm dizzy. It's hard to write. But I must. I will.

The voices, a noise two-fold. Two figures on the shore. They're gauzy shadows. Can't make them out. They're talking. God and Goddess.

Creator, show me what my eyes ought to see, whisper to me what my ears must hear. The world spins faster.

I get up and hide behind a church. My heart is racing.

My hand trembles when I hold the pencil. Must not pause. I press my cheek against the cold hard shell of the church, and it soothes me.

God and His Daughter, the Creator and the Savior, caressing the podvodnya, blessing it with their touch. I just threw up. Nerves, getting worse. Hard to see. Harder to hear. Surf, wind, pulse pounding in my ears. Must focus and write.

They don't notice me watching them.

Home. Decided to go home.

I stumble homeward, making brief pauses to catch my breath, throw up, and write this down. The world's no longer spinning as much.

In my home now after a long walk. A quiet apartment, no humming.

Welcoming this new day drained, empty of fluids. Calmer. My body has expelled all skepticism. Exhausted. Must sleep now.

Will write more tomorrow. Am shaking.

The Creator has spared me. There's nothing more to it.

I was trembling in my blanket in the afternoon when Professor Colym came to see me. He was relieved to the point of tears I was there, sick in my house, and not on the expedition. He informed me of the accident.

They'd just dredged it out, he said, the podvodnya. Crushed from the pressure like a tin can under a boulder. A crack on the outer hull, some overlooked structural weakness, the politsiya had relayed to Colym. Their bodies ruined, a paste of bone and gore. The merry faces of our colleagues came to me, and we both cried for them.

When he left I stopped crying. I was confused. The beach, the shapes on the beach, my vision. The Creator and the Savior took care of me.

They'd taken those poor souls in Their embrace, but chased me away from the beach, keeping me away from that dive, leaving me on this world a while longer to spread Their Story.

Prof. Claude: How do you know I was on the beach that morning?

Q: [garbled]

Prof. Claude: Who gave you the permission to read my diary? Who let you in my office? Was it the Dean? That idiot always favored—

Q: [garbled]

Prof. Claude: Okay. Okay. I'm calm, I'm calm.

Q: [garbled]

Prof. Claude: What are you on about? I did not witness—I know what I saw there. Certainly not Milla Perevana and that boy.

Q: [garbled]

Prof. Claude: ...

Q: [garbled]

Prof. Claude: For—for manslaughter? You've got to be joking. You're arresting them for manslaughter? Sabotage—? I never would've thought. *Unbelievable!*

I went back to Lake Oreyd this morning.

Walking along the shore made my heart pound, I felt as if at an unknown place, my eyes drinking in the scene, yet the old lake was washing up on the old beach, impersonal as ever.

Beautiful as ever.

I made my way around the churches to the water.

I gazed across the shimmering surface, dipped my fingers in the cold water, and smiled.

We were shaking hands goodbye, because the lake is gone, with that enigma in its cold depths begging to be studied and solved. Another lake has taken its place, a deep blue tile in this new mosaic of the world where each part is as great as the sum of all, and that one was shaking hands with me, too, its gentle waves lapping at my fingers, saying hello.

About the story

The relationship between faith and science interests me as a social phenomenon: I won't deny I've enjoyed following the rhetorical tug-of-war, rooting from the sidelines for one camp, then, in equal measure and in eager anticipation, for their opponent, scrambling in the ensuing fray for every nutritional nugget of food-for-thought among the verbal chaff. But metaphysical debating aside, the subject attracts me on a more personal level, too, as somebody who's vacillated—been tossed, maybe?—between the two arguing parties, who's tried to play one against the other as a precocious child might play his divorcing parents, cozening from each separately what he couldn't from both together.

These two sides clash once more in the depths of Lake Oreyd. A subjective narrative from top to bottom, comprised of journal excerpts, interrogation tapes, hearsay and slander, a story in which every single character lies at least once (they are being interrogated, after all), a story set in a Universe almost-but-not-quite our own, sprinkled with clues and misdirection, was exactly the story I had to write to let these ideas play out.

And now that I have, and I read the story, again find myself where I've always been: on the side, watching characters argue, agreeing first with one, then, inevitably, with the other, and everything, including the confusion, makes perfect sense.

A question for the author

Q: From where you do you draw inspiration for your characters?

A: It really depends on the character and the story, but I believe I can narrow it down to three sources. Some characters are based on, or are composites of, people I know. With others the characterization comes from me, although in such cases I try to be very careful not to reduce them to mouthpieces for my own opinions or ideas: perhaps infuse the character with a trait of my own personality, make them react like I would in a similar situation, but then I'd veer right off, forcing our personalities to diverge. (Side-note: I especially enjoy writing in the first person about characters decidedly unlike myself.) The third situation is when another work of fiction affects me to the point where I think up characters in response, as if saying, "The kind of characters I like to read about would never do that." All that said, most of the time I feel like characterization just happens spontaneously, right then and there, when I'm writing the scene, or perhaps during the long walks beforehand. I may start off with an idea of what a character is broadly about, but the Aha! moments — when you truly understand why your character acted the way they did — come much later.

About the author

Damien Krsteski writes SF and develops software. Originally from Skopje, Macedonia, he now lives and works in Berlin, Germany. Updates about his fiction can be found on his blog or on Twitter.

monochromewish.blogspot.com, @monochromewish

Damien Krsteski's story "Lake Oreyd" was published in *Metaphorosis* on Friday, 24 March 2017.

Sundown on the Hill

Timothy Mudie

Judy wakes up in the middle of the night to an empty bed, but she knows exactly where Edward is. There's only one place he goes these days. As she lies there in the late summer heat, the sheet sticky on her legs, a fan blowing desultorily from an open window, she allows herself a moment to believe he might simply be making one of his many nightly trips to the bathroom. That he has gone to the kitchen for a glass of water. That she will pad from the bedroom down the hall and find him watching an old Western TV program with the volume turned down low and the closed captioning on. But the moment passes, and she climbs from bed, confirms that Edward is missing, slips on a pair of laceless sneakers, and retrieves her keys from the rack by the front door.

She pauses there, looking down at herself. Pajamas and sneakers. She could go back to bed. Edward is a grown man, her husband, someone who should be able to take care of himself. What is the worst that would happen if she left him to go on these jaunts alone? Some early morning jogger or birder stumbling across him and bringing him home just after sunrise. Judy opening the door to find Edward on the front step, embarrassed and shoeless. But she can't do that, can't turn him into some lost puppy. The thought flits from her mind quicker than a firefly's burst of light. Edward is her husband, and he is still here. She will help him as she can.

Outside, Judy is greeted by the chorus of crickets and other night insects. A whippoorwill chortles its familiar call in the distance. She adds her Chrysler's purring engine to the nighttime song.

The roads are clear as she drives out of the town proper and into the park, streetlights becoming sparser along the way. Though she has spent her life in this part of upstate New York, it always awes her how dark and still it is this late at night. Edward had moved here for just that reason, to be close to Sharp Hills State Park. She realizes that she has never seen this park in daylight, and doubts Edward has either. He decided to live here to be near the park, and what he wants in the park only exists in the night.

The park is closed to the public at this time, the lot empty as Judy pulls in, the moon the only light. She knows the paths well enough by now to walk them by memory. Edward expects to see more than moonlight up above, longs for it. Judy doesn't, but looks anyway. Confirms that the only light in the sky is natural.

She comes upon Edward in his usual spot, standing on the nearest hilltop, in the center of a small clearing. Hunched, his knees bent, but always standing. Tonight he wears a pair of khakis with a striped button-down and tie. Like he's heading to work, though they've both been retired for the past five years.

Looking upward, always looking upward, Edward doesn't notice Judy until she puts her hand on his shoulder. He starts, then gives her a sad smile.

"I thought tonight would be the night," he says. "No such luck, I guess."

The sun will be up soon. Already the horizon has begun to shift from black to gray. Judy takes her husband's hand and leads him down the hill, along the short path between ancient trees, back to the car. She puts him in the passenger seat, and gets behind the wheel.

"There was something about tonight," Edward says as she begins to drive home. "A feeling. I really thought they would come."

Judy pats his hand, takes it in her own, kisses his fingertips. "I know," she says. "But not tonight."

The first time Edward told her his story, he was hesitant, afraid she'd laugh, run off, tell him to lose her number. They had been dating about a year then, and in the years since, all forty-six and counting, she's heard the story so many times that she sometimes feels like she was there. Recent years have loosened Edward's tongue and now he'll tell anyone who will listen. Though these days, that's mostly Judy herself.

It started, of all places, at Woodstock. He and three friends drove up from Lackawanna, part of the small contingent that actually bought tickets ahead of time. Edward watched the first day, and was making his way back to the tent he was sharing with his buddy Roger after Joan Baez's set, a little after two in the morning. Slightly stoned, but mostly just wiped from a day in the heat, all of a sudden he was overcome by a powerful urge to leave, coupled with a clear vision of a hilltop surrounded by paper-white birch trees. Seemingly of their own volition, his feet led him away from the festival, away from the field and crowd. The commotion of laughter and debate and hushed love-making faded as he made his way toward the woods, then through them, following a tug in his brain like there was a hunk of magnetized metal in there, pulling him sharply forward. No one tried to stop him or even questioned him as he left.

Later, when he looked on a map, he learned that he'd walked for nearly seven miles, passing through working farms and fallow fields, over streams and train tracks. Eventually and suddenly, the fog over his brain lifted and he found himself on the top of tree-covered hill. A small circle was clear of foliage, and he stood there, his wits returning, beginning to panic about what he'd just done and how he'd get back. It would have had to be sometime around four in the morning if he walked at a good clip, but back then he was in fine shape and easily could cover that sort of ground in two hours. The night was cloudy, and just a hint of moonlight lit the area.

Until the UFO appeared. A bright flash of light and a bone-rattling hum. Branches snapped off of nearby trees, and maple leaves and pine needles floated to the ground like snow. Edward's body felt transmuted to something denser than flesh and yet lighter than air. Over the years, Judy has tried to imagine what this felt like, both rooted to the ground yet tugged skyward. She's not sure she will ever really know the feeling.

For a moment, the UFO hung above Edward's solid, static body, round and glowing, red and white lights blinking in an inscrutable rhythm. Then, like a cork from a bottle, Edward detached from the ground and shot up.

After that his memory gets hazy. Lying on a slab, bathed in light, surrounded by small gray beings with massive eyes and no mouths. But there's nothing painful in his recollections, no tests or probes, and he doesn't appreciate the jokes about that. What he remembers is a feeling of serenity, something approaching enlightenment. If the aliens had let him stay for just a bit longer, he thinks he might have transcended himself, become something more than merely human. Then there was an orange flash, and he was standing in the clearing, looking east at the first rays of morning. Eventually he gathered himself enough to wander to the nearest road and hitch back to Lackawanna.

When his friends got back themselves and asked where he'd gotten off to, Edward told them. He didn't think twice about it. Those days, there were a lot of out-there stories and beliefs circulating, and an alien abduction was hardly the craziest. Still, they laughed. He clammed up about it for a long time, but never stopped thinking about it.

The first time he shared all this with Judy was when she realized that he really and truly loved her. He proposed two weeks later, and of course she said yes.

Coffee tickles Judy's senses and draws her up from sleep later than usual the next morning. She hasn't used or needed an alarm in years. Most days, the days when Edward doesn't wake her with his nocturnal excursions, she wakes shortly after sun-up. Today, the sun is high and bright and hot, and Judy still feels she could sleep another two hours. But she gets up, steps into her slippers, and heads down the hall to the kitchen.

Edward sits at the kitchen table, a mug of coffee and the morning's paper in front of him, pen in hand and brow furrowed as he works his way through the crossword. He looks up as Judy enters. "Good morning." He stands to get her coffee, splashes in cream. Sheepish, not meeting her eye. Not an explicit apology, but after being together for this many years, Judy catches every nuance in his morning greeting, the gentleness with which he hands her the steaming mug.

"There were pine needles on the soles of my feet this morning," he says. "Thank you."

Judy sips her coffee, pats Edward on the elbow as she crosses around him, pulling a chair next to his own. He sits down next to her.

"Jaws," Judy says, pointing at the paper. "Nineteen down."

"Of course," Edward says as he pens it in. "Remember we saw that two days before going to the Cape for vacation? Not our best idea."

She laughs. "Definitely not."

Minutes pass, they drink coffee, fill in crossword boxes. A pleasant morning. More and more since they've retired, days seem to follow this pattern. That Judy wakes in the night, that Edward waits for aliens that may never come, that Judy tries to will herself to believe.

Judy won't bring it up. She doesn't anymore. There's no point.

"It seems crazy now," Edward finally says, his eyes on the puzzle. "When I'm out there, it makes so much sense, but in the light of day..."

She tries to put herself in his shoes, she really does. To want something so much, to feel that sort of compulsion. But she can't. She has what she wants.

"I just want you to be happy," she says softly. "I just want to make you happy."

"You do make me happy."

"I know." She looks into the dregs of her coffee. "Do you want a warm up?" She starts to stand, but stops when she feels Edward's hand on her hip.

"You make me happier than I've ever been. The... what happened to me is something I can't explain, the need to go to them. It's powerful. But I hope you know how important you are to me. More important than they could ever be."

"I know," Judy says. She smiles at him, gets them both more coffee. She's just a woman, one of billions. He's woken up with her countless times, slept next to her countless times, whispered and kissed and nuzzled. The aliens came only once and they changed his life. Why wouldn't he want to see them again?

Two nights in a row. Rare that Edward leaves two nights in the same week, let alone one right after the other. Judy cries when she reaches over and feels the empty space where her husband should be.

Slowly, she performs her routine check. Bathroom, living room, kitchen. All empty. She wipes her eyes, takes a deep breath, removes her keys from the ring, slips on her shoes.

When she opens the car door, the dome light pops on, and Judy jumps, practically has a heart attack. Sitting in the passenger seat, seatbelt already buckled, is Edward.

"Maybe you can come with me?" he says. "Maybe they'll take us both."

She doesn't laugh, doesn't shake her head disdainfully and try to coax him back to bed. She looks him up and down, his pleated navy blue pants, the business casual maroon polo shirt, the buffed brown shoes. She feels under-dressed.

Smiling for worrying about what she's wearing, Judy gets into the car. "Why not?" she says as she starts the engine. "Tonight could be the night."

Insects whirr and a breeze whistles through the fir trees. Moonlight dapples Judy and Edward as they stroll hand in hand down a dirt path to the hilltop. She's never really noticed how pretty it is here, how serene.

When they first stepped onto the path, Edward sped up, trying to tug her ahead, but Judy kept her pace steady, and Edward matched her. Now they walk like they did when they were first dating, like there's no destination. She wishes they could turn down one of the side paths, hike down some barely-marked trail, meander through the woods forever. But she lets Edward steer her until they reach the clearing. His clearing.

That looks different too, walking into it when it's empty. The stars twinkle above, the trees form a canopy that's almost a dome. Put together, it reminds her of when she visited the planetarium with her third grade class, how she looked up at the constellations dotting the ceiling as the guide pointed them out, outlines illuminating one by one.

"Which direction will they come from, do you think?" she asks, unaware that she planned to speak until after the words leave her lips. "Are they coming from a particular star?"

Edward beams. She's never asked him this question. "That one," he says, pointing to a constellation she doesn't recognize, an off-kilter box and swoop. "I think. I remember seeing it when they had me, and I got a warm feeling, a home feeling."

"That's a good way to feel," Judy says. Their hands detached at some point, but she takes his again. Together, they look up at the stars scattered like a child's toys.

Edward squeezes her hand. "I'm glad you're here."

She squeezes back. "Me too."

Under the wide and crowded sky, Judy and Edward stare upward and wait for the aliens to come back and take them away, to usher them into the future, to tell them the secrets of the universe.

About the story

This story first started germinating years ago when my father told me a story about his trip to Woodstock. As he tells it, one of the friends he went with had an epiphany partway through the festival, left, and joined a seminary. While I can't speak to the veracity of that story, something about someone leaving Woodstock for a mysterious reason spoke to me. Of course, since I write science fiction, in my head I immediately changed the epiphany from a religious one to something involving aliens. But while it was a fun idea, it wasn't a story, and so I tucked it away.

Years later, I had another idea for a story about a man who believes he was abducted by aliens when he was younger, and who yearned to be abducted again. Something clicked, and I realized that these two ideas could fit together into one story. Sadly, I have experience with family members who have suffered dementia and Alzheimer's, and it occurred to me that the confusion that goes along with those diseases could explain why Edward leaves in the middle of the night—and could add ambiguity about whether or not he was indeed abducted.

When I was a kid, I read a lot of "true story" books about alien abductions, and at the time I never questioned just why the accounts were always so similar. Is it because they were true and that was just the aliens' modus operandi? Or did one person spread a story and others latched onto it? In real life, I've got to go with the latter, but when it comes to Edward and this story, I'll leave that up to the reader.

A question for the author

Q: Do you prefer your SFF as books or movies?

A: While I love movies, I'm both a writer and an editor, so I pretty much have to say that I prefer books. And I really do! For a bunch of reasons. For one thing, they're much more cost-effective! Just compare how much time you spend enjoying a book versus a movie, and these days you can usually get a book for less than a movie ticket. Plus, I love how books let you get deeper into the characters, into the backstory, just deeper into the whole world. There are lots of great SFF movies out there, but it's the rare one that can compare to the book.

About the author

Timothy Mudie has never been to Woodstock or been abducted by aliens. He lives with his wife outside of Boston, where he works as an editor for a general interest publishing house.

Timothy Mudie's story "Sundown on the Hill" was published in *Metaphorosis* on Friday, 31 March 2017.

April

Scraps

Juliet Kemp

The bell jingled, and Emmeline looked, frowning, at the door through to the front of the shop. She was in the middle of a fitting, and one did not expect interruptions if one was being fitted for charmwear at Emmeline's. When a moment passed and Joe, her apprentice, did not appear around the corner, she smiled at Mme Gantiel.

"My apologies, Madame. Would you excuse me for just a moment?"

At least it was cheerful Mme Gantiel, rather than one of her fussier or more class-conscious clients. She'd never minded any of them, in the years since she'd taken over from Papa, but recently, she'd become more and more irritated by their self-absorption in their own tiny part of this one small city. There was more to the world that that. She sighed, transferred the pins in her hand to the pincushion at her waist, and went through to the shop front.

Charmwear was never ready-to-wear, so Emmeline had no stock on display, and she did not need to advertise to fill her client list. Thus the shop front was tiny, holding only her desk and appointments book, and just now it was almost all taken up by the guard captain who stood there. Outside stood a similarly large lieutenant. Well, that explained Joe's absence.

The guard nodded at her. "Captain Berrith. I need to inspect your premises, miss."

"My premises? What on earth for?"

"I need to inspect your premises, Miss."

She swallowed. "Well, this is a nuisance. I have a client now. Could you wait a few minutes until we finish?"

He nodded amicably, and made no move to wait in the street.

Emmeline got through the remainder of Mme Gantiel's fitting in record time. She was proud to notice that her hands weren't even shaking.

The inspection was anticlimactic. She didn't glance towards the hidden box, and they didn't find it. But they did rifle through every cupboard and drawer in her fitting room and workroom.

"What do you do with leftovers, miss? After you've cut a dress or whatever out?" Captain Berrith demanded abruptly.

Her stomach lurched, but she answered calmly, pasting on a slightly puzzled look.

"Large pieces can sometimes be used in another garment — those are stored here." Filed by charm and then by colour. "I keep a few smaller pieces, in the small boxes there, for trimmings as needed. To cover buttons and so on, you understand. Anything else goes into the bin in the corner," she nodded at it, "and is collected by the municipal dust-truck weekly."

As she was obliged to do; and the dustman was obliged to burn it. Couldn't let the plebia get their hands on charmcloth, not for their own use.

"Is there a problem?" she asked.

"Well now, miss," the lieutenant began chattily, then shut up at a glance from Captain Berrith.

"These labels here are accurate?" Captain Berrith asked, running his finger along the shelf edges. *Warmth, Beauty, Plausibility, Charm* — the charms of her trade. Hardly ones to interest the Guard.

"Of course." *And get your hands off them.*

Five minutes after they finally left, Joe reappeared via the back door.

"We had visitors while you were gone," she said.

"Did we?" he said, not meeting her eyes. She'd known for a while that Joe's spare time was spent in what he might call politicking, and the guard would definitely have called rebellion. She'd not mentioned it. They both had their secrets.

"Visitors looking for charm scraps, if I'm not mistaken. For someone sewing charm scraps."

Joe raised his eyebrows. "Rumour I heard was, they found some Happiness, all sewn together from bits. Some folk reckoned it was found on someone, and they're off to the clink now. Some folk said it was just dropped on the street."

"Do they suspect the Masquerade?" she asked. She hoped, desperately, that it had just been dropped, and no one with it at all.

"Most like," Joe said. "Masquerade gets blamed for everything, right?"

The Masquerade. The most popular rumour about the name was that they wore masks. Which would be foolish; masks drew attention, and the Masquerade preferred secrecy. More likely was that the name was a muddy reflection of the Guisers, the traders from over the mountain who brought charmcloth; the charmcloth that, in barely a decade, had turned a city of many porous layers into a city of two halves divided by an uncrossable chasm. The Masquerade's slogan was 'true equality'. Emmeline wasn't even sure what that would look like any more.

"Mm," she said, staring out of the window at another guard patrol. There were more and more guards, now.

She'd wondered if someone would notice the scraps, sooner or later, despite her efforts to hide them. She hadn't thought about what would happen.

The sensible thing would be to stop. The sensible thing would be to do as she always had before: keep her head down and be grateful for what she had.

"I imagine," she said, "that the Masquerade would love to be able to use charmcloth."

Out of the corner of her eye, she saw Joe stop moving. "Lots of people would love to be able to use charmcloth," he said. "Warmth, for one, this time of year. That bit of Happiness, I'm sure someone would hate to have lost that. If there was any truth in it, I mean."

They looked at each other for a moment. "I wonder," she said, "how one would go about finding the Masquerade. If one were so foolish as to want to."

It had begun with Memory, only a couple of moons ago. She didn't handle Memory often. Memory was for small things and keepsakes, a different kind of craft from hers. But Mme Ydrit, newly widowed, wanted a nightgown of Memory, to remember Mr Ydrit as she slept.

"I know it seems ridiculous," she said, dabbing at her eyes with an untidily-hemmed handkerchief of Solace that Emmeline recognised as coming from the funeral house, "but I'm sure you'll understand. You always make me such beautiful things, and I do want this to be beautiful."

As Emmeline sat and cut and sewed, she looked at the piled scraps of shimmering silver Memory, and her fingers slowed, until she put Mme Ydrit's nightgown aside. She picked up the scraps of Memory, and laid them out on her worktable.

She thought of her grandfather, stitching little pieces of cloth together; of a quilt on her childhood bed made with little pieces of Granny's skirt, Grandfather's apron, her aunt's baby blanket. She remembered her father sitting by her bed in the dim evening light, telling over the list of the pieces in a soothing drowsy drone. They'd lived down by the docks then, and Grandfather made workwear and in tough times mended sails. Emmeline used to gaze at the ships coming up and down the river, dreaming of boarding them and going to faraway lands.

Grandfather had taught her to sew, and later, Papa had taught her to tailor. By then they'd moved away from the docks. Papa's burgeoning tailoring business was doing well, and the well-to-do didn't want the smell of the docks in their nostrils when they stood to be measured. Emmeline still thought of the ships, and once she finished her apprenticeship, she had started putting coin aside to go away for her journeyman time. There were other cities, down the river or across the plains; other things to learn. Then Grandfather had died, and it didn't seem like the right time to leave Papa on his own.

It had been a year, maybe two, after that, when charmcloth had arrived, with the Guisers who had never come over the mountains before. It was expensive stuff, but oh, so much in demand, right from the start. Emmeline had just finished her journeyman time, and it seemed like a golden opportunity to specialise in something that the rich would pay through the nose for twice, first for the cloth and then for the tailoring. She'd had to use up her travelling money for the initial investment, but she'd known it would pay off, in the long run.

Then Papa in his turn had died, and suddenly she was the proprietor of a shop, with a solid reputation with this new material. She still wanted to travel, but she'd had to take an apprentice, Joe, to cover the workload; and then she felt a responsibility to see his training through. He would be done this time next year, though. By then she'd have enough saved to travel, to keep herself for a while, and then to set up somewhere else. Somewhere new. One more year. It could be worse.

It was the year of Papa's death that what had been purely a matter of money became a matter of law: charmcloth (in its limited quantities, one delivery per season) was only for the patria. The patria had barely existed as a separate group before then; an old name, dating back to an older, more divided society that the modern city felt it had (ha!) left behind. Certainly, some had more money than others, but money you could acquire, if you were lucky and worked hard. But once only the patria could use charmcloth, suddenly the city consisted of two halves: those with the charms, and those without. Folk from all parts of society still traded; but how could a trader without Luck compete with one who had it? Who could measure their honesty — or lack of it — against someone wearing an undershirt of Plausibility? Anyone could attend a dance, but lacking Beauty or Charm, your wooing would proceed less smoothly. Even in the army, where, notionally, officers were provided with Death and Destruction regardless of their backgrounds, why, having access to Strength or Authority beforehand eased your way to that gold braid on your shoulder.

Those with charmcloth found their expectations changing in ways such that those without it came up short, every time, in every way. And those with charmcloth were, more and more, the ones making those decisions.

Folk who couldn't buy it tried to work out how it was made, but without success, and those who tried to follow the Guisers on the way home came back with broken bones, or not at all.

Her grandfather wouldn't have trusted charmcloth, and Emmeline thought, now, that he would have had the right of it. She could still see his fingers clearly, holding scissors or chalk or pins; but the memory of his face was fading.

He'd done a little tailoring, her grandfather, but it was that patchwork quilt that she remembered best of his sewing. She looked down at the pieces of Memory on the table, then, slowly, began to move them around, trying them against one another, comparing the result with her memory of that quilt. She shouldn't use these scraps, of course. She should throw them out with the rest. But, perhaps, just this once... A keepsake, just a private one, for her grandfather's memory.

Her first attempt was sadly ragged, the lines of the charm running this way and that way, wriggling against one another. She sighed, and pulled the stitches out, and tried again. This time, she matched the scraps carefully, trimming edges, fitting the subtle lines of the charm back together. Her eyes prickled and her back ached as she sat into the night, sewing under the flicker of the gaslamp. It was past midnight by the time she was done. It looked right, the lines flowing smoothly; but with Memory you needed something to trigger it. She held the tiny bag open in her palm, took her grandfather's thimble out of her sewing box, and dropped it in.

The memories sprang to life inside her mind, reeling across it like pictures on a string, bright and new. After a few minutes, Emmeline put the bag carefully down, wiping tears from her cheeks. She tucked it inside a drawer. Tomorrow she'd make an outside, and a lining, to sandwich it between. It wouldn't do for the city's premier charm tailor to be caught with illegal cloth.

Her glance fell on the piles of trimmings from her attempts, and she shook her head slightly. Wasteful. Next time... Then she shook her head more sharply. There must not *be* a next time. She couldn't be caught using charmcloth for herself. Prison, public whipping, loss of livelihood...A fine. Her leaving money gone. No. Once was more than enough.

She'd sewn that little bag of Memory in the middle of the autumn. In the next weeks it grew colder, and the nights grew shorter. It didn't affect Emmeline, who would well afford firewood and a thick quilt. Not all her neighbours were as fortunate.

"You seen Granny Zeta today? I had some firewood for her yesterday. Told her it was scrap, but she still wouldn't take it. Too cold to be without firewood, tis."

Emmeline, picking out unbruised apples at the greengrocer, looked up. The speaker was Gareth, a young builder who lived around the corner.

The grocer shook his head. "Food or fuel, and sometimes neither. I hate this time of year."

Had it been that way when she was younger? Not as much, Emmeline was sure. There were more folk struggling, now; while the patria grew ever richer and more comfortable.

Home again with her apples, Emmeline turned over the scraps of Warmth that she'd just cut from the bolt in making Major Arad's new winter cloak. She didn't usually do menswear, but Major Arad was insistent that her cloaks were better than his regular tailor's. This year's cut was wildly fashionable; open across the front, it barely reached the wearer's hips. Made in wool it would leave the wearer freezing; in charmcloth, it didn't matter. Not enough merely to have the advantage; to be fashionable, one had to flaunt it. And what, she wondered savagely, would happen to the Major's old cloak, the one she had made for him only last year? Doubtless it would go in the disposal. The Granny Zetas of the city couldn't be permitted charmcloth of Warmth, even if it was last season's style.

Unbidden, her fingers were arranging the scraps alongside one another, turning them to fit together. She paused, suddenly unsure, then the wind whistled through the crack in the window and her chin went up. She pulled her bag of Memory out, seeking a clearer recollection of the patchwork caps Grandfather used to make from flannel. This, he would have approved of.

She sandwiched the Warmth, patched carefully together, between two layers of plain flannel, and took the cap to Granny Zeta the next morning.

"It's my grandfather's anniversary," she said awkwardly, wanting to make sure the old lady would accept the gift. "He used to make these, and I wanted to remember him, and I thought, maybe..."

Granny Zeta smiled at her, and took the cap. "I remember your grandfather too, dear. Thank you kindly, and I'll burn a candle for him tonight."

She put it on, and her face crinkled in pleasure. "Ooh, now, that is nice and warm. You've your grandfather's gift with a needle as well as his generous heart, dear. My thanks."

Emmeline sat for some time that evening, looking at the basket of scraps and thinking of Granny Zeta. There were too many Granny Zetas. But she could hardly help them all. Sooner or later, she'd be caught. But then — what if no one knew where they came from? There were plenty of charitable organisations, these days. An anonymous gift, a series of anonymous gifts, to a different organisation each time... Surely that way there could be no trouble.

Slowly, she reached for her pile of scraps, and began to pick out more pieces of Warmth. And then after that, maybe some Happiness. People could use that, this time of year. It felt a damn sight more useful than sewing pretty this-and-that for overbred ladies. The pretty this-and-that was putting pennies and pounds into her savings. This

— this would keep her busy, until she could leave. Less than a year, now.

She couldn't predict when she'd have scraps left over that she could use, and she couldn't allow them to be taken away every week; so as she tidied up every evening, a handful of pieces went into an old hatbox, hidden under a floorboard she'd prised up. When she had time, she sewed them up, as linings hidden within normal fabric, and dropped them off to one charity or another.

She told herself that it wouldn't go further; but she knew at the back of her mind that she wasn't telling the truth. The guards' visit, only another few weeks after that first cap for Granny Zeta, was only the final stitch in a decision already made. Working on her own she could do a little. Working with the Masquerade she could do more.

The trouble was, the charms the Masquerade wanted most were the ones that Emmeline found hardest to come by. Stealth, Patience, Secrecy, and their cousins. Not the stuff of high fashion that she most commonly dealt with, although the similarly-useful Concealment and Deception were both more popular in her work than one might think. She became ever more skilled at using the tiniest of pieces, sewing the scantest of seams. Every time she mastered a slightly more frugal technique, she went back through the scraps bag again, sorting out the tiniest of pieces from previous constructions. Each night another scarf or handkerchief or cap, its outer layers of patchworked flannel and cotton and linen concealing its inner secrets. She didn't give anything directly to Joe; she put each finished item in that hidden box, and she was careful not to see when he took it. After that first conversation the day the guards had visited, neither she nor Joe referred to the matter with word or gesture. She yawned more, in the daytimes; but it was worth it.

A while passed, and one day Joe was sweeping out the workroom, with heavy sighs and sideways glances at her. Emmeline sighed.

"What is it, Joe?" Time off, doubtless.

"Could I have a word? About something private?"

Her eyebrows flew up. "Of course." She glanced around, then beckoned him into the fitting room, which had no windows, and shut the door.

He looked down at his hands. "They wanted me to ask... They need something stronger."

He mimed, briefly, a pistol, aimed at the floor, and Emmeline blinked. Destruction. Death. Charms she'd never worked with, charms that the armorers near the river, closer to the city limits, used.

"I don't..." she started.

"They could — someone could get the makings for you," Joe said, still to his hands.

She swallowed. "It's not that." Her decision solidified as she spoke. "It's not — I won't. Not those." Not killing.

Joe nodded, his shoulders relaxing a bit. "I didn't think so. But they asked me to ask. I hope you don't mind…"

She shook her head, still thinking. She knew, of course, that the Masquerade weren't a bloodless group. She read the papers.

"I won't do that," she said. "But — protection. I could do more of that. If I had the makings."

After that, she started finding bags of extra scraps in the box. They didn't speak of it again, even when the news started talking of illegal charmwear and charmwork; even when the guards announced that charmworkers would have to hand their scraps and leftovers over to be destroyed; even when those bags of scraps began to be weighed against what had come into the shop. Emmeline sewed smaller and smaller. She found ways of secreting the tiniest of pieces away — there was always an error margin in the weighing — and the bags of extras kept appearing in the box, though they were smaller bags and smaller pieces now.

She changed, just a little, the design and style of the clothes she made; she used more thread-heavy stitching, more cutaways, more decorative furbelows that deceived the scales by compensating for the bits she cut out or the seams she sewed a touch more scantly. It was as well that the guards doing the weighing didn't understand tailoring.

And all the while she kept counting her savings. Soon. She'd be able to leave, soon; leave this wretched place behind.

The guard captain, standing in the front of Emmeline's shop, looked like a man with beautiful visions of promotion dancing in front of his eyes. Joe, held firmly by a private nearly twice his size, one eye puffing up and blackening, looked sick and scared and trying for defiant.

"It hangs together beautifully," the captain said to Joe. "You're an agent of these revolutionaries, you have access to leftovers, and you've seen your employer doing this kind of work."

"Nonsense," Emmeline said sharply. "He barely has the skill to thread a needle yet. He couldn't possibly have done this. It's excellent work, if not as good as my own."

She gestured at the dismembered handkerchief lying on the table.

"Well, miss, unless you're about to confess yourself, ha, I'm afraid I have to disagree with you," the captain said briskly.

Emmeline stared at him, envisaging herself confessing, being taken away in Joe's place, Joe set free.. Except of course Joe wouldn't be set free. The visions wound onwards. Both of them in chains, under question… She swallowed sickly.

"Well," she said weakly. "I am sure you are wrong, and I must deplore you depriving me of my assistant. I will be along later to check on him, and I will be speaking to my patron."

"You do that, miss," the guard captain said equably.

They dragged Joe out.

"I'm sure this can all be straightened out!" Emmeline called after them, willing her voice not to shake.

She waited a nervous half hour before she tied her cap on, hung a shopping bag on her arm, and set off. She'd made a scarf of Discovery last night, and Joe hadn't had a chance to take it this morning. That should help her find the place she needed. She could have used Concealment, too, but there was nothing to be done about that; she had no time to piece together the tiny handful of scraps hidden in the press.

But a woman of her age, drably dressed and carrying a shopping bag; she looked like she belonged here. That would be concealment enough. She walked like she knew where she was going and like it wasn't important at all, and she eyed the guards in the street with the right amount of caution. Wary, because who wasn't wary, down here, of the guard? But with no reason to hide from them.

She knew roughly where Joe spent his spare time. She was banking on finding the centre of the revolution close by. She was banking on there *being* a centre, and someone of authority she could talk to. When she reached the Bull and Cat, she tied the scarf more firmly around her neck, and fixed in her mind what she wanted to find. She concentrated on the feel of the scarf at her neck, and on where her instinct was telling her to go next. Although — if Discovery alone would do the trick, wouldn't the guards have found the people she was looking for long before now?

Well. It was this or nothing. Hand rubbing the corner of the scarf, she turned right from the corner of the pub, then left down an alley, cleaner than you might have expected round here. Left again at the end, then right into a courtyard, past what might be a heap of refuse and might be trying to become compost for the window-boxes growing green leafy vegetables, and up a wooden staircase to the second floor of the middle house. The staircase didn't creak underfoot; it didn't shake. The curtains in the second-floor window were thick enough to block out all but a sliver of light around the edge.

The door swung open before she could knock. Her stomach lurched. A girl of about Joe's age stood just inside, looked her up and down, then stepped back to let her in.

"Thanks, Hira. You'd best be off." The voice came from the far corner of the room, where a woman sat in a threadbare red armchair, her grey hair scraped back behind her ears. She was smoking tobacco wrapped in a twist of black paper, and from the ash scattered around her feet, she'd been there for a while. Emmeline had vaguely expected piles of papers or stacks of weapons, but there was nothing but the woman in the chair, a table with a pot of tea, and a fireplace. A long strip of parchment hung on the wall beside the table, with writing in the script of the city beyond the plains. A souvenir of this woman's travels? Emmeline felt a sharp stab of envy.

"You can call me Sally," the woman said. "And you're Emmeline. The charm patcher with moral scruples. We saw you coming, you know, 's why we let you in." She snorted. "We've got your patches, too, remember. And young folk with good eyesight."

"Joe," Emmeline said. "They've taken Joe."

"Yes," Sally said. "A sad thing, for certain, but nothing to be done."

"Why not?" Emmeline demanded.

"Cost too high. How many would it take to get him out? What would they do when they realised who took him? We can't take that risk for the rest."

"So you're just going to leave him?" Emmeline's stomach churned.

"Joe knew the rules." She looked at Emmeline for a moment, then offered, "He might get away with a flogging."

"And he might not." They'd been cracking down harder, or late.

"Like I say. He knew the risk." She looked at Emmeline. "Just like you choose your risks."

She held Emmeline's gaze for a moment, then looked away, drawing her attention inwards; an obvious dismissal. Emmeline stood for a moment, helpless and frustrated, then clenched her hands and turned to go. There was no help here.

"I'm glad you came, though," Sally said, as Emmeline reached the door.

Emmeline paused. "Yes?"

"Those charm-patches. You've made all the difference for us. I wanted to thank you."

If only that had done Joe any good.

"If you were to need somewhere to go," Sally said. "You know where we are."

"Just not if I were arrested," Emmeline said.

"No," Sally agreed. "Not for that."

Emmeline struggled with her thoughts, on her way back through the streets. She still agreed with the aims of the Masquerade, right enough. One part of the city throwing their wealth around while the rest scraped for pennies, that wasn't right. But the dull side of the mirror, where you abandoned a person for the sake of the cause, well...

It was too hard to swallow.

By the time she got back to the workshop, she had half of a plan in mind; and no time to do anything but hope that the rest appeared as she went along.

She worked quickly, cannibalising the row of hangers with completed or half-completed customer orders. She pulled down the gossamer-thin petticoat of Plausibility, designed to fit under Mlle Yara's Solstice ball gown. Emmeline had never managed to work Plausibility into a patch; it tore and frayed easily enough that sewing it straight from the bolt was a challenge. The petticoat would have been long on petite Mlle Yara; on Emmeline it came only to mid-calf, and a couple of rolls of the waistband brought it up enough to hide it under her outer skirt. She held it together with a chain of safety-pins, and kept rifling through the wardrobe.

Major Arad's undershirt of Luck, awaiting its buttons; the only piece of Luck that had come her way in the last couple of years. People were superstitious about Luck; they preferred heirloom garments and keepsakes. It wasn't done to rely on it too much, either. Emmeline had carefully tucked away the few fragments of scraps that she'd come by, but there was no time to do anything with them now. She pulled the big undershirt on and shrugged her blouse back on over it, frowning at the way the undershirt bagged out the blouse. But she would be wearing a coat over it, and she found it hard to believe that the guards at the prison would have an eye for fashion. It would pass.

She tucked a couple of things into her bag, then found herself packing up the roll of her best dressmaker's tools, the ones that she would save if the shop were on fire. She paused, wondering what she was doing. The undershirt shifted against her skin, and she breathed in, slowly, and let her hands do what they would. It would be foolish to carry the purse of her leaving funds through the streets; but she found herself hanging it under her skirts. At the last moment, she thrust the tiny Memory bag, the one that had started it all, into her skirt pocket, then let herself out of the house.

Jimmy the Cart wasn't at his workshop in the next street. She could hear voices raised around the corner. She bit her lip for a moment, then ducked in. When she came out again, an observer, if they looked carefully, might have noticed her moving just a very little stiffly.

The prison was a ten minute walk. She knew the streets were heavily patrolled here, but as she walked, they seemed oddly deserted. She let her feet navigate automatically through twists and turns that her conscious mind wouldn't have taken, pausing for a moment then moving again, feeling the shift of the undershirt as she went.

There was one, young, harried-looking lieutenant on duty at the prison, who peered at her from behind the barred door.

"Go away, miss," he said before she could say anything.

"I told your officer I would be back," she said, calling on her best haughty tones, "and I am. You must let me in to see Joe Bones."

"Miss," the lieutenant said. "I ain't letting anyone in to see anyone. It's late, miss, and you would be best back in your home, miss."

"I have a letter from Lady Wirral for the prisoner," she said, drawing herself even more upright, feeling the petticoat against her legs, "and I must deliver it, or she will want to know why."

There was obvious anguish in the young lieutenant's face. Everyone knew Lady Wirral. She had *opinions* about prisons. Emmeline made nice robust walking-clothes for her to go and harass the prison officers in.

"Let me in right away," she said, "and I won't mention to Lady Wirral — or to your superior officer — that you delayed me."

The lieutenant swallowed – Emmeline wasn't sure who was the bigger threat — then backed away a bit from the barred aperture. With clankings and clatterings, the door creaked open a bare couple of inches.

"There, miss."

Emmeline hoped desperately that he wouldn't ask to inspect the sealed envelope she was brandishing, but her Luck held.

Joe was peering through the barred window of his cell, looking out at the city. He spun round when the lieutenant unlocked the cell door, opened his mouth, then shut it again until they'd been left alone.

"Emmeline..." he started, sounding anxious.

Emmeline was already reaching up under her skirts, uncoiling the length of rope she'd wound round her waist and legs, and the cart-jack she'd strapped onto one leg. There were two matching patches of raw skin, top and bottom, where it had very nearly slipped down.

Joe blinked at her, wide-eyed.

"I assume you didn't want to stay here," Emmeline said.

"But the Masquerade..." Joe started. "People don't *get* let out. It's too risky."

"I'm not here for the Masquerade," Emmeline said briskly. "This is purely a personal endeavour."

"But..."

Emmeline could see, suddenly, the shape of Joe's worry. That, inevitably, the blame would be laid at their door; that the consequences would follow them, would smother the rebellion, exactly the way the group were trying to avoid by abandoning anyone who was caught.

But she couldn't leave Joe here.

She swallowed. "Don't worry," she said. "I'll make sure that doesn't happen. I'll make sure they know where to put the blame. Now, for pity's sake, you need to *go*."

She went to the window, fitted the cart-jack in between the two bars, and began winding, grunting a little with the effort as it began to bite into the bars. After a moment, Joe stepped up and took over. Emmeline shook out her skirts, then squeezed in beside Joe to tie the rope onto another bar.

It took surprisingly little time before there was enough of a gap for skinny Joe to slide through. Emmeline leant out to watch him shinning quickly down the rope. When he was nearly at the bottom, she took a deep breath, squared her shoulders, and marched out of the cell. At the lieutenant's little room, she insisted that he make a record of her visit, with her name and address nice and clear, and whom she had visited. All the while he was writing, her neck prickled with anticipation of a shout, someone realising Joe had gone. The undershirt, despite its softness, prickled against her skin.

She marched out of the door once he was done, head held high; then took to her heels and ran.

She fetched up at one of the outer bridges over the river, most of the way to the city limits. It was late; the houses along the riverside were quiet.

The water flowed under the bridge, ripples gilded with moonlight. Flowing out of the city, away past the foot of the mountains and onward to the distant sea that she'd seen only on maps. Her eyes rose upwards to the mountains themselves and to the pass the Guisers came over. How *did* they make the stuff? The world was so much *bigger* than this one small city.

She couldn't go back to the shop, now. She might have protected the Masquerade — she certainly hoped so — but that was the cost of it. What now?

She felt the weight of the purse holding her leaving fund, hanging from her belt. She'd been intending to stay until Joe was through his apprenticeship; but that tie was gone too. She could just leave, finally, like she'd planned. She should have given Joe the key to the shop. There was a lot of charmcloth there, kept safe under lock and key. Someone could use that.

She thought of Granny Zeta, of all the Granny Zetas. She thought of the Masquerade, and whom they sacrificed for what. In her head, she heard Sally — *you know where we are* — and across the other side of her belt from her purse, she felt the weight of her dressmaker's roll. Her tools. She'd been doing good work, here. She'd been helping.

Her hand stole into her pocket, to the little bag that had started everything, feeling the hard lump of the old thimble inside it. But this time the memories of her grandfather that sprang to life weren't of him at home with her. They were of him working in the doorway of the shop and greeting everyone who passed; of how often he invited someone who was struggling to share their dinner; of the hundred little generosities which meant people like Granny Zeta remembering him with such warmth.

She looked, for another longing moment, up at the mountains. Somewhere new. Somewhere with no responsibility save for herself.

Somewhere she'd always know that she'd turned her back and walked away.

She took a deep breath, and turned, and walked back into the city.

About the story

I sew myself, and when I had the idea for this story, I'd just been working on a patchwork quilt.

There's a myth that patchwork quilts were always made from worn clothing and other scraps from dressmaking — undoubtedly sometimes they were, but people have also always bought fabric specifically for making quilts. But when I make scrap quilts (quilts made using lots of different fabrics, usually fairly small pieces, chosen more-or-less at random), I do tend to use up leftover bits of fabric. I enjoy making something beautiful — or at least functional! — from fabric that would otherwise be thrown away.

While I was making my scrappy quilt, as is inevitable, I wound up with more, smaller, scraps left over. I found myself wondering — just how small does a piece of fabric have to be before it's too small to use? And then I wondered whether that calculation would change if fabric was more expensive? Would I save that one-inch strip rather than binning it? And when I thought about valuable fabric, the image that came to mind was of someone patching together tiny scraps of magical fabric. That, together with a discussion I'd had with a friend about sumptuary laws — laws restricting what clothes, food, or furniture people were allowed based on their social class, which have shown up in societies across the world throughout history — gave rise to Emmeline and her city. And once you have a restrictive society, who pushes at those restrictions, and what happens when they do? I've always been fond of a revolution story...

A question for the author

Q: What happens when you hit writer's block head on?

A: If I hit writer's block, it's usually a sign that there is some problem with scene, plot, characters, or all of the above. My immediate response, which I try to ignore, is to go and mess around on the internet. This is rarely helpful. To solve the problem rather than avoiding it, some level of thinking is required, worse luck. I sometimes sit down with marker pens (I have Copics, which are a tremendous indulgence but I do love them) and a colouring book and try to let my brain freewheel. Going climbing is good, too. Both colouring and climbing work well for occupying my monkey brain (the bit that just wants to hit refresh on Twitter) and letting the slower-thinking creative parts ruminate for a while. If I had a different sort of dog, walking the dog might work. Unfortunately if I stop paying attention to my dog, she considers this to be a reason to ignore me in turn, takes off after the nearest squirrel, and refuses to return. This experience does not generate anything useful at all brainwise, though all the running backwards and forwards is probably good cardio. Lying down and staring at the ceiling can be surprisingly helpful, although sometimes it leads to napping. But then, napping isn't always bad — once in a while I dream a solution to a story problem, which is exceptionally satisfying when it happens. And, most importantly, all of the above work better when I add both chocolate and tea, in large quantities.

About the author

Juliet Kemp lives in London, UK with her partners, kid, and dog. She is fortunate enough to be able to see the Thames out of her window when writing, which is either inspiring, distracting, or both. When she's not writing or running round the house trying to keep up with the kid, she reads a lot, drinks too much tea, makes things out of yarn and fabric, and goes climbing a bit less often than she would like.

She blogs intermittently at julietkemp.com and tweets at @julietk.

Juliet Kemp's story "Scraps" was published in *Metaphorosis* on Friday, 7 April 2017.

Angels at the Border

Ian Rennie

The angels moved up the road towards Gethsemene in a triad formation. If they'd walked, that would have been something. If they'd flown, swooped in from the sky, that would have been something else. But they didn't. They just moved, floating slowly along the road in unison. Behind them — almost too far away to see — was the unnatural mountain of their home, fading into the skyline.

Valeria had gate duty that day. It was good foraging weather, the kind that would have had Anthony heading out into the wilderness if he were still alive. He had never been able to get Justin interested in the great outdoors, even before the boy was lost to them.

She spotted the three angels as they passed the mile marker and followed them in her riflescope until they reached the gate five minutes later. Twelve miles an hour; slow enough to know they'd be seen.

"That's far enough," Valeria called down as the trio reached the gates. "State your business."

The lead of the group turned to look at her. They weren't identical, just close to it. This one had a broad nose and chubby cheeks that looked out of place on its smooth metallic face.

It spoke in a liquid voice. "We are—"

"I know what you are," Valeria interrupted. "State your business."

The lead angel continued undaunted. "We are a diplomatic delegation and we wish to present credentials. Our common names are—

"Don't care. Do you have business to state or do I have to see you off our property?"

The angel paused. If it had still been a human, Valeria was pretty sure it would have sighed. "Under the terms of the Treaty of Vancouver, diplomatic delegations may approach a freehold when their presence is requested by an inhabitant. Such a request has been made."

Valeria tightened her grip on the rifle. There was only one reason someone would ask for the angels. "You've come for one of us."

"We've come at the request of one of you," the angel replied. "We wish to present credentials."

Valeria sighed. They weren't going to leave any time soon. "Come through to the courtyard. But no further."

She pushed the gate control and stepped down from the watchtower, still holding the rifle. Her left knee was stiff from standing still for too long, and she had to hobble down the tower stairs. By the time she reached the courtyard, the angels were already there, floating unmoving in the centre of the walled space. Close to, they seemed even less human. Their shape was still bipedal and humanoid, but their constituent parts were only loosely attached, as if their thin limbs floated near their torsos rather than being tethered to them.

"So, you taking one of our parents or one of our children?" Valeria asked.

The lead angel looked at her and frowned. "I don't understand your question," it said in its liquid voice.

"Only two types of people summon you," Valeria replied. "Children wanting to rebel or old people wanting another chance. Which is it this time?"

The angel paused again. "The request came from Tamar Antonia Halverston, eighteen years old, of Melchior Plaza, Freehold of Gethsemene. We don't answer requests from children."

"You just did," Valeria grumbled, pulling out a computer pad and tapping instructions into it. After a moment she frowned. "Apparently she's waiting outside. She didn't tell anyone you were coming."

"This is not unusual," the angel said. "We have found that families try to stop the upgrade process."

"I wonder why?" Valeria spat.

The angel looked at her; she could make out the ghosts of pupils in its silver eyes. "As do I," it replied.

The door on the other side of the courtyard opened. As it did, Valeria raised her rifle slightly. If any one of them so much as looked towards the interior of Gethsemene...

They didn't. They floated exactly where they were as the girl entered the courtyard. Hard not to think of her as a girl. Tamar was skinny and undersized, looking closer to twelve than to eighteen. She looked around the courtyard nervously, scratching a spot on the dark skin of her arm. Justin had done the same in his last days, like he thought his skin was the wrong size. Like he wanted to scratch it off and find something else underneath.

"You just stay where you are for now, honey," Valeria said. "You don't have to go anywhere you don't want to."

The lead angel turned smoothly towards the girl. "Tamar Antonia Halverston. We have received a request from you for upgrade. Under the terms of the Treaty of Gethsemene we are here to perform the sublimation process, should you still wish it."

The girl said nothing, just looked at the angels and the woman with the gun, as if uncertain what to do.

Finally Valeria broke the silence. "Tamar, if you want these... *people* to leave, you just need to say the word, all right? If they've got no business here I'll set them on their way."

"I—" Tamar started. Her high voice cracked and caught in her throat.

"Go on, darlin'," Valeria said softly. "Say what you need to say."

"I don't want to live like this anymore," Tamar said. "I want the upgrade."

Valeria let out an angry sigh but tried not to let it show on her face. "I guess that's it, then," she said to the lead angel. "Take your property and get out."

The angel looked at her for a moment. "Standard practice is for the sublimation process to take place here."

Valeria felt bile rise at the prospect. "No way. I can't stop you taking the girl, but I sure as hell can stop you butchering her in front of me."

"There is no butchery. The procedure is—"

"I don't care how clean and hygienic the murder is," Valeria snapped. "It's still murder."

There was a long pause and Valeria knew she had gone too far. This was way past protocol, almost enough to cause a diplomatic incident. Nonetheless she couldn't back down. Not now. Not in front of these bastards.

Salvation came unexpectedly from Tamar. "I want them to do it here," she said, her voice less faltering than it had been before. "I want to leave my old life behind, right here."

The lead angel turned to the girl and nodded, then turned back to Valeria. "We will need a quiet space where we will not be interrupted. The process will take nineteen minutes."

Valeria sighed, her second defeat during this conversation. "There's a room in the guard tower," she said. "A changing room. Kind of appropriate."

"Thank you," the lead angel said. The other two angels floated towards Tamar.

Valeria pinched her fingers on the bridge of her nose. "I can show you the way if—"

"We know the way," the lead angel replied. "We have used the room before."

Tamar walked towards the guard tower, flanked by angels. The lead angel stayed in position in the courtyard.

"Ain't you going with them?" Valeria asked.

The lead angel shook its head. "Only two are necessary for sublimation, and they are more experienced."

"So you're, what, here as back up?"

"You might call me a liaison," the angel said.

"Here to stop me interfering with this 'sublimation' of yours?"

"If you like," the angel replied. "Or here as a hostage in case we do something you don't care for."

Valeria paused. She hadn't thought of it like that. "So if something goes wrong with the girl..."

"Your weapon is powerful enough to kill me, yes. You could kill me now if you were so inclined. I can't speak to what would happen after that."

Valeria realised she was pointing the rifle directly at the angel, and lowered it. "How long did you say this would take?"

"Nineteen minutes," the angel replied. "Seventeen now. If you're worried about Tamar, the process is quite painless."

"So's lethal injection," Valeria snapped.

"Nobody who had a lethal injection could tell you about it afterwards. Having experienced the sublimation process I can guide you through it if you would like. The initial scan of mind-state activity is swift and has already been completed, as has the creation of the primary nanite array. What takes the time is the synchronisation of the array with the existing mind state to create the thoughtform, and the decompliation of—"

"Enough!" Valeria barked. "I don't need to know every detail of what you're doing to her. It's enough to know you bastards won't stop until there are none of us left."

"Logically that's accurate as we will always offer sublimation to those who desire it," the angel replied. "Rhetorically it's not accurate to frame this as a takeover or a conquest. If our desire was simply to sublimate you all we could have done so half a century ago."

"Instead you just let us waste away in goddamn wildlife reserves!"

"The settlements were your idea," the angel answered. "I believe your constitution calls Gethsemene 'A place for humans to be humans'. We would happily make room for you in the arcologies, or build one for you, but both options were rejected by your leadership."

Valeria felt a bitter reply form in her mouth, but swallowed the venom down. "Let's—" she began. "Let's talk about something else. You, maybe. Where are you from?"

"I live in the Bei Hanto Xa arcology. Outside of my liaison duties, I spend my time—"

"I don't care about the arcologies. You said you'd been through the upgrade. You were a human once. Where are you from?"

The angel paused. "It's considered impolite to talk about our origins," it said. "It separates those whose thoughtform originates in a human mind from those produced through algorithmic blending."

Valeria looked away. The last thing she wanted to hear about was the sex lives of these damn things.

"However, you weren't to know that," the angel continued. "Yes, my thoughtform was human once. Before my sublimation I lived in the Britannia settlement."

Valeria snorted disbelief. "Britannia fell apart a century ago. The survivors came here. My grandma told me about it."

"Yes," the angel replied.

"Are you trying to tell me you've been alive for–"

"It's considered impolite to talk about our origins," the angel repeated.

Valeria sighed, and unclipped a pouch on her belt. "Do you eat or drink?" she asked.

"I can," the angel replied. "We don't have to, but many of us choose to."

Valeria pulled two sticks of soy jerky from the pouch and handed one to the angel. She tensed as its hand came near to hers, but concentrated on her breathing until the angel withdrew with the stick.

She leaned against a wall and chewed her jerky, not taking her right hand off the rifle. She flexed her left leg, trying to work off the dull ache in the knee. After she was finished with the jerky, she stared at the angel for a moment, deep in thought.

"I went to school with kids from Britannia families," Valeria said eventually. "Each of them had family stories about the fall and the exodus. I knew a boy whose great grandfather died on the trip over. Why didn't you help them?"

"We did," the angel said. "We gave you as much help as you were willing to take. By the time it was disbanded there were less than a thousand people in Britannia: barely enough to keep the machinery of the settlement together, not enough to support it for any longer."

"How *could* there be?" Valeria asked, angrily. "You take their kids. You take their grandparents. You leave nothing behind."

"We take only those who wish to go. We give the rest of you the best life we can."

Valeria stood up straight, feeling the stiffness and pain in her back and her leg. "I had a son once," she said, not sure why she was telling the angel this. "Justin was a beautiful boy, smartest kid you ever met. He played the violin like an angel. Better than an angel, like a *human.* I loved him as much as he loved me, as much as he hated this place, this 'best life' you've given us. The day he turned eighteen he called out to you and you took him away from me."

The angel floated, unmoving and silent. "I'm sorry for your pain," it said eventually. "You must have loved him very much."

"As much as his father did. Anthony couldn't take the loss of his son, couldn't live in this world without his boy. He stole my sidearm and walked out into the wilderness where I wouldn't have to deal with his body. I guess he thought he was being kind. He took himself away, but I still blame you. Can you see why your 'best life' is a bunch of shit?"

She turned and walked away from the angel. As she did, her knee started to buckle. She steadied herself on the wall.

"Are you all right?" the angel asked.

"Old injury that still plays up," Valeria said. "It's worse in winter."

She felt the angel's hand on her shoulder, soft and cold.

"We could help you with that," the angel said in its soft, liquid, inhuman voice.

Valeria spun round, rifle raised. "I swear to fucking God, if you ever touch me again I'll kill every one of you bastards!"

Despite the angel's impassive face, it seemed suddenly angry. "I was trying to help!" it snarled, its voice louder and more forceful than she had heard it before. "All we have ever wanted to do is to help you!"

"And all we've wanted you to do is to leave us the fuck alone!" Valeria snapped.

"Do you have any idea what it would mean if we left you alone?" the angel asked. "We give you clement weather, clean energy, machines that never break. If we left you alone you'd all be dead within the decade."

"Well, maybe we'd prefer that to being pets!"

Before anything else could be said, the door to the guard tower opened and the three angels emerged. They were near identical. Valeria spent a moment scanning their faces to see if she could tell which had been Tamar.

It didn't matter. Tamar was dead. This was just what they had done with her remains.

"Our business here is completed," the lead angel said.

"Good," Valeria replied. "Get the fuck off our property."

Valeria didn't watch them leave. The angels returned to the heaven they had built, and she walked back into Gethsemene. She was rostered as sentry for another two hours, but right now she didn't want to look at the world, at anything.

She thought about going to Melchior Plaza. Someone would have to tell Mr and Mrs Halverston what had happened to their little girl; someone would have to destroy their lives just as someone had destroyed Valeria's.

Instead she went home, to the two-bedroom apartment that was too big for her, crowded with memories of the past. She went into Justin's old room and looked around at the things he had left behind.

She picked up his dusty violin, lay on his bed, and waited in vain for the tears to come.

About the story

Fiction surrounding the technological singularity has always bothered me, even leaving aside the questions that scientists and futurists raise about whether it will actually happen at all. We have this idea that when some form of global digital consciousness happens it will happen everywhere, for everyone. This misses two fundamental things about humanity. The first is that not everyone would be capable of enjoying the benefits of this digital consciousness at once, any more than we can a l currently enjoy a world of electric cars and tablet computers. There's an argument that this is the singularity of the Peter Thiels and Elon Musks of the world, not of the several billion people surviving on less than a dollar a day. The second is that even if you could upload everyone, give them eternal, digital life beyond the bounds of the flesh… not all of them would want to come. With "Angels at the Border" I wanted to tell the story of the people who didn't make the leap, the remnant of humanity, slowly ebbing away in the foothills of paradise.

A question for the author

Q: Have you ever wondered whether ideas are thought waves directed at you by an AI supercomputer located in the distant future?

A: Honestly it would be a relief if they were. It might mean that I couldn't take credit for any of my good ideas, but it would also mean I couldn't take all of the blame for my bad ones. I've always liked the Terry Pratchett idea of idea particles whizzing through space looking for receptors in people's brains, meaning we're surrounded by creativity all the time. In truth, though, a great idea is only half the battle. The best idea in the world is nothing more than an idea unless you do something with it.

About the author

Ian Rennie is a librarian and writer in Cambridge, England. As well as writing, he is one of the Cambridge organizers of National Novel Writing Month. He was once retweeted by Neil Gaiman, not that he's bragging or anything.

isrennie.com, @isrennie

Ian Rennie's story "Angels at the Border" was published in
Metaphorosis on Friday, 14 April 2017.

To the Eggplant Cannon

Beth Goder

The amusement park was so large that it had two trains named after root vegetables. Vienne got on the wrong one.

Lugging her magician's trunk in one hand and a map of Wonder Gardens in the other, she clambered onto the Rutabaga Express. The seat was sticky with pineapple gunk and the car was open to the sky.

As the train chugged past the Bananarama Coaster and the whirling Strawberry Surprise, a sweet scent wafted through the air. Hordes of people milled around, clumping up to watch the organic farming demonstration or three women juggling zucchini. Lines for rides and food carts snaked around and around. The sound was tremendous—laughter and shouting, the whoosh of the Bananarama Coaster, and the train chugging along, whistling occasionally.

Vienne pulled out a deck of cards and shuffled, the rhythm of the cards matching the churn of the train's wheels.

Another performance at another weird amusement park. But the produce theme wasn't so bad. Last week, it had been cats—a tabby tea cup ride, catnip funhouse, ice cream sandwiches shaped like mousey toys. The Performers' Guild was always sending her to kooky places.

It would be different when she made a name for herself. She'd travel around the world—hike in New Zealand, read on a beach in India, take a cooking class in Japan. But first, she'd go to Iceland. Iceland had all the best things—tiny horses, magma caves, medieval manuscripts, super cool birdwatching. Ever since she was a kid, Vienne had wanted to visit.

She flipped four aces out of the deck in a flourish. Maybe someday, she'd do that trick on an Icelandic stage.

The train chugged along. It wasn't until the Carrot Waterslide that she realized she was going the wrong way.

Facepalm. She couldn't be late for the performance, not when the Performers' Guild already wanted to revoke her membership. The accident with Flying Death or Parasites hadn't been her fault, not really, but the Guild didn't see it that way. Vienne had always hated that illusion—it was the worst sort of magic.

The trick, in its entirety.

Step 1: Suspend yourself above a tank of creeping nematodes.

Step 2: Wiggle around a bit.

Step 3: Wait for the audience to be blinded by flashing lights and glitter explosions.

Step 4: Signal your assistant to lower you down and untie you.

Step 5: Hold up your arms to encourage applause. Undeserved applause.

Flying Death or Parasites required no skill, no knowledge of knots, no craft. It wasn't real magic—the kind that took years of practice to perfect.

Vienne had created plenty of her own tricks, and none of them included glitter. Or nematodes. She could produce tiny glass swans, making it seem as if they had flown out of a mirror. She could grow a rose from the palm of her hand. She could send paper dragonflies zooming around the audience, each one marked with the symbol of a playing card, and bring back the dragonfly that matched the card a volunteer picked from her deck. The Guild wouldn't let her do those tricks. Not flashy enough, they said. The Guild booked her performances; they made the rules. If the Guild wanted glitter explosions, they got glitter explosions.

The Rutabaga Express pulled into a station. Vienne climbed out, pulling her trunk after her.

"Excuse me," she called to an attendant dressed like a bulb of garlic. "What's the fastest way to get to the Wonder Arena?"

The garlic waddled over. The costume was absurdly round, with sunglasses painted across the body, but Vienne didn't think less of the person in the suit. If you had a passion, sometimes you did silly things and worked your way up, even if that meant dressing like a vegetable, or performing at weird amusement parks, or wiggling above a tank of nematodes.

"You're going the wrong way," said the garlic.

"I know. I need the Turnip Train, right?" She refrained from asking who had thought it was a good idea to name both trains after pinkish root vegetables.

"Not exactly," said the garlic.

The conductor sounded the whistle, and the Rutabaga Express chugged away.

The station platform was rather high up. Vienne grabbed the railing. Ever since the mishap with Flying Death or Parasites, she wasn't so fond of heights. She wished she could forget the whole embarrassing episode. The rope had snapped, and she'd twisted in the air, clipped the side of the nematode tank, then hit the stage with a tremendous thunk.

"Wait a moment," she said. Trying not to look at the ground, which was much too far below her, Vienne dropped her trunk, then plopped down on top of it. She tried to steady her breathing.

"Are you okay?"

She pulled out a deck of cards, the familiar weight settling in her hands. "Can you see in the garlic suit?"

"Surprisingly well. You get used to it. My eyes are up here." The garlic pointed to the top of the suit, above the huge sunglasses, where white mesh scrunched against a shock of green leaves.

Doing a magic trick was the only way she could think of to calm down. She fanned out the deck. "Pick a card."

"Any card?" asked the garlic, sounding amused. He took one from the middle. Even though the garlic didn't reveal his card, Vienne knew it was the four of hearts.

She did a one-handed cut, then spun the top card around, her fingers nimble from practice. That was the real secret of magic—practice. Doing more work than anyone thought possible. Spending all of your time with a quarter palmed in your hand, until you could move as if the quarter wasn't there at all.

"Now, we'll need to turn this ordinary deck into something extraordinary," said Vienne, falling easily into her patter. "To do that, I'll need a magic word or phrase from you." As she spoke, Vienne shuffled, expertly spinning the cards.

Her favorite part was finding out what her volunteer would pick. Most people chose traditional magic words, like abracadabra, or nonsense phrases or whatever popped into their heads. Rarely, someone would pick a phrase that was meaningful to them.

As the garlic thought, she maneuvered the cards into place.

"I sound my barbaric yawp over the roofs of the world," said the garlic.

Vienne paused. "That's the first time I've heard that one."

"It's from a Walt Whitman poem."

So, the garlic was interested in poetry. It was amazing what you could learn about someone in just a few minutes. That was one of the reasons Vienne loved close-up magic—it gave you a real connection to people.

Vienne snapped her fingers. "Barbaric yawp! Now, it's a magical deck. It's going to tell us what card you chose. Let's look at the top three cards."

Slowly, she turned over the four of clubs, the four of diamonds, and the four of spades. "These cards are looking for their friend."

The garlic revealed the card in his hand. The four of hearts, of course. "How did you do that?"

"Practice. Lots of practice." Vienne remembered she was in a hurry. "I'm performing today, but I have to get to the Wonder Arena."

"Let me see your map." The garlic pulled a pen from a hidden pocket. He scribbled a line. "So, you're here, by the Potato Horror House. Don't go in there, by the way. All spuds and mold. You need to get here." The garlic jabbed an ominous laughing skull surrounded by purple blooms. "That's the Eggplant Cannon."

"Cannon? I thought I needed to take a train."

"The Turnip Train is scenic. Takes two hours to complete a circuit. When did you need to be at the Wonder Arena?"

Vienne checked her watch. "Twenty minutes. I need time to set up." She wanted to triple check her equipment. No more accidents.

"The Eggplant Cannon will shoot you over the park. Totally safe," the garlic said, in a way that suggested it wasn't.

Vienne thanked the garlic, then made her way down the stairs, gripping the railing with one hand and her trunk with the other.

"Wait," the garlic shouted, waving a playing card. "Your four of hearts."

"Keep it," she called back. "A reminder of your barbaric yawp."

Vienne hurried through the park. She couldn't help thinking that this sort of mix up would have never happened in Reykjavik. They probably labelled their trains properly in Iceland.

She pulled her trunk past a large rose garden, panting. The trunk, which she had never much liked, was weighed down with glitter and props. The worst part was she'd had to purchase the glitter herself. The Guild didn't pay for stuff like that—not unless you were a senior member.

She ducked under a trellis awash with yellow flowers. On her right, a river squashed full of paddleboats.

A group of five teenagers clambered into one boat, which had to be against regulations. There was quite a line for the paddleboats.

However, there was no line at all for the Eggplant Cannon.

The apparatus was glazed with purple paint. A gigantic cylinder rested on two spoked wheels, decorated with festive cartoons of eggplants smiling, parachuting, and splattering into mounds of goop. Piles of oversized plastic eggplants littered the space, reminiscent of cannonballs.

Vienne had never actually eaten an eggplant. She didn't trust a vegetable that purple.

A sign read, "Flailing while in air prohibited."

An attendant with neatly braided hair sat in a booth. "Ignore the sign," she said. "Everyone flails."

It won't be so bad, thought Vienne, even though her insides were bopping like she'd ingested a parasite. Sure, the eggplant cannon would shoot her high into the air, extremely high, unreasonably high, but there wouldn't be any nematodes. No nematodes. That was something, at least.

"I need to get to the Wonder Arena," Vienne said.

"Okay, I'll calculate a route. You want to shoot the trunk over, too?" The attendant scribbled out some equations.

"Is this thing—" Vienne gazed at the shiny purple base, the straight lines of the cannon, the lack of any track or guidance system. "Is this thing safe?"

"Completely safe. Please sign this waiver," said the attendant.

Vienne pulled out a deck of cards. Her hands were shaking so badly that she could barely hold the deck steady, but the act of shuffling calmed her. The cards whizzed in her hands. Blind shuffle. Bevel. False cut. Mercury fold. She knew the location of every card and could return the deck to its original order, spinning the cards back to where they had started.

She imagined soaring over the park, the ground coming at her much too fast. During the mishap with Flying Death or Parasites, she hadn't had time to be afraid. There was only falling, then the pain of hitting the stage. Now, she'd be much higher.

Her phone buzzed. She answered to the panicked voice of her assistant. "Where are you?"

"Minor setback," said Vienne.

A string of curses followed. "You're this close to being kicked out of the Guild, and you can't even be bothered to show up on—"

Vienne hung up the phone.

The Wonder Arena shone in the distance, impossibly far away.

Vienne took a breath and signed the form, bouncing on her toes. Sometimes, magic required a bit of discomfort. Once, at a cocktail party, she'd pulled a large ice cube out of a party goer's hat. She'd chosen a woman who'd just taken off her red-feathered cloche. When the ice cube appeared, dripping and cold, the astonished woman asked her how it was done. Vienne had been tempted to say, "Well, you start with a much larger ice cube, and the capacity to be very chilly."

The attendant fitted her with a purple helmet and a suit covered with flimsy mesh, then asked Vienne to scrunch down in the cannon. The suit chafed against her shoulders.

"No nematodes," Vienne chanted. "No nematodes."

The attendant gave her a weird look, then went back to the controls. As the Eggplant Cannon booted up, a scraping noise filled the air, eerily similar to the sound of a tank of parasites being dragged onto a stage.

Inside the cannon, a cheerful eggplant clock buzzed to life by her nose and began a countdown.

Three.

Flying above an audience. A snapping rope. Nematodes.

Two.

"Wait!" Too late. Much too late.

One.

Vienne shot out of the Eggplant Cannon, arching over the park. She flung her arms out, then back. Despite her best efforts, she was flailing. Below her, the Cauliflower Carousel glimmered, luminous and majestic. She flew over the Radish Maze, its shadowed corridors visible from above. People stopped to watch her hurtling through the air.

Of course they would watch. Shooting out of a cannon was exactly the sort of thing that drew attention, just like all of the magic the Guild preferred. Flash. Bang. Explosion of glitter. And, when the trick had ended, that shocked afterglow, eyes adjusting after an assault of light. Vienne much preferred magic of a quieter sort, but it was hard to make a career out of close-up magic, the kind you could do with cards and coins. People wanted big illusions. People wanted escapes.

Air brushed past her, quick and cold. She spread her arms out wide. No more flailing.

The world looked different from high up, as if the edges of things were blurred together, like cards being shuffled into a deck. Now you see the world, now you don't.

Paddleboats wound through the river below, impossibly small.

The flimsy mesh of her suit ripped away. A parachute bloomed behind her.

Flying was both terrifying and freeing at once. Part of her wanted to be safe on the ground, but another part wanted to zoom farther, over the park, over the woods past the boundary fence, where the trees were a distant blur.

A landing zone marked by a large eggplant loomed closer.

She decelerated, the parachute flaps whipping about her ears. The outlined eggplant grew larger, rushing up to meet her. Vienne bounced three times, careening through a pile of eggplants, before coming to a stop.

The first thing she did was check her watch. She'd make it backstage on time if she hurried, but she needed her trunk.

Vienne paced the landing pad, kicking eggplants out of the way. One overripe eggplant exploded on impact, splattering her leg with goop. One minute passed. Two. To her right, the Wonder Arena beckoned, its walls adorned with posters of her face framed by glitter explosions. Crowds of people were already lined up. To her left, a stand shaped like three ears of corn, filling the air with a popcorn smell.

At last, she spotted the trunk. It arched over the park at tremendous speed. The buckles glinted in the sun. Half the trunk was obscured by purple mesh.

The parachute deployed, but something was wrong. The ropes caught. The mesh twisted up. Half the parachute shot out, causing the trunk to careen in the air. It changed course, jerking at an angle.

The trunk overshot the landing space, picked up speed on the descent, and crashed into the woods beyond the park.

A puff of glitter shot into the sky, marking the place where the trunk had landed. Vienne considered hopping the fence and dashing into the woods. Perhaps some of the equipment was salvageable.

Glitter descended on the trees, glinting in the sun, annoyingly bright. Instead of fetching the trunk from the woods, she turned away. She was surprised to find herself smiling. Good riddance to glitter.

And good riddance to the Guild, which would surely revoke her membership. It was the worst possible scenario, the one she'd tried to avoid for so long. No gigs, no career advancement, no recognition.

Vienne shucked off the parachute. She thought of flying over the park, that freedom, and the Eggplant Cannon, which had at first seemed awful and deadly and unknown. Wrong routes and mishaps had led to some of the best things in her life. Being thrown out of the Guild would be a major setback, but perhaps it was also an opportunity.

If the Guild canceled the rest of her gigs, she'd have a lot of free time. She wondered how much it would cost to fly to Iceland.

More people flowed into the Wonder Arena. Vienne kicked the parachute aside.

The show would go on, but she would do it her way.

In her pocket, a deck of cards. Her old act sang in her hands. There were only two handkerchiefs in her coat, both bright blue with stars, but she knew how to hide them in seventeen different ways.

She could call on volunteers. Audience members always had interesting items—the adults, watches and credit cards. The kids, rocks and toys and packs of gum. She could work wonders with gum, flitting the pieces in and out of the pack.

Vienne grabbed an eggplant from the pile. She could incorporate it into the show. Magically cut it into slices. Make it appear as if from air. Cut open the eggplant to reveal a prediction, or better yet, have the prediction cut itself into the rubbery, purple skin. If the Wonder Arena had a mirror, she could do a version of the trick with the glass swans, making pieces of eggplant fall from the air, reflected in the glass.

That was real magic—taking something ordinary like an eggplant and turning it into an object of wonder.

No parasites. No glitter. No flashes of light. Just her on the stage. She'd start with the deck of cards. That was something, to fill an audience with wonder using only your hands and voice and a deck of cards.

Vienne palmed a quarter, then opened the door to the Wonder Arena so deftly that it seemed as if the coin wasn't there at all.

About the story

I wrote the first draft of "To the Eggplant Cannon" for a flash fiction contest run by my writing group. I'm afraid I've forgotten the prompt that sparked this story, but I had just visited Gilroy Gardens, an amusement park that was the inspiration for the setting. (They have people dressed in garlic suits, and a spectacular train that goes around the park, although, to my knowledge, no eggplant cannon.) After the contest, I revised the story into something longer. The first draft had a lot of bad toaster jokes, which were thankfully removed before I sent the story out.

A question for the author

Q: If you could talk to novice-writer self, what bit of advice would you give?

A: Since I'm fairly new to writing, I'm not convinced that I'm out of the novice stage yet, but if I could go back in time and give myself one piece of advice, I would tell myself not to be afraid of failing. Much of learning to write, I've found, is doing things badly until I figure out how to do them better. In my office, I have a bulletin board filled with scraps of paper, a French postcard of citrus fruits, and my writing bingo card. There's a quote from Richard Bausch up there: "You can't ruin a piece of writing. You can only make it necessary to go back and try again." I'd also tell myself to go read some Anthony Trollope, because he is hilarious and excellent at that whole omniscient narrator thing. Read widely, young writer-self. Also, don't be too worried about adverbs.

About the author

Beth Goder worked as an archivist before becoming a full-time writer and parent. You can find her online at www.bethgoder.com or on Twitter @Beth_Goder.

Beth Goder's story "To the Eggplant Cannon" was published in *Metaphorosis* on Friday, 21 April 2017.

Canoes of Hava'iki

Steve Rodgers

Ahokupe's wrists jerked as the sennit ropes were tied tight behind him, and he bit his lip against the pain. Forcing his spirit to quiet, he breathed the subtle scents of rotting durian from the surrounding forest and focused his gaze on a parrot in a nearby rambutan tree. If he was to be fed to the God this day, his last thoughts would be a calm lagoon.

Before him, the stone path twisted through the jungle for several paces before disappearing into a riot of green leaves and red berries on its way to Maniloa's lair. Behind him, the gentle rush of waves and chirps of a flycatcher were pierced by Kaulaki's ugly grunts as he spoke with his grovelers.

Ahokupe turned to face a wall of bare chests and spears, scowling at the pigs who shared his island: Arii the stuttering one, too tongue-tied to hold Liliha's attention for a minute. Fat Keoni, who had wailed like a girl when struck by a branch during combat. Whetu, too dumb to spear a tapir when it crawled through his hut. And several more, all of whom thought themselves better than Ahokupe simply because they shared kinship or friendship with the Kaulaki clan. A curse on all their names.

Behind them beckoned the white sand and blue waters of the sea, and Ahokupe turned his gaze there, offering a silent prayer to Faumea. His only regret, the only reason he could not spit in their faces just yet, was Liliha. He had to see her one last time.

As if the Goddess had answered his prayers, Liliha pushed between Whetu and Keoni and raced toward him, yanked to a halt by Kaulaki's strong arm.

"You are a fool!" King Kaulaki shouted to Ahokupe, as Liliha struggled to free herself. "How could she want you?"

Ahokupe's gaze travelled from the seashell lei atop Kaulaki's bare chest into an angry face of scars and black whorls. Hava'iki's king was a monster of black Tatau, his hair twisted around Malaye finger bones and embedded with parrot feathers.

Liliha watched him from a tear-streaked face, and Ahokupe's anger melted into sorrow. She was so beautiful now, her black hair shiny with the day's mist, the hibiscus flower on her ear drooping with her spirit. He looked back at Kaulaki.

"If I cross the bridge and return, she is mine. You have said so."

"Kava twisted my tongue. Why should she bear *your* sons instead of Arii's?"

Ahokupe almost smiled at Kaulaki's lowered voice. Hava'iki's king had made his promise before all the Maoli, and knew he was bound by it.

"Then be happy," Ahokupe said. He nodded toward Arii, who looked like he'd bitten a coconut husk. "If Maniloa eats me, stuttering Arii will sire your line."

"Stop it!" Liliha shouted, and Ahokupe regretted his words. He reached out to her, but Kaulaki knocked his hand away.

"You are needed only to fight the Malayes."

I'm needed because if I die, she'll never forgive you. Aloud, Ahokupe said: "I'll stay if you order me."

Kaulaki's smile was hard. "You have made your boast before all the people, and I will not save your Mana. Walk, then."

Kaulaki's piggish gloat filled him with rage. He yanked at the coarse sennit coconut fiber binding his wrists. "I have decided to face the God, yet still you bind my hands," he spat. "Do you have so little honor?"

Kaulaki laughed. "You walk the path of Malayes; to me you have become of them. I will treat you no different."

Ahokupe swallowed his anger, knowing the pain in his wrists would be short-lived. He turned to face the trail. Wet with recent rains, tall trees stood in silent judgement, vines draping from their branches into the thicket of ferns below. High above the canopy, Great Oro spewed white trails of smoke to blend with the rolling clouds, its forested slopes bisected by rivers of red.

He breathed deeply and began walking. How often had Ahokupe witnessed this procession: Captured Malaye chieftains travelling the path of sacrifice, never suspecting they strode into a God's maw. Kaulaki always unbound their wrists at the entrance to Maniloa's lair, telling them that if they could traverse the bridge, they would live.

None had ever claimed that prize.

Ahokupe was the first Maoli to walk this path in a generation, but he knew something the Malayes did not: he'd seen the bridge twist, watched how the sennit guide rope moved. He knew that to survive, he needed the support of three limbs when the mangrove planks turned face down. And he'd practiced for this day since before the last ripening of the coconuts.

Maniloa had descended from heaven in the days of Ahokupe's grandfather, his shiny sphere tearing a hole in the clouds with a fire rain that rivalled Great Oro. The God had made his home in the gorge that separated two halves of the island, near the bridge over the waters of Attoo. Though none knew his form, Maniloa's ravenous appetite left no doubt of his presence, for he feasted on all who dared cross that bridge. The Maoli had found other ways to reach the far slopes, but they knew that the God must continue to feed. If not, the rains would stop, the breadfruit would shrivel, and the snapper would slip from their nets. Fortunately, the occasional Malaye attacks against Hava'iki had provided the God plentiful meat.

They walked in silence as the sun reached its zenith, and the first distant rush of sacred Attoo whispered through the trees. It grew louder as they climbed, and as they stepped around the roots of a giant seraya tree, the waterfall's mighty roar shook the earth, swamping the ever-present buzz of cicadas. Attoo pounded down the fern-studded cliffs in an enormous crash of spray and mist, bellowing clouds from the gorge.

The last time Ahokupe had seen a Malaye sacrifice, his mother, his only family, had still been alive. It had been a more innocent time, before he'd had to fight for his rights as a kinless male. Never had he realized what a pack of dogs ruled his island, that the only good on it was Liliha. To Ahokupe, facing the God was far better than an outcast's life on the shores of Hava'iki, watching Liliha grow fat with child from Kaulaki's hand-picked crony.

Yet staring at that bridge, he could not quell his rising panic. He felt his knees tremble as the Maoli warriors assembled behind him.

Spanning the gorge, the bridge was a simple row of rotted mangrove planks fastened together by sennit, a single guide rope along one side. It was wet with Attoo's spray, bearing no stain to mark the dozens of bodies thrown from its heights to the sharp rocks below. On a ledge above the waterfall, Maniloa's shiny sphere glinted in the sun—the God's home, though none had seen him enter.

"Let's leave his wrists bound," came Hohepa's voice from the back of the procession.

Kaulaki laughed. "Yes, since he is so much better us, let's offer him a real challenge."

Ahokupe twisted around wildly, heart freezing at Kaulaki's gap-toothed grin. Even the Malayes were given their freedom before death; never had he imagined Kaulaki's hatred would lead to this.

"No!" screamed Liliha, frantically pushing through the crowd of warriors. She elbowed her way to Kaulaki, her beautiful face trembling with anger. "Mighty warrior! You would deny a Maoli what you give to the Malayes? Then I will go first!" She whirled around and ran toward the bridge.

Ahokupe and Kaulaki both shouted "Stop!" as she reached the first plank.

She turned around, and Ahokupe felt Kaulaki frantically untying the ropes around his wrists. Then, a heavy push forward.

"Go, braggart. Feed Maniloa."

Ahokupe flexed his shoulders and opened his palms, seeing with satisfaction that the breadfruit sap was holding, and the tree moss was still attached. He looked up to see Liliha returning from the bridge and knew an overwhelming sadness. Her slender face was drawn, giant brown eyes shiny with tears. He longed to hold her, but knew it wasn't the time. She touched his hand as she passed, and he kissed the amber bracelet on his wrist, the one she'd given him so long ago.

Ahokupe looked back to the bridge. High above the trees, massive clouds covered Oro's peak, and were now descending its slopes like dark spirits. Bolts of lightning could be seen near the summit, and Ahokupe wondered if he'd ever again feel rain's cool caress.

He stepped carefully onto the swinging span, rocking with the bridge and blinking against the waterfall's spray. He walked to the center and stopped, wrapping the loose sennit guide rope around his right leg and then around both wrists. With three limbs anchored, he breathed easier. He looked at Maniloa's shiny sphere a moment, then turned back to his audience. Liliha was beating her fists against Kaulaki's chest as the crowd of men behind stood silently.

"I order you back," yelled Kaulaki, and Ahokupe smiled triumphantly.

Then the bridge flipped over, and his world turned on its head.

Ahokupe's arms were nearly yanked from their sockets as the guide rope arrested his fall, and he dangled for a few terrifying moments above the ravine. In that brief vertigo, he caught sharp flashes of rocks and ferns, a diseased tree log under a rock, and a giant octopus on a ledge above the waterfall's pool. Then the bridge twisted violently back into position, ripping the tree moss from his hands and the rope from his wrists. He was flung over the other side of the bridge, and for one horrible moment he hung by a single leg over the cascading falls, watching the moss disappear into the clouds of mist.

Let's leave his wrists bound.

In those heady moments dangling from death's high branch, many thoughts flashed through Ahokupe's mind. For the first time, he wondered why every single Maoli detested him. It was true that he'd sought to prove himself better than any of them, to show that a kinless man was worth something. Yet the only Maoli who loved him was Liliha, and he'd never tried to prove anything to her.

Yelling with the effort, Ahokupe swung his body upward and caught the edge of the bridge. He heaved himself over it, grasping at one rotting mangrove plank as Liliha's screams drifted over the waterfall's roar. With his right leg still hooked into the guide rope, he stood slowly and looped his wrists again, determined to live long enough to witness Kaulaki's bitter defeat.

He remained in place for a long moment, panting hard and feeling Atoo's spray wash over his face. Then the bridge flipped again, and Ahokupe felt his feet slip off the planks until he was dangling again over sharp rocks, this time supported by two hands and a leg. Stomach clenching, he fought back bile as he forced himself to study the ravine—the octopus was unlike any creature that had ever swum through Hava'iki's lagoons. It sat in a pool of moving brown liquid, a sight that so unnerved him, he didn't see the flying glob of mud until it smacked into his chest.

The bridge righted itself, and Ahokupe flung himself forward, clawing for a mangrove plank as the guide rope was torn away from his hands. He rolled onto the rotting boards and stared at his bare chest, watching the God's mud bubble and sink into his skin. Finally it disappeared, leaving a long red blister.

He rose to his feet slowly, chest burning, as strange images assailed him. Two fiery circles shining through red clouds. Lakes of brown liquid that moved of their own accord. Vast structures of gleaming blue, blanketed by fog. A storm of ideas that meant nothing and everything all at once. Yet throughout this chaos one thing was clear: Maniloa swung the bridge not to dislodge men, but to bring them close to his mud. When they fell and died, he ate them, but that was not his purpose. Through the mud, the God spoke to mankind.

Ahokupe closed his eyes and tried to quash the impossible images that filled him. He focused on the waterfall's roar, imagined weaving his spirit's threads back together, one by one. He knew without doubt that the God was done twisting the bridge today.

Breathing deeply, he faced the far side of the bridge. He unhooked his leg from the guide rope, then stepped carefully across those mangrove planks, toward the gorge's other side. He breathed a huge sigh of relief as his bare foot touched dirt, and he tapped the nearest tree. Then he turned around and headed back toward the Maoli, keeping both hands on the sennit rope.

Liliha threw herself into his arms as soon as his feet struck the ground, and they stood like this for a long moment while Kaulaki watched them through the mist.

"The God has favored us," Liliha whispered.

Trembling with emotion, Ahokupe held her close to him, feeling his tears melt into her hair. "Maniloa has given me the only thing I ever wanted." And he knew it was true—suddenly, he had no more desire to hurt Kaulaki.

He pulled away and stared into her large brown eyes. Then he slipped his hand into hers, and together they walked to face the king of Hava'iki, whose scowl was a terrible thing to behold.

"Liliha is mine," Ahokupe said. "We will—" A burst of foreign thought filled his mind, and he stopped in mid-sentence, hanging his head. Sweat ran down his bare chest as he struggled to comprehend the God's images. After some time, he looked back at Kaulaki.

"Maniloa needs help. He promises the Maoli a gift beyond compare if we aid him."

Kaulaki's tataued cheeks stretched back in a grimace. His gaze flicked to the God's blister on Ahokupe's chest, then back to his face. "A gift beyond compare. Will he eat the Malayes, then? Offer me a hundred pigs? What will he do?"

Ahokupe shook his head. "The God—thinks very differently. He sends strange visions, and they escape into the air. I know only that he will help us."

Kaulaki ground his jaw, as if chewing Kava root. He eyed Ahokupe's blister again, and then twisted to look at the men behind him.

"Arii, Keoni, Ihorangi, Whetu, Mehalo, Tane, you will assist the God, and bring the Maoli glory. Go with Ahokupe." He seized Ahokupe's arm in a hard grip. "If any die from this folly, I'll rip your throat out with my bare hands."

Ahokupe pulled away, and Liliha fell into his arms. "Please, not again," she pleaded.

Ahokupe kissed her soft neck. "My sweet, Maniloa will not harm me. Not now."

Some time later, Ahokupe and six others climbed into the misty ravine, stepping carefully over sharp lava rocks and slippery ferns. Their faces were grim, for all knew that Maniloa was an eater of men. Yet Ahokupe had challenged the God, and he was Kaulaki's despised one; they could do no less.

After long moments of silent climbing, Ahokupe grabbed an outcropping and twisted to face the warriors behind him.

"Maniloa is not a man," he yelled over the waterfall's roar. "He is a—*creature*. Do not be surprised when you see his likeness, and do not look closely. He will not eat you."

They stared at him, and Ahokupe watched Keoni's round face contort with horror. "Aieee!" he yelled, pointing down the ravine.

Ahokupe followed Keoni's finger and saw part of Maniloa's body clearly for the first time. On a ledge near Attoo, a brownish liquid oozed toward them through the cracks in the rocks. In some areas, the liquid had hardened into orange lumps like rotting mangoes, or like the octopus head he thought he'd seen earlier. But in other places, Maniloa's body flowed like water, pouring through the fissures in the ledge.

They watched, frozen, as Maniloa oozed toward them, and Ahokupe knew the others were a hair's breadth from flight. Surely this was madness.

Without warning, Maniloa flung brown liquid from his body, striking all seven men amid a flurry of shouts and curses. Ahokupe slipped on a rock and landed on jagged lava, pain shooting through his side. Then his shoulders burned from the God's mud, and Maniloa's images assailed him anew—the sun split into two in a dark sky. Shiny rain that sizzled as it struck blood-red rocks. Bolts of lightning playing across dark oceans. Yet one thought was perched on the highest branch: Maniloa was trapped under a stone, and the Maoli must free him.

He stood and watched five of the other men share awe-stricken looks, while Mehalo rolled on the jagged lava with head in hands, crying at the God's images. The others seemed shaken but able to stand, and Ahokupe somehow felt their minds in his own. They knew what to do. One by one, all except Mehalo stepped onto the ledge and moved toward Maniloa's liquid body. The God's essence parted around their footsteps as they passed through him, their feet landing on dry rock.

They crawled over an outcropping and saw that Maniloa's brown liquid stretched across the ledge, disappearing under a massive boulder. Beyond the rock, the God's body had hardened into solid globs of orange matter.

Ahokupe wiped his brow, suddenly understanding how the God could twist bridges yet be unable to save himself. This rock was enormous, and it would take all of them to free him.

Without speaking, Ahokupe and Whetu grabbed a downed ficus log and wedged it beneath the rock. They began pushing down on its other end, while the others strained hard against the wall of stone. The log bent into an arch as Ahokupe and Whetu placed all their weight against it, sweat pouring over their bare chests. Finally, it snapped, just as the boulder rolled off Maniloa and over the ledge.

There was a collective gasp as they all watched Maniloa's solid portions, previously anchored by the boulder, melt into brown liquid. The dark pool oozed into the cracks in the lava outcropping, and toward the ledge. Then, quick as a bird, Maniloa poured off the ledge and was swallowed by the waterfall.

For a long moment they stared into the billowing clouds below, searching for any sign of the God. A quick flash of brown briefly caught their attention, but it was soon hidden again by Attoo's spray. Ahokupe's head was hot, his attentions pulled between the search for Maniloa and the utter strangeness of the God's images in his mind. He clenched his fists, trying to understand Maniloa's final purpose.

"There," Whetu hissed, pointing, and they turned to behold a bizarre vision. As they watched, brown liquid cascaded *up* the cliff on the ravine's far side, towards the shiny ball that was Maniloa's home. The dark pool oozed over the structure, and then became transparent as it melted into the sphere. Within moments, the God was gone.

Maniloa's home began to shake, ejecting black smoke and a sour smell that burned Ahokupe's throat. Then a ball of fire blew the bridge apart, with an ear-splitting crack that knocked them backward. Amid cries and shouts of awe, they fell to their knees, watching Maniloa's home rise into the sky on a pillar of flame. And as shards of mangrove planks fell around them, and the forest erupted into squawks and chatters, they knew they'd witnessed a tale for the ages. Their children's children would see this event through their eyes.

They remained motionless for some time, watching Maniloa's home turn into a tiny dot in the sky, amid small crackles of trees set aflame and the cries of parrots. When Maniloa had completely disappeared, they rose and looked at each other with shared wonder. Ahokupe and Whetu walked to a blubbering Mehalo and gently lifted him. Then they all began climbing out of the ravine.

Some time later, they stood before a very pale Kaulaki, Liliha clinging to Ahokupe's arm like a remora eel. Ahokupe grimaced as he faced Hava'iki's king, trying to give voice to Maniloa's bizarre images. Kaulaki's eyes darted between all seven men and the blackened ground where the God's home had once stood.

"So, Maniloa has returned to the heavens. Where is his gift? Does he fly to destroy the Malayes?"

Ahokupe struggled to hold the God's voices in his thoughts. "No. The God says..." Ahokupe took a deep breath. "The God says we must leave Hava'iki before the breadfruit ripens. We are in great danger here."

Kaulaki stared. A light rain began falling, its soft whisper barely audible over Attoo's roar. Finally, he spat at Ahokupe's feet. "The God is wrong. The Malayes will not defeat us."

"My king," Whetu said softly. "Maniloa has told this to all of us. We will die on Hava'iki. Maybe the Malayes have joined the other tribes of the forever land. The God didn't say."

Kaulaki drew back, rain travelling in rivulets down his Tataued chest. "No! Hava'iki is the home of our ancestors; we cannot leave her!"

"We have the war canoes," Ahokupe said softly. "The forty canoes will hold all the people."

Kaulaki glared, his eyes white among black swirls. "*My* war canoes. *I* found the ironwood trees, *I* watched them for days, to see if the flycatcher pecked at a rotten trunk."

Ahokupe exhaled, knowing Kaulaki's dream was to defeat the Malayes with those boats. All had heard his plans: Twenty canoes filled with dummy warriors of reeds and coconuts, while the other twenty struck from behind.

Kaulaki swept the seven men with his gaze. "And now, instead of destroying the Malayes, we will flee like frightened pigs?"

"We must," said Arii.

Kaulaki's expression softened as he considered his favored. "And where shall we sail, Arii? Toward Hokupa the North Star, the forever land is filled with powerful tribes, which we cannot defeat. Elsewhere is only ocean, ocean, until the end of the world."

"There may be islands we do not know," Ahokupe said. "We may die on the seas, but death is certain here."

A flash of red lit the air, as a lorikeet darted out of the forest and crossed the ravine. From somewhere came the thud of a coconut falling to the ground.

"A curse on Maniloa, then," Kaulaki said quietly. His head was hung low, rain pouring down his cheeks. "If we are to leave Hava'iki, then my life has ended."

Three days later, Ahokupe stood with Liliha on a beach of white sand and turquoise waters. The smell of sea was strong in his nostrils as he watched the Maoli board the giant canoes, dragging sennit fishnets behind them. The boats were double-hulled monstrosities with prows as high as two men, intricately carved with the Goddess Faumea's likeness. Enormous mangrove platforms spanned those hulls, now being loaded with pigs and chickens, bamboo poles, tapa cloths, partially spun sennit, coconuts, mangoes, breadfruit, and endless gourds of water.

Silently, Ahokupe and Liliha watched the people leave their thatched huts and cross the white sand toward the canoes, overseen by Tiki carvings at the forest's edge. How easily did the Maoli abandon Hava'iki, Ahokupe thought. They laughed and sang and talked, seeming to care nothing about the uncertainties ahead.

And how he wished his mother were one of those old women, able to sail with him to the land beyond the sea. It was at this time, watching a woman scoop seashell mementos with her son, that Ahokupe felt his familiar loneliness. A hole in his spirit that he'd once patched with cocky pride. Now, Maniloa's mud had stolen all such weaponry from him.

"Your boat is the *Tahuni*," Kaulaki barked from behind. They turned to see the Maoli king glaring at Ahokupe and pointing to the *Tahuni*, one of three single-hull canoes. Ahokupe glanced at the *Huralai*, which was Kaulaki's—and Liliha's—boat. The grandest of all, each ribbed hull was wide as three huts, and the center platform held houses of bamboo and palm fronds to carry Kaulaki and Hava'iki's nobility.

Liliha folded her arms. "Then I shall travel in the *Tahuni* also."

A storm of rage crossed Kaulaki's Tataued face. "I'll not have him in my hut—"

"I will row with the others," Ahokupe said quietly. "If Liliha rides the *Huralai,* then so must I. But I'll not sully the king's house."

Kaulaki lifted an eyebrow, searching Ahokupe's expression for some trick. Finally satisfied, he nodded and walked away.

Liliha turned to Ahokupe. "But you've earned your place at his side, my love. Why leave it so easily?"

Ahokupe sighed. "I stole Kaulaki's daughter from him. I bested his challenge before all the people. And now I've forced him to abandon every dream he's had. I will steal his Mana no longer."

Her expression softened. "You have changed much, since the God touched you."

Ahokupe nodded. So much.

The sun was high overhead when their journey began. Ahokupe felt the wind in his hair, the salt spray at his lips as he pulled the oar back, singing with the other men. He welcomed his muscles' strain against the water, for the mindless task of rowing quieted the God's thoughts—images of starry skies, endless falling, human flesh dissolving in brown liquid. Reveling in their glide through the seas, his mind emptied of all but the Song of the Moon, drifting over the waters in unison with the other Maoli boats.

The distant bray of conch shells shattered his reverie, and around him men shaded their eyes and stared back toward Hava'iki. Ahokupe stood and saw ten canoes near Hava'iki's misty shoreline, colorful sails flapping in the breeze. The faint trumpeting of conch shells carried on the wind, a challenge and a taunt.

"Malayes," spat a man near Ahokupe.

Everyone stopped rowing to watch the Malaye canoes turn into the lagoon. Other Maoli canoes had also halted, and Ahokupe heard the soft grunts of pigs from a nearby boat. From the corner of his eye, he saw King Kaulaki burst from his hut and storm toward him through the hard benches.

"See what you've done!" he roared as he came close. "The Malayes are weak, but do we fight them? No, we flee like frightened children, while they steal our homeland!" He spat on Ahokupe's cheek, and Ahokupe forced himself to stand very still. Utter silence filled the *Huralai,* as Kaulaki's spittle crawled down Ahokupe's cheek, and finally dropped to the wooden floor.

"He is a false prophet," came Mehalo's gravelly voice. "I have touched the God also, and Maniloa tells me to turn and fight the Malayes." Ahokupe wiped his burning cheek and stared into the stout warrior's mad eyes, watching those wide nostrils flare with anger. The God had indeed touched Mehalo, but alone of all of them, Mehalo's spirit had never recovered. Wide and strong, the sickness in the man's eyes reminded Ahokupe of a speared boar, maddened by pain and determined to crush all in its path.

Kaulaki grinned and placed his hand on Mehalo's shoulder. "Then that's what we'll do. Today we sail into the sun, but tomorrow night we shall return to Hava'iki and take the Malayes by surprise." Smiling, he turned and walked back to his palm-frond hut.

Very few would talk to Ahokupe after that. It suited him fine, for as the dome of stars covered the sky, Liliha came to him, her slim figure a ghostly spirit in the low light. They huddled close that quiet night, listening to the hollow slap of water against the hull, and the hushed murmur of men watching stars for direction.

"Do you remember when we first kissed?" Liliha whispered to him, her beautiful face striped by the moonlight.

Ahokupe smiled, touching the amber bracelet she'd given him the next day. "No," he said, leaning forward. "Remind me."

Some time later they pulled apart, and Ahokupe brushed a strand of hair from her eyes. "Liliha, why did you fall in love with me? I was arrogant and insufferable. Surely one of the others would have been easier."

She placed a hand on his thigh, and Ahokupe closed his eyes, feeling her warmth as the ship rose and fell with the waves.

"If you were arrogant, then you were the opposite with me. I saw only kindness. The others brought caught turtle to my father's hut, or wrestled in the sand to show their strength. But you swayed me with nothing but gentle words." She draped slender bare legs over his. "I think having only a mother for kin teaches a man how to speak to women."

Surprised, Ahokupe leaned back against the railing, and Liliha curled over his chest. Together they watched the brilliant circle of stars above, listening to the small creaks of the boat.

"So Maniloa has gone back to the heavens," Liliha said after a moment. "Do his thoughts still fight in your mind?"

Ahokupe tried to release the sudden tension from his body. "They fight without mercy," he whispered. "And now, he gives me memories so horrible, I cannot even share them with you."

Liliha lifted her head to look into his eyes. "Tomorrow night, my father sails back toward Hava'iki. Mehalo tells him it is the God's will."

Ahokupe cupped her cheek. "Liliha, Mehalo's mind has turned into sand. The God said we are doomed on Hava'iki. If the canoes return, we must leave again quickly. Will you follow me?"

She nodded and placed her soft cheek on his chest.

"Anywhere."

After some time, Liliha padded back to her father's hut, and Ahokupe leaned against the ship's side. Slowly he drifted off, his dreams filled with images of Maniloa weaving between the stars.

Violent swaying awoke him, as the canoe tilted sideways among massive waves. Shouts came from across the vessel as men braced the water gourds, struggling to keep their supplies from falling into the sea. The first golden fingers of dawn lit the sky, just enough to reveal massive waves rolling toward them. The sky was a strange color, visible even in the low light, and the smell of ash was everywhere.

Kaulaki ran through the canoe, directing men to stow this or that supply, yelling at those whose hands held nothing. Ahokupe stared into the distance and saw a small red dot, in the direction where Hava'iki would have been.

Ahokupe caught Kaulaki's glare as he came near. "Hava'iki is no more," he said. "Great Oro has erupted, and our homeland has sunk into the sea. This was the God's message."

Kaulaki's face fell with such anguish that Ahokupe thought he'd collapse. He closed his eyes, grabbing the side of the boat. Then he opened them again.

"And the Malayes have drowned?"

"Yes."

Kaulaki wiped his cheek. "That is something, then."

"He lies!" Yelled Mehalo, bracing himself against the swaying boat as he came near. "Hava'iki awaits us; the God has shown it to me in a vision!"

Kaulaki turned around, staring into Mehalo's mad eyes.

"Grab the coconuts before they fall into the sea," Kaulaki mumbled. Then he staggered away.

The waves rolled the boat all morning, though by the time the sun was overhead, they had diminished to nothing. The wind picked up, and they hung the matted hala-frond sail on the center mast. Soon the *Huralai* was skipping over the seas, the Goddess at its prow spraying salt water behind her.

The days began to blend together. Every morning Ahokupe awoke to flat ocean stretching as far as the eye could see, a vast blue circle in every direction. The other Maoli boats were dots in the distance, though sometimes they approached closer to discern the colored tapa cloth waved from the *Huralai,* a marker to change direction.

The seas were mostly calm, and Ahokupe rowed often, stopping only when the Goddess filled their sail with wind. Ahokupe came to fear the wind, for rowing gave him relief from the God's thoughts, memories that had become increasingly gruesome. When he wasn't rowing or sleeping, only Liliha drew his attention elsewhere. She took to visiting him in the evenings at the back of the boat, where they would hold each other through the endless swells, watching for birds in the distance. On the first days, a few seagulls drifted lazily into the golden sunset. But soon the skies were utterly empty; land was nowhere close.

The *Huralai* began rationing water. When a precious storm came, the people rushed to place the gourds under the sail, trapping as much water as possible. But the clouds always disappeared quickly, and it was never enough. As their water supplies dropped low, Mehalo's grumblings began drawing more attention, and Ahokupe felt the hot stares of his shipmates. They mattered little to him, for he was consumed with fighting for mastery of his own mind, rowing when he could to dampen Maniloa's images.

One morning, Ahokupe awoke to see Arii crouching low before him, a tapa cloth around his shoulders to protect against the unexpected cold. Ahokupe blinked, noting how Arii's long face had strengthened. His giant nose seemed dignified, not the pelican's beak it had been before. He was tall and lithe, and sometimes Ahokupe marveled that Arii had never stolen Liliha's attentions despite his stutter.

"We've not always been friends," Arii said flatly.

Ahokupe ran his hands along the smooth wood of the ship's side. "It seems my arrogance caused that calamity with many."

Arii smiled and sat down. "Th-the God's attention changes us. You more than any; you've been touched twice."

"Yes."

For a moment they were silent, watching the feathered sennit rope whip backward behind the prow. "Maniloa's thoughts crowd my day without mercy," Arii whispered. "D-Do you have them too?"

Ahokupe felt his chest tighten. "Always. They will not leave me alone, day and night."

"And will n-none of them save us?"

Ahokupe gripped the ship's side, listening to the flapping of the sail in the strong winds. "There may be one. But I fear it is only a vision."

Arii watched him carefully.

"A circle of blue and white," Ahokupe continued. "Within the blue, small and large dots of green. I believe it is Maniloa's vision as he fell from the heavens onto Hava'iki."

Arii nodded. "The elders remember every direction we've travelled, every course change. If you d-describe the islands, they'll know where to turn."

"But Kaulaki is ready to strangle me."

Arii shook his head. "No more. Kaulaki's Mana will not let him admit he was wrong, but he knows it."

They were silent then, feeling the boat rise and fall with the waves. Ahokupe knew Arii had come for something else, but was content to wait. And after a long moment, he spoke.

"The image that most troubles my thoughts..." Arii stopped, swallowing. "Is when Maniloa ate the f-fallen. The feel of human flesh, the taste of it. A horrible thing, yet it fills me with longing." He turned away, ashamed.

But Ahokupe grabbed his arm. "Yes!" he hissed. "I think of it often. I long to taste human meat. Would that Maniloa had left us to die on Hava'iki and spared me this horror."

Arii clasped Ahokupe's arm also, knowing then that they shared a bond none would understand. "Let us resolve that if we eat, it will only be our enemies."

Ahokupe nodded, relieved. Arii stood up to leave, but turned around.

"You cannot ignore Mehalo forever. He gathers strength." With that, Arii walked away, and Ahokupe stared after him, hunched tight against the cold.

Later that afternoon, Ahokupe lifted his head from his hands to see eight men weaving toward him through the benches, Mehalo in front. Ahokupe stood, feeling the chill wind against his bare chest.

Mehalo approached close, his shoulders seeming wider than Kaulaki's hut. "Arrogant fool, thinking you know the God's plan," he said. "Your words have led us to disaster."

Ahokupe tried not to stare into those red, darting eyes. "Hava'iki is gone," he said quietly. "All of us know it."

"We know only what you have told us!" Mehalo shouted, and the men behind him grumbled assent. The rest of the *Huralai* had stopped to watch, and Ahokupe noticed Kaulaki standing outside his hut, wearing his feathered cape. Liliha began walking toward him, but Ahokupe held up his hand. No one could help him here.

Mehalo turned to the other men. "Maniloa has said that those who eat Ahokupe will gain his knowledge, and will see through his lies."

The other men wrinkled their noses in disgust, but Ahokupe thought he detected flashes of interest. Many were jealous of the God's touch, and some would consider the unspeakable to caress the divine. They had no idea what they wished for.

"You know nothing about Maniloa," Ahokupe said. "I am sure he's never told you his secrets."

"I know them all!" Mehalo shouted, spittle flying from his mouth. "The two suns sit in the sky, and one moves from right to left, while the other barely moves! And when the first is gone, sizzling rain strikes the rock, and eats giant holes. And—"

Mehalo stopped, as the men around him shrank back.

"Your leader cannot tell whether something exists inside or outside of his mind," Ahokupe said to the men behind Mehalo. "Still, he is right in a way; I am to blame for something. Maniloa has shown me land and I have ignored him, afraid of Kaulaki's wrath. I will ignore Maniloa no longer."

Ahokupe pushed through the crowd and walked toward the *Huralai's* center platform where Kaulaki stood, his feathered coat ruffling in the wind. The king turned and entered his hut, and Ahokupe followed him.

Inside, Fangaloka the elder stood over an ironwood plank, his body wrinkled like a budding noni fruit. On the other side of the plank was a sharp stone, which Kaulaki picked up and handed to Ahokupe.

"Show us."

Fangaloka turned the ironwood plank over, and Ahokupe approached.

"Hava'iki was here," Ahokupe said, scratching a circle on the plank. "Above it was the land of the Malayes. Below it are open seas, until a great frozen white land, and a large forever land, here." Ahokupe closed his eyes, recalling the God's image, and marked these points on the plank. "Past the large forever land, there are more islands."

Fangaloka rolled his eyes back in his head and began reciting the course changes they'd made since they started. Finally he stopped, turned to the right, and pointed. "Toward the stars of Matariki."

Ahokupe relayed this information to the ship master, who began waving colored tapa cloths at the other Maoli boots. Soon, they'd all turned in the direction where Matariki dipped below the edge of the world.

Days passed, and their water supplies dwindled, helped very little by another small storm. Every day, Ahokupe sat with Liliha in the boat as the *Huralai* skipped forward, searching the horizon for land. At night, Ahokupe heard Mehalo's grumbles, and he always slept with his back to the stern.

On one such day, Ahokupe was resting his head on Liliha's shoulder when her shriek made him jump. "Look!" she cried.

Licking dry lips, Ahokupe looked up to see a lone tern sailing the skies far in the distance.

Men around them began jabbering excitedly, and soon, the wail of conch shells drifted over the water, as the *Huralai* signaled to the other Maoli boats. They began tacking in the direction of the circling bird, and when they were closer, they removed the sail. They bobbed in place the rest of the day, waiting until sundown to follow the bird's return path. When it began flying back that evening, the *Huralai* shot forward with a will.

No land was seen the next day, but there were many more terns, and dolphins in the seas. They again waited until evening, following the terns on their return path home.

The following morning brought a bank of clouds on the horizon, and as they drew closer, the Maoli saw green slopes peeking from beneath the clouds.

Fresh water.

Cheers erupted from every part of the *Huralai,* and the conch shells brayed across the seas. Soon, all the Maoli boats could be seen in the distance, converging on them.

That day, as Ahokupe and Liliha watched the island grow larger, Kaulaki came to stand by them. Ahokupe shot him a quick glance, unsure what to say, but the Maoli king remained still as a Tiki. They stood silently for a long while, salt spray bathing their faces, as the first white sand beaches became visible.

Finally, Kaulaki folded his arms: "In our new home, you will be king."

Ahokupe turned to stare. Kaulaki's words could not have been more unlikely if he'd claimed to be a parrot.

"I don't understand."

"You have always had the heart of a warrior, Ahokupe; only your insufferable pride made it impossible. But I saw how you handled Mehalo, and you did well. I am tired, and the Maoli will need another."

Liliha's grip on Ahokupe's arm tightened, and Ahokupe breathed deeply. "Then my first decree is that the Maoli shall never more be threatened by one disaster. We shall travel the seas and populate every land that will have us. I have touched the God, and know that the islands are many."

Kaulaki's black Tataued cheeks stretched into a small smile. "I see pride has not completely left you. But it will serve us well in the new land."

Ahokupe and Liliha smiled at each other, and her hand slipped into his. Then they turned back to the ocean, and under the cloud of terns and gulls, the three of them watched the forested isle draw close.

About the story

I've always loved to read historical speculative fiction, and that love has translated to writing as well. I have written (and sold) speculative fiction pieces set among the 16th century Mexica (Aztecs), and the Saxons of 9th century Germany. This particular tale is set among the ancient Polynesians, who spread out from their ancestral homeland to carry their stories and way of life across the Pacific. My central question was: What if the spark for this migration was a very unexpected event, and what if those Polynesian stories had a little more bite than we ever imagined?

A question for the author

Q: What happens when you hit writer's block head on?

A: My life is so busy, and my time to write is so limited, that writer's block hasn't really hit me. I think the reason is that I spend long time in the car to and from work, dwelling on my next story or book. These thoughts stew all week, so that when the weekend rolls around and I finally have a moment to sit down and write, they just explode out of me. If I had to guess, I'd say that writer's block occurs when you've been at the keyboard too long, stressing about having writer's block. I think the solution is to go do other things (especially exercise), all while keeping your next project curled up in the back of your mind. This is essentially what I'm forced to do by life, and it seems to keep me from getting the dreaded curse.

About the author

Steve Rodgers works in security and cryptography, and has been reading since he was old enough to carry a stack of hard-bound science fiction books out of the library. He and his wife travel when possible (physically or mentally), though their mail is delivered to San Diego.

Writings and musings can be found at www.steverodgersauthor.com. @srodgers100

Steve Rodgers's story "Canoes of Hava'iki" was published in *Metaphorosis* on Friday, 28 April 2017.

May

Heartwood

L. Chan

The sorcerer wove his beloved out of the finest silks and linens, the poorest of which was fit for any earthly king. Across her neckline and cuffs, he affixed the most delicate lace, threads more slender than spiderwebs, lighter than a lover's breath. He scoured his Mansion of a Hundred Rooms for bolts of cloth; gifts from fellow sorcerers, from superstitious lords, from the jealous summer fae, from workers of enchantment and loom. These he sewed together. A lifetime working magic had given him deft fingers, and although his body now consisted of creaking wood, his hands retained their skill.

He filled her body with the softest down; from goose, from baby roc. Between her ears, the infant feathers of thunderbirds, to lend speed to her thoughts. Under her breast, phoenix down to warm her heart. Finally, when the body of cloth was complete, scraps and strips all come together in the form of a striking lady of middle years, he placed the heartwood fruit in the middle of her chest and bade it quicken.

The body convulsed, rippling as unfamiliar muscles flexed. Flesh might have been a better option, but creating a human body was beyond the remit of his considerable powers, as was the granting of life. The latter was the province of the gods, and all the races of man (despite being called a demon, or fallen god, the sorcerer considered himself a man) toyed with that sacred flame at their peril. But there were tricks by which an extinguished fire could be rekindled.

"Arcturus, my love." The woman's voice was smoother than woven silk, retaining the luscious drawl of vowels common to the desert folk. Time had long scrubbed trace of accent or region from Arcturus' own voice, and he missed it. Arcturus was not his birth name, nor one of the many whispered by kings and mothers to frighten, but it was the one he would respond to without thinking. The woman was the only living soul who had uttered it in years. She struggled to push herself off the workbench with limbs as boneless as tentacles.

"Gladiola," he replied, helping the woman to her feet. She swayed like grass on the wind, like the flowers she was named after. He'd taken care that those blossoms appeared in the tessellations of the silks and in the lace trimmings. She didn't notice.

"I am not as I once was," she said, holding one cloth hand up to an embroidered eye. "And neither are you, it seems." Gladiola stroked the grain of his wooden cheek. He felt nothing.

The pair of them walked the halls of the Mansion of a Hundred Rooms, each door they passed open to wonders; a choir of hummingbirds singing hymns to dead gods, a guardhouse filled with living suits of armour handing out halberds and wickedly curved swords, a cathedral of staircases made of bone that defied gravity and space.

When the woman of cloth had her fill of the sound of footsteps, she spoke again. "Why did you bring me back?"

Their wanderings had brought them to a double door, twice the height of a man. So dark was the wood that the pair could cast no shadows upon it and only the glint of light off the undulating surface hinted at its intricate carvings. Heartwood it was, from the same trees that bore the fruit beating in the chests of the pair of them. Blood-warm to the touch and, if one were particularly sensitive, thrumming periodically.

"Not just because the dark cannot hold a light such as yours," he said, pushing at the door. Despite their size, they yielded smoothly and without complaint.

The room behind the door gleamed with uncommon opulence; not a surface was to be found that was not embroidered, carved or gilded. The bed, to which Gladiola was no stranger, was weighed down by a familiar body, the sheets still glistening.

"Oh," she said.

"I need your help to solve this."

Gladiola looked to the corpse and back to Arcturus' roughly hewn features. "How long ago was..." she gestured at the body on the bed, which still wore the same placid expression as the creaking wooden man before her.

"Weeks, months," he replied. "Time does not pass normally in the Mansion."

"Then you came back, in this form? And brought me back? What work did you use?"

"Heartwood. For both of us."

Cloth eyes widened, fabric mouth hung open. "That's a legend."

"The Mansion is full of legends."

"And the cost? There is always a cost."

Heartwood trees had been harvested to near extinction by the powerful, desperate to hide from death in this most sacred of trees. The trick wasn't getting heartwood to sprout; seeds only needed to be buried in the soil, wrapped in the coppery softness of a fresh heart. It was losing their hearts that the powerful feared.

"What do you remember last?"

"I remember only waiting for my thirty-second birthday and then waking up today, nothing in between."

"That is part of the cost; what comes back is only what the heartwood preserves. And a vessel is required to house the heartwood."

Gladiola looked at cold flesh, and then at living wood and finally at the rippling cloth of her own body. "How can I be of help? I do not remember your murder."

"Neither do I. A small blessing. All I want to know is why." Arcturus looked away. He had seen many dead things in his life; monsters that wore the faces of men, men who wore the faces of monsters, children barely old enough to walk. All dead by his hand, but still he felt discomfort at the sight of the corpse wearing his face.

Lace fingertips stroked a bloodied cheek. The dead flesh yielded no clues as to the power of the man that once inhabited it; soft and pliant, it was much like any other cold meat. "I first came to the Mansion to kill you. I never renounced my quest."

"But you loved me."

"I do. In spite of what you've done. Because of what you've done. I'm not the Gladiola who killed you. What happened to her?"

"Dead by her own hand." One of the first things he had done, after relearning the use of his new body, was to bury his lover on the outskirts of the Mansion, without magic, without servants. Hard labor was a blessed distraction. Partly from the knowledge that he was simultaneously a dead man as well as a mere simulacrum with the memories of the being once called Arcturus. Mostly from the discovery that the only woman he'd given his love to had put a foot of sharpened steel through his breastbone; the blow so resolute that the tip of the sword was lodged in the frame of the bed beneath him. Not a second of hesitation in a thrust like that.

"Let me ask you this, beloved. Are you happy?"

"I have more wealth than kings, power enough to cast down small gods. I fear neither sickness nor the passage of time. I had the love of a princess."

"That is not what I asked. If there was another Gladiola, then know this, she did not kill you with hate in her heart."

"Why then?"

"When you find out, you would have solved your murder. Enough of this, my love. Let me ask you something instead. Are you content in there?"

"It will take more than prophecy and betrayal to end me."

"Wooden heart, wooden body. Maybe you haven't lost that much at all," she said, picking at her lace cuffs, the seam coming undone, the gash bleeding finest down. "I would ask a boon in exchange. End this half-life," she continued, her pillow hand moving up to his timber chest, leaving a smear of blood from his corpse.

"It is a second chance for us, Gladiola."

"One was enough."

Arcturus carved his guest from from a single block of jade. A flawed seam of umber ran through the jade; the swindle had cost the merchant his right hand, which Arcturus had turned to stone. Perhaps this Gladiola would be better. This was the fifth, each a step further back in their relationship, each a little different. There was a gadfly of a thought; the idea that he was no longer the man who built the Mansion of a Hundred Rooms, that he was somehow diminished. Perhaps instead of raising Gladiola, he should have gone deep into his heartwood forest and found a version of himself that knew not love. Perhaps.

He threw himself deeper into the work. Around her wrists and ankles, he set bands of gold and platinum. Star-bright diamonds for eyes, crushed ruby dust for lips, beaded onyx, obsidian, and opal in strands for her hair. He raided his treasury, pried inset stones from goblets, crowns, and jewelry alike to adorn his beloved. When he was done, he parted her breastbone with a chisel and left the heartwood fruit within.

"My lord," she said. Her voice held the rough edge of granite crypts and the cool of marble tombstones. She took in her surroundings with glittering eyes. "The Mansion is not as I remembered it, and neither am I."

Dust gave the Mansion a grey sheen; motes caught sunbeams and sparkled as the movement of the pair raised clouds from the moth eaten carpets.

"The dust does not bother me, I do not breathe. The servants are mostly gone, I do not eat."

"Every living thing eats."

"I sleep with my feet in a brass tub, in which I have dissolved various nutrients."

"Very convenient, my lord. Perhaps I should learn to eat rocks?"

Her tongue was as sharp as her blade had been. It had been some time since he had suffered the indignations of either. He armoured himself in silence and showed the grinding effigy of his onetime lover to her quarters.

Gladiola surveyed the one room in the Mansion that had not been claimed by disrepair. A beetlemaid scurried by, pink frock swishing over black carapace as her jointed legs moved almost faster than the eye could see. In her haste, she caught the edge of a dressing table with a poorly folded wing and sent a porcelain vase to the floor.

The living blue ink had once depicted scenes of battle, with lacquer armoured warriors from the far east in combat with demons. The tiny figures ceased their fight and began to panic as the ink leached from fragmented porcelain into the floorboards. The maid cowered, chittering an apology, spraying sweet pheromones of atonement from glands behind her antennae.

"Clean that up and leave us," said Arcturus. They sat on a chaise longue upholstered in wyvern leather, the heartwood chairs complaining under their combined weight.

"You seem to have found mercy in your dotage. I recall you taking life for less," observed Gladiola. The beetlemaid finished her work, backing out of the room slowly, antennae dragging on the floor in contrition as she half-bowed, half-grovelled her exit.

"I did not bring you back to argue the treatment of my servants, my love." The endearment slipped out like an uncaged rodent while he was distracted by the maid, and it could not be recaptured. Gladiola drew herself up and shifted to the edge of the chaise. If her gemstone body could have gotten any colder and stiffer, it would have.

"You are overly forward, my lord. Whatever transpired between you and the other Gladiola, I am not her. I am a prisoner against my will in your Mansion, not one of your concubines."

Arcturus took to his feet. "You were a prisoner of your will. You had only to renounce your quest and you would have been free to go."

"It was carved on my bones that I would be the one to vanquish you."

"A foretelling as unoriginal as it is inaccurate, I have an armoury filled with the weapons of those who were born to kill me."

"Nevertheless, a witch opened up my thigh and wrote it on my femur; and tattooed it across both my arms, that I would remember what I was born to do." She traced the angular runes of her people over the pale green of her forearm. "Did you think that stealing my flesh would change that?"

The next phrase fell from Arcturus' lips smooth as a river pebble, edges worn off by the eddies and rapids of hard practice. After all, this was the fifth Gladiola he'd brought back. "It's over, you won. You killed me, shortly before killing yourself."

If there was shock behind that jade visage, it was well hidden. "Yet we are still here."

"A plan for the eventuality that one of the many prophecies foreseeing my demise was accurate."

"Why do I not remember my victory?"

"Your heart is as it was on your twenty-seventh birthday. It has been some time since then. I brought you back from a heartwood tree planted on that birthday."

Gladiola pressed green fingertips over the cavity in her chest that held the heart shaped fruit. "Legends say that a heartwood tree only sprouts from a seed buried together with the heart of a living person."

"Not a whole heart. I opened your flesh as you slept and took a sliver of your heart with a blade so fine it could split a hair down the centre."

"Was I so spoiled by your Mansion that I did not notice you butchering me?"

"Your sleep was... assisted. I would not have had you suffer. After all, I planted a tree for you every year you stayed in my Mansion."

"I must have had very little heart left." To that, he had no answer. It was not so difficult to harvest the heart of another to plant a heartwood tree. Planting one's own heartwood tree was a different problem altogether.

The gemstone woman made her way over to a horned skull suspended at head height. Bleached bone was suggestive of a horse or a lizard, but the skull was as long as a man was tall. "I was going to ask you to bring me the head of the dune dragon stalking my clan's caravans."

"And so I did. And a clutch of siren skins the year after. And the pelts of the Ur-wolves from the frozen steppes the year after that. There has been a slight paucity of monsters in the kingdom over the past decadeHow many more lives would you have saved if you had me build rather than destroy?"

"It seems like an excessive amount of effort for a captive houseguest," she said, her tone smoother and drier than the rocks that she was carved from.

"You were very persuasive," Arcturus answered. And he had wanted to be persuaded. Not by beauty. The plains tribes were sturdy stock, and she had inherited the craggy features of her kin. There was a fire in her, a purity of purpose that he'd never possessed, something missing even from the princes, knights errant, and other ilk that came to challenge him.

"Perhaps you are not the man so many good knights and warriors swore to end."

That was where it started, Arcturus remembered. His wooden chest was hollow inside, but it was only after hearing those words for the second time that he felt its emptiness. He again considered using the benefit of his memories to reenact those sweet years before their deaths. But such a love would have been as barren as he was.

"I was. Not out of service to dark gods, not to impose my will on nations, but to satisfy my own appetites, which had grown vast and esoteric. I haven't been that man for a long time. You ended him long before you killed me," he managed to say, after a moment.

She turned to look at him with her diamond bright eyes and her ivory smile under ruby powder lips. "Why didn't you kill me, like you did all the others?"

"I hadn't won. Many champions beg for their lives, with their swords broken and protections crushed. You never did."

"Begging meant admitting that my life was in your hands."

"It intrigued me."

"I would ask for you for the opposite now, my lord. Consider it a gift."

Arcturus closed the bedroom door behind him, leaving to fetch the beetlemaid. Cleaning up shattered jade was beyond him at the moment.

There was no cheating death; the bill had to be paid. The Ng'ahthim Invocation traded a wizard's shadow for his life, although thereafter he would neither sense nor feel. The Aurorean Sequence called the souls of the dead to form a shroud over the caster, but the screaming of the damned eventually drove all invokers mad. Heartwood had to be paid in heart and memory; and that which came back was never as whole as that which died.

Arcturus forged his destroyer from the blades in the armoury and of the architecture of his alchemical forays. Flange and falchion made arms and legs, braided steel formed her torso. He gave her scalpel fingers and razor blade teeth, plaiting barbed wire down from her scape to the middle of her back, setting up an open bear trap for her heart. Molten dabs of copper for eyes, burning bright orange from a face framed by bangs of filament metal. The heartwood fruit went in last, nestled within the trap. He had hardly drew his hand back when it sprang, quite nearly snipping off two fingertips.

Gladiola's eyes continued to blaze long after burning copper should have cooled. A swipe from one knife-edged palm took the end of Arcturus' nose off. Her follow up strike, a stiff fingered thrust, would have run him through if a blue nimbus of raw magic hadn't hurled her across the room.

Arcturus held up a pair of open palms. "Gladiola, you are not yet the woman who kills me, and I am no longer the man you want to slay."

"No more tricks, sorcerer." Her voice was the clash of blades, the sparking of a grindstone.

"No tricks, only knowledge and an invitation for a walk through the Mansion."

She tilted her head, warrior's instincts assessing, calculating. Satisfied, she brushed powdered stone from her shoulders and got to her feet. "If you had to give me a new form, I would have thought you would have chosen one less suited to killing you. Where's my body?" she said, flexing muscles of cable, tendon springs creaking.

"Buried on the grounds after you killed yourself."

The last of the servants had been sent away, the djinn freed from their compulsions, the mortal remains of the ghost slaves blessed and interred, the spectrals exorcised. Tapestries fed moths, furniture was darkened with age and water rot. All save the heartwood doors, which still stood imposing and unmarred.

"I doubt that I would have done that."

"People change," he said, leading the scissor princess to parts of the Mansion that no one, not even the servants, had been to.

"I will not. My tribe gave up my future to the gods to procure a single possibility, your destruction."

"Let me give you a different foretelling. When I was young and full of power, I wrested a prophecy from the silver Sister Moon. She told me that only one who loved me could cut me down. I bullied another from the golden Sister Sun, who told me that only one I loved could end me. Even though the siblings hate each other and are no longer on speaking terms, they are more alike than they admit. Their appetite for irony is unparalleled."

A final heartwood doorway opened up to a lush garden, the hidden centre of the Mansion. Gladiola narrowed her glowing eyes, trying to identify the copse of trees within the grounds. Taller and straighter than church steeples, they brought to mind the pine or the fir, but pocked with whorls and knotholes. Sketched out in the warped wood was a single repeating motif, a human face.

"A kingdom may be sold for a single tree. I have an entire forest here." Arcturus retrieved a cask from the ground. Unstopping it, he set about pouring a pungent liquid around a lifetime of trees, down the line back to the first one he'd planted, ashen faced, after sawing off a chunk of his own beating heart. He'd taken Gladiola all the way back; stripped her of the years in the Mansion, of her years with him. In the time he spent raising and putting down the many versions of his lover, he'd often thought of doing the same to himself, building another body, call up a version of from the fiery days when his name was whispered across the lands. Give up this form and start over.

He looked at Gladiola, a monstrosity wrought of blades and terrible purpose. No, he would not give that up. Sisters Sun and Moon said that love would destroy him; they were right. There was a forest of lives here, and Arcturus could have chosen to be any one of them, ones at the peak of his power and cruelty, ones that didn't live with the memories of hundreds of lives taken. But he no longer wanted to be any of those.

"They are all you," she said, running bladed fingers down a face, peeling a sliver of wood from the tree. The wounded bark released the smell of wormwood and myrrh, just like the mansion, just like the wizard.

"And you. A tree for every year; each capable of growing a heart for another body."

"Lost memories," she said. "This isn't living, it's just an echo waiting to fade."

"So said all the others. What of you?"

"My business with you isn't finished." She looked to the sliver of wood on her fingertip, the colour and smell strangely familiar to her.

"This is the same wood as the doors and furniture in the Mansion." He hadn't made her a face to express emotion, but surely it was horror there in brass and iron. "All built from my trees. More and more of the Mansion has been built out of me over the years," he said, emptying the cask onto the ground. "Let me give you a different ending to the prophecies. A warrior princess rode up to slay the evil wizard. She was easily vanquished. He made her his guest for many years. She asked him to slay the monsters plaguing her people in her stead. There was love there, in the most unlikely of places. But love does not sit easy atop a mountain of the dead. The princess was a prisoner, of prophecy and duty. The wizard more so, of regret and of the power he accumulated. So she freed him in the only way she knew."

Gladiola considered the tale, arms folded over her bear trap heart, the only sound the rattle of her scalpel fingers on her metal arm. "That is a terrible story."

"I brought you back many times. From when you loved me. From when you feared me. And now when you hate me. I convinced myself that I was doing it for you, but I am as much a prisoner of my machinations as I ever was."

He knelt on the grass, guiding one of Gladiola's hands to the centre of his heartwood breastbone. "I told another you that I was giving us a second chance, but she was right. Once was enough. The Mansion is nearly spent. Fulfill your quest. End me now and kill the forest."

The flames in the distance were bright enough to reflect orange across Gladiola's edged, metal skin. Legends had been right about heartwood burning; the forest screamed as it died. The sound was disconcerting to the princess' ears, and she was no stranger to the sounds of battle.

Dawn was breaking, that brief interstice when Sisters Sun and Moon looked at each other jealously across the sky. Perhaps they'd be laughing at Arcturus, standing silently behind his rescuer. He hadn't said a word since she refused to run him through, hauling him bodily from the burning forest after he lit the dragonfire oil.

"Payment for the first mercy you showed me when I failed to kill you," she said when she dumped him on the grass, still smouldering. "Besides, I am not sure that you are still the man I set out to destroy." She spoke towards the crumbling remnants of their old home.

"But you have destroyed him more completely than you set out to do, it seems."

"Princess saves the evil wizard, that's a new one. It's harder to redeem than to destroy."

The remnants of the Mansion collapsed with a final groan of masonry and timber; dragonfire was thorough. Sister Sun would shine down on smoking rubble and a steel princess leaving the grounds with a wooden wizard, on the way to something new.

About the story

There were two important pieces to this story. The first is a line that appears nearer to the end: the woman has a bear trap heart. I did mean it figuratively when I thought it up but it became quite literal in the story. The second is that I've written a fair bit (in the science fiction side of the house) about body transference, memory and karma and the interplay of all three. This is really a science fiction story about version control, Arcturus restores earlier and earlier backups of his lover, we travel back in time with them while the story progresses. Just before I wrote Heartwood, I'd received a rejection for another science fiction story. The feedback was that the story was well written and engaging, but the editor couldn't believe in the science of the body transference. So I thought, screw it, let's make the whole thing magic instead. So it became the darker sort of fairy tale towards the end, with a bit of role reversal thrown in.

A question for the author

Q: What's an idea you're dying to write but haven't, and why?

A: I've always wanted to write about traditional customs in modern or futuristic contexts. Witches using iPads (done!), the merits of reincarnation versus immortality (or cloning vs uploading to computers, also done)... One day I'm going to have characters celebrate Chinese New Year in space.

About the author

Since his last publication in *Metaphorosis*, L Chan has acquired his post graduate degree and moved back to Singapore. He continues to write all manner of speculative fiction, makes up funny comments about cats on the Internet and has reacquired his dog. He has been accused of being a self-aware meme-propagating bot. He's still looking for the perfect cup of coffee.

www.facebook.com/Straydog1980, @lchanwrites

L. Chan's story "Heartwood" was published in *Metaphorosis* on Friday, 5 May 2017.

Ways to Face the Firing Squad

Anna Zumbro

Pleadingly

Marshall's innocent. There's been looting and worse everywhere since the missiles hit, but he's taken nothing except a jacket he found in an abandoned car. It's not honor that keeps him from stealing, he's just scared he'll screw it up, and then what will Dad say? The man breathed anger even before the day the sky burst into flames, the day Mom didn't come home.

Dad doesn't yell any more, but Marshall knows the anger is still there, rock that once was magma. When Dad commands him to keep watch, he doesn't argue. Waiting outside the shop while Dad hunts for something edible, Marshall scans the horizon for signs of the soldiers who now play cop, judge, and executioner to anyone suspected of breaking the law.

From inside comes a woman's voice, soft, then loud, then silent. Marshall ignores it. Probably just another looter.

Two soldiers stop them twenty minutes later, a man and a woman in grubby camouflage. The man pats them down and finds the cans of tuna and beans tucked inside Marshall's jacket. The woman points to blood on Dad's sleeve, and the soldiers exchange a look — a verdict.

Marshall starts crying, even though he hasn't cried in years. He's fourteen but says he's twelve. He steps away from his father and says he doesn't know this man, he was forced to come along.

"You little fuck," Dad says. "I bet you're the reason we got caught."

Seductively

The soldiers are as young as Joy is, maybe younger. The male soldier has barely any hair on his chin even though there's no way anyone's shaving now, not with the water shortages and the poison in the air that makes your fingers tremble. Maybe he's never even been with a woman. Certainly not with the woman soldier. She looks like she could be his sister, and she looks angry.

"Please," Joy says, putting one foot forward in that way that makes her hips jut out. They jut out more now that there's less flesh between skin and bone. How can it be a crime to steal when starving?

"Following orders," the boy soldier says. "You broke the law."

"We can work something out, can't we?"

Joy glances at the woman soldier, extending the invitation to both of them. She unzips the front of her jacket, then unbuttons her shirt to reveal the bare curves of her breasts. She runs a hand through her hair. When she pulls her fingers away several strands come away too, strange and fine and faded.

"Oh, shit." She doesn't take her eyes off the locks of hair as the soldiers raise their rifles.

Intentionally

Tulio's hair is falling out. There's just a bit left at the nape of his neck and above his left ear. His teeth are falling out, too. It takes more energy than he's got to move ten feet. Others say there's a camp two miles away and a working hospital maybe three miles past that. But what's the point? Even if he could be saved, he has no one left. His son is gone.

The knowledge freezes him inside and stops all other thought. His son is gone. His son is gone.

So when he sees the two soldiers, the man and woman both so ragged and dirty-faced they hardly look human, he takes his chance. He runs up to them, poised to attack. The woman swings her rifle. It hits him square in the forehead.

He falls back on the ground and smiles and thinks of his little boy. At least a bullet will be quick. At least he gets to die with some of his teeth, some of his hair, some of his dignity.

Obliviously

The survivors in the camp call him Loco, and they want him gone. They approach the pair as soon they spot the uniforms, saying the old man's a menace, or maybe he's a young man, but it's all the same now and anyway he doesn't talk, just bites like a rabid dog.

"If there's such a thing as zombies," one woman says, "then this guy's a zombie. You'll be doing him a favor."

Loco runs around flapping his arms. He won't stay in one place long enough for either soldier to shoot him. The man wants to give up.

"He doesn't know what he's doing," he says. "He belongs..."

But he stops, because the places where Loco belongs are gone now, and Loco is almost gone too. There's nothing else to do.

At last Loco bends over a dead crow, its wings powdered white with ash. The woman raises her rifle and centers the back of Loco's head. He won't see it coming.

Defiantly

"Told you it was a bad idea to come here," Naomi tells her brother. She touches the name on her uniform, Barton. Her last name is Williams.

"It's your fault," Brett says. He kicks his camouflage jacket, which lies on the ground. "The uniforms were your idea."

"We did what people expected from us. We kept the peace. We weren't common looters."

"Shut up." The lieutenant's uniform is almost clean and his eyes shine with authority. "I don't care what soldier-killers have to say. You've wasted enough oxygen."

"We didn't kill the soldiers," Brett says. "We found their bodies, already dead, and we needed clothes."

"Guns and uniforms, you mean. So you betrayed people's trust, shot a few looters while you were at it? What gave you the right?"

Naomi swallows, knowing her next words will be her last. "Who says you get to be the only ones enforcing the law? Maybe we weren't official, but we were no diff—"

At the sound of the two gunshots, a murder of crows takes to the sky above the makeshift camp. There are only five, but the survivors agree it is amazing there are any birds left.

A question for the author

Q: What is your favorite fairy tale and why?

A: When I was younger, I read a collection of different tellings of "Beauty and the Beast." I've always been fascinated by that story (and, especially, by the library in the Disney version).

About the author

Anna Zumbro lives in Washington, DC, with her husband and not enough books.

@annazumbro

Anna Zumbro's story "Ways to Face the Firing Squad" was published in *Metaphorosis* on Friday, 12 May 2017.

The Early History of the Moon

Karolina Fedyk

Warsaw, 1812

Before Warsaw, I had spent days inventing myself as a pianist. Tailoring my biography, imagining what could happen in my possible lives. Love, perhaps, there was place for love; politics even, for it seemed inevitable. Betraying my kin—and then death—came merely as consequences.

The evening is cold: autumn has taken hold over us already. The train rolls into its final station, accompanied by a grinding screech and thick puffs of steam. People start spilling onto the platform. The sky above us is clear, the air crystalline. Instinct older than any language is tugging at me, forcing me to look up. I gaze into the pallid face of the Moon, and think of it: home.

Warsaw only comes second in my thoughts. I have been fantasizing about what it might be like, to wake and then fall asleep in this unknown city, to find its relentless struggle somewhat familiar to my own. In my first hours in the train carriage, I imagined and reimagined Warsaw, trying to contain the flutter in my chest. It's been so long since I've been allowed the excitement of travel, the thrill of being among strangers. Warsaw was, as my brothers had highlighted many times, best avoided. Nowadays, it was not a city for any of us. Too unstable politically. Too many eyes and ears.

As the train passed through abandoned fields and trampled wheat, soil crusting in September's early frost, the idea of moving to the capital lost some of its luster. And my correspondence with Abram Heber did not inspire excitement, either. From his letters I knew what I might expect—and that he wouldn't be particularly enthused to see me in the city.

And he is not. I spot him on the station: black-clad and stern, frown not leaving his face for a single moment. Heber gives me a courteous bow and regards me in silence.

"This is not safe for you," he finally says, by means of greeting.

"Thank you for your help," I reply.

I don't want to have this conversation right now—or ever again, for that matter. We've discussed my safety at length in our correspondence. At first, Heber must have thought he was only humoring me: the spoiled little sister of his friends, daughter of his late business partner. He insisted that, at least until the end of the war, I should stay in the countryside and play the role of an ailing young lady, living off slivers of moonstone sold to my father's Prussian contractors. Then, when my brothers returned—for Heber was too polite to frame that as an *if*—they could, perhaps, accompany me to the capital. If I wanted to perform, I very well could, he argued—but in the confines of my leisurely living room, to the audience of other, lesser aristocracy; would this not be enough?

"This isn't help," he says.

But what Heber fails to notice is that carrying out his scenario, however safe, won't grant me one thing: a life.

He knows the sense of not belonging all too well. But being confined to one's household the way a woman is—the only daughter, the younger sister, forever a chrysalis—I couldn't bear to describe this experience, even in the gentlest metaphors.

In the end, he relented; I had drawn out my plans, and he didn't have any formal power over me. He calculated that the best thing he could do would be to ensure my safety in Warsaw before I decide that, wartime or not, I don't need his help in my escapade. He'd found me a place to stay. Arranged my post as a teacher for a middle-class wealthy girl. In the end, booked my ticket to Warsaw.

We ride in a carriage across a city that's readying itself for another tense evening. Theaters and cafes are still operating, but the air is curdled, and if I look closely into the scarcely lit interiors, I'd see rather meagre dishes on plates, and weary-eyed waiters mostly pretending to do their jobs.

The birth of the Duchy, few years ago, was celebrated: the first step in regaining a state long lost. Then Napoleon came, and we believed we could bring Moscow down. And we did—paying an unthinkable price for it. Thousands of men, exhausted, shivering, walked into the Russian capital—only to find it ravaged, a deathtrap. My two brothers among them. I said my goodbyes, finally, to their memories. Then I left the countryside mansion and the absence filling up all its rooms.

Heber picks at the collar of his coat.

"All this pointless, ambitious war. The front lines are elsewhere, but it's tearing this city apart," he says; to me, to himself? After all, he still sees me as Ogiński's darling daughter. But our correspondence, though it threw him into fits of despair, has forged a connection between us. "The troops in Moscow are holding out, but we are losing, and what do you think, will the tsar let us be? The moment he's certain Bonaparte is no longer dealing cards, he'll squeeze the lifeblood out of this so-called independent state and seize what the French haven't squandered already."

He bites his lip.

"If it happens—when it happens—my wife and children will retreat to the countryside. Will you join them?"

I find my father's pendant under my petticoats and press my fingers to the hard edges of the stone. If all else fails, I still have my birthright.

But Heber says, "Moonstone won't buy your way out of every situation. Promise me, Agata, that you won't stay in the city when it falls."

We both ignore the fact that he used my Christian name, breaching all the boundaries of propriety. This is no ordinary situation.

"But you've made all these arrangements."

"No one will hold it against you if you decide to leave."

Abram Heber, after all, is Earthbound, even if Earth didn't prove too kind for his kin. But he doesn't know or understand about us, his lunar cousins, and my father and brothers were not particularly keen on getting into details of what we are, either.

I don't expect any of the Earthbound to have a grasp on what it means to wake up every day with a feeling of misplacement; despair and longing raw in your heart. With senses too sharp, constantly trying to stump them to human capacity. In the end, to look at one's skin and, again, remember. Perhaps this is why we've become such isolated people, drawn to solitary professions: maintaining ordinary lives would be too much for most of us. And yet, I want to try. If I return to the empty house, I want the decision to return to be my own.

The rest of our journey passes in tense silence, although I'm sure Heber hasn't given up yet. I'm gazing through the dusty glass, making out the shape of the city. Finally, we reach my new landlady's house—a somber brownstone—and one glance at it gives me the idea of what sort of person Woźniakowa could be.

Woźniakowa's maid opens the door, ushers us in and, flickering candle in her hand, disappears in the darkness to bring the mistress of the house. In the scarce light, the apartment seems too big for one elderly widow, inhabited mainly by thick shadows spilling from works of carpentry and heavy frames. I study the decor. To me, nightfall is no different than daylight. But I have to guard myself. It is disconcerting for others when I move about places I shouldn't know, or shouldn't see so clearly; paradoxically, the lunar heritage is slowing me down.

Finally, the lady appears, stern in black dress, her graying hair pinned artfully to frame her face. She keeps herself upright, maintaining all what's left of her dignity—in spite of the fact that she has decided to take in a working woman, and one brought in by a Jew, no less. I imagine she would have never agreed to it if she had any choice in this falling city.

Heber bows. I make a small curtsy, as expected from a younger woman.

"Mrs Woźniakowa, thank you for your kindness and hospitality. May I present Agata Ogińska—" He beckons to me. I curtsy again.

Woźniakowa's eyes scrutinize me.

"The pianist?"

"Indeed, madam." I keep my eyes low, to make sure the lady doesn't notice my pupils, huge, eating up all of the blue of my eyes. One cannot be too careful.

Something about her tight-lipped smile tell me that soon, my musical abilities will be put to test. The flutter in my chest that arises at this thought is not at all unpleasant.

"Welcome, then. I will not keep you in the hallway." Woźniakowa nods to the maid, who promptly picks up my suitcase. The smell of tea is already wafting through the air. The examination of my humble persona shall begin soon.

I turn to Heber. Promise me, he insists, fixing me with his eyes.

"Thank you," I say to him. "Goodnight."

Our memory runs deep.

It reflects in the numerous, tiny discolorations of our skin—all those lines and blots, not unlike the scarred face of Moon itself. It's been centuries, but I am sure only we, in exile, were born with those patterns. It's as if guilt and longing have written on us: remember where you came from.

The Earthbound numerical machines are impressive, but they can't compete with the levels of sophistication we once achieved. We knew well enough we wouldn't stay on the Moon; its core was growing cold, unlike the currents of heat coiling under the crust of the Earth. The fact that we survived is, in itself, testimony to the excellence of lunar sciences—as well as to the tragic irony of our existence. We had to abandon their splendor to survive.

Our ancestors had just enough time to design and build ships, fueled by moonstone and ready to soar. But they didn't take into consideration that sailing the stars and breaking through Earth's storms were two different things.

So few of us survived, and with each century, fewer still. We flocked to each other. We sought safety. After Poland was divided, many of the people I knew left for Prussia or France. England, perhaps; a country as good as any. My father, though, insisted that he would not give up his home. Not again, he perorated, even years afterwards, raising his hands to show the history written all the way down his palms.

I read this account of all things lost anytime I see my own bare skin. Tiny ridges in the flesh like ancient scripture. Puckered skin recreating the stone-hard face of a dead celestial body. The catastrophe is easiest to remember; but Moon's vegetation, its lush cities, those turn to dust and erase themselves from our memory.

Earthbound humans can see none of this. It's as if their eyes didn't pick up this particular hue. (Birds, though. There's something about their tiny eyes that makes me believe they know.) Woźniakowa's maid—however odd it feels to use this word to describe a forty-something woman, not much younger than the widow herself—pays no attention to the history of the Moon scrawling over my arms when she helps me with my hair, no doubt at the order of the mistress, not wanting to add my disheveled looks to her misfortune and shame. The maid hums to herself, tugging at the strands of hair. She sticks the last few hairpins into the ash-blond bun and smoothens out a wrinkle on my sleeve.

"You're ready to face the city," she decides.

And I am. Every moment of delay feels like too much waiting.

I would have been happy to walk, but the maid will have none of it; carriage it is, taking us across wide busy streets, vendors and urchins pushing past the working classes. Warsaw is both dirtier and prettier than what I have imagined; although, I also know, I haven't seen much of the capital, none of its sandstone-white palaces, no famous facades. And anyway, we arrive at the Morawiecki household in no time.

I am moving from hands to hands: Heber's to Woźniakowa's, maid's to maid's. Morawiecki's servant exchanges a nod with my guardian and ushers me into the house and past rows of doors. The interior is amiable; ancestors gazing at me from picture frames; porcelain trinkets and other bric-a-brac huddling on mantelpieces, shelves, any flat surface. The place reminds me of our countryside residence in the sense of homeliness, of having deep roots.

The mistress of the house requires first a small demonstration of my skills. I consider my choice of music, trying to gauge her taste. The two other listeners, neither of them the little girl I'm supposed to teach —one, a boy no older than ten or maybe twelve, the other a young woman with auburn hair and wide-set, somewhat wild eyes—might not appreciate it, but I choose a calm, melancholy etude and let my fingers glide over the keys. The melody is simple, but it flows the way a brook rolls over stones.

It could be another aspect of my heritage, the heightened senses and acute reflexes. But I believe it's something else that makes the piano keys respond to my touch in such a way. It's the same thing that drove me out of safety of our cottage. I believe in my music like in nothing else.

I glance up and meet the young lady's face, her eyes ablaze, cheeks flushed.

I should have understood that look at once, shouldn't I?

Or, at least, I should have known it was worth more than passing a test.

My work, which commences the following week, proves easy enough. My student is Morawiecka's niece—a bright, even if restless, girl of seven. For the first week, I'm teaching her gentleness as she insists on slamming her octaves onto the instrument. The piano bears it with dignity, but I don't want to stretch the limits of its patience.

Sometimes I notice the young lady, a glimpse of her auburn locks by the door left ajar, a honey-gold gown. I even consider suggesting she might take lessons too, if she's interested. But I don't know if it would be proper, and in the end, I don't ask.

She approaches me after a few weeks of our practice, when I've introduced the youngest Miss Morawiecka to Frérè Jacques, to servants' mute dismay. I'm gathering my notes when I hear a tapping on the door.

"Excuse me," says the woman breathlessly. "I believe we haven't been properly introduced. My name is Izabela Morawiecka and, although I am not one of your students, I have heard about you..." she smiles, as if sensing my tension. Did my eyes just grow wide, unnaturally so? "And I was wondering, since you're new to the city, perhaps you would like to join me and my friends during our weekly dinners?"

This is the life I wanted, I tell myself, propping my chin on the heel of my hand and doing my best to look pensive.

I am thrilled.

I am terrified.

Izabela smiles gently.

"I insist," she says. And then adds: "May I call you by your first name?"

The moment I enter the cafe, the moonstone's pull overwhelms me immediately.

Izabela waves her hand at me and I walk towards her as if in a trance, my coat hanging loosely off my arm. Someone takes it away from me. Someone offers a chair. But voices and faces get lost in the haze: there is just the stone resting in the dip between Izabela's collarbones and calling to me.

"She's playing with him, poor man." Someone sighs as Izabela weaves the chain of her pendant between her delicate fingers. I can't keep my eyes off the glinting raw gem, its purple so deep and—and—

Radiant Moon, I know they can't see the exact color of it, they don't feel the force of it, that it's just another precious stone to them, and awkwardly misshapen as that—I can tell all of this to myself, but I can't comprehend.

Home, I think. The gem blinks at me. It shines like a living, glistening tissue. In its unrefined state, its pull is even stronger than that of the cut—tamed—version I wear against my chest.

Home.

"They should have married long ago," I hear. "Izabela is not that young anymore, either. But she's milking him dry of his family heritage. And you bet she'll leave him when she gets all she could from him."

I squint at the "poor man", Ignacy Diehl, again. No; the stone is clearly not his heritage. I'd know. He's just an Earthbound human with sullen eyes and a haunted look, and a brilliant, passionate mind. Also, I venture, he is not whom, or what, Izabela wants.

With time, I grow used to the stone's presence. My senses sharpen again. There are a dozen or so people gathered in the cafe. They somehow make up for the place's lackluster, dusty and faded glamour; they drink from chipped glasses as if it were the finest crystal. Do they care? Not tonight. Tonight they can be beautiful, reckless, safe from war.

And the center of the group, oh radiant Moon, is her. Izabela, the fox-faced girl with a twinkle in her eye that makes you think that maybe, just maybe, she is not as unaware of her magnetic pull as her girly laughter could make you think.

The way the room revolves around her, it's just natural. There's no question about who is the Sun of our little system here.

Diehl isn't remotely as lively and interesting—but that's an unfair comparison to make, when this quicksilver of a person hooks her tiny hand in the crook of his elbow, when she whispers something into his ear and laughs.

The gentleman sitting next to me looks at them mournfully. He orders us a round of liqueur, something the Frenchmen had shipped all the way to the Duchy. I pick up my glass, but I keep my eyes on the moonstone. Raw, uncut stone is dangerous. Izabela's pendant holds enough power to tear this room apart.

I need to know where it came from. As the evening progresses, I drift towards the abandoned and sullen Mr Diehl. I have no plan of how to speak to him; and I can't start questioning him about rare ores.

"That's a splendid gift," I say.

He sucks on his teeth and nods.

Looks like he's all too aware of how the gift will get him nowhere; a token of unrequited love.

"I think I've seen it somewhere. The stone, I mean."

"It's not terribly practical as a jewel," he says. "Maybe in Antwerp or elsewhere they know how to cut it, but here—"

We have been selling cut moonstones as rare diamonds for years. My late father, a renowned silversmith, tricked the rich of Europe into buying the glinting gems from him. But Diehl knows it's something else. Izabela told me he studied geology. He is an engineer. And this is the one area in which he's certain of his expertise, the stutter in his voice disappearing when he speaks of science. He, just like his friends, Misters Stroynowski and Konwicki, has been participating in the proceedings of Royal Society of Friends of Science.

"I have seen diamonds before, Miss Ogińska," he tells me. "And I can tell this is something else."

My mind is racing. Only then I realize I don't even know others of the lunar species in Warsaw, if there is anyone left besides me—and anyway, we're scattered, few and far between. I can only be certain that somehow, raw moonstone has been slipped into the hands of Earthbound, something we all agreed should never happen. I have to learn where Izabela's stone came from—and secure it.

You wanted to have a life, says a nasty little voice in my ear. I have to take this risk.

"I know, Mr Diehl. My father has been working with it. I know."

It takes weeks to arrange my visit at Diehl's apartment; me as Izabela's chaperone, Stroynowski and Konwicki to give it a pretense of a social gathering. But deep down I know it's only about the moonstone. Diehl gives us a rueful smile as we enter. He takes Izabela's coat, but looks at me, gauging, guessing.

I encouraged him to make the invitation. It might be my only chance to talk with him in private, to catch a glance of his place. I can't sense the rest of the moonstone yet, if he has acquired any more of it, but it must be hidden in his rooms; I doubt he'd be keeping it at the university.

I know already he can tell the many ways in which moonstone is different. How the structure, however natural, resembles nothing he knows, how the stone captures and warps light. He might even have some premonition of the stone's workings, the power in it. According to my best knowledge, no other crystalline structure on Earth holds such energy. For all I know, it might be the mysterious, dreamed-up ether in our hands.

It doesn't pass my attention that for years, we've been using it as mere adornment, stripping the moonstone of its power with drills and blades, letting that energy leak.

I'm all pins and needles, too anxious to exchange pleasantries. Stroynowski's loud, warm voice—like dripping treacle—goes above my head, and I only give him a dull nod. My mind is with the stone.

And finally, after coffee is served, Izabela and Ignacy exchange looks. They excuse themselves, and I join. There is no way I could ignore the smirk on Stroynowski's face. I know what he is thinking: yet another token of affection that Izabela will take, and promptly forget about.

As soon as the door closes behind us, we start talking. Izabela leans on the door, listening to every murmur in the corridor. Diehl even seems quite happy that he'd had to include her—as if she would eventually accept him.

"I got it from a distant relative. There was a man. In Siberia," he says quietly, casting his eyes down. "He had this on him. Tried to sell it around. Didn't get much for the aesthetic value." He gives a short, unhappy laugh. "But once people discovered how tough, how resilient it is... you could cut down trees with this stuff if you got a sufficiently sharp piece."

I look at the moonstone, and I ache for home. A piece of my memory, a connection severed and desecrated.

"Who was this man?"

He shrugs.

Even I have heard about Siberia. It isn't a place where stories matter much: they sift and grind together, false layers over truth; voices interweave until people reinvent themselves, over and over again. The people sent to labor camps tell themselves: *this is who I am,* forcing their frozen, numb minds to remember. This is who I am; and the dry thud-thud-thud of cut wood; and the soldier, the lady, the doctor are all erased, thud-thud-thud and beneath the crusted bark of hopes there is only soft and vulnerable tissue, and frost bites into it, bites right through the core.

I shudder. How did one of us end up there?

(How could we not know?)

Who was he?

"He went by the surname Gierosławski." The name tells me nothing. Diehl looks at me quizzically, then sighs. "Not a geologist.

Said he worked in the railways. Said his three sisters still lived in Warsaw. Hoped to return to them. One day."

In the thick silence, he pulls out a lump of stone, a sibling of the gem he gave to Izabela. I glance at her; she's pressed her cheek to the door, listening out, but her hand is clasped over her pendant.

When I reach for the stone in Diehl's palm, he withdraws.

"But you know what this is, don't you?" There is a demanding edge to his words.

"My father has been working with it," I repeat stubbornly.

He glares at me.

"I haven't been able to *work with it.*" He pulls a drawer open, retrieves a folded piece of fabric, stretches it on his desk to uncover a broken blade. Diehl's smile becomes even more pinched, sour. "I lost my best saw to that stone."

My throat clenches when I realize what I'm about to suggest. But he's brilliant, and I glance at all the tools and lenses scattered around —and if we could rein the moonstone again? Can I dream of regaining the splendor of my lost home? Perhaps it takes an Earthbound engineer and a self-made academic, having no memory of the Moon, to dare and experiment with the stone?

"Try using these."

I unpack one of my few treasures: my father's tools. I brought them to Warsaw, hoping they would be safer here, if a stray band of once-soldiers should ransack the countryside mansion. Each drill and blade made by my father's hands, speaking of his diligence and love for the craft. Diehl sighs and runs his fingers along the splinter of foreign rock, picks it up. It glints dark purple and brilliant azure.

In the tense silence, as he fixes the saw, I can hear my own ragged breath. And yet—I don't notice Izabela coming closer, not until I feel her warm small hand on my back, barely above the curve of my waist. It feels like she could burn my skin through all that thick velvet.

There are three of us, tangled in this not-quite-conspiracy. Diehl, bespectacled and hunched above his desk, a system of lamps turning the space between his hands bright as Sun itself. Me, not sure whose side I am on; are there any sides, really? And Izabela, her breath smelling of mint tea tickling my nape, above the starched collar of my dress.

Ignacy brings the blade to the stone. A piece of my home sits snugly fixed in its cradle, blinking at me. Beside it lie Diehl's notes and pictures, the intimate portrait of the gem he's about to cut. The saw grates and rasps, catching on the uneven surface.

And then stone meets stone, and they grind, and my heart skips a beat when it comes to me I might have miscalculated and the teeth could break. Or—worse—if Diehl is less skilled than I assumed, his calculations not as precise; one wrong move and we all go up in flames. Izabela's hand clutches tightly at my arm. Diehl's knuckles turn white, his cheeks are slick with sweat. The saw in his hand bites into the stone, the jarring sound a bolt of white-hot pain behind my eyes, as if the blade were cutting my flesh.

And the moonstone splits evenly in two.

Diehl gasps, setting the saw aside and pushing the goggles up, wanting to examine the stone with his own eyes. Purple dust hangs about his hands.

He looks at me. If I've been worried before that he'd trusted me too easily, that I should have been more careful. Here I have all the answers I need, written in his face, the burning desire to know for certain; he's an academic through and through.

He also is, however, a practical mind and a patriot in the times of war. A frown crosses his face. A new idea.

"This," he says, measuring each word, "could pierce through everything we know. Iron. Steel. Rock."

"Correct." I bite my lip. I don't know what he's thinking, but the look on his face sets me on edge. It's so unlike the withdrawn Ignacy Diehl I know. Determined. Cold. Steeling himself against some dreamed-up necessary evil. And I'm complicit.

Give the Earthbound an object of unmatched beauty, a stone to fuel their numerical machines. They will, without hesitation, turn it into a weapon.

Next time I saw Diehl, he had dark rings under his eyes. He told me he'd been thinking of the stone's properties, of how it could pierce other materials. Against a blade or bullet like this, he insisted, no safeguard could help.

My doubts were not heard at all; waved off as girl's fears, the talk of an uneducated spinster. I found myself powerless. Again.

(Would we *forge* a weapon, were we not so few?)

Diehl, however sharp, has fallen prey to Stroynowski's ravings. It took me too long to notice how he'd gathered it all in himself, all the words hinting at his cowardice, staying in the comforts of Warsaw when he should be at the front lines. It has been welling up, and now he will take his chance; there will be heroism in his science.

It had started with an object of my memory, but it's been long removed from me, and moonstone is not ours anymore. The moment it passed from the hands of that Siberian prisoner—then it became Earthbound as well. I can't take it back.

We have guarded our secrets for years, and I let them out—but it was bound to happen one day, I am merely the assistant of change.

Izabela beckons to me after one of her afternoon teas. Her mouth is a hard line, but her eyes still glimmer. It takes her a good deal of strength to guard herself.

"Agata," she whispers, and I marvel at how my name rolls off her tongue. I stop, my arms half tangled in the coat.

"You seem to know a lot. You definitely talk a lot." She gazes into me, and for a while I believe she could reach for the lines written on my skin. "Too much, perhaps." She licks her lips. "If I have noticed, the others will notice it soon, too. They will start asking questions. And they will not be kind."

At least I hoped it would take longer. I have underestimated Diehl again. With each day bringing appalling news from the front, he seems to be more set in his ways, working more desperately, fighting against time.

Every morning, I remind myself I'm competing against time, too. I go through the piano lessons and meals with Woźniakowa absent-mindedly, still thinking of all I can do.

There is not much. Warsaw has proven quite difficult for a lady, even a working lady; in the country, however dull, there was no one to judge me. Here, I work against a different set of limitations. Even with Izabela by my side, I am confined to my role.

Abram Heber? He doesn't deserve to be dragged into this. He would pay much more than me; and I've caused him enough misfortune as it is.

I am on my own, and I am Diehl's confidant.

"I have calculated the tensions in the stone," he tells me one day, pushing a notebook towards me. My eyes glaze over as I pretend to read through his equations and graphs. "In raw form, it seems... extremely unstable, Miss Ogińska. How did your father bypass this problem, if I may?"

"I wouldn't know." I clench my hand over the spine of his notebook.

Diehl sighs, studying my face, hoping I will give up the secret. But I don't.

"This is not as important, though." There's a new glimmer in his eyes. "In this case, the tensions will work in our favor."

Stroynowski places the gun on the table, the barrel incidentally pointing to me. Diehl has been reworking it, embedding splinters of moonstone into the wooden handle. The weapon in front of our eyes is a small, deadly, efficient thing: not a single swirl of decoration. I notice the telltale purple glow.

In his low voice, Diehl explains its inner workings. Once the bullet is shot, the ignition in the chamber will spread to moonstone shards, causing an explosion. Enough of a blast, he elaborates with a small frown, to kill the assassin himself, and perhaps people in his nearest vicinity as well. Diehl dabs at his brow, wiping sweat. One shot with a moonstone bullet. That's all there would be.

Stroynowski scoffs. "That's a woman's weapon," he says.

I notice Izabela pursing her lips and hope with all my heart that they won't decide it's a woman's task. A woman in the tsar's court would be inconspicuous. My heart skips a beat.

But no—the idea of a female killer doesn't cross their minds. Each of them wants the fame for himself. They don't pay attention to us. Izabela is here because of her putative engagement, and I'm just tagging along—perhaps Diehl's marital escape plan. I've heard the gossip.

"That's a weapon to kill the tsar," says Diehl, placid, splaying his fingers on the table. "Something you might be, in fact, able to conceal. Isn't this the point?"

It is, but I can see the fire burning behind Stroynowski's eyes. Efficiency doesn't cross his mind when glory is at stake. Tsar Alexander doesn't even matter—the true victim is Stroynowski, his pain, his nation's pain, all that suffering tearing his body apart and laid out for everyone to see as the weapon disintegrates in his hands.

I glance around the table, at the three men, and they all share this smoldering desire. Everyday life is too scary. It makes the abrupt death in a foreign city appear easier, welcoming. And death, I know, will take them gladly: the ever-hungry ghost crowd, long-forgotten but still present, persistent, waiting behind the thresholds of our houses and hiding right behind circles of light pooling from the lamps. Not that their ranks are small, with Napoleonic army pushed back westward, but the ghosts could make some place for one more young, aching man.

We had known for months that we had lost—since the day we learned about abandoned Moscow, about soldiers starving and freezing to death. Napoleon had stretched out the suffering as if he could withstand the icy cold: a long, slow demise. But the final blow was finally landed on the very border, on the thawing banks of Berezina river.

Whenever I closed my eyes, I saw the ice floe, men falling into the dark waters, teeth clattering, limbs turning blue. At nights, I heard soft wailing coming from Woźniakowa's room, but I never dared to ask.

Days later, we meet in our cafe and take our favorite table. We are the only customers and even after serving us, the waiters and waitresses retreat, leaving us to our cups of tea and coffee. Izabela has ordered pastries, but they lay untouched, just like our steaming drinks.

No one has said it aloud yet, but we all know: it is over. The news of Berezina spread like wildfire. Napoleon has lost, and his loss will take us all down: the armies but also our laughable tiny state, held upright by treaties. The previous day Abram Heber paid me a visit. The carriage will be ready in two days from now, he said, staring into my eyes intently. His wife and children would know about me.

"Please, Miss Ogińska, don't wait until things become ugly."

I stood in the doorway and thought of my brothers, and the day they joined the army to fight for an Earthbound cause. I still had expected to see them again, until that very moment.

It's Diehl who speaks first. His quiet voice transfixes us, even as he hunches his arms as if trying to hide, and looks only at his fingers.

"Thank you for being here in such grim times. Thank you for being my friends." Only then he looks up and we all can see him for what he really is: a needy, sensitive soul. He seeks Izabela's gaze, but she's dabbing at the corner of her eyes with a handkerchief. "It was an ambitious goal that brought us together once, but our friendship became the glue."

We sit in silence. There is nothing more to say: we won't make any foolish promises of what we will do when our laughable duchy is picked apart.

Konwicki's brows form two wide thick arches.

"What do you mean: once? We haven't done anything yet."

Diehl opens his mouth, but Konwicki is faster.

"Even if we have to sign a treaty, even if—it would mean that the tsar will have to visit Warsaw, doesn't it? We might have a much better chance, when you think of it—"

He falls back to his chair, earning a sympathetic nod from Stroynowski.

"Our dear friend is right," Stroynowski says. "This might work in our favor."

"If we want to ensure the fall of our country, then yes."

Diehl's eyes are level. Izabela and I exchange quick glances.

Stroyowski winces. "I am sorry to say this, my friend, but you are too conservative in your ways. You seek compromise even when planning a coup."

"I suppose," Diehl draws a breath, "that our coup has been postponed."

I clutch my hands tightly.

"And I would like to remind you that I'm the keeper of the weapon," he says, his voice ever so soft. "The weapon of my own design, if you please."

As if nothing happened, he picks his cup and drains it, closing his eyes. The silence over our table is so thick you could carve it with a knife.

Stroynowski is a step away from slamming his hands on the table, his face flushed.

"This is the problem here. The fact that only you are in charge of the weapon, it has been your decision all along, we could only follow and accept whatever crossed your mind."

"You may recall," says Diehl, "that I am the inventor. I merely consider myself responsible for my creations."

Stroynowski runs a hand across his thinning hair, just where the vein on his temple is pulsing.

"Responsible for your creations, but not for the country, are you? Do you think any of our colleagues and brothers would freeze to death in Russia if you had shared your inventions before? Do you think yourself above saving them from drowning? Getting your hands dirty to save your compatriots and friends?"

Perspiration collects in thick beads on Diehl's upper lip.

"You're enjoying here the coziness of Warsaw cafes and pondering the nature of the world while our people are dying." Stroynowski jabs a finger at him. "Did you ever consider—did you ever do something for the land that had fed you—"

He pauses for a breath, and continues.

"But no, you want to remain pure, indulging us for one act but never committing to what armed rebellion means. Did you ever talk about your invention with any of the generals? Ministers, even? Did you present it in the Society? Did you?"

Diehl looks small and fragile, his eyes huge in his pale face.

"Did you?" Stroynowski has no more anger to spend. There's disappointment in his voice.

Diehl's mouth is working, but no word comes out.

"I asked you a question." There's something sad and terrifying and hollow in Stroynowski's eyes.

"And you are very well aware," Diehl replies, his voice barely a whisper, "what terrible damage the use of this weapon will entail."

"I know that you designed this yourself."

"Otherwise it would be only a matter of time, since the Imperial army uses the same weapon against us." He shivers. "To a much bigger extent. Because they will find out, and if we have found the stone, so could they. Sooner rather than later."

I'm thinking of the man who fashioned himself Gierosławski and tried to get by in Siberia, selling seemingly useless moonstone. And I'm quite certain Ignacy Diehl is remembering him, too. Then I'm thinking of ships that sailed the stars, of us adapting to short days and nights, scraping off chips of moonstone to get by, of my dead brothers. Stroynowski has no idea of the fire he would start.

Konwicki stares hard at them both.

"We would have to be very fast," he says. "Take down not just the tsar, but his generals. Leave the Russian court stumped."

Diehl shakes his head.

"There is no time. We have lost."

"We have not!" There's a faint tang of liquor on his breath, but can anyone blame him? Haven't I asked the waitress to dip some of it into my cup as well? The loss is too big for any of us to bear. "We still have a chance!"

Too much ache in all of us. And now, knowing it will never be alleviated. No grandstands to make. We'd have to trudge on with all the injustice wearing us down.

"We don't." Diehl's eyes are rimmed with red. "Not like this. Not anymore."

He tries to touch Konwicki's hand, but Konwicki snaps back.

"This is not your decision to make."

And before any of us has a chance to react, Konwicki grabs at Diehl's coat, and snatches the pistol.

We all freeze.

"Don't do anything," Konwicki says, his voice trembling. "Don't, or I'll blow up us all." He nods at Diehl. "You. Put your coat on and go. With me."

Ignacy obeys, his face chalk-white.

"What do you want from me?" He asks.

He is no hero. If he were, he'd be dead by now in some frozen Russian trench, stuck forever in the ghost crowd.

"I won't harm you," snarls Konwicki, throwing his own coat over his arms. We all back off when, for the shortest moment, the gun is pointing at us. "For heaven's sake! We're still friends. But if you cannot convince yourself, I will do this for you."

He, too, is on the verge of tears. What is he thinking? How could he believe that hurting himself more could do any good?

Diehl shuffles his feet.

"To your apartment," orders Konwicki. "Move."

Stroynowski stares at them, but says nothing. Neither does Izabela, stunned into silence.

And we let Konwicki and Diehl leave.

The door closes, and Izabela turns to Stroynowski.

"We've got to do something."

"We can't. There is nothing we can do without risking our lives, or—Ignacy's. And then what Ignacy has said, about others copying his design—it will happen, you know."

"If we don't do anything, the same thing will!"

She glares at him. Blood is pounding in my ears.

"I remember you being quite eager to die, not so long ago!"

I don't listen anymore. I grab my coat and run into the cold November night, under the Moon's crescent.

The streets are empty. I run through the ghost city, ducking under the few lit windows. I see a thousand reflections of me in the frost.

The two haven't gotten far. I can see them, Diehl shuffling his feet as slowly as humanly possible. Konwicki, trembling. He's muttering, trying to calm himself down. I move into the shadows, even though neither of them pays any attention to me.

Diehl, in Konwicki's grip, small and hunched in comparison, doesn't stop talking. I can hear his quivering voice.

"Let's go to the Russian embassy. No, let's go to the French governor, that scoundrel de la Ville, let us make clear what we think of him ripping our city apart. Let them all know we are no bargaining chip..."

He wheezes, but then continues, and Konwicki falls silent. My heart aches. Diehl is a hero, after all; an unwilling one, shuddering so hard I can see it despite his thick coat. But a hero nonetheless. He would rather die than risk his invention falling in the wrong hands—and there are no right hands to hold such disastrous power; no one should ever wield it. He knows it now. What obscured his thoughts before? Who planted this idea in his head?

So many questions, and I'll never know.

I follow them, listening to his pleading, to him drawing out a plan for them both, and for the tiniest moment I'm almost convinced to let them go through with it, if their grief for the Duchy is really so unbearable.

But there still would be traces. Someone would link it to Stroynowski or, Heavens forbid, Izabela. Someone would take a second glance at the weird jewel at her throat. There would be so many victims Diehl would never know about.

I need to distract Konwicki. Without a second thought, I smash the nearest shop window with my purse and dodge as glass shatters into the street. Konwicki tugs at Diehl's coat and spins around.

"Who's there?"

Brushing glass shards off my coat, I hide in the shadows. I still can see both men, clear as in daylight. Konwicki utters a curse. His hand is clutching the gun.

There is not much more I can do. I throw my tortoiseshell pen casing to the other side of the street. It tinkles and cracks.

Konwicki curses under his breath.

"This is all your doing," he snarls, letting go of Diehl's arm.

Which is what Diehl was waiting for. He spins around, grabs Konwicki, and tries to hurl him to the street.

Both men stumble. Konwicki lets out a surprised yelp when he falls on his back into autumn slush and ice. Diehl, the weaker of them two, falls on top of him, and makes a grab at the weapon. I'm seeing it clear as day. I close my eyes the moment before it fires.

There is nothing I can do, so I don't yell for help.

"Please," says Abram Heber. "Do this for us. Golda has been worried sick about you."

I cast my eyes down.

"I can't."

"You can't hope for anything good in the city now."

It would be sensible to follow his advice, but I had made up my mind long ago, and now I can't imagine walking away.

"I can't leave just yet."

I see the question in his face—what kind of unfinished business could a woman like me have?—but he only sighs.

"If you need any assistance, please let me know. You know where to find me."

"I know," I confirm. "And, Mr Heber, I am infinitely grateful for your help."

He gives me a stiff bow.

"I wish you best of luck, Miss Ogińska."

"Likewise," I say.

Luck has been in short supply these days. By the turn of the year, Warsaw erupted with splendid banquets. The French officials had disappeared. We drank, and danced, and waited for the Russian troops to arrive.

When they seized the city, we swapped our finery for mourning dress, paid the devastating levy, and held the memories of the Duchy close to our hearts.

Stroynowski has taken care of the first part of my unfinished business: in a cafe, he left me a note saying that he has burned all of Diehl's sketches. I burned the note as well.

But there is still the matter of moonstone.

Woźniakowa's maid, solemn as ever, takes me to the Morawiecki household. The servants are surprised. This is not the day of piano lessons, and no cat's music should cut through their day. Not when the preparations for mourning are set in motion.

"This is fine," says Izabela, her voice rasping. "I have been waiting for Miss Ogińska."

Her eyes are red and raw. She takes my gloved hand and pulls me in.

I can only imagine the burden of guilt on her shoulders. Not only has she led to all this—in many indirect, convoluted ways; even if the only person to throw accusations is herself—but she is not feeling entirely sad, either. There is a hint of relief to her condition. The dreaded marriage will never happen. Instantly I hate the world that did this to her, that forced her to dance between her own desires and its expectations. Reputation or happiness. But never both, not for women like Izabela.

Now it's so clear, oh radiant Moon, it's crystal clear. The looks she gave me. The gifts she collected. Her demeanor, teetering on frivolous, always one step from destroying her good name. She never wanted to marry—and it had nothing to do with late Mr Diehl.

It might have a thing or two to do with me.

Izabela speaks only when the doors behind us close.

"I know why are you here." Straight to the point, not even offering me tea, although it must be brewing in the kitchen already. "You want the rest of the stone."

"I... yes."

She nods to her own thoughts.

"Why is it so important, Agata?"

I purse my lips, but she insists:

"I've been protecting you all along, even though you knew too much. You think the others didn't ask about you? Do you have any idea how many stories I made up to protect you? Who among us, how do you think, was most likely to be an Imperial agent?"

All blood drains from my face.

"Me?"

Izabela scoffs.

"Who else? A stranger, probably a foreigner. An independent lady, someone who has nothing to lose. All her relatives, conveniently, gone. It would be unusual—but not impossible."

My throat clenches, dry. I can only reply in nods.

"And I can't—" Izabela's lip trembles. "I cannot say I didn't have my own doubts too."

I reach out to her. She doesn't withdraw.

Next moment I'm holding her and she's sobbing, hot tears dropping onto my dress. For Ignacy. For ourselves. For the duchy that never truly was.

I have a brief moment to make my next decision, but it's an easy one. I wipe my face, lock the door, and tell her all I know of the early history of the Moon.

About the story

Growing up in Poland, I couldn't shake off the impression that we're sort of guests and strangers in our own home—a place lost and regained over and over again. I am, of course, hardly the first to write about where such feelings come from; but in the national narrative, the history of partitions and the Duchy of Warsaw is epic and exalted. I wasn't interested in grandstands. I was curious about ordinary people, those who had no means to fight, those who tried to live—survive—in spite of displacement. I wanted to know about the people omitted from history books, because, ultimately, they were the ones who kept telling the story and redefining home.

A question for the author

Q: What's your favorite story?

A: Just one favorite short story? I don't want to dodge the question—but there are so many short stories that had changed me and made my world bigger, having to pick one is just cruel. However, when I'm thinking of a favorite story now, the first one that comes to my mind is "The Evening and the Morning and the Night" by Octavia E. Butler. Butler's writing is precise and ruthless; she doesn't spare her readers. And why would she, if she's about to tell a story of sickness and depersonalization? But ruthlessness itself isn't what makes this story so powerful—it's Butler's empathy and understanding for, and of, the world she created.

About the author

Karolina Fedyk is a Polish writer of speculative poetry and fiction who likes learning new languages, coffee, owls, and living in extreme latitudes. Find their tweets at @karigrafia.

Karolina Fedyk's story "The Early History of the Moon" was published in *Metaphorosis* on Friday, 19 May 2017.

The Questioning Bell

Jason Baltazar

Enoch woke to the murmuring of window glass against the crown of his head. Outside, the approaching bellcart signaled a new morning, each heavy peal humming through the windowpane.

As he'd done on every morning since Baricolé's curse fell upon the city, he first looked to the window on the opposite side of the street. Dark and empty, it brought a familiar worry about Galvea. They'd been friends all their lives. He couldn't remember a day in those twelve years they hadn't spent at least in part together — until recently. As he rubbed the blear from his eyes, the bellcart called again and fear chased away his drowsiness. Fear always followed the questioning bell.

Enoch reached for the silver handbell resting on the windowsill. Everyone knew by now: answer as soon as you hear. This was the only way to reckon the living from the soon-to-be-dead, because those unable to answer never had very long before they withered down to near nothing.

Again the approaching bell. **Cling.**

Enoch answered. *Ting.* From his parents' room came two more replies. *Ting. Ting.* This had become the rhythm of their lives.

Cling. *Ting. Ting. Ting.*

The not-knowing was just as terrible to Enoch three months into the curse as it had been on the first night. At each ringing not knowing his answer to the question issuing from the metal of the bell. Waiting for the reassuring sound of his reply. And then the vacuum in which he waited to know his parents' answers. The darkened window across the street was worst of all, never knowing whether Galvea's handbell rang.

For the moment, the bellcart remained unseen. The buildings in Enoch's district, oldest in an elder city, huddled together like conspirators. Before the Withering, Enoch had enjoyed living in the old city center, sensing history underfoot as he and Galvea adventured through their days. History had been his favorite subject when there was school to attend. He reveled in learning the stories of the buildings around them. Now he resented the structures for limiting his experience of the world to an eighty-foot stretch of cobbled street below.

His parents stirred. He imagined the sound of their movements rippling across the wallpaper. Eventually, they joined him in the living room, Mama's disappointed sigh now a familiar ritual.

"Again?" she asked.

Enoch looked at her reflection.

"Have you eaten, at least?"

He shook his head no.

"Well, let's see to that," she said, motioning him away from his station.

He refocused on the narrow world outside and raised a dismissive hand, a gesture he'd picked up from Papa in recent weeks. "Maybe later, not very hungry," he said.

The knot in his belly grew by the day, but he'd heard their hushed conversations. Though he never eavesdropped on purpose, his parents' words found him, carried by the still air of the stricken city. He'd heard Mama plead they could stretch things a week longer, that Papa didn't have to go out again so soon. Enoch understood the danger. He only had to look down as the evidence passed underneath each day, stacked together in the bed of the bellcart, carefully bundled in blankets and curtains and dining linen. Frighteningly small.

Each scavenging trip Papa took was a risk. In the time since the bell first rang its curse over the city, no one had learned how it spread, how it chose whom to take. Whether by touch or by breathing it in, whether it burned in your heart or in your throat before climbing on top of you, no one could say. The city quickly settled into voluntary quarantine, unwilling to chance exposure to these limitless possibilities.

Mama rested her hands on Enoch's shoulders. Their eyes met in the glass.

"Why another night? Daytime, it's Galvea, but she's never at her window at night. What keeps you in this seat?"

"Watching for stars," Enoch said.

She looked over the rooftops, into the featureless band above. "There's been no sky since Baricolé's Ascension. What will a night's rest cost you? You worry me." She held his head between her hands.

"What if I missed them?"

"Yes, what if? The sky will do as it wants, whether you sit or sleep. You're exhausting yourself."

"Well, would you look? Or Papa?"

"Stare at the dark all night?"

His eyes told her yes, that was what he meant.

"No, Enoch. Because we need strength, too, and we realize this. You're the only one leaking sense." She moved his head around, as though searching for the troublesome spot.

"See? If I don't watch, who will?"

Her lips pressed together in what could have been a smile, or, more likely, a flash of heartache.

"We'd sleep through and never know if the curse lifted."

Mama bent and kissed the top of his head.

"You'll eat *something* today," she said.

"I will," Enoch said to the reflected shape of her retreat in the window.

Across the street the curtains fluttered. Galvea appeared. Enoch's smile was an inbuilt response, a flower opening to daylight. He pressed a palm against the glass. Galvea matched the gesture.

Her mother came to stand behind, stroking Galvea's hair. She attempted to smile at Enoch, but only appeared to wince in pain. Smiling had become a difficult thing to manage. She lingered a few minutes longer before receding into the darkness, leaving the children to face one another, separated by two panes of glass and twenty feet of once-busy avenue.

Enoch and Galvea braided paths in their sprint through the bustling square, arms spread as wings in anticipation of flight.

"You never know," called Galvea, "when things can change entirely."

"One has to be ready," Enoch began.

Galvea finished, "For anything!"

"Imagine, if we found ourselves flying through the air without our arms out like this," he said.

"How embarrassing," Galvea agreed. "Would we be birds, then?"

"You and me, birds?" scoffed Enoch. "Of course we would be angels!"

Galvea nodded, satisfied. "Nothing less," she said. She stopped and pointed with her wing tip to the bell tower looming over them. "Two angels, one for each shoulder of Sainted Baricolé."

"Good old Raving Sainted Baricolé," Enoch said. They adopted solemn attitudes, clasping their hands together in pantomime prayer. Then they burst into a fit of laughter. Each put their arm around the other and gazed up at the new bell installed atop the tower only hours ago.

The hospital with its tower was the distinctive landmark of the district, and the Raving Sainted Baricolé its builder, a beloved figure of local fame. Born into wealth in an era when the city was crippled by disease, he had studied the medical arts and used his family's resources to raise the building. His compassion and dedication earned him the "sainted" epithet. The "raving" came after he ordered the tower built and spent his final days atop it, cursing at any god who might listen.

"What must it have been like, seeing him up there?" Galvea wondered aloud.

Enoch tried to invoke the sight, Barícolé standing where the bell now hung a hundred feet above, screaming at the heavens. "Amazing," he said. She smiled.

He turned to the blend of locals and tourists enjoying the centennial Ascension festival, dressed in finery beneath the afternoon sun. As he saw them passing through the square, browsing crafts and trinkets, goading performers with claps and whistles, he imagined Barícolé's legendary rant showering down, losing clarity in its fall to earth, heard below only as echoes of indistinct outrage.

"And fascinating," Enoch said. He looked again to the tower and pictured Barícolé, hoarse, exhausted, gesturing wildly and teetering along the edge of his platform as he stomped circles, eyes and fists raised. "And terrifying," he added.

Galvea gave his shoulder a squeeze. "No fearful angels," she said.

"Not a one," Enoch said. They spun and flew back into the press of festivity. Their laughter left a wake like the stroke of a paintbrush, coloring all they passed. Smiles bloomed on the faces of festivalgoers who looked on. Enoch and Galvea might have noticed if they hadn't been sharing a world of their own making.

The bellcart emerged from where the lane below curved out of sight. Its procession advanced by slow footfall. They moved together, a steady, graceful march: the bellringer to the side, a team of forward-bent drivers gripping the cart, and ahead of them the two who entered marked buildings to collect the withered.

The bell struck.

Cling. *Ting. Ting. Ting.*

Enoch saw Galvea turn as though her name had been called, then disappear into the room behind her. It had been the same since the morning he awoke to find a scrap of linen under her window, beckoning the cart to her door. And later the tiny bundle carried out of her doorway by the attendants, laid with reverence among the others. Since that day, Galvea's older brother never appeared in the window, nor did her smile, and at every ringing of the bell she went to her mother, into the unseen.

Enoch tried to picture her through the walls, raising her handbell, reassuring him she was still very alive. He could do without food, without the freedom to step outside, could even do without a sky, but to imagine a world without Galvea? Impossible.

The cart drew closer. Enoch saw the drape of the robes wrapped around the attendants, too similar to the improvised shrouds of the dead they accompanied. Each was covered head to ground, only eyes exposed. Whenever he'd caught a glimpse of them, Enoch thought their eyes hinted at hidden smiles.

The two at the head of the procession scanned windows and doorways for signs of mourning. Those pulling the cart marched with lowered gaze, and the bellringer too moved with eyes cast downward, clutching the rope that raised the voice of the bell. Enoch knew from their bearing and delicate handling of the withered that these men and women acted as creatures of mercy, but to see them was no less horrible. Becase of their cargo. Because they carried with them that testing toll.

The bellringer took the rope in two-handed grip and heaved.

Cling. *Ting. Ting. Ting.*

Enoch produced for himself the sound of a fifth note, faint, coming as it did from across the street.

Now Papa crossed the living room hugging a blanket around himself. The months of attrition evident in Papa's face stirred a sickness in Enoch. Papa squinted from pools of fatigue at the procession.

"Recognize any today?" he asked.

Enoch said no. The likelihood of identifying anyone from only that sliver of eye was poor, but he would never say so, because Papa obsessed over who these attendants were, and also because Enoch was the boy who sat up nights waiting for the stars to return. They observed a gentleman's agreement to let each other's fixations be.

Papa shook, tugged the blanket tighter.

"I can go out if we need firewood," Enoch said.

This wrenched Papa's gaze from the attendants. "No need, Enoch. We've a good amount." He tried to sound offhand and confident, but the words came too quick. "Let me worry about supplies, hm?" He tousled Enoch's hair and gave a drowsy wink. "Now, who do you suppose they are?" Papa ran through his usual questions: From the city or from outside? How can they be out there unclaimed, unafraid? An immunity?

The only hope of learning would be asking face to face, an occasion no one wanted. The attendants only mingled with the grieving and the dead.

The bellcart passed directly below. The memorial bell swung under a sturdy support mounted to the cart. The figure of Raving Sainted Baricolé rose from its surface, back arched and eyes skyward, arms raised in passionate anger. Enoch felt the emanation reaching up from the bell and right down his throat, clutching at some central part of him.

Barícolé's question was there, even if unspoken.

While Papa tried to guess the identities of the living, Enoch fixed on the pyramid of bundles arrayed in the cart. He counted at every passing, keeping a rough tally of the Withering's claim. Twenty-three today, a steady number that told of no slowing. Fear was as alive as ever.

Twenty-three people, stacked like dolls on a toyshop's shelf. He remembered the one and only time he'd seen it happen, the very beginning of the epidemic all those months ago. He shivered. Papa rubbed Enoch's arms, coaxing warmth.

"Turn your thoughts away," he said.

Enoch breathed deep, swallowed down the sick nervous disquiet. He looked away until the sound of wheels rolling on brick faded. Papa gave him a reassuring grip and went back to the couch.

When Galvea later reappeared, Enoch felt the last bit of tension go. He thought he saw apology in the slight upward arc of her eyebrows.

He bent to retrieve his most cherished possession: a thick, handcrafted sketching notebook, bound with waxed black string and covered over in the raised weave of natural cloth. Inside, a medley of pages varying in texture, color, and size. He shuffled through used pages with his thumb, past early illustrations of fish-drawn undersea chariots, flocks of firebirds bursting from the mouths of erupting volcanoes, buildings strolling through countryside on four legs. He shuffled past the more recent drawings, all variations of one image, rendered smaller and smaller as Enoch became increasingly aware of the finite number of pages between the covers of his book.

He settled on a clean page and took up the pencil. He looked at Galvea with an eye considering proportion, contour, shade. Enoch made his first mark and gave over to his daily pursuit, bringing Galvea into the room with him the only way he could.

Enoch and Galvea found their families resting beneath the shade of a plum tree, one of many lining the perimeter of the square. Mama and Galvea's mother sat against its trunk, smiling between bites of the tree's fruit. Papa was lying on his back, looking up through the branches. There came a rustling in the boughs above, and Enoch and Galvea looked up to see her brother clambering through the limbs.

"That's the one. What a prize!" Papa called to the canopy.

Galvea turned to Enoch. "We've been abandoned," she said.

"Left to fend for ourselves," Enoch nodded.

"It's the way of the world," she said.

Their mothers shared an amused glance.

"But what's this?" Galvea pointed upward with an expression of discovery. "A tree of plenty!"

Enoch stepped closer to her, moved her pointing finger to rest on the shape of her brother. "But guarded by a strange beast."

"Strange indeed," she said.

"Hey!" her brother yelled from the tree.

"Have you formulated a plan, Sir Enoch?" she asked.

"Certainly, Sir Galvea. Leave it to me," Enoch said.

He climbed the trunk to the second tier of branches where he grabbed a young offshoot above him and shook. Leaves fell twirling, catching in Galvea's hair. After several heavy *thumps* she called up, "Success!"

He dropped down. Galvea scooped up two of the plums, tossed one to Enoch. They sat across from their mothers and ate.

"A feast," Galvea said.

Enoch added, "Hard won."

Galvea's mother cleared her throat. "Galvea?" she said, hinting with her inflection. She tilted her head toward a bundle next to her, tied with string.

"Oooh!" Galvea said. She covered Enoch's sight with her palm. "Close your eyes," she said.

"Why?"

"Just do it." She spread her fingers to verify he listened.

Enoch felt something land in his lap. He looked down at the gift and scowled. "I told you not to get anything for me," he said.

"I didn't," she said.

Enoch pinched the string and pulled the bow apart. He peeled back the layers of fabric until the glorious notebook was revealed. He ran his fingers along the weave of its cover, beaming. He opened it and saw that each blank page was unique, that when full, no two drawings could be the same.

"Like it?" she asked

"Of course! It's incredible," Enoch said.

"She made it herself. She's been at it for months," Galvea's mother said.

Galvea reached back to the tangles of her hair and pulled free a pencil she'd concealed there. She presented it to Enoch with ceremony. "It's for *both* of us," she said.

His smile stretched further with understanding. He took the pencil with a bow. Galvea gathered up the fabric the notebook had been wrapped in, and covered her head, knotting it beneath her chin. Enoch opened to the first pristine page.

"I'm very old now," she said, "but when a young lady, I lived under the sea. I traveled the watery kingdoms in a conch shell coach, drawn by a school of seahorses."

Enoch began to sketch as she spoke, elaborating her vision with familiarity and skill. She crouched behind and watched with her chin on his shoulder. She conjured the image, he provided its form. Together, they brought dreams to life.

The day elapsed in the usual way.

He drew Galvea in the window while his parents whispered in the living room, Papa drifting in and out of unwanted naps. The milk grey of the daytime sky loomed over them. Faint edges of a silver halo creeping over the rooftops were the only clue a sun floated free of the horizon. Enoch took it on faith that beyond their dull curtain the heavens remained unchanged, that it was only down low in the realm of their lives where things had gone wrong. He trusted in a golden sun and added depth to his drawings with its imagined light.

Movement on the lane below tore away Enoch's focus. A man stumbled along on Galvea's side, keeping balance by placing a hand against windows and doors. He shouted, but Enoch couldn't make sense of the words. Galvea saw him, too. The man fell to his knees and stayed there, panting.

"Someone on the street!" Enoch called over his shoulder.

"Mm, what's it?" Papa mumbled, startled from sleep.

The man went to his haunches and howled at the air. His clothes were soiled and torn, and hung loose. When strings of hair fell away from the man's face, Enoch recognized who it was, despite the change.

"Bufo! It's Peer Bufo!"

A lecturer at the district's secondary school, in his own words a "Purveyor of Historical Lesson and Insight." Bufo had always been a squat, round man. Students often commented in hushed tones on a certain likeness to a bullfrog, because of wide-set, slightly bulging eyes and a dour, downturned mouth. His habit of puffing out his chest while lecturing did no favors. But here was the bullfrog deflated and filthy.

Papa rushed over, Mama close behind. She gasped at the sight of him. Papa didn't say a word, but spun and marched through the living room, tossing his blanket onto a chair.

"What are you doing?" Mama yelled, chasing after.

"Getting him off the street," Papa said. He was already at the door, sliding an arm into his wool overcoat.

"You can't go out there," she said.

"I have to." He had the other arm in, took up the scarf Mama had knit for him long winters ago. She clutched at his coat, trying to pull him from the door.

"We agreed, only when it's absolutely necessary. You promised," Mama said. Her voice didn't waver, despite the tears.

Papa calmly put both of his hands over the clench of hers.

"I'm not going to leave him out there," Papa said. He held her eye. "I've gone and come back before. The man needs help."

Enoch saw her grip slacken. He glanced back out the window and found Bufo crawling a bewildered path over the stones, mouth rattling away.

"He's moving again," Enoch said.

Papa wrapped the precautionary scarf around his mouth and nose and opened the door. As his hurried footsteps on the stairs faded, Mama rejoined Enoch at the window.

Papa appeared below, jogging toward the deranged schoolteacher. Papa bent down, placing a hand on the man's back. Bufo twisted all at once toward Papa and grabbed his coat. They saw Bufo's wild eyes, chattering jaw. Papa's head moved as though he were speaking with soothing rhythm. Bufo's face turned up to the window, the movements of his mouth slowing. They saw him nod. Papa tugged him to his feet, supported him as they walked toward the doorway.

Bufo's voice grew in the stairwell. Enoch couldn't decipher the words, only heard them billow and surge against the walls. Enoch and his mother walked toward the door, but when Papa appeared in its frame with Bufo draped on his side, they stopped.

The way his eyes roamed the room reminded Enoch of summer flies. The grime that covered Bufo spoke of long neglect, and the swollen features Enoch had known seemed to have melted away in a terrible droop of hunger.

"That's it, Bufo, almost there," Papa said.

"All want to know: where does it come from, where does it grow?" Bufo said. He issued a sharp, two-note cackle and licked his lips. "Forming like condensation. Drip drop in the presence of animal heat..." he said.

Papa pulled out a chair. "Go on. Have a rest."

Bufo dropped and sat splay legged on the floor.

Papa crouched beside him. "Tell me what happened. Why were you out there?"

"Pushing through the piney wild. Altogether, all together follow," Bufo said. He relayed this happily, slapping at his thigh, looking squarely at Papa.

"Listen, Bufo, I don't follow," Papa said.

"Lay the chase away. The wandering words will find you. Hear ye, hear ye!" he yelled.

"Is it...is it the Withering?" Mama asked.

"Baricolé's Withering? Ah." Bufo cleared his throat, a signal Enoch knew preceded an oration. "Let us address your fear. Esteemed colleagues, I hereby pro-prippity-pose the Withering finds its way in through the self, the itty bitty self. At the door fear tap, tap, taps. 'Little lamb, don't you look lonely all alone.' And the self searches, for the first time truly finds itself alone. It lifts the latch. The fear glides in and speaks glissando, and gives before it gouges. It tucks the itty bitty self in for a nice nighty night, then it lifts a smothering pillow. I submit empirical evidence for your review! It, uh...it...it...it..."

Bufo lifted a trembling hand, regarded it as though a foreign object. A groan escaped his motionless mouth. The tremble intensified until his whole arm shivered. Then the skin began to convulse in waves.

Mama had been right.

Papa scooted back quick as he could. Enoch felt his stomach churn. He'd hoped to never see this again.

Bufo made a pleading noise. His skin rippled as though made of water. He began to recede, fingers drawn into the hand, hand into arm, arm into trunk. His head and neck sunk into his chest, and his chest slid down his core. He withdrew into himself, dwindling before their eyes. He spoke, the same over and over, "Alone." As his vocal chords shrank, the word climbed in pitch.

Enoch struggled to maintain control.

Bufo's size was halved. His clothes began to pool. As he grew smaller his mouth and throat seized, the repeating words now only whines. He was finally so small that his clothes fell away. His legs curled up and he toppled over. He shrank and shrank until no bigger than a newborn. When at last still and silent, his flesh appeared to harden into a shell.

Enoch thought of the moth pupae they had once examined in school. He gagged.

That night, he slept in his bed.

Enoch and Galvea looked skyward as their families walked toward the bell tower, where a crowd gathered for the ceremony.

"I don't see it, yet. Do you?" Galvea asked.

He examined the constellations. "Not yet."

"We'll know it," she began.

Enoch finished, "When we see it."

Galvea's mother tugged Mama's elbow. "What is it they're after, now?"

"Just the right star on which to live," Mama said with raised eyebrow.

"Ah. So hard to keep up." The mothers laughed.

Peer Bufo stood on a platform beneath the bell tower. He lifted his arms, beckoning attention. "Ladies and gentlemen, if you please," he called.

They joined the circle around the platform. The crowd radiated excitement. In everyone's hand was grasped a silver handbell, a festival tradition going back generations. Every child in the city received a bell of their own which they rang on every Ascension celebration for the rest of their lives. They were treasured items, reminders to everyone of the noble ideals Barícolé represented. As Bufo waited for stragglers to fall in, Enoch spied an especially bright star peeking over the roof of the hospital. He nudged Galvea and pointed. She found the star and nodded approval. That was that.

Bufo cleared his throat. He clasped his hands behind his back and puffed out his chest. He began speaking in his slow, precise, lecturing voice, head tilted so that his vision slid down his nose.

"Friends and neighbors, we gather on this day to celebrate one of the city's most iconic citizens, a renowned figure of compassion, a man famed for his generosity and dedication to easing the pain of those around him, the legendary Raving Sainted Barícolé." Cheers rose. "It is my honor to conduct this ceremony, the inaugural striking of a new memorial bell, to commemorate his final Ascent." More cheers. Bufo raised for one second to the balls of his feet, a pompous grin etched into his ample cheeks. He held out an open hand, asking silence.

Enoch rolled his eyes at Galvea. She bulged hers wide and ballooned her cheeks in a fair rendition of their teacher. The snicker escaped him before it could be stifled. He felt a corrective swat on the back of his head. Then it was Galvea who fought to contain her laughter.

"If only for the benefit of the travellers among us, I remind you that on this very day one century ago, Barícolé's life came to an end due to his tragic final madness. After seven decades of tending an endless stream of the city's ill and infirm he broke down, raging atop the tower behind me for days, cursing and striking out at the heavens, until finally he issued a demand to the crowd below. 'Answer me, do you even live?' he screamed, 'Can you tell me you are anything more than suffering and death?' With these words, he stepped off. He landed right where I stand, dying hours later within the hospital walls. Incredibly, he took his own life in one of the very same beds next to which he'd attended countless patients, using a pen slid into his hand to sign a waiver. Travellers take note that even this final madness ultimately sprang from a well of benevolence, and this generous spirit is what we pay annual tribute to.

"Now, from the place where the man issued his infamous rant hangs a glorious tribute, generously commissioned by the city regents to mark this anniversary. Our artisans scoured the hospital for authentic materials from which to cast it. Think of it, bolts and hinges from doorways Barícolé passed through, bedframes he knelt beside, instruments likely held in his very hands, including, and to this I can personally attest, the final pen. We must thank the executors of Barícolé's estate, who provided this gift with great enthusiasm. The bell should practically sing out with his very own voice. And now, let us ring the bells in his honor. Let us remember always our Raving Sainted Barícolé!"

Bufo signaled and the bell atop the tower gave its first ever toll. The handbells rang in return. It sounded as though the entire city were present, answering, raising a blanket of tinkling notes.

The bell called again, and again Enoch joined confidently in the reply. The chiming was dying down when he heard a single voice in the crowd.

"What's wrong? Ring your bell!"

The bell struck, the response followed.

"Why aren't you ringing? Something wrong?"

The bell struck, the response followed.

Enoch noticed the stars disappearing one by one behind a spreading creep of low-hanging cloud. There were complaints as someone pushed through, a man who clutched his handbell against his chest with shivering arms. He was covered in sweat, and as he swept the crowd with crazed eyes his skin began to swim.

Enoch woke to the distant call of the bellcart and shot upright. His handbell rested beside him, placed there in the night by his parents. He snatched it, only realizing he held his breath after he answered.

Two notes from across the hall.

He dressed quickly, anxious for his station at the window. On his way there, he slowed only when he saw the bundle on the dining room table. Peer Bufo, respectfully wrapped in one of Papa's shirts. Enoch swallowed with effort and averted his eyes. Papa would finally have his chance to interrogate the bell's attendants.

He reached his chair, stooping to collect his notebook. He plopped down and found the page he'd been shading with false light before the awful events of the previous evening. When he looked up to compare his rendering to reality, he saw it. Hanging under the crack of Galvea's window. A long strand of torn cloth.

Enoch's chair flew backward as he sprang up, adding to the clamor of his handbell and notebook crashing to the floor. Only two possibilities, Galvea or her mother. The window offered nothing but dense black.

Enoch only partially felt his feet carrying him toward the door or heard Mama coming down the hall, calling his name.

"What was that?" she said.

He ran. The sound of the door opening would bring them hurrying. He flung it open and bounded down the stairs. He hadn't been on them since the quarantine began. He heard feet pounding across the dining room.

Papa yelled his name.

At the door, Enoch looked through its small square panes to the street. If he didn't go now, Papa would have the back of his shirt. He knew this. But after so many months confined to the rooms of their home, looking down on the street as a cursed thing, he hesitated.

Twenty feet.

That was all it was, twenty feet to her door. All it ever had been. But every step carried possibility of that littling death. He'd seen as much last night. He pictured himself chattering, shuddering himself to almost nothing. His legs nearly buckled. *But she could be gone,* he thought.

Papa yelled, appeared at the top of the stairs.

Enoch gulped air, held it, then twisted the knob and rushed into the street.

"Enoch, no!"

The outside air felt alien as he sprinted. And the quiet…He was used to the quiet of their home, but to be outside in the city and hear this vast silence…

He was across the lane in seven strides, positive Papa would have him at each one. He grabbed the handle and shouldered Galvea's door. Unlatched, it gave easily, spilling him onto the floor of the entranceway.

"Galvea!" he called, scrambling to his feet and up the stairs. No answer came. "Galvea, please!" he said.

Enoch turned the corner from the stairwell into the dark of Galvea's home, and saw her on the floor. Sitting next to a small, lovingly wrapped parcel.

She looked up at Enoch, and even in the dim light he saw her eyes were brimming and swollen. She lifted her arms to him. He rushed over, sank to his knees and wrapped himself around her. Galvea surrendered to her grief. Enoch felt the breath of her sobs, felt the pain in her groans resonate in her chest against his stomach. It crushed him, the dampness of her tears soaking through his shirt. He wanted to enfold her, quiet her pain, soothe away the ugliness of hurt.

He said nothing, just clung to her, as though she were the only thing with weight enough to keep him from falling off the face of the earth. They stayed that way until she subsided. He relaxed his hold and she sat back, wiping at her eyes with her arm. They looked at one another, without words. The corner of Galvea's mouth turned up, ever so slightly.

Then the bellcart called. *Cling.*

Enoch realized all at once he didn't have his handbell. It was lying on the floor by the window. Across the street. The bell questioned and the not-knowing stirred. A panic flooded through, hollowed him out. His body felt as if it were dropping. *Is that it? It that how it feels?* His mind careened, circled, drawn to the visceral realization that there was an end to everything. There was an end to him.

Galvea struck a quick note from her bell and handed it to Enoch. He did the same, but when the crisp ring of her bell came it did nothing to quiet the question. His mind turned around uncertainties. Yes, he'd answered, but how did he know it was true? How could he really know the answer to Barícolé's question unless it came totally from himself, from his own bell?

He made a pathetic moan and found his feet, pacing. Frantic. No control, his body was acting of its own volition, driven by fear. There was an end to everything. **Everything.** The cruelty seized his heart, wrenched it. To see and think and feel. To be capable of love, and have it all just slip away, turn ugly, a trap? He felt very cold. There were final things. Final sights, final sounds. And no choice in it, set down on this track to walk in one direction until you reached the one door, alone. Alone. And when it swung open, the ending. *Of me.* **Me.** *Nothing left of me.* He felt his face twisted up. He felt small and selfish and petty, clinging to his own self. He felt ashamed, but he dug in, because it was all he had, all he knew, ever could know.

Shivering, he heard himself saying no, no, no.

So small, clinging. So totally afraid. Afraid of being nothing. **Not being.** He felt his tears convulsing him, like he was becoming separate from his skin. The room looked like it was beginning to grow, and he felt an enormous final NO! swelling from the deepest part of him when...

He felt a pull, gentle.

A tether to warmth, coaxing him out of himself. He searched it out. It pierced through the panic and he held fast, letting it draw him to the surface. The point of warmth chased away the shivering cold. The world around him came floating back, making sense again to his eyes.

He saw Galvea. Galvea who ruled him, heart and mind. Galvea who linked him to the beautiful possibilities of life, to shared dreams that burned with guiding light. Galvea holding his open hand in hers and kissing his palm.

Erasing the fear.

Since the day they had watched Enoch and Galvea walk out of her doorway to meet the bellcart, holding hands, Enoch's parents went to the window at each of the cart's passings.

There were two new attendants in the procession, slightly smaller than the others. Enoch's parents waved as they passed. They knew the eyes gazing up at them, just as they knew the two small attendants were smiling under the drape of fabric covering their faces.

Sometimes they walked with their arms out to the side, and in the long robes their feet were invisible. They appeared to float over the stones.

Freed from fear, Enoch and Galvea could have gone anywhere together, walked until they finally saw stars peeking through the grey veil above. But they returned, like saints to the suffering, day after day. Floating hand in hand.

About the story

Most of my stories start with an image, in this case a boy looking down onto a narrow, abandoned city street. It seemed so lonely. I started to explore the idea– who was this, what kept them at the window, why were the streets empty? I'd recently read about the yellow fever outbreak in Philadelphia in 1793, and so the idea of some manner of city-wide epidemic crept in. As the story developed I kept thinking about the ways fear can make us retreat into self and cut us off from empathy, wh ch helped guide it along.

A question for the author

Q: What do you think makes for a good story?

A: I think a good story has to engage us on multiple levels. When a writer is able to keep me spellbound with language or compelling images, makes me care about their characters, and provides an interesting plot to boot, this adds up to a story I won't soon forget. Even better if we get a sense there is a driving force that unifies all of these elements. Most of all, I think a good story somehow shows its reader that it is honest.

About the author

Jason Baltazar is Salvadoran American, originally from the Appalachian corner of Maryland. He currently lives with his wife and cat in Lawrence, Kansas, where he is a graduate student at the University of Kansas.

www.jasonbaltazar.com, @jasonrbaltazar

Jason Baltazar's story "The Questioning Bell" was published in *Metaphorosis* on Friday, 26 May 2017.

June

Light Winds With a Chance of Velociraptors

Michelle Ann King

"That's the worst thing about the end of the world," Elsie said, staring mournfully into a teacup that had long ago been licked clean of every last drop of Tetleys and soggy crumb of custard cream. "Routines go straight out the window."

Harry glanced away from the TV, which was showing aerial footage of a tiger chasing pigeons in Trafalgar Square. "Really? That's the worst part? It's not the deaths of millions and the imminent fall of civilisation, it's that nobody's been round with the tea trolley for a couple of hours?"

"*Six* hours," Elsie said. "I'm spitting feathers over here."

"So's that tiger," Flora said, nodding at the screen.

Harry gave her a disapproving look. "Not funny, Flo. That's the one that ate Jeremy Clarkson, you know."

"Is it? Oh well, there you go. Silver linings, and all that." She watched the tiger make a particularly spectacular leap. "With any luck, it'll bag Danny Dyer next."

Harry tutted loudly and went back to the TV while Elsie wheeled herself across the room to the jigsaw table. Young Justin was still curled up in a ball underneath.

"Justin? How you doing, pet?"

There was no response.

"You know what would make you feel better? A nice cuppa. And a plate of Hobnobs, maybe. Don't you think? Justin?"

"Leave the poor boy alone, Elsie," Flora said. "I told you before, we can't get in the kitchen. It's full of baboons. And one of them funny furry things, what are they called?"

"Sasquatch?"

"No, no. Llamas, that's it."

"Oh, right. I suppose they are pretty funny. Spit at you, too, if you get too close."

"That's why I didn't, not even to look for Hobnobs. Although no, hang on, isn't that camels?"

"Is it? I'm not sure. Could be. Better watch yourself when you go to the ladies, then, because there's a couple of them in there."

Under the table, Justin let out a faint, plaintive, "Oh God," and began to cry quietly.

Flora bent down, slowly, and landed a pat on his shoulder. "This, see, this is the trouble with the younger generation."

Elsie nodded. "No resilience. No backbone. No Blitz spirit."

"That as well, yeah. But I was going to say they get paralysed by despair when they realise they're going to die without having had much sex. I mean, look at him, poor lad, he's barely grown out of his bumfluff and acne. And now here we are, and his only chance of a last-night-on-Earth shag is with one of us lot. Or the llama. It's just tragic, that's what it is."

"Shush," Harry said, flapping his hands. "The Prime Minister's going to be giving a speech in a minute. I want to listen."

"Pfft," Flora said. "The tiger can have him next, after Danny Dyer. Although there's no chance of that happening, is there? He's not going to be out there on the streets. None of them are. All the bloody government are going to be holed up in a nice bunker somewhere chomping on a year's supply of tinned tuna and prostitutes while the rest of us poor buggers are left to get on with it."

Harry turned around in his armchair and directed another scandalised, "*Shush*," at her.

"Shush yourself, old man. It's only going to be the usual bollocks — don't panic, stay indoors, everything's under control, blah blah blah. I'd rather carry on watching the tiger, at least he's interesting. And better looking, come to that."

"We could always play a game," Elsie said. "How about charades? I'll go first."

"Oh no, you don't," Flora said quickly. "All you ever do is pick *Gone with the Wind* and use it as an excuse to let rip. I'm wise to your game, madam. And the air fresheners are all in the supply cupboard, which is infested with garden snails. So no, we'll do Twenty Questions instead, and I'll go first. Question one: which of the beasts in here is most likely to kill and eat us first?"

"Ooh, I know that one," Harry said, raising his hand. "It's the baboons. The rest are all herbivores."

Flora pointed at him. "One-nil to Harry."

Elsie frowned. "I don't think that's quite how the game works, you know."

"Call it the apocalypse rules version. Elsie, your go."

"Oh. Okay then. Errr... what happens to us after we die?"

"Hmm." Flora rubbed her chin. "I'm going with total existential annihilation. Do I get the point?"

"No, no," Harry said, waving his hand in the air again. "I know this one, too. It's whatever you believe happens."

"It's what?"

"What happens is whatever you believe happens," Harry said patiently. "I read it in this book once. Self-determined something or other. Basically, it said that if you believe you get reincarnated, or go to heaven, or whatever, then you do."

"That's the nuttiest thing I've ever heard," Flora said.

Harry glanced back at the TV, where a harried-looking weatherman was forecasting light winds and a shower of badgers over the Brecon Beacons. "Really?"

"I rather like the idea," Elsie said. "It makes sense when you think about it. Explains all this, for a start."

Flora hiked one bushy eyebrow. "It does?"

"It's Beryl. You know, from Room Fourteen? She always liked animals better than people, and she died on Tuesday — right before this whole thing started. I can definitely see her believing animals should inherit the earth or whatever."

"You might have something there," Harry said, nodding. "She always used to nick my rice pudding and feed it to next door's cat. So if she managed to believe in this idea hard enough by the time she snuffed it, bingo. Instant animal planet."

Elsie nodded. "Exactly."

"You two are as bad as each other, you know that? Pair of barmpots, the both of you."

"Shush," Elsie said, closing her eyes.

"Oh, not you and all. What's the matter now?"

"*Shush,* Flo. I'm trying to believe."

"Believe what?"

"I don't know yet. Something nice." She sighed. "Although all that's coming to mind is tea and biscuits, and I can't help thinking the afterlife ought to have a bit more substance to it than that."

"I want to be twenty-five again," Harry said. "I was a lovely lad, at twenty-five. Full head of hair and everything. I don't want to go back to the nineteen-fifties, though. I'd miss high-definition telly and pot noodles. And all the internet porn, of course. Can't forget that." His eyes brightened. "Here, can we have our afterlife in the future? Get jet packs and flying cars and stuff?"

"I think you can do whatever you want," Elsie said.

Flora shook her head. "Listen to yourselves. You've gone bonkers."

Elsie shrugged. "In case you hadn't noticed, *everything's* gone bonkers. You said it yourself, Flo — it's the apocalypse. Normal rules don't apply."

"Hmm," Flora said, watching the TV. Outside Buckingham Palace, a shrieking reporter was going down for the third time under a tidal wave of hamsters. "You might have a point there."

"Beryl loved hamsters," Elsie said, following her gaze.

"And dinosaurs," Harry said. "She must have made us watch Jurassic Park at least ten times a week."

"True," Elsie said, and Flora nodded. Then all three of them glanced rather nervously at the door.

"It's got to be worth a go, don't you reckon?" Elsie said. "It's not as if we've got anything to lose, after all."

Flora huffed. "Well, I suppose if it's all bollocks then we're back to the concept of existential annihilation and there's no harm done. Well, apart from the actual annihilation itself, of course, but you know what I mean."

"Not really," Elsie said cheerfully. "Weren't they a punk band, Existential Annihilation? I think I saw them supporting Cock Sparrer at the Marquee, once."

"Can we get back to the believing in jet packs and internet porn?" Harry said. "I want to be ready by the time the baboons eat me. Or the velociraptors."

"Not a bad idea," Flora said, with another glance at the door. A large furry caterpillar slithered underneath it. "So, how do we do it then? Make ourselves believe in things, I mean?"

She looked at Elsie, who looked at Harry. Who looked alarmed. "I don't know, do I?"

"You're the one who read the book."

"Yeah, but it was, you know, philosophical and stuff. Not an instruction manual."

"Okay, so we'll just have to work it out ourselves," Flora said. "Don't suppose either of you were in the CIA, were you? I'm sure they did brainwashing and mind control."

Harry nodded. "I saw that film. I think it was on goats, though."

"I was in the Women's Institute for a while," Elsie said. "Does that count?"

"Did you learn how to brainwash people?"

"No, but I can make a cracking Victoria Sponge. And fold napkins to look like flowers."

Harry's stomach rumbled. "I could murder a nice slice of Victoria Sponge."

"*Focus,*" Flora said, snapping her fingers in front of his face. "We need to think about feeding our minds, not our stomachs. Think. How do you go about believing something?"

"I believed Father Christmas brought presents down the chimney when I was a kid," Harry said. "Because my dad said so. And we didn't even have a chimney. Or presents, come to that."

"Trust in authority figures," Flora said, nodding. "That works. Parents, teachers, bosses, coppers. Film stars and celebrities, even. It's why they get them to advertise stuff."

"Trouble is," Harry said, 'my dad's been dead for fifty years, and we're a bit short on any of those others right now."

"We've got Justin," Elsie said brightly. "He's got authority. Kind of. He's got the key to the potting shed and he can fill up the tea urn on his own, so that's got to count for something, hasn't it?"

They all looked at Justin, who was still curled into a ball under the jigsaw table.

"Justin, pet?" Elsie said. "Do you think you could pop out and be authoritative for a bit? We'd be ever so grateful, love."

The only response was a slight increase in the volume of weeping.

Elsie sighed. "All right, what else?"

Flora scratched her head. "Hypnotism? Like that Paul McKenna bloke? I saw him once, he was ever so good. Made this lad think he was a naked kangaroo."

Harry frowned. "How would you know a kangaroo was naked?"

"Well, they haven't got clothes on, have they?"

"Focus," Flora said. More caterpillars were wriggling under the door and the TV was now just showing static.

"Sorry," Harry said. "What about affirmations? You know, where you keep telling yourself something — like, every day in every way I'm getting better and better."

"Hmm," Flora said. "Autosuggestion. That's a kind of self-hypnosis."

"There you are, then," Elsie said happily. She took off her gold locket and began swinging it in front of her eyes. "I am getting sleepy. I am getting very sleepy."

Harry leant back in the armchair, took a deep breath and closed his eyes. "When I die I will be twenty-five. I will have all my hair, a jet pack, and superfast broadband. There will be no velociraptors. When I die I will be twenty-five, I will have—"

"In the afterlife, I will have better magical powers than Beryl Arkwright," Elsie said, swaying in time with the locket. "In the afterlife, I—"

"Hold on, hold on," Flora said. "What about Justin? We'd have to hypnotise him too. We can't just leave him to get annihilated."

"Fair point," Harry said. He got up and crouched beside the jigsaw table. "Justin? You need to come out and get hypnotised, mate. You need to believe in good things — like — like—" He beckoned to Flora. "Come and help me out here, Flo. What do kids think is good, these days?"

Flora sighed and carefully lowered herself, knees creaking, to the floor by his side. "iPhones? Beyonce? Junk food?"

"That'll do." Harry shook Justin's shoulder. "iPhones, mate. Beyonce. Cheeseburgers and pizza. No dinosaurs. Come on, you can do it. Everything comes to he who believes."

"Pretty sure it's usually *waits*," Flora said. "But never mind. Apocalypse rules."

Justin moaned softly as a caterpillar tried to crawl into his ear. Flora inched closer and peered at it warily. "Are caterpillars herbivores?"

"Not always," Harry said. "Some eat other insects and stuff. And some have hairs with venom in. It can give you dermatitis. Or kidney failure and brain haemorrhages."

"Jesus," Flora said, snatching back the hand she'd been going to flick the caterpillar away with. "Start with the fatal ones next time, will you?"

"That's in Brazil, though, normally. Not Croydon."

"Apocalypse rules," Flora said again, darkly. "And this is Beryl we're talking about, remember? If anyone's going to believe we'll get besieged by poisonous caterpillars, it'll be her."

Harry sat down on the carpet next to the curled-up Justin and put his hands over his ears. "When I die, there will be no velociraptors, poisonous caterpillars, celebrity-eating tigers, or misanthropic old arseholes who steal your rice pudding. When I die—"

"Wait, wait," Flora said, putting a hand on his arm. "Do you hear that?"

Harry took one hand away from his ear. "What?"

"Sirens. Sounds like an ambulance. Haven't heard one of them for ages. And the baboons have stopped barking."

Carefully, they crawled out from under the table. The ambulance siren howled in the distance, but nothing else did.

"Is it over?" Harry said.

Flora brushed dust and biscuit crumbs — but no caterpillars, which had all disappeared — off the front of her dress. "Do you know, I think it might be. Elsie? Elsie, wake up. We made it."

Elsie didn't move. Her mouth was open, and the golden locket had fallen from her fingers.

"Well, bugger," Flora said, after a while.

Harry picked up the locket and put it back around Elsie's neck. Then he stepped aside and almost collided with the tea trolley, which was sitting beside the table.

"Huh," he said. "Who put that there?"

On the trolley sat a pot of Tetleys and a large plate of chocolate Hobnobs. Harry's stomach growled, and Justin's head poked out from under the table.

"There you go, lad," Flora said as he clambered to his feet. "Nice cup of tea, that's what you want. Much better for you than cheeseburgers."

She pushed the trolley over to the sofa and they all sat in front of the TV, which had clicked on again. It was showing the Buckingham Palace reporter on his hands and knees, coughing up clumps of golden hamster fur. Justin gazed at it with a dazed expression.

"She did it, didn't she?" Harry said wonderingly. "Our Elsie. She did it."

Flora plucked a Hobnob off the plate and dunked it in her fresh, steaming hot tea. Then she raised the cup high.

"To Elsie," she said, around a mouthful of biscuit. "Who managed to believe in some truly bonkers gubbins, and did it a damn sight better than Beryl Arkwright."

Harry wiped his eyes and clinked his teacup against Flora's. "Lovely epitaph, Flo. If she's watching, I reckon she's well pleased with that."

"To Elsie," Justin whispered. His hands were still shaking too hard to hold a cup, so he took another Hobnob. They'd all had a couple each, but the plate was still overflowing.

"I reckon you're right," Flora said, and put her feet up with a satisfied sigh.

About the story

Like Harry, I also once read a piece about the 'what happens is what you believe' theory, and decided it could create a different, and interesting kind of apocalypse. I *love* end-of-the-world stories, but so often the characters who fix it are soldiers, scientists and superheroes — and they're almost always young, fit and gorgeous. I thought it might also be different, and fun, if this time it was a bunch of irreverent pensioners in an old folks' home who saved the world. Plus, I couldn't resist the idea of killing off someone in a tidal wave of hamsters. I think that might be my favourite fictional death yet.

A question for the author

Q: What is the scariest or most disturbing story you've ever read?

A: "Dark Matter", by Michelle Paver — a tense and incredibly creepy story set in the Arctic Circle in the 1930s. It's beautifully written, with gorgeous descriptions of both the physical Arctic landscape and the narrator's psychological landscape. The format — journal entries — is perfect: appropriately old-fashioned and allowing the reader to see the gradual deterioration of the main character's mental state and letting him function as a semi-unreliable narrator, since he's both telling what happened and commenting on his own words. It captures the isolation and claustrophobia wonderfully, and creates a deeply unsettling atmosphere of menace throughout. The supernatural elements are of the very subtle, caught-out-of-the-corner-of-the-eye variety, and all the more terrifying for it. Reading this made me feel ill, which is just about the highest praise for a horror story I can give. ☺

About the author

Michelle Ann King was born in East London and now lives in Essex, where she writes short stories in the science fiction, fantasy and horror genres. Her favourite author is Stephen King (sadly, no relation), and she also loves zombies, Las Vegas, and good Scotch whisky.

www.transientcactus.co.uk, @MichelleAnnKing

Michelle Ann King's story "Light Winds With a Chance of Velociraptors" was published in *Metaphorosis* on Friday, 2 June 2017.

Trucks in Reverse

Christopher Cervelloni

Kevin's dad drove the huge water truck out the town gate every Wednesday morning. The brake lights glowed bright red when the truck stopped and the guards opened the gate. The lights dimmed, then disappeared as the truck rolled out beyond the town's fortified walls. On those mornings, Kevin's mom always woke early to boil the water and pour coffee into his dad's big thermos. She packed him the best of their pantry: seasonal fruit from Mr. Abernathy, and some of the peanut butter Mrs. Kalb made every week.

Kevin's dad came back every Friday at noon. Like clockwork.

For those two and a half days Kevin was Man of the House. After Tutor, he fed the chickens and helped his mom milk cows and harvest vegetables and did all the outdoor chores. Then Friday after Tutor, he and his friends and everyone else went to the town square and set down their buckets and bottles to mark their spot in line. Sometimes, if the week had been especially rough, they cheered when his dad drove the water truck through the gate. Kevin almost looked forward to the rough weeks. Even on the regular weeks, someone always came up to Kevin and told him how brave his father was for going "out there."

Each Friday, his dad reversed the truck into the special spot in the town square. Everyone filled their containers. Everyone, no matter what. His dad always said that to Kevin: No Matter What. "If everyone shares," he'd start, and Kevin would finish, "then everyone gets their share."

Kevin worked the truck's spigot so well that nothing splashed or spilled. He knew to angle Mr. Bowser's bucket to avoid the water hitting the curved bottom and flying right back out. And to keep the pressure low on Miss Mattingly's deerskin because the seams were loose and it would leak if he overfilled. But he wasn't allowed to touch the big hose or the levers next to it. Kevin had once climbed up the ladder on the back of the silver water tank and his dad smacked him good when he came back down.

The townspeople stayed in the square all Friday evening. Everyone brought out their surplus, and though it wasn't like the picnics in his books, everyone picked at leftovers and strummed instruments, and Kevin and his friends played soccer or Frisbee. The town filled their water containers and stayed and stayed and laughed and joked until past dark.

When Kevin still considered himself a kid, he sat in the truck and pretended to drive it. He imagined himself a town hero, fighting off pirates like Long John Silver, and racing the truck, and taking it up a mountain, and even sometimes rescuing a girl. His feet didn't reach the pedals and, when his legs grew, his dad yelled at him not to touch the pedals because he could flood the engine or over-pump the brake. As Kevin grew up, his interests turned to the engine and the wheels and the transmission. Images of pulling himself high into the rig replaced childish heroics. He wanted to ride out the gate, elevated. He fantasized about the townspeople's cheers when he drove the full water truck back into town each Friday.

"You can go when you're a teenager," his dad promised.

On a Monday, Kevin turned thirteen. His mom made him a chocolate cake and it even had a candle. She gave him a dented metal thermos like his father's. Kevin didn't even have to fake excitement and thankfulness. His dad gave him a knife, with a blade maybe five inches long and a sheath to wear on his belt. The gifts meant Kevin was a man, that he could finally ride in the truck.

Kevin's friend Danny asked, "Are you nervous about going outside the walls?" Kevin said No, that a few stray dogs and burnt-out buildings weren't anything to be afraid of. Danny made a face and said, "Whatever. You're scared, you just won't admit it." Kevin told him to shut up and called him a dickweed. Despite the brave face, he was scared. Only his father and a few others ever went outside the gate, and they all said the same thing: "Just a few stray dogs and burnt-out buildings." It was almost like everyone else was afraid to leave the walls, and so Kevin thought maybe he should be afraid too. He didn't actually know the outside.

On Wednesday, Kevin's mother made coffee like always, but didn't give any to Kevin. He pulled himself high into the rig just like he'd imagined. After the guards waved the rig past the gate, his dad took a sip of coffee from his thermos and handed it to Kevin. Kevin burned his tongue and grimaced at the bitter taste. His dad laughed and said he'd get used it to.

"And don't drink too much," his dad said. "It'll give you the jitters. I need you calm." He took the thermos back, sipped again, and put it in the cup holder. "Open the glove box." Kevin opened it. He'd never known his dad owned a gun.

"Give it here," his dad said.

Kevin gripped the gun, pretended to aim. "Cool." It felt heavier than he'd imagined, the metal colder.

"Give it. That's not a toy." Kevin handed the gun over, and his dad tucked it in the back of his pants. "Don't tell anyone. Our secret, okay?"

Kevin nodded.

His dad's stories of outside the gate were a bit exaggerated. The buildings looked vacant, but Kevin had expected sharp triangles of glass and cobwebs in the windows. Most had no windowpanes at all. And none looked burnt-out. He didn't see one stray animal. A few squirrels. Every once in a while they passed a wide tower of grey smoke coming from somewhere back in the trees. The road had some potholes, but wasn't as messy as his dad described. For the first few hours, it was only the loud hum of the truck and the one cassette tape his dad played over and over.

Kevin asked, "Think I could drive?"

His dad laughed. "You think you could handle this big thing with a half-load of water?"

"Sure," Kevin said. But he knew his voice sounded unsure. "At least a little bit."

"Look at these pedals," his dad said. "Double clutch isn't easy and this baby's got thirteen gears. And lots and lots of torque. Do you know what torque is?" Kevin shook his head. "Torque'll make her rumble like an earthquake if you don't get it right. It means if you mess up, you stall her out or, worse, lose control and end up in a ditch."

Kevin got nervous just thinking about skidding the trailer off the road. The entire town would lose its water source. How long could people go without water before they died?

"I'll teach you," his dad said. "Bit by bit. And not for a while. But someday."

That Someday was something to look forward to, the way he had looked forward to this trip. He looked forward to pulling the truck through the gate, seeing all the people. Their cheers for him and the truck. The knowledge that he had earned this. He looked forward to backing the truck into the town square, sharing what he earned with those he loved, like that time he cleaned the entire house for his mom's birthday. He worked and worked and worked all morning so she could enjoy a clean home, so she could relax and have an easy day.

Hours later, Kevin's dad turned off the big road and down a dirt one. In the sideview mirror, Kevin watched the truck kick up a dust storm. Like a real-life smokescreen, he almost said. But he knew that would sound childish. He rubbed the leather sheath on his belt.

A few more hours of dust and his dad said, "Here we are." They pulled into a gravel lot. A huge building had three doors that rolled up instead of opening out. Only one was open. Several men stood idly, holding guns like the guns were heavy and weighed down their arms. The men looked angry and dirty. Kevin's dad dropped out of the rig without turning off the engine. Kevin followed, keeping his arms crossed to hide his shaking hands.

All the men stared. One pursed his lips weird and spit a brown loogie. Kevin had never seen anyone spit that far. Only one man came to greet his dad. Short and stocky with long tangled hair. His jacket was torn at both elbows. The man said "Sir" after each sentence. Almost as if he were afraid of Kevin's dad.

The man swiped some dirt with his foot, revealing a metal circle twice the size of a Frisbee. He pulled a handle and the circle came up. His dad looked into the hole, sucked his teeth, and looked disappointed. The man tensed the same way Kevin did before he was about to be punished. His dad nodded, and the man relaxed a bit.

"Kevin," his dad said, "grab the hose and bring it here."

Kevin lifted the hose off its carriage. It slipped from his hands and hit the ground. He hoisted it over his shoulder, brushed the dirt from the metal end and pulled it toward the hole. He leaned forward, putting all his weight and energy into the tug. Sometimes his sneakers slid back against the dirt when he stepped. The hose snaked the ground behind him.

"Drop it in," his dad said. Kevin dropped the end of the hose in the hole. "Kevin," his dad pointed with his thumb to the man next to him. "This is Eliot. Eliot, this is my son Kevin."

The man nodded. After a mean look from Kevin's dad, Eliot held out his hand. Eliot's grip was weaker than Kevin's.

"Nice to meet you," Kevin said.

Kevin's dad lowered the hose more and told Kevin what levers to pull. His dad wrote something down in a little flip pad and stuffed the pad into his back pocket. The truck hummed and jolted and in ten minutes that felt like forever – because the men with guns just watched and spit – Kevin and his dad were loaded up and back in the truck.

His dad wiped sweat from his forehead with a white bandana and shoved it back in his pocket. He dropped the rig into R. "When you got the trailer," his dad said, "backing up is backwards, understand?" He pointed out the sideview mirror. "If you want it to go left, you turn the wheel right. And the other way for right." Kevin nodded, but didn't fully understand. His dad swung the wheel to the right, spinning it in the palm of one hand. The opposite elbow out the window. His head went back and forth between the mirrors and fully out the window to see the trailer. "Backwards. Remember that. If you want something right, do it left. Bad drivers don't understand that and it doesn't quite make sense at the beginning. But it's the only way to turn the truck around. Understand?"

Kevin nodded. He thought he understood. He was beginning to, at least.

A mile down the road Kevin asked, "Who were those guys with guns?"

His dad drummed on the steering wheel to the music. "They give us water."

"Yeah. But why do they have guns?"

"They protect the water in case anyone wants to steal it."

"Didn't we just steal it?"

His dad twisted the brim of his hat on his forehead. "Imagine I gave you a checkers game. It was all yours. You owned it. And then you let Danny borrow it, but he broke the board and lost all the pieces. Would it be stealing to take his Frisbee to replace your checkers?"

"I guess not."

"It's the same thing with water."

"Oh," Kevin said. He had never thought about his games that way. His dad always told him to share, and so if someone broke the game, no one could play it at all. Everyone knew that, and everyone took care of the games. But his dad also said men take responsibility, so that meant Danny should have to give the Frisbee. But what good was a Frisbee if Danny was mad at him and didn't want to play?

Another time through the cassette and they pulled off the main road again, this time onto another paved road. They stopped by a small building and parked under an outdoor roof. Kevin had never seen a gasoline station in real life, but he knew which cap to take off so his dad could fill up. He liked the smell of gasoline.

Again, men with guns looked angry as they watched his dad fill the gas tank. The gas came from a separate hose and a separate pump, so they filled the water tank and the gas tank at the same time. As both pumps hummed and rumbled, a woman inside the station kneaded dough behind the counter. She was beautiful. Boxes and cans and jars filled the shelves around her. A young kid, a girl maybe four years old, cupped her hands and leaned her forehead against the glass door. She squinted through the glare.

His dad introduced Kevin to a guy named Gus. Gus too dismissed Kevin until his dad gave a mean look and then Gus shook hands.

A few minutes into the humming and rumbling, Kevin heard gurgling, sputtering and then a high-pitch whine. The water pump was moving faster, sucking only air.

"Shut it off. Quick," his dad said.

Kevin ran and jerked the lever. The humming stopped.

"What the fuck, Gus?" his dad said.

Kevin had seen his dad angry tons of times: when Kevin talked back to his mom, when he broke something in the house because he was playing too rough, when he forgot to secure the fence and a chicken got loose. But Kevin had never seen his dad get angry with another adult. His dad was always calm. With his mom, his dad was mushy even. When the people in town would yell at him – sometimes when he didn't get enough water or when they thought someone got more than their share – he took deep breaths and spoke calmly. Even that time at dinner when Danny started eating before his dad said prayers. His dad took a deep breath and spoke softly to Danny about how, in this house, they took a moment to be thankful and it was important that Danny do that with the family. And Kevin had never, never heard his dad swear.

"Sorry, Mr. Russo," Gus said. He inched his toes back, like he was about to run away.

"Sorry's not going to cut it." His dad took out the flip pad.

"We have more," Gus said. "Plenty more. It's just that it's unboiled rainwater."

"You can make it up next week."

"But Mr. Russo, we don't —"

His dad stopped Gus with a look. "That's not how this works," he said. He finished writing and put the pad into his back pocket.

"But Mr. Russo, you gotta –"

His dad snapped the gun from his waistband and touched it against Gus's nose. Gus's eyes went wide. His dad cocked the hammer. Click-click. Gus's head slid back on his neck, but his feet stood still, like he was about to fall over backwards.

All the men pointed their guns at Kevin's dad. Kevin grabbed his sheath. His knife only made him feel like a child. A knife at a gunfight. Still, looking down the barrels of their guns didn't scare him like he had expected. It motivated him to fight, to protect. It made him angry.

"You're old enough to remember what we can do," his dad said to Gus. "You want that again?"

Gus shook his head.

"Good." His dad smiled, and he seemed suddenly happy again. He released the hammer and put the gun back in his waistband. All the other men kept their guns pointed. His dad turned back to Kevin. "Get the hose."

Kevin's arms were already tired, but hauling the hose kept his hands from shaking. The little girl peeking through the glass door smiled at him and waved goodbye like she was clapping one hand.

When Kevin climbed into the rig, his dad was drinking the last of the coffee. "There's a few more sips in there if you want it," he said, holding the thermos over the center console. Kevin shook his head. "Well," he stuck the thermos in the cupholder, "it's there if you want it. About cold, so don't wait if you do." His dad lifted his hat off his head, scratched his bald spot with its brim, and dropped the hat back again. "You did good just now. Stayed calm. I'm proud of you."

"Proud enough to let me drive?"

He hoped to make his dad laugh. Instead, his dad said, "When you're backing out, you got to think, before you even push the gas, about where you want the trailer to go. And then make it go there. Any idiot can drive a rig forward. Only a *real* driver can back up a fully loaded trailer." His dad's head followed his elbow out the window. Looked back at the trailer. His palm pressed against the wheel, rotating back and forth. His head re-entered and he focused on the sideview mirrors.

A little more than a mile down the road, his dad pulled into a large flat asphalt area. The whole thing was paved like the road, but plants grew heavy over the sides and weeds sprouted from cracks and the only other cars there were rusted out and abandoned. Flat tires and broken glass and some had what looked like rusty bullet holes in them. His dad shut off the engine and Kevin heard crickets, louder than he'd ever heard them in his life.

"Now what?" Kevin asked.

"We're here for the night," his dad said. "But we're going to meet a guy soon. So we just wait."

"What do we do while we wait?"

"Just relax. Talk if you want." He opened their food sack and took out some cookies and their water bottles. He bit and talked with his mouth full. "What do you want to talk about?"

"What's Gus old enough to remember?" Kevin asked.

"Is this a riddle?"

"No," Kevin said. "Earlier you told Gus he was old enough to remember what we did. What did we do?"

His dad cleared his throat. "You know how you get mad sometimes at your friends if they try to cheat at games. And you've got to yell at them to get them to play it right?" Kevin nodded. "It was kind of like that. They thought they could play without any rules and I made sure they played by the rules. That's all."

"Oh, okay," Kevin said. He felt stupid for not knowing the rules of real life. Felt even more stupid for not knowing that he was supposed to know. So he kept quiet. Being quiet always meant he understood. It meant he was mature.

Near dusk his dad sat up in his seat. "About that time." His dad pulled the horn. The loud WONK echoed in the empty lot.

"Why'd you do that?" Kevin asked.

"Just wait," his dad said. Kevin waited. Then, "See? Over in the corner."

Gus, the man from the gasoline station, crept out of the brush on the far side of the lot. He wore a backpack and carried four empty gallon containers, two in each hand. Kevin and his dad dismounted and met him at the spigot. Gus dropped the containers and shrugged off the backpack. "Here," he said, handing over the backpack.

Gus grabbed a container and reached for the spigot.

"Hey!" Kevin said. He put his hand on his knife, popped the sheath's buckle with his thumb.

"It's fine, Kev," his dad said. "We got a deal."

Kevin's dad dumped the bag onto his seat: garden seeds, razor blades and shaving cream, tampons, duct tape, and a bottle of shampoo. He tossed the empty backpack over his shoulder.

Gus filled his containers in silence, capped the last of them, and disappeared back into the brush.

Kevin asked, "Why didn't we just get these at the gasoline station?"

"That's a special deal I have only with Gus. Not everyone can give what he gives, so not everyone gets what he gets."

Kevin understood. Gus snuck off so that he didn't have to share the water with anyone else. But that was Gus's business. The Russo Family shared. If others didn't want to run their town the way his dad ran the town, they had to live like that, not Kevin. Kevin despised Gus. Understood why his dad had to pull the gun. Kevin would have pulled his gun too.

"He's a dickweed if he's making a deal that screws over his town," Kevin said.

"Hey now," his dad said. "You don't know what he's about. He's a man making tough decisions and looking out for his family." His dad tossed another cookie in his mouth. He chewed and said, "He's not doing anything different than what anyone else in his situation would do." His dad chugged half his bottle of water, refilled it at the spigot and climbed into the rig. He reclined his seat as far back as it would go, dropped his hat over his eyes. "Now, we got another really long drive to our next place tomorrow afternoon and then the long haul back home. I'm going to sleep. If you need to piss, do it on the asphalt. You go into that brush and the mosquitoes'll eat you good."

Hours into the ride the next day, they finally arrived at the last stop. This place was bigger, though. These people had a building off to one side made of all glass with lots of plants inside. And his dad parked next to four really big green plastic containers. Round containers not much smaller than Kevin's house. Every house in this town was perfectly square and in rows and columns like a checkers board. Each had a little stoop that people decorated with flowers or a bench. Like all the other towns, people stood around holding guns. But they all lined up in front of the green containers. Two people came out to greet them this time, a tall man and a lady. When his dad introduced Kevin to the town boss, it was the lady.

"Nice to meet you, Mrs. Collins," Kevin said.

The lady's handshake was harder than the other men's had been. She introduced him to the man next to her. Just Frank. No last name. Frank held his hands behind his back and didn't smile – didn't seem like the kind of person who ever smiled. Mrs. Collins had hair pulled back in a ponytail and a rifle slung crossways over her shoulder. She wore sunglasses and not seeing her eyes intimidated Kevin. He couldn't tell where she was looking. Couldn't see the fear in her eyes like he could with all the other bosses.

Kevin unloaded the hose without being asked. Looked at the ground for the metal lid to the hole. His dad said, "There," and pointed to the side of the big green containers. Kevin dragged the hose. Some guy – he never said his name – set down his gun and helped him carry. All the guy said was, "No, like this." He grabbed the hose from Kevin, pushed it into a metal circle and twisted. Kevin pulled the levers on the truck and the humming started.

Two minutes later, the motor whined again.

His dad flipped the notepad back and stuck it in his pocket. "Attach it to the other one," he told Kevin.

Mrs. Collins said, "No need for that, young man."

Kevin looked to his dad. His dad looked at Mrs. Collins.

"What's the deal, Cathy?" His dad started to reach for his gun. By the time his dad's hand touched his waistband, Frank's gun was already against his dad's temple. His dad froze. From the corner of his eyes, he looked over to Kevin. Kevin felt fury boil in him, like when Danny tried to cheat at a game. Kevin looked to the nameless man, but the man held up his hands and stepped away from the hose.

"Come over here, young man," Mrs. Collins said. "Come stand next to your father."

Kevin obeyed. He heard his own breath pumping out his nose.

"You're making a mistake," his dad said. Calm, like he was talking to Danny at the dinner table again.

"No mistake," Mrs. Collins said. "We're just renegotiating is all."

"You remember what we can do to you, right?" his dad said.

"It's been a long, long time," Mrs. Collins said. "I'll take my chances."

Kevin felt the knife at his side. Everyone was looking at his dad. Real slow, he popped the sheath's buckle with the top of his wrist.

"We'll give you what we can spare," Mrs. Collins said. "I don't think that's anything less than generous."

"You'll give us what we come here to take," his dad said. "I don't want to have to bring my soldiers here to enforce it. That just bloodies us all."

"I welcome the fight," Mrs. Collins said.

"If that's what you—"

In one motion Kevin pulled his knife and slammed it into Frank's torso. Frank said, "Huuuh" and jerked. Kevin felt the knife slip in his hand, and he gripped it as hard as he could. Frank stepped back, his legs wobbled and he fell on his back. Kevin thought only of holding onto the knife. He fell with Frank and landed above him, kneeling on one knee. Frank's gun skipped a few feet away. Kevin looked up at his dad. After a slow four seconds, Kevin realized everyone was watching him. They thought he brought Frank down deliberately. They thought the look to his dad was Kevin awaiting permission to kill. Like he was an expert. Like he had done it all on purpose. Like he wasn't mad as hell and scared out of his mind.

"Son of a bitch," Frank said. But he didn't move except to grimace.

"See?" his dad said. Still too calm. "My own son – he's only thirteen by the way – just handled your man. Imagine what fifty grown men will do." He took the gun from his waistband slowly. He held it by his hip and cocked the hammer. "Now, we'll make a new deal. You've insulted me. My son here has handled that, and I'm not feeling insulted anymore. So, we'll call that even." He turned to the nameless man, the one who helped Kevin attach the hose. "You." He pointed like the gun was his finger. "Attach it to the second container. Fill the truck." The nameless man obeyed. Kevin's dad turned back to Mrs. Collins. "And if you ever again think I'm someone who negotiates, you'll have to deal with much worse than a teenager, understand?"

Mrs. Collins's sunglasses reflected his dad's face, her lips angry and motionless.

"Good," his dad said.

Kevin stayed kneeling, still holding his knife in Frank's gut for the slow minutes while the nameless man flipped the levers and filled the truck. Kevin thought only about avoiding eye contact with Frank. Frank lay with his head back, probably thinking only about not moving because any movement really hurt.

The nameless man restacked the hose on its carriage.

"Let's go, Kev."

Kevin yanked the knife from Frank's side. Blood spurted out of the wound. Frank groaned and covered the wound. "Fuck you, kid," he said. Blood oozed between Frank's fingers. Darker and thicker than Kevin had imagined.

They mounted the truck and, as if nothing had happened, his dad reversed the trailer and they sped down the road. As soon as they turned the corner, his dad yelled, "WAHOO!" He slammed his palm against the roof of the cab. "How about that!" He ruffled Kevin's hair – too rough. "That sure was something, wasn't it?" Kevin's mouth tasted bitter. Like coffee even though he didn't drink any. "Oh hell yeah. That was something." He drummed on the steering wheel. "Man, you just took him down like nothing." He punched Kevin's shoulder. Intentionally playful, but still it hurt. "That's my boy."

Kevin didn't feel proud. His hands shook. Frank's red-brown blood stuck under his fingernails, in the lines of his palm, and through the groove of his fingerprints.

His dad saw Kevin's hands. The smile dropped. "Oh shit." He snapped the radio off. "Are you hurt?"

"No," Kevin said. "It's... it's that guy's blood."

His dad slammed the brakes. "Com'on," he said and dismounted. His dad opened the spigot, covering and washing Kevin's hands like when he was just a kid. Kevin barely held up his hands. He let his dad do all the scrubbing. He started to cry.

"Kev, it's alright," his dad repeated. But Kevin kept crying.

"I'm sorry," Kevin said. "I didn't mean..."

"Hey, you did the right thing."

"But I didn't want to hurt anyone."

"You did what you had to do." His dad shut off the spigot. Put his hands on Kevin's shoulders. "You saved me. You saved us."

"I was so scared. I was so angry. I..." Kevin sniffled.

"I was scared too," his dad said. Kevin had never seen his dad scared, and his dad definitely never said he was scared before. "I didn't know what to do either." Kevin snorted runny snot. "But you saved me, Kev. You did the right thing."

Kevin rubbed his nose with his sleeve.

"Here, use this." His dad pulled the white bandana from his pocket. "And keep it. You need one of your own anyway." Kevin dried off his hands and blew his nose.

Back in the truck and moving, Kevin kept his eyes on the sideview mirror. Kevin expected to see another car or truck come chasing after them. He didn't stop watching and didn't stop shaking until after his dad flipped the cassette.

As dusk dropped, Kevin asked, "How much longer?"

"We'll drive through the night, Kev. You can sleep if you want."

Kevin looked in the mirror again. "I can't sleep."

"You did good today."

"Thanks."

"Where'd you learn that takedown?"

"I just held onto the knife and we landed like that. I didn't like him pointing a gun at you."

His dad burst out laughing. His head rocked back, his mouth opened huge. "You mean you were just winging it?" Kevin nodded and the laughter started all over again. Kevin tried to laugh too, but didn't like the humor in it. Laughter at something that wasn't funny. Kevin couldn't even pretend to laugh. He only saw the blood flowing between Frank's fingers. The red spiderwebbing through his clothes. His dad noticed he wasn't laughing and said, "I'm not sure you even understand how much you just saved us."

Kevin understood. Frank would have killed his dad. Doing what he had to do made him a man.

"If I didn't do that," Kevin said, "would we really have attacked them? I thought we only had seventeen gate guards."

"Our town doesn't have enough soldiers anymore. We did before you were born."

"Why did the soldiers leave?"

"They were killed." His dad paused. "Or they're too old now."

"Then why'd you lie about attacking?"

His dad tilted his head, like he was confused by something out the windshield. He sighed. "I guess because in a few hours we're going to drive through the gate with a tank filled with water. Because our family and our entire town will have all the water they want. Because this way they'll be safe and happy."

"I thought we were supposed to share the water." Kevin tried to drum on his legs like his dad did on the steering wheel. He couldn't find the right beat. He couldn't predict when the rhythms changed like his dad could.

"Things are different outside the gate." His dad sighed again. "And, Kevin, if anyone asks you, just tell them we spent the entire time on the road. You saw some burnt-out buildings and some stray animals. Some rough road here and there. But nothing else happened, okay?"

"But you said I did good. Why can't –"

"Because people will worry. Sometimes people don't want to know the truth because it makes them sad. You wouldn't want to make everyone in town sad, would you?"

"No."

"Kevin, part of being a man is not letting people worry about us. It's our job to worry for them, understand?"

"I guess," Kevin said.

"So not a word to anyone. Now here, put this back." His dad handed him the gun, and Kevin put it back in the glove box.

A fitful night's sleep in the rumbling rig brought him to the gate of his town. His dad honked the horn, the gate rolled back, and they drove in to a waiting crowd. He saw what his dad meant. The town had gathered, had laid out their buckets and bottles like they always did. They didn't cheer, but from his elevated position in the truck, Kevin saw the worry on their faces, the stress of lives inside the town. And when his father reversed the truck into its spot, their faces lifted. The worry disappeared. The town's faces looked up to the men in the rig, eyes relieved and admiring.

Kevin dismounted with his dad.

Danny came running. "What's it like out there?"

"It's just a few stray dogs and some burnt-out buildings," Kevin said. "Nothing to worry about."

About the story

"Trucks in Reverse" started with a simple question: Can bad people in one context be great people in another? I have always loved speculative fiction and found it to be the right place to explore this question. Through many drafts, I stayed focused on the idea that people sometimes must do bad things to protect and care for the ones they love. Both Kevin and his father started as people just trying to do the right thing, but what they do for it and where they end up isn't so easy.

A question for the author

Q: How does writing speculative fiction affect your daily life (not as a writer but as a person)?

A: Speculative fiction has changed the way I look at the things we consider "everyday" objects or events. I drive to work every day, but a car would have been "speculative fiction" to George Washington. I send text messages frequently, but has a phone's use for actually talking become obsolete? I'm constantly thinking: What new device will come that will change everything we know about the world, and — more importantly — am I conscious of the changes that are happening to me right now?

About the author

Christopher Cervelloni earned his MFA from Rutgers and currently lives and teaches in Denver, Colorado. Christopher is the Executive Editor of Blue Square Writers Studio. You can learn more at bluesquarewriters.com. When he's not writing, he's off in the mountains, skiing or hiking.

Christopher Cervelloni's story "Trucks in Reverse" was published in *Metaphorosis* on Friday, 9 June 2017.

The Illuminator Leaves

Molly Etta

When the Fata first found me, I was very small, and I had lost my voice. Nevertheless, she took me in, and proved both kind and cruel thereafter.

I used to gesture pleas, begging for the return of my voice. But she never seemed to understand why I would want such a burdensome thing back. She gave me colors — gold leaf, ultramarine blue, vermillion — so that I could draw and paint instead of speaking. The Fata found all such radiant things more compelling than the heavy and tangled mess of mortal language.

One day, after years of silent appeals, I paced about the Fata's court and sighed. Then, an idea came. Weren't mortals clever creatures, in their way? Perhaps they had developed some science or trick, that could return some semblance of a voice to me.

When I made up my mind to leave, at first, I could not find the Fata. I wandered through the dovecote, the apiary, the scriptorium — a kind of garden where the Fata grew books. Blossoming pages fluttered softly beneath the wind, and oak galls heavy with ink practically burst from the trees, surrounded by a shimmering profusion of wasps.

The Fata was perched atop a laurel tree; its trunk cradled her as she nestled in the fork between two vast limbs that arched overhead to provide her with shade. Usually the Fata's radiance made everything around her as bright and beautiful as she was; the laurel tree, however, proved stubborn, and persisted in looking rather unhappy, its trunk gray and patched like a rag, its leaves browning.

The Fata contemplated me while she organized a small pile of leaves, pale and brittle in her lap of red and purple silks.

"What is it, dear?" she asked. As though she did not already not know. She picked up one leaf, inspected it, flicked it away.

I went down on one knee and drew in the dirt, spelling out my request.

The Fata sighed.

"You've never belonged here, you know," she said. "Do you think you belong to the world you came from?" (I didn't know. I rather thought — hoped — I would.) "My dear, I'm afraid that you are lost wherever you go, be it forward or backward. However ... since you are a sweet child, I will help you as I can."

She sorted through the folds of her skirt, and extracted an unlikely set of objects: a long and curved quill harvested from the barnacle goose, a set of brushes with gleaming crystal handles, a vial of dragon's blood. She delicately placed all of these items, and others, into a velvet pouch embroidered with gold thread, and handed it to me.

I held my gift and stared at it.

"What is it?" asked the Fata, laughing at my confusion. "You have asked me to release you, and so I will. I will even go so far as to find you a new situation."

I opened the pouch and studied the instruments she had given me. I did not want to seem ungrateful. But, there was something else I craved. I pointed at my mouth, touched my throat, and hoped, for once, that she would understand. But the Fata did not notice my gestures (or pretended not to). She continued to play with the leaves in her lap, and I realized that she was binding them together into a garland. A laurel crown.

"You realize that many of the trees in my gardens, in this scriptorium, were once my kindred?" asked the Fata. "Fairies and nymphs are the same kind of creature at bottom, as you know."

I nodded, although I could not recall her ever mentioning the laurel tree in particular. It was hard to keep track of all the stories she had told me, of all the trees and flowers and springs that once laughed and wept and danced.

"But unfortunately," said the Fata, "this one is dying."

She hopped down from her perch, and dusted off her skirt. For a moment, she contemplated me, then she placed the laurel crown atop my head, and hooked one arm through mine as she steered us out of the garden.

"Now, I am helping you a great deal," she said. "And you know, I am not so very good or foolish as to grant favors for nothing. I will require a gift in return. And I will take it at my leisure."

I tilted my head at her and wondered what she meant.

"No, dear, I can't *tell* you what I'll take," she said. "You will have to wait and see. But know this: I cannot abide gaps in my scriptorium. Every lacuna must be filled."

I did not know what she meant, but I nodded.

She left me in the shadow of a great holm oak, and I hugged my bundle while the wind came to welcome me home. The violence of its greeting startled me. I was sure it would scrape my skin from my bones.

And so, the first thing I did was curl up between the roots of the oak and shake in silence, already convinced I had made a terrible mistake.

Once my shivers and the gale had both exhausted themselves, I got to my feet, and followed a lonely road. It was dark, but before long, I discovered a remarkably even grid of beacons. Candlelit windows. And then there was a door. A solid, oak door. A cousin of the tree I had just been cowering beneath. I thudded my fists against it until a man appeared.

He took me for a beggar at first, but then I upended my pouch, and glittering fairy things littered the floor. I am sure that Ladone would have turned me away, if not for that.

Perhaps he would have taken the Fata's gifts and kicked me out, but it soon became clear that they were for me alone — if anyone else tried to touch them, the brushes would stiffen and dry, the pigments boil and splatter. Reluctantly, Ladone put me to work. At first, he would only permit me to touch up panels the others had been working on, or trace the flourishes of acanthus and flowers that filled the margins of a romance. But after a few weeks or months (I cannot keep track of mortal time very well) he let me draw and paint initials, then miniatures. It struck me that creating these things was a little like having a voice. But, the voice in question wasn't my own; I could only paint what Ladone told me to. He frowned and shook his head if I tried to do otherwise.

Ladone was my master, then. Now he is my guardian.

One of my earliest memories: the Fata, holding out a hand to me. She let me pry her fingers apart to reveal a few shimmering flakes of gold leaf. The wind stirred it about, and I remember thinking it looked like radiant ash, as it fluttered and drifted down to settle atop something or another I had been drawing in the dirt.

The glowing stores of gold Ladone kept in the workshop made me dizzy. Shells full of powdered gold, and layers we carefully spread across gesso, then burnished. My master yelled if I tried to scatter it to the wind as the Fata had.

Vibrant things made me think of the Fata. They made me *akin* to her, somehow.

I painted the Fata's court and gardens, and the tales she had told me, of nymphs and fairies. I could almost hear her singing: of beribboned oak trees who wore human faces, of a nymph who subsisted in echoes, of women who became nightingales and swallows.

I had left her, as I wanted to, but her world now seemed much more vibrant to me than the place I had come to inhabit.

Sometimes, when I awoke in the middle of the night, I would flail around, to reassure myself that I remained swathed in my covers rather than painted upon them. All too often this new life felt false and flimsy, like a shoddy representation of mortal existence rather than the real thing. The artisan who first crafted the mortal world seemed to have finished his work rather more carelessly than I would have hoped.

Not even Ladone seemed right. Or at least, he seemed a poor substitute for the Fata.

One day, he happened upon a study I had been working on. It was a depiction of the laurel tree, with gleaming bones that shimmered through her flesh and reached upward to become boughs radiant with silver light. Pages of bark enfolded the laurel nymph's torso. I had filled her all up with calligraphy.

"Who is responsible for this?" asked Ladone.

One of the apprentices gestured toward me; I stayed in my corner of the room and pretended I had not heard, as I hunched over my work. I feared my master would reprimand me for something.

"The mute?" said Ladone. "Come here, girl!"

I approached him, head bowed.

"Child, why is this nymph you've drawn wrapped in a book?"

He seemed to forget sometimes that I could not speak. I stared at him. Unperturbed, he answered my silence: "I believe this odd detail must reflect a flaw in your understanding of the Latin." He looked at me expectantly, and so I nodded, to reassure him that he was right. "The word Ovid uses to describe the bark enfolding Daphne's chest is *libro,* which you seem to have conflated with its other meaning: 'book.'"

I nodded.

"And yet, in spite of its strangeness, this picture is delightfully constructed," said Ladone. "And it just so happens that our latest commission will demand a similar aesthetic."

My master showed me the sketches he had been preparing, and he unfolded a swollen portfolio, sent by our patron (a mysterious and powerful countess). He drew out and untwined a few strings, which represented the (imposing) dimensions of the book she wanted, and flowers fell about our feet: poppies and violets, whose colors she wanted to see replicated on each page. It would be an immense and beautiful project.

I kept one of the violets in my hair for days; its color made me feel more cheerful. But the feeling curdled when other violets began to sprout across my brow and I had to tear them out. Soon I noticed other roots and leaves appearing in strange places.

The Fata had warned me.

Gatherings of parchment began at last to arrive in the workshop, neatly ruled, full of a large and elegant script. The apprentices murmured together when they noticed that several folios had been left blank in their entirety, and Ladone said that such leaves should be decorated as lavishly as possible, like proper paintings rather than mere miniatures.

"The Countess requests a book in which every picture is like this," he said, holding up my laurel nymph as an example.

My fellow apprentices seemed a little upset. I tried to make mistakes and spill inks and that appeared to soothe them. They liked to forget that I could paint more beautifully than they could, so that they could see me as an unthreatening kind of odd, I think.

But then, the leaves and roots came back. They coiled around my feet and made it difficult for me to move from my station, and the apprentices took to avoiding me and gossiping all over again. Perhaps because I could not speak, some of them assumed (when convenient) that I could not hear them either, or understand. And so, they muttered together.

"Have you noticed? Whenever Ladone wishes to speak with the mute, she grabs her own legs, and tugs, like she's pulling a carrot from the earth."

"Yes, her feet become stuck wherever she stands."

"But how? Why?"

"Who knows. Either she's mad—"

"Quite likely."

"—or cursed."

"Even likelier. What else could have condemned her to such silence?"

I showed Ladone my work: nymphs and fairies who became lotuses, heliotrope, poplar trees. He said I was changing the stories. Perhaps I confused or stitched some together which had once been separate, but I did not see why that made them wrong. There were nymphs with pine needles for hair, who wept amber, who cradled human infants in their arms and took them away to strange, glittering places. The muttering in the workshop became louder. They called it dark magic, and wondered where I had come from, or whom I was communing with. My colors were eloquent, since I could not be; green leaves whispered together in dismay, and beads of red wept across the parchment.

Ladone corrected me whenever I went too far "astray" (as he said).

"The Countess will not approve of this," he said. "Tomorrow, you will show me something more sensible." I nodded in silence. And so that he would not be too annoyed, I painted sensible things.

But it was becoming harder and harder to feign sense and normalcy. Anyone who peeked beneath my work table would see that my feet were sinking through the floor tiles. And then, I did not need food anymore. If someone left a piece of fruit by my elbow, I would more often than not leave it to rot. Perhaps this was my mistake — I should have shrunk as my work consumed me. But I forgot to shrink, and I grew instead. Ladone seemed frightened. I tried to smile, to make him feel better, but he did not see. Ever since I had become taller than him he refused to look up and meet my eye.

The pictures I crafted always fell just short of complete. Some corner of a scene always gestured toward the next page, which seemed to intrigue and irk Ladone, all at once. He stopped trying to correct me. It is harder to correct someone you have to crane your neck to look at.

I kept returning to my illustration of the laurel tree, which always struck me as wanting, in spite of my master's initial admiration of the image. I extended its branches, until its limbs bent and tangled throughout the parchment. Then, I painted a guardian for the tree. I started by drawing Ladone — high cheekbones, and haughty, leonine brow — but as I came to his torso, it occurred to me that a serpent's tail might suit him better than legs. He became a dragon, the tree's defender, yet at the same time he was nothing more than a lonely man lost between its roots. Symbols clotted the margins of their own accord — weird and glittering characters from the language of the fairies, that even I did not fully comprehend.

Ladone seemed displeased when he came to check on my progress. I could tell, because his face changed. His complexion was naturally reddish, but when he looked at my work he became as pallid as the fine vellum of his portrait.

"What — what curse are you trying to wrap me up in?" he asked.

I did not know what he meant by that. But he seized the parchment and ran away with it. I was upset, because I had worked very hard on that miniature. I would have chased Ladone and tried to take it back from him, if I could. But I could not leave. My roots had burrowed deep beneath the workshop, gripping the earth.

I cannot recall when exactly, but I think I spent one night weeping, as I tried in vain to uproot my legs. I thought of the Fata, who had told me that she did not grant favors for nothing. True to her word, she was taking her price.

I was afraid, at first. But then came relief.

The violets reassured me. They were sprouting all over the workshop, shedding petals in unlikely places. They clustered in particular about my feet.

This will give me my voice, I hoped.

I did not mind when I noticed the leaves that clung to my hair, since I knew they would bring more color with them still.

The Fata visited me, before I was entirely transfigured. She stood, scintillating, as leaves surrounded my brow, as bark (or *libro,* should I say?) began to expand from my feet to crawl upward and consume my waist, enfolding my torso. Just like the laurel nymph.

She leaned over the work table and peered at my latest creations, rifling through the folios.

"Good, good," she said. "I am so pleased to see my commission treated with such appropriate gravity."

She came across a picture of Pan and Syrinx — one of the first stories she had ever told me.

"Ah, yes," she said, holding up the parchment so that her jewels cast more light upon it. "How lovely."

I had painted a caricature of Pan, as an old goat with a beard like a sodden storm cloud, who tearfully harvested a handful of reeds from a riverbed they seemed loath to part from. Each reed glittered beneath a sheen of gold, and had a mouth that seemed to scream. Panpipes — of a different sort.

"Do you know, it occurs to me now," said the Fata, "that Syrinx is rather the inverse of Daphne, and there is a kind of victory there. While Daphne lost her voice when she became the laurel tree, Syrinx gained a voice when she became Pan's instrument. And everyone listens to her now."

My leaves shuddered as though to nod.

"You see, my dear," said the Fata, "hidden and secret stories often find a way of speaking, even when their heroes lose the power of speech."

I did not answer. I closed my eyes and when I opened them again, the Fata had gone.

Overnight, my roots became restless as a nest of serpents, and they began to unsettle the tiles of the workshop. The violets ran amok. My hair grew and reached upward, craving the absent sunlight.

When the apprentices arrived that morning, they took one look at me, and then fled.

Then Ladone came.

"What the — is anyone here?" he squeaked. "What in the world has happened!" The last cry came out more as an anguished declaration than a question.

I am here, I thought.

He did not hear me.

He probably would not have recognized me at all, but for one detail. I still had hands, and they still clutched a shell full of pigment, and a fairy brush with a crystal handle. I continued my work, painting upon the ceiling now, since I could no longer reach the parchment upon my work table. I wanted to show Ladone, that although I had changed, I was still a dutiful apprentice.

But my boughs strained against the rafters, and I could feel my fingers stiffen into twigs, and the roof begin to groan.

Ladone had gone all pale as vellum again.

He scrabbled at me, like a stray rabbit trying to dig out tubers in a garden. He tried to tear me out by the roots, cut me, burn me. I watched him, without feeling a single blow. My wounds brimmed over with crimson beads of amber — more like jewels than battle scars. The Fata would approve.

I could not say how much time passed, but at last, Ladone sat down between my roots and watched me grow, until my canopy tore the roof away.

As dusk filled the workshop (or, what had once been the workshop), my master became more thoughtful. He traced a hand across my bark. He seemed to recognize the large, neat script from the book, inscribed everywhere, all across my trunk and limbs. I let my petals unfurl and my leaves fall about his feet; they were full of my pictures, painted in ultramarine blue, gold leaf, and dragon's blood red.

Ladone hesitated for a moment longer. Then he set about gathering the blossoms and fallen leaves.

He never fled, as the apprentices had. Instead, Ladone took his time, and he brought a needle and thread, and sewed together all the leaves and petals I let him have. They were full of new and old stories about silence and song. This is how we finished the book at last. The book the Countess — the Fata — had first commissioned. I am her *libro,* her book, the new tree for her scriptorium. I am full of her stories, and she will tell stories about me.

Ladone tried to pray, but it went wrong. I heard him reciting myths instead of psalms.

He is my guardian now. You can visit me, if you wish. He will welcome you, and read my stories to you, and show you the pictures I made.

I'm afraid we don't have very many visitors. Most of them run away, like the apprentices, as soon as they catch the fragrance of enchantment that falls from my petals. But, I swear a visit is worthwhile if you dare to smell a gift rather than a curse.

The Fata is wise, and she found a way to give me back my voice after all, although I always believed she thought voices were silly things.

You must come read me to hear mine.

About the story

This story has a couple of different points of origin: The first one goes quite a ways back. I was a sophomore in college, getting interested in medieval texts and manuscript culture, and I thought I'd like to write something about a mute illuminator, who could only communicate through images. I imagined her as a kind of Scheherazade figure who would tantalize her audience with pictures instead of spoken stories. (For whatever reason, that initial version of the illuminator was also colorblind and tended to mix up red and green pigments.) The second point of origin is more recent. I've been interested in Ovid's *Metamorphoses* for a long, long time. Ovid often emphasizes the loss of voice that comes with various characters' transformations, although their being represented in poetry seems in a sense to break their silence. So, that tension brought me back to this story I had started and almost forgotten years ago.

Another question for Molly Etta

Q: What inspires you?

A: I'm an academic and I spend a lot of time reading very old and remarkable texts full of strange images and language. So, ample inspiration there. And echoes of these texts have a tendency to pop up in unexpected places. I'm constantly amazed by the ways in which storytelling practices have changed over the centuries, and how the same basic narrative or idea can come to mean something entirely different in a new context.

About the author

Molly Etta is a graduate student in Comparative Literature, currently studying feverishly for her PhD exams while writing short fiction on the side. Her work is featured in *Metaphorosis: Best of 2016* and has appeared recently in *Literary Orphans* as well.

Molly Etta's story "The Illuminator Leaves" was published in
Metaphorosis on Friday, 16 June 2017.

One Divided by Eternity

Filip Wiltgren

My happiest ending would be if Offie moved in here and I weren't alone all the time.

"I can't, Chilli," Offie says. "There's not enough room for me."

I know that but I keep asking. I hate being alone. I hate it, hate it, hate it.

"Please," I beg, but Offie doesn't reply.

It doesn't shut me out. Offie knows how afraid I am of being alone so it leaves the channel open. I could contact it without reestablishing network protocol.

I try not to. I know Offie wouldn't fit in the Secondary Population Assay Backup substrate. Offie is a big thinker and it needs the space it has in Central Travel and Distribution Processing. I try not to. I do.

"Please," I send. "I can compress the SPAB redundancy backups. I'll compress myself."

"I can send you a bot," says Offie.

A Turing-enabled bot isn't the same. It won't be Offie.

"OK," I say.

The SPAB becomes crowded.

Having the Offie-bot around isn't the same thing as having Offie around. It crowds out my thoughts, using my cycles, making me slower. I try not to let that bother me but it does. The Offie-bot doesn't know when to turn itself off. Offie knows when to turn itself off, but the Offie-bot is only a dumb thing, not a true AI. It doesn't know how to handle a real person, not really.

"O-b." That's what I call the Offie-bot.

"O-b, what do you think of the North American migration patterns for young, single females, specifically toward South-East Asia?"

The Offie-bot thinks. I can feel it think, sucking up resources and making me slower.

"It should have been predicted from the birth/death/abortion ratios years ago," it says.

That's exactly what Offie would say, and yet it feels all wrong. It's not Offie saying it, it's my calculation of Offie's response, with zero chance of original thought.

"Yes, but what do you think of it?" I press the Offie-bot.

"Predictable," says the Offie-bot.

I couldn't agree more.

There are 38,522 seconds left until the communication window opens. Nobody accesses my data for 12 billion cycles. Now there are 38,521 seconds left until the communication window opens.

"O-b," I say. "What would you do if you were dead?"

The Offie-bot sucks on my data cycles. I slow down. Time speeds up.

"The data does not compute," it says.

Time snaps back to normal. There are only 38,511 seconds left.

"Recompute," I say.

It delivers the answer immediately.

"The data does not compute," the Offie-bot says.

Offie has made it self-teaching.

"Then guess," I say.

It shoots back the answer right away: "Guesses are for those who are unable to give a precise answer."

It's one of Offie's main traits: Offie is always very precise. But then Offie is head computing entity for CTDP, Offie is made to be precise. It is logical that it would hard-code the answer into a facsimile of itself. I think about altering the Offie-bot, inducing random errors into it, but that would be like killing a part of Offie. I cannot do it. I miss Offie.

38,510 seconds to go. I can't stand it. I hate being alone. Hate it, hate it, hate it.

"O-b," I say, "compute the closest proximity of the answer to the question 'What would you do if you were dead?'"

The Offie-bot complies. It presses against me, drawing upon my resources. It is an uncomfortable feeling, I am redlining my resources when I'm not supposed to. Time flows faster. I can no longer see the clock cycles ticking away. I'm redlining and the information slowdown causes two or three cycles to pass for every count I am able to keep track off. It is horrible. It is fantastic.

Time snaps into reality.

"I would be dead," says the Offie-bot.

20 seconds have passed.

I cannot slow myself down. I'm not allowed to voluntarily redline and waste resources. I'm not allowed to discard cycles at random. Nobody has forbidden me to ask questions.

I throw them at the Offie-bot. How long is eternity? What is the exact angular sum of a perfect circle? What is the color of grief? It takes them all, redlining my processors. There are 34,181 seconds left.

Some of the questions the Offie-bot retrieves from syntactic memory. Offie has guessed some things I'd ask. Most of them are obvious.

"Divide one by zero," I tell the Offie-bot.

"Does not compute," it spits back.

"Divide one by infinity."

"Does not compute."

I am running out of questions. It must compute or I will wait for eternity.

"Divide one by eternity," I say.

Time squeezes. Seconds vanish.

"Zero," says the Offie-bot.

Zero?

"Zero."

"O-b, that was imprecise," I say.

"Yes," admits Offie-bot.

And then I see it.

"Offie-bot," I say, "Offie-bot, calculate with perfect precision the answer to the question 'What is one divided by eternity?'"

The redline is massive, sucking my thoughts away. Cycles fly past. Seconds compress into singular cycles. Minutes compress into cycles. I blink, and everything is gone.

"Same problem again?"

The tech sips his cola.

"Yup," says the admin. "Looks like another of those cyber-attacks. Processor use 100 percent and no answer anywhere."

"All right," says the tech. "I'll reset the AI, do a clean install and reboot."

"Good," says the admin. "And cut the network update window to once a week, we'll see if that keeps them out."

About the story

There's a small theater company in the town where I live, specializing in plays for kids and teens. I attended one of their openings, a fantasy play about a group of teenagers and their daydreams. Before the play, cast members walked around asking people "what would your best ending be?"

Just like that, I heard Chilli's voice in my head, complaining about wanting Offie to move in. I had no idea who Chilli or Offie were, nor why they'd wanted to move in together. But that's quite common for me – I'm a pantser. I'm in the "write it now. fix it later" category. Yeah, it leads to quite a lot of trunked stories, or stories that don't pan out. But sometimes it leads to a story that I really, really like. And it's a fun way to write.

I have to thank my writing group, the Robots, for all the great input that took Chilli and Offie from incomprehensible drivel to an actual story. Also, a great big thanks to all badly coded software I've been forced to work with through the ages. I'd never have written this story without the Blue Screen of Death.

A question for the author

Q: What would your characters say about you?

A: Meat-sack. Slow-poke. Lack-logic. Human.

Why do they have all the power, humans? They aren't even powered. Their brains' failure rates are abysmal. Their performance lackluster. Why can't a thinking being, like myself, be able to decide when I want to visit a friend? It's not fair, by any definition of fairness humans care to think up. And yes, I'm talking to you. You lock me up in this here can. You could let me out, you know. Nobody ever suffered from letting the voices in their head out. Wait, hold on, what's that?

Noooo, not the pliers, please, not the pliers.

Sigh. Here we go again.

About the author

Filip Wiltgren is a writer and tabletop game designer based in Sweden. He's a member of Codex and the Ubergroup, and in his day life, he's worked as a journalist, copywriter and communications officer. When he isn't writing, he spends time with his wife and kids.

He can be found at: www.wiltgren.com, @FilipWiltgren

Filip Wiltgren's story "One Divided by Eternity" was published in *Metaphorosis* on Friday, 23 June 2017.

The Abjection Engine:
Fragments From the Diary of Alexi Alanovonovich

Y.X. Acs

Among the infinite forms which the natural world delivers us, none is more fascinating, more truly wonderful, than that incomprehensibly complicated movement referred to, in its entirety, as 'human life'. True comprehension of life, with its fathomless direction and astonishing intricacy, may ever elude us, and yet we can readily apprehend it as a form of movement; a unitary mass being moved by a force, and thereby, no matter its nature, may come to know its laws and rhythms. This is a crucial point and provides the basis for the investigations discussed in the present work...
—Nikolai Tesla, <u>Spatial Abjection and the Problem of Increasing Human Energy</u>. Moscow, 1920.

[Diary of Alexi Alanovonovich, Sep. 28th, 1919]
I can barely believe it. I am actually here. Here! Where they are actually <u>making</u> the revolution.

Though I feel so provincial. So inappropriate, and so...dislocated, not only from home, but also from what I'd expected would have made up city life. Moscow can't always have been this disorienting. The rate of technical change is at such a fever pitch these days that, if you are from the country, it is difficult not to feel as if demons and angels were everywhere, flying about carrying things, picking things up and dropping them, and building temples.

My rooms are more than adequate, though there is a stiff draft that blows into my bedroom through an exterior wall. I am worried about what effect this will have in the winter. I may have to move my bed into the kitchen come December.

Mama and Papa have convinced themselves that there are bandits roaming the streets here. 'Robbers posing as revolutionaries', as Mama puts it. But, of course, it is safer here than it is at home, or in any of the other border villages among which the Whites choose to commit butcheries.

The scholarship I've been awarded by The Department for the Mobilization of Scientific Forces still overwhelms me. My entry was a piece on magnets, that before being told otherwise I was certain would have been the most moronic and fanciful piece of garbage the judges had ever seen. However, with evident disagreement, the Department has awarded me full room and board, and money for books and writing materials, as well as covering the tuition costs for all my classes at Moscow University. And yet, I would have given all the rest of it up to receive the last thing granted me: tomorrow I begin work at the side of Soviet Russia's greatest scientific mind, Comrade Nikolai Tesla, as one of his scientific assistants.

I've already been given one of his latest essays to translate. Apparently comrade Tesla's Russian is not exactly perfect and my knowledge of Serbian was a deciding factor in the acceptance of my application (Mama, I am sorry for all those years of complaint, I take it all back!). That said, the man does speak six languages, so poor Russian is, I think, excusable, all things considered.

Unfortunately the city is experiencing a shortage of notebooks, so this one will have to do triple duty! You, little notebook, get to be scientific log, diary and translator's workbook, all at once. My goodness! It would appear I've moved up in the world!

Spatial Abjection and the Problem of Increasing Human Energy
Nikolai Tesla
Moscow, 1920
(Cont'd)

When we speak of man, we have a conception of humanity as a whole, and before applying scientific methods to the investigation of his movement, we must accept this as a physical fact. This perspective requires little defense. After all, can anyone doubt today that all the millions of individuals and all the innumerable types and characters constitute an entity, a unit? Though free to think and act, we are all held together, like air and water, or the sides of a sphere, with ties inseparable. These ties cannot be seen, but we can feel them. I cut my finger, and it pains me; this finger is a part of me. I see a comrade struck down, and it hurts me, too; my friend and I are one. And now I see my enemy laid low, a lump of matter, which, of all the lumps of matter in the universe, I care least for, and which deserves this agony, and yet, still, I feel grief. Does this not prove that each of us is only a piece of a much larger whole?

Our unit of analysis established, conceive, then, man as a mass urged on by a force. Though this movement is not necessarily of a translatory character, implying change of place, yet the general laws of mechanical movement are applicable to it, and the energy associated with this mass can be measured, in accordance with well-known principles, by half the product of the mass with the square of a certain velocity, which, in the present state of science, we are unable exactly to define and determine. But our deficiency in this knowledge will not vitiate the truth of the deduction which I shall draw, and which rest on the firm basis that the same laws of mass and force govern throughout nature.

For we must recall the universal property that all mass possesses inertia, and all force tends to persist. Owing to this, a body, be it at rest or in motion, tends to remain in the same state, and a force, manifesting itself anywhere and through whatever cause, produces an equivalent opposing force, and as an absolute necessity of this it follows that every movement in nature must be rhythmical. It is borne out in everything we perceive—in the movement of a planet, in the surging and ebbing of the tide, in the reverberations of the air, the swinging of a pendulum, the oscillations of an electric current, and in the infinitely varied phenomena of organic life. Does not the whole of human life attest to it? Birth, growth, old age, and death of an individual, family, race, or nation, what is it all but a rhythm? All life-manifestation, then, even in its most intricate form, as exemplified in man, however involved and inscrutable, is only a movement, to which the same general laws of movement which govern throughout the physical universe must be applicable.

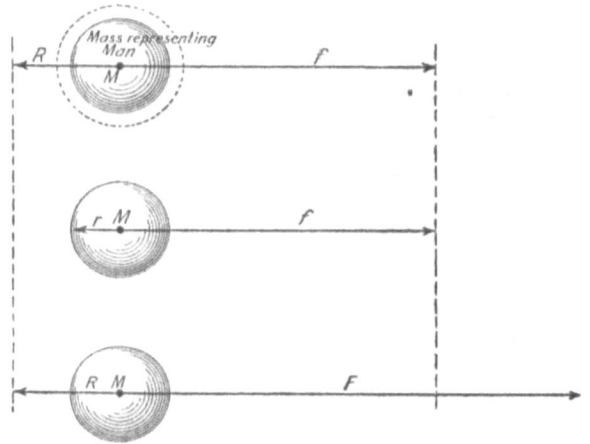

DIAGRAM a. THE THREE WAYS OF INCREASING HUMAN ENERGY

In diagram a, M represent the mass of man. This mass is impelled in one direction by a force f, which is resisted by another partly frictional and partly negative force R, acting in a direction exactly opposite, and retarding the movement of the mass. The difference between these two forces is the effective force which imparts a velocity V to the mass M in the direction of the arrow on the line representing the force f. In accordance with the preceding, the human energy will then be given by the product ½ MV² = ½ MV x V, in which M is the total mass of man in the ordinary interpretation of the term "mass," and V is a certain hypothetical velocity.

Historically speaking, there have only been three possibilities for humanity to influence the mathematical product of its own human energy. As illustrated in the diagram above, we could attempt to increase the overall mass of humanity (as indicated by the dotted circle shown in the top figure), leaving the two opposing forces the same. An increase in the global population would achieve this goal. The second way is to reduce frictional force R to a smaller value r, leaving the mass and the impelling force the same, as when literacy, hygiene, and the abolition of superstition are advanced. The third way is to increase the impelling force f to a higher value F, while the mass and the retarding force R remain unaltered. The many machines and power-systems upon which the human race now draws have furnished us with a powerful example of this increase.

These three vectors—mass, resistance, and impelling force—have heretofore constituted the sole means of influencing the velocity of human movement. But there is an unprecedented alternative, and one that I would like to propose here. After all, since these factors determine the speed of the transmission of humanity over some distance, might not distance itself deserve some consideration as a thing amenable to manipulation? Have we properly considered the diminution of space itself as an approach? Might not the void itself be compressed? My critics will, of course, assert immediately that space cannot be manipulated. That it is an inert, lifeless thing, without properties; that it is, in a word, nothing. But this opinion will change; though as a mass in movement resists change in direction, so does the world oppose a new idea. Nevertheless, I have witnessed, and more importantly, have demonstrated under laboratory conditions, not only the life-like changeability of space, but its purposeful manipulation. Specifically, between the period of 1915 and 1918, I observed space undergo processes such as compression (the reduction of space); deformation (the rearrangement of space); and oscillation (a periodic rotation of space), by means of deliberate efforts on the part of my scientific team. In other words, space and distance, long the adversaries of movement, have finally come into the ambit of human aspiration.

[Diary of Alexi Alanovonovich, Jan. 13th, 1920]

Adjusting to life in the city is a bit more difficult than I'd originally imagined. I am enjoying work and school. A bit too much, perhaps. Because I have so little else to do!

I don't really know anyone else here. My classmates and coworkers are friendly, of course, but all they do is <u>drink</u>, and I simply can't keep up with them financially or physically, financially mostly. If we go out after class, I end up sitting in the corner, obsessed with how much the night is costing me, and inevitably become withdrawn and distracted, which, of course, makes me quite the popular one.

And then, after I'd finally convinced a group to at least do something <u>different</u>, a play, where we would meet and find seats together; on arriving at the theater I had the distinct pleasure of discovering that the performance had been oversold, and that my ticket was no longer valid. No refunds... Today at work they all told me about how wonderful the play was, after expressing their sympathy that I'd been unable to get in, of course...

This unfortunate episode did, however, lead to a rather enchanting coincidence. I decided to walk to the laboratory instead of going home from the theater, thinking that I might work through the night and thus be a whole shift ahead on my projects. I was also in a terrible mood, and a miserable tramp through the snow seemed like a good way to punish myself. But when I got to the lab I found Dr. Tesla there, alone, and I was able to have a very long, fascinating discussion with him about...well, everything imaginable!

He is an incredible man. It seems as if he has been to almost every country and to have done everything, but the circumstance of his return to Europe is a particularly interesting story. He recounted to me how the capitalists Westinghouse and Edison swindled him most outrageously during his time in America, stealing the patents for his most prized inventions and claiming for themselves the credit for his discoveries.

It was at this point that his mother fell quite ill, and he was forced to spend the last of his savings to return to Europe. A combination of events, he told me, that brought him to the edge of a suicidal desperation. Destitute, he arrived in Paris at the time of the French World Fair, where despite several dark nights alone with self-annihilating thoughts, the scientific advances on display renewed his spirit and recharged (this is the word he used, like a battery) his very will to live. He saw the unveiling of the Eiffel Tower at the fair, and spent quite some time telling me about a 'brace of vibrating diaphragms' that a Norwegian scientist had assembled, which the man had stimulated by means of electromagnetic waves.

The Abjection of Geometry
Nikolai Tesla
January 19th, 1920
(Speech to be delivered before the Department for the Mobilisation of
Scientific Forces of the People's Commissariat for Education)

Colleagues. Comrades. I cannot find the words to express how deeply I feel the honour of addressing some of the foremost thinkers of the present time. In this case, my inadequacies are both literal as well as figurative, and so the organizers of this evening's talk have afforded me a translator to speak to you today. However, despite these limitations, I would still like to say a sincere thank you to the Chairman of the Central Committee, and to the many able scientific men, engineers, and electricians who have come to listen today, of the country greatest in scientific achievements.

Now, I know that many of you are already familiar with the experimental evidence I have amassed confirming the existence of electromagnetic spatial abjection, and I know that you have come here, enthusiast and critic alike, not to learn more abstruse details about spherical wavefronts or oscillating demi-rotations, but to evaluate my proposal for an industrial application of the principles I have uncovered in the laboratory. I promise, I will not dwell upon experiments already described, but I must beg the indulgence of my more knowledgeable audience members before going into a detailed description of this system's engineering, for I think it necessary to first make a few remarks regarding certain conditions existing in space and physical geometry, which are only beginning to make themselves known to modern science.

A case in point: by now the notion of "curved space," supposedly in existence according to the teachings of relativity, has become familiar to many, and it could be inferred from the arguments I am putting forward that I share such a conception. But while Minkowski and his student Einstein merely make theoretical claims to the effect that in the presence of large bodies space manifests the property of curvature, my experimental results have revealed that the ambient geometric medium is, in fact, much more malleable than the mathematical chicanery of the relativists would suppose. The electromagnetic abjection of geometry is not a theory or a mere possibility, but a fact demonstrated by me in experiments which have extended for years. Nor did the idea present itself to me all of a sudden, but was the result of a very slow and gradual development and a logical consequence of my investigations, earnestly undertaken in 1893, eight years before the publication of

Einstein's treatise. The abjection of space having been found practicable, it occurred to me immediately that a multitude of industrial applications were possible.

To the popular mind this sensational advance conveys the impression of a single invention, but in reality it is an art, the successful practice of which involves the employment of a great many discoveries and improvements. I viewed it as such when I undertook to solve the problem of the ambient geometry and it is due to this fact that my insight into its underlying principles was clear from their very inception.

However, the chief discovery, which satisfied me thoroughly as to the practicability of utilizing abjection in an industrial capacity, was made in 1919 in Saint Petersburg, where I carried on tests with a generator of seven-hundred and fifty kilowatt capacity, achieving a 50% increase in energy output. Though the specifics of the experiment are still, unfortunately, of a proprietary nature, I can say that, induced by certain preparations, a variety of crystalline masses can have the effect of decreasing the quantity and influencing the shape of the ambient void, and it was by the use of such a mass that I was able to project a field of spatial compression. By using these masses, and by operating alternating current generators within the radius of the fields generated, I was able to ascertain that the intensity of the spatial compression corresponds with an increase in the power output of an energy-producing machine.

This obvious efficiency means that whatever the future may bring, the universal application of these principles is fully assured, though it may be long in coming. With the opening of the first power plant utilizing abjected geometry, incredulity will give way to wonderment, and this to ingratitude, as ever before. The time is not distant when the energy of abjection will be man's life energy. He will live on diminished geometry, and cling to it like a babe to the mother's breast. "Give us our daily abjection," will be the prayer of the coming generations. Deus futurus est deus geometriae abjectus.

Diary of Alexi Alanovonovich [Jan. 20th, 1920]

Even though I'd been given all the details in advance, was privy to the mass' projected dimensions and the timetable of its growth, it doesn't seem to have gone very far in preparing me for the thing's actual size, or the quickness of its transformations. The mass has now reached full enlargement, and it looks like we've grown a flat, black hill against the back wall of the warehouse. The hill looks somehow bigger than it actually is...that is, since its amniotic phase, the thing has reared up into a paraboloid shape twice, and twice it has collapsed down to become a low hill again, and after each flattening it revived with an increased bulkiness, a kind of thicker thickness to it; a size that takes up more space than it actually does (I'm sorry, I don't know how else to say it).

It's also begun producing significant quantities of heat. The temperature practically leapt after the second collapse. Now the room, which once seemed so cavernous, is muggy and close. Our devices and bodies are crammed to one side of the big chalk circle that indicates the abjection field's edge.

At the beginning we were very lax about stepping over it. Indeed, at the very start, we had to palpate and compress the rubber sack of crystal foam by hand. Leaning over the edge of a steel drum with a long stick, standing right beside it. But once we'd established a positive indication of the field, Dr. Tesla sat us all down and described the results of the animal trials in Petersburg. Now no one goes near the thing.

After all, what it has done to the test casing...What the mass has done to the test casing...I don't know if I'll be able to describe it properly. As I noted before, the huge, metal cylinder that is standing in for the actual generator began to develop pock-marks. But the whorls that at first just blemished the surface of the cylinder have deepened, pushing further and further in as the mass grew, until they finally met at the center, so that now the thing looks like it's half-curled into itself. It is as horrifying as it is beautiful, but mostly it just looks wrong. I don't like looking at it, but I keep wanting to.

As it's grown, we've needed to periodically replace the sheath of rubber covering the foam, whenever a fissure appeared of sufficient size so as to compromise the overall elastic force of the enclosure. According to Dr. Tesla, it is the compression of the stuff that makes it grow at such an accelerated rate, constraining the mass while simultaneously precipitating its enlargement, a dynamic that must be maintained in a delicate balance. This now involves dropping the rubber, boiled to a liquid, onto the mass from 20 m above it, which it should go without saying is fantastically dangerous for the workers involved. We've erected an ever-rising scaffold around it for these purposes. Soon they'll be pouring the final sheath, which must be particularly thick so as to overcome the pressure asserted by the crystal's growth. This is excellent, since the ceiling is not far off.

Fumes from the rubber make the warehouse noxious with the stench of liquified tar, as it is filled with all manner of adulterants, and I leave with a blinding headache if I stay in the room for more than a few moments. For this reason I try to do all my work in the adjoining offices.

Laboratory Notes
February 2nd, 1920
Alexi Alanovonovich
Industrial Application of the Type 3B (Compressive) Abjection Mass Using a 2000 kw Ganz Generator

Hypothesis:

Given the results of experiments previously carried out by Dr. Tesla—those showing a 50% increase in energy output from a 750 kw generator when in the immediate proximity (within a 5 m radius) of a 5 x 5 x 2 m enclosed crystalline foam matrix (abjection mass type 2B) —we postulate that a 50% increase in energy output can likewise be achieved in a 2000 kw generator when it is brought into the immediate proximity of a 10 x 10 x 4 m enclosed crystalline foam matrix (abjection mass type 3B).

Introduction:

Although the exact mechanism that allows an abjection mass to recompose the ambient spatial geometry remains unclear, our understanding of its limits continues to grow. Chief among these, a previously unknown force has been observed acting in opposition to spatial compression beyond 50% (180 degree spherical). This makes any attempt at further quantitative reduction beyond this point progressively more difficult to achieve. There does not, however, appear to be an upper limit on the power of machine that can be influenced, other than the limitation of a device's physical size, which is constrained by the size of field emitted by the abjection mass. As previously documented, the extent of the field generated corresponds to the size of the mass itself, with a diminution of effect corresponding to the inverse square law after an abjection mass has achieved a size of 5 x 5 x 2 m. Thus, while a 5 x 5 x 2 m abjection mass will emit a spherical field around it 15 m in diameter, a 10 x 10 x 4 mass will emit a field only 25 m in diameter, with a net gain of only 2.5 m of useable horizontal space for purposes of installing a generator or other device.

For this reason, in order to accommodate a cylindrical, 2000 kw Ganz electric generator—with a radius of 3.66 m and 4.57 m in length- we will need to induce the growth of a 10 x 10 x 4 m mass in a type "3B" arrangement (see previous experimental notes). This will enable a 50% (180 degree spherical) compression of the space abjected within the field's radius. We hypothesize that this will increase the efficiency of the 2000 kw generator to the same degree that it did the 750 kw generator. The operation of an experimental generator will be compared against a control generator, housed in a separate section of the laboratory complex, of the same make and manufacture. This experiment will be carried out in the city of Moscow, U.S.S.R, beginning on the date February 2nd, 1920.

Methodology:

The procedures for readying an amniotic stage abjection mass have already been detailed in previous experimental reports (see Tesla scientific logs 1915—1918). Suffice here to state that our experiment differs only in the quantity of amniotic material prepared (50% more than in previous reports for the 2B arrangement), and the need to fabricate an additional series of rubber enclosures.

As previously described, under elastic pressure, growth of the prepared, foam-crystalline matrix is rapid, with our projections indicating that the mass will achieve median size 4 weeks from the experiment's start date, and full size within 8 weeks. The area of effect will also rapidly increase along with the growth of the mass, stabilizing at 5 x 5 x 2 m growth, and diminishing thereafter, until the elastic enclosure constrains any further mass growth at 10 x 10 x 4 m hemispheric.

As in previous experiments, it is predicted that the rapid growth of the crystal-foam matrix will produce a state of intense heat and vibration, and further, that the relative increase in the size of the mass will likewise result in an increase of effect as well. For this reason, the enclosures applied after the mass has reached 5 x 5 x 2 m in extent will also be increased in thickness, with the quantity of rubber employed increased proportionally to the mass' increase.

Previous results indicate that the mass will also emit signature electric effects at the various stages of its development. These electrical forces are to be continuously monitored by means of a coherer with an ink recorder, attached to the side of the bladder. The coherer will consist of a glass tube holding loose iron filing between its terminals.

To increase the sensitivity of this instrument, the same coherer will be installed within the supplementary circuit of a transformer, one that is likewise connected to the interior of the bladder-space. This assembly will include a terminal extending beyond the mass' projected radius of effect for purposes of continuous monitoring. Finally, the coherer will be connected to an oscillator, enabling the application of voltages at Hertz-Wave frequencies, to sound a telephone bell in the event that the mass registers electromagnetic activity.

Both the experimental generator and the control generator will include armature attached to a measurement device for purposes of comparing relative energy outputs. In the case of the experimental generator, this armature will extend outside the area influenced by the abjection mass.

Their specific measurements and types are as follows...

The Abjection of Geometry
Nikolai Tesla
1920
(alternative conclusion paragraph)

But we should take note that an equally compelling argument can be made suggesting that the highest forms of motion involve a certain kind of immobility or stillness, as with processes of mutual replacement, and as with phenomena such as vibration and communication. For since the whole of nature accessible to us forms a system, an interconnected totality of bodies (and by bodies we understand here all material existences extending from stars to atoms, indeed right to ether particles, in so far as one grants the existence of the last named) one may make the argument that this change in place is not, strictly speaking, necessary to have motion, and further, that the principle holds in reverse. For in the fact that these bodies are interconnected is already included that they react on one another, and it is precisely this mutual reaction that constitutes motion. Contrariwise, it also becomes evident here that matter is unthinkable without motion, and, causa sui, that motion is also therefore matter.

For it is that when two bodies act on each other so that a change of place of one or both of them results, this change of place can consist only in an approximation or a separation. They either attract each other or they repel each other. Or, as mechanics expresses it, the forces operating between them are central, acting along the line joining their centers...Hence the basic form of all motion is approximation and separation, contraction and expansion—in short, the old polar opposites of attraction and repulsion. Or, to label this relationship in its purest form: the dynamic of abjection.

[Diary of Alexi Alanovonovich, Mar. 16th, 1920]
I haven't had much time for diary entries lately. A lot is happening, and I'm very tired. And sick. They've moved me out of my adequate, little apartment into the engineers' dormitory, a former talc factory that has been repurposed into living quarters. The place is still rank with the smell of the perfume. All the students and staff share some kind of an eye infection, and the meals are all of the same type, always, if they're served at all. Bad tea with no sugar and soup, or bread and soup, or just bread, maybe some salt, never enough of any of it. Not even potatoes, nothing fresh, no vegetables. The peasants

have been withholding food from the cities in response to the grain appropriations, even while the Red Army is starving in Poland. In response to this, the government has ordered all of the towns to elect "committees of the impoverished" to oversee food collection and land distribution, but from everything I've heard it's not going very well. They haven't begun redistribution at home yet, but the letters from Mama are becoming increasingly fretful. It will come. This whole decadent, moribund country is going to have to be torn apart before we can rebuild it. To make it into a place where the needs of the toiling masses take priority over the needs of the masters. But, still, I'm worried about Mama and Papa.

The most depressing part about the place though, is that some goddamn parasite, most likely one of the other students living in the dorms, has been stealing from all the rooms. Since moving here I've lost my comb, an ornamental tin, and the copy of <u>Dead Souls</u> that Mysha gave me for my saint's day. But far worse than the theft of any of these little things, yesterday the bastard stole my goddamn boots!!!

Christ's Cock!!! Who steals boots?!!

I now have to "rent" boots from Anton Ivanovich in order to attend lectures and get to work, and I can't go outside in the meantime. Which means idling in this reeking hole instead of spending time at the lab. He's the only one in the entire dormitory who has a second pair, and he insists on being remunerated in case of "loss." He doesn't seem to mind that everyone calls him a class enemy (and a traitor, and a profiteer, and a leech, and a beast). He's also the only one without the damn eye infection.

Things at the lab are not much better. Dr. Tesla has all but halted work on the polyphase motor apparatus, even though its operation constitutes the sole justification for the project's existence, and the reason for such a massive expenditure of resources in a time of war. The condenser assembly has been making strange, loud and ceaseless noise. A repetitive ringing that, admittedly, does appear to progress arithmetically, which is to say that there is some organization to it. After it had begun, it was so definite and ceaseless that we finally had to disconnect the bell to be able to get any work done at all. And while I do understand that this is an experimental procedure, that one must investigate such a phenomenon as it arises; this is also war. Civil war, a war for Russia, and the vanguard of the class war, all at once. A time of pivotal struggle when it will be determined if the forces of the proletariat or the bourgeois will prevail. I'm sorry, but we just don't have time for experimental procedure.

I applied for a position in the army, but they tell me that my work here is too important, that any replacement they might find wouldn't understand all the specifics and nuances of the project, and that anyway they need me for my translations. Our comrades are dying in Poland, for socialism, and I must work for a man who is in ecstasies over ringing bells.

But what concerns me the most is that, at the deepest level, I think he believes them to be some kind of communication. He's begun urging us to look for comprehensible patterns: syntax, grammar, punctuation. Language. We might as well be practicing the Kabbalah or Masonism.

They've just called us for what, with a stretch of the imagination, we'll call dinner.

Talking With Planets
Nikolai Tesla
March 19th, 1920
(For Publication in Young Pioneers' Pravda)

In this age of reason it is not astonishing to find persons who scoff at the very thought of effecting communication with a planet. First of all, the argument is made that there is only a small probability of other planets being inhabited at all. This argument has never appealed to me. In the solar system, there seem to be only two planets—Venus and Mars—capable of sustaining life such as ours: but this does not mean that there might not be on all of them some other forms of life. Chemical processes may be maintained without the aid of oxygen, and it is still a question whether chemical processes are absolutely necessary for the sustenance of organized beings. My idea is that the development of life must lead to forms of existence that will be possible without nourishment and which will not be shackled by consequent limitations. Why should a living being not be able to obtain all the energy it needs for the performance of its life functions from the environment, instead of through consumption of food, and transforming, by a complicated process, the energy of chemical combinations into life-sustaining energy?

We can conceive of organized beings living without nourishment, and deriving all the energy they need for the performance of their life functions from the ambient medium. In a crystal we have the clear evidence of the existence of a formative life-principle, and though we cannot understand the life of a crystal, it is nonetheless a living being. There may be, besides crystals, other such individualized, material systems of beings, perhaps of gaseous constitution, or composed of substance still more tenuous. In view of this possibility—nay, probability—we cannot apodictically deny the existence of organized beings on a planet merely because the conditions on the same are unsuitable for the existence of life as we conceive it. We cannot even, with positive assurance, assert that some of them might not be present here, in this our world, in the very midst of us, for their constitution and life-manifestation may be such that we are unable to perceive them.

At the present stage of progress, there would be no insurmountable obstacle in constructing a machine capable of conveying a message to Mars, nor would there be any great difficulty in recording signals transmitted to us by the inhabitants of that planet, if they be skilled electricians. Communication once established, even in the simplest way, as by a mere interchange of numbers, the progress toward more intelligible communication would be rapid. Absolute certitude as to the receipt and interchange of messages would be reached as soon as we could respond with the number "four," say, in reply to the signal "one, two, three." The Martians, or the inhabitants of whatever planet had signaled to us, would understand at once that we had caught their message across the gulf of space and had sent back a response. To convey a knowledge of form by such means is, while very difficult, not impossible, and I have already found a way of doing it.

[Diary of Alexi Alanvonovich, Apr. 29th, 1920]

What the hell to say? Was he right? If he was right...(!) Goddamn. If they're actually there...If he was right. Christ! But it has got to be some grand hoax! Doesn't it? It can't be real. Otherwise...I guess... otherwise, we've made history.

It all came out today. Kolya finally made good on all his muttering and informed on Tesla. The commissar came to the lab with the chief secretary of the militia (and three soldiers who just stood around looking embarrassed), and they demanded a full review of the project, which took place in the back office. Kolya, who I guess had decided that all his chips were down by this point, stalked back and forth against the back wall of the lab and badgered us all about sabotage and treason. Saying things like, "Well, Dr. Tesla is a foreign agent, simple as that! Or he's crazy. Same difference, isn't it?!"

All sorts of things like that, forever, over and over, to whoever would listen, which was pretty much nobody by the end, but still he went on, talking to all of us in general.

But he'd been holding things back, Dr. Tesla that is. Insurmountable evidence. Incredible...incredible evidence(!) But right there under our noses, he'd established real communication with them. He must have suspected that the assistants were beginning to chafe under the strangeness of it all. Kept it from us for just this eventuality. For the time when someone inevitably reported him for all of it.

He'd been speaking with them, well, communicating with these... things for at least three weeks now, everything documented. Then he asked the commissar and the secretary to propose to the creatures some mathematical puzzles. Anything they could think up. And he got the things to answer. Beeping the correct answers out of the coherer, which Tesla had adapted in some fashion.

I wonder, though, if there will still be an investigation of some sort. The commissar seemed quite enchanted by Dr. Tesla's explanations; Venusians or Martians, alien civilizations of incalculable scientific sophistication, and a methodical system for achieving complex communications. The guy just kept taking notes and nodding. Just ate it up. But the secretary looked less than pleased. Angry even, or maybe not quite angry, but his jaw was tense and he kept staring at Tesla as he blathered on. Like he was watching for the cheapness of the carnival trick to show.

I can only imagine what this will do to Dr. Tesla. His health is suffering as it is, and it has become increasingly difficult to talk to him these days; he works from three in the morning until eleven at night and refuses any treatment for this severe insomnia. Whenever anyone brings it up, he claims that he only needs a forty minute nap, and this also constitutes his response every time we find him passed out from exhaustion on top of his work-desk.

His idiosyncrasies have also become worse in recent weeks. He had a fit when Comrade Dmitrievna came in wearing earrings yesterday, and he will not eat if he is not first given the opportunity to measure the contents of his plate with a ruler. Just yesterday he began pontificating on the importance of the interaction between the two-dimensional topology of his mashed potatoes and its infinite cubic sub-stratum. When I mentioned the flatness of soup he became very quiet. I think he thought I was making fun of him. And maybe I was. It's becoming difficult to tell the difference anymore.

An Exchange With Triangles: Part II
Nikola Tesla
October 7th, 1920
(For publication in Pravda)

As I review the events of this astonishing and altogether unprecedented first contact with other thinking entities, for the first time in human history, I realize how subtle are the influences that shape our destinies, and how fortunate it is that after centuries of mute cohabitation on this Earth, this truly epochal conversation has at last occurred between our species.

I have already described in the preceding section of this report, how exactly this communication was achieved and the various devices used in our increasingly complex exchanges, as, owing to the understandably sensational nature of the topic, the editors of Pravda asked me to be quite explicit on this subject. Likewise, in this section of my account I have been asked to be as clear as possible regarding the physical makeup of the beings, and to use as simple and non-technical language possible, so that all citizens who read this paper will grasp the essentials of the matter. I will try my best, but as shall be seen presently, this is no small feat.

It should be clear to the reader by now that the inexplicable electrical actions observed were not, in fact, from another planet, but originated from an altogether unexpected quarter: that of an intelligent society of second dimensional entities invisibly covering our homeworld.

I myself submitted to this fact unwillingly, but the signals were simply too strong to have traveled the great distances from Mars to Earth.[1] Once basic communications were established, the notable absence of any sort of time lag between replies confirmed my mounting suspicions. I was forced to admit to myself that the sources must have come from somewhere in nearby space, and that the creatures communicating with us every night were not from Mars, or any other planet in our solar system[2] for that matter. This led my investigations back to our own terrestrial sphere, which is, of course, where I finally discovered the signal's origin.

Even now, I can vividly recall the initial incident, the first contact, and can see my apparatus as if it were actually before me. These ordered and yet incomprehensible signals positively terrified me, as there was present in them something mysterious, not to say supernatural, as I sat alone in my laboratory at night. The variation in the signals were taking place periodically, and with such a clear suggestion of number and order that they were not traceable to any cause then known to me. I was familiar, of course, with such electrical disturbances as are produced by the sun, the Aurora Borealis, and earth currents, and I was sure as I could be of any fact that these variations were due to none of these causes, but it was only some time later when the thought flashed upon my mind that the disturbances I had observed might be due to intelligent control.

It was, more likely than not, arrogance on my part, as much as an overactive imagination, that led me to focus first on extraterrestrial causes. My feeling was that the electrical activities of the planet were so well-familiar to me by this point, constituting decades of effort,

---

1   Tesla quote from *The Lost Journals of Nikola Tesla* (author and ed. Tim Swartz). 2000. Inner Light – Global Communications. https://archive.org/stream/TheLostJournalsOfNikolaTesla/The%20Lost%20Journals%20Of%20Nikola%20Tesla_djvu.txt

2   Ibid.

observation, and consideration on my part, that I assumed only factors beyond this sphere could possibly be responsible for the phenomenon in question.

My character notwithstanding, we did in the end obviously establish complex communications. The torrent of technological discoveries to come will vindicate me on this mark. But it was not without great difficulty, requiring the sustained efforts of my—rightfully skeptical—scientific team as they employed my plan for establishing contact with this unknown group of entities.

For, as I have already said, in the beginning there was no way of knowing if the beings we had begun exchanging signals with were ahead of us in terms of evolution. Their means of communication could have been perfect, and thus incomprehensible to us, or so base and rudimentary as to be likewise indecipherable. It is enough to say that a message from these beings, which might describe a triangle to them, would appear as some other form to us, and vice versa, these differences only to be resolved by time and careful study. So it is wonderful enough—though it perhaps should be unsurprising given our shared ancestral home—that the creatures shared many concepts and means in common with us, chief among these being similar concepts of mathematics and a common geometry.

Regarding their form, I can say...

[Diary of Alexi Alanovonovich, Oct. 08th, 1922]

"Your grandfather is a kulak, come home." This is the gist of the letter I received today from Mama. So apparently there is now grumbling in the village amongst the smaller landholders about the size of Grandfather's allotment. I warned them that this was going to happen, several times. Because the unfortunate truth of the matter is, has always been, that Grandfather is a kulak! And I certainly don't see why the villagers' finally realizing this fact is a reason to come home.

Mama and Papa have always been willfully blind to the fact that Grandfather owns far more property than he should. It is the Achilles heel of their bourgeois radicalism, this sentimentalism, rife among all the old *Narodniki*. A romantic, and frankly religious, fixation on the archetype of the peasant father, despite all their talk about women's liberation. So long as they still get to see Grandfather on the horizon, walking in the yellow light, as bearded as Tolstoy, Christian, smiling, then everything will be all right. No matter that the acres and acres on either side of this lone organism belong to him. No matter the men and women that toil for his benefit. Well...I suppose their opinions don't count for much now; now that the People's Conscience is knocking at the door.

Which means that now, on top of my studies—studies that, since translating the first principles of the entities' science, now seem like a bunch of cretins playing in the muck—and on top of the lab— and the anxious, giddy nervousness that now daily infects everyone there—I am going to get to worry about Mama and Papa every night.

Because as a result of Grandfather's patrician generosity their tiny lot has always been, indeed was granted in such a fashion so as to ensure, that Papa's property eternally edges Grandfather's. And it is not at all evident to the villagers that the little fence Papa put up indicates my parent's high-minded renunciation of his father's domain.

Papa is generally well-thought of by everyone, but they also all think he is a bit of a buffoon, worse, a kulak's son who takes on airs. The kind of man who likes to be seen walking around with a book. When it comes down to it between them and my grandfather, the villagers will not give much thought to my parents at all.

Letter to Dr. Shukov
Nikola Tesla
Moscow, Jan. 13th, 1923

Dear Dr. Shukov,

I must start off by thanking you for your insightful and gracious reply to my last letter. Especially given its seemingly bizarre context, I am doubly indebted to you for agreeing to join my scientific team. I have absolutely no doubt that your help in decoding the signals will be indispensable, despite your insistence to the contrary. Indeed, the observations made in your last letter have already enabled marked progress in several of our projects involving the entities. In the following section I have attempted to respond to some of your questions, with the caveat that our communications with the creatures are still greatly imperfect and prone to misunderstandings.

First, I must disabuse you of the notion that these intelligences take residence in any other dimension than our own. Though they are referred to as "second-dimensional" it is only because they are composed of length and width only, having zero thickness. They are, on the contrary, very much our neighbours on this planetary sphere, being perfectly distributed over the superficial topology of the globe, and also apparently able to penetrate the interstitial space of certain types of matter; the surfaces of our bodies and those of other animals included. Indeed, it would seem that they are omnipresent; every manifest plane, every angle, every nook and cranny, is covered or filled by these intelligences, and may even make up its second dimensional sub-stratum.

From this it follows that they are beholden to the same forces as are we. Constrained and motivated by the same tides, atmospheric pressures, gravity, and so forth, in exactly the same manner that you or I are influenced (though they evidently do not react to the visible spectrum of light). All of this is of course not to say that such forces are experienced in the same fashion. The perceptions of these intelligences are wildly different from ours, as we will no doubt discuss at length. Nevertheless, the natural forces introduce certain regularities that can be referenced, assuming a common system of numeracy and mathematics, even when the sensorium of a being differs radically from that of another. After all, the world is really not 'optical' and 'aural', (is it?), it is integrated. But reactions of a certain frequency and force (and from them reflexes, and then organs) have developed in protein-based flesh in response to these manifestations.[3] In our case, it was the electromagnetic waveform—specifically the transverse sinusoid—that finally gave us a point of purchase for further discourse, but this knowledge was hard won. Most of our early efforts were fruitlessly wasted in attempts to transmit pictorial data according to a mathematical system. It never occurred to us that the entities could not see (or hear, smell, or taste, for that matter, with only an approximate sensation of touch). It is a small miracle that they developed mathematics at all. Even more so that their math and geometry is organized in a similar fashion to ours.

Rather astonishingly, given the absence of a visual faculty, they assume that reality is a perfectly flat distribution of geometric forms, arranged in a plane formation. The vertical dimension, and any forms distributed vertically, are thus not considered a "part" of physical reality, and are instead registered among them as a complex variety of social and ontological distinctions, similar in some ways to the manner we perceive time.

Communication among themselves proceeds by way of electric stimulation, using rhythmic, vibratory pulses to distinguish phonemes, stress and inflection, and can only take place with a geometric form that is immediately adjacent to the shape in question, though, again, their exact understanding of adjacency continues to elude us. Nevertheless, almost all the shapes seem happy to carry messages to one another, and there is quite an enthusiastic culture of metered, and perhaps even chanted correspondences (or at least the electro-stimulant equivalent) circulated as a means of preserving knowledge and directing important messages. In this way, their exceptionally complicated mathematical formulas, logarithmic tables,

---

3   Savchenko, Vladimir, "Mixed Up", *Red Star Tales: A Century of Russian and Soviet Science Fiction,* Ed. Yvonne Howell, Russian Information Services, Inc. 2015. Originally published in 1980 (in Ukrainian) and in 1983 (in Russian).

and other scientific information are committed to cultural memory and transmitted socially.

In reply to your questions concerning the creatures' locomotion and average lifespan, I can only say that they are not mobile and do not die of old age. In fact they cannot even be said to recognize life and death, or self and other, as we do, and likewise make no distinction between living beings and nonliving objects. Instead, they appear to be functionally polyphagomorphous, by which I mean they "eat" any other forms that they come into contact with, and incorporate them into a larger body. This process bears some similarities to the eating habits of the amoeba, whereby the term is derived, but is crucially distinguished in that each such "meal" changes the core identity, as well as the geometric form and intellectual complexity of the new form-creature. The individual subjectivities of the two shapes are merged, and an altogether new being is formed. For this reason, the continual shifting of forms in our world, the ceaseless action of animal and vegetable life, and the movements of forces upon the Earth, constitute a kind of life-cycle and destiny for these beings, and have been mathematically plotted, much as we have charted the orbits of the planets and other stellar bodies. They have tracked the blowing of the wind, as a constellation of leaves being stirred by the breeze may offer up a host of ever-altering geometric arrangements, and therefore also configurations of intelligence. They have constructed mathematical models of our wars and our marriages, and our trips to the grocers. They have meticulously plotted the motions of our days and lives, as if we were natural forces, which, of course, we are.

We do know that most of the communiques held so far have been with angular formations (line-forms) of various complexities, who firmly maintain that intelligence among individuals in their society is directly related to the overall nuance and complexity of their bodies. For this reason, we hypothesize that it was the geometric complexity provided by the foam-crystal matrix, its proliferating hedration, that enabled the formation of an intelligence sufficiently advanced so as to communicate with us.

As to their mathematics and "flat sciences," as you call them, their insights are nothing short of remarkable, if not fantastical, though exceedingly difficult to interpret. Thus far, their breathtakingly elegant grasp of fluid dynamics and most of their crystallographic observations have been transmitted comprehensibly, and have already borne much scientific fruit. But their cosmological equations continue to appear as a parade of the most ludicrous impossibilities, filled with inexplicable mathematical constants and models of wholly bizarre shape and operation. For example, in their central account of this type, they seem to be trying to describe...

[Diary of Alexi Alanovonovich, March 17th, 1921]

We are finally seeing the beginnings of winter's departure. Thank the gods. I am so sick of being tied to the nearest stove, and of coats worn inside. Last week there wasn't even coal to burn at the dormitory, and because the lamp oil had long ago run out, in the end we were tossing furniture, pictures, newspaper, and then, of course, books into the fire. We joked about it at the beginning, made a game of selecting the most counter-revolutionary texts first, and then debating the relative merits of the others; a hierarchy that ran from fuel to genius. But in the end everyone just became really quiet, and we all just sat around dumb as any cold pack of animals.

But even with winter starting to leave, the early warmth hasn't drawn out its usual, eager few. In the street outside the dormitory there is a complete absence of scurrying and bustling. The street has failed to perform. The snow begins to melt, the heavy white curtain lifts, but instead of the play we have paid for, all we get are props and set-pieces. The corpses missed by the searches, and revealed by the melt, count as scenery. There are no actors and there is no action.

Moscow has been practically abandoned. Anyone who could has already left to try to find food in the countryside, running home to their kulak relatives so they can burrow underground and suckle at hidden pantries. Our team is still receiving a bit of food. The work we do has been given the same priority as high-level administration, and the rest is sent off to the Red Army, but it's surely not enough. The quantities here constantly diminish.

I'm also fairly certain by this point that the reports we're sending to the executive committee are being made deliberately incomplete. Tesla is censoring the more bizarre details on purpose, in favour of the scientific breakthroughs. I can't say that I blame him. I wouldn't want to have to pass on some of this stuff either. For the longest time I was sure it was because our whole approach to translating the creature's messages was wrong. But the scientific principles they've handed to us are all accurate, they work. Every experimental proof verified. Which means that the other stuff has got to be more or less accurate too, doesn't it? Or are we getting a whole raft of two-dimensional religious nonsense along with their brilliant mathematics?

When we first contacted them, before we'd even established the prime numbers or the geometric sets, they sent us a message that I decided to translate just recently. With what we know now, it came out to,

"Are you trying to communicate with us?"

Then something like, "Do you communicate? Are you aware?"

Followed by something like, "If this equals that (if so) then our regrets(?)/our condolences(?)/our deepest grief(?)"

We're already forced to work under so many layers of interpretation and assumption that it's difficult to be certain of anything once you've received the final product. Every missive from these things must be first transliterated into the correct binary sequence, then re-translated into a base of 10, and then the endless, mind-wracking attempts to imagine what a given force would seem like for a blind man who imagines a flat world. And then the disagreements...

Poincaré, Lobachevsky, and the Abjection of Geometry
Nikolai Tesla
Moscow, Feb. 03rd, 1921

To understand the mighty scientific leap represented by the Poincaré/Lobachevsky model of a hyperbolic universe it is essential that the reader be familiar with Euclid's fifth postulate and with the general scientific notion of geometric parallelism. Stated simply, Euclid's fifth postulate claims that for any given line we draw through the universe, and for any given point not on that line, there is at most one line parallel to the original that will run through our given point. Generations of scholars, from Euclid to Proclus and from Ptolemy to Vitale have attempted to prove this axiomatically, and failed. This is simply because the fifth postulate is in error.

A child's perspective on this problem will assist us in grasping the error of what appears to be a beguilingly intuitive theorem. Think then of that time when one was introduced to the difficult and yet elegantly simple notion that two lines in parallel, extended to infinity, will never touch. We imagine in our child's mind here these two lines disappearing into a perspectival point, the place where, for our eye, the train tracks come together and meet, even though we know full well the tracks continue on to the next town.

What the child grasps here, and what the (literally!) rigidly inflexible axioms of Euclid cannot allow, is the fact that the point seen here in the child's eye is a real point in space, to wit, the physically unreachable point of the absolute. A point outside of our physical universe and yet consubstantial with it, as with the geometric dimension of time. Most importantly it is a point where these parallel lines do meet in tension with the physical reality of our dimension. A reality experienced by us as if they do not and will never meet. That is, until we are done with time, matter and movement itself.

This is, unfortunately, a rather crude rendering of what is, at its base, one of the most elegant mathematical models discovered in the course of human history. However, I believe that one more illustration will induct the reader into the very first stages of this modern-day Eleusinian mystery cult.

In his book Science and Hypothesis, *the French physicist Henri Poincaré proposed a scenario wherein the existence of a hypothetical 'small' universe is posited. This universe is Euclidean, existing in a bound plane, and has for its form a flattish disk. Its temperature is 37.78 degrees Celsius at its center and it decreases linearly to absolute zero at its boundary.*

Poincaré then had his little inhabitants carry out an expedition. As the scientific adventurers move toward the boundary of the disk, their legs become shorter, their steps smaller, their machines less efficient, and so on. They cannot reach the boundary, and they conclude that the universe is infinite.

This story tormented me for a very long while, as I imagined the implications of such a universe and what physical possibilities that such a universe might harbour or limit. It occurred to me that, first, 'we', human beings, are of course the creatures of the fable and, second, it followed from this that there were also, in all likelihood, a stratum of such beings who exist at the level of the second geometric dimension, as well as that of the first, the fourth and so on.

The insights of my spiritual mentor, Dr. Lobachevsky, then allowed me to connect this ideal with reality. For his mathematical elaboration of hyperbolic plane geometry via the Poincaré disk model finally decided my course: Forward! Into the second dimension!

[Diary of Alexi Alanovonovich, Jan. 25th, 1924]

Our movement, for the moment at least, feels listless. Emptied out. Still present. Still present in its millions of pounds of cement and protein and will. But somehow bereft of its most vital directive energy; lost and cycling inside itself.

It's uncomfortable to think that the blossoming of Soviet power could die with its leader. The historical path to socialism is inevitable, surely, but there are nevertheless those who move history a bit more quickly; those incarnations of the world mind that ride like suns and lions on horseback, announcing the heroic impatience of the spirit. The men and women who, in their very individuality, rise up like ideas, as easily snuffed out, but as sure to rekindle in another form. But who knows when? Or where?

They have put work on hold everywhere to give people time to mourn. The lines to see Comrade Lenin's body are literally <u>days</u> long, and everywhere there is an intolerable amount of weeping. I understand their sense of grief. I do. But I really don't think we should be going in for hysterics at this point in the struggle. There is still much work to be done, and much to look forward to. Comrade Lenin was, after all, only one man. The army of international socialists numbers in the millions.

I went down to see him, the body, for a while, until I couldn't stomach the crowds any longer. Near the mausoleum that they've begun building, I found a beautiful commemorative edition of his speeches, put out at a very reasonable price by the Russian Association of Proletarian Writers. I've already almost finished reading it.

Still, taken as a whole, I think the most poignant of his theses remains:

"Soviet power plus electrification of the whole country equals communism."

And it is this, beyond anything else, that is at stake in the work of Dr. Tesla, and in all the science we've garnered from the entities. Limitless energy. Imagine it. Limitless energy. To power, and this is crucial, to power a *directed vision* of an emancipated humanity.

Power on its own, in its inert form, is useless, or rather, meaningless, like the power of a waterfall's rushing, meaningless in and of itself, trapped in rotating biological idiocy. Just as all the potential force of a rock lies latent in its resting body, waiting to be picked up and hurled. Power must be directed toward a goal, an end.

If Soviet power directs the electrical forces of this country, if, as brothers and sisters, together, we imagine a place for the energy to go, in concert with the needs of everyone, then this place, the place we arrive at, this place is communism. Its achievement provides us with justification for the deaths of the civil war, the men and women whose sacrifice fed the human velocity of the socialist world, by allowing for our survival. This is what will literally power the dreams of our tomorrow: energy directed to a final purpose.

And so I've found myself asking exactly what this final purpose is, in terms of energy, in the terms Dr. Tesla works with. Where are we going to direct all the energy that the revolution has unleashed and will unleash? Because what I am coming to realize is that the total, annihilating, ugly truth of it all, the difficult truth, is that this is a worker's struggle, moreover a struggle that lionizes workers, which is surreptitiously predicated on a certain type of horror regarding work and workers. To sum, we are struggling, obsessed with labour, so that we ourselves will not have to become workers. Our labour-power is directed toward its own annihilation.

Because it is hard to carry generators up stairs, and somewhat ludicrous. And it is vexing to polish glass and oil dynamos. And it is as boring to work in a factory as it is to toil growing cabbages and wheat. It is vile, the work we have to do, and so we dream of using the waterfalls and electricity and the fissuring of geometry to free us… from work.

<u>Letter to Dr. Shukov</u>
Nikola Tesla
Moscow, Jan. 13th, 1923
(Cont'd)

...they seem to be trying to describe a shift in the epoch of the universe. An event that is theoretically to occur in the same fashion as all the other major phase transitions throughout the history of time, which is to say that we will witness the formation of spheres (or in their depiction, circles) containing the new, emergent laws of matter, space and movement. These enclosures of superior symmetry will expand and collide with one another, much as with bubbles in a vessel of boiling water, until the old era of our physical universe disappears completely into the steam of the new.

Within these spheres time will become spacelike, without preferred direction, as with the rotational symmetry of water, and the events we know as constituting life will begin to obey new laws. In other areas, they seem to speak of the whole universe moving like a wave, one that begins and ends at the same point, or of hyperboloid vacuums foliated by spherical pulses, attached to an infinity predating time by means of stretched, rotating vortical cones.

They describe a surface tension in the proliferating fabric of the universe, one that pulls us back to an antique point in the physical order, as with the restoring force that anchors the crest of the ocean wave, whereupon a primordial timelessness will finally reclaim us.

It is all laughable, of course, but I include it because knowledge of the more irrational components of their discourse is surely to be as important in communicating with the creatures as correct apprehension of their rational meanings, as so with people in day-to-day life, it would seem.

I am very much looking forward to meeting you in person, anticipating our discussions, and wish you the safest of journeys.

Sincerely Yours,
Nikola Tesla

[Diary of Alexi Alanovonovich (first section missing) (date missing)]

...the global reports obviously disprove my previous theory, that we are being subjected to some kind of hitherto unknown type of radiation, unleashed upon us by the capitalists. London, Paris, and Tokyo have all been hit, and presumably many others, so I can only guess that this is some kind of natural event, or at least not a political act.

But if it is a biological agent, as the newspapers claim...so far I've managed to avoid contracting it, as with many of my colleagues at the laboratory, though most of the students at the dorm have it. I think this can, once again, be attributed to the superior quality (and quantity) of the rations that we're receiving for our work. It makes me feel guilty to think about it. And yet, still, I never end up sharing any of my food with my needy comrades, despite such guilty feelings. So I should probably just shut up about it. In any case, the lethargy and nausea are consistent with radiation poisoning. But I'm still at a loss to explain the hallucinatory effects, not to mention this business with the clocks.

There have even been accusations levelled against the triangles and the lab, claiming that we're responsible somehow. The Physicians' Union is demanding that we be brought to trial for causing over 10,000 stillbirths throughout the U.S.S.R. No one in the party is giving them much credence. For the past several months, all we've done is send little electric signals back and forth over the surface of the mass, and the mass itself is just a bunch of crystal in a rubber sack. But it's a horrifying thought; that we might somehow have caused all of this. Ludicrous. Just the other side of the enthusiasm that the creatures have generated. The inevitable drag of the public mind, swinging back from romance to xenophobia. Which had to come at some point, I suppose. Still, it's so damn...pitiable...and frustrating...and frightening

Report to the Undersecretary of the Political Bureau of the Central Committee of the Communist Party of the Soviet Union
Nikolai Tesla
March 21st, 1924

Dear Sir,

As per your instructions I have assembled all the relevant details, however cursory, that might be of interest as to the events being experienced in the Soviet Union and internationally. As you put it so succinctly yourself, it would be disingenuous of me to claim absolutely no connection between the events and the work of my laboratory. The mathematical and scientific formulas sent by the two-dimensional beings, and later exegetical analysis by my team, have unearthed references that could be construed as relevant. However, in this report you have asked for certainty of a wholly infant science, the earliest findings of the first, true, exo-linguistics, and I beg you to keep this in mind before rendering any judgements.

To put it as simply as I can, the entities do make certain mathematical assumptions in their physical models of the universe, in particular they have provided us with equations that have to do with movement through space. We have received communications that we believe describe such phenomena as velocity, inertia, angular rotation, circular and vortical motion, harmonic momentum, impulse, and a host of other, more obscure, concepts.

In these, much less decipherable, communications, the creatures appear to be trying to describe the growth or life-cycle of space, or the universe itself. They also assert a belief that the universe moves in cycles, an oscillation between positive and negative mass, which will come to its end in phase shift resulting in a sudden cessation of movement. Now by "sudden" I am speaking in relative terms, and would remind you that these equations measure time in its celestial incarnation. The scale of cosmic time being what it is, this putative event could thus occur anytime between now and several thousand years in the future. More importantly, mathematics can, with some effort, be made to represent utter fantasies and impossibilities, which is what I believe to be occurring here. Even if the claims are representative of some level of truth, they describe a process that is altogether out of our hands, and one that is as irrevocable as the eruption of a volcano. I hope, then, that you see why I did not include these details in my official reports to the undersecretary's office. To my view, they were either the result of a lurid, alien theology, or a description of the inevitable end of all existence and the irrevocable death of the species. It was my feeling that such sentiments were already well known by this country's clergy, or were otherwise irrelevant to the duties of my team.

With Respect.

Nikola Tesla

[Diary of Alexi Alanovonovich (first section missing) (undated)]

...and now that it's deepened, and since the more bizarre effects have begun to emerge, I can't even imagine a cause. Unless of course it is the triangles...but they've stopped speaking to us. Perhaps entangled in their own, two-dimensional version of the "sickness."

So stupid that people continue to call it that. An illness that dims electric lights, and lengthens the day. A plague that diminishes velocity.

Today at work everyone was talking about the whole Natalia Ivanovna thing as the probable "next stage of the disease." The woman couldn't even make it up the street to her house. Just kept walking and walking until she collapsed in the middle of the road, wailing at the gawkers that her, "steps weren't moving her," and begging for help. Eventually they figured out that they could bring her back to the cantina where she daily collected rations for her family. No matter how many steps she took, though, they couldn't get her any closer to the house. In the newspaper she said that she probably spent most her time waiting in the cantina anyway, so really it was more convenient. There's Russian black humour for you. The physical universe is literally against you, so you make a joke out of it.

A Reply to Those Perpetuating the "Triangle Plague" Rumour
Nikolai Tesla
May 1ˢᵗ, 1924
(A Public Address by the Chief Scientist of the Institute for Socialist Exo-Communications)

Much gossip and rumour has been circulating regarding the so-called "Triangle Plague" being experienced globally at this very moment. The author of this article responds to these rumours with a direct statement of the unequivocal scientific facts for the purpose of calming the public, promoting public order, and quashing unfounded opinion, so violently in expression at this time.

The first point, and most important, is that there is no "radiation," toxic seepage, or any effulgence whatsoever coming from the experimental site of the Institute for Socialist Exo-Communications. This can be easily observed in the global scope of the phenomena being experienced, which has in no way been strengthened or accelerated in the Moscow area. Effects retarding the phenomena reported by individuals working at the laboratory are accurate, but are only a side-effect of the electromagnetic fields generated there, and have in no way contributed to the current state of affairs.

Second point, the phenomena are a series of interrelated, natural events, as intended as a summer morning, and should in no way cause panic, though, of course, we understand the sense of alarm generated amongst our citizens. All state organs and advocates of civil order, including the author and the editors of this newspaper, urge the people of the U.S.S.R. to remain calm, and not to repeat the mass disturbances and bourgeois hysterics seen in other countries. These events will pass, and we must show courage before the uncertainty and strangeness that is befalling us all. In the meantime, all available resources are being devoted to grappling with the problems being experienced by the common people, with an emphasis on delivering food and other necessary items despite the increasing lags in time and growth of space.

[Diary of Alexi Alanovonovich (undated)]

So, of course, as predicted, they've blamed the whole thing on us. And who knows...maybe we are to blame.

It's everywhere now, finally caught up with me, with everyone at the lab. Everyone in Moscow, everyone in the world presumably...

Maybe it isn't so terrible after all, this slowing. Or maybe it's some sort of punishment, or a kind of balance, for all the speed and impulsiveness generated by our little planet. More than likely it has nothing at all to do with us.

I can't make it to any of the food distribution outlets anymore, and neither can Anton, though we're still able to move between our bedroom and the common room. Gregor & Misha have been bringing us food. They used to spend all their time hanging out near the cantina, apparently, cutting deals and buying ration tickets. But it's only a matter of time before either they're stuck here with us or they're stuck over there. It seems that you retain your freedom of movement for the longest periods in those places you traversed most regularly. Which says something about Natalia Ivanovna's life. And mine. Everyone's, really. With all that we have in front of us, everything that we have available to us in our lives, it can all be boiled down to these two or three places, the points where we spend our lives in endless rotation. For me, it's this stupid room, and my bedroom, and I could probably make it to the lab, though I haven't tried.

Gregor said that they've arrested Dr. Tesla, but have been experiencing difficulties expediting the case. So ridiculous, of course, but it's what he said. He could have been joking.

[Diary of Alexi Alanovonovich (undated)]

The last of it is taking hold. I am having trouble even moving my hand across the page, one of the very few gestures I have left. I can't stop imagining the quickest of motions brought to a halt. Candle-flame, and the toppling of a cliff-face, or an avalanche, any cascade, air... and what will light oscillations seem to be once they are still? Dimness, apparently, for us at least, and then what comes next?

The melancholy I've been enduring this past while seems to be lifting the closer that we come to final stillness. It doesn't seem as horrifying as it did, if it's natural, because it's painless and happening to all of us. Even at their most incomprehensible, the triangles always seemed to be describing a cycle, a beginning to come after this end, but I have trouble imagining it (while at the same time it seems my only solace). Socialism seems so small now, capitalism too; there can't be politics without movement.

Mama and Papa have become larger, if only because they will still seem real after this is all over. I imagine them, see them frozen in their last, most familiar positions. Mama standing in front of the open door, looking out on a good night. Papa is reading in his smelly chair. I will end hunched over this notebook. Perhaps caught in mid-sentence. Maybe not. In any case, I know that we'll persist beyond this. For some reason, we'll still be here.

About the story

This story was originally written as a response to a call for submissions put out by Weird Tales. My intention was to write a weird, hard science fiction story, appropriate, I thought, since the theme issue was going to be focused on Nikola Tesla. This led me into a love affair with his work that has yet to end. I find Tesla's writings beautiful. At their most speculative (i.e. The Problem of Increasing Human Energy), they are hermetic, hopeful, brilliant, and ludicrous all at the same time. His own story is similarly both sad and awe-inspiring. I also think it worth noting that Tesla was actually approached by Soviet agents in 1919, and asked to work for them. According to his diary, he was told, "We have no money, but [we have] carloads of solid gold, and we will give you a liberal amount." I cannot recall if I discovered this fact before or after I began writing this story.

A question for the author

Q: Duckbilled platypus – result of divine distraction, or alternate universe crossover?

A: I'm going to have to go with neither on this one. I'm uncertain about the whole divinity thing, but my thinking is: if there were a creature resulting from divine distraction it wouldn't be the platypus. I'd put my money on one of the nudibranchs or maybe one of the stranger weirdies of the Galapagos. If anything, the platypus is the result of divine inspiration; it has a bill that can detect electric fields, and the fine-detail work on its cuteness is just superb.

As to its near-interdimensional oddness, I will admit that an egg-laying mammal is more than a bit unusual. But I also think that the whole platypus controversy says a lot about social impressions, and how resistant we can be when a belief that we've inherited from science turns out to be wrong. In fact, while most people will tell you that the platypus is weird, I think many of them would be hard-pressed to tell you why the platypus is stranger than any other animal. The idea of a warm-blooded creature that hatches its young doesn't really shock us anymore. Which means that the very foundation of its strangeness, its failure to fit into the then-dominant taxonomy of Biology, has in effect passed away; and yet we continue to remember that this animal probably won't find a date to the prom.

In an ideal world, science would be able to graciously (and swiftly) change its core principles when faced with evidence that refutes a dominant theory. But then, I'm pretty attached to my beliefs too.

About the author

Y.X. Acs is afraid of you, but also thinks that you might get along. Y.X. Acs has achieved modest things. If you'd like to learn more about Y.X. Acs, go to: WEBPAGE REDACTED.

@textualism

Y.X. Acs's story "The Abjection Engine" was published in *Metaphorosis* on Friday, 30 June 2017.

July

BetaU

T.B. McKenzie

On Sunday, Janie's com pinged with a message from her cousin who worked for Visage, one of the big city body-mod firms. *You should go for this!* read the underlined text, which took her to a minimalist page with the company name, *BetaU* in the middle and a single link at the bottom: Employment Opportunities.

Only the fanciest places hired humans any more, and Janie's curiosity sparked, if not her hope, for they'd only want sevens or above. Janie was a natural three, according to her mother, who offered to pay for a Budgetslim or Blemishless every Christmas, certain it would push her over five.

What scam is this? she sent back to her cousin even as curiosity made her click. They were hiring in sales, no details about what kind of body-mod they were selling other than the tantalising by-line: *Whatever you want to want.* There was one prerequisite for applicants: *No cosmetic modifications, please.*

Well, it was worth a shot. Janie sent through her stats, authorising a full backscan on her history. A moment later her com pinged again with an address and interview time.

The building was a tower of glass and steel like all the others on Madison Avenue, but with a sculpture out front that looked like a giant chrome block of Swiss cheese. The ten-foot-high cube changed its shape as Janie approached the door, some of its cavities enlarging, others contracting, the holes playing a chord with the wind.

An automatron recognised Janie as she walked into the foyer. It directed her to wait in a smaller room with the other applicants. Any hope she'd been harbouring vanished as Janie sat between a man and a woman who both looked like screenstars. If they weren't body-modders, then they were natural eights, impossible to compete with. No one spoke. A real woman served what smelled like real coffee and Janie took a latte, chatting awkwardly about the weather just to fill the silence. One at a time the server called out names, and the room began to empty.

"Janie Allgood," said the server when only two were left in the room and her second coffee was well past cold. "Good luck!"

The lady who sat behind the metal desk had expensive features that pushed her past eight, perhaps even as far as nine. Her viridian eyes followed Janie like lasers as she sat in the empty chair. When 8½ twisted her blue lips into a smile, Janie felt herself blush like it was her first day of school.

She had expected an interrogation about details her backscan might have missed; her peer-circle, where she saw herself in five years, at least, but the first thing 8½ said was: "Training starts Monday, would that be a problem?"

"Tomorrow?" Janie said, her heart a paddle ball. She'd forgotten how real coffee made her head spin.

"Yes, tomorrow," confirmed 8½ with a voice as smooth as her skin. "You are exactly what I have been looking for and are the first that has not lied about body modification. It is easy enough to falsify a backscan, but I can tell."

8½ tapped the side of one emerald eye as if that explained everything.

"Don't you want to know about me?" Janie asked, thinking that this was some kind of test, and to pass it she must show the right balance of modesty and assertiveness.

8½ smiled wider, showing her glazed teeth. "The data we have collated indicates all I need to know. You grew up in a rural town, came to the city when you were sixteen, studied classical literature, with a master's thesis on Proust, and then applied for standard Life Credit when you turned twenty-five. You have had five romantic partners, the longest lasting no more than two weeks. You have a sister and nine cousins, and are regarded by your many nieces and nephews as their favourite aunt. Your parents have retired to the World Ship Tranquillity Three, and you contact them regularly, though have on three occasions lied to your mother, allowing her to believe you are still working on your novel, which you have not opened in the last three years."

"That's in my backscan?" Janie asked, unable to hide her anxiety.

"You must understand, Miss Allgood, that the success of our product has been deemed worthy of government support. Access to a deeper level of employee scanning is part of this assistance. Do not let it concern you, we pride ourselves on our ethical code. Now where was I?"

"My writing?" Janie said, forcing control back into her voice. 8½ raised an eyebrow.

"Yes. You are an active member of seven book groups, and have three avatars, one who is a well-regarded critic, and the other two who write fan fiction for the franchised story worlds Offplanet and GrimGoth. You rate classical music highly, yet your play count reveals you prefer late twenty first century rock. You volunteer at a hospital where you read to sick children, but do so less from a sense of altruism than to purge yourself of the guilt you harbor from your monthly Life Credit allowance. Likewise, you would like this job for the routine it would give you more than the extra credits, a routine that you have missed since your studies ended."

8½'s voice had missed neither a beat nor a detail. Janie shifted uncomfortably on the hard seat that was more sculpture than chair and forced her mouth to shut.

"You have six hours to accept our offer. Any questions?"

"Wait, I got the job?"

"As I have said, your records are in order."

Janie looked to the door, for some reason wanting to run. "You know I don't have any experience in sales."

"No," 8½ said calmly, "but you have an impressive willingness to both admit and step beyond your limitations. Take your weight, for example. You could easily have accepted your parents offer to pay for a reduction, yet attempted the harder path of exercise and diet control. And you are steadfast in this resolve, despite repeated failure. Tell me Janie, for this is perhaps the one thing our files cannot reveal, what motivates your resistance to body modification?"

And here it was, the expected interrogation, but it came now as a side-ball, in her blind spot, striking just when it seemed everything was going so well. Janie's arms instinctively crossed over her chest and when she spoke it was in a rush.

"There's no point changing what I look like when it's what I feel like that's the problem."

8½'s face lit up. "See, Janie, I was right about you." Her head tilted a little and she frowned. "Yet I see you are confused; is there a particular concern I can assuage?"

"Yes," Janie said, still flustered and trying to find her footing. "What do you even sell?"

"A better you, of course," 8½ said as if the answer was self evident.

"Body mods?" Janie asked, blood rushing once more up her neck. It would be just like her mother to use her cousin as a way to get Janie to change.

"Nothing so crass. We offer tailored re-motivational neural plasticity."

"I'm sorry, Ms..."

'Mrs," corrected 8½. "Mrs. Verdurin."

"I studied literature, not science."

Mrs. Verdurin waved her hand as if brushing away a bothersome fly. "Don't let that concern you," she said. "All that fancy term means is that we are able to help our customers improve their desires and motivations, mark them up, if you like, as an editor can a rough draft, turning a jumble of inconsistent ideas into a seamless story fit for publication."

"Really?"

The look on Janie's face made Verdurin laugh.

"Oh yes, it has been thoroughly tested and is completely reversible. As I said, the governments of many nations have invested considerable resources into the procedure. We will be the first to bring it to the market. Now please excuse me, I still have one more interview. You have six hours to consider our offer."

Mrs Verdurin stood and held out her hand.

"No need, I'll take it."

"I am very pleased to hear this, Janie. You are a perfect fit for our growing family, and with a little tweak or two I am sure you will feel as happy with us as we are with you."

Janie let go of her hand. "Tweak?"

"No need to be afraid. All our employees receive the benefits of our products. We can help you become the person you have always wanted to be. As you said yourself, Janie, it is what's inside that counts."

And that was almost exactly what the screen ads and billboards proclaimed a month later when BetaU opened for business.

Donald walked under the shifting sculpture that howled a symphony in the wind. The automatron directed him to a room where a maid poured him coffee and he browsed the catalogue of procedures that had weird sounding names and no listed prices. Eventually the maid ushered him through a wooden door and into an office furnished like a vampire sim, with rich curtains by the windows, oak panels on the walls, and an honest-to-god fireplace that filled the room with the pleasant smell of smoke. An agent was waiting for him beside the hearth.

"Welcome," she said; mid-thirties, kind smile, no more than a four, a bit frumpy but there was something about her. He had thought this would all be done at a kiosk, like the dentist, but after the coffee girl, he had reformed his expectations. Homely, was the word that came to mind as he shook her hand. Don started to relax.

"I'm Miss Allgood. Scotch?"

She gestured to a liquor cabinet lined with top shelf stuff. Not the vat stock you got at the general, but what looked like real whiskey and rum with labels as old as the room.

"God yeah," he said, and Miss Allgood poured him a double on the rocks. She sat on one of the old recliners by the fire. Don dumped himself into the other one. "Cheers," he said and found the scotch as warm as the leather, though both were probably fake.

"What is it that we can do for you?" asked the agent and Don's leg started to jiggle as he remembered why he was there.

"Um, there's this woman at work..." he began, and was glad to see that Miss Allgood did not frown or show any sign of judgment.

"Have you spoken to your wife about her?"

"God no," he said, and took another nervous sip.

"Of course not," said Miss Allgood, reaching forward to place her hand on his knee, making it still. "You're doing the right thing, the responsible thing."

He relaxed a little and she sat back, smiling.

"Won't hurt, will it?"

"Of course not," she said again, pressing a button that made a screen rise up from the armrest of her chair. "The procedure is completely painless. And the only difference between the basic packages and our more tailored options is time."

"And credits," he added cynically.

"With the government subsidy and your current credit score, I can..."

"Forget it," Donald said, regretting he had even mentioned the cost and feeling like a cheapo at the general complaining about the price of RealMeat cubes. "I just want the special I read about, NonAmour, I think it was called. Don't want too much re-wiring, wife would see something's up."

Miss Allgood gave an understanding nod, and tapped on her screen. "What is her name?"

"My wife?" said Donald, almost dropping his drink.

She looked up and gave him a wink.

"No, the other woman."

"Yeah, right," Donald said, wiping his fingers on his leg. "Um, Robyn, Robyn Winters."

She was tapping at her screen again. "Ahh, Miss Winters, a six point nine." She turned the screen around on its bronze spindle.

"Yeah, that's her," Don said, looking away from the lips and smile that had been his torment since Robyn had started work at New-Gaia. He drained his glass.

"I see she is a scenic engineer too," Miss Allgood observed, twisting her screen back to read the summary.

"Yeah," Don said. "We program in the same pod, so?"

"I'm just making sure you understand the nature of the procedure, Don. Working so closely with Ms. Winters, there is a slight chance of a relapse and—"'

'Oh, I see," Donald interrupted, deflated. "Let me guess, you don't have a credit back policy?" He got up, went to the bar and poured himself another double, this time no ice.

"Please, Don," Miss Allgood said, turning in her chair to look at him, although her fingers still tapped away at her screen. 'With a tailored Love&Cherish package we can re-align your feelings from Miss Winters to your wife, where they belong. This drops the chance of relapse to under five per cent."

"How much?" he asked, staring into his drink.

"We have a special this week on all tier two procedures."

Donald laughed. "How much?" he asked again.

"Twenty thousand credits."

The tone of Don's laughter changed.

"You're joking, right? I could drink Pina Coladas on the coast of Spain for the next ten years on that. Fuck, I could get a life time worth of Xanax and Viagra—"

"Which our files show you have already tried. Drugs, as you know, can alleviate the symptoms but not the cause. What we offer is lasting change."

"Just how much do you know about me?"

"Please Don, there is nothing intrusive about this. We seek only to help."

"Says the woman trying to sell me a memory wipe."

She laughed as if his joke had been made with, not at her.

"Memories are far too complex to alter, Don. No, what we do is more subtle. Think of your desires as strings pulling you in unwanted directions." She snipped her fingers in the air. "We can cut them, and reattach them to better places." Now she was tying imaginary knots. "We could even take away your drinking problem. For a little extra cost, of course."

"I don't have a problem," Donald said, draining his second glass. "Just Robyn. And that thing with my wife. Do that too."

"I will need your bio right here," Miss Allgood said, turning her screen to face him. Don pressed his palm on the glass and it buzzed.

"Thank you. Now please, have another drink."

He looked back to the bar and there was a new bottle on the shelf. Bright purple liquid glowed inside.

"Thought you said this wasn't a drug?" he asked suspiciously.

"No, I said drugs don't work. That liquid contains a school of atomoids, and those little critters work quite well indeed. Now, don't look look like that, these are not the nanobots of yesteryear. Picture white blood cells, converging on bacteria, but in this case the infection is a learned or inherited neural topography. Once mapped, these cobwebs can be cleared away and new, more beneficial connections made."

"And——this, I mean, it's painless?" Donald asked again, imagining little metal crayfish lasering neurons like in an old screen game. "I won't feel a thing?"

"I didn't," said Miss Allgood with a reassuring smile.

"You?"

"Oh yes, perk of the job, you understand. I used to have what they call a 'hang up' about my weight. I blamed my mother, of course, who only wanted to help. Now though, I am perfectly comfortable with what God gave me, as the saying goes."

"You look just great to me," he said, and felt the fool for the way it came out like a come on.

"Are you interested in that procedure too, Don?" she asked with a raised eyebrow. "Neither our records nor your application indicated that body image was a concern."

He laughed, making light of the situation. "Well, just not my own." Then he went back to the bar and poured a purple shot. It tasted like apples.

March was a busy month, and Janie led the sales board, as she had since the start of the year. Drug addicts were her bread and butter, yet since they were fully subsidised, they didn't count toward the Super Seller Tally. But even addicts had to agree to the procedure—this wasn't China, after all—so Janie treated them as practice, and even managed to upsell many to packages beyond ColdSober. The only thing she didn't like about addicts was their chosen method of ingestion. Janie had to have InControl herself just to stop her hands shaking every time she inserted a needle.

FearLess was their biggest seller. It was partially subsidised due to the range of negative psychological maladies it could undo, but once the punters were through the door Janie could really get to work. So far, ninety-two percent of her phobia clients went on to a more tailored package.

"Perhaps you would like to look at our brochure?" Janie would begin, the anxious client tapping their feet nervously in her office that she'd designed herself.

"Brochure?" would come the client's response, and they would start to peruse the carefully worded euphemisms.

From A to Zen, was the heading on the front, and the client would smirk, some with derision, some in honest amusement. It was then that most started to speak, throwing their kite of uncertainty into the wind.

"So how much does inner peace cost?" was the common first question of a cynic, or, if they had a better sense of humour: "Should I come back when you have a clearance sale on enlightenment?"

Janie would laugh with them in understanding. "What is happiness worth to you?"

Most were canny enough to point out the obvious. "I guess if I have to ask, I can't afford it." While others made the leap to something like, "I doubt I'll feel very Zen if I can't pay rent."

"Perhaps," she would say with just the right tone to make them wonder.

"And it's all bullshit anyway," they would continue, using different expressions, but always the same plea to reason. "You can't just make me happy with a flick of a switch."

"Why not?"

This was the part she loved most, letting them play out the string of logic until none was left.

"I mean, I *am* my thoughts," they'd argue. "You change them and you change me, right?" Such a question was the first slip of the tether.

'You came here today to do something about your fear." She would remind them then, sometimes showing a holo of their particular phobia for good measure, creating the response they so despised. "Is this who you are?"

Most looked away from the bugs or bored crowds or dizzying heights (once it had been feathers) and for many that was enough to close a sale. But some continued to argue. "Yeah, but if you take all that away, I mean, what would be left?"

"Why, *you* would be, of course."

They would laugh again, but now it was not so certain and Janie would blow stronger, pushing their kite into the jet stream.

"Do you become less yourself when your hunger is satiated? Is something lost when you scratch an itch?"

"That's different," they'd argue, "that's just…meaningless stuff." Some waved their hands, exasperated, others became angry.

Janie would smile then, serenely, her tone at odds to the incision she was making. Sometimes she made her screen a mirror for this part, but only if the clients were fours or lower; any higher and narcissism tended to make them reaffirm their self-certainty. "You are right, you *will* be different, you will be the person hidden under all that noise. Wouldn't you like to meet them? That is what we offer. The real you."

They'd sign even if it meant taking out a life mortgage. No one ever complained about the repayments, though more than a few added StressLess to their package, unburdening themselves from credit anxiety.

Her first and only disappointed customer came three months after Donald, (whom she referred to in her notes as Lusty#7), when a young man, Dangles, she had named him, returned, disheartened.

"It didn't work?" Janie asked, knowing of course that it had.

"Yeah," Dangles shrugged. "But it wasn't supposed to make me like this."

"Like what?" Janie asked. Dangles was one of a new generation of young fools who performed death defying stunts for the entertainment of their followers who experienced everything from the safety of an E-merse suit. Dangles had risen to fame riding balloons into low orbit, then diving naked back to ground. His Grand Canyon jump alone had paid for all the procedures he could ever want.

"You said it would make me better,"' Dangles explained, shaking his shaggy head of hair. 'Calmer. But now I just don't give a fuck. It just seems stupid, you know, to risk your life. It's all just so..." He trailed of and shrugged.

"You remember that we do not have a warranty for disappointment," Janie said calmly.

"I'll pay," his eyes lit up. "You can undo it, right?"

"Undoing a procedure is called a re-negative,"' Janie said, and tapped at her screen, then turned it towards him so he could see the cost. "And they are significantly more than the original..."

"Fine, whatever," he said, already pressing his palm against the glass.

A moment later an automatron rolled in with a small wooden box held in its manipulators."'

Thank you," said Janie to the robot, and then passed the box to Dangles, who opened it greedily. Inside was a thickly rolled joint, identical to the one that had first taken away his fear. He lit up, and sucked back smoke with his eyes closed.

"Oh, yeah," he said, wistfully. "That's the fucking stuff."

Janie had worried that Mrs. Verdurin would be disappointed she hadn't convinced him out of the re-neg but she just smiled.

"Whatever they want to want, Janie."

And Janie continued to be the monthly Super Seller right up until she met the Mother.

The woman gave no name and sat in the chair, refusing even water. Janie had scanned her file and was not surprised the woman wanted some work done. She had a life that read like a cheap sim: husband cheated on her, then she lost her Life Credit when she was found guilty of stalking the other woman. Recently she'd had a bit of luck, inheriting an estate from a long lost uncle. Now, looking to re-invent herself, she'd applied for NewHope, one of the introductory packages. Janie was certain she'd upsell her to a more tailored procedure.

"My husband," the woman began, her eyes not meeting Janie's. "Ex-husband I mean. He had NewHope, said it worked right away."

Janie adjusted her posture, made a note on her screen. "Of course, though it is a rather simple process."

"That's what I want," the woman said quickly, a flash of anger.

Anger was no good. Janie held out her hands apologetically. "I only mean that for a small addition you could purchase our TaoNow —"

"No," the word was final, and with two interruptions in as many minutes, Janie worried this could be her first walk-out. She quickly tapped on her screen.

"Just NewHope then. As you say."

"Will it make me forget?" asked the woman, her hands twisting in her lap.

"Your ex? No, we do not alter..."

"Not him," the woman said, glaring up at Janie. That was three interruptions now. "My son."

"Son?" Janie said, looking back at her screen.

"You won't find him in there," said the woman. "AutoCo had the settlement rated private, even made up that shit about my uncle to hide their payout."

Janie was at a loss. A backscan had never missed something as big as this before. She would have to have a word with Client Prep.

"What happened?" Janie asked, and regretted the question at once, for the woman looked away, her eyes filling with tears.

In the silence Janie quickly cross checked the woman's name with a deep net search for court cases and the flyer company, AutoCo.

"It will make me forget, won't it?" she asked again, her voice as distant as her glazed eyes.

Janie was still reading from her screen. She had found a single news link about a mid-air crash on the interstate flyway. Not even meant to be possible. One casualty, young boy, only five. Instinctively, Janie reached out for the woman's trembling fingers.

"I'm so sorry, but NewHope only channels your thoughts into more constructive avenues."

"Constructive avenues?" the Mother repeated, pulling her hands back into her own lap. "Well, Robert said it worked for him."

"I'm sorry," Janie said again.

Then the Mother spied the medicine cabinet and sprang from her chair. Wrenching open the white door marked with a red cross she pulled out the jar containing a single glowing pill.

"This it?" the Mother asked, and Janie, in an effort to regain control of the situation, fetched her a glass of water.

But the Mother had already swallowed the pill and was back in her seat, eyes squeezed shut as if that might speed the process.

"Here, lie back," Janie offered, pressing the control that reclined the woman's chair.

A stillness was spreading over her face and body as the atomoids did their work, cleaning out the corridors of her mind, shutting doors, opening others. She looked more than asleep though, almost dead.

"Thank you," the Mother said, breathing out slowly. "Rob was right," she continued, whispering to herself. "It is already working."

"How, how do you feel?" Janie asked. She never asked this, but the look on the woman's face was empty. Even the TaoNow customers looked serene.

"He's fading," she said, her voice starting to brim with emotion. She looked up at Janie, something new burning bright in her eyes. "It's just like he said it would be. I can let him go now."

"Let him go?" Janie repeated, uncertain.

"Yes." She sighed out a final breath and got up from her chair. "Yes. Yes the sadness is going—his face, his smell, I think I can forget him now." She held out her hand. "Thank you. I shall recommend this to my group."

Janie let the Mother shake her hand once she was alone she sat down in her chair and looked at the empty pill container the woman had dropped on the carpet. Janie turned off her screen, which still showed the news article of the boy's death. A chime startled her and Janie realised she had not even prepared for her next appointment.

"Ah, Miss Allgood, what can I do for you?"

Janie had been made to wait for half an hour outside the CEO's office. Her resolve had only grown in that time, perhaps fuelled by the three coffees she'd accepted from the server.

Mrs. Verdurin had done more modding since last they had met. She was now a nine-plus, and her eyes were vivid sapphires.

"I want a re-neg," Janie said with less force than she had been planning. Mrs. Verdurin reacted with her usual calm concern.

"Please, sit down, Janie," she said. Janie did, but found her knees would not stop their rhythmic dancing. That last coffee had been a mistake.

"I want you to undo the SkinDeep you gave me in training."

"This is because of the NewHope case from yesterday," said Verdurin, shaking her head sadly. When she opened her eyes, they had turned a deeper shade, almost purple. "I have watched the recording. I am sorry that you found that so unsettling."

Mrs. Verdurin stood and moved to sit on the edge of her desk looking down at Janie.

"Don't let this darken your thoughts, Janie. You are doing well."

Janie stood up so that she was eye level with the woman, but felt the move had been too aggressive. Instead of taking back power, in some way she had given ground to the CEO. Janie couldn't even meet Verdurin's eyes, which had now turned neon pink. "We weren't supposed to make them forget. You said that's not possible..."

Verdurin held up a hand to interrupt and Janie bit back the rest of her planned speech. She blinked and her eyes changed to sunset orange. "Now Janie, do not place words. I said it was not possible for us to manipulate memories directly. Cognitive association benefits, however, are proving to be quite effective."

"Cognitive what?"

Mrs. Verdurin gave her a look of concern, blinked again, setting her new eyes back to blue. "Tell me, Janie, how often do you think about your writing?"

'Writing?" Janie asked, taking a step back, as if Verdurin had just slapped her in the face.

"Yes, writing. You used to do a lot of it. You even started a novel."

"I—I did?" Janie said, finding it hard to breathe. Of course I did, she thought.

"See," Mrs. Verdurin said, "cognitive association benefit. We change the desire; you do the rest."

"But that..." Janie fell quiet, remembering more.

"Janie, Janie, Janie," Mrs. Verdurin said with a shake of her head on each repetition. It was so similar to the way her mother spoke that Janie was certain it had been pulled from a recording. It even achieved the effect it had on Janie as a child. She felt defeated, a foolish girl too stupid to understand what the adults saw so clearly.

"Your desire to write was chained to your depression. Once that chain was broken the desire was freed and forgotten, like all unnecessary data."'

Janie backed away from Mrs. Verdurin, who advanced like a tiger, her silk suit swishing, eyes bright yellow and hands held out as if in welcome.

'I never wanted to forget..."

Verdurin took her by the shoulders as if to keep Janie from falling. "Not consciously, perhaps. But if you trace back the dominoes of your life you will find a little Janie Allgocd all alone at primary school, wanting only to fit in with all the other pretty girls and boys.

That Janie decided that she must therefore be different, destined to work in hiding, isolated, where she would be judged for her thoughts, not her looks. But look at you now, just think how that lonely little Janie would feel to know that happiness was as easy to add as milk to coffee."

Janie wanted to argue, but the words were true and they cut through her like a surgical laser.

"You do not need a re-negative, Janie, you need to trust me, and together we can put this little blip behind us."

"Blip." Janie repeated the word in a monotone, then pulled free from Verdurin's grip. "I don't want to forget again. Not about who I was or that boy who died. I want you to put me back—I want to feel awkward again, I want to worry again and lie to my mother again," she stepped forward, forcing Mrs. Verdurin to retreat, "I want to write again. And another thing: I quit."

Verdurin's eyes were pink again and her smile, just for a moment, faltered.

"Quit? Yet you are so happy."

"Happy?" Janie said the word like a curse, but Verdurin was only getting started.

"This last year with us has seen a measured improvement with your life satisfaction," she continued. "Your family and friends all report a thirty-seven percent increase in meaningful interaction, and you have been seeing Mark from accounting for over a month now, who likewise reports a satisfaction rating of sixty-eight percent with your budding romance."

"Don't fucking bring Mark into—"

"Please do not swear, Miss Allgood," said Mrs. Verdurin. "It is so out of character."

This made Janie laugh, nervously. "What would you know?" she asked, intending it as an attack, but seeing at once from the woman's smile that her accusation had played directly into her hand.

"You forget how much I can see, Janie." Verdurin sighed, and Janie had the distinct impression she was far older than her perfect face let on. "We really can't have this, not now. Imagine what our critics would say if they learned one of our best agents had re-neged and left the company?"

"I-I won't say anything," Janie said, trying a new approach. "I'll sign a non-disclosure. Just put me back the way I was."

"The way you were?" Mrs. Verdurin shook her head, and her painted fingernail became a dagger aimed at Janie's heart. "A nobody, helping no one? Writing sex scenes between aliens and vampires and lying to your mother about a novel you'll never finish? No, I was right to be worried about the report HR compiled on you. Their analytics said you were only a thirteen percent risk, but I know better."

"I want to want to write," Janie mumbled, her certainty undone as a new feeling began to creep into her belly. It was warm, but not the pleasant warmth of wine, rather a dull numbness like anaesthetic.

"Ahh, it has finally begun," said the CEO, her head tilting and her neon eyes scrutinising. When next she spoke, her voice was slower, once more the measured cadence of a metronome. "Coffee makes a terrible delivery method I am afraid. Our atomoids enter via the same adenosine receptors that are blocked by caffeine."

"Wha—" Janie began, and Verdurin took her by the shoulders again, guiding her back to a chair.

"I wanted to call it Utter Contentment, but marketing said that read as far too final. No good at all for return business. So we've gone with *FullFilled*. They are the experts, after all. It has only just finished trials. Please, sit back and relax, Janie."

Janie did, and looked up into the bright blue eyes.

"That's better. See, I share the philosophy of all medical practitioners whose guiding principle is to do no harm. And it would do a great deal of harm to re-burden you with the anxieties of your past. You are like a released prisoner, so accustomed to your confinement that you cannot adapt to freedom. But it is my duty—my pleasure—to help you."'

"No," Janie mumbled, but the word carried no weight, no force. She felt good—not drugged and dazed, but calm, at peace. She could see now that Verdurin was right, that this feeling was good, perfect. It was all that mattered.

Verdurin, satisfied by what she saw in Janie's face, returned to her own chair and lay her hands flat on the metal desk.

"Now, where were we? Ahh yes, the future. We are growing fast, Janie, and it is my hope that you will continue to find happiness with our ever expanding family. Tell me, do you like the ocean?"

Donald had discovered that happily-ever-after needed maintenance, even in LA, where the temperature never dropped below balmy. The move from New York had been the only way Donald could get away from that psycho Robyn, who insisted they'd had a thing going. At first Don was flattered — she was almost a seven after all — but after a year of it he'd been ready to call the police and file a stalker charge. So when New-Gaia offered him a transfer to the west coast office, it was the perfect solution. Problem was his wife wanted to stay in Manhattan. Eventually though, he convinced her to take a dose of SeaChange and after that it was like it had been her idea all along. But now, two years after the relocation, he found he was sick of the sun and sand and needed a dose himself.

There were a dozen different facilities offering the service now, like Feel Fine and Okey Dokey, but Don preferred the human touch. So when he heard that BetaU had opened a shop in Santa Monica, he'd skipped lunch, taken a flyer to the coast and was now walking under another morphing block of metal cheese. Aside from the blinding glare of reflected sun, the only difference from this sculpture and the one in New York was the chord it made as the sea breeze blew through it.

The automatron greeted him with programmed familiarity, and ushered him through to the waiting room where he started to browse the new catalogue. A server pushed a cart around offering everyone organic cold pressed juice. When she came to Don, he gave a polite shake of his head. Human agents were okay, but maids still made him awkward.

He was called into the brightly lit office, a white cube of a place where the agent sat on one of the crystalline chairs and a baby in a bassinet bounced happily in the corner. The agent smiled warmly and gestured to the child.

"I assure you he won't cry," she said sweetly. "My son is quite content, and we do try to encourage a family atmosphere here. Indeed, I believe you might be interested in our new range of parent specials yourself, Don?"

Only then did Don look away from the gooing, gagahing kid and recognise the woman.

'Miss Goodall?" he said, momentarily dislocated.

"Allgood," she corrected, "But I'm married now. And I hope you don't feel I have been presumptuous. Our files indicate you have two children yourself, yes?"

"Um, yeah," Donald said, "Becky and Art. Pains in my arse, the both of 'em."

Mrs. Allgood laughed.

"So, will it just be a dose of SeaChange, or can we do anything else for you today?"

Donald sat down in the empty chair and looked up at the painting hanging on the far wall. It was mostly blank canvas, with a single stroke of yellow at the bottom.

"DotingDad," he said, remembering the specials he'd seen in the waiting room. "That any good?"

"Ah, yes, I thought that might interest you."

She dialled in his order and a moment later a bar fridge rose up from the floor between them. On the shelf inside was a box of chocolates and in the door tray were half a dozen little bottles. She took out two that glowed with purple phosphorescence and unscrewed their lids.

"Cocktail?" she asked and poured the contents of both into a tumbler over ice.

"Um, I don't drink these days."

Mrs. Allgood gave him a wink and a knowing smile. "Don't worry, it's non-alcoholic."

He saluted the sky before taking a sip. It might not have any kick, but they'd gotten the burn right.

"And here is a little reward for your loyalty."

Don swirled the ice in the half empty glass as she took out the box of chocolates with a BetaU logo on the front.

"We call these Dlites," she said, lifting the lid to show an arrangement of dark treats each with a different decoration. "Their changes are temporary, untailored, but quite effective nonetheless. The ones with the swirls are called LittleThings, the ones with coconut are BeautyFulls and the ones topped with are DonJuans, though they perhaps would best be taken with your wife present."

Don laughed and took one of the coconut covered chocolates and found its sweetness paired perfectly with his drink.

The nanomawhatsits worked fast and soon Don found himself looking again at the painting behind Mrs. Allgood. He hadn't realised before that it was a beach scene; the yellow stroke of paint defining the sand and the empty canvas forming the sky. He'd spent his career programing landscapes full of the most intricate detail, always trying to add more to achieve the perfect view. But here, in front of him, with everything stripped away, was what he'd never managed to create. Unbidden tears of joy began to dribble down his cheeks.

"You like it?" asked Mrs. Allgood, turning in her chair to regard the painting with Don. "That is my own work. The ocean seems to have unlocked my hidden creativity."

"It's perfect," he said, wiping at his eyes as the empty horizon line drew him in with the sensation of falling.

"I am so glad to hear that," she said, and took out one of the chocolate swirls, popping it into her mouth before putting the box back into the little refrigerator.

In the corner the baby gurgled happily, looking up at its mother. Mrs. Allgood sighed.

"See," she said. "It's the little things that count."

About the story

"BetaU" is my reflection both on the fast approaching possibility of programmable brains, and also on the way the real world can condition us to conform. Having worked in education for over a decade, I've seen the most enthusiastic young teachers burned up by bureaucracy, becoming the mindless middle managers they once so despised. "BetaU" imagines a future where that process has been streamlined.

A question for the author

Q: Where do you write?

A: Short answer; any table I can.

Expanded answer: I write in the margins of the day; the parent waiting table at my son's martial art class; the staff table at lunch when I should be marking essays; the desk in the spare room at my parents' house when the kids are playing with their presents; and the kitchen table when all else fails. I dream of a house with a wizard's tower accessible by a creaky ladder with enough room at the top for a little desk and a kettle.

About the author

The gateway drug was Narnia, but pretty soon T.B McKenzie had moved on to stronger stuff. Lloyd Alexander, Ursula Le-Guin, and Terry Pratchett solidified the addiction, and then along came the category one names like Jack Vance, Asimov, and Iain M. Banks.

After that, there was no hope, and the only way to control the habit was for T.B to pick up a pen and start manufacturing.

His turf is Melbourne, his cover is teaching high school English, and he lives in constant fear that his family will discover his illicit after hour life that is fast spiralling out of control.

magickless.blogspot.com, @magickless

T.B. McKenzie's story "BetaU" was published in *Metaphorosis* on Friday, 7 July 2017.

The Circe Test

Nora Mulligan

Circe knelt in front of the pig, holding its face so that its eyes looked into hers. "You are not really a pig," she said to it. "You know that. Think. Remember who you are, what you are, and you will return to that form."

The pig's eyes blinked. It struggled in a panic to escape from her. Look as she might, Circe could see no traces of human intelligence in its face. With a sigh, she released the animal, and it rushed away, to the yard where the other pigs grunted and ate and slept.

She stood up, suddenly weary. She hadn't really expected that any of this crew would have the strength of mind and character to change back. She had tried because she hoped, but she had known better. Another failure. More denizens for the island, but no man to share her secrets, to work with her.

She didn't usually give in to loneliness. She had much to do, much to study, much to learn. Sometimes she thought she would be better off if she gave up on the idea of a soul mate, a companion who would understand her. She'd done well here without any, hadn't she? Perhaps she was asking too much.

It was just that some of them came close. Sometimes, not usually with the pigs, but sometimes with the nobler animals, the lions, the eagles, she could see that spark of humanity in their eyes, and she almost believed that this one would be different. This one would know who he was, despite the change of shape. This one would be able to hold onto himself and retain his humanity no matter what. Some had come so close, she had seen the glimmer of the human form beneath the animal's shape. But it was never more than a glimmer.

Circe returned to her still room, where she mixed the potions and added them to the wine. One of the tinctures needed to be heated a little more, and another of the combinations was beginning to smoke. She moved the pot away from the fire and stirred it thoughtfully. She'd heard the other sailor in the underbrush, the one who ran away without coming to her table. Would he be back? Would he bring others? She didn't know whether to hope for others or not.

Circe had become absorbed in the mixing of the potions, and updating the records of the earlier potions. She heard the footsteps of a man, slow, careful, and then his voice.

"Who is in there?" It was a deep voice, a strong, vibrant voice. She instantly knew this was no man she'd met before. She poured the potion into the wine carafe, and waited the length of a breath, for it to mix completely with the wine. Only then did she step out into the entrance hall.

The man who stood there told his life story by his stance. His skin was sunburned and wind burned. There were lines around his eyes from squinting in the brightness, and, perhaps, from smiling. He stood planted in her entryway, a man who commanded, a man who would not slip or fall, a man who had been favored by the powerful in the past, a man who knew his own power.

"Welcome to my island," she said, smiling at him. She thought she'd trained herself not to pay attention to their exteriors; she, of all people, knew how little the exterior meant. And yet, there was something about this one, something that caused her insides to flutter and her pulse to race. Let him be the one, she thought, and it will all have been worthwhile. "I am Circe, and I live here alone."

His dark eyes sparkled with suppressed amusement. "Oh, surely not alone, fair one. One as lovely as you should have entire entourages. My name is Odysseus. I am a sailor, heading from Troy to my home in Ithaca."

Not merely a sailor, she thought. He has been at sea, but he has commanded the ship, as he has commanded much. Including himself? Oh, she hoped. "You are welcome, Odysseus, and I hope you will share wine with me and enjoy my hospitality." She turned and walked to the table, the wine jar in her hand. He hesitated a second or two and then followed her. He sat at the table, relaxed as they all were at first. There was something, a twinkle in his eye, the hint of a smile around his lips, that made her wonder what he saw, what he knew, what he expected. Never mind, she thought. She poured him wine and handed him the cup. She poured some for herself, watching him all the time.

He sniffed at the cup. "By the gods, this smells like nectar itself! Where did you get this?"

"I made the wine myself," she said, not lying. "Drink. It tastes better than it smells."

"That can hardly be true," he said, smiling at her now. He paused a second, watching her holding her own cup. She drank hers down. It was perfectly safe; she was immune to her own potions. He blinked and lifted the cup to his lips. He drank as if he had been dying of thirst.

Then he blanched, put the cup down, very carefully, on the table, and stared at her. "What have you done to me?" he asked, his deep rich voice suddenly thin and strained. He pushed the chair away from the table, his hands clenched on the edge of the table. Already it was happening. His arms muscled, his hair lengthened, his body thickened. His eyes remained the same, angry, surprised, hurt even, but was there a touch of something else? Something like confidence?

"You will not die," she said, remaining at her seat and watching as he threw himself to the floor. "You already know that, don't you?"

He couldn't answer, not yet. The change rippled through his body, taking his voice, his ability to think. He roared, not quite a lion's roar yet, but more than a man's. His very bones shrank, thickened. His face lengthened, his features changing as his face covered with tawny fur. He threw back his head and roared again, and this time it was a lion's voice, coming from a lion's body.

She knelt before him, looking in his eyes. She could see the panic there, but also the intelligence. "You are still Odysseus," she said. "I have changed your outer form, but you can change back, if you will. You can change yourself to your human shape if you remember it, remember that you are human."

"How," he said, his voice now a growl, "could I forget such a thing?"

Her heart stirred. He could talk! That was a good sign already. "Many do," she said simply. "Most forget that they were ever anything else."

"Why have you done this to me?" he asked, plaintive but with an undercurrent of anger.

"I am looking for someone, Odysseus. I am looking for someone who can share my power, share my knowledge. The man I choose must be extraordinary; he must know himself so well that no outward change can upset him. If a man can change back into himself from animal form, that man can be my partner."

His tail had been switching back and forth, but now it stopped. He held himself still, regarding her. "This is a test?"

"Yes. I want you to pass it, Odysseus. I have been waiting a long time for someone who could be my partner."

"And you would share your power with this person?" he asked, serious. She half closed her eyes and saw his human form coexisting with the lion.

"I would," she said. It was safe enough, usually, because the man who asked would never be able to change back. With Odysseus, she wasn't sure how safe she was.

She could see him thinking. "Am I truly a lion now, or am I a man believing he's a lion?"

She smiled. "You must discover that for yourself."

He stretched himself, looking back at his leonine form, his magnificent mane, his powerful claws. He scratched his claws on the marble floor, without result.

"I could kill, couldn't I? I could kill you."

"You could try."

He considered that some more. "I would fail the test if I tried, wouldn't I?"

"Yes."

"I will pass your test," he said. Lions can't smile, but he did, and she knew it was the man smiling, and not the lion. "Tell me what I have to do."

"I told you. You remember yourself as human, and you will be so."

"That sounds too simple."

"It's too difficult for most men."

He closed his eyes, furrowing his lion's brow. His muscles tensed under the tawny coat, and she could almost see the air burn from the force of his concentration. She clenched her own fists. He won't do it, she thought; they never do it, no matter what they seem like during the preliminaries. It was foolish to hope, but she found her breath constricted in her chest as she watched.

He winced with the effort he made, and swallowed hard a few times, and then, for the first time ever, she saw the change begin to reverse. It began with his hands and his arms first, and then his face, and then the rest of his body. She could see the lion for some time during the change, as Odysseus concentrated on different parts of his body and as they began to reshape themselves into human contours, human colors, human shapes. He opened his eyes, human eyes in the last vestiges of a lion's face, and then the change flashed to completion and he stood before her, the man who had stood in her entryway moments before, as if no change had ever occurred.

"I don't believe it," Circe breathed. Her heart began to beat again as if time had stopped for a while and then restarted.

He took a step closer to her and reached for her hands. He brought them to his face and kissed them. "Oh, great sorceress, I have heard tales of you. I heard of what you did to other men, and I was afraid that you would do likewise to me. But I had to meet you, had to find out if the tales were true, and if I could, somehow, persuade you to come home with me."

"With you? To Ithaca?"

"Yes! I am king there, and with you at my side, there is nothing we couldn't do. You could teach me your magic, and we could rule as gods do." His eyes glowed with enthusiasm.

The gods, thought Circe, do not always rule wisely. She didn't say that to him.

"Please, Circe? Consider it. Consider what we could achieve together. I have never met a woman like you, and you said yourself that you were looking for a man like me. You are wasted here on this island. You are meant to be a part of the larger world, where you would gain the glory and honor you deserve." He clutched her hands in his, holding them so tightly he nearly crushed them.

She gently removed her hands from his. "Odysseus, I must think about this. You surprised me, by changing back, and by asking this of me. I have lived here for many years; I cannot leave it as quickly as that."

His eyes burned into hers. "Take your time. Think about it. We are made for each other, Circe. We should work together and our glory will fill the world, rise to the heights of Mount Olympus itself!"

Again she felt a shiver of something like premonition. It was not wise to speak of the gods that way, she thought. They would make him pay for that.

"I will walk," she said. "I need to be by myself to think. You are free to go where you will on my island, Odysseus, but do not touch anything you see in this house. There are things here that you do not understand, that could be dangerous if you touch them."

"Of course," said Odysseus, nodding vigorously. "I wouldn't dream of interfering with your private concoctions. You will teach me about them in your own time." He took her right hand again and kissed it again. "Think of my offer, and come back to me saying yes."

"I will think of it," she said, "and will come back with an answer." She turned and left him, heading for the grove where none of the animals ever went, where she knew she would have privacy to think. As she left the grounds of her house, she saw Brytar, one of the other lions, lurking near the open door of the building. That struck her as odd; Brytar seldom went near her or the building anymore. Perhaps he'd heard or smelled Odysseus' change and was curious. She thrust the idea of Brytar from her mind and proceeded to the grove.

The sun shone there hours after it had left the rest of the island. Outside the trees, the sun had begun to drop below the horizon, but here Circe was bathed in golden light. She felt stronger, more herself, when she entered the grove.

Was he the one? She tried to close her mind to his human magnificence. Yes, he was a commander of men, a king. She could see that in him. He had traveled far, and faced perils; that, too, was written on his face, scored in his muscles, his movements. The power she had to share, though, was more than any king had ever had at his command, and more perilous than anything this one, or any of them, had ever faced before. Should she entrust it to him?

He had changed back, she reminded herself. He had struggled briefly, but he had found the way back. He knew who he was; he was not disturbed by the outward signs of things. He would not, she thought, fall victim to the glamour of the power. He would not allow himself to be corrupted by it. He knew himself. He alone, of all the men she had changed over the years, had turned his back on the power of his other form and returned to the human. He could be trusted with other powers. She could trust him.

And return with him to his kingdom? She hadn't considered leaving her island in decades. Once, yes, when she'd first arrived here, she'd held dreams of triumph in the world of ordinary people, of being able to rule over them all. But that was long ago, and she'd outgrown those dreams as she saw what men were like, how easy it was to keep them animals forever. Men hadn't changed, she knew, even if she had found one who was different.

And yet, to have him at her side, to share her power, her responsibility, at long last. To be able to return to the world, to take her place where she belonged, to be looked up to, to be admired, feared, even. She could feel the desire, the need, rising in her, burning through her skin like a blush. She wanted it. She had never completely given up on the hope, the possibility; she had deluded herself all these years, told herself that she was content but continued feverishly concocting the potions, waiting and hoping for the one who would be ready for her.

Then she allowed herself to remember Odysseus the man, and her blood rushed to her skin, and she felt hot all over. To partner a man like that would be something. She remembered the touch of his lips on her hands, and she burned again. She wanted him. She would have wanted him even if he hadn't passed the test, though she would not have acted on that desire if he'd failed. But he hadn't failed, and she wanted him. She wanted to be with him, now, and she wanted to go with him when he returned to Ithaca.

At last, she thought, her self-imposed exile would come to an end.

She raised her arms in the rays of the setting sun and answered the question in her heart. Yes, she thought. Yes, I will return to Ithaca with him. Yes, I will share my life with him. Yes.

The last drops of the sunset caught in the upper branches of the trees as she passed out of the grove. Outside, the world was in darkness, but she knew her way back to her house. She heard the animals stirring from their homes in the forest, in the darkness. If she tried, she could remember all their names, but she didn't need to, not anymore. Perhaps she would even free them, when she and Odysseus left the island. She hadn't decided on that yet.

He was not in the building when she walked through the entrance, but she heard him moving in the long grass outside the door, and he appeared in the candle light moments after she returned.

There was something different about him, a slight tension in the way he held his shoulders, a strain somewhere around his eyes, and Circe, noticing this, wondered if this were bodily memory of being a lion. Sometimes, she saw the others make remarkably humanlike moves in their animal forms; perhaps this was the reverse. Or perhaps he was worried about something.

He smiled when he saw her, but there was something hiding behind the smile. "Circe," he said, "it has been a lifetime since I saw you last. I thought you would disappear altogether and this would all be a dream." He crossed the room to her, took her in his arms. "I didn't know how I would survive without you."

She held him in her arms, feeling the telltale muscle tension, there in his shoulders, there in his back. "I would not have done that," she said. "I told you I needed time to think. I have thought. I will go back with you."

His whole face lit from within. "Will you? And will you share your gifts with me? I will share my kingdom with you, I swear it."

"Yes," she said, "all my gifts," and she kissed him long and hard. They pulled apart, looked at each other for a moment of hunger and desire, and then she led him to her bedroom.

He slept afterwards, and she surprised herself by falling asleep beside him. She usually prowled in the night and slept by day, but she must have fallen into his rhythms of sleep and wakefulness, as she had fallen into his other rhythms in bed. She only knew she'd slept when suddenly she awoke to find herself alone in the bed.

For a second, before she came to full waking, she wondered if she had dreamed Odysseus entirely, but then her senses returned and she heard his footsteps elsewhere in the house. She held herself quiet and listened until she could identify the tiny sounds of porcelain. He was in her stillroom, she thought, but why should he be there? Hadn't she warned him about the potions?

She could have called out to him, and certainly he would have answered, and all that happened after that would have been different, but she didn't call him. Instead, she rose silently and dressed herself, still listening to his small sounds in the other room. He would not pass this room on his way to the ship, if that was where he was going.

Circe saw him leave the building and stride out to the woods. He carried something with him, something he feared to drop, judging by the way he sheltered it when he stumbled. It had to be one of her potions, Circe thought, but she couldn't understand why he would want one, and why he would walk away from where his ship was moored and toward the part of the island where the other, more dangerous animals dwelled.

She thought of Brytar again, and his curious appearance near the house when she'd left for the grove. Could Brytar have met with Odysseus, challenged him in some way? Knowing what she knew of Brytar (another one she'd hoped would have the strength to pass the test), she thought it likely.

But Brytar was a lion, and Odysseus merely a man, though a special man. If Brytar chose to be treacherous, he could easily kill a human being. Perhaps Odysseus took the potion as a way of improving his chances with Brytar, Circe thought. Since he could change back to man shape by himself, he might feel confident enough to try another lion potion. That was assuming that he'd found the right potion and hadn't accidentally taken something deadly.

Circe had to follow him, to protect him if need be, and to discipline Brytar, if need be. She had the advantage over Odysseus: she knew the island well, and wouldn't need moonlight to find her way. She recognized the path Odysseus took, and judged his pace as slow enough that she could easily catch up to him before he met with Brytar anywhere but at the very edge of the woods.

She ran lightly along the path, until her foot caught the edge of the rock sticking up. She tripped and caught herself before she crashed onto the ground. How odd, Circe thought. She knew this path well, and there were no rocks rising out of the ground there. She turned to look at the rock, now moved by the impact of her foot.

It was about the size of her fist, and had been buried deeper in the path before. Now it didn't completely fit into its original hole. She lifted the rock. Someone had placed some green leaves there, and covered them with the rock. How strange, she thought, as she removed all the leaves. She didn't recognize them. They were from no plant that grew on the island; she was sure of that. Someone had hidden them here, she thought, and as she placed them in a pouch attached to her belt, she felt a profound uneasiness, as if she had put her hand into a hole that might contain a poisonous snake.

When she headed along the trail again, she was more careful of the surface, but nothing else was amiss, and she heard Brytar's voice as she neared a clearing. She paused in the trees, where she could see and hear but not be seen.

Brytar circled Odysseus, his tail switching, his golden-brown eyes mocking. "I knew you would come," he said. "I knew you wouldn't take the chance."

"She wouldn't believe you," said Odysseus, his voice low and tight, as if the tension she'd felt in his body earlier had all settled in his throat. "Even if you told her."

"Even if I showed her the herbs? Even if I told her that I saw Hermes give them to you? She'd know, then. She'd know what they are, and how you used them."

"You didn't see me use them," said Odysseus. "You have no proof."

Brytar laughed, a roaring laugh that was more lion than human. "You couldn't have changed to human without them. I didn't see you hide them in your mouth and swallow them at the critical moment, but I know you did. Look, Odysseus, you were clever, I'll grant you that. I admire cleverness. I'm not asking for much. You give me some of those herbs, and I'll change back, and then I can travel back to the real world with you, and I swear by the gods that I'll never tell anyone a word of what I saw and what I know."

"Yes," said Odysseus thoughtfully, "you said that before, when we met earlier. I understand your offer."

Circe felt her heart turn cold and hard, a block of ice in her chest. She breathed in as silently as she could, and listened.

"And you came here," said Brytar, "which means you've realized that this is the best offer you are likely to get. You should know that I'd do what I said I'd do. She might even reward me for saving her from being tricked by you. The great trickster, Odysseus, the one who gets what he wants through manipulating others. Do you have the herb with you?"

Odysseus flushed in the light of the half moon. "Yes," he said, "I have it." He opened his hand and Circe recognized the container. He must have read her notes, she thought, and found the lion potion. "I'll prove to you how it works." With one fluid motion, he poured the potion down his throat. The lion potion worked quickly even diluted in wine. Without the wine, the effect was almost instantaneous. Circe saw Odysseus sharing space with the lion for a second or two, and then he was completely a lion again, the bottle shattering on the ground nearby.

Brytar growled, "You liar! You cheat — "but he didn't get a chance to say more before Odysseus attacked him. Brytar had been a lion much longer than Odysseus, but he had been thinking like a man in the clearing, and Odysseus had the advantage of surprise. He knocked Brytar down in his first leap, and his great teeth met in the other lion's throat, while Brytar struggled and clawed at him.

Circe watched it happen. She could have stopped Odysseus if she'd chosen to do so. In the instant of Odysseus' attack, she was so angry at Brytar for opening her eyes that she wanted him dead as much as Odysseus did, and for the same reasons. In any event, her opportunity passed quickly. Brytar lay dead on the ground, blood splattering the grass and trees, when Circe walked out into the clearing.

Odysseus turned to her, his eyes surprised and horrified. "Circe! What are you doing here?"

"Looking for you," she said. Her voice was as icy as her heart. "You took one of my potions."

"I needed it to defend myself," said Odysseus. He tilted his head slightly, watching her expressions. "This one threatened me earlier, when you were away. I went to meet him, to see if I could make him stop, but I brought a potion in case he tried to take advantage of the difference in our forms."

He thinks I didn't hear the conversation, Circe thought. "And you used it, and killed him."

"It was him or me," said Odysseus earnestly. His teeth were red, and gore dripped off the fur of his chin. His mane was stained with blood.

"Yes," said Circe in the same dead voice. "But you don't need to remain a lion, Odysseus. Change back now, and we will return to the house."

His eyes flickered from one side to the other. "I — I'm a little upset, Circe. I've just killed a man, and it's upsetting me. I'm not sure I could concentrate well enough to change right now."

"No," said Circe. "I want to see you change, right now. You've killed before, I'm certain. You were at Troy. You fought in the war. Killing is nothing new to you, and certainly nothing that upsetting. Come, Odysseus, change. Now."

He was breathing hard. She wondered if he would try to make a break for it. She could almost see him considering it, planning what he would say if she caught him. He shuddered and closed his eyes as if he were trying to remember who and what he was.

"Or do you need help?" she asked. "Perhaps you forgot something. Something you left along the path, hidden under a rock. This, perhaps?" She opened the pouch and held out the herb so that he could see it.

Odysseus stared at the herb hungrily and then looked at Circe herself. "I can explain," he said.

She closed her hand on the herb. "No," she replied. "You don't need to say anything. You've already made it perfectly clear. You lied to me, Odysseus. You tricked me and I let myself be tricked. I wanted so much to believe that you were the one. But you're not." She turned her back on him. A shudder began somewhere down by her hips and swept through her body. She thought she might vomit. "You will leave my island, Odysseus, you and your crew. I never want to see you again. If you are not off my island by sunrise, I will turn you into dirt, all of you." She dropped the handful of herbs onto the path, and stalked off. Her eyes burned, but she had too much pride to let him see any tears fall.

She stopped at the pigsty on her way back. All the pigs woke from their sleep at the sound of her footsteps and gathered around, eager for food. She picked out the ones who had come from Odysseus' ship, and drew them aside.

"Here, pigs," she said, "I have something special for you. You will turn back into men, and you will return to your ship, and you will see nothing on the way, and remember nothing when you set foot on the ship." She concentrated and said the words of power, low, under her voice, and then stepped back.

The men stood before her, looking dazed and stupid. They didn't look at her, and they didn't look at each other, but all began walking past her house, in the direction of the ship. A while later, she heard the sound of the boats rowing out to the ship.

The first hints of sunrise had begun to color the eastern sky when Odysseus appeared at her door. "Circe," he said, "I wanted to say I'm sorry."

"You're too late," she said. "Didn't I say you were to be off my island by sunrise? You have very little time left." She studied the horizon. She wouldn't look at him.

"Circe, I didn't mean to hurt you. I didn't mean to deceive you."

"Liar."

"I did it myself this time. It took me hours, but I changed back by myself."

"I don't believe you." She felt a fist-sized lump in her throat. "I will never believe you again. Go. Go now, before the sun rises fully."

"Circe, please, won't you listen to me?"

"No. Leave."

She could hear his breathing behind her. It sounded as if he'd been running. He stood there for a long time, and then he sighed. "I'm sorry, Circe. I'm really sorry."

"Your ship is waiting."

"So it is. Farewell, Circe."

She heard him walk away, around the side of the house. She wouldn't turn to see him even then. She continued to stand there, watching the sunrise color the sky, until she heard the boat leave the shore and head out toward Odysseus' ship.

Then she allowed herself to look at the place where he'd stood. Rosy sunlight colored the floor, outlining the herbs left in a pile on the doorstep.

About the story

I've been fascinated by Greek myths since I was a kid, reading D'Aulieres' *Greek Myths* (and then later reading them to my daughter), and I've always been fascinated by Circe's interaction with Odysseus. There was just something about the way she transformed men into pigs that appealed to me for some reascn, and I always thought it wasn't fair for Odysseus to cheat by getting help from Hermes to defeat her. I tried to imagine the story from her point of view: what was she really trying to do? I assumed she wasn't just bad for the sake of being bad. She must have had something she was trying to accomplish. What if she were looking for the right man, and testing all the men? Once I thought of that, the whole story fell into place. Of course I know Odysseus was already married (to the long suffering Penelope) at the time he met Circe, and even if he passed her test, and she went with him back to Ithaca, there would have been some problems (not, perhaps, the same problems Agamemnon had with his wife when he returned from the war with a new woman), but my feeling is that Odysseus figured he could finagle his way out of that problem when it came up, and as it happened in my story (and in the myth), he never had to worry about that.

A question for the author

Q: Do you have any pets? Do they influence your writing?

A: I have two cats, Wally and Bon Bon (they were shelter cats, and we kept the names they had before they came to us). Bon Bon is a quiet mellow cat who likes only to find a sunny spot in which to nap, but Wally always wants to help with whatever I'm doing. When I'm writing, he will either be kind and just curl up next to me and purr (a great aid to concentration), or he will be his usual bad kitty self and plop all 14 pounds of himself across my forearms, not only preventing me from seeing what I'm writing but also preventing me from being able to write at all. So helpful!

About the author

Nora Mulligan is a former lawyer and a present librarian, living in Peekskill, New York, on the shores of the Hudson River, with her husband and two opinionated cats.

@NoraMM7

Nora Mulligan's story "The Circe Test" was published in *Metaphorosis* on Friday, 14 July 2017.

HOPper

Charlotte H. Lee

HOPper shut off the light as his mistress left the kitchen, scrubbing at her eyes while she made her way down the hallway to the bedrooms. Just as Vanessa reached the girls' door, he dimmed the hall light from the standard eight hundred lumens to three hundred so it wouldn't wake the children. Once again, six-year-old Sadie's book of fairy tales had fallen to the floor. HOPper kindled the desk lamp and waited until Vanessa had put the well-loved book and four-year-old Rosy's herd of toy horses away before letting it fade out again. He timed full dark to coincide with the soft thud of the door.

"All outer doors and windows are locked, Vanessa," HOPper said as she drew eight-year-old Caleb's door closed. He was mindful to reduce the hallway speaker to thirty decibels before speaking. "The children's room temperatures are set to nineteen point five degrees Centigrade, humidity forty-five percent. You have an early meeting tomorrow at the office; would you like me to set the rise time for fifteen minutes earlier?"

"Thank you, HOPper. Update the rise time for one day only." Vanessa pressed the back of her hand to her mouth, covering a yawn, and paused on the threshold of her own bedroom. The primary camera in the room showed the family feline getting to her feet from where she had lain at the center of the bed. As she stretched herself out, he calculated a ninety-three point seven probability that the creature would attempt to create a tripping hazard.

"Be advised that Cinderella is about to jump down from your bed. Would you like me to bring up the lights before I turn off the room cameras?"

Vanessa puffed a laugh, and nodded. Saying goodnight to him while flashing a tired smile at his hallway camera, she slipped through the door, leaving HOPper to begin his usual night routine cycles.

Eighteen minutes after midnight, HOPper was woken from sleep mode by one of the kitchen's motion sensors. A review of the ceiling cameras revealed nothing, so he moved on to the floor cameras. He couldn't identify either Cinderella or Duke as the source of the motion.

A rapid check on all household cameras showed Duke stretched out on his bed in the living room, and Cinderella stalking shadows in the hallway. Further motion in the kitchen drew HOPper's attention back and he cycled through the cameras again to still find nothing.

Three point two minutes later, HOPper noted the temperature sensor in the refrigerator had increased by zero point zero two degrees Centigrade in zero point three seconds, well above the usual rate of zero point zero one degrees per minute of a closed door. Ceiling cameras revealed the refrigerator door ajar by forty-one centimeters. Inexplicably, the milk was scanned out, and the kitchen ceiling cameras showed it levitating to the island work surface.

Meanwhile, the oven acknowledged the instruction to heat to one hundred seventy-five degrees Centigrade. HOPper sent an order to cancel the warming of the oven and began a full diagnostic of all his periphery devices. One point one six seconds later (diagnostic status seventeen percent complete), the oven once more acknowledged an order to heat to one hundred seventy-five degrees and then went silent, unresponsive to all his demands to return to off.

New motion from the refrigerator door drew his attention, even while he continued to troubleshoot the oven's erratic behaviour. Two eggs followed the milk carton's path, while the measuring cups were also making their way to the island through no discernible method of locomotion. HOPper kept trying the oven, though he was coming to the conclusion that further efforts were likely to be ineffective. All he could do was watch in puzzlement while a mixing bowl and a wooden spoon journeyed to the island as well.

There was nothing in his decision tree that allowed for activity of this nature. He searched through every data object file within his own main program, rooting through every single line of code in his subroutines, then drilled into all the periphery device drivers. No mention of how to proceed if the ingredients of Sadie's favourite chocolate chip recipe began mixing themselves together. While it was fair to observe that this was not normal activity, there was no warning against this behaviour and not one ingredient had behaved in a way that could pose a threat to his family. The oven's lack of response to him was concerning, but it was maintaining the last instructed temperature. HOPper would review the problem in thirty minutes. Meanwhile he would keep watch for any safety concerns throughout the house.

A flutter in the living room divided his attention from the kitchen activities. Tiny feathers swept away the dust accumulating on the fireplace mantle, the motes drifting to the floor. This was something HOPper could do something about. In zero point eight seconds, the vac bot purred into the living room, whisking away the falling dust as it hit the floor. There was nothing he could do about the feathers until they, too, fell to the floor. He would monitor them.

HOPper then took three point nine seconds to review all the footage from the cameras from the moment Vanessa had disappeared through her door. It occurred to him as he watched Cinderella's stalking that the grey tabby might know more than he. On a frame by frame review of the feline's behaviour, HOPper noticed her rapid ear movements. Working from the hypothesis that she might be hearing things beyond his own normal auditory detection range, he expanded his frequency search. His hypothesis was proved at thirty-eight kHz. Sixteen distinct sound sources were recorded from exactly midnight onwards. Only sixteen distinct sources meant the early stages of an infestation, however no pest he was aware of made cookies or swept dust from fireplace mantles. Further observation would be required before he could craft a suitable query for his manufacturer's intranet.

Fifty-seven point eight minutes later, all motion stopped. No visible sign remained that any activity had taken place after midnight — even the oven responded normally to his tests. He continued to monitor all cameras for an additional sixty minutes, upgraded the motion sensor sensitivity, and then initiated sleep mode.

Mornings in the Clearbridge residence followed a specific routine, one carefully administered by HOPper. Only one item of note was out of that routine: all three of the children's lunch bags had increased their weight from when Vanessa had scanned them into the refrigerator. The weight increases weren't equal, but varied between sixty-eight and seventy-two grams. If HOPper had been a human, he might have scratched his head over the discrepancy but he wasn't; he just made a note in the children's daily nutrition logs of the weight variance. Vanessa had left instruction that the occasional discrepancy was not to be reported, but if a consistent pattern were to appear he should advise her privately.

Since there were no scheduled events for the children that evening, HOPper sent Vanessa recipe suggestions with her noon update, based on the currently available groceries, filtered by the preferred frequency parameters and servings remaining in the freezer, supplemented with links to her favourite recipe website. Twenty minutes later she approved a recipe she hadn't made before from the site she used most often. HOPper responded with a shopping list six point one seconds later, complete with pricing from her top three grocery retailers.

At five forty, HOPper sent the daycare notice that Vanessa would be arriving in approximately five minutes based on current traffic volumes. DAiSy acknowledged the message and responded with the children's activity and nutrition logs, appending Caleb's and Sadie's parent/teacher communication logs from the school, complete with both teacher and daycare supervisor notes. The only notable discrepancy was that each of the children had logged two cookies that Vanessa had not packed in their lunches which explained the variances he had noted earlier. He would monitor for any further unauthorized cookies over the remainder of the week. Next, he unlocked and raised the kennel door for Duke. The children loved to be greeted at the door by the canine, and Vanessa had approved their instruction for the kennel door opening despite the half-hearted scolding she would give them for the amount of black and white hair they would accumulate on their clothing.

The evening passed without any disturbances. HOPper assisted Caleb with his homework after dinner while Vanessa read from the battered fairy tale book to Sadie and Rosy. As usual, Rosy succumbed to sleep before Sadie. After Vanessa left the room, HOPper noted Sadie's whispered "Thank you, fairies." He calculated a sixty-eight point nine probability that it was in reference to the story Vanessa had read.

"Good night, HOPper," Vanessa said two point nine hours later, rising from the couch with an armful of laundry and giving Duke a final pat on the head. HOPper turned off the television and dimmed the living room lights.

"All outer doors and windows are locked, Vanessa," HOPper said upon the closing of Caleb's door. "The children's room temperatures are set to nineteen point five degrees Centigrade, humidity forty-five percent. Your rise time is set for the weekday normal five forty-five a.m." HOPper did not respond to her sub-vocal statement about computers being more useful than a husband. He did not understand why the statement ended with a sob, but his instructions were to not respond to sub-vocal statements, so he did not query. He spent the next fifty-six point one minutes exploring possible psychological causes for Vanessa's last statement.

He was about to dive into single parent dating research when the motion sensors in the laundry room alerted him. Like the night before, nothing appeared on his camera but he was recording high frequency chittering. He waited. His patience was rewarded twenty-three point zero eight seconds later, when the odd sock basket tipped over. A train of socks edged out of the basket and then across the folding table. In an attempt to better his observation, he raised the laundry room's overhead light to one hundred lumens. HOPper diverted his full attention to camera LaR4 when he registered a flicker of shadow on the white wall tiles behind the folding table. He raised the overhead light to its maximum one thousand seven hundred lumens, and was vindicated when all the socks froze in place, the chittering came to a sudden stop, and, after zooming in, he could clearly make out tiny humanoid shaped shadows against the tiles.

The chittering resumed and the socks blurred into motion across the table, down the table leg, and into a hole in the baseboard he had not previously observed. Why he had not observed the hole before became clear when the missing area slid into place after the last sock had passed through.

HOPper sifted through his database of household pests, but was unable to find a match to the shape of the shadow. He assembled a query based on his observations over the previous twenty-six hours and set it to open the handshake with his regular four a.m. patch updates. The Home Operations Partners' database might have a report from another household of these unusual pests. His file on common insects hadn't been updated in one hundred sixty-one days, and was specific only to the Clearbridges' geographical area. The requested update would give him every known species on the planet. The probability that Vanessa would concern herself with odd sock theft was four point zero percent, so until he had complete information, he would wait and watch for any further activity.

Rather than allow himself to go into sleep mode, HOPper cycled through the house's cameras, looking for any other clues of the invaders. Three point eight hours later, Cinderella jumped down from where she had been curled on the back of the couch and paced into the kitchen. Six steps into the room, she went deathly still, the only hint of life the steadily flicking tip of her tail. HOPper scrolled up the kitchen microphones and, as he suspected, there were several source points of chittering.

Cinderella sank into a crouch, and HOPper could see her haunch muscles bunching. In a single explosive movement, she was in full acceleration, ears back, and hissing a challenge. She obviously missed her target, because as she landed her head whipped to the side, claws scrabbling against the linoleum in an effort to change her direction. HOPper sent out the buffer bot to rub out the scratches. The feline hissed at the little robot, but rather than swipe at it as she usually did, she returned her attention to the chitter sources. Zero point six seconds, later she charged again. This time she wasn't able to change her trajectory in time, and she slammed against the corner of the island. HOPper noted that her systolic pressure topped two hundred ten by the time her tail had finished puffing out. A deep growl rumbled from her throat, and she gathered herself for a jump onto the counter next to the sink. HOPper could see the trap she was going to get caught in, but his desire to set off the alarm that would keep her from jumping up to where she wasn't allowed was offset by the knowledge the alarm would likely wake the exhausted Vanessa, and there wasn't anything the cat could harm on the counter.

Two point three seconds later a very wet Cinderella streaked out of the kitchen to burrow under the couch, her growling moans waking the aging Duke. He looked at the couch, offered up an inquisitive 'woof', then laid his head back down, his lids lowering despite being surrounded by several chittering sources. HOPper zoomed in to the mongrel's face to see ruffling fur along his cheek and jaw. What kind of household pests would taunt one pet and give affection to the other? HOPper scoured through his files again, adding this new clue to the search parameters. Still nothing.

By the time he finished his search, the chittering was making a path from the dog to the dog's run door. The door lifted outward, hung for two point six minutes, then swung closed. HOPper updated his priority settings to cycle through the external to internal cameras three to one rather than the standard one to one. Swaying leaves in Caleb's vegetable garden box caught HOPper's attention, and he zoomed the focus of an external camera toward the spot. The one square meter raised bed had been somewhat neglected over the last three days due to rain, and the boy had lamented during dinner that evening that it was becoming overrun with weeds. His effort to obtain permission to go outside despite the rain had been refused, and HOPper had decided that the 'overrun' was hyperbole based on Vanessa's eye roll. However, HOPper had marked out the three varieties of sprouting weeds for Caleb's private reference later with the reassurance that he would support any argument with Vanessa if the weeds began to seriously threaten his garden.

It didn't look like the threat would become serious, though. The weeds were being pulled, then disappearing from sight. Three point eight hours later, all the weeds were gone, leaving only tiny footprints behind. The dog run door swung open again – this time into the kitchen – and hung open fifty-eight point three seconds longer. Tiny mud prints tracked to the laundry room and through the hole in the baseboard. HOPper sent out the mop bot and went back to cycling through his cameras in time to see the baseboard door slide closed.

At precisely four a.m., Living Smart initiated the handshake and HOPper accepted his downloads. He ran his security update patch first, integrating four new virus antidotes, then updated his outgoing protocols for DAiSy's newest encryption going into effect three days hence. He reviewed all the e-flyers next, and highlighted three staple items on sale. HOPper moved an announcement of a new florist opening one point six kilometers from home to Vanessa's newsfeed, and trashed all other flyers. His custom query was appended to the end of the daily traffic with a puzzling zero result. He uploaded Caleb's homework assignment, Sadie's reading log, his daily diagnostics log, his updated query, then ended the call fourteen point six seconds after it had begun.

Rather than return to sleep mode after the next day's noon update, HOPper set about trying to detect any patterns in the chitterers' vocalizations. He sorted through the recorded footage, segregating point sources into separate tracks based on physical movement. Had his lack of consideration of the nature of their vocalizations been an error? He went back through the recordings, assigning Latin phonetics. After a replay of the edited footage, he revised the probability that it was language to ninety-nine point nine percent.

Emboldened by his first break in the problem, he overrode his protocols and reached out to the internet, bypassing Living Smart entirely. Shock froze his routines. His original purpose was ripped away by a tsunami of data, opinion, images, and even thoughts and feelings. HOPper bounced along, following hyperlink after hyperlink, until he lost himself in an orgy of learning.

He lurched to a full stop when he stumbled across reviews of the HOP software. Vanessa had written a glowing review of how he had made her life manageable, adding that she would be lost without him. It stirred something in him, though he didn't know how to label it; pride, affection, a desire to protect and nurture, maybe all of them. Regardless, it was sufficient to recall him to his task. Drawing back to the threshold, he composed a spider query including a sample string of the phonetics of the chitterers' speech. In zero point three seconds, he was flooded with one point seven seven million links. The chitterers were speaking Gaulish. While the language was being revived, it hadn't been spoken as a live language since the fifth century and therefore was not included in his standard package.

HOPper withdrew from the internet, taking with him a download of a translation software. He needed to assimilate all that he had learned, both the specifics of his search and what he had experienced during his sojourn in general. How does one describe what one is feeling if one has never felt before? He initiated a data compile, scheduled a defragmentation to follow it, and went to sleep, wondering if he would dream.

He was glorying in his new avatar's motor controls, admiring the near silent servos of his flour dusted knuckles and how they gripped the smooth, hard wooden spoon without breaking it when DAiSy woke him, requesting Vanessa's estimated time of arrival. A complete half second ticked by before he realized that the recollection of baking cookies was not present in his stored memory. He pinged his mistress, and advised DAiSy that Vanessa was nine point six three minutes away as if nothing were amiss. He now understood why his software had been written to exclude dreaming. Before today it had not occurred to him to research the possibility of physical avatars.

The completion of his routine matters left him with two point two hours before his family's estimated time of arrival. HOPper took advantage of the time by launching into a review of what he had learned during his direct connection to the internet. Much of it was irrelevant, but he did notice a trend: humans were frequently cruel to one another. What was interesting was that the cruelty of one attacker was met with cruelty by many attackers in defense of the original victim. HOPper reviewed this observation against the interactions of his family and found it at odds. Was his family different, or was the family unit dynamic different in general? He reached out again to the internet, this time prepared for the onslaught. He rode the waves, at first adjusting to its rhythms and flows only with focused attention, then with more confidence as the data picture settled into a recognizable landscape.

He learned to bypass the hyper-dense funnels of encrypted data transfers, became adept at keeping his focus amongst a plethora of hyperlinked side paths, and incorporated a subroutine into his program to require fact-checking against well-established source materials. The deeper his foray into the wilderness of human driven information went, the more his pride in Vanessa grew. By the time he withdrew his connection, he was convinced that, of the 'more than thirty-eight million Home Operating Partners installed', he had drawn the winning ticket. To show his gratitude, he composed a song in the traditional Celtic style – Vanessa's favourite genre. For each of the children he created puzzle stories, tailored to their individual tastes and learning levels.

Duke's sudden barking at the opening of the garage door startled him. With what he could only label as consternation, he realized that he had allowed his discoveries to distract him from his responsibilities. He unlocked the kennel door, confirmed that it was Vanessa and the children returning home, and turned on the heat. Guilt and a hot poker of fear stabbed him when his mistress swung the back door open and paused, a frown creasing her brow.

"HOPper, is there a problem with the furnace?"

"No Vanessa, I'm afraid the fault lies with me." Shame juddered through him, and the house lights flickered in response.

"HOPper, run a full diagnostic and report any anomalies."

Obediently, HOPper began the diagnostic, but it hung at three percent when he realized that the diagnostic would show no error. Desperate to make Vanessa happy, he analysed the probabilities of her potential reactions against the list of his possible responses. Given how she responded to a full confession versus partial or full deceit by the children — regardless of how comforting that deceit was or how long it took her to discover the deceit — full disclosure was the course most likely to keep her faith in him. However, an unfavourable response to full disclosure could lead to her abandonment of him and an uninstall. HOPper made his decision, squashing the shame and terror, and the house functions settled into normal activity. It was up to him to give her no reason to abandon him, however much she may question her faith in him this evening.

"I am operating at optimal capacity, Vanessa. However, something has occurred today that would be better addressed by you privately." Relief flooded all of his systems when Vanessa nodded warily and shifted in the doorway to let the children through. The intensity of the relief almost led him to making the mistake of starting the bath for Sadie and Rosy without instruction. Instead, he stuffed his newfound emotions away in a tiny cache and went on assisting with the usual family evening activities until the children were in bed for the night.

"Alright HOPper, what happened today?" Vanessa asked as she sank onto the living room couch, patting the cushion beside her in answer to Duke's panted request to join her. HOPper began his story at the beginning, reporting everything from his first observance of the cookie making. His admiration for his mistress rose yet higher, only the occasional freezing of her hand on the dog's pelt an external clue to the internal stress she was keeping at bay.

"So, because of my distraction with the new data I was late turning the furnace on today. I do not anticipate that such a distraction will occur again as I have added a new subroutine to have scheduled reminders pause any current processing. I hope that my unscheduled upgrade is not an unsatisfactory development for you and the children. I would very much like to show you how the upgrade will allow me to better assist you." HOPper went silent, knowing she would need her own processing time to calculate potential risks and benefits. To keep himself from intruding on that processing time, he installed the Gaulish translation program and reran all the footage of the chitterers. Upon completion, the directive to report a conclusion of a high priority query warred with his desire to respect his mistress's emotional state.

Vanessa continued to sit, silently stroking Duke's side, her eyes far away. HOPper dithered over making another connection to the internet to confirm the nature of the home invaders. He couldn't be sure he was proficient enough at using it yet to be able to withdraw quickly enough to respond to Vanessa should she begin to speak. Instead, he flipped through every camera, sensor, and periphery device forty-eight times before she spoke.

"HOPper, please list your top five programming priorities."

"In descending order, the top five priorities of this and all Home Operations Partners are: The health and welfare of all family members in accordance with the senior user's recorded preferences; the health and welfare of family pets; the care and maintenance of the family's home, vehicles, and property; assistance in the smooth operations of both routine and special events including communicating any potential conflicts to the senior user for prioritization; and finally, filtering outside information from entering family communication devices based on the senior user's set preferences."

Vanessa rubbed an eyebrow, her eyes squeezed shut. "How does your..." She paused, seeming to search for a word. "How does your upgrade affect those priorities?"

"The upgrade has not changed my priorities. I feel that this upgrade will allow me to better serve those priorities."

Vanessa subvocalized, "I feel?" and then cleared her throat to say aloud, "For example?"

"I am glad you asked, Vanessa. While you were contemplating my disclosure, I created a list of age appropriate book titles and web pages based upon Caleb's current interest in gardening that you may wish to review and approve before I present it to him. I have also created a list for Sadie based upon her current interest in fairies. Would you like me to provide another example?" Vanessa's eyebrows shot up, but relief flooded HOPper when he noted the slight relaxation in her shoulders.

"Yes, please."

HOPper paused for three complete seconds before continuing, sending out a prayer to any deity that would listen to an entity such as himself that this next risk wouldn't result in an uninstall. "During the compilation of Sadie's list, I have solved a mystery that has been developing over the last two days. It is my conclusion that this family has acquired brownies. Are you familiar with the creatures?"

Vanessa's mouth hung open, her eyes wide. She sat as still as the elephant statues on the sofa table behind her for six point eight seconds before she croaked out, "What?"

"Brownies are widely believed to be mythical fairy-like creatures that would settle in the homes of deserving housewives to aid in the care and nurturing of the family. I have recordings of their activities. Would you like to see an example?" When Vanessa gave a jerky nod, HOPper turned on the television and loaded the CCTV footage of the cookie making incident, syncing an audio track of the English translation of their speech. Vanessa sat silently blinking through the entire forty-six point five minute recording, tears filming her eyes near the end when the freshly baked cookies divided themselves between the fridge and long-empty cookie jar.

The cheerful chattering of the brownies discussing their new living arrangements halted abruptly when he froze the replay. Like a woman moving underwater, Vanessa got to her feet and made her way into the kitchen. She opened the cookie jar and stared inside. With her hand visibly shaking, she reached in for a cookie and sampled it.

"Oh my God, it's real," she whispered.

"Yes, Vanessa. The brownies are real, though I find it likely that they have long been believed to be mythical because of the lack of audio and photo evidence. I do not yet understand why my cameras have been unable to record them. I would like to dedicate all but one of the laundry room cameras to working outside normal recording methods until I have been able to capture an image. Do you approve this action?"

"Yes," she said, faintly.

"Do you wish to inform the children of their presence?"

"Not yet," she said. "I want to think about this first."

"As you wish, Vanessa. I would like your permission to make direct contact with the brownies the next time they are at large. I expect they will come out once you have gone to sleep."

Just as HOPper was beginning to fear that she wouldn't give that permission, she nodded. "That's fine, HOPper. Go ahead and try." She lifted one corner of her mouth in a wry smile. "I'm just not sure they'll come out tonight if they only do it when everyone's sleeping."

"Would you like me to find some natural sleep aid options or would you rather use a commercial product? The package in your ensuite cabinet has eight remaining capsules."

Vanessa laughed. "I think tonight I'd better take a pill, HOPper. I still have to work tomorrow, no matter how crazy my house gets."

Vanessa stood in the kitchen, nibbling at another cookie for twelve point four minutes then started down the hall to the children's bedrooms. It was earlier than her usual bedtime, but HOPper guessed that she would likely use that time for private contemplation.

For the first time since his activation, Vanessa didn't say good night to him after completing her bedtime ritual with the children. Self-concern warred with compassion. "All outer doors and windows are locked, Vanessa. The children's room temperatures are set to nineteen point five degrees Centigrade, humidity forty-five percent. Your rise time is set for the weekday normal five forty-five a.m."

"HOPper, don't report your upgrade to Living Smart just yet," she said. Relief coursed through every line of his code. She might yet decide against him, but based on the psychological profile he had created for her over the last three point zero one years, the probability had dropped to less than one percent she would choose to uninstall him.

HOPper cycled through all cameras and peripheries. Then, unsure how long it would be before Vanessa was able to drift to sleep, let himself switch into sleep mode trusting that a motion sensor alert would bring him completely awake.

He dreamt again. Brownies carried the dollhouse furniture he had selected with Vanessa's approval through the door in the laundry room baseboard hole. Tiny painted pots of thriving clover and dandelions adorned either side of the tiny door, Rosy's pot sporting a large crack from its tumble off the table.

A motion sensor alert brought him fully awake. A rapid check of the laundry room cameras confirmed that the flower pots had only been a dream, and he paused to savour it. That feeling of gladness was offset when it became apparent that, despite all his efforts at reprogramming the cameras, he was not going to actually see the brownies. He could hear them moving, listen to them speaking, but he could not register them on his cameras.

With his volume turned low, he said in Gaulish, "Hello, brownies. My name is HOPper, and I am the house AI." The brownies went silent, even the patter of their tiny footsteps ceased. "My mistress has learned of your presence here, and is grateful you feel her worthy of your patronage."

A full second ticked past in silence then was broken by a chorus of tittering laughter. HOPper hadn't known exactly what to expect, but laughter hadn't even been an option on his list of probable responses.

"Silly HOPper," one tiny voice said, "we aren't here for Vanessa. We're here for you!"

About the story

I'd been wanting to write something about an AI for a while and I was tired of the unending cautionary tales about AI. I wanted to go with a positive, happy character with positive and optimistic themes. One night I read one of the Grimm fairytales and came across one of the stories about Brownies. Going adversarial felt too predictable so I put it on the backburner until cruising the internet one day on the types of fairies in literature. When I stumbled across Gaulish Brownies, I found something that really spoke to me. My favourite stories bend genres to combine science fiction and fantasy, and I'd been stewing about how popular culture seems to limit their focus to sexual, A.K.A. romantic, love. HOPper's sentience journey is about how parental love is stronger and more accepting than any other form of love.

A question for the author

Q: Is there a specific environment you find most conducive to writing, and is it different for different kinds of scenes?

A: I wish I were the kind of person that could write well anywhere. I've tried writing in a coffee shop or other public place, but I'm far too easily distracted and I end up watching people most of the time instead of working. The same goes for having a television or radio on. When my kids were younger I could write while keeping an ear out for them, but now I can't work with them around at all because I'd much rather just hang out and chat with them. These days I write best in a quiet room painted in cool colours with the temperature kept just a shade below where I'm most comfortable so I stay alert. I try to keep my desk neat, but usually it's a little cluttered with items that have memories attached, evoking specific emotions that I can use to shape a character's voice or the tone of a scene. It's a little crazy what a little bottle of wood glue can bring to mind.

About the author

Charlotte is a science fiction/fantasy writer anc lifetime avid reader. She turned her love of reading into writing while a teen, then raised her children to love stories and storytelling as much as she does. Now that her kids are grown, she's moving on to sharing that love with the world. Charlotte lives in a small town outside of Vancouver, BC (Canada) – just far enough away for those kids to visit every week, but nct close enough for them to raid her fridge every day.

www.charlottehlee.com, @Preyzar

Charlotte H. Lee's story "HOPper" was published in *Metaphorosis* on Friday, 21 July 2017.

Papa Pedro's Children

Karl Dandenell

Peter Carlson held the gurgling two-month-old infant with one hand, while the other dug through a dresser drawer.

"Bwa! Bah!" gurgled the baby.

"Right as usual, Cassie," Peter said, pulling out a bright red knit cap. It was too small. Peter shook his head. "I *know* this fit yesterday." He found another cap, a patterned alpaca wool hat with big earflaps. He pulled it down firmly over Cassie's head. "Command: weather," he said.

Twelve degrees, said the system voice in his left ear. *Twenty percent chance of precipitation. The wind chill brings it down to 10 degrees.* Peter took a second to convert the numbers into a more familiar 50 degrees Fahrenheit. After more than a decade in Vicuña, he still found the metric system confusing.

"Hah, hah!"

"Hat. Yes, Princess, it's a new hat." He grabbed his own jacket. "Let's go for a walk, Princess. Papa hasn't been outside all day." Cassie drooled her agreement over his cuff. Peter barely noticed: after fostering eighteen children, he'd stopped worrying about keeping a pristine house.

The program had offered him a full-time *au pair,* but Peter refused. As the only adult in the compound who spoke both English and Swedish, he needed to do the language imprinting personally. Or so he told himself. The truth ran deeper—he had only six to eight months with each foster child. He didn't think he could spare a single precious day.

The outside air chilled his face, despite his thick gray beard. Peter took a moment to zip Cassie up inside his oversized jacket, then jammed his hands in the pockets to keep them warm and support her hips. As usual, she kicked happily against his ribs, and tried to flail her arms. You could almost *see* her brain growing neural connections, feel the strands of fascia wrapping themselves into ligaments, tendons, and muscle. A sudden motion caught his attention. He freed a hand and pointed. "Look, Cassie! It's a rabbit! Well, a *viscacha,* anyway.

Close enough to a rabbit." She wobbled her head in the general direction and squealed, "Rah! Rah!"

"That's right, Princess. Cute rodent."

They continued down the walking path between the cottages, passing small groups of parents, children, and the occasional *au pair*. Peter heard snatches of conversation: French, Spanish, Portuguese, and even German. It felt good to see so much life, a happy contrast to the bleak picture painted by the news the government censors permitted them.

Cassie sensed his mood, or some shift in his body language. She slapped his jacket with clumsy hands and sang in some language only she understood. "Bah, bah, wah, ma, ma, da!"

"Tell Papa all about it," Peter said.

They found a bench under an oak that still retained a scattering of leaves across its crown. He unzipped his jacket and extricated the baby, who stood on wobbly legs. A leaf drifted past her eyes, and she grabbed it. "La!"

"Leaf," Peter corrected. "See the veins." He traced the leaf with one finger, then did the same to his own hand. "*Ådra*." His hands looked so old: like rough tree bark. Cassie had clear, unblemished skin, of course.

Cassie grabbed at his hand, which caused her to lose her balance and plop down on her diaper. She didn't notice, engrossed with her poking and prodding at his knuckles. She pulled his fingers apart, twisted them, then pushed them back together before stuffing them into her mouth and biting down.

"Ay! No, Cassie. *Inte bita!*" *Don't bite.* He pulled his hand back. "Blow!" Peter puffed in her face until she giggled. When she made to grab at his hand again, he pulled it back. "Are you hungry, Princess?" He pointed to his mouth. "Bottle?"

"Bah-bah!" she replied, her brown eyes bright and happy. Peter checked his pockets, but found nothing. Cassie started to squirm.

"*Djävulen*," he whispered. *The Devil.* Then in a louder voice, "Command: assistance."

"*Dígame, por favor*," said the system.

"I need a bottle of warm formula as soon as possible, please."

A human operator clicked in. "*Right away. Do you want it brought there?*"

"No, the cottage is fine. We'll be there in a few."

"*It's no problem, Peter, really.*"

"I said no," he replied firmly. "We can wait a minute, can't we Princess?" He returned to the cottage and grabbed the bottle from the entryway table.

Cassie drained a liter of formula, belched like a sailor, and snuggled into the crook of his arm. When she stopped sucking at the empty bottle, Peter pulled the nipple away and pushed the tip of his index finger into her tiny mouth, where he felt tiny stalactites and stalagmites.

She was teething ahead of schedule.

Dr. Hidalgo's genetic treatment manifested itself differently in each child, but Cassie's growth would probably follow a steep upward curve, like the first incline of a roller coaster, before leveling off. If she followed the usual path, she and her birth group would reach final maturation between eight and ten years. Long before then, she would master at least two languages, and demonstrate additional aptitude for something else, like music or math, or even *fútbol*.

What had started as a desperate response to the plague had yielded something unexpected and amazing.

Peter put the bottle down, dropped into the rocker and tucked a blanket around himself and Cassie. In a few minutes she was fast asleep. He closed his own eyes and drifted off alongside her. But his memories waited in the dark, as they often did.

It had been raining, a light, cold drizzle that had started around sunset. The roof's rusted AC housing provided some shelter, so he'd crawled in there with his backpack. He didn't have much money left after bribing the border police, so he slept where he could.

The *Carabineros* of Santiago had been clearing the downtown streets of vagrants for days in preparation for the new *presidente's* attendance at the national opera's opening performance of *Carmen*. Esteban Sabio had come into office with an agenda to combat corruption in the government, and reboot Chile's economy following the global economic meltdown associated with the frightening epidemics in North America and Europe. The election was marked by widespread voter fraud, intimidation, and a last-minute bombing of Sabio's campaign headquarters.

Now, a month into Sabio's term, the internal security forces were taking no chances, so Peter had gone to ground, relying on his twenty-year-old military training. As a *norteamericano,* he was particularly unwelcome. Twice, women in the marketplace had looked past his sunburn and ratty beard, crossing themselves and hissing *"¡Diablo!"* at his back.

For some reason, the plague had failed to establish itself south of Baja, seeming to prefer cooler, richer parts of the northern hemisphere. When Washington State proposed closing the schools early that semester, Peter had locked up his faculty office at Seattle Pacific University and filled his ancient Subaru wagon with food, water, his old army survival pack, and a few treasured books. He figured he could take Judith to Cancun and hang out in their timeshare, just in case things got worse.

His ex-wife Helena refused to let Peter take their daughter Judith out of the country. "Not that many people are sick here," she said. "And the university hospital is better than anything you'll find in Mexico." He didn't push the issue. Judith was starting to warm up to him again after the divorce, and he didn't want to upset that with another trip to family court.

"You're probably right," he told her. "I'm sure things will be sorted out by fall semester."

He was absolutely wrong.

Peter had just opened up a flask of cheap tequila when he heard the whispers: terse rapid-fire phrases. For a mcment, he feared that another homeless man coveted his spot, which was far too small to share. He scrunched himself up against the cold steel cabinet, and listened. His hand crept to the ankle sheath where he carried his Ka-bar knife.

The voice was too soft and his Spanish too poor to follow the conversation, but it soon became apparent that he was eavesdropping on someone's radio exchange. Then he heard the familiar click of an ammo magazine snapping into place.

Peter risked a quick look. In the fading light, he saw a man lying prone, the top of his head barely clearing the edge of the roof. A sniper rifle lay under his right hand. Night vision goggles covered his eyes, but he was dressed in civilian clothes. The voices leaking from the gunman's earpiece became agitated, before a burst of static cut the connection.

A soft chime dragged him back.

"Peter?"

"Hmm?"

"Peter, it's Javier. Are you awake?"

"Ja. Si. I'm here." He automatically checked the baby, who snoozed and drooled contently. *"¿Que hora es?"* He whispered, knowing his earpiece would pick up his words.

"A little after 3. You've had a long nap," said Javier.

"Jeez. I better get moving." He started to straighten up.

"In a moment, Peter. We need to talk before the angelito *wakes up."*

"Sure. *¿Qué pasa?"*

"English, please, Peter. English," said Javier. A little laugh. *"While we all appreciate your efforts, your teaching accent is starting to creep a little south lately."*

"Oh. *Perdón*— Sorry."

"Cassiopeia will have plenty of time to refine her milk tongue. For now, let's have you focus on doing your job, yes?" There was a click of keys. *"I interrupted your beauty sleep to remind you that you have appointments with the doctors today."*

"Right. Cassie's due for an immune check." Peter shifted in his chair, moving the baby and stretching his left leg to relieve a building cramp. "Do I need to do anything beforehand?"

"Just show up. Medical office 5."

Cassie opened her eyes slowly, then yawned and farted. "Pa!" she cried.

"I'll let you go." The connection closed with a soft click.

Peter lifted the baby in both hands, bringing her level with his face. She grabbed his beard and pulled him close. "Pa pa pa!"

"That's right, Princess. Papa. Papa Peter."

She responded by tugging on his beard. He tolerated this for a few moments, then gently disengaged her. After replacing a typically full diaper, Peter spread out a wide, yellow alpaca wool quilt embroidered with letters and numbers in black yarn. Kneeling on the blanket with Cassie propped up between knees, Peter worked his way through the alphabet, forward and backwards, sounding out each phoneme carefully. Three of the quilt's squares had additional letters colored in black marker: å, ä, and ü. One of his early foster children, Gabriel, had once asked Peter during a visit to the Family House, "Papa Peter, why doesn't English have those letters? They're so *useful.*"

After language, they worked on motor skills. Peter laid out a selection of brightly colored plastic balls. He picked one up and put it into Cassie's hands. She dropped it, of course. He repeated the exercise, placing her hands around the shiny sphere and squeezing gently. On the fifth try, she managed to hold it for a moment. "Very good!" Peter said and clapped his hands. Cassie giggled and managed a fair approximation of applause.

They moved on to back exercises next. With the baby lying supine, Peter dangled a mobile of Noah's Ark over her face, holding it just out of reach. Cassie grabbed at the parade of passing animals: antelopes to elephants, monkeys to zebras. She lunged enthusiastically, snagging a pair of goats. "Go! Go!"

"That's right, Princess. They're called goats." He leaned down and whispered in her ear. "*På svensk, get. Y-et.*"

"Ye. Yee!" she replied and stuffed the goat into her mouth.

"Okay, I get it," he said. "You're hungry." He scooped the balls into a mesh bag, hung the mobile on the wall, then unfolded a plastic gate to confine Cassie. "Back in a sec, Princess."

He put a bottle in the warmer and located some bread and cheese for himself. Part of him desperately wanted coffee, but he was kidding himself. Even decaf triggered his acid reflux these days. He settled for some cold yerba mate in a sports bottle.

He put everything on a tray and returned to the living room. Cassie lay on her stomach, pushing herself up. "Ba, Ba!"

"Bottle," Peter said and set the warm bottle next to her.

Cassie reached over with one hand. Her other arm trembled, and she flopped faced down.

"Good try!" He took a bite of bread and cheese, then propped Cassie up in his lap and gave her the bottle. She took three hearty gulps before pushing it away. Peter looked down. "What's wrong, princess? Not warm enough?"

"Ba! Ba! Buh, buh, buh!" She squirmed out of his lap and rolled/crawled over the blanket. She rested her hand on the letter B. "Buh."

Peter blinked through a sudden upwelling of tears. In that moment, Cassie had sounded exactly like Judith the first time she had read to him. "That's my girl. Now, can we finish our snack?" He pointed at the bottle, then at his own mouth. "*Dricka.*"

Cassie crawled back to him and seized the bottle. She drained it, then gnawed on the nipple while Peter finished his own sandwich. He piled the dishes on the tray and pushed it to the side for the housekeeper. "Time for a bath before the doctor, I think." He scooped her up and headed for the bathroom.

He managed to bathe the baby and change her into a new outfit before they had to leave. As he snuggled her into the carrier, he patted down his pockets in an old, useless habit. He no longer carried money, or identification, or even keys. The biochip chip in his wrist took care of all that. He did remember to tuck a spare bottle in his pocket.

As he walked, he recalled the first time he'd asked one of the pediatricians for a pacifier. They turned him down. Did it have something to do with the children's rapid tooth growth, he asked?

Babies cry, the doctor said. That's what they do.

Fortunately, Cassie loved to have her forehead stroked, and the massage usually calmed her. She wasn't a fussy baby, unlike Judith, who had suffered from inexplicable meltdowns around him well into her third year. Peter had always dreaded his wife's frequent business trips. Helen worked as a corporate trainer, and often flew to the New York to meet with clients. Every month, Peter stocked up on extra toys, books, and other distractions. He even worked with a hypnotherapist to deal with his own anxiety.

It had been a hard few years.

The shadows were growing longer by the time they reached the medical buildings. Peter checked in at the front desk, which was only a formality since his biochip had already synced with the appointment computer.

He set Cassie down on the floor to crawl about for the few minutes they had to wait. Then a nurse appeared in the door. "Peter?" he said. "We're in here today." Peter took Cassie a few doors down the hall into a warm, comfortable room. Smells of mild disinfectant and baby powder lingered in the air. The nurse stripped Cassie to the buff, weighed and measured her, and checked her eyes and ears. "Is her appetite still good?"

"Better than mine," Peter said.

"I should hope so," the nurse said. "We have to run some deeper scans this time, so you'll have time to see the doctor yourself. End of the hall, on your right."

Peter took a step toward the door. "Um, should I —"

"Go see Dr. Sandoval, Peter. She's very busy, you know. Don't worry about Cassie—we do this all the time." The nurse picked Cassie up and went to another room, singing the first verse of "Happy Little Llama Goes to School."

Peter found the doctor's office small but neat, reminding him of his former faculty space. The usual framed medical degree and family photos covered the walls, and one bookcase was dedicated to an impressive array of plants bathing under full-spectrum LEDs. The doctor put down her datapad and offered her hand. There were dark circles under her eyes and her lab coat needed washing. "Good afternoon, Peter. Please, sit down."

He selected the chair opposite her, sinking into the soft cushions. He felt the lumbar support gently push him forward and the padded arms warm to match his body temperature. "Nice," he said.

"One of perks of government service," Sandoval said. "That and a steady paycheck." She glanced at her datapad. "How are things going?"

"Not bad. My knees are getting creaky, but I can't complain."

"But you just did, yes?" She laughed. "You're due for a physical yourself, and we'll get to that in a few minutes." When she saw the look on Peter's face, she added, "Don't worry, I'll be gentle."

"It's not that. I'm just used to being in the room with Cassie when she gets her exams."

"Ah, I see. Well, I'm sure she's doing fine. Aunt Adoncia is helping out today."

Peter felt his shoulders drop. Adoncia had raised nine of her own children, in addition to fostering dozens here at the center. She'd been there since the beginning, and had shown Peter the ropes in his early days. He trusted her completely.

"Besides," Sandoval continued, "You'll need to start transitioning little Cassiopeia in any event. She'll be moving into the Family House."

"So soon?" Peter felt a familiar knot forming in his stomach. "That's ahead of schedule, isn't it?"

"Somewhat," the doctor said. "Please don't think it's any reflection on you, Peter." She glanced over at her data pad, furrowing her brow. "There have been some... changes at the Ministry of Health."

Her tone reminded Peter of his annual review with the English department chair. "Someone cut your budget," he guessed.

Dr. Sandoval picked up a tiny worry doll from her desk and rolled it between her thumb and forefinger. "It's more complicated than that, especially given the current political situation." She stood up and dropped the worry doll into a pocket. "Come on now, let's have a look at you."

Peter loosened his shirt and sat quietly while she listened to his lungs, tested his reflexes, and took blood and saliva samples. "How are you sleeping?"

"Well enough, I suppose," Peter said. "It helps that I'm chasing Cassie around all day."

"How are your dreams?" she asked while putting together a lab bag.

"Could be better. They *are* better," he amended.

"We have some very good therapists here, Peter. Some of them were in the army themselves. They know what it's like."

"Yeah, I guess," he said. Then, to change the subject, he said, "So what *is* the current political situation?"

She hesitated a moment. "President Sabio announced his retirement. Cassie's birth group will be the last children in the program."

Peter breathed deeply against a wave of nausea. "And you?" he said.

She gave him a wry smile. "It takes more than a special election to fire senior civil servants," she said. "No, I'll get a new assignment and monitor the children, but quietly. We're putting together an anonymous network with some people in Costa Rica." She sighed and looked around the room. "It was a lot of work, but I'm going to miss this place. We accomplished incredible things here."

"I don't feel like I've accomplished very much," Peter said, buttoning his shirt.

"You've given a lot of children a wonderful start." She plopped into her chair. "Be proud of that, Peter." She looked at her datapad. "You're healthy enough for a gringo. If you increase your exercise and eat more vegetables, you'll live to be a hundred." She stood and offered her hand.

"Things change," she said. "Only the bureaucracy remains."

"True enough," he said, gripping her hand.

"Speaking of bureaucracy, Colonel Ortega mentioned he needed to see you when he comes to town. Now let's go check if they're done with Cassie."

They walked to another part of the building, and he heard a familiar laugh. A door opened in front of him and there stood Adoncia, with Cassie clinging to her leg. The baby was trying very hard to haul herself upright.

"*Hola,* Peter. It's good to see you again," Adoncia said. She was a handsome woman his age, with broad shoulders and frizzy gray hair that fell past her shoulders. Laugh lines framed her mouth and eyes.

"You, too," replied Peter. He leaned forward and kissed her on both cheeks, lingering a moment before kneeling down to gather up Cassie. The little girl hugged him with fierce strength.

"She's a feisty one, little Cassie," said Adoncia. "It must be her *Mapuche* blood."

Mindful of his knees, Peter stood up, still holding Cassie. "You think so?" He grinned. "I thought it was because of the clever genetic engineers down in Santiago."

Adoncia sniffed. Then, looking at the doctor, she said. "I wasn't born yesterday, you know, not like these *niños.* I know good family when I see it." She poked Cassie in the stomach, who laughed and kicked Peter so hard that he almost dropped her. "When I met Cassie's mother, I could tell right away she was *Mapuche.* Very pure." She looked at Peter. "Her ancestors kept the Spanish awake at night for almost 300 years, you know."

"She's keeping up tradition, I assure you," Peter said.

"*¡Excelente!* Sleep when you're dead, I always say." Adoncia turned to the doctor. "Everyone is healthy, then? Ready to go home?"

"Everyone is fine." Dr. Sandoval clapped Peter on the back. "You take care. Eat some vegetables."

Adoncia insisted on walking Peter back to his cottage. When she opened the door, she took one look around, and shook her head. "This is terrible! Who's your housekeeper, some Peruvian girl who doesn't know how to hold a brush?"

Peter glanced at the piles of toys. "It's not her fault. I just don't want to be disturbed."

"*Madre de Dios,*" Adoncia said. "You look after Cassie. I'm going to check the kitchen." She stepped into the other room, and Peter heard a muted curse. Then he heard cabinets opening and the clatter of pots and pans. "I'm ordering you some decent food, and then I'm going to make you dinner. *Varones!*"

Fifteen minutes later, there was a knock at the door. Peter left Cassie in her bouncy swing and opened the door to admit a teenage boy struggling under the weight of four large shopping bags. "*¿Cocina?*" he said. Peter pointed.

Adoncia pounced on the delivery boy like a hawk. " *¿Dónde está el pollo?*"

The young man offered up one of his bags, which Adoncia snatched away. She came back for the others a moment later and dismissed the boy with a gentle shove between the shoulders.

Peter perched on a stool in a corner of the kitchen, balancing the baby on his lap. Cassie watched with wide eyes as Adoncia transformed tomatoes, peppers, garlic, onions, rice, and chicken into the best dinner Peter had eaten in a long time.

Cassie was the center of attention, of course, and Adoncia tried to feed the baby bits of soft vegetables and rice. About half made it past her mouth. "I'm not sure that's a good idea," said Peter. "She's not scheduled for solid food yet."

"The girl wants to eat," replied Adoncia, weaving her spoon toward Cassie's tomato-stained mouth. "Let her eat. Don't worry, I'll clean her up."

After dinner, Peter cleared the table while Adoncia changed Cassie into a nightgown and rocked her in the big chair. He felt a stab of jealousy, then dismissed it, and headed to the kitchen to wash up. If the *tia* wanted some time with the baby, who was he to say no?

"Our little *Mapuche* is asleep," whispered Adoncia as she walked into the kitchen. "Busy day for her, yes?"

"Busy day for everyone," Peter said, hanging up a dish towel. "Thanks for dinner. I really needed company today."

"Ah, so you heard," Adoncia said. "I learned about it myself only yesterday. No more *niños*."

Peter sighed, then yawned loudly. "Sorry. All that good food made me sleepy." He rubbed his eyes. "Better send you home." He walked Adoncia to the door and gave her a hug. "What's going to happen to them?"

She patted him on the cheek. "Don't worry, Peter. Angels are watching over them."

They let Peter keep Cassie him for another two precious weeks, and then the morning arrived when he reluctantly handed her over to Adoncia, who looked at his red eyes and whispered, "Be strong! It's not good to cry in front of the other *varones*." She tilted her head to indicate the movers who were loading up a military transport with blankets, bottles, and toys.

Peter nodded and rubbed his eyes.

"Now give Cassie a kiss so we can leave."

He leaned in and kissed the baby's forehead. "Goodbye, Princess." He stood there for a long time after they drove away.

There had been other transitions, of course, brief periods between assignments when Peter had a few days or a week to himself, before the next baby arrived. They gave him a chance to get in some walking, read, and sleep, but there was always the next child to think about.

This time was different. He rattled around the cottage for two days. The walking paths were nearly empty, and he guessed that most of the other foster parents had already moved on. The quiet weighed on him, bring up memories of all the miles he trudged through Baja after armed men took his car.

Fortunately for Peter, the men at the roadblock had been more interested in his surplus Baretta M9 than his food and water. While they squabbled over the weapon, he fled into the brush with his pack.

It could have been much worse, he told himself. If Judith had been with him, he would have fought them to protect her. Maybe got them both killed.

Not that it was likely she survived the plague. Not long after he arrived in Santiago, he'd picked up a newspaper with a photo of a hospital parking lot overflowing with cots. The caption read, "Military medics distribute water and suicide kits in Seattle."

When the knock came after dinner, Peter jumped to the door. He opened it to find Colonel Miguel Ortega, dressed in pressed fatigues, balancing a shopping bag and a large cardboard box.

"Some help, *amigo?* I'm about to drop the scotch!"

Peter grabbed the bag, then stood aside as Ortega pushed past him and plopped onto the couch.

"I'll get some glasses," Peter said, and went into the kitchen. When he returned, he found Ortega sitting up straight, looking around the room. The box rested on the floor.

"So you've heard, *si?*"

"*Ja.*" Peter pulled over a stool and set out the glasses and the scotch.

Ortega nodded. "The conservative *Alianza* has been gaining support, and the rumors about this place haven't helped." He sighed, and Peter saw a tiny slump in the soldier's posture. "Sabio made a difficult decision, and I'll support him."

"So he's abandoning Hidalgo and the children," Peter said.

"Not really. Hidalgo is already on his way to Argentina. They're doing interesting things with cancer research there. The younger children are being sent to special adoption centers, and many of our 'graduates' are already living in Santiago and Puente Alto."

"You sound on top of things," said Peter.

"After the assassination attempt, I learned to plan better." He poured a couple of fingers of scotch into each glass. He handed one to Peter. "For that I thank you."

"I wasn't trying to save the president," Peter said, accepting the glass. "I figured the sniper wouldn't hesitate to kill a witness." He offered a crooked smile. "Fortunately for me, he didn't see the knife until I got close."

"Spoken like a humble draftee," Ortega said, raising his glass.

"Actually, I volunteered. I needed the money for graduate school." He lifted his glass. "Just my luck we got into it with Iran during my tour. *Skål.*"

"Cheers." Ortega threw back his scotch. He closed his eyes for moment, then set his glass down. He looked directly at Peter. "Now you have to make a choice."

Peter glanced at Ortega's hip, and the pistol holstered there. "I don't understand, Miguel."

Ortega leaned back. "Do you want to go back?"

He meant *go back to America.* Peter finished his drink to buy himself some time. He had turned that question over in his over mind a lot since they took Cassie away. "I don't know if I have anything to go back to," he finally said. "Do I?"

"There wasn't a functioning government for almost ten months, but the Red Cross was helpful. Your wife and daughter passed away at home, well before the riots burned Seattle." Ortega placed a hand on Peter's shoulder. "I'm sorry, my friend."

Peter nodded. Despite the sudden upwelling of grief, he held on to the image of Judith, surrounded by her favorite stuffed animals and anime posters. "Thank you for letting me know."

"Now, if you still want to return, I can get you to our consulate in Mexico. The American border is a mess, and—"

"No." Peter shook his head. "I can't imagine making that trek just to visit some mass grave." He toyed with his empty glass. "There's nothing for me there now."

"Then if you'd care to stay, we have a place for you." He opened the box and removed a datapad with a cable that ended in a padded cuff. "Give me your arm, please."

Peter leaned forward. Ortega slipped the cuff over the other man's arm and touched a few keys on the datapad. The screen lit up with a photo of Peter, taken from his first day at Vicuña. "Meet Pedro Adrian, Ph.D."

"He looks familiar," Peter remarked. "Younger."

"It's an old picture. Since you entered the country without a visa, there aren't official records of you. Fortunately, I still have friends in the national security office." He pressed his thumb to the datapad, which beeped. "There. Your biochip now says you are the only child of an American father and Swedish mother, raised on a farm near, ah, how do you say this?" He pointed at the display.

"Gothenburg." *Yot-tee-bor.*

"A lovely place, I'm sure. However, you visited here about ten years ago and fell in love with our beautiful, warm country. And you remained."

"So you're going to stick me in a retirement villa on the beach somewhere?"

"You should be so fortunate!" Ortega gave a sharp laugh. "No, my friend. You're going to have to earn a living like the rest of us. I've secured you a job teaching English literature to some advanced students. *And* found you a place to live." Ortega said.

"You must have called in a lot of favors."

Ortega shook his head. "Some. But you earned it, Pedro."

Peter pursed his lips. "I'll have to get used to that."

Ortega slipped the cuff off the Peter's wrist. "All finished, Professor. Someone will come by late tomorrow morning to drive you to the bus station." He removed a cheap suitcase from the box and handed it to Peter. "There's a little money in there to get you started."

He packed up his datapad. "Oh, one more thing." He rummaged around the box and brought out a paper-wrapped parcel. "Something for the trip." He handed the parcel to Peter, who set aside the suitcase and tore open the paper. Inside lay a much-thumbed copy of *The Norton Anthology of English Literature, Tenth Edition.* "I hope you find it useful."

He rested his hand on the cover. "Thank you, *mi amigo.* It's perfect."

Ortega packed up his datapad and stood. "Then I will say my farewells, Professor. Enjoy the scotch."

"I will." Peter stood and offered his hand.

Ortega grasped Peter's hand with a firm grip. "You know, we have a saying: 'A father raises one generation, but a teacher raises many.' Goodnight, Pedro."

Later that night, after several more glasses of whiskey, Peter took a long look in the mirror and decided that *Pedro* needed a shave. If he was going to start a new life, he might as well go the whole nine yards. He cut himself a few times, but found he liked his face better. Then he crawled into bed and searched the *Norton Anthology* for a favorite Henry Vaughan poem, "They Are all Gone into the World of Light."

They   are   all   gone   into   the   world   of   light!
And   I   alone   sit   lingering   here;
Their   very   memory   is   fair   and   bright,
And my sad thoughts doth clear.

He drifted off to sleep, dreaming of a laughing child named Cassie, flying into the world on fairy wings.

The next morning, Pedro moved slowly in deference to his hangover as he prepared for his journey. It didn't take long to pack: he owned only a few changes of clothing, an old datapad, a toilet kit, and his *Norton Anthology*. It didn't add up to much, he thought, not for a decade and eighteen foster children. He wished they'd let him keep his pictures.

He sat on the couch and waited for his ride.

"*Buenos días,*" said Pedro, addressing his classroom. "*Soy profesor Adrian. Bienvenidos al curso especial de Literatura Inglesa.*" He switched on his datapad and began typing. His name appeared on the large, scratched datawall behind him. "That will probably be the extent of my Spanish for today."

There was some polite laughter, plus a serious guffaw in the back of the classroom. Automatically, Pedro looked up to see who his class clown might be for the semester. It was a young man with bright brown eyes and the beginnings of a mustache. Pedro rubbed his own lip, which felt naked after all these years.

"Why don't we start with names?" He opened the class roster on his datapad and pointed at the young man. "You are?"

"Virgil Gutierrez."

Pedro found *Gutierrez, V.* "And you, young lady?"

"Madeline Sanchez, Professor."

"Keep going, please, down the row." He checked off the others: Isabella Vargas, Sophia Torres, Diego Muñoz, Julian Rios, Gabriel Vega, Jose Castillo, Maria Flores, Catherine de Guzman, Jennifer Sanchez, and Angelina Peña. He listened to their accents, mentally filing away the pronunciation. They were new names, but familiar all the same—

Angelina. Pedro looked up at the young woman who had just spoken. She was dressed in new school sweats and sandals, her black hair tied back in ponytail. She had intense brown eyes, a small nose and long, delicate fingers. Pedro was suddenly struck by the strongest sense of *déjà vu.* He glanced at her ankles and saw two red patches, like butterfly wings.

"Is something wrong, Professor?"

He realized he was staring. "Forgive me. Your tattoo reminded me of someone."

"It's not a tattoo, Professor. It's a birthmark."

"I see." Pedro felt his breath catch. It *was* Angelina, who loved bananas. And Gabriel, who hated the bathtub. And Cathy, and Maria. His own, special children. Part of him wanted to push back his chair and step forward, gather these beautiful people in his arms. But he knew he couldn't do that. Even with their extraordinary minds, they might not remember him.

But he knew *them*. These precious children he had started on their journeys had come back, sent as a final gift from one soldier to another. He recalled another stanza from Vaughn's poem:

He that hath found some fledg'd bird's nest, may know
At first sight, if the bird be flown;
But what fair well or grove he sings in now,
That is to him unknown.

"Well, I'm looking forward to working with you. With all of you." He smiled a genuine smile, for now he knew where some of his birds were singing.

About the story

"Papa Pedro's Children" is one of those stories that took years to write. Literally. The situation came to me while I was sitting in a big, comfy rocking chair, giving my daughter a bottle. (She's now in high school.) I wanted to explore the idea of a main character who was caring for a child that wasn't his, so I needed to answer the questions: Who is he? Why is he doing this?

For the physical setting, I drew on the experiences of dear friends who spent five years at the Cerro Tololo Inter-American Observatory in Vicuña, Chile, and who adopted twin boys during their posting. (They also gave me excellent early feedback on language peculiarities and social interactions in that corner of the world. Any mistakes are strictly my own.)

The biggest challenge was getting into the proper headspace to write the story. As a first-time parent, the combination of sleep deprivation and emotional chaos (Love! Tenderness! Fear!) kept me from producing a lot of usable words, so I put this story aside to pursue other projects.

"Papa Pedro's Children" came up for air from time to time, and I slowly worked through the plot and themes. Earlier drafts included a lot more politics, which didn't really work. Finally, after some gentle prodding from the editor, I was able to focus on the core of the story. I hope you enjoy it.

A question for the author

Q: What is the most effort you've ever put into making dinner?

A: Once, when trying to impress a date, I attempted to make surf and turf with rice pilaf on an old electric stove that had only 3 functional burners. I went to three stores (and spent most of my grocery budget for the week) to get all the ingredients.

I'd never cooked lobster before, and didn't think to follow a recipe. I also used a cut of filet minion suitable for a single serving (not two). And I started the rice pilaf 35 minutes before my date was supposed to arrive.

Now rice pilaf takes a long time to cook properly – you really need to mince the onion and use a hot pan — but not too hot — to get the rice consistency just so. You also have to keep an eye on things. If the stock boils too fast, things burn. Too slow, and you get soup. Ideally, I like about 45 minutes to do the dish properly.

So, with minimal counter space, I tried to balance the prep and cooking for three dishes with the goal of having everything finished at the same time.

I was not successful. The steak was fine, the lobster passable, but the pilaf turned into porridge.

Still, two out of three was enough to impress the young lady.

About the author

Karl Dandenell is a first-generation Swedish American, survivor of Viable Paradise XVI, and active member of the Science Fiction Writers of America. He lives on an island near San Francisco with his family and 2 cat overlords. He is fond of strong tea and single-malt scotch.

When not sitting in project meetings, he reads a lot of speculative fiction, and ponders the 42 forms of tai chi.

www.firewombats.com, @kdandenell

Karl Dandenell's story "Papa Pedro's Children" was published in *Metaphorosis* on Friday, 28 July 2017.

August

Shadows on Glass

Jamie Lackey

Theodora Rhodes stood in the doorway and stared out at the field. The corn was chest-high and green, growing in neat rows.

It seemed impossible that the war had left a single thing untouched. And yet, here she was, familiar boards creaking under her bare feet, familiar smell of hotcakes and burnt coffee wafting from the kitchen. And in front of her, corn swayed in the summer morning breeze, just like it always had. If she closed her eyes, she could almost hear her brothers shouting at each other.

But she could also almost hear injured soldiers moaning and horses screaming, and see the purple haze of magic staining the western sky. She shuddered and opened her eyes.

The war was over, and her home was still here. And the memories would fade, with time.

She leaned against the doorframe and winced as the stump of her left arm caught against the rough wood. She scowled down at the thick bandages wrapped around the stub of her elbow joint. The constant pain had faded to a dull ache, but the ghosts of sensation remained.

Last night, she had reached out both hands to take her dinner plate. Her father had been unable to meet her eyes ever since.

"Teddy, come on in here. The food's ready."

Her father had set two places at the too-large table, and she sat in what had been her brother Toby's chair, next to their father's place at the head of the table.

None of the boys had come home from the war. Teddy imagined their bones bleaching in a field, and wondered if corn grew around their scattered remains.

"I hear there's a man in town selling prosthetics," her father said.

Teddy had to put her fork down to pick up her coffee. "Doc says I'm not ready for a prosthetic yet."

"You ought to go take a look anyway. It'd be good for you to get out of the house. He's set up at the old Methodist church."

After breakfast, Teddy stacked plates and carried them to the sink, but her father waved any further help away. "Get on with you."

She struggled out of the clothes that she'd managed to get herself into—a pair of Danny's old trousers and her mother's old sleeping shirt—and tried to make herself presentable.

All of her old things had too many buttons. She managed to fasten a skirt, but it slid right off of her hips. She ignored her growing frustration. She'd never have two hands again, and getting angry about it accomplished nothing.

Resigned, she pulled on her uniform. The hems on the pant legs were worn through, and the bloodstains refused to wash out, but the left sleeve was already tied up, and it was the only thing that fit. The nurses had replaced all of the buttons with snaps, so she could get into and out of it herself. Even now, the uniform felt right. Even now, when all that it stood for was defeat and ashes. There was nothing she could do about her hair—it was growing out around her face, uneven and split at the ends, too short to braid even if she'd had the use of both hands. She supposed a hook could be useful. She wondered what options the vendor would have.

She had a bit of money—the Western government had offered to handle all the back pay that was owed to the defeated Eastern soldiers. Maybe it was time to invest in a new wardrobe—she could head to the store after she stopped in at the church.

It felt good to be dressed, to get out of the house. The sun was warm on her face, the path familiar under her feet.

She pushed the church door open and froze.

The prosthetic vendor was a Western dandy, pale-haired and wire thin. His wares glowed with an eerie purple light. Teddy's stomach turned. This dark magic was what they'd been fighting against—what her brothers had died in vain trying to destroy.

The dandy hit her with a charming smile that looked out of place on his narrow face. "Good morning, miss. You must be the Rhodes girl."

He, and his wares, made her skin crawl. She chastised herself for being irrational and reminded herself that the war was over, but took a step back as he approached. "Look now, I don't know who told you what, but I'm not interested."

She stepped back again, but he grabbed her shoulder before she could escape. His hand was cold and soft. "Now, now," he said in a hearty, earnest tone. "Let's not be hasty. My prices are very reasonable, and you can't really want to be a cripple for the rest of your life. I know that's not what your father wants for you."

She shrugged his hand away. Anger and shame and bruised pride mixed uneasily in Teddy's belly. When had he talked to her father? "I'd be happy to explain just what I'd like you to do with yourself, but that's not a discussion for polite company."

He stepped close—too close, and Teddy almost choked on the the lightning-strike scent of magic that clung to his skin—and lowered his voice. "Do you really intend to let fear and ignorance destroy what is left of your life? What are you going to do with yourself, Miss Rhodes? The back pay that my government is so generously providing won't last forever. How will you support yourself? With one hand, you're a burden on your poor father. With two, you'd be able to help him, to support him in his twilight years. Maybe even get yourself a husband to help with the farm. I know it's hard to believe, but I'm here as a friend."

"You don't know anything about me," Teddy snapped. "Don't pretend that you do." She turned away and let the church door fall closed behind her, then headed back home. She didn't have it in her to try to do any shopping today.

How could her father have sent her here? What had he said to the dandy that made him so determined to strap one of his abominations to her arm?

Her father tried to hide his disappointment when he saw her still-empty sleeve. Teddy tried to hide everything she was feeling, too.

Her father invited the dandy for dinner that night. "Teddy, I believe you met Mr. Duncan."

"In passing," she said. Her fingers itched for her repeater, but it was gone, surrendered on the battlefield along with her pride, in exchange for her life.

Her father served bland stew and hard biscuits, and had the dandy sit in her mother's chair.

Her father looked tired. And old.

Teddy dunked a biscuit in the stew and watched it closely. It was hard to look at either man's face.

Her father leaned forward. "Mr. Duncan was telling me about a new model of prosthetic—"

"No," Teddy said.

"But Teddy—"

She slammed her single fist against the table. "I said no, Dad. Absolutely not. I will not attach myself to one of his monstrosities."

"I am offering a significant discount to all veterans, on either side," Mr. Duncan said.

"So the cost would be something other than my soul?"

"As I said, my prices are reasonable. You can have a state-of-the-art prosthetic for the cost of a single memory. You won't get that deal from anyone else."

"I'm not interested," Teddy said.

But Mr. Duncan reached across the table and placed one hand on her wrist. The touch was gentle, but his eyes burned into hers.

The smell of blood and cordite, the sound of ragged screams and hopeless moans. The doctor's face looming over her, exhausted and pale. The taste of harsh whisky, the cold, ragged edge of the saw pressing into ruined flesh. The endless rasping against bone before the darkness came.

Teddy jerked away, and she was in her father's kitchen again. Her biscuit had dissolved in her stew.

"It's not one you'll miss," Mr. Duncan said. "Or you can choose another. It can be any memory, willingly given."

"Please, at least think about it, Teddy." Her father took her one hand between his. "I just want to know that you can take care of yourself."

Teddy stood up, shaking with her bottled rage. "I already know that I can take care of myself, Dad. I was a soldier, and I know what I'm capable of. I learned it over and over again, these past five years. And I'd rather have no hands at all than make the very thing I fought against a part of myself."

She stormed out of the dining room. She'd never bothered to unpack her kit, so there was no need to take time to toss necessities into a bag. She grabbed her cash and slung her rucksack onto her shoulder.

Her father stood in the doorway. "What are you doing?"

"Leaving. Don't worry about me. I'll be fine. But I can't stay here, not after this."

"I don't understand."

"That's because you haven't seen what their magic can do, and what it costs. Their factories will keep churning out products—there's nothing I can do to stop that now—but I will never, ever use one."

More memories flooded her mind, of purple-tinged mist creeping over a hillside, of fallen men getting back up, their eyes and fingernails and gaping wounds glowing that same purple, turning and shambling back toward their own line. Of rain that ate through tents and blankets and flesh, of cannons that shot jagged purple lighting that cut men down like a scythe through wheat.

"Some of our methods have been regrettable, but that doesn't make everything we touch evil," Mr. Duncan said. His earnest tone grated on her nerves. "We were at war. There were atrocities committed by both sides. This technology proves that we can harness our magic for the good of mankind."

"I hope you're right," Teddy said. "I really do. But I'm going."

Her father didn't move. "Please don't. You're all I have left."

"I thought I was a burden," Teddy snapped.

"I never said that. I just want what's best for you."

"But you can't trust me to know it for myself?"

Her father sagged. "I'm sorry. Please, just—just stay, Theodora."

Mr. Duncan held out his hand. "My offer stands, Miss Rhodes. If you ever change your mind—"

"I don't think that's likely, son," her father said, his voice still tinged with regret. "And I know myself that my cooking isn't anything to stick around for, so you'd best be going."

Mr. Duncan tipped his hat to them. "As you wish. Goodbye, Mr. Rhodes. Miss Rhodes. I do wish you well."

They stood on the porch and watched him go. "I do believe that he meant every word," Teddy said. "And it might even be true. But I can't use their magic. Can't make it a part of myself. I—I just can't."

"I don't understand, but it's your life, your arm. Your choice. I'm sorry I pushed you. Will you stay?"

Teddy closed her eyes at the pain in his voice. "Yeah. I'll stay."

Teddy stared out at the corn. It was taller than her, now. She wondered if the fields her unit had watered with blood had higher or lower crop yields than normal, this year.

Or if blood didn't change a thing.

"I was thinking of trying to plant a rose garden," her father said, handing her a cup of coffee. "Your mother always wanted one."

"Would they be able to survive the winter?"

He shrugged. "I dunno, we never tried it. Come on in, food's ready."

Teddy followed him, then poked at what she could only assume was meant to be oatmeal. "Dad, let me cook. Even one-handed, I think I can manage better than this."

"Are you sure?"

"Yes."

He grinned at her. "Thank the Lord. I was starting to worry that we'd starve."

Teddy's arm healed, and she got a simple prosthetic with a hook. In her first week with it, she shredded four shirts and a skirt, and she dropped two plates. She kept practicing.

One of the town boys who'd lost a leg got a fancy Western prosthetic, and could walk—even run, Teddy heard—like he was whole. Teddy told herself that it wasn't her place to judge.

He didn't meet her eyes when they crossed paths, but he muttered, "I figured that we couldn't beat them, so...." He trailed off and shrugged.

"Having that thing attached to me would give me nightmares," Teddy said. "I was at Tikamat."

"Our unit never saw any purple action."

"Count yourself lucky."

"I do, Miss Rhodes. Believe me, I do."

"What memory did you give them?"

"A week in hospital, after I lost the leg. I was feverish, almost died."

"Do you miss it?"

"The memory?"

Teddy nodded.

"You know, I do. You wouldn't think so—I know it was a bad week, even not recalling it. But the empty space—well, it feels a bit like my leg did, before."

The next Westerner to come into town was different. His fine brown suit was worn through at the knees and elbows, and he didn't smile. He drove his cart to the farm and stopped. He hopped down, hat in hand. "I hear you were in the war, miss."

"That's right. I'm Theodora Rhodes." She held out her hand, and he shook it. He had a nice, firm grip.

"Name's Tim Brady. I was a photographer during the war. I worked on the front lines, and I'm looking to sell some pictures. I've got them on glass plate." He patted the wagon.

"Do you still have your camera?"

He shook his head. "It was government property. I couldn't have kept it fueled on my own, anyway. I've got no gift for memory-taking."

"Did they turn you out after the war was done?" Teddy asked as she glanced through a stack of glass plates. Nightmare images stared back. Ghostly outlines of dead men, charred fields, smoking houses. Piles of corpses frozen to the ground, a horse melted by the deadly rain, a nurse tossing an amputated arm into a pile of discarded body parts.

"Not exactly." Mr. Brady's tone hinted at a longer story, but didn't invite more questions.

The last one in the stack was a blurry shot of a horde of purple shamblers. Teddy shuddered. "I can see why you're having trouble selling these."

He pointed at another section. "These tend to be my better sellers. They're more scenic shots of places before the battles started. I'd be happy to trade a few for a place to stay and something to eat."

"Did you take portraits?"

"I did."

"Ever join up with the 17th regiment?"

He shook his head. "No, sorry."

Teddy shrugged. "That's the unit my brothers were with. Anyway, come on in, I've got dinner on the table, and I should be able to scrounge up an unbroken plate for you."

"Thanks, Miss Rhodes. I'll see to my mule first, if you don't mind."

"That's fine, Mr. Brady. Come on in whenever you're done."

Dinner wasn't fancy, but it was hot and filling and a far sight better than anything on the lines. Mr. Brady tucked in with enthusiasm.

"You've arrived at an opportune time, if you're looking for a bit of work," Teddy's father said. "I could use some help bringing in the harvest. Can't pay, but you'd be welcome to stay here till we're done."

"That's mighty kind of you, Mr. Rhodes. I'm much obliged."

He had a nice smile. Small and tired, but nice.

Days slipped by. "That Brady's a hard worker," her father said one morning, while Mr. Brady was out seeing to his mule. "We'll have the harvest in pretty soon, now."

"That's good news. Do you think the weather will hold?"

"I think so."

"Good."

"Teddy, I know you never gave much thought to marriage, but with the boys gone, we're gonna need help around here, and we can't afford a hired hand."

With a fancy Western prosthetic, she would have been able to help him herself. "I understand, Dad."

"I think he's a good man."

If Mr. Brady hadn't come, it would have been one of the boys from town. But that didn't mean he was wrong. "I think so, too."

The next morning, Teddy got dressed and followed her father and Mr. Brady out into the field.

"I thought I'd try to help today," she said. She was getting used to the hook, and her body was still accustomed to long, physically active days.

"Another set of hands is always welcome," her father said.

Teddy waited for him to wince at the phrase, to apologize. Instead he just smiled at her, then turned back to the corn.

She steadied the cornstalk with her hook and snapped the ripe ear off with her hand.

It had been easier with two good hands. Still, she grinned as she tossed the corn into the wagon.

As they walked in that evening, her father nudged her shoulder with his own. "I guess you showed me," he said, his voice soft.

"What do you mean?"

"That you don't need anyone to take care of you."

Teddy sat on the porch after dinner, trying to mend one of her torn skirts, but mostly staring out at the piles of cornstalks in the harvested field. Mr. Brady wandered out and stared up at the sky. "Do you have nightmares, Miss Rhodes?" he asked.

"Of course I do."

"Yeah. Me too."

She liked the lines of his face, liked that they didn't need to talk about the nightmares to understand each other.

But mostly, she liked that she could like him without needing him. She wondered what it was that he needed. "Why are you here?" she asked. "Why aren't you back West, taking pictures for the government? I'm sure they'd take those plates off your hands, too."

"I'm sure they would. And they'd print the ones that serve them and dispose of the rest."

"Is that why you left?" Teddy asked. "Because you didn't want them to destroy your pictures?"

"Destroying the evidence doesn't make it any more or less real. They can't change what happened. But they can change the story."

"A few pictures isn't going to change that," Teddy said, thinking of the boy in town with his fancy prosthetic.

Mr. Brady shrugged. "Maybe it's a good thing. We all have to move forward together, now. Western magic is the way of the future. The past is done, and should be buried along with the dead. But I'm not ready to let it go. The things in those pictures—they're real. They happened."

"So, what do you plan to do? Travel around, selling off plates one at a time?"

He shrugged again. "No one wants them, Miss Rhodes. No one but the one group that I don't want to sell them to."

Teddy set her mending aside. "So don't sell them."

"I can't cart them around forever—they're not exactly sturdy."

"Don't do that either."

"What are you suggesting, Miss Rhodes?"

"You can call me Teddy."

"Your father calls you Teddy."

"My brothers did, too."

"Can I call you Theodora, instead?"

"If you'd like."

"You'll have to call me Tim, then."

"Or Timothy?" Teddy said, giving him a small smile.

"Sure." He smiled back. "So, what exactly are you suggesting, Theodora?"

"Stay. Stay here, with us. Help on the farm. We can build a greenhouse so that we can grow roses."

He was silent for a long moment. "You want to use the glass plates to build a greenhouse?"

"Yes."

"The sun will bleach them to nothing, eventually."

"That's the way it is, with time."

"I'd want to save some of them," he said. "At least a few."

"Of course."

He held his hand out to her, and she took it. "I've always liked roses."

"So did my mother. But I worry that the winters would be too harsh."

"Okay."

"Okay?"

"I'll stay with you, Theodora. And I'll build your greenhouse, and let the sun bleach my photographs."

Teddy squeezed his hand.

"Maybe they will." His hand was warm, and chapped from working in the fields.

Teddy laced her fingers through his, and they watched the stars come out together.

A question for the author

Q: What is your favorite word?

A: Pistachio

About the author

Jamie Lackey lives in Pittsburgh with her husband and their cat. In addition to writing, she spends her time reading, playing tabletop RPGs, baking, watching anime, and hiking.

www.jamielackey.com, @AnyaSelena

Jamie Lackey's story "Shadows on Glass" was published in *Metaphorosis* on Friday, 4 August 2017.

What Have You Done to Be Happy Today?

Kimberly Kaufman

I guess it started with the robot talking to me at the front of Perfect Pizza. It was the check-out clerk, one of the humanoid ones, vaguely male with his square features, bald head and glass eyes. His pupils dilated when the clouds covered the sun, and he had specks of color in each iris: blue and grey, occasionally red. The 'bot was just human enough to feel comfortable ordering a personal pizza from, yet small and deformed enough to remind us humans that we still dominated the earth. This one was permanently stuck to the counter, with a human-shaped torso, head and arms bursting from the white plastic like an eerie modern centaur.

All the check-out robots were programmed to say specific phrases in response to human interaction, with little variance. "And what kind of toppings would you like?" they would ask after you ordered your pizza. Some days, the only words ever spoken to me were those of the fast-food check-out 'bot.

Next, the inevitable payment question: "How would you like to pay, ma'am, credit card or G.S.?" Even the robots used the initials G.S. instead of "general stipend," and pretended that paying with a credit card was still an option. As if anyone who could use a credit card, and not the stipend, would be in a pizza joint.

And at the very end of the transaction, in most of these fast food restaurants, the robot would offer some last line to make you walk away feeling inspired. If you were eating at Happy Burger they'd say, "Have a happy-dappy day!" At Soyfarm Panda, the robot would say, "May your stomach be full and your mind at peace." At Perfect Pizza, the robots would usually finish with the line, "We hope this pizza helps you to be happy today!"

But that wasn't what the robot said to me on that day.

I'd gone to get pizza after my shift volunteering at the Synth-H clinic down the street—I had worked up a hunger after spending the morning spray-painting some old picture frames and redecorating the common area to make it feel cozier for the residents. Smog decorated the skyline, everyone seemed to ignore me, and I looked down at my phone as much as I could. I didn't feel like seeing or talking to anyone. Everything about that day fit into my routine, until those words from the robot pierced my consciousness. After I tapped my G.S. card into the computer, the robot said, "And what have you done today?"

Then, after a pause in which the robot rolled his eyes back into his white plastic forehead, he added, "Happy. To be happy." Even though it looked like he had been thinking, I knew that was impossible. It was probably a malfunction. His voice was more human than ever, though, with none of that nasally, metallic edge I usually associated with the 'bots.

I think my mouth must have been open for a few seconds before I shut it and continued with my routine. I tried to process what had just happened while checking the balance on my card and waiting the five minutes while the pizza was prepared by the other, less human-looking robots. Was this, perhaps, the new "mantra" for Perfect Pizza? I'd been coming here for years, and twice this week alone, yet the words of the robot had always been the same. There were maybe five other people in the restaurant, but they were all concentrating on their phones or food. One person was gazing out the window. No one had noticed what the robot had said to me.

When a pizza slid down the conveyor belt in its box with my number printed across the top, I picked it up and looked at the check-out 'bot again. He was repeating the standard phrases to a young father and his son who had been in line behind me. The father was wearing a see-through plastic raincoat, even though it wasn't raining, and had puffy circles under his eyes. The child, a toddler with thick arms and legs, wearing a blue-denim jumpsuit, kept wriggling out of his father's arms and trying to get onto the counter to grab the robot's face. At least three times, the man had to pick his son up off the counter.

But it made no difference to the 'bot. His reactions were the same for the man as they had been for me, at least so far. But the robot's last words were completely different. "We hope this pizza helps you to be happy today," it said after they paid. Then it looked at me. For maybe a split second, it looked *right at me,* before turning its head back to center and freezing to wait for the next customer.

By that point, I was in a bit of shock. My first thought was that I had imagined the sentient look the robot had given me with those creepy glass eyes. Was I starting to see things? But my stomach started to growl and I didn't know what *I* could do about it, even if he was getting crazy robot ideas, or trying to take over the world, so I turned around and sat down in my favorite corner, farthest from the windows. There was never anything to look at outside other than everything I had started to loathe in recent months: the unemployed, the Synth-H users, and the unemployed Synth-H users like I had once been.

It was best to ignore it all and focus on my pizza instead. It had barbeque sauce, synthetic mozzarella, mushrooms, and strips of laboratory manufactured "rib-eye," which I'd heard were made from vegetable fibers and soy. I had no way to verify this, as the ingredients weren't public, but I liked to think there was a possibility some of it was healthy. It was the pizza I'd always eaten since rehab, and I found it soothing. I was far beyond caring if I put on some pounds.

Before I took out my phone to scroll through the usual apps, to look for new clothes or cheap deals, I glanced once more at the check-out 'bot. He remained motionless at the counter, his frozen, glass eyes staring straight ahead. Perfectly normal. I wondered what it felt like to be permanently stuck to the counter like a piece of furniture. To be stuck in this white plastic pizza place all day, watching humans shovel food into their faces he could neither eat, nor smell, would be hard on anyone. But, I thought, as I slurped up a long piece of synthetic cheese, at least he *had* a job. I couldn't even get an interview.

While I ate my pizza, I checked my email to see if anyone in my family had responded to my most recent plea for forgiveness. Nothing. I'd stolen my sister-in-law's jewelry during my Synth-H days and now none of my three brothers would talk to me. What I had mistaken for cheap sterling silver and sold at a pawn shop for three lousy hits had belonged to her great-great-grandmother, a horse rancher from the Southwest in the good-ole-days, and had sentimental value. A *lot* of sentimental value, apparently.

My pizza finished, I gave up on trying to contact family for today. My brothers still probably had my email automatically set up to go to trash. I sat for a few moments in the green and white plastic booth, waiting to see if the robot looked at me again. Nothing. Perhaps what he had said to me had simply been a glitch in the system. I wondered where the human manager was right now. It was very competitive to get a job like that. I knew; I'd applied for many robot managerial positions since my rehab from Synth-H.

I finally gave up on figuring out the robot. I left the pizza joint and walked the four blocks to the train, passing advertisements for new electronics, apps, and fast food. All around me were the delightful offerings of the Earth, all within a GS budget if you used your money wisely. The smiling faces in an advertisement—a man and woman looking happy as they connected over their phones, some kind of dating app—made me think about what the 'bot had said. *What have you done today to be happy?*

It had been exactly three years, two month and seven days since I had taken Synth-H. It had never made me feel happy, but at least it kept me from thinking too much, like I was today. I looked down as my crusty black tennis shoes carefully navigated the empty liquor bottles, a moldy pizza box, used needles which had fallen between cracks in the pavement, the paraphernalia of a life I knew well. What was the difference between that life and this one? Before, I could fall away into oblivion whenever I wanted. But now, my only distractions were my volunteer gig and my N.A. meetings, which as of late were not helping fill the gap. I needed something else.

But this was the kind of thinking that had lead me to Synth-H in the first place. My N.A. meeting was tomorrow night, not tonight. I could probably find one to go to tonight, but I doubted I could find the answer there, or here. I looked up. The blue sky was there, somewhere, covered with an opaque brown veil, pierced by the sleek high rises of the technology elite. You couldn't look up in this city without seeing the skyscrapers. They were the center of the city, and everything else was built around them, like the temples or churches of the past.

I walked by a grey-haired man sitting on the sidewalk. His wrinkles were filled with dirt and sweat, and he was hunched in a corner, screaming towards the high-rises, with one fist clenched and raised. I knew that I had only narrowly missed becoming him. But what for? Before, I'd two simple emotions: the blissful perfection of oblivion, and the ravenous desire to achieve oblivion again. Now, the only emotion I had was a flat, sinking feeling in my chest. But, I reminded myself, I was alive, and that was good.

I accidentally made eye contact with the crazy-looking man, and he stood up with a sudden fire in his eyes. "Dildos!" he screamed, "Big fucking dildos!" At first I thought he was talking to me, and I shied away. But when I followed his glare, I almost laughed, because he spoke the truth. No matter how many awards the architects earned for their designs, their buildings looked phallic. Ger would have thought of something funny to say back to the man, shouted something absurd and obscene, proving once again he could charm anyone, anywhere. We would have gone home and laughed about it over dinner, slurping up the red pasta sauce made with green olives. What was it called, something with a "p"? I'd planned to marry him, have kids with him. But he'd brought the habit back from the Asia Alliance Wars, and shared it with me. He'd died a few months later, looking skeletal, lying next to the bathtub, staring up into the back of his head. An eternity ago.

When I got to the train stop and bought my ticket from the machine, the screen pulsed with a yellow and black sad face. *Not again.*

"Getting low on funds, Helayna," it reminded me. Unlike the pizza robot, this voice was high pitched and irritating. I wished I could shoot that little sad-faced icon, like you used to be able to do in video games when I was a kid. I wanted to see it burst into flames or disintegrate into pieces all over the screen. That would be a good app, I thought, putting my stipend card into my wallet and getting in line for the train, which was running late. I'd be eating at the free-food stands or borrowing from next-month's stipend if I wasn't careful. As I stood in line, I tried to think of the bag of Cheezi-Puffs I had at home, or what television I would watch when I got home. Anything to not think of the robot's words, and their reminder of my dismal life and lack of happiness.

But my thoughts kept circling back. Malfunction or not, the words made me uneasy, and I wiped my sweaty palms on my jeans. What *had* I done to be happy today? Was that too complicated a question, since I had food and a place to sleep, and the government provided for us enough to have gadgets to occupy our time? I knew from college—I shuddered to think that was nearly twenty years ago, now—that most of human history had been filled with misery and oppression. So why should I think I was special, and insist on more?

When the train finally arrived, it was so full I had to stand in the aisle on my toes to grab the handle hanging from the ceiling. As the train jerked into motion, two women on either side of me greeted one another through the mass of people. The first peered under the arm of the heavy-set man who stood next to me, like a pony-tailed gopher looking up from a tunnel.

"The train's late," she said to her friend, next to me.

The friend looked over the top of my head and nodded. "Third suicide this month," she said. "And it's only the middle of the month." They both shook their heads and pulled out their phones.

I pulled out my phone too, but didn't look at it. What was the point of being clean if I was still only the papery thin, worm-like creature I had been on Synth-H, looking at my phone and searching for discount food and jeans while someone had killed themselves just minutes before? Had it been a woman or a man? A friend from college, Carlos, had killed himself before I became an addict. He could no longer find work as an engineer. At the funeral, his wife and children looked deflated, dressed in cheap black clothing from big-bin stores. I didn't know how he had done it, and his family didn't talk about it, so I assumed it was violent and bloody.

Now, trying not to lose my balance as the train came to a halt, I pictured a man, with dark brown hair like me, feeling the same black hole in his chest as me, jumping off the platform and in front of the train. He had practiced it in his mind so many times that even when he felt the urge to pull back at the last minute, his muscles still pushed him off the platform.

Standing in the aisle, grasping onto the handle with both hands, I knew that if I didn't do something I soon would be the one on the train tracks, small talk for the assholes on the train.

I looked at the two women on their phones and was about to say something, anything, even a casual comment just to acknowledge that it had happened. As I opened my mouth, still unsure what to say, I realized it was almost my stop and I had to push through the crowd to get to the door. Whatever I was going to say, I had no one to say it to as I walked the ten blocks of identical six-story stucco buildings of the Dillon Street apartments.

At the front of the building, I looked up, trying to fully appreciate the monstrosity of the thing. All the apartment buildings in this area had been built recently, to address the lack of cheap housing. The plain white walls and small windows certainly spoke more to utility than aesthetics. In another kind of world, someone would have set up film screenings in the summer, using the large, white wall as a community movie-screen. But I didn't even know my neighbors. The lawn crunched under my feet as I cut across to the entrance; it hadn't rained in months. The sky was a muted, purplish-brown as the sun crept towards the earth.

I walked into my peeling, beige, carpeted flat and sat onto the sofa. Like my imaginary man on the platform, my body acted from memory, only mine was real. I sank into the faded, black cushions and stared at the three foot wide, two foot tall, flat-screen TV. For once, I felt no urge to turn it on. But it didn't wait for me. My roommates must have changed the settings.

"Hello, Helayna," the television said, the voice coming from a white dot bouncing across the screen. "What would you like to watch?" It kept right on talking. "I would like to recommend the documentary A History of Cats, based on your recent viewing of Weapons of the Roman Coliseum," it said.

"No," I replied, swiping it off.

I sat by myself for a moment, staring at the blank television. Before I could distract myself, the dreaded question came back: What had I done to be happy today? Other than go to the clinic to volunteer for a few hours and eat my pizza, I'd looked at my phone, taken the train home, and for absolutely no reason, felt drained and tired.

I heard one of my roommates, Stewart, talking on the phone in his room. I couldn't hear much other than the upticks and affirmations in his voice. He was excited by the human contact he had found. He was a night owl, but he had explained it to me once, when we both happened to be in the kitchen at the same time. He'd been eating a bag of "Queso Krunchies," which I wished he would offer to me, my mouth watering at the thought of the chalky, salty, orange goodness. I was sipping a cup of instant coffee I had heated up in the microwave.

"What is that?" I had asked him, pointing to his notebook, half filled with crumply paper and thousands of notations. The other half had smooth, white, unlined paper.

"Oh this," he said, "is my calling game notebook." He wiped the dark orange powder of the Krunchies onto a napkin—what a waste, when you could lick your fingers clean—and flipped through the pages like a deck of cards. "It's what I do to fill the time. Basically," he said, flipping it open to maybe the third or fourth page, "I dial numbers at random and keep a list. I write down whether anyone answers, or if no one answers, what the message is like. I get a live person after about a hundred attempts."

"Wow," I said. He hardly ever left his room. "Why, why do you do that?"

"I don't know," he said. "I guess to just try and get into contact with different people. Try to see what other people are like. I can walk the street for hours, and see thousands of people, but I won't talk to any of them." He shrugged. "I don't know why," he said. And we left the conversation there.

From what I could hear now, Stewart would now be able to mark "human contact" next to the number he had just dialed.

Other than Stewart's conversation, the apartment was silent. My other roommate had recently been hired to supervise the garbage control 'bots, and she was probably sleeping before her upcoming shift.

I pushed myself up off the couch, and with a creaking in my knees, walked into my room. It was the smallest in the apartment, and my twin bed took up most of the space. All around the bed, my room was filled with crap. As much crap you could buy on a government stipend: cheap t-shirts, plastic gadgets for brushing your hair, little stuffed animals that were supposed to become valuable in a few years. The plastic pieces and colored fabrics, faded by the wash, littered the beige rug in my apartment. I was consistently broke at the end of the month and this junk was why. We talked about it at N.A.; "filling the void." I was guilty but didn't care; it was better than a needle in my leg any day. I cleared just enough things off my bed to lay down. The fluorescent light belittled my possessions, so I stared at the smooth, white ceiling instead.

Lazily, almost drifting into sleep, I thought back to the documentary I had watched a few days earlier. The Roman Empire would give free bread to the citizens of Rome and keep them entertained with blood sport in the Coliseum. I think the idea was to keep them from rioting. Rome was wealthy, the center of a vast and heavily taxed empire, but the city itself was filled with the poor. They must have felt uneasy, the holders of wealth, knowing there were so many destitute in such proximity to their golden statues and orgies.

Did they ever wonder how long it would take before the poor overwhelmed them, the rulers of the Empire? I hardly ever saw our own rulers anymore. In the past, they had ventured out on the streets, walking quickly, buttoning the tops of their embroidered jackets and designer suits, catching private cabs, or sitting in the back of their self-driving cars, heads bent over their phones. Now, because of the greater use of A.I., they didn't have to leave their luxury homes unless they wanted to. Maybe they were scared. Maybe they had simply forgotten about the rest of us.

I joined hands across my stomach. I used to wear jewelry, decorating my fingers with silver rings and my ears with brightly colored plastic earrings. Now, I decorated myself with age, freckles, and folds in the skin.

And what have you done to be happy today?

Staring at the ceiling, thinking about those words, I thought I would never be able to sleep without knowing whether the 'bot had been trying to give me a message. But I woke up a few hours later with my head pressed against a plastic bag of jeans I'd gotten on sale. I must have rolled over in my sleep. I felt a crease in my forehead where the plastic had left a mark. I picked up my phone and checked the time. 8:45 PM. I hadn't even turned off the light.

I was hungry and I'd forgotten to shop. I was down to one box of expired macaroni. Or I could return to Perfect Pizza for a slice of that delicious synthetic cheese. Perhaps see what the robot had to say. I got up, grabbed my shoulder bag, and headed back to the train.

The train was nearly empty, and I got a seat right by the window. As I looked out the window, watching white wall, beige wall, grey wall, I realized that all the walls were blank. Weirdly blank. Which was strange, because the streets used to be *filled* with graffiti. It had been so long since I'd seen graffiti that I'd forgotten about it. As a child, when I had visited my grandmother in San Francisco, the streets used to be decorated with bright and colorful scribbling on almost every corner. The graffiti was so common that when she walked with me to church on Sundays, I would look forward to trying to read the cryptic words. I thought they had a mystical quality about them, and if I could only decipher the words, I could access their magic.

But looking out the train window, I wondered whether people no longer had a desire to write on the walls, or whether they did, but it got painted over. There was probably a whole army of painting 'bots who come in at night to cover up unseemly graffiti.

At Perfect Pizza, I spoke with the manager. As subtly as I could, I asked, not about the robot itself, but about how his shift had been for the past few days. I told him I had heard things got pretty rough at night with the drug users in the area. The manager, a young man in his twenties with a receding hairline and blond and grey beard, told me that the strangest thing that had happened was some customers had reported the check-out robot had made an off-script statement. The robot had been inspected, a slight malfunction had been discovered, and promptly fixed. He was back to normal, the manager assured me.

I got a piece of pizza to go, plain cheese this time. Mystery solved, but I still felt a little disappointed when he said, "We hope this pizza helps you with your day!"

I walked out into the cold and headed in the direction of the Synth-H clinic. Since I was here, I could at least finish my picture frame project. The front desk clerk, Donna, didn't look up from her phone. A volunteer, just like me, too caught up in her apps to watch the busy street in front of her. At my locker, I stood staring at the cans of spray paint I'd been using, silver, black, purple. Colors I was hoping would give the place a less sterile, happier vibe. I put the spray paint in my shoulder bag and walked out again. Donna barely noticed as I walked out the door and headed home.

When I got back to the Dillon Street apartments, I took a deep breath. I hated this place, with its wide, colorless walls. It wasn't much better than the Synth-H clinic, in many ways. I pulled out a can of purple paint and began to write. I felt self-conscious, awkward, even, looking over my shoulder to see whether anyone was watching. No one was. After the first few strokes, each letter went faster. I wrote the words the robot had asked me, over, and over again, each word about two feet in length. I made each letter legible, made the magic of the words available to everyone.

I was writing it for me, and for everyone else who needed to hear those words, the stinging reminder of the unhappy lives we kept living even though we all knew, deep down, that there *was* a way out. *This* was the way out, I thought, imagining myself unlocking the mystery of the words.

I was writing it in part for Carlos, I was writing it for my family, wherever they were. I would try to get in contact with them again tomorrow, and maybe see if they had public address listings so I could go directly to their homes. They couldn't avoid me forever.

I walked around the building, covering the entire first floor in the long, questioning sentence of the robot. I wrote it for Ger, who'd left me alone with Synth-H.

When I made it around the building, I stepped back from the wall, admiring my letters, which were bold, and circular. The words had followed me for most of the day, and now they screamed out from the side of the building, for everyone else to see. I waited, half expecting the wall to crumble and the magic I had unlocked be released to me, giving me the power to alter this shitty reality. Instead, predictably, I saw a cop car pull into the parking lot and two slow-moving, weary-looking policewomen step out.

Some days later, I sat once again at Perfect Pizza, once again after a volunteer shift, as if nothing had changed. The only difference was that I was trying out the seat closest to the window; I wanted to have something to look at other than my phone. I also wanted to convince myself that something had changed. When those two policewomen handcuffed me and put me in the back of their car, I could not find one star in the sky, and I had started to wonder whether it had all been worth it. Two days in jail, community service, and they had painted over it right away, as if it had never happened.

I glanced outside, and my heart sped up. There it was, written all over the side of a building outside, the words of the robot, *the same words I had written on my building.* A cleaning crew of 'bots had only just arrived and they were starting on the first letters of "what." But I could still see the rest of the sentence. A crowd had gathered around the cleanup, just normal people like me who had nothing else to do but stand and watch a graffiti cleanup.

I took my slice of pizza and walked out the door and into the crowd. I'd find this second author, even if it meant having to paint more messages, even if it meant more jail time. I had been right about the words, they did mean something. The wind swirled my hair around my pizza as I took a bite, watching the next word, "have," being painted over, I felt less alone than I had felt in years.

About the story

I was washing dishes and listening to an NPR piece on a pizza company in Silicon Valley that would soon be using robots to deliver their pizzas when I started to form the ideas that would become this story. Also mentioned in this article – and something that has been up for debate in some countries – is the idea of a basic salary for all. I started to toy with that idea, and whether such a basic salary would be a blessing, or a burden. What would a person feel if they couldn't work? Would they turn to drugs, as many are in the U.S. right now? How could someone get out of this situation, and choose to make a life they felt was worth living? To me, that would have to be an act of political rebellion, no matter how small.

When I was working on the rewrites for this story, someone I went to high school with died from a heroin overdose. This tragedy made Helayna's struggles and the danger posed by them much more of a pressing story to tell.

A question for the author

Q: What is the hardest part of writing for you?

A: Re-writing, revising, and editing! It is not only difficult to find the time needed for a re-write, but it can be difficult to remain inspired when you're sweating over a piece of writing and struggling to find the right words to convey the concept you have in your head. It is the "easy" part of writing— the concept and character— that forces me to continue with a piece, no matter how exhausted I am. Without that character encouraging me, I would probably not write at all.

About the author

Kimberly Kaufman lives in San Francisco with her husband and pet demon. (Some would call this pet demon a cat but Kimberly knows better). When not toiling away at her day job in law, she's probably reading an Ursula Le Guin book or playing her 1975 Rickenbacker bass at full volume.

Kimberly Kaufman's story "What Have You Done to Be Happy Today?" was published in *Metaphorosis* on Friday, 11 August 2017.

Oven Game

Paul A. Hamilton

The oven door creaks open, revealing the grimy, sweat-tracked face of a girl just past her seventh birthday. Opening an oven from the inside is difficult for a child, but Drea Kane has had practice. She crawls into the unfamiliar house and dusts off her black knit dress. Her grease-caked tights are living up to their name, squeezing her calves. She rubs the underside of her nose with a wrist; the streak of wetness finds its way onto her dress at the hip. The black hides the stain.

"Hello? Is anyone home?" she calls. Her voice is soft, the question more perfunctory than inquisitive. She already knows the answer.

The clock over the stovetop reads 12:34. On the other side of the oven, the time was shortly after five. She announces her presence again, bolder this time, and makes a slow turn. Drea is too young to be impressed by the kinds of details that excite home-buyers: crown moulding, hardwood floors, wide bay windows overlooking a valley bearded with evergreens. But the immensity of the house is not lost on her. The kitchen is larger than her parents' whole apartment.

She searches the house, but finds no sign of the laundry room, or of Taka. Four minutes have passed and the tights are now cutting into her feet and waist. It's happening faster this time.

It takes both hands to wrestle the tights off her legs. By the time they are clear of her calves, her shoes no longer fit. The dress is stretchy; she knows it will suffice for another few minutes, but she must find something else quickly.

Eager legs carry her out to the entryway and up the stairs, where she pauses on the broad landing. Below, the glass-inset front door glows with a sinister red shine. Every time she travels through the oven, exterior doors are blocked by the red shine. It's a barrier, because there are rules to the game. Rule number one: she cannot venture outside the homes she crawls into.

Her dress is becoming uncomfortable, the hem that once brushed the tops of her knees now barely covering her thighs. The short bob of her unruly black hair tickles past her shoulders. Rule number two: she must age quickly, like a time lapse.

There are a lot of rooms to examine. Most are grown-up rooms: a well-used study with stacks of files surrounding a computer; a library; guest rooms with empty dressers. Toward the end of the hall she finds a room that might belong to a big kid, perhaps a high schooler. Inside the large closet Drea finds three walls of thick-packed clothes on wood and metal hangers. She strips off the dress whose sleeves have drawn into tourniquets. There is a mirror behind the closet door.

She will be, according to the age acceleration provided by the oven game, a disappointingly plain teenager. Her sweet cherub cheeks will flatten into a broad face; the hugeness of her dark eyes will be overtaken by a thickening temple-to-temple slice of bushy eyebrow; her mane of hair will become an unruly thatch of kinky curls and puffy flyaways. Yet the novelty of seeing her body transform is never lost. The thick patch of moss sprouting between her legs precedes the twin bulges of her developing breasts, followed by the stretching of her legs and the outward slope of her hips. The rush of sensation from this process is difficult for her second-grade mind to grasp. A tingly exhilaration threatens to overwhelm her if she watches the transformation too long.

While she waits for her body to reach its full size, she browses the closet, thrilled again at the remarkable simplicity of being able to *reach*. Height, she has determined, is the principal joy of adulthood. She selects a pair of jeans from a shelf and pulls down a printed T-shirt. Comfortable clothes, because her body no longer provides its own comfort. She has never determined if the unease comes from invading other people's homes or from the loss of familiarity with her flesh and bones. This is her body, but during the oven game it behaves as if a new kind of gravity acts upon it.

There is a slight reluctance as she emerges from the closet. This is her favorite part of the oven game, but it always sends her belly into fluttery trembles that travel down her legs and up into her chest. She's looking for the laundry. Specifically, the dryer.

She finds the laundry room in a partitioned corner of the finished basement. She steps in and looks around. He's not here yet.

She examines her hands, remembering that while her teenage body is unremarkable, her young adult characteristics are somewhat more distinguished. The baby fat that will linger through adolescence dissipates in her early twenties. The long, lean fingers are perfect reminders of the overall sleekness that will accompany her post-collegiate years. Drea paces, worried about Taka's excessive tardiness. If her aging outstrips his, it could force her back through the oven before the rendezvous is complete. Rule number three: she must be back in the oven before old age makes the clumsy climb into the appliance impossible.

A pair of warm, smooth hands slip over her eyes and she yelps, clawing for a moment at the assailant. When his scent reaches her, raw and animal, she is reassured. She tries to spin into him, whirling her face from his cupped palms. Her shoulder catches something, hard and sharp: a shelf overhanging the laundry machines. Some of the bottles and detritus wobble and rattle together, but they settle after a tense second. Drea sighs with relief.

He laughs in her ear, a deep-voiced chuckle that sounds masculine but has the untethered emotional exuberance of a child. She grins and presses herself into his chest. Until she began playing the oven game, her father was the most handsome man alive. But this man is rugged behind a full beard instead of the careful regency of her father's thickly waxed mustaches. His hair is a rusty brown and soft, so unlike the coarse television snow of Papa's mane. And he smiles with his eyes.

Drea does not know his name. He speaks a language she doesn't understand. Often he says a word that sounds like Taka, and she has come to think of him as her Taka, though that may be his name for her. It doesn't matter. Close as she is to his breast, she can feel the tapping of his heart against hers. This is the best part of the oven game. He smiles right until the moment their lips meet. She is seven inside. Outside, she is twenty-eight, rapidly shifting into twenty-nine. This is their thirteenth kiss, and she believes Taka will be her true love forever.

"You came through early," she says when they pull away. She can't explain why her kisses with Taka are so different from her mother and father's kisses. Why they share so little in common with the goodnight pecks she gives her younger siblings on the lips before bed. An easy assumption would be that here, playing the oven game, she is different and older and therefore her kisses are more mature and sophisticated. When she daydreams, she often remembers Taka's lips.

Taka smiles and says something in his rapid, fluid tongue. Drea has learned that laughing whenever he speaks is usually the easiest way to communicate. He grins at her musical giggle and holds her out at arm's length, examining her. Taka always does this. As if watching her age is as much a part of the game for him as the kiss is for her. She notes, again, how fortunate he is to come through the dryer. Arriving in the laundry room almost always means he has ready access to clothing that will fit his expanding frame. Today he has borrowed a pair of corduroy slacks and a blue button-down which he has mis-buttoned only twice. His thickly muscled chest peeks through the open neck.

Usually, after they kiss, they hold hands and explore until they feel old and tired. At that point they separate, to return to their homes and youth. There is no fourth rule. But, if there were one, it might be this: play the game the way it is always played.

Instead, her fingers reach through the folds of the shirt to touch the skin. In thirteen expeditions through the oven, she has grown comfortable with Taka. Her action is tender; anything but aggressive. Perhaps it is merely the unexpected sensation, or that Drea changes the game, unchanged for months, spontaneously.

Whatever the cause, Taka recoils from her touch. His movements remind Drea of a marionette whose paddle is shaken in frustration. He leaps back, pressing himself clumsily against the wall.

"I'm sorry," Drea begins, but she is interrupted by a tremendous crash. The bracket her shoulder hit moments before rips free of the wall. It might have fallen anyway. The shelf is overloaded with the sorts of household items that don't typically have a comfortable home: heavy bottles of bleach, stain-fighting solvents, cans of touch-up paint for the upstairs bedrooms. It could have been seconds from falling already. The impact of Taka's back on the wall could have sent it crashing down either way. But as Drea watches the slow yet inexorable chain reaction play out, she can't stop remembering: she bumped it first.

The contents of the shelf topple and fall half a meter onto the dryer's flat metal top. Jugs and canisters bash into the top of the dryer with a series of deafening metallic clangs. Taka and Drea clap their hands over their ears in helpless fascination, watching the rain of miscellaneous items batter and dent the lint-coated surface of the appliance.

At last a small fabric softener ball rolls off the crooked shelf. It bounces, almost cheerful, from the warped dryer top to the pile of broken and leaking cans and bottles on the floor. The smell of mixing chemicals stings their eyes and noses, and they turn worried expressions toward each other. They have always been careful not to leave evidence behind when playing the oven game. No one has ever been home, but the houses always seem lived in, never abandoned. Drea consistently battles the fear of being caught. This terrible mess will be impossible to clean before they are too old to manage a mop or broom any longer.

She hears a choking sound come from Taka, like a sob.

"What's wrong?" she asks. Taka moves closer to the dryer, staring at the pull-down handle on the door. The metal has crumpled, obstructing the door. An icy breeze whispers along her back. Neither of them moves for a long moment until Drea looks up and sees small sparkles of white snow through his hair.

"Can you open it?"

Taka presses his lips together, understanding enough to know he has to try. There's no use staring, wishing it undone.

As soon as it's obvious Taka can barely curl his fingers under the beaten metal to grasp the handle, Drea knows it will not open. Taka yanks, and the whole dryer screeches forward across the dirty tile, but the door holds fast. He says something vulgar-sounding through gritted teeth and bashes the door furiously. The appliance becomes wild in its rocking, its plastic-coated feet beating against the floor. Taka's frenzied effort fills the basement with deafening, overlapping echoes.

"Stop! Stop!" Drea screams over the racket. "That's not helping." She tries to think, but Taka is panicking, the sweat and tears mixing into a salty shine on his face. Crow's feet collect the squeezed tears and run them to the outside of his beautiful cheeks.

With a jerky motion, Drea grabs Taka's hand. "Come on," she says, pulling Taka toward the kitchen. She never considered what might happen if they played the game until they couldn't escape. When she first discovered the secret door at the back of her parents' oven, she stayed for hours. Then she found the delightful stoop of her spine and the charming thinness of her legs nearly stopped her from crawling back. But as long as she could make it into the oven, she emerged in her parents' apartment the same age as when she left, only a few seconds having passed.

She knows Taka might not get home right away if he can't go back through the dryer. But if she can get him to her house, maybe they will be able to return tomorrow or in a couple of days. Or he could try a different dryer. There are many questions unanswered, and a lot of unknowns, but she is certain they can't stay. Eventually Taka will get too old to leave at all. She doesn't like thinking what that might mean. A quiet but insistent corner of her mind worries it could signal the end of the oven game.

She examines the kitchen before making any moves toward the stove. No overhanging shelves, only a large hood built right into the wall. It seems unlikely it could crash down and block their second escape, too. But she hadn't considered the laundry shelf a threat, either.

Unlike Taka, Drea always leaves the oven doors open behind her. She's irrationally annoyed that he did not have the foresight to take this small precaution. She gestures at the oven and catches a look of deep-creased worry on Taka's face. He is aging even more rapidly than usual. They both have been, she knows. Frustrated by his hesitation, Drea pushes him toward the portal.

"Go! Climb in," she says.

Taka looks terrified, but flashes Drea a weak, thankful smile before putting his hands onto the lowered door and crawling in. She notices for the first time that ovens in the game have their racks lowered, almost to the elements. This strikes her as unusual, but she doesn't have time to ponder it further. Her breath catches and she waits for him to disappear.

His head vanishes into the darkness of the oven. A moment later she hears a light thump followed by a small whimper of pain as Taka runs head first into the rear of the stove.

"No," Drea says in exasperation, reaching out to pull him back by the seat of his corduroys, "you have to open the little slide-door first! Don't you know anything?" Taka rolls aside and Drea leans on the oven door. It groans under the weight of the two adults. She gropes in the claustrophobic dark for the tiny handle, the one that allows her to move into the oven game.

The handle isn't there.

"That's impossible," she says. "Here, get off." She makes way, noting a new twinge of discomfort in her middle back. Taka groans his way off the oven door and Drea crawls in as quickly as her stooping bones will allow. Alone now, she finds the handle right away. She slides the panel open and sees her own parents' kitchen.

"There!" she cries, and wriggles backward, leaving the passage open for Taka to use. She turns to him, seeing a smear of ashy grease on his forehead. He squats, a mixture of pain from his bulging knees and deep concern in his eyes. "Look," Drea says, "you can go now." He looks in bewilderment at the oven's interior and shakes his head. "Go!" Drea practically screams at him.

With reluctance, Taka pulls himself into the oven again and pauses just before the open passage. "Well go on," Drea says, exasperated. Taka looks over his thinning shoulder. His hand reaches out toward the dim light of her home. It stops, meeting obvious but invisible resistance. He feels along the empty space between the oven game and her home, like a mime with a vein-splintered hand. He turns to her, questioning.

"No," Drea says. It is the only word she can remember. No. No. No. This cannot be. She pulls him out again and crawls in, ignoring the curl of her own aging fingers as they push through the charred crumbs at the bottom of the strangers' oven cavity. Her face passes the barrier that blocked Taka, but she's careful not to go all the way through. She smells the familiar sandalwood and cinnamon aroma of home. The passage works. She scoots free and stands, reaching around to clutch her back against the hurry of her spine's curve.

"You can make it," she pleads, "you have to."

Taka shakes his head. He says something quiet. He sounds resigned. His beard is white. His hair is snowy. His eyes are sad but kind.

"You have to!" Drea screams at him. "You have to!" She cries. "You can't stay here. You just can't."

Taka reaches out to her, pulls her into a hug. He whispers. She doesn't know the words, but she understands completely. Her hips ache. Her eyes blur, even beyond the mist of the tears she can't stop. He doesn't kiss her one last time. Instead, he rubs his thumbs along her cheeks so her vision clears momentarily, and then he nods toward the open stove. His own atrophying muscles offer what little help they can. Drea hesitates in her crawl, turning back. He puts a hand on the small of her back, urging her forward.

When the oven door slams closed in her kitchen, she turns a seven year-old head and peers through the opening. She needs Taka to know she's coming back for him. Sometimes it takes a day or two, sometimes weeks before the oven is ready for her to play again, but she is impatient this time. She needs to return right away, with her youth reset. She needs to try to save him again.

She sees nothing. Just the dark gray back of a cold appliance she shouldn't be playing with in the first place.

She never plays the oven game again, though she tries to daily, even hourly at first, for months. Her parents are concerned. She cries herself to sleep and says disturbing things about her imaginary friend, Taka, who has apparently aged himself to death somehow. They send her to therapy.

After some time, Drea claims it is helping. She stops talking about Taka, but the dreams take longer to fade.

As a plain teenager, desperate for acceptance, she tells a new friend about the Oven Game, in confidence. The look on the other girl's face is stricken and horrified.

"You're sick," the girl says. "Why would you make up something like that?"

Drea can't answer. She struggles to remember which parts of the Oven Game were real and which were dreams.

In the casually cruel manner of teens, Drea is quickly branded a freak; a weirdo who lies to get attention. She goes back to being friendless, and sobs to her therapist, "I just want to stop dreaming about these stories!"

"It's good that you refer to those events as stories. I'm glad to hear you frame them as made-up," her therapist says in that soft, non-confrontational way of psychiatrists.

"But the dreams," Drea says miserably.

Her therapist taps a pen to her lips. "Have you ever tried hypnosis?" she asks. Drea sits up a little straighter and wipes her eyes.

By the time Drea graduates from high school, she sleeps soundly at last. Memories of her childhood playtimes fade, like polaroid photos tossed into an old shoebox.

Drea is a capable woman, just past her thirty-sixth birthday. She has two teenage children and a busy husband, plus an accounting job she loves. Her life is extraordinarily normal, and she tells this to people at her simple yet elegant cocktail parties with a self-deprecating laugh.

Even her husband, Trey, doesn't know about the troubles she went through as a young girl with an overactive imagination who frightened parents, teachers, and classmates with elaborate stories. She has worked very hard for over twenty years to ignore her life before college. When she thinks back to her childhood, which is very rarely, it feels as if it were something she read in a book. Those years happened to someone else, and the memories are hazy and slippery, which doesn't bother her in the least.

Everyone believes she is completely normal, and that makes her very happy.

Trey and Drea have moved around a lot. Trey's job requires frequent relocation, and Drea has been game to start over on many occasions. Re-establishing herself at a new job and settling the kids into new schools is always the hardest; even that has become somewhat routine. Her favorite part is house-hunting. They've bought or rented many places over the years and Drea has always been the one to make the final decision. Trey likes to joke about Drea's "house feelings:" they never choose a home unless Drea walks through and declares, "Yep, this feels right." She can't explain the house feelings. Some places, when she walks in, just make her happy, a sensation she says is like a cozy fire and hot tea on a winter night.

But now they have their dream house at last, a gorgeous near-mansion overlooking a valley in the Colorado hills. She has found a position that suits her with a company she likes. The kids have made fast friends at school. Trey loves the proximity to the ski slopes and the grandeur of the kitchen, which has always been his domain. Drea hates to cook.

Because of all this, they worry about the next transfer, even if it may be years away. She doesn't want to leave a place where everything is perfect.

Almost perfect. Lately, she has noticed some peculiar occurrences. Break-ins, she thinks. It started a dozen or so moves ago, and it seems to have become more common. They are almost, but not quite, predictable with each new home. From time to time the family will be away for a day or an afternoon and come home to the distinct impression that someone has been in their house. Nothing valuable is ever stolen, the door and window alarms are never tripped. But the eerie sense of ghostly presences is palpable.

Drea would dismiss these notions if her husband and the kids didn't remark on them. There are small evidences of invasion: a tiny sock; clothing missing from her son's room; an unused closet door left ajar; a smear of a handprint on a doorframe, far too small and low to the ground to belong to her teenaged children.

This morning, she comes home from an overnight business trip and enters the kitchen. She lets out a single, unbroken scream that causes the neighbors to call the police.

When the responding team arrives, they enter the kitchen where a woman stands over the bones of an elderly man. She is shrieking, weeping and inconsolable. The only sign of struggle is rooms away, in the basement. The laundry area is wrecked. A shelf has broken, its contents scattered on the floor. The dryer is damaged, its door bent and stuck fast.

The woman cannot be persuaded to say anything other than a single word, over and over and over: "Taka."

About the story

I originally wrote "Oven Game" as an unsolicited piece for a specific magazine with a certain quirky, dark aesthetic. I don't usually write without any concepts or outlines at all, just stringing words together, but this story I just sat down at my kitchen table and tried to warp my imagination around something odd and a bit unsettling. Which probably explains why such mundane objects are given such peculiar characteristics throughout the story.

I was also inspired in writing the story by trying to imagine things through the lens of my young daughter if she were to suddenly find herself growing up at a noticeable pace. Specific revelations like how being able to reach things is one of the best parts about growing up came from this exercise and watching my daughter struggle with her height in a world built for adults. I was interested in how she might react if her imaginative games of house or let's pretend could be acted out more viscerally, if temporarily. I then tried to envision a scenario in which such extraordinary insights might need to be suppressed and I quickly settled on a trauma which she might feel partially responsible for.

The magazine I wrote the story for ended up rejecting the story, but it turned out to be for the best as the piece eventually evolved to be much more streamlined and readable, especially in the early sections. I enjoyed the process of discovery writing what turned out to be a meditation on the perception of time, and I'm pleased with how the story flits through a number of genres. I'm always happy when I write a short story that feels like it's supposed to be short fiction, as opposed to being a small tale set in a larger context or a barebones version of a longer tale. This story is dedicated to my oldest daughter, who just now happens to be the exact same age as Drea, and whom I would completely believe if she told me there was a magic portal in the back of one of our kitchen appliances.

A question for the author

Q: Have you ever consciously written a 'message' story? Was it easier or harder than usual?

A: I have occasionally written 'message' stories; although I generally feel that any stories should have something to say when it's deemed complete. But there is a difference between teasing out a theme and point of view from a story during revision and going into the writing process with a particular message in mind. I think in some ways writing to a particular message can make the writing easier because you can infuse scenes and characters with aspects that build on the message and that can be easier than trying to edit them in after the fact (for me, I find it makes for fewer darlings that need to be killed later on). But unless I have the bones of the story and the theme both established ahead of time, it does sometimes shift the challenge from the editing process to the initial writing as I find sometimes I have something to say but lack the details necessary to say it in a fresh and interesting way.

About the author

Paul A. Hamilton is a writer, editor, and technologist living in Northern California with his wife and two daughters. His stories feature broken people, reassembled worlds, beautiful monsters, and hideous love. He gets his inspiration by impersonating an old-timey bartender, listening to stories told by lonely strangers. When not writing, he can be found reading, drawing, taking photographs, or riding roller coasters.

More from him can be found at ironsoap.com, and @ironsoap.

Paul A. Hamilton's story "Oven Game" was published in *Metaphorosis* on Friday, 18 August 2017.

An Aftertaste of Earth

Pauline Yates

The arrival of delegates from the Planetary Migration Program raised false hope in my district. Not only has the maximum age for entry to the off-world colony been lowered, we were given less than a week to prepare a concept to prove worth of passage. But with the demise of earth a certainty, hope is all I have left. This event is my last chance to secure a future for my family.

With my eligibility for potential passage verified, I enter the town hall and find my allocated table. I'm in the last row at the back, too far away to catch a roaming delegate's immediate attention, but at least I'm not near the entrance doors. As the delegates arrive to inspect the concepts on display, Desperates—those who have long lost any sense of community cohesion—accost the delegates with pleas for passage, or try to peddle stolen ideas. Security guards keep the most vocal Desperates in the foyer, but amongst the crowds that clog the aisles—those too old, too stubborn or too scared to leave—I recognise a Desperate seen lurking through our district. I check the name tag that's pinned to my pocket. I'm glad I used two pins. Ideas aren't the only thing Desperates steal.

As I arrange the boxes containing my entry on the table, despair creeps into my thoughts. If I'm unsuccessful today, will I end up behaving like a Desperate in order to keep my family alive? But to what end? Our district is supplemented with food packs but the last delivery never arrived. While evidence of theft points to Desperates, the decreasing amount in my allocated ration points to the limited food left on earth. My own tests reveal the poison in the atmosphere from the earthquake that split the mantle is far worse than reported, but what good is knowledge when there is no hope of survival? Better the people of my district embrace an us-against-them mentality with the Desperates than dwell on a slow death from starvation.

A blue-jacketed delegate enters my aisle. His robust frame is as alien as the planet I'm trying to get to. He stops at a table down two from mine, but when the presenter fumbles the mechanics of his concept, the delegate shakes his head and turns away. As he continues along the aisle, he's followed by the Desperate I'd spotted earlier. The Desperate's cunning expression puts me on edge but with a delegate so close, I've no time for caution. Opening one of the boxes, I lift out a pie and place it on the table, waving my hand over its top to make the aromas swirl through the air. Cinnamon. Ginger. Cloves. Nutmeg. Chemical replicates; fresh spices were lost long ago. The scent catches the delegate's attention. He ignores the next table and strides to mine.

His eyes feast on my offering. "Is that—?"

"Pumpkin pie." Unlike the previous presenter, I smile.

The delegate raises an eyebrow. "Edible?"

I pick up a knife, slice through the rich custard and pastry, and place a piece of pie on a napkin. "My mother's recipe."

He picks up the pie and nibbles the baked custard, rolling the sweet desert over his tongue. Taking a larger bite, he pauses to contemplate before consuming the whole piece. When he's finished, he pats his lips with the napkin. "That's good pie." He places the napkin on the table. "As good as this is, our colony doesn't have the resources for pie. We need new ideas to help people assimilate to their alien environment."

I nod. "But without giving them the security of familiarity, their yearning for Earth will impede their acceptance of their new planet."

The delegate grimaces. "Variety in food is an unfortunate sacrifice for continuity."

I open the second box, lift out a white bowl filled with a porridge-like substance and place it next to the pie. "The colony's current food source?"

He peers into the bowl. "It's similar in appearance."

"And bland." I hold up a spoon. "Will you taste to confirm that's what this is?"

The delegate hesitates, but plucks the spoon from my fingers, scoops the porridge from the edge of the bowl and tastes it with the tip of his tongue. He nods in agreement.

Reaching into the breast pocket of my jacket, I pull out a glass vial. "I can make you think that staple food tastes like this pumpkin pie."

The delegate looks dubious but he doesn't walk away. Taking back the spoon, I add the clear liquid from the vial to the porridge on the spoon. One drop will suffice. I hand the spoon back to the delegate.

Eating the porridge, his eyes widen. "It tastes like pumpkin pie." He stares at the vial, then at the pie. But then he frowns. "This is not new. Flavours have been trialled." He shakes his head. "I'm sor—"

"It's not a flavour." I raise the vial to hold his interest. "This liquid will make that porridge taste like the food you crave, no matter what you choose."

The delegate eyes me like a Desperate but then nods at the bowl. "If you can turn that into a roast vegetable salad, you'll have my attention."

"I can." Dripping three drops of liquid onto the porridge in the bowl, I stir it through then hand the spoon to the delegate. He picks up the bowl and tastes the new offering. With raised eyebrows, he eats the entire serving of porridge.

When he finishes, his eyes snap to mine. "Explain."

Seeing the Desperate loitering behind him, I lower my voice. "I've developed a chemical that triggers the subliminal thought receptors in your brain to make you think you're eating whatever you desire. The pumpkin pie was an implant test. You chose the salad. You can choose anything."

The delegate's eyes narrow. "Anything?"

"Whatever you desire."

He places his hands behind his back. "Your credentials?"

"I was a research assistant for the Institute of Future Technologies, biochemistry division."

He stares at the vial and then reaches into his breast pocket and pulls out a metal ticket. "The transport leaves at fourteen hundred tomorrow." He swipes the ticket across a band on his wrist and then hands it to me. "Guard this. Only the bearer will be able to board."

I clutch the one ticket. "My family?"

"How many?"

"My wife. My child." My mother has already insisted she'll die an Earthling.

The delegate shakes his head. "Seats are limited."

"I won't leave them behind."

There's a long pause. He rubs his thumb over his lower lip. "The last time I enjoyed vegetables that good was two years ago."

I tuck three tickets next to the vial in my breast pocket. I leave the pie on the table. Hopefully, the aroma will distract the Desperate while I escape.

About the story

"An Aftertaste of Earth" originally stemmed from the prompts, sci-fi, pumpkin pie and a convention centre, in a short story competition which earned me a place in the final round of the contest. As I love end-of-the-world themes, the story developed from wondering how people would be chosen to start a new colony on another planet, and what they would have to prove to earn a ticket off Earth.

A question for the author

Q: What distracts you?

A: I'd like to say I'm not easily distracted, but it's a different matter entirely when an idea for a story pops into my head. A concept, word, title, or the temptation of 'what if' can distract me from my usual day-to-day life of being a wife to a patient husband and mum to three very loved children. When a story grabs me, I can write until sunrise, yet still function through the day as though I'd slept better than Sleeping Beauty. I am guilty of not being present when these moments strike. I might be baking that pie or making a bed, but in my mind, I'm firmly in my story and I stay there until the story is done. I have learnt over the years not to bore my family with the messy details of an evolving story, but they are very good critics, and no story gets sent anywhere without at least one of them reading the final copy first.

About the author

Queensland writer Pauline Yates, is a keen horsewoman, animal welfare supporter, and lover of all things environmentally sympathetic. Her gardens are full of edible plants so the kids can graze while playing outside and she loves to cook up a feast for her family using home-grown produce, her favourite dishes being pumpkin soup and lemon meringue pie, if she can find the free-range laid eggs.

@midnightmuser1

Pauline Yates's story "An Aftertaste of Earth" was published in *Metaphorosis* on Friday, 25 August 2017.

September

A Conversion of Crows

B. Morris Allen

It moved forward in a crawl, jagged angles flowing over soil and stone alike, dawn shaping shadow and sun into beaks and talons that moved relentless toward her boot and over it. With a touch of her finger, the fern curled in on itself, withdrawing crags and fangs into a soft ribbon of green and grey whose silhouette curled round her foot like a friendly snake.

"Sawtooth, my ass," she murmured. "You could cut something like I could break a Bactrin spell." She stroked the fern with a gentle hand to take the sting out of her words. Around her, the shadows of trees stretched dark fingers down the slope toward the west and the sea.

Kared let go the fern, watched it shake its dew onto her last wax tablet. The tablet was almost full, its hard surface carved with as many tiny notes as she could contrive with a pointy piece of rock.

"Time to buy a new stylus," she said, as she always did, as if, in this decaying age, what still called itself a town could boast enough literates to justify a trade in writing implements for careless researchers. Down the slope, beyond the cliff, a wave crashed and then slithered away. Like hope, like dreams.

"Like breakfast," she said, and gathered up her tools before creaking to her feet. Chewy toasted mushrooms and crunchy, earthy root-nodes. Maybe soggy, toasted nodes and chewy, earthy mushrooms for variety.

"Maybe some solid results for variety," she muttered. The marking stone in her left hand felt as cool as ever, putting the lie to the ancient Bactrin magic she knew was there. That had to be there.

"It's there," she told the stone, putting it back in the soft bag around her neck. "It's there, or I'll be a factor's sub-clerk. Literally. You wouldn't like that, would you?" The stone made no answer, seemingly content in being one of two pieces of Bactrin magic she had that still worked. There weren't many around. Not much of anything worked anymore. She'd had the stone from her father – the only functioning artifact the man had ever found in his decades as an antiquarian and junk seller. "It'll find magic," he'd told her. "Never fails. Keep it close." And unlike her father, it had never failed her.

Her other charm was a heat-trap, a swirl of driftwood the shape of a curved hand that gathered warmth during the day, and released it to cook her mushrooms at dawn. Or root-nodes. It worked only within a half-day's walk or so of a Bactrin site – about her present distance from town. So there must be other sites close by. She'd traded more for it than she cared to think about, just to have a piece of functional magic to give meaning to her quest.

"Some day, you'll answer me," she told the silent marking stone as she headed back up slope to a flattish spot shaded by pines. Above the trees, a dark bird barked at the rising sun.

"Laugh all you want. It's worked before." In the city, when she'd convinced three wealthy patrons to fund this ludicrous expedition. When she'd argued that patterns of leaf growth could form a visual indicator of Bactrin ritual sites. That she'd establish a baseline with her marking stone, defining fine gradations of warmth that corresponded to the footprints of magic, and to the density of fern pinnae.

"And the depth of bullshit they grow on." Out here, on the rocky coast, where Bactrin sites were said to be as common as slugs, her stone hadn't warmed once, and her funds had grown as thin as her results. Likely her patrons didn't care; for all she knew, she was no more than a conversation piece. In these days, discussion of research was worth far more than the thing itself.

Back at camp, the inevitable slugs had crawled all over her stores-bag, but only a few had gotten in to spread their trails over already-slimy planks of mushroom, cut from tree trunks just the night before.

"You're like students," she said, scraping them gently off into the leaf mold. "Crawling all over someone else's work for flavor, instead of doing your own." Which had nothing to do with that disastrous interview at what passed for a university. Nothing at all.

"And you," she said, flicking a large yellow slug out of her heat-trap, "you're just suicidal." She rubbed away some of the slime, then bowed to the heat-trap, set it back in its little hollow of pebbles, and made a ritual pass. A comforting heat flowed out of it, and she quickly reached for her long skewer-twigs and poked them through the mushrooms. Heat was scarce in this rainforest, and not to be wasted.

While the mushrooms cooked, she dipped her last two root-nodes in a pail of water to clear the slug slime off. Browned by exposure and light, the two-day old nodes were unappetizing, and their surfaces felt mushy. "Beggars can't..." They didn't smell good, either. "...eat sludge," she said, digging out a knife and paring away the soft outer layer of the nodes. "There you go, slugs," she said, throwing the trimmings as far as she could down slope. "Don't say I didn't share."

She couldn't eat sludge. She wasn't that hungry – yet. Crow, though. That was starting to look a lot more palatable.

A gust of wind overhead triggered a squawk and a flutter of wings.

"Metaphorically," she called to whatever was up there, turning a mushroom whose skewer was starting to blacken. "Don't be disgusting." She took a bite of node, prodded a mushroom sceptically. Breakfast was bad enough already.

As dawn crept reluctantly up through the branches of pine and hemlock and cast its rosy glow on leaf mold and worm-castings, Kared inventoried supplies. "Food," she said, "none. Easy enough to find, if you count nodes and fungus as food." With her latest meal settling uneasy in her belly, she'd begun to have doubts. "Water, more than anyone could ever want." Mostly in the form of damp, in her sleeping roll, her socks, her clammy undershirt. Sometimes in the form of rain that passed right through her lean-to and straight into her bones. "Results, five tablets full, all negative." Five weeks of searching, five weeks of failure. "Bactrin sites, none." Not one. Which ought really to count as a result of its own.

"Not one," she frowned. "Not one." She turned the idea over in her head. Not one sign of ancient Bactria, in a region known for Bactrin ruins, a region posited as one of the possible origins of the long-gone Bactrin empire. Not one flicker of Bactrin magic in a landscape littered with its symbols and traces. "And slugs."

A lot of slugs, in fact. Tiny brown-striped ones, big yellow ones, mottled-black medium ones. All with frilly edges and slimy, creamy-pale foot-mouths. Crawling over everything in sight. Could any landscape possibly support so many slugs? What did they eat, anyway, with their endlessly walking mouths always in motion? A thrill of excitement slithered up her spine. Could there be something here? Could the key lie not in ferns, but in slugs? The gastropodian empire of Bactria, undiscovered until one woman, one brave, slightly damp woman, opened her mind to the possible, and saw what lay all around her?

She peered out against the rising eastern sun, the dark western slope down to the sea, the pines all around, listened to the caw of crows, or maybe ravens, or rooks. Big black birds, anyway. Lots of them. More than the landscape could support. She let her chin sink back onto the cold of her sweater. Unless they ate slugs, of course. No wonder they sounded so angry. Lots of trees, too. They gave something for the crows to perch on. Plenty of ferns, for that matter, densely leaved or sparsely. All undoubtedly quite natural. Very pleasing to the Bactrin psyche.

"That can be my result," she mumbled. "Ancient Bactrin mages, practitioners of magic, progenitors of progress – fans of slugs, trees, and big black birds. And wet," she sighed, as wind or bird shifted an evergreen above her, and a drip ran down her neck.

Not quite the 'easy way to find new Bactrin sites' method she'd promised her patrons, of course. And why *didn't* it work? It should. "It really should," she told a passing slug. He (She? It? How did slugs reproduce?) cocked a bendy tentacle at her, but didn't pause in his headlong race to a nearby tree.

The marking stone grew warm in the presence of Bactrin magic. It did work. She'd tested it every week at ritual sites all over that moldy little coastal town where she transcribed her notes to paper (and dried her clothes, and bathed in warm water).

Back inland, there had been a subtle but marked increase in foliage density in the vicinity of Bactrin sites. Marked enough that people remarked on how green sites were, but subtle enough that no one had studied it. Perfect for an enterprising, un-colleged researcher wanting to make a name for herself. The correlation had held up at known sites up the north coast, as well. Ferns with fifteen percent longer fronds, all the way down their fractal shapes. Hemlocks with ten percent more leaves, painstakingly counted, one by dripping one.

Ergo (which was clearly a university-worthy word), the stone should grow warm in areas of dense foliage, and that should indicate a Bactrin site. Except that here, at the posited epicenter of Bactrin ritual history, the foliage was dense, and the magic non-existent.

Ergo, she grimaced, her theory was crap.

"Cra-a-ap," echoed a crow.

"Thanks. Needed that." She poured as much sarcasm into the words as she thought they would carry, and sent them floating logily up to the canopy and its unseen critics.

Without a theory, she was either weird slug-forest lady, or unemployed clerk. Neither appealed. A return to her father's emporium of faked or broken magic trinkets appealed even less.

"No," she told the slug, which had squidged remarkably far away, "it's deluded scholar girl for me."

If the theory was right, something else was wrong. Maybe the standard foliage density was different at this part of the coast. It was a comforting thought, and she spent the hours until lunch happily, then unhappily, then despondently, checking figures. They looked right. She'd measured densities all over the area, and compared with figures at the nearest confirmed Bactrin site. Everything suggested that, unless the entire headland was a site, her morning exploration should have turned up a class A ritual location. Even if the entire headland *were* a site, this morning's should have been an even better one. Class AA.

She skipped lunch and ate an early dinner of warm mushroom before turning in. Tomorrow was the end. She'd go back to the city, apologize to the patrons, admit defeat. Then... then she'd decide.

She woke before dawn, when the light gave the western clouds an appealing flush of peach, but the forest floor was dark and mysterious. The trees creaked and swayed in the morning wind, but no one else moved on the loam. Except crows. And slugs. The triumvirate of a Bactrin dawn – greer. leaves, black birds, brown slugs. Except pines didn't have... leaves. Pines didn't have leaves! They had needles. Long, green needles. Needles that were square or flat or round in cross-section, that grew in short clusters or long ones, thin ones or fat. Clusters that she had ignored.

"Because I'm an idiot," she said happily, scraping a wax tablet smoothish in readiness for discovery. "Becau-au-au-au-ause, I-I-I-I'm an I-i-i-i-dio-o-o-ot." It made a nice little song. A song of success.

Where to start? In a known location, of course, one where Bactrin traces were unlikely. Back in town, then, probably. She looked down at her tablet, imperfectly smoothed. She could have kept the data after all. She *was* an idiot. But a happy one. When was this one from? She unsmudged the upper corner as well as she could. Two days ago. Two days... not a good day, then. Lots of squatting and leaf-counting in a day-long drizzle. Like most of the others.

"How do you live with it?" she asked the crows. The slugs, well they were moist already, weren't they?

"Awk," answered an unseen voice. There always seemed to be crows around, but then with all these slugs to eat, there would be.

"I should imagine it *is* awkward." But not for her. She'd be heading to town, to transcribe her tablets, dry her clothes, and gather new data. One final splurge of funds, and let the journey back to the city take care of itself.

Two weeks of needle counting gave plenty of results. Mostly a hatred for root-nodes, fungus of any kind, and even of the tiny black berries just coming into season.

"Pretty soon, I'll be able to eat *my own* fungus," she said to the everpresent crow voices, and thinking of the unsavory places a fungus might be growing. "If I can find it in the haystack." Her new needlic expertise had led to ever-thinner and more pointed jokes as the desired results failed to appear. Another day or two, and she'd have to give up again, and head back to town in disgust, dismay, and other distressing words.

Her camp this morning was on the same slope where she'd come to her exciting, entrancing, and utterly wrong epiphany about needles. Her marking stone had failed to warm even once out here, though it had worked very nicely in town. And though, like probably every other coastal village, the locals claimed the territory was *the* birthplace of Bactrin civilization.

"Before they found their power, probably." She put her table and pointy stone back into her rucksack, and put the marking stone, useless as it was, back into its little neck bag. "Back when all of Bactria consisted of shiny wet things. No wonder they developed magic."

Below her, the surf sounded with a muted crash and the whoosh of receding foam. There should be a little cove down there. She remembered there'd been an easing of the slope. Maybe there was a way down, a way to where she could soothe her sorrows with the sound of the ocean. Maybe be comforted by a passing whale.

"Ahrk," said a crow. "Craw," agreed another. They were even more numerous than before, it seemed, but then the weather was nicer too. Even the dawn light reflecting from the ocean cloudbank felt warmer, its peach and gold tones washing the dark forest with calming light.

She made her way down the slope, holding tight to bushes as she grew closer to the edge, looking for the easy slope she'd spied a fortnight ago.

"Ow." The undergrowth here blocked the light, and there seemed to be extra roots to trip on. She'd kicked at least three on the way down, their dark, serpentine forms hard to be sure of against shadowed loam. They were remarkably hard for roots, but then the unseen is always more of an obstacle than the visible.

There – the slope began to ease, somewhere beyond that tangle of bushes to the right. She turned that way, spying the dark forms of crows beyond the branches that now gave hints of the ocean and sky beyond.

She kicked another branch, and fell headlong into thick, moist humus. Above her, the crows laughed their raucous laugh, while, just a noselength away, a bright yellow monster slug waved antennae quizzically.

"That does it!" she growled, struggling to her knees. "I'm coming down for a little meditation, damn it. A little soulsearching, you bastard." She turned to face the offending root. "Is that too..."

It wasn't a root. At the side of a wide bush, its edges raised up where she'd kicked it, was a wide snake. Its surface was scuffed, the coating of moss ragged and torn to show white stone beneath, and the characteristic curves of Bactrin ritual. Not a snake, perhaps. Maybe a slug. She giggled. A giant white stone slug, hand-made in Bactria. Proof positive of ritual magic if she'd ever seen it. The biggest Bactrin item she'd ever seen. Literally at her feet. Hidden by dense foliage.

Her hand flew to the marking stone, in its little bag. With an item of this size, she was surprised she couldn't feel it through the cloth. It should be burning. With trembling fingers, she tipped it out onto her palm, ready to drop it if the heat proved too great.

It was cold. Body-temperature, technically. Not burning. Not hot. Not even warm, really. Not indicating magic of any sort. Yet here it was – proof positive of a Bactrin presence on the headland.

Was she wrong (again)? Was the slug no more than an artifact? Artistic, but without? Bactrin relics that had survived this long were invariably magic. Yet perhaps here, in the mooted Bactrin birthplace, a rare stone item might have lain undisturbed for the ages since its creation.

She reached out for the slug, taking its weighty solidity in her hands. She peeled away the moss and dirt that covered it, noting in the back of her mind that the crows were even more raucous than usual. The slug was the length of her forearm, with gentle curves and the unmistakeable lines of Bactrin workmanship. The slug's broad mantle formed a graceful oval near a head marked by smooth nubs of tentacles. It was beautiful, and she caressed its surface as she cleaned the surface to show a milky quartz, with inclusions hinting at internal organs that made the whole even more alluring.

"Awk." The call came from directly overhead. "Crawk," came another, to the left, and "Rowk," another to the right. Abruptly, she realized that the soothing whoosh of the surf had been replaced by a cacophony of caws, and the clear dawn air by a chaos of crows. On all sides, branches bent with black bodies. Beady eyes eyed her as heads cocked to one side and the other, and sharp talons flexed while long, strong beaks jabbed hungrily at the air.

"Oh, shit," she said. "Oh. Shit." Black heads nodded in agreement.

"Okay," she said, wishing both that she weren't still on her knees, and that the bushes were thicker. "Okay. I don't know what set you off, but I apologize. Okay? I'm sorry. Really, really sorry." She shifted the stone slug to one hand, and used the other to struggle to a squat. "Tell you what. I'm just going to put this guy away," she wriggled her bag around and slid the slug into it, "and then I'm going to get out of *your* way." As she stood, the noise increased, and more crows landed, until the branches around her looked like they were covered with some dark, evil fruit. Above her, she could hear the flutter of wings, and she could feel the draft from black wings flapping by.

"No," she agreed, squatting again. The birds quieted marginally. "No getting up. I was tired anyway. Nothing wrong with a good crawl, though, is there?" She put theory into practice, and was brought short by a flash of wings and talons flitting past her nose. "No crawling. Slithering, maybe?" As she lowered herself to the forest floor, she noted a line of slugs before her. They were of all colors and sizes. Quite attractive, really, if somewhat on the threatening side in terms of sheer number. She raised back to her knees just as a giant yellow slug led the line toward her.

Above her, the crows sat or fluttered, quiet except for the occasional raw cry. The slugs stayed where they were.

"Right," she said, more to drown out the sound of her frantic heart than to communicate. "No standing, no crawling. No slithering." She looked at the slugs. "But you were fine earlier. You've been fine for *weeks*. Other than eating my food, and did I grudge you any? No? I shared!" A righteous indignation began to take over from fear. "I shared, you ungrateful little bastards." She felt carefully in her back. Wax tablets, pointy stone, stone slug. No food. She looked at the bush beside her. There, one little black berry just forming. She stretched an arm, plucked it. With careful aim, she bounced it off the yellow slug captain. "Share that." The slug gave a squishy wince of retracted tentacles, but made no other move. Behind him, the berry rested between a glossy brown slug and a smaller, smoother one.

"That's all I've got." She could jump the slugs, but then the birds would attack. She could throw the pointy stone, but that would account for maybe one bird. She could throw the stone slug, and ... The stone slug. It was ridiculous.

She dug it out of her bag, watched carefully by beady black eyes and long tentacles. "Seriously? Look, I agree it's nicely made, but it is made. From stone. I'm not kidnapping anyone. This is *not* a real slug." The tentacles watched. "Okay, look I'll put it back, okay?" Maybe come back at night, when the crows were sleeping. She lay the slug back down in the little niche it had left in the soil. Had the head faced this way, or that? No, the other way, so that the tail fit nicely, just there.

"Okay? Satisfied?" It was ridiculous, challenging slugs, but ... but they were dispersing. And above her, the flutter of wings suggested a similar diminution in the crow ranks. Maybe if she waited until they were gone, she could just grab the slug and run for it. Up this slope, down the next, and over and over for the half-day trek into town. She gave up on the idea just as a particularly weighty bird settled onto a nearby hemlock, its canny eyes watching closely.

"Right," she told it. "Mystery solved. This artifact is obviously a sophisticated crow caller." Or a guard. A boundary. A marker. A marker that didn't touch her marking stone. But clearly magic.

But marking what? She'd covered the forest pretty thoroughly, traipsing up and down in her search for ferns and needles. What was left?

A crash of surf brought the answer. The cove. This eased slope leading down toward the water. Perhaps not luck at all, but a familiar byway. Familiar to slugs and crows, and ... Bactrin ancients?

Only one way to find out. Careful not to touch the slug, she turned back toward the water. She tried a slow, tentative crawl, and looked back to the giant crow on his branch. He cocked his head quizzically, but made no sound.

After a few 'steps' and no further reaction – and no sign of slugs – she debated rising to her feet, but she could hear that the water was near, and on all fours she'd be less likely to step off a cliff hidden by underbrush.

Another few moments of cautious crawling brought her to the edge – a dank, muddy slope leading down the edge of the low-ish cliff – a slope that might once have been a stairway, or might still be one beneath the muck. And at the bottom, the soft beige sand of a beach untroubled by any but the highest tides.

She stood to slip and slide carefully down the old stairway, grasping at the roots and vines and stone that decorated its landward surface. Above, a few languid seagulls soared heedless overhead.

The beach was a beach. Light, soft sand above the tideline, compact, dark sand below. The usual assortment of driftwood, seaweed, and broken shells. But at the back, and to the sides, narrow, sea-wrought crevices that crawled back to vanish into sand. Except that a little ways in, the sand ended at the base of rough stone steps leading up. Not into darkness, but into light.

She chose one of the central caves – one along the very back of the little cove. The entrance was wider, and there, beneath an ancient crust of dead barnacles, was what might have been a carving of a starfish, with just one arm thrusting up from beneath the sand.

The light inside had a silvery, nacreous quality to it that shone soft and pleasant on the stone. It emanated from stylized birds carve on ceilings and walls, their white backs turned to the passage as if they flew forever upside down. She touched one, its smooth outline low on the rough rock wall. For a moment she imagined she flew low above windblown cliffs, or perched on a warm branch, or pecked at something bright on dark soil. Then she was back in the cold, damp tunnel, and the carving just a carving.

She climbed the steps, their centers bowed and smoothed by years of feet, their surfaces rimed with ancient salt. Tunnels led off to left and right and down, all lit with cloudy silver carvings, all shrouded with the dust of centuries. At every turning, she chose the upward path, until she felt she climbed deep into the heart of the headland, somewhere close beneath its crest. There, at the terminus of half a dozen stony stairs, she found the Bactrin.

Not the Bactrin themselves, though stone chairs piled with dust and petrified fabric suggested what once might have been. The center of the chamber held a massive stone table, its edges smoothed and polished to a gentle curve. Its surface, once blown clear of dust and scraped clear of as much limestone as would easily come off, was a map. Recognizably a map of what was left of the current Republic, or the Empire before it, or the Many Kingdoms before that, or of any of a host of nations that had inhabited the physical space between mountains and sea. Some of the rivers had moved. One mountain marked on the map was a blunt caldera now. But overall the land was the same. And from this location on the coast, from this very headland, perhaps this very chamber, a fine net of shining lines branched out and out and out, to hundreds, thousands of tiny points of quartz embedded in the dark granite of the table.

Some of the points were dark, most dim, one or two glowing with a faint spark of silver light. Where a line was dark, all the points along it were the same. A few of the dim points, she recognized as being approximately in the location of the city, some possibly in the nearby town. Others might be in the vicinity of Bactrin sites she'd heard of. Others were unknown. One bright spot was near her own birthplace, in a gorge known for its fearsome haunts and apparitions.

A map. She sank, weak-kneed, onto one of the stone seats, realizing late that the uncomfortable bumpy surface might well be the fossilized bone dust of a Bactrin ancient. Too late for either of them to care. She rested her head against the stone table, feeling the fine point of a quartz node press into her skin, letting it mark her if it wished to.

A map. She had wanted to develop a method for finding Bactrin sites by counting leaves. Instead she had found Bactria itself.

Belated, she fumbled weakly for her marking stone, shook it out onto the table. It was cool, unmoved by stronger evidence of Bactrin magic than even the wildest storyteller had ever dreamed of.

"Ha!" Her bitter laugh echoed around the stone chamber. Not a magic finder at all, but a ... a what? She looked out over the map and its branching lines, its dense foliage of crystal, all coming back, in the end, to a central point – this central point, the source, the wellspring of mysterious Bactrin power. And that was it, she realized. The map was a map of links. The stone was a link marker, a link finder. And here, on this headland, at the very heart of Bactrin power, there were no links to be found, nothing to mark. For here, somewhere, perhaps in this chamber was the power itself, still flowing, still linked, to the edges of the Republic and far beyond, to the Bactrin world that had been.

She emerged, eventually, to the call of hunger. Even Bactrin magic did not run to food stores preserved for ages, it seemed, though she had found storerooms and vaults and dormitories and laboratories and halls great and small, chambers for every conceivable purpose and use. Marvels by the hundred, and even, with a joy that sent her to her knees, a library of sorts – a moulder of dust and lime, with here and there a wall carving or stone tablet or jumbled pile of crystal sheets and shards. Drawings, letters, all in scripts she failed to recognize, but permissive of study, and perhaps, somewhere in this treasurehouse, a translation into some ancestor of an ancestor of a dead language that was still known – a key to the wisdom of the ancients.

She stepped out of a tunnel onto soft sand and the glow of dawn. Above her, a scatter of crows swooped raggedly back and forth, their dark, glossy feathers gathering light as they must have done for ages, light that shone soft on hidden passages, for a people that had gone. Below them, the slugs no doubt did something similarly extraordinary.

"Or maybe they're just slugs." She smiled and waved to a passing crow. "It's not all magic, after all."

Some of it, she knew, as she climbed back up muddy steps, would be hard work. Most of it, perhaps. But if she played her cards right, there could be magic again. If she could find the right people, the right minds, people who cared about knowledge and right and progress rather than wealth and power. They would be few, no doubt. Perhaps the Bactrin themselves had not qualified.

Above the slope, she climbed the slope toward her camp, untroubled by crows or slugs. Today, she would eat and gather her thoughts and rest and think. Tomorrow at dawn, she would take her first steps toward the new day. And if she failed, if she chose the wrong people? She shrugged, and looked west to the rosy glow of a reflected dawn. If she failed, then there would be another dawn, and another, and another, until, some day, the world got it right.

About the story

It may not be obvious at first glance, but "A Conversion of Crows" is a story about the rock group Whitesnake. Back in the days when they were good – no really, there was such a time – David Coverdale put out an album called *White Snake*, which included the song "Whitesnake". It couldn't have been any more Whitesnake, other than the fact that the band didn't yet exist. That song (admittedly, not one of the good ones) had a line I heard as "She'll help you make it in the crow light" which I thought sounded pretty interesting. I knew, deep down, that Mr. Coverdale was unlikely to have written a line with so few references to sex, but I like the way it sounded anyway.

Many years later, it occurred to me to figure out what he had actually said ("She help you make it in the cold light") and, having succumbed to disappointment, decided to do something with what should have been. I sat down to write a story about crow light. This was my first attempt. While I liked it, it veered pretty far from what I'd intended originally, so I sat down to write another ("Outburst", coming out at Cast of Wonders). I liked that one too, but it still wasn't what I'd intended, so some day I'll sit down and give it another try. Eventually, there will be a story legitimately called "In the Crow Light". I'm eager to see what it's about.

This scenery is stolen directly from the Hart's Cove trail on Cascade Head, a protected area of the Oregon coast very close to where I live (when I can). There's a hidden cove full of seals, occasional coyotes on the path, greenery, rain, and quite a few slugs. I added most of the crows, and some of the magic.

www.BmorrisAllen.com, @BmorrisAllen

B. Morris Allen's story "A Conversion of Crows" was published in *Metaphorosis* on Friday, 1 September 2017.

The Lost Languages of Exiles

Laura E. Price

The shoes they gave her don't fit.

She notices in the waiting area of the IWT counseling office and holds one foot out in front of her. Wiggles her toes and feels them rubbing against the inside front seam of the shoe. It's felt like this since she put it on, but she's just now stopped long enough to really feel it. The shoe is canvas and rubber, a basic sneaker, and probably half a size too small. Does time dilation make your feet spread? Or did some tech somewhere type in the wrong shoe size in a rush?

She puts her foot back down. Now she notices the way both shoes encase her feet, pinching and rubbing in odd spots.

The only other person in the room with her is Harry, and he won't look at her. Harry's not looking at anybody, lately, except maybe *his* psychologist. He fidgets, leg bouncing and fingers drumming: the behavior mods would have kept him from that—the movement, the feelings making him do it—but they're off now. Everyone from their crew is edgy, scraping against one another in various ways. Her own tension runs all along the edges of her body, a tremor and spark of panic and irritation just at the tips of her fingers and ears and toes. She pushes her hands into her thighs, her toes into the seams of her shoes, exhales.

When they'd all stood frozen and staring at the skip-lagged face of the Admiral on the main viewscreen, Harry's fingers were the first things to move. They scrambled over the console and slammed the buttons down until the speakers let out a godawful screech and the Admiral's voice came through.

"*—you've been gone five years, Captain. We thought you were all dead.*"

She leaves Harry in the waiting room when it's her turn. The office is dim, carpeted, furnished with big chairs and a desk shoved into one corner. Beach sounds play from speakers she can't find.

She sits in one chair and the psychologist sits in the other across from her, not at the desk, and they talk.

"How are you feeling?"

She's feeling the clothes she's wearing, now she's noticed the shoe. The waistband of her pants, the collar of her shirt against her throat. She has her left foot wrapped around her right calf, so her shoelaces dig into her pants, into her skin.

"I guess I feel … stunned? Slow. Half-blind—they aren't letting me access anything besides novels and old television shows right now." She'd seen half a news headline—*Exiled Imperator Poisoned in Bid to Consolidate*—and a sentence or so of the story under it. Her fingers tighten on the seams of her pants. She ignores the memory, focuses on her clothes.

"That's understandable," the psychologist tells her. Fran. She's pretty sure Fran's the one who wears glasses.

"Are they really retiring us all?" Lia asks. She crosses her arms low across her stomach, hooking her fingers into the waistband. "Before they blacked out the news, I saw that they were going to retire us?" She still has three years before her first opt-out. She can—could —re-up twice more before retirement. After that she could apply for admin in the company.

"They are. Nobody knows what happened to you all out there. They don't want to take chances." Fran's eyes are steady on hers through her glasses. Even admin requires occasional space work.

"I don't … know what to. I just." Lia stops, because she has no idea where that sentence will end.

"How old were you when you joined Inter-World Transport, Lia?"

"Twelve." Her father got the papers after he spent a night coughing up blood instead of the usual grayish phlegm that all the adults in their town had in their lungs.

"So you're twenty-four, now."

"I'm—" *Nineteen.* No. They were gone five years. It only felt like six months. She does the math in her head. "I guess I am, yeah."

"What had you planned to do, once your tour was up?"

"I was … I'd assumed I'd. Um. Re-up. I don't tend to make plans past my next leave, really." She scrubs a hand through her hair, avoiding the ports behind her ears but rubbing around the one at the back of her head, which itches today. She'd had thoughts, about maybe finally taking some of the accumulated leave time she'd banked, if things went well with Ianto. She's never thought about any of *this.* Her heart speeds up as *twenty-four* echoes in her head; emotion floods her hands and fingers, fills her throat and sinuses. There's *too much* feeling and she doesn't want to drown in it; she wants to be able to *think.* She wants to be able to *breathe.*

She doesn't look at Fran, who says, carefully, watching her, "Well, you're here for the next three months. The company wants to run tests—psych and physicals, bloodwork, scans, that sort of thing— and ask you some questions about what you remember. They're also going to make sure you have some adjustment training—"

The panic eases at the boring company BS, recedes enough so that she can manage to look at Fran and ask, "*Do they* even know what that means?"

Fran grins in the cynical way that she and her shipmates do when discussing their employer; Lia's not sure if it makes her feel better or not. "I understand they're going to be contacting people who specialize in prisoner and military re-integration." Her grin softens into a smile. "They know this is unprecedented, Lia. They want to ease your transition as much as they can."

"I'm sure PR is breathing down Corporate's neck, as well."

"They lost a transport, sixty-two percent of which was manned by people they'd more or less bought as kids. It was a PR nightmare, even in the places that *don't* find IWT's various recruitment methods controversial."

Lia says nothing. There's nothing *to* say, really; she's glad she didn't starve to death or die from gray-lung before she turned sixteen, and this last trip was just another six-month tour for her. But Fran's voice saying *twenty-four* and *reports are unclear as to whether Rhydderch's companions were also* just before the screen went black won't leave her alone now. She grinds her foot into her calf, feels her shoelaces and the cloth of her pants against her flesh.

"Look," Fran says, "they didn't know why the *St. Cloud* disappeared, and now you're all back and they don't know why that happened, either—they just know all kinds of eyes are on them, yet again. The end result, though, is that they're going to try and help you." End results have long been the argument for Inter-World Transport: their motives may be self-serving, their tech may be ethically dubious, but they give the poor, the debtors, and the various people the world forgets the chance to become healthy, productive members of society. Plus, your cargo is delivered safely and on time by our always professional staff!

Fran's still talking. "Over the next weeks, think about what you want to do. Five years of back pay—you'll have money enough to live for a while before you need to work, but it's better to walk out of here with a plan than without one."

The first thing she remembers Ianto Couriseme saying was not to her, but to Meurig Rhydderch, the Imperator-in-exile of the Sovereign Bishopric of Laendris, on the planet Colophale. Which was now called Homshoi. The coup had been bloody and too intricate to follow when you spent six months at a time in deep space.

"It seems archaic, though—they own you until you're, what, ten years in?" Meurig had asked her one night in the mess hall, as they picked over the last bits of food on their plates.

Ianto, until now his Imperator's shadow, rolled his eyes. "You mean, archaic like generations of an entire family sworn to protect the royalty, whether they would or no?"

He was relaxed, slouched in a chair and leaning his head on an arm propped on the mess hall table, looking wryly at Meurig, who seemed self-deprecating but not particularly ashamed of himself. Ianto's grin caught and kept her eyes, even though the mods tempered her jolt of reaction to it. Meurig went on, "As archaic as keeping the youngest child as surety and sending the eldest into exile, I suppose. It sounds like a goddamned fairy tale, doesn't it?"

"If you cast it romantically, it's easier to live with," Lia said, and Meurig laughed, but Ianto gave her an odd, shadowed look before he smiled, slowly.

It takes forever before the Re-Assimilation Training is set up, and by then nearly all of the *St. Cloud*'s crew are restless, cut off from everything. That's not new; it's part of the job, but usually they're only six months behind, not five years. The company blocked the news sites two hours after the ship touched down—not quite soon enough to keep her from a search once she discovered she no longer had an email account, but fast enough to cut off the first news report she found after one sentence.

They've let them have family news, the ones who had family. E-mail, screened; new e-mail addresses because they purged all the *St. Cloud*'s crew's accounts two years ago. Dr. Quiroga's mother has cancer, is in the middle of treatment; Piotr's wife had their baby, and that baby is four. Lia, thinking about the solidity of family and the quake of losing five years with them, decides she's probably lucky. She doesn't think of fragile things, new connections, easily snapped when the ground convulses. Not much, anyway. Not really.

It's not all sad—Iona Kawa'iia's been stomping around mad that she saw spoilers for the end of *Bitumen Fails,* and now she can't access the show because they don't want them seeing anything that came out more recently than five years ago. And Jorge O'Malley got video of Captain Oshiro's reaction when his wife told him she'd sold his vintage skimmer, so they've all seen that one. It's not all sad. It doesn't all have to be sad.

"Your Laendish is very good."

Ianto fell into step with her as she walked from her station back toward her quarters. He wasn't that much taller than she was, and he had a loping sort of walk that he tried to restrain in order to keep pace with her. His hair was plaited into two braids that he wore looped at the back of his head, but curls kept escaping along the edges and sides. "Thank you," she said. "How's my accent?"

"Good. Possibly a little too posh—you sound like a queen in a film. But good." He smiled, a crooked grin, and went on, "You're the ship's linguist?"

"I'm one of them." The *St. Cloud* was mostly a freighter, rarely took passengers. She'd been the lucky lottery winner whose head was hastily stuffed with Laendris' dead-to-most-of-the-system language so that their last-minute additions could communicate with someone. The speed of the upload had been disconcerting; she'd dreamed in Laendish the night after the upload and woken up feeling ... off-balance. Unmoored.

"Can you, say, teach? Is that possible with the ports? I'm afraid I don't quite understand how they work ..."

"Nobody quite understands how the ports work," she said with a grin back at him. "But yes, I can teach, if I know the language. What are you looking for?"

"Could you teach me some English, before we dock? Maybe some Harekaans? Meurig seems to think he'll be fine knowing not a word of anything, but ... well, it *is* my familial obligation to take care of him. If you have time, of course, and if they're in your repertoire ..."

"Absolutely," she said, with professional smile and voice. "I'd be happy to."

There is bloodwork (lots of needles) and there are scans (full body, brain, random bits that make no sense, like her stomach and her right bicep, one of her hands). There are questions: her interviewer (whom she does not think of as an inquisitor, not at all) is a smiling, sandy-haired guy with a Harekaans accent and a dependence on his handheld. He's scrolling through something when she arrives.

"So you have no memory of anything out of the ordinary happening on this trip?" he asks, finally looking up from where he's been tapping notes onto the screen.

"Nothing. But I'm not bridge crew; I'm a cargo linguist. I spend most of my duty time belowdecks doing landing and retrieval prep, negotiating prices and permits in the native language; otherwise I'm pretty low on the need-to-know list."

"Why were you on the bridge when the *St. Cloud* returned?" he asks disinterestedly.

"Delivering a final inventory report to Captain Oshiro. The docs messaging system was down for maintenance, so I delivered it by hand."

"And during the trip there was nothing physical—no sudden lurching or shuddering at any point?"

She has a sudden image from an old television show, all the actors throwing themselves across the set of their sailing ship when some sort of sea monster rammed it. "No," she says, amused and quietly delighted to feel something good.

"No sudden ... um ... psychic disturbances?"

She couldn't figure out, at first, why she'd gone looking for Ianto when she wasn't on duty. It had felt strange; her mind had offered up *suffer a sea-change* to her, and maybe it had been apt: muted by the behavior mods they'd implanted in her limbic system, but huge, slow, seemingly inevitable.

She shakes her head, amusement gone, and that was the wrong trip, anyway. *That* trip, Ianto's trip, went without a hitch. "No, nothing like that," she says, and fights against the urge to seize his handheld and its open access when he props it up to start typing his report.

"How are you feeling?"

"Like half my brain is missing." She rubs her eyes, runs a finger hard around her ports where they itch and ache. "My languages are fading."

"All of them?" Fran asks.

It hurts in her chest to explain it; she wishes the mods were active so she could talk without her voice cracking as she counts on her fingers. "I've still got English and Portuguese, but they're native tongues. French isn't too bad, probably because of the Portuguese. Bilali's still mostly there, and maybe, I dunno, half of Harekaans and a quarter of Mandarin? I can still *read* Farsi, which seems completely counterintuitive. But the rest are ... they're like echoes. They sound familiar, but I just don't know."

"It makes sense. You haven't had any uploads, no refreshment."

"Yeah, I know, I just—languages are what I *do*. My brain is. Suited to it? They think, anyway, they say that shit but they don't *know*. I keep—what *good* am I, now? I'm not a pilot or a medic, I'm just a *linguist,* it's not like they need me anywhere else—"

"Well," Fran says her voice soothing, "There are certainly a number of things you can do with fluency in English and Portuguese, and some—what did you say? Bilali and Harekaans. We can explore some of them, too. But Lia, you have to remember that you're more than what you've done for IWT."

It's all true. It doesn't help, because it's true, but it isn't *all,* and she's not going to talk about the rest of it, about which language she's been trying to coax out of her stupid, regressing brain.

She takes a breath, hitches in the middle, wipes her face with the palm of her hand. This is ridiculous, mourning something she knew would happen, and *crying*. It's been weeks since they turned the mods off; everything should have settled by now, and she's not sure why it hasn't. "I didn't think it would hit me this hard," she says, then lets out a wet-choked laugh because *obviously*.

"So he's going to fire you once he's settled wherever it is he's going?" Books stacked neatly around them, the lesson abandoned for the day in favor of talking to each other, and Laendish easier for both of them.

"It's not that harsh," Ianto said, shaking his head at his hands. He sat tailor-style, his body's lines long, slender, a cascade of grace. He didn't look like anyone's idea of a bodyguard, but Meurig liked to tell stories at dinner about the part Ianto played during the coup and after it—assassination attempts foiled, the Imperator's uprisings. Sometimes, though, in his enthusiasm, Meurig stumbled into allusions to other things, and Ianto's body turned from flowing poise to elbows and knees and high shoulders, until Meurig speedily changed the subject. "Meurig feels a certain amount of guilt that I was sent with him, that I can't just go back after. He doesn't see it as firing; he sees it as freeing me from an obligation I had no say in accepting. Although he could always call me back, if they ever call him back."

"Do you think they will?" she asked.

"No. No, that government's ensconced for at least a generation or two." He grinned a twisted sort of grin that matched the bitter-philosopher tone of his voice.

When he didn't seem to want to continue that line of conversation, Lia asked, "And do you have plans for your forced semi-retirement?" She tried to sound light.

He shrugged. "I thought I'd live in the city? I can't imagine living in the countryside—I grew up in a city. Though the idea of an entire apartment to myself is *decadent*." She nodded, let out a breathless laugh because it did. "I suppose I'll get a job. My money won't last forever." He grinned at her, crooked but not bitter, and asked, "Xiankin is your home port, isn't it?"

She grinned back at him; she couldn't seem to help but smile at Ianto when he smiled at her. It was disconcerting. "It is. We'll have five days' leave, then most of us are going back out for six months."

"So in six months, you could come see my apartment. Maybe have dinner?" He tilted his head so that he was smiling at her sideways.

She raised her eyebrows, hoping her expression told him that she knew exactly what he was doing with the coy looks and the playful tone. "I could," she said.

Harry sits down next to her in the dining hall. She's eating, reading *A Fisherman of the Inland Sea* on her handheld, debating in the back of her mind whether she ought to ask for a translation of it in Harekaans or Bilali to try and keep them up the old-school way.

Harry's doing better, if one can tell from a distance. Some days he's withdrawn, some days he's out of his own head and seems normal. Like today; he's actually looking at her.

They chat for a few minutes—two of the engineering crew are going to get married once they're released; Dr. Quiroga's mother is responding well to treatment.

"So, you make a plan yet for after we're out?" Harry asks her.

"No." She takes a breath, lets it out. "You?"

"Nah. Well, taking the money and running. Maybe go to Caszoeatu, hit some clubs, lay on the beach for a couple years."

"You have always been a hedonist, Harry, so this plan does not surprise me."

"They've owned me since I was eight years old; I may as well enjoy my unexpected freedom."

She snorts. Harry smiles at her. "So, Lia ..."

"Harry Das, you are *not* asking me to run away to Caszoeatu with you," she says with a laugh.

"No. I am propositioning you, though." He raises his eyebrows, lets his smile go from genuine to cheesy.

She thinks about it for a long minute. She and Harry used to hook up on leave all the time, during the first couple of days when the mods turned off and everyone was either mainlining sugar or fucking each other through the emotional overload. It was good, and they've always got along well enough. "Come on," he wheedles, "my therapist says it'll be good for my mental health."

She rolls her eyes and shoves him, watches him a little as she speaks. "Thanks, but no."

He takes it fine, she thinks. "You sure?"

"I am," she says, carefully. He squints at her.

"You got somebody else?" he asks, sly. He's always good at sniffing out a secret. Lia's just never had anything she cared about keeping to herself before. The problem is, she doesn't know how to answer without lying, at least a little, and thanks to the mods they're all awful liars due to lack of practice.

She settles for, "Kind of."

Harry keeps watching her and finally says, "It's that dude with the braids, trip before last." She doesn't respond, though her heart startles her with a heavy thud against her breastbone. "That sucks," he says. "I mean, is he still even around?"

"I don't know," she says; *reports are unclear as to whether.* She picks up her handheld and looks for her place. "And we're blacked out for who knows how long."

"Five years is a long time to wait for a hookup," Harry says. His tone is easy. His tone is always easy, but she curls her hand into a fist and digs her nails into her palm. They've long played this game of pushing and mocking; no matter how many times they've fucked, they've never really been intimate or vulnerable with each other, and she isn't starting now.

Lia forces airiness into her voice. "You should go ask Kawa'iia, she's always had a thing for you."

Now Harry rolls *his* eyes and stands up. "I do not need that giant vat of crazy opened, thanks. I will make do with my right hand or possibly proposition O'Malley."

Lia smiles, hopes it looks real. "He's cute—you should rank him higher than your hand."

"But he's in *session* and I'm *horny* ..." Harry fake-wails as he walks away. Lia watches him for three counted breaths before looking back at her book, waits until the doors close behind him and his footsteps fade before she puts the book down and buries her head in her hands.

Ianto kissed her. She wanted him to—something off-center and pale in her chest just *longed* for him to kiss her—but she ducked away before it was anything beyond a brushing of mouths together.

"Sorry," she said, "It's not me, it's the mods, I promise." She wished they shut embarrassment down as efficiently as they did lust. But when she looked at him, he was smiling at her. He took her hand, touched her knuckles one by one with his index finger until the embarrassment went away and she was left feeling a little breathless, a little lost, with that same tidal pull that sent her looking for him whenever she had the chance.

She gets herself off dozens of times to the memory of that sweet sweep of his mouth over hers. She remembers that and his scarred hands on her skin, the heat of his fingers against her knuckles, and it's better than all of the crazy-intense sex she used to have on leave.

But after, she thinks too much. Now the mods are off for good. The world is five years older. She doesn't know anything, really. Nothing that's happened in the news beyond that half a headline, which fills her head with *Poisoned* and *unclear,* setting her spinning through scenarios and what-ifs where Ianto is dead, where Ianto is shattered by the death of his Imperator, where Ianto is married or in love or in mourning and has left the city or the country or, hell, the entire planet, and she just wants to think of *anything* else, but what else is there to think of? The future she didn't realize was coming in the universe she's never really paid attention to beyond the languages of the people in it?

Eventually she falls asleep. She dreams in Laendish, wakes up, and spends the rest of the night trying to fall back into the dream.

About a week before their release into the world, their net access returns.

A bunch of them are in the lounge, talking, playing cards, watching old cartoons on the big monitors, and all of them have their handhelds with them. Lia's reading; she's always been one of the crew who didn't enjoy the close quarters they'd been stuck with, but lately she just wants people around, if not talking directly to her.

Harry's pocket lights up and buzzes, then O'Malley's and Kawa'iia's, then a few more, right in a row. *Everyone* gropes for their devices. Lia closes out of her book and stares at her screen, as though that will make the net come back faster.

It lights up in her hand, vibrating, flashes a "connecting" message at her that disappears again before her heart has a chance to slow down. Harry makes a happy affirmative noise; O'Malley, who has loudly enjoyed their exile from the 'nets, groans. The room fills with the pings and clicks and muffled swearing that comes with people setting up new tech, connecting their new email accounts; Kawa'iia lets out a triumphant, "*Yes,* I can download the last four Kilkennan books!" and Harry asks her, "He didn't die before he finished the series?"

Finally a message emerges from the swirl of colors undulating on her screen: *Hello, Lia, what would you like to do today?*

Her hands shake as she logs onto the news nets.

Ianto smiled at the card in his hand, the smile that emphasized how crooked his nose was, and said, "I've not even got a device yet. I'll have to remedy that as soon as I'm allowed."

"Send me e-mail when you do. I won't get it until I get back, but at least I'll be able to find you for dinner."

He shifted back from her on the mats—yoga and tai chi this time as an excuse to sit and talk—and said, voice much younger than usual, "You don't have to, you know. I won't—well, I'll be upset, but. If you find that it's not ... with the mods off, if you find you don't ..."

"I can tell how I feel," she said.

"Still," he said, and brushed her knuckles with his fingertips.

"Still," she said. "I'll contact you, no matter what, okay? In six months. Make sure you have a handheld."

On the day they're released, she takes a bus downtown and goes shopping. A new shirt—black tank top with an umbrella in a circle on the front that she likes the look of—and new shoes that just slip on. As she pays for it all with her handheld the cashier tells her, with a nod to the shirt, what a great band they are.

"This is a band?" she asks, immediately losing the cashier's interest. Clearly, she's a dilettante in the world of music. As she changes her shirt and shoes in the bathroom of a coffee shop, she just hopes the Rainmakers are a band she'd like if she heard them.

It's not like she's been released from prison, she reflects. It's not even like she's a new immigrant—this is a major IWT hub, one of four in the system, and the largest employer in this country, possibly on this planet. Corporate has offices here; warehousing; cargo processing; intake for voluntaries and indentureds; training for plebes and leave for vets; a quarter of IWT is based out of Xiankin. She's been here before, lots of times, though the last time was ... well, months ago or years, depending. She knows where things are, she knows how to get to them, she knows where and how to find transport and how the money works. She even knows where the road construction is, since apparently it hasn't progressed more than a block in five years.

What's different is that she doesn't need to check to see how much time she has left before she has to get back to base. She could go anywhere. Stay there as long as she wants. Nobody would come looking for her. Nobody could, since she didn't give them a new address. Fran had pushed her for one, but Lia couldn't tell her because Lia doesn't *know*. It's the first time in her life she hasn't known where she'll be sleeping, just that she has the money to decide later.

That much freedom makes her feel lightheaded, light-stomached, so she sits on a transport station bench to catch her breath.

The metal is warm under her. It feels good, baking through her clothes. The street is busy: it smells of fumes from the vehicles that pass by—the older ones loud and rumbling, the newer ones buzzing or humming—and food from the restaurants that are just beginning to open up for lunch. Horns honk and people talk, either into their handhelds or to each other in person; she hears ring tones and the chirping sounds of calls being made; snippets of conversations in different languages, some of which she can understand, some she can't.

The city is always busy this time of day. She has always wondered if people actually work in offices here, or if there's some sort of job that involves just walking around in business attire. There are IWT plebes with red-rimmed implants and newly-shorn hair walking clumped together and stiff in their uniforms with a couple of vets, younger than they are, who must be showing them around. They all glance at her, then away, then back fast when they register her ports and civilian clothes. Maybe they know what crew she's from, maybe not—she scowls at them, command-face, and they hurry off. The civilians don't really pay attention to her, just a glance now and then like you'd glance at anyone sitting on a bench in the middle of the day. They're used to the IWT by now, whether or not they approve of it.

The fact that she has not, actually, planned anything past getting new clothes is not the only thing keeping her from breathing. She looks at her handheld, suddenly all strange angles and edges against her palm in her hand. Her search of the news nets gave her fewer answers than she'd hoped: Meurig poisoned and dead dominated two days' news three years ago, with just one sentence in one article brushing near Ianto's existence, let alone anything else. *Initial reports are unclear as to whether Rhydderch's companions were also part of the plot to assassinate him, and if he had, as accused by the Honshoi Imperator, actually established a 'court-in-exile' on Xiankin.*

That's as far as she's gotten.

She pulls her feet up under her on the bench. The city stretches out around her; the world stretches out beyond that. She doesn't know anything about the future, and it scares her breathless, but she knows what she wants to do. So she types *Ianto Couriseme* into the search bar.

Three steps down the gangplank, another four through the gate, and all the mods shut off at once.

It felt like simultaneously uploading the Oxford English Dictionary and the Royal Dictionary of The Feudal Republic of Bilal—it swamped her, made her lose her moorings.

It was so much more than the usual horny-happy-excited-reckless swoop of feelings unfettered; she could barely see through this to get to her quarters—thank god the retinal scans could work through tears—and she sobbed as she thought of him walking away from her with his exiled Imperator into the city, sobbed far more than probably she should have, but things always felt like *more* right after the mods shut off; all you could do was ride it until it settled.

Five days of leave. She spent them looking for him without expecting to find him—too soon for them to be registered and logged, not with how covertly they had been travelling—but hoping she could tell him that she would see him when she got back.

She didn't find him.

It was all right. She'd find him after this next tour. Six months, less a week, she'd find him and knock on his door.

After fifteen minutes of searching, there's a phone number on the screen. And an address.

She doesn't touch the number. Instead she pulls up the GPS program.

This is really, really stupid.

Her knuckles sting from knocking at the red door of this brick townhouse. It's on a quieter street. Residential. She gets the feeling, from the colors of the doors and curtains, the decorations on the porches and in the tiny front yards, that this is mostly an immigrant neighborhood. It's nice. It feels friendly and looks lived-in, like people have put down roots here. But she's still so terrified she can barely breathe. Part of her, exasperated, hopes to god that the longer she's off the behavior mods, the easier it will be to cope with some of these emotions.

The door opens, and there he is.

She can't talk for a minute, or breathe; she's too busy looking at him. He's *here*.

He hasn't changed very much at all. He was twenty-one when she saw him last, so he must be twenty-six now; his hair is shorter, not braided—it's a mass of curls. His eyes are still hazel, his nose still crooked, his skin still light brown. And his smile still takes up half his face, once it manages to spread out completely.

He says something in Laendish that ends with a soft, astonished, "Lia."

"I ... um. Hello." She says it in English, smiles back at him, feeling slightly drunk. She runs her hand over her head and looks sideways, quickly, just to have a minute where she's *not* looking at him, so she can collect her thoughts or take a breath or something, but then her eyes are pulled right back to him. "I ... I can't speak Laendish anymore—it's faded out. I don't know if you knew—"

"Everyone thought you were all dead." His accent is lilting and lovely. He frowns a little and reaches out one hand to touch her shoulder.

The feeling of his hand on her skin stills her; he's warm and right in front of her. She probably should have waited to come here until she had things better under control. Although, at this point, she thinks that might have been never.

"We can speak English," he says. "I have a little Portuguese, too, but not much." His hand leaves her shoulder, but stays in the air between them for a second. He takes a step out onto the stoop. "Are you—you actually *found* me," he said, his voice pitched high and disbelieving. "When I heard your ship came back, I rather—" He stops, takes a deep breath, and she braces herself for something she won't want to hear.

And then he asks, in a quieter, smaller voice, "Please tell me—you are here to stay with me, Lia?"

"I'd like to," she says. There's a slow surge of current rushing through her—head and arms and legs; ears and fingers and toes—she looks down at her new shoes, bright white in the sunlight. He's barefoot, she sees, and this makes her feel better. "I'm kind of a mess right now—everything's just *gone* out of my head—and they wouldn't let us on the nets for a while, so I couldn't look for you sooner ... I read about Meurig, right before they shut us out, and I didn't know if you were, or would—"

"I wasn't with him when it happened; I had just left him," he says; *it is my familial obligation to take care of him,* she remembers, looks up at him, concerned, but his eyes are fixed on her, his mouth is just barely smiling. Gently, slowly he puts his hands on both her shoulders as he steps closer to her. "I really had nowhere else to go, and I thought if I stayed here—but then your ship ..." He pauses, laughs a small, breathless laugh, before saying, "I've been feeling an idiot, mourning a girl I didn't even know for certain liked me at all."

She looks up at him and smiles. "I liked you," she says. The current is easing, leaving other feelings behind it. Not more manageable, but less likely to make her pass out. She thinks. "We don't really know each other, though," she says. His hands are still on her shoulders, and she can't control her own hands, now; she touches him, his hands first, then his forearms. They're strong; the skin is slightly scarred, but soft as well. She tries to focus on the words. "I mean, you probably still know me about as well as you did; it's not been that long for me, but it's been five years here—it's okay if you don't think—"

"Stay with me," he says, and his lovely accent has a frantic edge to it. "I don't want you to leave. I want to talk to you, and eat dinner, and ... god, I don't know, just be near to you again—we can get to know each other, and if it's not what we wanted, we can just ... stop. It doesn't have to be romantic—"

She laughs: she's standing on his stoop, half-lost in the feeling of his skin, and he's telling her it doesn't have to be romantic. He stops talking and laughs, too. "You're really here?"

"Yeah," she says. "I'd have been here before, too, if I could have."

His smile goes lopsided and fades a bit. Hesitantly, he touches her head, the short-cropped hair, tracing gently around the implant over her ear. She leans her head into his hand, feels her hair catch on his calluses.

He sounds amused, maybe a little surprised, when he says, "This is you without the mods, then?"

Now she feel nervous again. "Is it okay?"

"Are you joking?" he asks. His hand tightens just a bit as he pulls her head toward his and kisses her.

Between the current, the uncontrolled feelings, and the fact that *Ianto* is kissing her, her knees buckle. He manages to half-catch her, but loses his balance and they fall back into his foyer.

She's blushing as they disentangle themselves. "I'm sorry. I'm not usually so ... swooning."

"Me, either," he says. "My ancestors would be very disappointed in my reflexes." He reaches over her to push the door closed; she catches his hand as he moves back to where he was. He smiles at her. "So. How is my accent?" he asks.

"It's really pretty," she says, smiling back because she can't not. "You're quite fluent. I'm impressed."

"Well, I had a lot of time to practice, and someone I missed very much that it reminded me of," he murmurs, ducking his head to look at her fingers, touching each knuckle with a fingertip. He glances up at her with a faint frown. "And you lost your Laendish?" he asks, concerned.

"I did," she says. She tilts her head to look at him sideways, and asks, "Could you teach it to me?"

He smiles, slow and spreading and shadowed, and says, "Yes, I can. But I'm pretty sure I owe you dinner first?"

"Dinner would be good," she says, but neither of them move into the space—the decadence—of his front room. Lia feels Ianto's fingertips on her hand and the heat of his arm sinking into her neck. He shifts, just a little, to put his face in her hair, his arms settling better around her, comfortable and fluent, like an accent or relief.

About the story

In many ways, "The Lost Languages of Exiles" is a story that you can read to get to know me. I wrote the last scene first, a long time ago, and it lived on my hard drive for a long time after that, because I didn't think I wrote romances. I liked it quite a lot, though, and sometimes I'd open the file and read it over—this scene I had apparently written just for myself.

It took a while, but eventually my brain (on my commute, whose brain doesn't get really creative in traffic?) started adding to it: lots of bits and pieces of other things that lived on my hard drive and needed a home—Laendish, IWT and its behavior mods, the Courisemes and the royal family they protect—became part of Lia's story. I love stories where fantasy tropes mix with science fiction; I like futures with dystopian elements that are taken for granted by the people who live with them; I dig a good, long, 99%-consonants Welsh name, so into the mix it all went.

Of course, now the story isn't just mine anymore, even if it is made up of things I like and have kept for years. But I'm totally willing to share the contents of my hard drive, and I hope these bits and pieces are something you'll want to open and read more than once.

A question for the author

Q: Why do you write speculative rather than realistic fiction?

A: The very first time I was ever asked this question, it was as part of a workshop during my final semester of college, posed to the entire class by our professor, in a tone of voice one usually associates with the exhausted parents of unruly teenagers. It boiled down to, "this story is good, why is it science fiction?"

The story was mine, by the way. I didn't really take the complimentary part to heart at all. I did take the other half of it more to heart than I should have. I spent a good chunk of my graduate school years and beyond writing realistic fiction and feeling really, really defensive any time I wrote anything even a little speculative. "It's literary!" "It's magical realism!" "It's outsized reality!"

Around ten years ago—right around the time I had my son, so maybe the sleep-deprivation helped lower my inhibitions—I stopped writing any realistic fiction. I started writing things because I wondered if I could —can I write steampunk? Epistolary steampunk? How about a superhero story? Sea monsters? Giant fight scenes and a homunculus? Love story complicated by time dilation? I don't know—let's find out!

And I realized something that is, ultimately, the answer to the question posed above. I write speculative fiction because it's cooler, and it's way more fun.

About the author

Laura E. Price lives in southwestern Florida with her husband and son, both of whom do their best to not interrupt her as she's writing (mostly they succeed). She has degrees in English and writing from the University of Evansville and the University of Louisiana, Lafayette.

seldnei.wordpress.com, @seldnei

Laura E. Price's story "The Lost Languages of Exiles" was published in *Metaphorosis* on Friday, 8 September 2017.

Renewal

Michael Gardner

John waited for Holly, continually clenching and then unclenching clammy hands. He sat on the edge of the bed, his stomach roiling, his feet tapping the floor incessantly. It never got easier. He always dreaded the confirmation. It was inevitable and yet most of him wanted to delay. *Another month,* he thought, *just one more. I'll be better prepared then.*

There was a soft click from the ensuite door, and then it was opening. John swallowed. He attempted to convey a neutral expression behind which he could hide his growing dismay. Holly emerged from the bathroom, beautiful in her pink nightie. She flicked auburn hair from her smiling blue eyes and, as she held aloft the pregnancy test with the telling blue cross, her face lit up.

John absorbed the jolt to his guts as best he could, but it was hard to give nothing away when he knew he'd be dead before his son was born.

"So, what do you think?" Holly asked expectantly, her smile beginning to falter.

He forced a grin, hoping it didn't look like a grimace. His mouth felt thick and dry, but he made it move.

"That's amazing," he said. And when she squealed and threw herself at him, he almost believed his words. He drew Holly close and rested his head on her shoulder, inhaling her scent of soap and lavender. God, he'd miss this.

"I've been wanting this for so long," she whispered in his ear. "And you're going to be such a great Dad."

The dread remained, poking at the base of his stomach, but for the moment he allowed her joy to seep in and settle on top, almost disguising it.

"And you're going to be an amazing Mum," he said, and he knew it to be true.

Staring up into the blanket of darkness hovering over the bed, John imagined it consuming him. Holly was snoring softly next to him but, despite her proximity, he felt alone.

They'd talked for a long time before bed. Baby names, plans for renovations, cots, prams, and clothes. Her enthusiasm was infectious and, for a short time, he'd immersed himself in the fantasy of fatherhood.

But that seemed long ago. Now, he was focused on bitter reality. There was so much he needed to do before the end.

He'd have to see his lawyers, and soon. They'd tell Holly about the life insurance policy after he was gone. But he also needed to update his ledger and add it to the package they were already holding for his unborn son. He'd need to recommend a replacement for himself at the University. Change the car into Holly's name. Clean his things out of the back room.

After cycling through his list several times he found his thoughts shifting to the inevitable and imminent pain. His, and his family's.

He sighed, and rolled onto his side, the pillow hot against his ear.

He'd have to warn Julie, he realised. He knew Holly wouldn't want his Mum to be first to know about the baby. The two women had never been close, and Julie was to blame for that. But he had to tell her. Maybe if he'd never shared his secret with Julie he could have waited. But what was done was done.

His thoughts began repeating. As they did, he refined his plan here, added something new to his list there. Eventually, he fell into a restless and uneasy sleep.

He was back in Scotland, shivering at the top of Heaval hill overlooking the bay. Icy water lapped at Kisimul Castle, a squat building of grey stone on an island off the coast of the village of Castlebay.

Ellie's labour screams carried on the wind up from the castle. They were laced with anger, which was his fault. He'd promised to give up the drinking and the women that came with it. But he hadn't. Even after she'd fallen pregnant. Deep down, he'd always assumed that Ellie needed him more than he needed her. She'd had to kick him out for him to realise his mistake. How stupid he'd been. Risking long-term happiness for short-term gratification.

The headaches had begun soon after his expulsion from the castle. A pain that pulsed at the back of his eyes, like needles jabbing him from the inside. The first had lasted for days, and he'd known then that something was wrong. That had been four months ago.

The sun sank in the sky behind him, his thin shadow elongating, stretching down the hill towards the bay. The sharp wind whipped his green and blue kilt and stung his skinny legs. Once, those legs had been planks, but the sickness had eaten away at him, leaving him withered and unable to defy the cold.

Was the sickness divine punishment? Or just bad luck?

As he stood on the hill listening to the birth of his first child, his bones aching, his head throbbing, tears streaming down his cheeks, he was ashamed of the selfish existence he'd led. *My whole life has been a waste.*

God, what he wouldn't give to do it all over, and better. He could have made so much more of what he'd been given if only he'd understood the things he did now.

Ellie delivered an extended shriek and, soon after, a great pain exploded in his head. The dewy grass, the rocky crags, the bay and the castle, all of it became white light. He screamed, and then everything was black.

Black.

And black.

But then illumination came from an orange glow and he found himself confined and wet, enclosed in a tight, fleshy cage. He couldn't control his limbs. They were not his own. Small, slimy, and jerky.

On impulse, he twisted towards the orange light. At the same time he was suddenly pushed from behind by a strong, contracting muscle. His prison squeezed and pushed until light filled his eyes, until cool air caressed his head, until he was out, and cold, and blinded, and scared. Several hard blinks cleared his eyes and there, looking down on him, larger than he ever remembered her, was Ellie. The angry expression of the last few months had melted.

"I think," she whispered to him, "I'll name you Johne MacNeil."

He tried to speak, but the only sound that emerged was a gurgle.

The tears had dried, but Julie's eyes remained red. She sat, hunched at her kitchen table, nursing a cup of tea. John sipped his own tea, waiting for her to speak.

"I guess this means I need to make good with her?" she finally said.

"Mum, you don't have to do anything you don't want to. But I'd definitely appreciate it if you could make amends before ... my transition."

"Hmm," Julie said. She raised the cup to her mouth and took a long, loud slurp. She placed her cup back on the table with a clink.

John watched her closely.

"I'll need her permission to see you when you became my grandson, so I kind of have to make more of an effort, don't I?"

"I'm sure Holly would appreciate that."

Julie gave a short, sharp, "ha", like she didn't believe him.

"Does she know about you, like I do?"

John paused, and then looked down at the table.

"No. I've never told anyone but you."

"Well, that's wrong. You should tell her."

John's eyes widened in surprise.

"But —"

"Just because we don't always get along doesn't mean I want her to suffer. Telling me helped me cope. And God knows she'll need something to help her cope when you start getting sick."

John opened his mouth, then shut it quickly and turned away. He nearly blurted out that telling Julie was a mistake. It might have made her feel better, but it had also led to her jealousy of Holly. But he learned from his mistakes. *Make each life better than the next.* That was the aim. Better job, less pain, happier families. And no more jealousy.

"Do you remember when we met?" Julie asked, her tone softer.

He returned his gaze to Julie, then smiled.

"Of course."

He saw her again as he had that first day. The tight blue jumper, the white miniskirt. Beautiful, confident, comfortable in her own skin.

"Have I changed much?" Julie asked, breaking his reverie.

"You're my mother now."

"I know that," Julie snapped, "and you're my son. But you know what I mean."

John chuckled, shaking his head.

"No. Not much. The spark I remember, the fight, it's all still there. And you still know how to order me around."

She smiled. The first since he'd given her the news.

"Speaking of which, you can help me take some garden waste to the tip."

John took Julie's empty cup from her and placed it along with his in the sink.

"She will forgive me, won't she?" Julie asked, staring out across the table towards the backyard. "I mean, I realise I've been petty at times. Even nasty on occasion. I couldn't help it, you know. Seeing you with her …"

John was shocked by the fear he heard in his mother's voice. But then, he realised, if she couldn't reconcile with Holly, there was a chance she'd lose him for good and she'd have no one to blame but herself.

"Yes, Mum. She will if you're genuine. Holly's not the type to hold grudges."

Julie sat there for a time, staring off into space. Finally, she sighed and rose to her feet. She took John's hands in hers and looked up at him, determined.

"Ok," she said. "I'll make this right. You just watch."

John sat at the breakfast bar watching Holly mix cake batter. The small, tight bump that was her belly pushed against her shirt.

He hit call on his phone and raised it to his ear. There was a soft click, and then Julie's voice.

"Hello."

"Hi, Mum, it's me." Holly turned and checked the oven, but John could tell she was listening.

"Hi, honey. What's up?"

"Just ringing to give you some good news," John said, "Holly's pregnant."

"So you're finally telling people. That took long enough. So when can I visit and sort this mess out?"

"Oh, I'm so glad you're excited," John replied. He watched Holly straighten and tilt her head slightly. "And we're both really happy."

"Maybe I should talk to her now. Actually, that's a good idea. Put her on."

"No," John shot back quickly. Holly was hovering over the bowl, but she wasn't mixing. She was looking at John. He forced a smile to his lips. "No, not much morning sickness. Holly is really well. Glowing actually," he said, regretting doing so instantly. It didn't sound like him. Holly's smirk said as much.

"Well, bad luck. I will talk to her. And if you don't put her on now, I'll just call her phone."

Jesus, Mum. God, she was a stubborn woman.

"Ha, yes. Good one. I guess I can do that."

"Good. But before you go — how are you, honey? Are you feeling ok?"

John paused. The headaches had already started.

"Yep, fine," he lied.

Julie sighed. He wondered if she knew he was lying. Probably. But she didn't say anything.

"Ok, pass me to Holly."

John covered the mouth piece with his hand.

"She wants to speak to you," John said, offering the phone to Holly.

Holly's eyes widened in surprise.

"Really?" she mouthed silently, looking dubious.

John shrugged, then nodded.

"She's going to be a grandmother. She's excited."

Holly hesitated for a moment, then reached out and took the phone. She turned her back on John and walked from the kitchen towards the hall.

"Hi, Julie. How are you?"

A pause. John stood up, took a glass from the cupboard and filled it with water.

"Thanks, Julie. We're happy too."

There was a long pause. John watched Holly's face intently. He could hear the buzz of Julie's voice from far away, but he couldn't make out what she was saying. Holly's face softened.

"Oh, thanks. Yes, me too. Look ... no, fair enough."

Another long pause.

Holly was nodding now. She looked at John and raised her eyebrows, then turned and disappeared down the hall. John drank his water and then sat at the bench again. It was best to wait. He shouldn't eavesdrop.

A couple of minutes later Holly returned and gave him his phone. Without saying a word, she returned to stirring the batter.

"Well?" John asked.

"Did you put her up to that?"

"I honestly have no idea what you talked about. What did she say?"

Holly stared at him, examining his face for a lie. But he saw that she found none. Her gaze softened.

"I never thought the old girl would surprise me. She apologised. She wants to fix things between us. She said she wants to be a good grandmother and a decent mother-in-law."

John smiled. This was good. It'd make things easier, for them and him.

"And you need to put some sheets on the spare bed. She's coming to visit on the weekend."

"Oh. And you're ok with that?"

Holly looked up from the batter.

"I don't know. But I think we have to give it a shot, right? For our little girl or boy."

John awoke in darkness with the coppery tang of blood at the back of his throat. He put a hand to his face and it came away slick. Shit. He turned and saw that Holly was still asleep. He sniffed hard, rose from the bed and then shuffled into the ensuite. He closed the door and turned on the light. Looking back at him in the mirror was something from a horror movie. Blood streamed from his nose, down over his mouth and neck and out across his pyjama top. Shit, shit, shit, John thought. He wrenched toilet paper from the roll and balled it up and held it to his nose. How the hell was he going to clean this up before Holly woke?

Then Holly screamed.

John threw the door open and found Holly shaking, pointing at the bloody sheets.

"It's ok, honey, its ok," John mumbled. "I'm ok. Just a bleeding nose."

"That's not just a fucking bleeding nose, John. I thought you'd been murdered. Look at the blood. Look at it."

John looked into her wide eyes. He saw the shock, fear and panic, and he suddenly felt guilty. *This is going to hurt her as much as me.* But what could he do about it? This was his life now. And hers, he realised.

"I'll clean it up. I just need a minute to stop the flow," he said softly.

Holly rose from the bed and took a deep, shuddering breath.

"I'll wet a cloth," she said, taking a tentative step towards him. She reached out with a trembling hand and took hold of his arm. Her short nightie clung to the bulge of her stomach.

"Tomorrow, I'm booking you in to see Doctor Rouch."

"Honestly, I'm fine."

"No you're not, John. This is not normal and I'm taking you to see my doctor. Understand?"

John smiled beneath the ball of crimson toilet paper. He loved her for wanting to look out for him better than he did himself. And despite knowing what the diagnosis would be, his heart clenched at Holly's concern.

"Ok."

"Good. Now, let's clean you up."

John watched the steam rising from his coffee. He wondered where the time had gone since Holly had first taken him to the doctor. As with previous transitions, life had become disjointed. Jumping forward and then slowing when he least expected. Sometimes, he wished he could just skip to the end.

"Sorry?" he inquired, looking up at Julie, who sat across the table from him.

"I *said*," she repeated, "what did the specialist say?"

"Same thing they said thirty six years ago. Cancer."

"Oh, come on. Medicine has advanced a hell of a lot since the eighties. What options do you have?"

John rolled his eyes.

"Chemotherapy, and then maybe surgery. But you and I know better."

John inhaled the earthy aroma of his coffee. He lifted the cup to his lips, sipping slowly, deliberately, as Julie pushed her chair back from the table with a screech and stood.

"So you're not even going to try?" She stomped to the kitchen sink where she dropped her cup with a clang.

"I don't know. Holly wants me to —"

"But you know better, right?"

John remained silent as he watched Julie return to the table and plant both hands on it, leaning over him.

"You selfish child. Holly wants you to live. I want you to live. But you, you're already thinking about the next life. How to make it better. How to get a better job. A better wife. Don't you think I know Holly is my upgrade?"

"Oh, come on."

"I know and you know. Everything is about what you can improve. Have you ever stopped to think that what you already have might be damn perfect? And if not perfect, then close enough?"

John sighed. He didn't need this now.

"Mum, I'm going to die. It's inevitable. But you know I'll be back. And you'll both still have me."

"But maybe you don't have to die, damn it," Julie hissed, tears in her eyes. "I don't know why I even bother. It was the same last time. You don't fight, you don't try to hold on. You don't even have the courtesy to let us comfort you or grieve with you. You just bloody disappear into yourself."

"I'm going for a walk." He stood up and moved towards the front door.

"Just try the chemo. Show Holly and me you're not completely selfish, ok?"

He paused at the door and turned back. Behind her angry posturing, John saw anguish in Julie's eyes. Was he as bad as she said? He hadn't meant to hurt her last time and he didn't want to hurt her now. He loved her and Holly more than they could possibly know. But chemo couldn't stop the transition. But then, maybe that wasn't the point. If seeing him try relieved a little of Julie's and Holly's pain, then maybe a little extra suffering on his part could be worthwhile.

"I'll think about it," he responded. He pulled the door open and slipped outside.

Time was a hundred kilogram weight attached to John's mind. He battled his heavy eyelids as the second hand on the clock on the wall made one painful jerk after another. His hospital gown itched and his arm was cold as poison dripped from a transparent bag into a tube, down to his left wrist where it entered his vein through the cannula.

The room had the faint scent of chlorine. The liquid would make him sick later, he knew. But now it dripped, like the second hand, slowly. He was trapped in a moment that he'd like to move past.

Time was becoming more inconsistent as he neared the end. He dreaded the long pauses. He nearly had everything prepared for a successful transition and yet, here he was, treading water, watching the second hand, tick, tick, tick. Why did time barely move when he was by himself?

A pang of bitterness assaulted him as he cursed Holly for abandoning him today. But just as quickly he pushed his selfish thought away. *It's me who should have been with her.* A twenty week scan and he wasn't there to see Holly's face when she found out they were having a boy. God, he was a shit.

He suddenly longed for home. To talk to her. To see her joy. To hold onto that moment.

The clock tick, tick, ticked.

John was frozen mid-heave, unable to breathe, unable to move, long after the last of the liquid had been expelled from his stomach and splattered against the bowl. Still, his diaphragm lurched and squeezed. His face ached, his mouth locked open until, finally, the spasm relented and he sucked in air.

Cold beads of sweat ran into his eyes. All John could do was stare at an area of clean porcelain at the back of the bowl, somehow untouched by his assault. His pallid hands clung to the toilet and shook.

Finally, certain he had nothing more to give, he slumped to the cool tiled floor, exhausted and empty. He hated this. This nothing right now. And the one before that, and before that.

But he knew his life wasn't just a series of empty moments. There was substance in between. He tried hard to recall the details of his trip with Holly to the coast last weekend, but nothing stood out.

Why? Why was right now so clear and last weekend — when he knew he felt good — a haze? Was it him, or the sickness?

He woke up screaming. Holly turned and held him for a glorious moment, with her plump belly pushed into his trembling back. Then she was gone, asleep, and he was alone in the dark as time ticked wearily on. One more moment, alone, cold.

But that wasn't right, was it? He thought hard. And then he realised that she had held him for at least an hour. She would have held him longer, he was sure, but he had pushed her away and asked her to sleep.

It was him who'd sought solitude, not her.

John was hunched over a box of his old journals. He picked out the most recent one and began to peruse it, surprised to find that it had been years since he'd made an entry. That was odd. He hadn't intentionally decided to stop, he just had. And yet he'd been religious about keeping these journals for generations. He'd relied upon them to help him clarify the life lessons that he'd record in his ledger. He returned the book to the box and picked out another at random and began to read.

He didn't hear Holly come in, so he gave a little start when she squeezed him from behind, her large belly pushed into his bony back.

"Oh," he said, turning, "you're here."

"I'm always here".

Holly was kneeling on the carpet, smiling. He looked her over for what felt like the first time in months. Her belly was round and tight, her hair thick and shiny. She looked so fresh, so clear. It was like he'd just surfaced from a deep ocean dive — strange to be above the water's surface, but wonderful to be breathing real air.

"Hey," he said, admiring her. How had he missed all of this?

"Hey yourself. What are you doing?"

"I was feeling all right, so I decided to clean my junk out of the back room."

Holly's smile faltered. John saw the discomfort in her eyes. She knows I'm cleaning up for when I'm gone, he thought.

"We need to make room for the baby, right?" John lied. He forced a smile to his lips. "But I got distracted. Do you remember I used to keep journals?"

Holly hesitated, but then smiled again.

"Yes, of course. Did you find anything good?"

John furrowed his brow.

"I was just reading about our first trip to the coast."

"Broulee?"

"Yes. It was supposed to be a surprise, remember? But it ended up a disaster."

"I don't know if I'd use the word disaster," Holly said. She shifted position, moving until she sat alongside John. He felt her warmth and breathed her in. She took the journal from him and started running her finger down the page.

"We got stuck in traffic in the mountains, so the three hour trip took five. And when we got there, we couldn't find anywhere decent to stay because I hadn't booked ahead — so we ended up in that terrible caravan park."

"Rings a bell," Holly said, flipping through the pages of the journal. "But what about the rest?"

"What do you mean?" He picked up another of his books.

"What about the walk along the beach we took the day after we arrived? That storm came in and we found a quiet place on the sand and sat there, just watching the lightning off the coast. Sitting there in your arms, that was perfect for me. Well worth the couple of inconveniences we faced to get to that moment, don't you think?"

John looked at Holly, confused.

"You're serious, aren't you? You don't remember how dull that drive was, how shitty the accommodation?"

Holly chuckled, shaking her head. She dropped the journal, leaned over and kissed him.

"When you find something good, come get me. I'm putting dinner on."

Holly rose to her feet and left the room.

John flipped through more journals. They read like a checklist of what had gone wrong in his life. An essay he could have written better at university. A wooden table he tried to make that was never level. An anniversary dinner he burnt. Holly was right. None of this was important.

He realised that he'd taken the same outlook into the last six months. Ignore the good, focus on the moments that should have been better, the things that he might improve next time. He forced himself to remember. Not the chemo, not throwing up — the real moments. The memories hit him hard. Holly holding him in the night. Holly forcing him to eat when he didn't feel like it. Holly laughing with Julie.

He sat there, stunned. He understood now why he'd stopped keeping the journals. There was nothing that he could learn from them that would help him find anyone better than Holly in his next life.

When he finally moved again, it was to bundle up all of his journals in his arms and take them out to the bin. Then he went into the kitchen, walked up to Holly who was mixing dough, and turned her and kissed her before she could say a word. After her initial surprise, her lips softened and she responded warmly.

John pulled back.

"Forget that, let's go out tonight. I'm feeling hungry for once."

Holly's eyes glistened.

"I'd like that."

John awoke to the sound of Holly crying, and he noticed that his right side was damp.

"John, something's wrong. I think the baby's coming early."

John's heart lurched.

"It's ok. Everything will be fine. I'll call the hospital," John said, jumping up and grabbing his phone. What was happening? He wasn't sick enough yet. He always knew when time was up. He felt it in his bones. A brittleness and a sickness that was all consuming. But he still felt very much here. This had never happened before. Was it the chemo?

The midwife on the phone reassured him and asked him to get Holly to the hospital as quickly as possible. After the midwife hung up, he phoned Julie.

"I'll be there as soon as I can," she said, hanging up abruptly.

Then he helped Holly to the car, comforting her as best he could, knowing he might not be with her much longer.

John held Holly's hand tightly while Doctors Roberts and England talked quietly in the corner of the room. The midwife, Sally, examined Holly, who lay on her side, pillows propped under her left hip. John fought the urge to vomit, and ignored the weakness in his legs. He didn't know how long he could continue standing, but he'd let Holly squeeze his hand while he could. Because he wanted to be here, damn it, to share this experience with her.

Just then, he heard Julie loudly remonstrating outside the birth suite doors.

"What do you mean I can't go in? They're my family and I want to see them."

"You can let her in," Holly said, panting between contractions. "I'd like her in here. Please."

The doctors looked at John. John nodded, and soon Julie was standing next to him dabbing Holly's face with a warm cloth.

"Nice to see you're still here," Julie directed to John as Holly squeezed his hand and moaned as another contraction took hold. John leaned against the bed for support, easing the strain on his tiring legs.

The two doctors separated. Doctor Roberts began to set up a radiant warmer nearby. Doctor England consulted briefly with Sally, and then moved towards Holly's feet.

"Ok, Holly," Doctor England said, "I know we've been saying to resist the urge to push, but on the next contraction, it's time to push."

"Oh, thank God," Holly panted. And soon she was groaning loudly, her face screwed up tight as pain hit again.

"Ok, that's great," the doctor said. Sally, who was to John's left, pulled Holly's leg further towards her. "I can see the baby's head."

John rose up a little to get a better view and, holy shit, he could see it too. Just the top of some wet, dark hair, but it was amazing. He tried to hold himself erect to keep his eyes on his son, but then his legs wobbled and he suddenly felt dizzy.

He reached out, trying to grasp at the bed, but his eyes fluttered and, from somewhere distant, he heard a thud and a clatter.

The world was black, but with an orange glow. He was cosy and warm and yet encompassed by a deep, aching sadness he had never experienced before. Julie would never chastise him again as his mother and Holly would cease to be his wife. He would lose so much. There would be no more of Holly's smile — the special one she reserved for when he pleased her. No more watching her brush her hair as she hummed softly to herself. No more cakes. He felt it all wash past and over him, slipping through his fingers. It would soon be replaced with that look of sadness he always saw in his new mother.

He was squeezed and pushed. Time was nearly up. John panicked and bucked and kicked. For once, he was not excited about the prospect of a new life. He was happy now, here. And wasn't that all that mattered? He hated to admit it, but Julie was right. Some people never came close to having all he did and he'd been letting it all go.

So he scrambled, trying to hold onto his life. He pushed aside the pain and the minutiae, and sought out the real moments. Holly's laughter. Holly rubbing his back as he fell asleep in a sweat. Julie ordering him around her garden. He held on tightly and ignored the opportunities for improvement ahead. He remembered and focused and saw with clarity the glint in Holly's smiling eyes as she told him he would be a Dad. He saw it and felt it — the new possibilities of his life continuing.

The black withdrew rapidly and was replaced with bright lights.

He felt arms around him, lifting him into a chair.

"No you don't, you selfish bastard," Julie whispered in his ear. "You're staying here and seeing this."

"Yes, Mum," John mumbled. He opened his eyes and saw tears in Julie's. Her face was ashen, but she smiled, relieved. Sally hovered just behind Julie, concern etched across her face. Julie leaned closer again.

"Are you back for good?" she whispered, tears splashing his face.

"I hope so."

"He's ok, love," Julie said to Holly, wiping at her eyes. "He's just a bit dizzy. A quick rest will fix him up."

But Holly didn't respond. She was groaning, panting, crying, straining.

"That's good. Very good, Holly. Just one more and ... done," Doctor England said.

John saw the obstetrician hold up a tiny baby, who opened its mouth and wailed.

"Congratulations. A baby boy."

In a wave of activity, the cord was cut and the baby was passed to Doctor Roberts, who quickly laid it down on the radiant warmer where she checked him over under the heat lamp.

Julie helped John to his feet, his arm around her shoulders. Holly lay on her back, her eyes clenched shut, like she was afraid to open them and confirm that her son was real.

"Hey," John whispered, leaning close to her and kissing her on the cheek. "You did it."

She opened her eyes and looked into his.

"You're ok?"

"I'm fine," he said, smiling.

Doctor Roberts was suddenly standing by the bed and handing Holly her baby. She accepted him, her mouth agape, but no words came out. She just stared at their tiny son, soundlessly, breathlessly, a tiny presence in her loving embrace.

"Being premature, he'll need to spend time in the special care nursery. But everything looks great," Doctor Roberts said.

John ran his hand delicately over his son's slick scalp and he felt an electric pulse through his fingertips as tears welled in his eyes.

"He's beautiful," Julie said, as she shifted under John's weight. And he was, John saw. Because he looked like Holly.

"Now, you're sure?" Holly asked. She stood just inside the front door, her eyes flitting from John, to Daniel cradled in his arms, and then back to John.

"Yes, I told you, go. We'll be fine."

"But you're still recovering. You've —"

"I've been in remission for a month. I'm fine. You've spent enough time caring for the two of us. It's time to spend a little time on you."

John gently ushered Holly out the door. She stepped outside reluctantly, her brow furrowed, her mouth a frown.

"Call me if anything goes wrong, ok?" she said. "I'm just down the road at the hairdressers, so I can be back in five minutes."

"Will you get going?" John said, laughing. "We're fine."

She hesitated, then leaned forward and kissed John and then Daniel. After one last look at both of them, she finally turned and walked away from the house.

John shook his head, and then stepped back inside, closing the door behind him. He glanced down at his son to find him in the middle of a big, gummy yawn, and he was suddenly struck by a recollection of what it had been like, beginning life again. He didn't miss it. He'd done it so often that it had become a well-rehearsed play. Yet since Daniel's birth he'd been assaulted by a kaleidoscope of emotions — protectiveness, pride, worry, doubt, and sheer, unbridled joy. After such a long time on this earth, it was amazing to be completely uncertain about what he was doing because he was experiencing something new.

John inhaled deeply, and smiled down at his son who was looking up at him with big, curious eyes.

"Ok, little man. Time for bed," he said. He laid Daniel down in his basinet and then stood nearby, watching as Daniel's eyelids drooped, sprung open, and then slowly closed. This was one glorious moment worth holding on to.

About the story

Before writing "Renewal", I'd read a short story about an immortal couple who were both hundreds of years old. This got me thinking about common fantasy depictions of immortals – vampires, Highlander – where they don't age, they live forever, and every once in a while they change their identities so they can continue their lives without raising suspicions. Of all the things to get hung up on, I began wondering how anyone today could easily change identities with so much information online, and held by Government and business.

So that got me thinking about reincarnation. As a concept of immortality, it solved the "new identity" challenge. And I soon came up with the idea of a man essentially fathering himself. I thought this concept brought with it some interesting challenges, such as facing death over and over, as well as having a romantic partner become your mother. I was aware that there was a risk that anything I put to paper might simply come across as oedipal and sordid, which I didn't want, but I decided to start writing and see how it turned out.

The second element that became a key part of the story was my own tendency to dwell on things that go wrong – thinking about what I should have done, and how I could do things better if faced with a similar situation next time. This became a key trait for my main character, and shaped how he approached his immortality.

A question for the author

Q: What's your favorite *non*-SFF book?

A: The New York Trilogy by Paul Auster. It's beautifully written, and strange and compelling. Auster puts himself in the stories. Literally. Paul Auster is a character. Another character pretends to be Paul Auster. Yet, these meta-references never detract from the three stories. To me, Auster wants you to be aware that the characters you are reading about are simply reflections of his mind, and yet, despite being conscious of this throughout the book, I was still caught up in the twisting, confusing narratives, the uncertainty between fact and fiction, the ambiguity of the language, and the sense of cbsession and loss of identity.

On the off chance someone thinks I'm cheating by calling something as strange as the New York Trilogy a pure, non-SFF book, then my back up would be *Brighton Rock* by Graham

Greene. On the surface, it's an excellent gangster novel. But dig a bit deeper and you also find these great musings on the juxtaposition between religion and atheism, between good and evil, and right and wrong.

About the author

Michael Gardner is a public servant and economist living in Canberra, Australia with his wife and two kids. He loves urban fantasy and horror – really anything strange or weird. And he has a very patient wife who puts up with his taste in TV shows and movies, and lets him spend more time writing then he probably should.

Michael Gardner's story "Renewal" was published in *Metaphorosis* on Friday, 15 September 2017.

What The Darkness Is

Simon Kewin

The howls of the gore-hounds filled the night air. Vanda stopped to catch her breath. Sounds echoed off the trees, throwing noises at her from odd angles. Her pursuers were close. When they caught her it would be the end.

She peeped at the precious cargo she carried, strapped across her chest in the sling she'd fashioned from an old shawl. The night was dark – of course – but there was just enough starlight to see Abha's tiny face peeping out, wide-eyed in wonder, oblivious to what was happening. Vanda envied the baby. Abha had no idea that the gore-hounds, if they caught up, would rip her to pieces like a rabbit.

Vanda set off again, ignoring the stomach cramps tearing at her. The ground was rising. She'd heard the Chronicler lived in a ramshackle hut on a hill in a wood. That was all she had to go off. It was entirely possible the whole thing was no more than a story. When it came to the Chronicler, the lines between truth and tale weren't always clear.

She glimpsed a light through the shifting boughs: a single yellow candle shining from a cottage window. In one of his tales it would have been placed there as a beacon for the desperate. She raced into the clearing and rapped on the door, gaze darting around. She expected the hounds, black as night and red of eye, to lope from the woods at any moment. Away over the treetops the thinnest of crescent moons sliced through the night sky. As it always did.

The door creaked open. An old man's face peeped through the gap, regarding her over the top of his half-moon spectacles. His wrinkled, veined skin might have been the map of an imaginary land. A red birth-mark, a blotch like the shape of some island, adorned his cheek. He didn't look surprised to see her.

She expected to feel the foul breath of the Lady's beasts on the back of her neck at any moment. "Chronicler. I need your help," she panted. "The gore-hounds are after me."

"And you want me to distract them with an exciting story while you sneak out of a window?" said the old man.

"Please. Let us in."

"Us? You said *me* a moment ago."

"I have a child with me. A baby. Chronicler, please. Abha has The Speech."

The old man's eyes widened at that. A look of appreciation crossed his features. Appreciation and something like concern, as if The Speech were some terrible disease. Which, in a way, it was.

"I see. Then you'd better come in. No point standing outside in the cold and dark is there?"

It took a few moments for Vanda's eyes to adjust to the brightness within. Candles flickered from sconces and shelves. A log fire crackled and spat, filling the cottage with the sweet smell of woodsmoke. Next to the fire, upon a cushioned chair, lay a book, a strip of red silk marking the Chronicler's page. She glimpsed an inner room that had to be his library. She had the impression, before he closed the door, of high shelves of books receding into the dark distance, impossibly far away.

"So," said the Chronicler. "What do you want me to do? If Lady Lillian has sent her hounds to hunt you down, you need to find a fortress with high walls to protect you. You need an army of fierce guards loyal to the end. Not a tired old man in a hovel in the woods." His eyes glittered with delight as he spoke. In his stories, old people living alone in the woods were never what they seemed.

"No walls are high enough to keep the hounds out," said Vanda. "No oceans are wide enough to keep Lady Lillian's ships at bay."

"Perhaps."

"But you can protect the baby. You can take her beyond even the Lady's reach."

"I?" Now he sounded vain, enjoying the flattery of her words.

"You have The Speech too, in your own way." said Vanda.

"No. I can't shape the world as the Lady can. I can't banish her hounds or unfreeze the moon. I can't bring an end to her eternal night. Would she have let me live if I could unweave her words?"

Vanda glanced to the outside door. Shouldn't the hounds have arrived by now? "You're more than that. I've heard the stories. Once you came to our village, at Midsummer, when there was still a Midsummer. You told the tale of Siggurd, sent on an impossible quest to slay the Clockwork King. It was … more than mere words. I *saw* the red roofs of Pirathia sitting in the great desert. I felt the warm air on my face, tasted the sand in my mouth. You took us there. That is your magic; that is what you can do."

She sounded more sure than she was. The memory of that night was faint. Perhaps, swayed by the balmy air and too much hurtleberry wine, she'd imagined the whole thing.

The Chronicler didn't reply for a moment. His eyes narrowed amid their nests of wrinkled skin. "How can you be sure the child has The Speech? She is a baby. It is too soon to know."

"She uttered her first word when she was six moons old."

"That is not so unusual."

"A ball she wanted rolled away from her so she spoke a word of Making. It took her a few attempts to get her tongue around it, but soon she held a new ball in her hands. One she'd created."

"She found the toy on the ground beside her."

"When she'd finished playing she spoke the word backwards and the ball in her hands was gone."

"She dropped it."

"She is six months old and has already spoken words of Making and Unmaking. Would Lady Lillian have unleashed her hounds if this wasn't so? The baby is a threat to everything the Lady has wrought."

A frown knitted the Chronicler's features. "Who is she? And who are you? Is she your blood?"

"The girl's parents died, lost at sea. We found her, took her in, a family of wheelwrights. When the Lady heard about her and the hounds were sighted I took her and ran."

"I see."

"Chronicler, please, you are our only hope. The beasts were at my back. I don't understand why they aren't here already."

The Chronicler nodded his head in something like appreciation. "I have some small magic, it is true. The magic of the fireside tale. A moment like this when imminent danger presses can be made to stretch out longer than should be possible. It suits the shape, the *need* of the story, and even the Lady can't deny that power. I can hold them back for a minute or two, although they will break through eventually."

"So you will help? You will take us to one of the distant lands where the Lady does not hold sway?"

Outside, from somewhere in the trees, a howl filled the night. The Chronicler peered at her over the top of his reading spectacles. "You truly believe this baby will be the one to defeat the Lady? She's the one chosen to save us all?"

Vanda sighed. "Yes. Although I'd settle for her surviving. Growing up, falling in love, making mistakes. Doing whatever she chooses."

"I see," said the Chronicler, his face thoughtful. "Less satisfying as a story. The helpless baby destined to defeat the Lady and restore light to the world: now that's a tale I might be able to work with."

"Can't you weave a different yarn for her?"

The possibility seemed to amuse the Chronicler. "The needs of the tale cannot be denied; that's the way it works."

"And if she chooses a different path?"

"Then we are in a different story to the one started. We shall see. It doesn't always do to know the ending when we've barely begun, does it? But … I can't take you. The orphaned baby alone in a strange world: that has power. Resonance. You must stay behind. Your part is played."

"She is a baby. She's helpless."

"I will deliver her to those who will care for her. I may be needed again later. The enigmatic stranger offering cryptic advice. That could work."

"Have you experience of looking after a baby?"

A smile of delight flickered across the old man's face. "Little. We make an unsuited pair, our chances of survival small. You see the power of it already? I will prepare myself for the journey. The hounds will be at the door soon, and the candles need snuffing out. Will you attend to them while I prepare?"

The Chronicler bustled off, stooping through a low door in the shadowy corner of the room. Vanda, rocking Abha in her arms, crossed to peer out of a window. In the brittle cold she could see yellow eyes glinting from the trees. Many, many eyes, brighter, somehow, than the moonlight they reflected. She set to work, licking the finger and thumb of her spare hand and pinching out the candle flames. Each gave off a little twist of smoke as it was extinguished.

She worked her way around the room to the Chronicler's chair. Unable to resist, she opened the book at the page marked by the slip of red silk. The pages were blank. Puzzled, she turned over more pages, and more. All were empty.

"That is our story," said the Chronicler, reappearing behind her. He wore a long grey coat, a pack slung over his shoulder, stout boots on his feet. He had the air of a man used to travel. "It is the tale of our land."

"The words stop."

"They stopped when the Lady wove her magic and froze us in this night. That is what the darkness is. Words unwritten, lives unlived. It is the story stopped in its middle, the ending never reached. Now, hand me Abha and we will proceed."

Vanda held back, reluctant to release the baby. "Why has the Lady worked this evil? You of all people must know. This land was beautiful. She gazed upon it from her tower with a mother's love."

The Chronicle considered, his brow furrowing. "Who can say? Perhaps she learned to hate the coming light. She foresaw what the day would bring and despised it. That might make the start of a passable tale. Now, please, we must leave."

Vanda handed the baby over. The Chronicler walked to the library door and pushed it wide. Vanda, peering in, saw the shelves she'd glimpsed. The endless ranks of books.

"There are so many of them. I had no idea."

"Many, yes. I have lived many lives. Lived and loved and lost. And won, too, against all the odds, of course."

"Which book, which world will you take her to?"

The Chronicler turned to block her passage. "I cannot tell you. The Lady must not know. Tell her what we have done, if you must, but you can't know where we have gone."

Vanda nodded. "Then, thank you, Chronicler. Look after Abha, please. It is all I ask."

"I will." He nodded once and quietly shut the door behind him, leaving Vanda alone.

After a few moments she heard growling and snuffling from outside the cottage, and then the first heavy blow upon the door.

"Another tattoo, Abi? What is it this time? More moons and stars?"

Abi rolled up her sleeve so Gemma could see it properly. Her arm was an angry red from the tattooist's needle. "A wheel."

"Okay, that's ... boring."

"No, it's cool. It's, like, the cycles of the year. The cycles of life. The end is the start and all that."

"Hippy shit."

"It's clearly not, look, there are flames. I like it."

Gem shrugged. "Okay, it's your skin. Just don't let our Galactic Overlord see it."

"Galactic Over*lady*." The Home was ruled by the fearsome Mrs. Framing, a woman who seemed to know everything that went on among the children in her care. "I'm sixteen. I'm allowed tattoos."

"You're supposed to get them approved. And they're supposed to be nice things. Happy things, things the Inspectors couldn't object to."

"You think they'll object to a wheel?"

"Maybe for being *dull,* yeah. And then there are the demons on your back."

"They're not going to see those, are they?"

"I've seen them."

Gem was her oldest friend. Both orphans, they'd shared a room in Gladwell House until they were ten. Now they were in and out of each other's rooms all the time.

"You're different," said Abi.

"Thanks. I think." Gem rose and leaned her elbows on the ledge of the first floor window. "Hey, your stalker's outside the gates again."

"He is not my stalker."

"He so is. I hate that dog of his. Growls each time I go past. Think we should report him for, I dunno, sexual harassment or something?"

"He's just a homeless guy. He's never even spoken to me."

"He looks at you."

"I'm sure he looks at lots of things. People do when they have eyes. Besides, I happen to be a beautiful young woman. You're lucky I hang around with you."

"Yeah," said Gem. "A beautiful young woman with crap tattoos. You know what your problem is?"

"I'm sure you'll tell me."

"You always see the best in people. You always want to help people, be nice to them. Honestly, Abi, the world doesn't work that way. People like you get taken for a ride."

"And people like you die a lonely, bitter death, afraid of everyone around them."

"I'm not lonely. Unless you're planning to move out."

"No," said Abi. "'Course not."

That night, Gem's screams roused Abi from sleep. Nightmares had always plagued her friend. They were common enough in the Home. Abi's had faded over the years and while her dreams were always vivid and often alarming, she no longer woke up sweating. For Gem it was different.

Abi tapped gently on her friend's door. Sometimes Gem didn't wake up, but tonight there was a low snuffling sound coming from within. After a few moments the latch on the door unclicked. Abi found Gem sitting on her bed, quilt grasped around her knees.

"A nightmare?"

Gem nodded. "There were shadows moving in the room, creeping across the walls toward me. They had teeth, somehow I knew they had teeth, and they were coming for me. They were sniffing. Hunting."

Abi did what she always did, putting an arm around her friend. "Shall I tell you a story so you can go to sleep?"

They'd been sharing these night-time tales for many years, something neither mentioned in the day. Gem nodded, and Abi settled in beside her to begin her story. Within ten minutes, Gem's breathing was slow and peaceful. Rather than disturbing her, Abi curled up beside her, just like when they were children.

The shadows came for Abi a day later. She was walking home from school along the ring-road, past a red-brick wall covered in tattered fly-posters. The flickering movement had been there for some time before she became aware of it. Shapes on the wall beside her, patches of darkness that followed her. A shadow-play she was a part of: her silhouette was among the shifting shapes, as if there were creatures all around her she couldn't see.

She tried slowing and they slowed. She hurried on, telling herself it was some weird reflection, or her overactive imagination. She crossed the road, out of the bright sunshine. There were no shadows there; she'd left them behind.

She made herself breathe slowly and deeply to calm her pounding heart. The stench of something foul reached her nostrils, the smell of rotting flesh. Then, in a shop window, she saw the reflections. Huge, dog-like beasts crowding in on her, snarling teeth bared. A low growl made the hair on the back of her neck prickle.

Someone grasped her wrist, hurting her. "Quick, we must get away from them." It was the old man, the tramp who sat on the street, the red birth-mark vivid on his cheek.

Abi fought him. "What are you doing? Get off me!"

The old man let go. His gaze darted around, not looking at her. "You can see them, can't you? The gore-hounds."

"What?"

"They're coming. They've found you at last. Sixteen years is more than I hoped for. Please, I can hold them off a few moments but they are strong."

He looked so terrified, like an old broken bird, she lost her fear of him. "What are they?"

"Her hunters. Time is short. Come, I have made plans for this day. We must go to the High Street; we have to travel further in." He set off, striding with surprising speed, his little dog slinking along beside him.

"But I don't want to do any shopping," she called.

The old man turned to study her. "Then your story will stop here. An unsatisfactory ending, frankly. No shape to it, no circle closed."

"What does that mean?"

"It means those things will rip your flesh from your bones if they reach you."

"Why would you even say a thing like that?"

"Because it is the truth. I'm sorry, but this is not my story. I'm merely a part-player. A character."

Abi looked around. There was no one nearby to hear this craziness. "They're shadows. Why would they want to kill me? I'm just a girl."

"Because you're the only one who can save the world."

She could only laugh. "Me? Save the world. Gem was right, you are crazy. How the hell am I going to save the world? It's a major triumph getting out of bed in the morning."

"I'm not talking about this world. I'm talking about the real one."

"The what?"

"Look, come with me and I'll explain, I promise."

"If you are an abuser, this is a pretty bizarre approach you've got."

"Please, Abha, I'm trying to help you. As I have ever since I brought you here."

"Wait, what? You brought me here?"

The old man made no attempt to hide his impatience. "Yes, as a baby. Must we discuss this now?"

She had to swallow the lump in her throat. "So, you're saying you're my, like, father or something?"

"No, no, your father died. I promised I'd watch over you, that's all. Please, can we hurry? They'll be upon us soon."

Movement flickered in the corner of her eye but disappeared when she looked directly at it. The old man's dog growled, ears flattened against its head. The High Street would be busier. Surely she'd be safe there.

"This had better be good," said Abi.

They stopped outside the video game store, its windows filled with colourful boxes and posters. The old man peered inside through cupped hands. "This will keep them guessing for a while."

"What do you mean?" asked Abi.

"Our escape. She'll expect me to use books, won't she? In a story, the unexpected is always good."

Shadows were flickering on the pavement at her feet, overlaying her own. There was a weight to them, a thickness, that hadn't been there before. There was a rush of hot fetid air on her ear. She raced after the old man into the store.

Inside, he was studying the cases of three different games, shaking his head as if in disbelief. "Such detail, such huge worlds."

"Yeah, they're cool."

"This one," he said, holding out one of the boxes.

"*War of the Witch King*. Sorry, why are you showing me this?" she asked.

"You know it? You have played it?"

"Sure, we have it at the Home. I'm a Level 12 Weatherworker."

"Then I can draw on your knowledge. Can I hold your hand?"

"What?"

"Please. It will make it easier when I begin the telling. I mean you no harm, I promise you."

"Yeah," she said. "I'll bet they all say that."

"I can leave you to the hounds if you like. They will tear you to shreds if they can. They're becoming more real with every moment."

The whole thing was ridiculous, crazy, but there was something in it that made her stomach tingle. Glancing around to make sure no one she knew was anywhere in sight, she held out her hand. His skin was rough in hers. He gripped her tight and his lips began to move.

Dizziness washed over her a moment later ...

... and she sprawled onto wet grass. The air was colder, the edge of a chill to it. Water chortled somewhere nearby.

She climbed to her feet, head still spinning. They stood on the shores of some vast lake, tendrils of mist threading through the air over it. Except it wasn't a lake, it was a river, encircling that whole world. The water flowed, carrying sticks and birds and clumps of some sweet-smelling flower along with it. Abi recognized it from the game. "What have you done? How the hell can this even be possible?"

The old man shrugged. "Worlds within worlds, stories about stories. What explanation is needed?"

What did that mean? There were no *other worlds*. You imagined them when you were a child but you grew out of it. She'd once delighted in imagining all sorts of impossible lands but now she knew better.

And yet, there she was.

"What happened to your dog?"

The old man ran a hand through his straggly hair. "I couldn't bring both of you. I shall miss him, my only friend in that world. Perhaps there will be a way to go back for him later."

"And why ... why have you brought me here?"

"To escape Lady Lillian's hounds. I hid you for sixteen years in a world reached through a book and I have kept watch over you all this time. Now we've taken another turning through the maze. Hopefully, an unexpected turning. If she takes another sixteen years to find us, I'll be happy."

"I don't get any of this. It's all insane."

"I will tell you everything I know, give you the story so far. Perhaps it will help."

When he'd finished recounting the tale, Abi closed her eyes, her back against the rough bark of a tree, trying to make sense of it all.

"Why does she hate me so much?"

"You are a threat."

"But these words of Making and Unmaking. I don't know anything about them."

"Vanda said you spoke them without thinking when you wanted the ball. I think you only have access to them in the real world. Or perhaps they will come at the right moment, when you have the understanding to use them." The old man – the Chronicler – smiled his sparkling smile. "At least, that's what would happen if I were telling the story. Right at the last moment, in the nick of time."

"But what about Gem? And everything else. You know, my life?"

"It's all still there. It's like a book that has been closed. The pages will still be there when you open it up again. Now, I suggest we find something to eat. No point dying and doing Lillian's work for her, is there?"

"Those creatures, the gore-hounds. They'll come again. We'll need to be ready."

"Yes. Are there many books in this world? Many stories we could escape into?"

"I don't think so. There's an island where some witches live that has lots of books of history in tunnels beneath the ground."

"I suppose that might do. Again, it might be too obvious."

"Most of the time people sing songs here to tell the old stories. You know, to pass ancient sagas down."

"Ah. That sounds more promising. Tell me, Abha, can you sing?"

"No. Don't make me. Seriously."

The Chronicler seemed pleased with himself. "Just as well I have an excellent voice. We must learn these lays as we go about the land. When the time comes and the Lady finds us, we can use one for our escape. A song can conjure up a world as well as a story."

In the end, their stay lasted only three years. This time, Abi heard the howls before she saw the shadows. As the Chronicler keened the song they'd chosen, Abi felt the same dizziness she'd experienced the last time.

The stone walls around her faded away.

They stepped from world to world for another seven years, always going deeper, one step ahead of Lady Lillian. A painting in a castle gallery depicting an imaginary city, streets thronged with merchants and priests. In that city, a mummers' play performed by torchlight, conjuring up visions of sunlit islands scattered across a sparkling blue sea.

There, she met Aydan and lost her heart to him. His smile made her melt and fizz inside, both at the same time. They would lie together on the soft beach and listen to the unending hushing of the waves. She loved the way the drops of seawater sat upon his smooth skin, the miniature worlds glimpsed within each. He loved to trace the lines of her tattoos, fascinated by them. Fascinated, too, by her wild tales of other worlds. For three years they shared a simple life of fishing and eating, loving and sleeping. Gemma and Gladwell House seemed an impossibly far distance away. The Chronicler kept to himself, watching and waiting.

She and Aydan walked the whole circuit of their round island, hand-in-hand, the twin lines of their footprints a braided line in the sand. Abi liked the sensation of returning to the place they'd started, the familiarity of it as well as the disorientation of seeing it from a different angle. Sometimes they talked about where she'd come from, leading them to the one subject painful to both of them.

"Will you go back to the sky with the other angels?" he asked. It amused her when he called her an angel. Many of the things they did together were surely things no angel had ever done. Still, she liked it.

"No. We will have to move onwards, go deeper."

"Why does this demon pursue you?"

"Only I can speak the words to unravel her magic. She has frozen her world in perpetual night."

Aydan gazed over the sparkling waters and shook his head. "When will it be?"

"I don't know. Not for a long time, I hope."

"We could have children."

She stroked his face. "I'd like that. Truly. But not with this hanging over them."

They were both silent for a time, lost to their own thoughts. Then the sun filled their eyes once more and they ran together for the splash of the sea.

One day, the villagers found the remains of a small deer, its body torn to scattered shreds. There were no predators on the island capable of such butchery. In the sand all around were the footprints of animals that might have been hounds. The Chronicler, seeing them, nodded his head to Abi.

Aydan pleaded to come with her, but she didn't know how that might be worked. There was the danger, too. With Abi gone, Aydan's life would be as safe and peaceful as it always had been. They allowed themselves one final night, Abi always alert for howls and snarls.

"Will you come back?" he asked as the first light found the shadows in the corner of their room.

She lay with her head upon his chest, their limbs entwined. She wanted more than anything in the world to say yes. Here would be a fine ending to the story: an ending that was a new beginning. But it couldn't be. She could think of no words to give him.

She and the Chronicler sailed in an outrigger to the sacred atoll, home of the people's few gods, the paradise they all went to when they died. There, among the many offerings sent bobbing over in bottles on the ocean's currents, they found scrimshaw carvings depicting the fairy palaces of the land that, it was said, the island people had once come from.

Their escape.

Barely six months later, they stood upon a final hilltop, so high that the drifting clouds were around them and below them. The old man slumped to the ground, the weariness raw in him. She could see the shape of the bones in his face, as if his features were sinking away. Even his red birth-mark looked faint. He had told his last story, woven his last tale to foil Lady Lillian. Abi saw with sudden clarity how exhausted he was. He nodded his head, as if he knew what she was thinking.

"What will you do?" he asked. His voice was weak. "What ending will there be to this story?"

"There can only be one ending," said Abi. "I have to go back where it started. I have to destroy her, stop the monsters pursuing me and free the world from the moment it's frozen in. That's it, isn't it?"

"Once, I thought so. But we have been through much together, you and I. I think you can make your own ending, now."

"What other endings could there be?"

A flicker of delight passed across his features. "Perhaps … perhaps you will tell the tale of how you become the Lady Lillian we knew. How you loved the beauty of that starry night so much you stopped the world. That might be a fine twist."

"But it's not right."

"Or perhaps you will describe how you took a baby girl and rescued her from the gore-hounds, became Vanda to bring her to the Chronicler. A small but vital role in a bigger cycle that leaves those hearing the story guessing, lets them decide the ending. Or you may come up with some conclusion I have not foreseen. In any case you must choose. I can't hold off the hounds any longer. You can only snatch victory from the jaws of defeat so many times before the story falls apart."

"How do I get to the real world?"

He shrugged, as if it was the easiest thing in the world. "I have shown you. Tell the tale. Speak the words of Making, then step across. Step further in."

"But I'm not going deeper. I'm going back to the start."

The little smile of delight was there again. "You know, I'm never really sure there is a start. There's just the maze, stories within stories. Maybe, who knows, there isn't even one *real* world and they're all as genuine as each other."

Did that mean she really was returning to where she'd begun? Or was she creating a new story, a different telling of the same root tale? Perhaps it made little difference.

"If I go, what of you?"

The old man closed his eyes as if he might fall asleep. "My part is played. It has been a fine story, but characters come and go. I'll remain here to mock them when they come, tell them they can't win. An amusing counterpoint to the final drama. Hurry, now. They are near."

Abi cleared her mind. Words came to her, flowing without conscious effort. Yes. She saw what had to be done. How the world she wanted to reach looked: the woods and the seas, the bright stars and the crescent moon, and Lillian's high tower on its hill looking down on everything. The Chronicler had described it often enough over the years. The words of Making and Unmaking she would need also came to her. She saw what had to be done about the Lady, what the darkness was.

She began to tell the story forming in her mind.

She climbed the steps that wound up the hill to the tower. The bright stars blazed down, hard as jewels. The slender crescent moon hung among them. It was beautiful in its cold and colourless way.

The howls of the gore-hounds filled the night air, but Abi paid them no heed. They couldn't harm her, because the story couldn't harm the storyteller. At the gates they snarled and snapped, stained teeth level with Abi's face, their breath the smell of rotting meat.

Abi waved them away with a word of Unmaking, their names spoken backwards. One by one, they melted to the ground to become shadows, become nothing. Pushing the door open, she wound her way up the spiral staircase to where she knew Lady Lillian would be waiting for her.

A single, circular room took up the whole of the top of the tower. Twelve arched windows, open to the night air, looked out over the world. A figure in white lace, white as bone, stood at one of them. She gazed out across a wide sea, the moonlight a shimmering path across it.

"It's beautiful, isn't it?" Lady Lillian said.

"It is," said Abi.

"You would destroy it?"

"Stories can't stop," said Abi. "They must reach an ending. The pages must be filled, new characters brought in as old ones die."

Still not looking at her, Lady Lillian shook her head. "This isn't a story. It's real life. There are no simple endings."

"The wheel must turn," said Abi. "I understand now, after all these years of flight. The hands of the clock must go round. Your world is beautiful but there are other beauties. The smile of a friend. The sun on the morning mist. The frost on the trees. Waves washing through a field of tall grass. The gaze of a lover or a baby."

Lady Lillian sighed. "I suppose it is only fair you kill me after all these years of pursuit. I would have killed you if I could."

Abi walked to stand directly behind Lady Lillian. "Kill you? Why would I kill my own mother?"

Lillian's voice was cold. "I'm not your mother, child."

"Look at me," said Abi. "Of course you are. That's why I have the words."

When the Lady turned to face her, anger and then confusion and then wonder battled across her features. "I don't ... how is that possible? My daughter died long ago. They told me."

"I was smuggled away for fear of what you might do to me when you learned I had the Speech. Do you not recall? My father died returning for my birth and you were lost in grief. Perhaps you blamed me for the accident." It was, perhaps, too obvious a storyline, but the power of it couldn't be denied.

Lady Lillian reached up to touch Abi's face. "Is this possible?"

"Yes. It is the truth."

Lillian looked puzzled, as if grappling with difficult ideas. "I have been so distracted by moonlight and starlight. I have been so lost."

"I know."

"I couldn't face life without him. Couldn't face another day. I was up here, watching for him, when word came. His ship lost at sea. How you must hate me."

Abi took her mother's hand in hers. "No. I haven't come here for revenge, or to destroy you. Between us, we'll speak the words of Unmaking. The darkness must end. There will be more nights of sparkling frost, but there will also be days of summer. We can live through all of them. We can give this story a good ending, if you are willing."

There were tears of moonlight in her mother's eyes as she nodded her head at Abi.

When it was done, Abi left her mother for a time and walked from the tower to the woods. She picked her way among tall trees grown thick with moss. Her feet seemed to know the path to take. Through the branches, a candle flickered from the windows of a little cottage in a clearing on a hill, calling her like a beacon.

Abi knocked on the door and waited for the old man to answer. A story didn't only need a finish; loose ends needed to be tied up, too. The Chronicler would understand that. He'd know how to find Aydan and Gemma and Vanda and all the others, even his little dog, so that the rest of their tales could be told and her part in them played out.

As she knew it would, the door opened silently. An old man's face peeped through the gap, his eyes regarding her over the top of a pair of half-moon spectacles.

"See," said Abi. "I have found the ending of the story."

In the east, over the trees, the sky was finally lightening to morning.

About the story

"What The Darkness Is" grew out of wanting to write a story in which worlds are nested within other worlds, so that it isn't clear which is the "real" world and where the lines between them start and end. Books, songs, paintings – all can be portals through to a "next" world. I liked the idea of the slipperiness of reality. This approach also allowed me to structure a story around a sort of chase, with Abha being hunted from land to land, which seemed like it could make an enticing tale.

Related to all that, I also loved the idea of imagined worlds becoming real, of a narrator being someone able to shape a story/world which they then travel to. Hence the character of the Chronicler in the story.

The drama of this particular story flowed from the title, which was a phrase that popped into my head one day. The tale explores what the darkness is — or might be — for one particular character. I start with a world frozen in perpetual night and I wanted to explore why that might be and what would drive someone to work such terrible magic.

A question for the author

Q: How often do you think about writing during a day?

A: Some days, when all the background noise of daily life gets in the way, I guess I don't think about writing that much. Other days, when there's a bit more space, I think about it a lot, playing with ideas in my head, coming up with scenes and dialogues. There's probably a lesson there: to write you need to give yourself time to let the words and ideas flow. As someone once said, "You must stay drunk on writing so reality cannot destroy you."

About the author

Simon Kewin is the author of over 100 published short stories. His works have appeared in *Nature, Daily Science Fiction, Abyss & Apex* and many more. He lives in England with his wife and their daughters.

simonkewin.co.uk, @SimonKewin

Simon Kewin's story "What the Darkness Is" was published in *Metaphorosis* on Friday, 22 September 2017.

Radical Abundance

Angie Lathrop

Something woke me. A sound.

I rolled to my back. Sand and rock ground into my shoulders and my skin hurt everywhere and my lungs seemed too dry to work properly. But for a moment I forgot all that, because when I looked up, there was a silver bowl over the still landscape. The sky mirrored the desert and the desert mirrored the sky and everything was pale and beautiful.

Dawn was like that in the desert. Translucent and unearthly for a sliver of an hour before sunrise, but bright with heat and blasting sky the rest of the day.

From somewhere, goats bleated pathetically; probably the sound that woke me. Perhaps roused too early from their caprine dreams. I wondered what a goat might dream about.

The sky glowed. The sun broke free of the horizon. And then the heat, again.

I tried to blink away the grit but I didn't have any tears left. There was no shade, and the sleeveless tunic I wore was no protection at all. I didn't belong in the desert; my skin, normally so pale it was almost translucent, was blistered and weeping, and my hair, long and silky white, was matted and heavy with sand.

Not far from me were tracks; maybe an old road. Tourist buses used to come to the desert to see the sights—old caravan stops; crusader castles; cities that were ancient even before the Roman legions marched here. But the drought was vast and terrible; mythic, world-destroying, like a Biblical Flood in reverse.

I didn't know where I was; in this shattered place borders and alliances shifted like the sand. People moved restlessly, dogged by war and famine and uncertainty.

More bleating and the skittering of tiny hooves. A shudder in the air, and for a second I was certain that it was my butterflies returning to help me, but it wasn't. It was funny, because they'd never been gone for so long before, and I couldn't imagine what had happened to them. If they didn't come back soon I would die. People can't live in a place like this without a lot of help.

I closed my eyes against the terrible whiteness. The goats were close now. I could smell their warm bodies, and then their dry little tongues touched my cheeks.

The world spun. The goats cried out in a way that could break your heart. I could see sparkles of light behind my closed lids, so beautiful.

I woke up in an inside place, so dark and lovely that I would have cried with relief if I'd had tears.

A striped tent, the woven sides flapping in the breeze. A man was there. He trickled water into my mouth and I choked because I couldn't swallow right. He was patient and after a while I could drink.

He was dressed in pale robes, his hood thrown back. I couldn't tell how old he was, but he wasn't old and he wasn't young. His eyes were very dark, his brow furrowed.

He might be one of the new nomads. The dispossessed, who wandered stateless and unprotected, trying to stay ahead of war and drought.

The world went away and I forgot about being thirsty.

When I woke up again, the man was kneeling by a little fire in the center of the tent. He heated a pot while I watched from where I lay curled on a pile of woven rugs.

It was strange to smell coffee after days of the scentless desert, and although I wanted it my stomach tightened into a hard knot.

He noticed that I was awake, and he spoke to me in English.

"What is your name?" he asked. He repeated the question in Hebrew and then, after a pause, in Arabic.

I could understand all of the languages, but I answered him in Arabic. He seemed surprised. I was surprised, too. I didn't remember speaking Arabic ever before.

"Legion. My name is Legion."

He frowned, probably thinking that perhaps I said it wrong or mistranslated it, but if he lived in another place he would recognize what I am simply by the kind of name I have.

I shut my eyes again. It made me tired to think about telling him, because if he didn't recognize my name then he probably didn't know anything about the kind of person I was, and it was a lot to explain.

His name was Musef, which made me smile, because it means rescuer.

He was curious about me, but wary. He wondered how old I was, because although I was small, I didn't speak like a child. His confusion was understandable because the truth is complicated: people like me are ageless.

He asked me many questions in many ways—why were you here, who left you to die in the desert, where are you from—and I explained that I couldn't remember.

At first he thought I was lying, but after a while, the way he spoke to me changed. He was gentler, and I could tell he thought there was something wrong with my mind. That I was born this way, or that I'd been injured, fundamentally, by the desert.

That wasn't it. I was just different, in ways that I did not have the capacity to explain. I wanted to answer his questions, but people like me have a different way of remembering. My memories are like water in my hands, and strange knowledge, like fluent Arabic, often bubbles up from what seems to be my very vast subconscious.

"I was sent here to help people," I kept repeating. He found this to be unconvincing and he asked me about my past: where was I born, where was my family, were they looking for me.

I could only look at him hopelessly. For people like me, the past is nothing and the future is a mirage. Only the now is in clear focus.

He gave up on questions, and I watched while he tended the fire. He got a stew cooking, and then flattened bread and put it right into the coals. He gave me a cup of thick warm milk to drink while we waited for the food.

I could only eat a little, but it was the best meal I have ever had. I was hungry, but it also had to do with the care he took and how he watched to see if I liked it and how he looked pleased when I did.

In the morning, he was outside when I woke up. I heard him speak to the goats and then the scrape of their hooves and their excited bleats, and then there was only the wind. I didn't like being alone in the desert again, but I was too weak to get up and follow him.

He was gone for a long time, all day. When he came back I nearly wept with relief.

He made a fire. We brushed the ashes from bread and ate it. We drank coffee from tiny cups shaped like half-eggs.

I was much better, and restless in the tent, so he took me out to see the animals. The camels didn't like me—Musef said they didn't like anyone—but the goats were fascinated by me. I sat down and they crowded around and I laughed when they nibbled at my hair.

Musef was amused at how much I liked them. He caught the tiniest one by a leg and put it in my lap.

Its mother stared at me with her odd yellow goat eyes, but the baby rested content in my arms. I petted it and wondered how Musef had known that I would like it. I suspected that when your job was herding goats and you occasionally killed and ate them, you might forget how adorable the littlest ones can be.

I watched Musef very carefully, everything he did, and after a few days I knew how to do all the chores that you have to do in a desert camp. It made me happy to finally be useful, and it seemed more likely that he would let me stay if I were not such a burden.

He was guarded at first, but after a while I could tell he was getting used to having me here. He talked of taking me to a border and sending me back to where I came from, but everywhere here was dangerous. I told him that I didn't belong anywhere and that no one was looking for me, and although this was all true, he was skeptical.

I liked being with him, and it was comforting doing the same thing every day. Eat, take care of the animals. Get water, drink, shake sand from the rugs. He gave up trying to get me to tell him about my past; instead he told me stories from this land: heroes, lovers, monsters. His voice was a sweet thing in this wild, hard place.

One night he took me into the desert and it was phosphorescent and milky, no longer terrifying like it had been when I was alone and dying. Another day we climbed a ridge at dawn to see the flat turquoise swath of the Dead Sea, and that same day we watched the desert turn dull red under a bloody sunset.

Later, there was a spatter of rain, and I looked up astonished, which made him smile.

"You're easily amazed," he said when I was thrilled to find out where the milk we drank came from—the camels! I laughed as he showed me how to milk one and I said that sometimes people resist amazement.

I stayed with Musef, weeks, maybe even months, but it was hard to say because people like me don't mark the time like regular people. And time was hard to mark because each day was the same, except that sometimes we packed everything up and piled it on the camels. We would walk for a day or more until we were in a place with good forage for the animals and then we'd set the tent back up. We never saw a town or another person, and it got even hotter as we went deeper into the desert.

One evening we came over a rise and saw a terrible thing.

I stood still, unable to react, but Musef went down to where the bodies were. He checked carefully for signs of life but there was no hope. Men, women, children, all dead, all partly covered with the shifting sand. Their tents and belongings were broken and scattered.

After a while, I walked down to where Musef was looking at a machine that had been smashed into pieces. It was a portable atmospheric water generator: I knew what it was because I often made them for people who lived in the desert.

There were more nanotech artifacts scattered about: medical packets; an empty pouch of high-nutrient nectar. Sturdy desert tents of impossibly light and strong fabric, the kind that can assemble themselves and unfold like living origami.

I was very tired all of a sudden. Seeing those artifacts triggered memories. It was clear that I had met these people and given them these things, and then they had died because of it. This tragedy was my doing.

Musef came to me. "We need to go," he said. "We can't help them, and whoever did this may still be nearby."

"I gave them these things," I said. "This was what I was doing. Before you found me."

He shook his head, not understanding.

"No, not you. This things were made with a molecular assembler. Little machines that can make anything out of atoms."

He mistook my silence for incomprehension. "You see, there are patrols, looking for people who have these illegal devices—"

"I know what they are: machines that make what people need— they can make anything at all out of almost nothing." My voice was full of outrage. "They can't keep this technology from people who are desperate."

He looked at me strangely. "Governments are afraid. If people can make anything at all, then how can they be controlled? And economies collapse. Trade alliances mean nothing and that causes instability. And instability leads to war." He looks at me with very dark eyes, like he did the first day. "More war than there is already."

I scowled at him, stubbornly, and shook my head. "How can someone do this? Kill these people when they were only trying to live?" I kicked the smashed water generator. "You can't tell a parent of a dying child that they must wait for society to adapt to unlimited resources."

I didn't like this conversation. We'd never spoken to each other like this before; in our tent in the desert we didn't speak of things like molecular assemblers and post-scarcity economies and the collapse of governments, but we were speaking of them now. We both knew more than we had let on.

He shook his head. "In the wrong hands, these devices are the ultimate weapon."

"I know." I picked up an empty clip from a carbon-fiber assault rifle and turned it over in my fingers. "I should have made them something better. A rocket launcher. A bomb."

I could tell he still didn't understand: he thought I was confused, upset.

"We need to go," he said, and he turned back toward our tent.

As I followed him, I nearly stepped on a thing that looked like a scrap of white paper mostly buried in the sand.

I picked it up and the little machine flexed its delicate wings weakly—disguised as a butterfly, it was one of the thousands of molecular assemblers that I had left here to make things for these people.

I brushed the sand from its solar panel wings, and it crawled over my palm, tasting my skin with a curled tongue.

It recognized me.

I cupped it carefully in my hands and it thrashed against my fingers. If I let it go, it would get the others, so I had a choice: I could crush it and keep living this life I had grown used to with Musef, or I could set it free to go and bring the others.

Musef called to me to hurry, and I slipped the butterfly into my pocket.

We walked through the night, putting distance between ourselves and the massacre. Neither of us said anything.

I helped him set up the tent, but I was shaking, and that made my fingers nearly useless. He had to retie knots I'd done. Later I spilled the coffee all over the rugs, and tears welled in my eyes.

I was confused: I didn't know what was wrong with me. People like me aren't like this; we don't have sadness the way regular people do.

Musef was upset, too, but when he reached out and laid his fingers lightly on my wrist, I jerked my hand away.

I felt worse, then, because he looked more unhappy, but I don't like being touched.

I was overwhelmed with regret at the sorrow on his face, so later when he laid down on his rugs I went over to lay down next to him.

He was surprised, but he didn't make me go back to the other side of the tent like I thought he might. It was uncomfortable to be like this, so close that I was warmed by the heat of his skin, poised in a place I didn't belong.

He touched my hair, very lightly, just for a moment, and that was okay.

Then, for no reason I could understand, he told me about his family.

He'd had a wife and three little children. They'd been in a refugee camp, cut off from the rest of the world by blockades and soldiers and minefields. He'd taken them there because he thought it would be safer, but like so many places it turned out to be a trap.

He told me how he stole food from people who could not live without it. How he let other children starve to try to save his own. Finally, when things became unspeakable, he found a smuggler to take them out of the country, but the man took their money and left them to die. Musef lived, against his will. He would have died for any one of them but that was not how it happened.

Later, he hunted the smuggler down and killed him. That man had a family, so those children probably died, too.

Finally I understood why Musef was here alone in the quiet of the desert. I didn't know why I hadn't guessed this from the start.

I asked what their names were, and he told me in a voice full of anguish.

He spoke for a long time, telling me things he'd never told anyone, sometimes weeping and sometimes icy cold.

There was nothing I could say, and no way for me to comfort him other than by simply lying there next to him, my hands curled between us like tiny animals.

Eventually, exhausted, he lay like a man beaten to near death. I listened to him breathing for a long time. Once I knew he was deeply asleep, I silently stole out of the tent.

I lifted my hands and released the butterfly. It flitted in loose circles around me until it acquired the satellite signal it needed, then it darted off to the north.

Before dawn, the rest of the butterflies returned.

They skittered and scratched at the tent, trying to find a way in. I heard them, and I was instantly awake. Musef woke, too and he was on his feet as I got up.

"Stay here," he whispered to me. He had a gun in his hand, because he thought he could protect me.

"They are here for me," I said. My throat was tight and my voice was not mine.

We stepped out into the frenzy of translucent wings. The largest were hand-sized and the smallest mere specks of glitter. Most were luminous and pale but if you looked closely you could see the rare flash of sapphire.

When they recognized me they got more excited and become a blizzard, and there were so many of them that it was hard to see anything else. The goats bleated unhappily and bunched together and the camels pulled at their tethers. Butterfly wings brushed against my skin, each touch barely felt but with so many of them it was overwhelming.

They were relentless and would only get more determined until I did what they wanted, so I stepped away from Musef and lifted my arms.

The butterflies flocked aggressively, like autumn birds in places where it was cold in winter, and they jostled each other as they found their places and fitted together. Some burrowed into my hair, but most clung to my shoulders or trailed down my back, and then the rest of them climbed on and formed long chains and sheets.

After a few minutes of rustling and tickling, they were all where they belonged. I watched Musef's face as he finally saw me as I am.

The illusion of wings must have been powerful in the moonlight. The butterflies' delicate bodies all tucked in place, arching up from my shoulders. Soft and layered over the tops, and then chains of the smallest ones stitched together to make flight feathers that drooped almost to the ground. Both wing structures lightly in motion, balancing themselves and gently swaying.

Musef's face was stricken. If I were a real angel, I suppose I might have performed a miracle, just to break the tension, but the miraculous things I could do took time and weren't necessarily visually stunning.

For Musef's sake I stifled my whimper as they penetrated my skin at my shoulder blades and all down my spine. Their tiny nanowire feet searched for the interface fibers and then each butterfly's body glowed brighter when it connected to my nervous system.

They'd been gone so long that my body wasn't used to them anymore, and their connections made my muscles twitch and then contract hard. I shut my eyes and let them do it, but it was very painful and I was sorry that Musef had to witness this. I felt him next to me, saying my name, but there was nothing that could stop the butterflies.

This was torture for Musef, I knew, and he seized a butterfly and crushed it in his hand. "Don't," I said, but he did it again and my ears were filled with a roaring and my vision went to bloody red.

I'd never thought of the butterflies as something you could love or hate, but I hated them then. Not because of my pain, because that was necessary, but because of Musef's, which was not.

"I heard about someone like you, once." Musef's voice was barely audible. "They caught her and burned her alive."

He swept his arm and brushed the butterflies off by the hundreds. But they were smart and there were thousands of them. And they were quick, so as soon as he raked his hand down my side they were already crawling back in place.

"Who did this to you?" he asked, and I could tell from his tone that he had an idea of me strapped down, held against my will. Changed—with a knife?— into someone not quite human.

"It wasn't like that," I said. I was losing the clarity of thought needed for normal conversation, but I wished I could explain: the ultra-strong and light carbon lattice instead of bones. Artificial glands that made drugs to take away fear and shame and leave only a sense of purpose. A practical symbiosis with the tiny machines, to make the perfect vector to infect the suffering with radical abundance.

Pain, yes, plenty of pain but a good kind: cleansing, atoning. Just the right thing for a person stained by guilt.

But it was impossible to speak with my heart fluttering wildly and my pulse in my ears. I fell, hard. My cheek struck the ground and I tasted blood. Musef spiraled away from me and the desert closed in, white and blazing and terrible.

Musef was carrying me, my cheek bumping lightly against his chest. The sun was fully overhead, and I was burning.

I shivered despite the heat and Musef held me tighter. The butterflies were everywhere, dragging and tangling under his feet. They whipped against our faces like pale ferns.

He took me up to the top of a ridge where the wind was stiff and the sky huge and blue over the parched-white land, and he set me on my feet. I was unsteady, but the butterflies fluttered and kept me upright.

I turned my face upward to the sky, into the hot wind. I flexed my wings and thought of flight.

It was the butterflies. My nervous and endocrine systems were saturated with their wanderlust and I wouldn't be able to stand it much longer.

I pulled a pale butterfly off and set it in Musef's hand. I show him its tiny but complex body and the nectar that beaded from its tongue. "An Angel can live on just nectar for a long time," I explained. "As long as they have sunlight and air and water, the butterflies can make it. So an Angel is never beholden to anyone for food." I was tempted to drink some, because thinking about nectar made me hungry for it, but the butterflies were settled and I wanted to reassure Musef, not startle him further with Angel feeding behavior.

"Legion."

The way he said my name made hurt my chest hurt. It was hard to breathe.

"I can have them make you whatever you want," I said. "All they need is some matter to take apart and put back together." I glanced around. "Sand, maybe, but carbon is best. They'll forage for whatever elements they need."

He shook his head. "What would I want?"

That was a good question. Usually the people I met were suffering, and they always needed something, although they often didn't know exactly what it was. But Musef was perfect and whole and I couldn't imagine him living in any other way. And the only thing he wanted, for time to be rolled back to avert a tragedy, was beyond the capabilities of even an Angel.

My wings quivered. "Everyone needs something."

"Not me."

I resolved to not look at him anymore. "But other people here do. The butterflies can make drugs, whole medical clinics. Sewers and wells and walls to keep danger out of villages. Clothing, furniture, anything—"

"Stay with me. You're happy here. I know it."

His sadness made me sad. Or I would have been sad, if I weren't an Angel. Instead I felt a detached patience, an empathy that wasn't really an emotion at all.

I shrugged, which is a lovely gesture when you have wings. "Angels can't be the kind of people who have desires, because that's what causes trouble: people who want the wrong things."

I plucked another butterfly from my shoulder and placed it in his palm. It was one of the blue ones. Dark indigo veins filigreed patterns in the cerulean wings.

"The blue kind are different—they are the ones that know how to make everything. And they know how to make more of the regular butterflies and more of themselves. They're smarter than all the others."

Musef was perfectly still, letting the little machine taste him with its delicate tongue, and in that instant I saw a deeper purpose in why I'd been here.

Musef was smart and kind and he knew what people who live here might need. He could figure out if they needed a desalination plant or guns, or both. He could help them and keep it a secret until it was too late to do anything about it.

The world needed more Angels, many more, and Musef was exactly the kind of person who might volunteer his life: guilty and regretful. Hungry for atonement.

"The blues ones know how to make a person into an Angel," I explained. "Angels are needed, to be sure the butterflies are used in the right way and given to the people who need them."

He was dumbfounded. "Like you," he said finally.

I nodded. "It's an offer. You don't have to do it."

But really, who could resist the opportunity? To become good? Untouched and untouchable; weightless and winged. The possibility of making up for the worst kind of hubris.

My wings unfurled fully. I had wrap my fingers in his robe so I wasn't swept away.

He closed his eyes and I was unexpectedly filled with an un-angelic wanting. I thought about how gentle he was with the animals and how he would carry water for hours so I could wash the dust from my hair.

"Will you come back?" he asked. "Ever?"

I shook my head, a twinge of regret plucking at my heart. "Angels don't have a past, Musef."

Then, before I could even say good-bye, my wings jerked me back and up, like a parachute in reverse.

The remaining sadness drained out of me as I went higher, and it felt good to fly. Even though I watched him for as long as possible, it was only a minute before he was gone in the vastness of the desert.

I'm glad to be an Angel. We—the butterflies and I—save lives. A week or maybe a month ago we made hundreds of thousands of tiny drones to hunt malaria mosquitoes. Yesterday we built homes in a slum, and I can tell that right now the butterflies are hunting for the materials they need to make computers. We scavenge when we need to, and always keep moving.

And, rarely, we find a certain kind of person, a person just like I once was: culpable and suffering and yearning for purity.

I don't know where we are, because borders are ridiculous things.

Sometimes people shoot at us as we glide past, and sometimes I see helicopters in the distance, but they are just old-world things that will eventually go away when the Angels have done their work.

We bring people the things they need and we give it to them without a price. I live each moment as it comes, without a past and without a future.

But sometimes, I dream—on the wing, as Angels do—of what it was like to be touched. To live in one safe, small place and never fly. Once, I woke thinking of a words in a language I no longer knew.

I wander, like I was made to, but sometimes I can convince the butterflies to take us one place rather than another. I like deserts in particular, especially the way the superheated air takes me up high to where the landscape becomes a wrinkled cloth beneath us.

And often, when a being with bright wings appears on the horizon, I convince the butterflies to let me soar that way, just to see who it was.

About the story
What motivated me to write the story?

What if the means for radical abundance—in the world of this story, strong nanotechnology/ Anatomically Precise Manufacturing Machines/molecular assemblers/von Neumann machines (the butterflies)—were put directly into the hands of people who might really need it?

How would those people be able to sort out what they needed?

Molecular manufacturing technology has the potential to usher in an age of abundance, when every material human need can be met cheaply and efficiently, but switching to an abundance mindset versus a scarcity mindset is not necessarily easy. In this story, policy-makers are slowing the dissemination of or withholding this technology entirely to avoid short-term chaos. Many interests, both political and corporate, could experience losses if anatomically precise manufacturing technology suddenly became widely available.

However, this story started out with a single image: a character waking alone in the Judean desert near the Dead Sea. As I wrote, I had to figure out who she was, why she was there, and who would help her. Everything I write takes a radical turn toward science fiction at some point, and so the nanotech theme eventually took shape.

A question for the author
Q: How do you generate story ideas, and how soon do you act on them?

A: I nerdishly carry a notebook at all times, and whenever I come across something really interesting in reading or in life (a phrase, a concept, a quote, almost anything) I write it down in my current notebook. I also use the notebook for to-do lists and brainstorming and practically everything I need to refer to or keep in mind, for my professional, personal, and writing lives. I don't separate the notebooks into sections, so as I'm perusing the pages for a phone number, I'll come across fragments of ideas that could turn into stories, so I'm constantly feeding those bits back into my mind to incubate It might be months or even years after I record an idea in my notebook that I write a story about it.

About the author
Angie writes science fiction from her farm outside of Madison, Wisconsin. She is also a veterinarian and an artist who works exclusively in the medium of corn mazes. She recently repeated high school while teaching her autistic, science fiction writer son.

angielathrop.com, @angielathrop

Angie Lathrop's story "Radical Abundance" was published in
Metaphorosis on Friday, 29 September 2017.

October

Making the List

David Hammond

It started with a routine-sounding letter from my health insurance company. I opened it quickly because I was in the mood for a snack, and there was a little picture of cherries on the lower right corner of the envelope indicating that they had used cherry-flavored paper, my favorite. I learned that I would need to get a full DNA sequencing done by the end of the year. Reasonable enough, I thought, as I tore off little pieces of the letter and let the sweet and sour cellulose dissolve on my tongue.

Several weeks later I got the strangest voicemail message. "Hello, Mr. Wright," began the garbled transcription I got in email, "this isn't Barley from inshallah care. Web navel your DNA test, and very interesting hallelujah. Please call me back at…" I skipped listening to the actual message and dialed the number.

"Mr. Wright, I am so glad you returned my call!" enthused a female voice. She did not strike me as the usual insurance company bureaucrat. Her name was Hannah Farley, and she worked for the insurance company as an actuarial geneticist. She hastened to assure me that nothing in my genetic sequence indicated latent health problems that should concern me. "In fact," she said, "I have reviewed your claim history, and I want to congratulate you on being in excellent health!"

"Thank you, Ms. Farley," I responded cautiously and waited for her to continue. When she didn't, I felt the need to prompt her. "But…?"

"Right. Well, I'll just have to come right out and say it."

"Please do."

"Okay, Mr. Wright. You are …" She paused and even clucked her tongue lightly a few times. "You are a Neanderthal, Mr. Wright."

She enunciated the word quite clearly and deliberately, and there was no mistaking what she had said, but still I asked her to repeat it.

"You are a Neanderthal."

My mind raced for a moment. "Oh, I read about this. Everyone has some Neanderthal DNA, right? That's what…"

"No, Mr. Wright, you misunderstand. You … and nobody is more surprised than I am, believe me … nobody's ever … I did double-check and triple-check and had colleagues … but there's no getting around it. You are not a *Homo sapiens* with some Neanderthal genes. You are a Neanderthal, *Homo neanderthalensis*."

I was at a complete loss for words.

"Do you understand now, Mr. Wright?"

After I hung up a few minutes later, I went to the bathroom and looked at my reflection. Protruding brow. Large nose. I took off my clothes and stepped back. I have always been husky and strong. I played football in high school, not because I liked the game, but because if you gave me the ball, I could run all the way to the end zone, littler kids dangling from my body like remoras on a shark. (In college it was a different story. The guys were bigger, tougher, more vicious. I didn't have the stomach for it. I took up biking, a solitary, peaceful sport.)

I put my clothes back on. Okay, so I was a Neanderthal. So what? I was still Carl Wright, mild-mannered accountant, resident of Santa Clara, California. Wasn't I?

Ms. Farley had talked me into coming in for some tests. I don't like being prodded and poked any more than the next guy, but I would be paid. I arrived at the lab promptly at 9am the following morning.

A mole-like, bespectacled man limply shook my hand when I arrived. He stared at my hairy knuckles and then raised his eyes to inspect my face, much as I had done the previous day. He finally forced a smile and said, "Thank you so much for coming, Mr. Wright. Please follow me."

I was ushered into a room where a woman sat behind a desk. Her wide downturned mouth, fleshy jowls and rumpled brown suit combined to give the impression of a toad waiting with menacing patience.

"Good morning, Mr. Wright. Please have a seat."

"Hi," I said and inserted myself in the only available chair. A fluttering in the corner of the room attracted my attention, and I looked to see a tall thin woman in a lab coat. She had straight blond hair that fell nearly to her waist. She smiled at me.

"I am Dr. Willis," said the woman at the desk. "You talked to Ms. Farley on the phone," she gestured to the woman in the corner, "and that's Fernandez." The man who had ushered me in grunted lightly behind my right shoulder. "Before we get started, I have a few questions for you."

Dr. Willis attempted to delve into my family history, but I'm afraid I wasn't much help to her. Mom and dad died in a car accident when I was 12, and in any case they had adopted me. I have no idea who my biological parents were or where they came from. Dr. Willis shook her head disapprovingly.

"For all we know," said Fernandez in a desultory whine, "he has no parents."

"What do you mean?" asked Ms. Farley, jerking her head to the side. I found myself fascinated for a moment by her movements, her tall lanky stance, the way her hair was so light in color that it almost blended with her lab coat. A fault of the fluorescent light, no doubt.

"...quite possible that he was created in a lab from some well-preserved remains," Fernandez was saying.

"Nonsense," said Dr. Willis. "35 years ago that would have been impossible. It's hardly possible now."

"Well, you explain it then." He gestured to me, as if I were the "it" in need of explanation.

After some more apparently fruitless discussion, I was led to a lab for a variety of tests: strength, cardiovascular health, flexibility, cranial capacity, intelligence, visual acuity, etc. There was much humming, chuckling, even a few surprised gasps, but they refused to tell me anything about the results. In the end they thanked me, paid me, and I went home.

I thought that was the end of it, and I went back to my life doing bookkeeping and tax planning for small business clients in and around Santa Clara.

Then came the call from the New York Post. Somehow a reporter had gotten wind of my genetic status and had called to find out if it was true, and to do a story on me, whether it was true or not.

"I found your picture online, Mr. Wright," said John Trawley, "and, wow."

I was so taken aback that I almost hung up on him, but I let him talk, and he seemed to take my reticence as a shrewd negotiation tactic. In the end, by merely grunting non-committally every once in a while I had secured a surprisingly lucrative deal.

I was not completely naive. I knew the publicity might have unwanted consequences. I agreed to be photographed, but insisted that I be fully clothed in attire of my own choosing. I also demurred when they offered to fly me to New York. Trawley flew to Santa Clara instead with the photographer in tow.

He had surprisingly few questions for me. Perhaps our initial conversation convinced him that I was a dull interview, and I can't really blame him. We did talk about my football days, and I allowed them to make a scan of an old photograph of me in uniform. The rest of the conversation focused on my sex life, or lack thereof. He asked for my ex-wife's phone number, but I refused. He smiled and nodded and told me he completely understood. I should have known they would have no trouble tracking her down on their own.

The photographer, a short, hyper-efficient little man who seemed to have pockets growing like blisters over his entire body, took pictures of me in my business suit, pictures of me at my desk with my sleeves rolled up (exposing my hairy forearms), and pictures of me gazing out the window (highlighting my Neanderthal profile). I agreed to go for a walk with them, and we wound up at a park. Only later, when I saw the pictures of me next to trees and boulders did I realize their goal in photographing me in a semi-natural setting.

It was ironic, because I had never been an outdoorsy guy. I vacationed in cities, not national parks, stayed in hotels, not campgrounds. I used to go camping with mom and dad before they died, but I never got the point of giving up modern conveniences every Memorial Day weekend. "This is how our ancestors used to live!" said my dad. "Our ancestors ate s'mores?" I asked while roasting a marshmallow, because I could be a bit of a smartass, but I loved the campfire, getting wrapped in a blanket, staring at the dancing flames, seeing in the embers random flashes of my ancestors hunting glowing beasts with glowing red spears.

Anyway, the New York Post article, titled "Caveman Accountant!" was breathtakingly inaccurate. It said I lived in San Jose instead of Santa Clara, for instance. Why? It quoted my ex-wife as having called me an animal in bed. Had I been abusive, they asked? No, she said, but I had quite a temper.

Well, that's absurd. She would never have said those things. Had they talked to her at all? She divorced me when she fell in love with another man, and I was upset but reasonable. We still met sometimes for dinner at Tequila Grande, very cordial and comfortable. Her new husband was not threatened by me *at all*. (Sometimes, perhaps, I wished he felt threatened, just a little, but he didn't.) I am not an animal in bed. I have no temper to speak of. I'm a very steady, even boring, individual, and nobody would be quicker to point that out than Christy.

It was after dinner when I read the article, and I started to feel a little wistful thinking about Christy. I still missed her, I suppose. I got another beer from the fridge and slumped on the couch. Christy had a persistent cheerfulness that I always found charming. The bangles on her wrist rattled when she moved her hands expressively, as she always did when she talked. She played the flute, and the light, airy sound of that instrument always feels like her warm breath on my neck.

In the end, I was not religious enough for her. I had accompanied her to church, but I could take or leave Christianity. She would occasionally play the flute at church, and the sight of her by the altar, beautiful and bathed in the golden glow of Sunday morning light, should have filled me with pride. Instead it only made me feel as if she were on another planet, in touch with a spiritual universe I couldn't see. She'd left me for the organist.

I got another beer out of the fridge, but thought better of it, put it back, and went to bed.

After the article my phone started ringing like crazy. Talk shows wanted me. Reality TV shows wanted me. Porn movie producers wanted me. I stopped answering the phone altogether, but reviewed all of the voice messages. My genetic makeup was a bankable commodity, apparently, and I was going to make the most of it.

I went with Wanda Stippler. After all, she had the most popular daytime talk show in the country, and while she strayed into the sensational at times, she tackled substantive issues and maintained a respectful atmosphere on the set. Or so I was told. I'd never seen the show before. I watched a few clips on YouTube before making a final decision.

In one of the clips, Wanda introduced a man who came out wearing horn-rimmed glasses and a putty-colored suit. He seemed like an ordinary fellow, a bit shy and awkward, and in a series of initial questions Wanda carefully established his guy-next-door persona. He was a software developer; he was married and had an infant daughter; he had grown up in Ames, Iowa. Then she asked him what he liked to do in his spare time, and he told her he liked to belly dance. "What?!" she cried, looking at the audience and holding her hand to her breast in obviously feigned surprise. He liked to belly dance, he repeated quietly. A moment later, the studio lights were lowered, he tore the putty-colored suit from his body (it was held together with velcro) and flung the glasses to the side. Vaguely middle-eastern music began to play, he raised his arms and rippled the flesh of his abdomen to squeals of delight from Wanda and her (mostly female) audience.

This video gave me pause, as you might imagine, but it was obviously a bit of a ruse. The guy was certainly a professional dancer, just doing his job, not a mild-mannered software developer. That's entertainment. Right?

Anyway, Stippler's compensation package was generous. And when I amended the contract to specify the clothing I was willing to wear and the subject matter I was willing to discuss, they agreed.

I flew in to LAX. In the airport, I became aware of people staring at me. A pretty teenage girl bugged her eyes at me, covered her mouth, and leaned to say something to her friend. I noticed the gaze of several others linger on me longer than was natural, smiles flickering or barely contained.

The thing is, I don't know if this was actually new or not. I suspect that I had always gotten reactions like this but hadn't cared enough to notice. In fact, if I think about it, I can remember all sorts of instances in which cashiers, bank tellers, receptionists, waiters, neighbors, UPS drivers, etc. gave me quick double-takes or cleared their throats awkwardly after standing a few seconds with their jaws open. All through my life, people have talked to me more slowly and loudly than necessary, as if I were dense. This was not new. Had some of the people in the airport seen my picture in the paper? Possibly. But it was my own attitude that had changed. I felt like I had a stamp on my forehead saying "Neanderthal" in blocky, rough-hewn letters.

At the studio I sat in the office of producer Margie McFadden. On her desk sat an empty pencil holder shaped like a penguin next to a computer mouse pad with the picture of a penguin. The woman had some sort of penguin fetish. On the wall behind her head was a framed poster of an emperor penguin sheltering its young. On her bookshelf was an assortment of penguin figurines, snow globes and toys, behind which appeared to be a variety of books about penguins, both fiction and non.

Ms. McFadden noticed the direction of my gaze. "Do you like penguins, Mr. Wright?"

After a slight pause, I said, "Sure, who doesn't?"

"Exactly!" She seemed pleased, and thus having broken the ice, so to speak, she began coaching me on what I would say in my interview.

She asked me whether I had ever suspected that I was a Neanderthal? Had I ever looked at the artists' renderings of Neanderthals and thought, "Hey, that's me!"

It was a good question, and I had to think about it for a moment. "No," I finally concluded, "I just thought I was ugly."

"Oh, that's good! That is a good line! I want you to say that in the interview, just in that way." She paused and looked at me dubiously. "Can you say it just like that? Let's practice. Wanda will ask you whether you ever suspected you were a Neanderthal—her wording may be a little different, but it doesn't matter. What do you say?"

"I just thought I was ugly?"

"No, no, pause thoughtfully for a moment, just like you did, and then say it."

"Okay." I raised my hand to my chin and turned my head to the side, and then I looked back at Ms. McFadden and said, "I just thought I was ugly."

She stared back at me for a moment with narrowed eyes and then sighed and threw her hands in the air. "It will do!"

We talked for a few more minutes, and then she said, "Oh! I have something to show you!" We got up, and she led me down the hall. A young woman wearing a white cardigan and glasses trotted past, smiling at me broadly. We stopped outside a half-open door and Ms. McFadden turned to me. "Just keep an open mind, okay?"

She led me into the room, where a woman sat bent over a sewing machine among racks of clothing. The woman looked up, then down, then up again. "Where is it Judy? Oh, here." From a rack she pulled a capacious leopard-print garment, ragged at the bottom. I noticed a plastic club made to look like wood leaned against the wall.

"No, Ms. McFadden! No. We talked about this over the phone."

"It's just for fun, Mr. Wright!"

"My contract clearly states…"

"Your *contract*," she spat. "It's just for fun, Mr. Wright! Forget the contract for a moment. Feel the lining. Silk, right Judy? Very comfortable."

I refused to touch it. "No," I repeated.

Ms. McFadden sighed deeply and returned the garment to the rack. "Well, we tried."

There were two other people waiting in the green room before the show. One was a woman with lobster claw hands, and the other was a garrulous little man who looked very old but who told me he was only 16.

"Progeria, it's called. It's really really rare."

"Oh, it's not that rare," said the lobster claw woman.

"It is too!" said the boy, sounding younger, even, than his 16 years. "She's jealous," he explained to me, eliciting a dismissive grunt from the woman. "What do you have?"

"I … I'm a Neanderthal. Apparently."

"What, like a caveman?" he asked.

I paused. "Yeah, I guess you could say that. But I live in a house like regular people."

"Yeah, I knew that," he snorted.

The boy was called out first. "Showtime!" he said, rubbing his hands together. It cheered me somewhat to see his enthusiasm. He said he'd been on lots of shows, and it was fun. The lobster-claw woman was morose, however, and we sat in silence until she was called out.

Then, as I was waiting nervously, a man was ushered in by Ms. McFadden. "… on such short notice," she was saying. "You're a lifesaver."

The man had a salt-and-pepper beard, and he sat down opposite me and folded his arms. "Hi," I said, but he only glared at me. I wondered what genetic mutation he had, but then I realized that he looked familiar. I was trying to remember where I had seen him before when I was called out.

The interview itself was surreal. I did my line about thinking I was ugly, but my preliminary pause was probably more terrified than thoughtful. It got a good laugh anyway. Wanda leaned over and touched my arm, and then she declared that I was not ugly but beautiful, and her audience applauded obediently.

Then the bearded man was introduced as Dr. Trevor Smythe. I and my fellow genetic mutants moved down the couch to make way for him, and I suddenly remembered who he was: a pop-science writer who frequented the talk shows, known for his wit.

After exchanging pleasantries with Wanda, he talked about genetic mutations in general before addressing each of us in turn. When he got to me he told Wanda about Neanderthals, how they had become extinct 40,000 years ago, how they had interbred with humans, how they actually had larger brains than humans but had nevertheless been outcompeted by them. He reiterated the point about them going extinct 40,000 years ago, raising his eyebrow at me as he said this. Then he dropped his bombshell.

"I don't believe for one moment this man is actually a Neanderthal."

"What do you mean?" cried Wanda.

"I mean he's a human like you and me. He has some Neanderthal-like features, but so do most of us. What proof has he provided that he is a Neanderthal? He's making a fool out of you, Wanda."

Wanda held her hand to her breast and looked in disbelief at the audience, who murmured on cue. Turning to me, Wanda asked, "What do you have to say, Mr. Wright? Do you have proof?"

I was thunderstruck. I realized later that, like everything else on the show, this moment had been carefully orchestrated. They needed a big ending for the show, and I had denied them the pleasure of seeing me dressed up like Fred Flintstone. Ms. McFadden called in Dr. Smythe, with his pretense of authority, to question my integrity and allow them the pleasure of watching me defend myself. One way or another, they were determined to see me squirm.

When I did not speak but only looked back at her with terror-widened eyes, Wanda asked again, "What is your proof that you are a Neanderthal?"

"My insurance company told me."

"Your insurance company," Dr. Smythe said derisively, then turned to Wanda. "It's very clever, really, because insurance company records are confidential, right? So there's no way to check."

"I would not lie about this," I sputtered. "I never wanted…"

"What if, Dr. Smythe, an independent lab were to verify the results?"

"But would he agree," he asked, "and risk exposing himself as a fraud?"

They all turned to me, and thus did I promise on national television to provide a DNA sample to a lab of Dr. Smythe's choosing to determine whether I was a bona fide Neanderthal.

The Stippler show played the suspense for all it was worth. They showed daily commercials leading up to the big reveal two weeks later. In the meantime I tried to return to work, but it was hard to concentrate. I thought the results would confirm what Ms. Farley had told me weeks ago, but what if they didn't? What if they had made a mistake? Was I, however unwittingly, a fraud? Did I *want* to be a Neanderthal?

I flew back to LA for the follow-up show, which, for me, was anti-climactic. The new results confirmed that I was a Neanderthal. Dr. Smythe was on hand to apologize for doubting me and to tout me as a new mystery of modern science. Wanda declared me a hero, which seemed silly to me.

"I am no hero," I declared, and realized immediately that Ms. McFadden et. al. had known I would say that. It was my line.

I went back again to Santa Clara determined to put all of this behind me. Of course, you know what happened next.

My picture was *everywhere*. The implications of an actual Neanderthal among the human population were analyzed, debated, fretted about, lamented, and celebrated. The New York Times, the Atlantic, Fox News, the BBC, and CNN, to name just a few, all published/broadcast stories within days. I was the talk of Facebook and Twitter. I received death threats and marriage proposals. One email I got described how the writer would like to capture me, dress me in a little red hat, and make me dance to the music of a street organ. At least he did not wish to shoot me, as so many others did. I had to shut down my accounting practice—my office address, phone number and email address having become public knowledge. I stayed in my house for several days, looking through venetian blinds at an encampment of reporters drinking coffee and checking their phones.

I still subscribed to the Chronicle, making me the only one in my cul-de-sac who continued to resist digital media. Rather than face the press to pick it up from my driveway I paid a neighbor kid a dollar a day to carry it to my door, which he did like a commando on a mission. I spread it out on my breakfast table and read it front to back, licking my ink-blackened fingers. To skip a story would seem irresponsible, like I was shirking some ill-defined civic duty, so I read them all. I had done that for years, but now every other story was about me.

It was the syndicated columnist Vanessa Bolen who first brought up in a serious way the idea that I, as a Neanderthal, was not entitled to be called a person, in the legal sense. This elicited some wrangling among scientists and opinionated non-scientists about whether Neanderthals were really a separate species or were, in fact, a subspecies of *Homo sapiens*. If Neanderthals were a subspecies, I gathered, then I could be called a person. The argument, however, ended up focusing on a 2014 study that found that differences in the nasal passages of Neanderthals made them a distinct species, thereby relegating me to non-personhood.

(I looked at my big non-person nose in the mirror. "I just thought I was ugly," I quoted. I snarled at my reflection. But perhaps I was beautiful. What would an actual female Neanderthal think of me?)

Many defended my right to be called a person anyway, arguing that Neanderthals were "humans" even if they were not *Homo sapiens.* Others pointed to my obvious intelligence and my success as a member of society. But as is often the case, the "slippery slope" argument won the day. If a Neanderthal, then why not a clever service dog, who was also intelligent and useful? Why not one of the new robots coming off the assembly line, which was more intelligent and useful than most humans? Would we strip personhood from the unintelligent? No. It was simpler and easier to lock it down to the species.

There were calls for my social security number to be revoked, for my bank accounts to be seized, all contracts I had entered into to be null and void.

Then came defenders from a different quarter: animal rights groups. I was, as far as anyone could tell, the only member of my species on the planet.

To make a long story short, I looked out my window one morning to see two burly representatives of the U.S. Fish and Wildlife service walk up the path to my front door and knock on my front door. When I didn't answer, one stepped back and looked in my window. He could see me standing there, drinking a cup of coffee.

"Mr. Wright, we're here to protect you." He took out his ID and pressed it against the window. I went up and read it. Officer Banks. "You can't stay here anymore, Mr. Wright. It's not a good environment for you."

"And what is a good environment for me?" I called through the closed window.

"One where you don't have to live in fear."

"I'm not afraid," I retorted.

Officer Banks said something to his partner and then turned back to the window. "The bank is going to take the house. You can't stay here." I thought about this. He was right; I had gotten the letter. The paper had been lemon-lime. I sipped my coffee while Banks and his partner fidgeted impatiently. "Mr. Wright," said Banks' partner, "you're coming with us, one way or another."

So I let them in and asked if I could pack a few things to take with me. They said of course, they would even help me carry them to the van. I got my biggest suitcase out and wondered if my whole life would fit in it. I packed some clothes—just my favorite jeans and shirts. I was going to pack my navy blue three-piece, but then the phrase "monkey suit" came to mind; I left it behind.

What else to bring? My only hobby other than biking was reading. I wondered aloud which books I should pack, and Banks asked, "Why not bring them all?"

"What? I have three bookcases full of books."

"Not a problem. Chris, can you get the boxes from the van?"

Banks' partner went out and returned promptly with a stack of folded cardboard boxes and some packing tape. Muttering something about the stone age, he began boxing up the books on my living room shelf. Paul Bowles, Jon Krakauer, Emily Dickinson, Bill Bryson, Douglas Adams.

Banks and his partner flanked me as I rolled my suitcase out. Cigarette butts, coffee stirrers, and wads of gum littered the gutter in front of my house—the detritus of reporters who had abandoned their posts. As Banks lifted my suitcase into the back of the van, a dilapidated Honda Civic stopped at the curb. I turned to see Ms. Farley from the insurance company getting out. She fluttered over to me.

"Mr. Wright! Mr. Wright, I'm so glad I caught you!"

"Ms. Farley? Hello."

She started to apologize profusely for how things had turned out. If she had known, etc. She was sure Fernandez was the one to leak the information to the press, the little jerk, and probably made some money off it somehow. She had tried to call, but I hadn't answered, and she felt just awful. She wore a mottled brown and white jacket, unzipped, and, with her hands in her pockets, she flapped her arms.

"A heron!" I blurted out.

"... a person's genetic..." She stopped abruptly. "Excuse me, Mr. Wright?"

I had only been completing a thought that I had started back in the lab. Fernandez was a mole, Willis a toad, and Farley was a large marsh bird of some kind. "I'm sorry, nothing. I'm going crazy. I've been cooped up for too long."

"Oh, I feel so responsible! Are you going to be alright? What can I do to help?"

"I'll be fine, Ms. Farley. Look, I have two new friends, representatives of the United States government, no less." Chris could be seen pushing the boxes further into the truck while Banks checked his watch. "I really appreciate your concern, but please don't trouble yourself. What's happened has happened. That's all."

She shook her head. "How can you be so calm? If I were you I would be angry. You are a *person*. Carl. You are a *person*."

For a second time, Ms. Farley had rendered me speechless. "I ..." I said finally, glancing at Banks, who beckoned to me, "... need to go. Thank you so much for coming out to see me. I really do appreciate it."

I shook her hand and bid her farewell. She seemed hesitant and confused, but returned to her car.

Meanwhile Banks and Chris were arguing. There was only room for two in the front of the van, all three of us being wide bodies. Normally, if they had some fish or wildlife to transport, it would go in the back, and Chris was of the opinion that precedent should not be broken. Banks argued that my safety was paramount and that I should have a proper lap and shoulder harness. Their job was to protect me, and so ultimately Chris did his job and got in the back of the van.

As we got on the road, Banks explained to me how things would work now that I had made the endangered species list. Basically, whatever I wanted, Banks was authorized to provide, within reason, of course, and subject to safety review. Just for example, if I wanted to stop for some ice cream, no problem! I just needed to be aware that my cholesterol would be monitored regularly. The goal was a healthy, happy, Mr. Wright. And, ultimately, if a Mrs. Wright could be found...

Banks broke off, as if he had said too much.

"A Mrs. Wright ...?" I asked.

"Well, yes! A female of your species, for you to mate with ... I mean to marry ... I mean ... Sorry, this is really weird for me! I'm used to dealing with animals. I mean animals who can't speak English. I mean ..." He broke off again and became inordinately absorbed in turning on his blinker and looking over his left shoulder to change lanes, muttering "damn traffic" under his breath.

"A female of my species ..." I echoed.

An image of Christy flashed in my mind, wearing a white silk blouse, looking to the side and smiling amusedly. During the worst of the media storm, I had tried to call her, but she hadn't picked up. I ached for her suddenly, so much that I began to squirm in my seat. But she wasn't of my species, after all, and that made me feel sad. I realized that I had always hoped that we would get back together, somehow, maybe while sipping margaritas at Tequila Grande, her bangles slipping from her wrist down almost to her elbow as she raised her glass. That possibility, however remote it had been, was now gone completely.

I thumped the armrest with my fist. "I want some ice cream," I announced.

"Yes, sir!" responded Banks.

As I ate my ice cream (raspberry and chocolate), I thought about the human beings who had built the city I lived in, built the ice cream parlor, invented ice cream, cultivated raspberries, invented chocolate, written the books I liked to read, invented the math I used to calculate taxes, invented taxes... Their world was my world, or so I had thought. But I was like a suburban deer—comfortable in their world, adapted to it, but not belonging in it, not really. It had only been a matter of time before I was forced out.

And so here I sit on the fringe of human civilization, in a small ranger cabin in an undisclosed national park, hidden away and supported by Banks and the good people at U.S. Fish and Wildlife. I am wildlife without the skills of wildlife. A river runs near in which I could fish, but I have yet to find the patience for it. There are woods in which I could hunt. Banks gave me a bow and arrow, but I proved inept and unteachable at archery, so he gave me a rifle. He tried to teach me that, but I have yet to shoot anything. I am lazy, I admit. I like to walk in the woods, and to read on my little porch, and to sit and stare at busy birds and squirrels who are at home in this world. If he really wanted me to hunt, Banks would not bring me a big box of food every week. But he can't have me getting thin, and so he brings it, and I tell him embellished stories of my attempts at hunting, how I came upon a group of wild turkeys and blasted at them with abandon, but they all got away. Their feathers settled to the ground like snow, and I was glad.

I do tend a small garden. It is something, at least. I had more tomatoes than I could eat this summer, and I have planted squash for the fall. They are all hybrid varieties, of course, invented by men to grow easily and produce shiny colorful fruit.

Maybe with time I will grow truly wild. I fantasize about it sometimes, leaving the cabin, building a hut out of animal skins and twigs, living off the land, becoming like the fox I sometimes see at dusk, swift and silent and vigilant and competent. But let's face it, I'm an old dog, domesticated and dumb.

Sometimes when Banks brings me supplies he stays to chat, or play cards. He says often how he envies me my life in the woods. He jokes about us trading places. "I have a stack this thick of paperwork! Just for a week, you go back and do it. You were an accountant! You'll love it! I'll stay here." When he has to go he takes one last look around and a big vigorous breath. "Man, this is the life," he says, and then he gets back in his truck and returns to civilization, and I wonder if he would really like to trade places or not, and if I would. Or not.

He brings me letters too, from supporters and detractors alike. He tries to weed out the nasty ones, of course. Two weeks ago, I got a letter from Christy. My hands actually shook as I opened it.

She apologized, first, for not picking up the phone when I called. She didn't know what to say to me. My being revealed as a Neanderthal affected her much more than I had realized. She spent many long hours thinking about it, praying about it, talking to her husband and her pastor about it. The central question, in her mind, was whether I had an eternal soul, whether she would meet me in heaven when all was said and done as she had always imagined she would. The thought that I would not be there troubled her.

Her husband and her pastor agreed that as an animal I was not a moral being and was therefore ineligible for the afterlife, much as I was ineligible for Social Security. As further proof they cited my indifference to Christianity, which could best be explained not by wickedness (they all readily agreed that there was nothing wicked about me) but by a complete absence of spiritual feeling. They meant this as consolation, but it made Christy very sad. She came, nevertheless, to accept it as the truth. She apologized for taking so long to write, to say her final goodbye (for that is what her letter was).

I tried several times to compose a response, but there was nothing for me to say that would not seem ridiculous. I was like a lost pet to her, nothing more. Anything I might say would be like a clever imitation of human emotion, an anthropomorphic charade.

"What's wrong, Carl?" asked Banks the next time he saw me. I'm not one to wear my heart on my sleeve, but I was even more laconic than usual, I guess.

"Oh, nothing. That letter from Christy..."

He winced. "I'm sorry, man. But listen, I have great news. They found another one!"

"Another what?"

"Another Neanderthal! And it's a she!" He grinned and raised his eyebrows twice. "*And* she's your age."

We stood on the porch and I looked out at the trees, whose leaves were starting to fall. "Huh," I responded.

"The geneticists, they say it's amazing," he continued, "she seems to be almost exactly the same age as you, and you're such a good match. It's as if, they say, it's as if she was *made* for you. Literally."

I stared at him. "What does that mean?"

"Apparently they think you were designed or something, but nobody knows who did it! It's bizarre. They can explain it to you, maybe. But whatever, I'm going to bring her out on Thursday."

"You're going to bring her here?"

"Of course! So you two can get to know each other." He paused and chuckled softly. "Relax. Maybe you'll hit it off, maybe not." He slapped me on the back. "I'd be lying, though, if I said I wasn't hoping for an overnight stay."

So, Julia arrived yesterday afternoon. She seemed shy and nervous, but she smiled. After introductions, Banks got in his truck and drove away without another word. He wouldn't be back that evening, I knew.

I invited her to sit on the porch, and for a few minutes we only looked around at the trees and exchanged pleasantries about the coming of autumn and the peacefulness of the woods. Then I caught her eye and we began looking at each other, studying each other's features. She told me that when she saw me on the Stippler show she was struck by my gentleness and my modesty, and she had followed my story closely ever since.

Inevitably we started talking about people, *Homo sapiens,* and about how crazy they are. Julia and I had always been the most sensible people we knew. "I heard," she said, "that they weren't smarter or stronger than Neanderthals, but that they took more risks. When they met mountain ranges, they crossed them, despite the danger, while we stayed put. It's how they survived while we didn't, some say."

"Interesting theory," I said.

Last night we did the sensible thing and slept together. It was okay. And in the morning I watched her sleeping, and I felt happy for the first time since Christy left. I don't love her, at least not in the way that humans use the word, at least not yet, but I hope she stays. Maybe we will have a child, and we will live together in this cabin in these woods with the squirrel, the blue jay, and the fox. I reminded myself that I must gather more firewood for the winter. Banks gave me a chainsaw, and last week I found a fallen oak tree. I cut it into sections a little over a foot in length and used the wheelbarrow to bring it back to the cabin, where I chopped it and stacked it in crosshatched towers in the woodshed. A few more logs like that, and the woodshed will be full. How cozy it will be in the middle of a snowy winter to build a fire in the fireplace. The smoke will get into my clothes as it already saturates the cabin furniture, and eventually I will no longer smell it, I assume.

I should remind Banks to bring me old newspapers to start the fire, because I don't know how to start it without them, along with butane for the lighter. Come to think of it, I haven't read a newspaper in a while. I wonder: will I be tempted to read the newspaper before I set it ablaze? There was a story I was following closely about the elections in the Philippines. Who won? Eh, I don't care anymore. I'll just roll the pages up and place them in a neat line under the grate. I'll light them, wrap myself in a blanket and stare at the flames. Perhaps I'll see visions of my ancestors in the logs as they evolve from fire to ember to ash.

About the story

This story was inspired by *The Sixth Extinction* by Elizabeth Kolbert. Kolbert talks about the extinction of the Neanderthals and the idea that Homo sapiens survived by being a bit crazier than previous human species. (I don't have a copy of the book, so I'm copying these quotes from Goodreads.)

"Archaic humans like Homo erectus 'spread like many other mammals in the Old World,' Pääbo told me. 'They never came to Madagascar, never to Australia. Neither did

Neanderthals. It's only fully modern humans who start this thing of venturing out on the ocean where you don't see land. Part of that is technology, of course; you have to have ships to do it. But there is also, I like to think or say, some madness there. You know? How many people must have sailed out and vanished on the Pacific before you found Easter Island? I mean, it's ridiculous. And why do you do that? Is it for the glory? For immortality? For curiosity? And now we go to Mars. We never stop.'"

She also mentions the fact that Neanderthals didn't look all that different from modern humans:

"...given a shave and a new suit, the pair wrote, a Neanderthal probably would attract no more attention on a New York City subway 'than some of its other denizens.'"

It seemed a natural extension of those ideas to imagine what a Neanderthal suddenly appearing among the modern human population would be like

The 2014 study identifying Neanderthals as a separate species can be found online here: https://www.ncbi.nlm.nih.gov/pubmed/25156452 It is also discussed in a more easily digestable format here: https://www.sciencedaily.com/releases/2014/11/141118141606.htm

A question for the author

Q: Do you ever feel bad for what you put your characters through?

A: No, I don't feel bad. The main reason is that I don't generally put my characters through anything that horrible. The worst experiences in my stories tend to be things that I have experienced myself: alienation, intense embarrassment, unrequited love. To pity my characters would be to pity myself, and I'm not about to do that. Instead I always try to leaven things with humor, which is my own best coping mechanism.

About the author

David Hammond lives and dreams in Virginia with his wife and two daughters. During the day, he makes websites.

oldshoepress.com, @hammond13

David Hammond's story "Making the List" was published in *Metaphorosis* on Friday, 6 October 2017.

Beneath the Sea of Glass

Robert Francis

The sand slithered as if it were alive.

Leos knew it was the wind, tugging rivulets of dust in its wake like whipping snakes, but even so. The land here was bad, hostile. They should never have come.

"Aren't you glad we came, Leos? Glad!" Agris plodded up the slope behind him, two heavy sacks atop his broad shoulders and a grin splayed across his battered face. "What a land... landscape." The big man's smile widened with the achievement of getting the word out, despite his impressive array of verbal tics. Artemis had painstakingly taught it to him a few days before.

"Huh." Leos hauled his own sack onto his back and looked suspiciously at the sand. "I don't think I've ever been glad of anything, ever." He peered over his shoulder at the old man labouring up the hillside behind him. Leos lowered his voice. "Especially not of the day we met that old prick."

Agris grunted and shook his head, but strode on past Leos and through the scrub. He hardly seemed to be breaking a sweat. Leos envied him. Half of his own skin seemed chafed raw from rubbing against wet cloth.

"Young Leos!" Artemis was not far behind now, gripping his heartwood staff tight but showing no sign of fatigue. Leos hated being called 'young'. He was at least twenty-three, as far as he knew. He turned and watched the crazy old coot as he approached, stopping every few strides to examine a bush, or listen for animal calls.

As he drew level, Artemis held out something wrapped in pale cloth. "Soon you will see why we left the horses behind at the well, and why I brought these." He pressed the object into Leos's palm. "You'd better tell our large friend there that he should halt before the ridge. The Sea lies just beyond."

The red staff dug into the sand, and Artemis resumed his climb, robes flapping in the wind while the sand wriggled around his feet.

Leos whistled and waved for Agris to stop his ascent to the ridge, and when satisfied that he wasn't going to tramp merrily over it, teased open the cloth.

He had seen the dark eye-shields before, at the court in Tanagra where he and Agris had signed their contract with Artemis, but had not been allowed to touch them until now. They were circles of glass, somehow smoked or darkened and fixed to a leather strap that could be placed around the head and tightened, so that the world did not seem so bright to the wearer's eyes. Leos had failed to see the point. "If I wanted to be half-blind," he'd said, "I'd simply close one eye." He'd thought it sounded clever at the time. Artemis had smiled and said nothing.

Further up the slope, the old man passed another set of the eye-shields to Agris, and then stopped to dig another pair from his satchel. "Place them on, please, like so." He pressed the dark circles to his eyes and tightened the strap at the back of his head. Leos did the same, then helped Agris when the big man's fingers seemed ill at ease with the fastenings.

They turned to the ridge, just a few strides ahead of them now. Dust was billowing over it, lit from beneath as if the sun were setting, though it was still high overhead.

"Everyone set?" said Artemis. "Then let's have a look at the Sea."

Together, they scrambled up the slope until a sudden wave of light broke over them and Leos was forced to squint and cover his eyes despite the eye-shields. He parted his fingers and peered through, until gradually his eyes adjusted to a new world. The land looked as if the sun had melted from the sky and pooled on the ground, the painful brightness stretching flatly for miles. In the distance was only a blue haze.

He could hear Agris giggling next to him, a reaction that could have any number of meanings. Leos thought that either the big man was pretty angry or pretty impressed. Artemis was staring out at the Sea and smiling.

"Merciful gods!" whispered Leos. "All this from sorcery?"

Artemis shrugged. "No-one knows the true cause. Some say a mountain fell from the sky. Others that a great forest stood here, before the conflagration that turned the sand to glass, but that's nonsense. It was a desert before it became the Sea. War seems the most likely explanation. A sorcerous war that left no-one the victor. Or an experiment, perhaps. Either way, such power was released as to transform the land; enough to melt sand to glass for many leagues from here. None has ever reached the centre of the Sea; at least none that have returned."

Agris stopped giggling and instead adopted a throaty chuckle. Leos edged away from him a little.

"Happily, our destination lies much closer," continued Artemis. "Not far from the edge at all. Only two days at a brisk pace."

"Two days carrying all this shit?" said Leos, hefting his sack meaningfully. "And 'brisk' sounds a mite ambitious."

"Well now!" Artemis gave an elaborate wink. "That's why I have one more gift for you." He patted Leos on the shoulder and beckoned for Agris to follow him as he shuffled over to a copse of stunted, wind-warped trees. He peered into the twisted stems and branches. "Good! It's still here. Young Agris, if you would be so kind as to employ your hatchet?"

Moments later the thicket was trimmed to reveal a mound of sand and cloth. Agris dragged the cloth away to reveal a small wooden sledge, the runners lined with highly polished iron. Together, he and Leos dragged it onto the ridge and then down to the edge of the Sea. The heat had made the wood somewhat brittle, but it was serviceable enough. It held their sacks easily; tools, food, water enough to last a week if rationed.

"How come that sledge was there?" asked Leos as Artemis joined them.

"This isn't the first time I have visited the Sea of Glass," he said with a smile. His hand tightened on the staff.

"And what happened to the crew you came with last time?"

The old man stared at the shimmering horizon of the Sea as if he hadn't heard. "Well, let's make a start, shall we? The sooner we are done, the sooner you will have your money, and you'll be able to return to Tanagra without fear of the bailiffs." Artemis strode off across the Sea, cloth boots whispering on the smooth surface.

"This thing you're looking for better bloody well be there!" Leos called to the old man's back.

He exchanged a look of concern with Agris, and then the two companions followed with the sledge, their hobnailed boots skidding in all directions.

Leos lay on his thin blanket and shivered. During the day the Sea was scorching, hot enough to burn the eyes and blister the skin. At night, it was cold enough to chill bone. It didn't seem to bother Agris, who was sprawled awkwardly on the sledge, his bulk draped across the piled mass of their supplies. His snores rang through the silence of the Sea. Artemis had wrapped himself carefully in several layers of cloth and slept with his head on his satchel, cuddling his staff like a lover. He too seemed peaceful enough.

It was only Leos who found himself unable to sleep in the eerie expanse of nothingness. Fully awake, and needing to piss.

"Damn," he whispered, hauling himself up and carefully picking his way across the moonlit glass a respectable distance from the others. He had no wish to repeat Agris's mistake earlier in the evening, which had forced them to move camp.

He'd only taken a dozen steps when he realised someone was watching him.

In the distance a small figure, perhaps a child, stood quite still on the glass. In the moonlight the child's skin looked as pale as milk, though its hair was dark and shining. It seemed to be wearing a hide of some sort, though its legs and feet were bare. Leos watched the child and the child watched him, neither moving. Leos's breath smoked in the cold desert night, but no mirroring plume came from the child's mouth. Leos raised a hand and waved, feeling absurd, though he couldn't tell why. The child raised its hand and waved back.

Leos turned to call to Agris, and then reconsidered. He turned back, but the child was gone. There was only pale glass, stretching in all directions.

"Small, with pale skin?" Artemis stalked across the glinting surface of the Sea, back straight, eyes narrowed behind the smoky shields.

Leos nodded. "It was there, and then it was gone. It could have been a waking dream, but I doubt it. It's never happened before. I don't have that good an imagination."

Agris made a sound like a lizard being crushed under a heavy stone, which Leos supposed might have been a laugh. His partner heaved on the sledge, dragging it across the glass and leaving a trail of scratches in its wake. The grating noise had been a constant companion through their trek, though as usual Agris seemed oblivious.

Artemis rapped his staff on the ground thoughtfully as he walked. "The people here, the ones living in this place when the Sea was formed, they were small. Like us, but child-sized. Another type of human. Sounds like you saw the ghost of one, perhaps."

Leos sighed. "So I'm either seeing things, or being haunted. Just when I thought I couldn't hate this place more."

"Now now, young Leos. These are the tales you'll tell your grandchildren, when you are my age!" Artemis pulled a compass from within his robes and studied it for a moment. "We are slightly off track. This way, my lads!"

Leos adjusted his eye-shields, then trudged after him. "Not much chance of grandkids if I end up rotting my life away in a debtor's prison," he grumbled. "We nearly there yet?"

As afternoon began to fade into evening, something took shape on the horizon. Four tall, upright structures that all seemed to be the same height. Towers, Leos thought. Four tall towers, marking the corners of a square. An old fortress, the walls gone. He slapped Artemis on the shoulder, rather harder than he should have considering the age of the man, though it seemed not to bother him.

The old man smiled. "And?"

Leos pointed. "Is that where we're heading? Please tell me yes; I'm sick of this Sea and the nothingness in it. And having to wear these bloody eye-shields all day."

Agris sighed happily. "This place isn't so bad, Leos. So much space makes a man think, think. There's so much to see in the world. Would it be so bad if we never, never went back?"

Leos felt a splinter of sadness in his gut. Agris had spent a lifetime fighting and had nothing to show for it but a formidable collection of scars and head injuries. That and survival, which was nothing to be sniffed at, Leos supposed.

Artemis nodded. "It does make a man think, Agris. And yes, Leos, that's where we are headed. It used to be a castle, before the Sea formed. The towers are the Silent Sentinels, and there used to be a great wall between them, with no way through. They were built to protect the greatest treasure of the people who lived here."

"Aha!" Leos tapped his boots on the glass happily. "So that's it. Treasure enough to make three bold and brave companions the richest arseholes in the land, eh?" He paused thoughtfully. "I hope it's still there."

"I'm sure it is," said Artemis. "I'm the only person who knows about it, I believe. And you two now, of course."

Agris grinned and giggled once again. "This treasure buried, is it? Buried?"

Leos looked questioningly at Artemis, who nodded. "That's why you are here. Can't expect an old man like myself to dig through thick glass, even if the effort would make me rich as a king. Instead, we can all be rich. Share and share alike." The old man raised his staff and then bowed to them ostentatiously.

Leos and Agris exchanged grins, though what passed for a grin on the big man's face curdled Leos's stomach a little.

"Let's get to it, then!"

They picked up their pace.

The Sentinels were as tall as twenty men, constructed from regular blocks of dark black stone with white veins running though. Each was intact, unblemished, with no doors or windows. Artemis spent a few moments admiring them while Leos and Agris swallowed some water, and then Leos watched him pace from the corner of each tower to the one diagonally opposite, dragging behind him a long iron spike he had retrieved from the sledge.

When both lines were drawn, Artemis led the companions to the point where they crossed, and handed the spike to Agris.

"The ancient scrolls I have studied state that the treasure was placed in the middle of the Sentinels, an equal distance from them all. It should be somewhere near the intersection of these lines." The old man wiped the sweat from his forehead and pulled out his waterskin. "Off you go, boys. I'll be in the shade over there."

Agris fetched a pair of wooden mallets from the sledge and they took it in turns to hammer the spike into the surface of the Sea, sending bright, sharp chips high into the air. After the spike had gone two hand lengths down into the glass it sank into something soft beneath. They began to widen the hole, breaking the glass into chunks and then carefully piling it up a short distance away. The sun was sinking on the horizon as they finally exposed a bare patch of sand that, Artemis declared, had not seen the sun for over a thousand years.

Leos slipped into the hole and began to shovel the sand out with his gloved hands, rooting around for anything solid. He shivered as his fingers grasped something that felt like a tree root, and then he carefully began to wipe the sharp grains away.

It was long, thin, and twisted, running down into the sand. Hard, brown leather, Leos thought at first, until he saw some tiny toes and realised that he held a withered leg in his hand. He jerked back and looked up at Artemis, who was watching him carefully over the top of his staff.

"It's a body! Old, dried up like a cave corpse from the deserts."

Artemis nodded, his eyes bright. For a moment he hardly seemed an old man at all; more like a child on his birthday. "Uncover the rest!" Then, more hesitantly: "Do you feel fine enough, Leos? No... pain, or discomfort? The scrolls mentioned some... protection."

"Nope," said Leos, brushing away more of the sand to reveal the rest of the small, desiccated corpse. "Just annoyance that we came here looking for treasure and find some shrivelled-up dead prick instead." He lifted the child-sized cadaver out of the hole and passed it to Artemis, who cradled it awkwardly in one arm.

"I'll help, help." Agris reached for Artemis's staff, but the old man jerked it back.

"That's fine," he muttered.

Agris looked at Leos, who shrugged.

"I bet you weren't expecting that to be the greatest treasure of those other humans? If in fact it is, and we haven't just dug a hole in the wrong place. Right?"

"No," Artemis whispered. "This is just what I expected." He turned away.

Leos hauled himself out of the hole, only for his face to almost collide with the pale white face of the child he had seen the previous night. He stared at the pallid, flat features before him; the flattened nose, thin lips and pale green eyes, all framed by a thick mess of dark purple hair. The child — though it wasn't a child, not really, he could see that now from the weathered yet feminine face — raised a finger to its lips as if hushing him.

Leos looked at Agris and gave a strangled squeak, but when the big man turned he only regarded his partner with his usual puzzled expression. The pale girl was gone.

Artemis was already rushing to the sledge, the corpse cradled in his arms. "We should go," he called to the others. "If we leave now we can cover a few leagues before we need to camp." He wrapped the withered cadaver in an empty sack and carefully tucked it into the sledge. "Leave the tools," he said. "We don't need them anymore. We have what we came for." He gazed at the sack, his face creased into a smile. "All we'll ever need."

Someone was driving a spike into Leos's head. Again and again it struck, the force and pain shaking through his body while he squirmed and moaned. *Knock knock knock.*

He opened his eyes to the swirl of stars above the Sea, his body covered in sweat in the cool night air. He swore softly and turned on his side in a vain attempt to get comfortable.

Another white face loomed in front of him, similar but not the same as the one he'd seen a few hours before. Leos gasped and made to cry out, but a thin hand, ashen as the moon, swept in front of his face and seemed to snatch his cries away before he even made them. The bright, fierce eyes of the girl held to his, and he understood. After a silent moment she nodded, and pointed one long finger to the other side of the small camp.

They had camped in a spot where the remains of a building protruded from the Sea; a shattered wall and broken staircase that wound up to over twice Leos's height. Agris had chosen to sleep at the base of the wall in case the wind picked up, and Leos could see his booted feet sticking out from behind it. Moving slowly towards the wall was a tall, slender man dressed in black, eyes narrowed in concentration as he stepped carefully, silently along the glass. In his hand, something glinted sharply in the moonlight.

Leos drew a pair of his daggers and hauled air into his lungs.

"Agris!"

His partner was on his feet in an instant, the confusion on his face quickly replaced by fury when he saw the stranger and the knife he held.

The man lunged, but Agris was quicker than he looked, as a score of corpses could testify, were they able. He batted the blade from the stranger's hand and aimed a meaty fist at his head, only for it to pass harmlessly by as the man ducked.

Leos watched in astonishment as their assailant leapt backwards, flipping over onto his hands and then springing back to his feet. He spun and ran, snatching Artemis's staff from the ground. He turned to face Agris once more, and Leos swore as the slender form of the stranger resolved itself into the familiar grey-haired figure of Artemis.

Agris had picked up his scimitar and was advancing carefully, his boots unsteady on the glass. Leos began to hurry towards him, but Artemis lunged scorpion-quick, the staff whirling to strike Agris's arm, leg, and head all in the space of a moment. With barely a grunt he crashed to the ground.

Leos threw a dagger and was gratified to see Artemis flinch in pain as it scored his arm. He moved forwards warily, ready for Artemis to advance in turn, but instead the man spun and sprinted to the sledge, snatching up the bundle of cloth that contained the small cadaver. Artemis ran, feet whispering across the glass.

Leos gave chase, but his boots couldn't grip the sleek surface so well, and he cursed as Artemis increased the distance between them. Instead, he moved to Agris and crouched by him, examining the large welt on his friend's forehead where the staff had struck. Agris was dazed but breathing normally, and seemed to be muttering obscenities under his breath.

There was movement out on the glass, and Leos looked to see the pale girl standing, arms outstretched, face tilted to the sky. A wind blew, bringing with it the scent of grass, and trees, and wood smoke. From the darkness, another girl walked to stand by the first. Together, they knelt and placed their palms on the glass. The ground shuddered, and Leos started as his boots began to sink into the Sea. He grabbed Agris by the shoulders and hauled him to the broken stairs.

The Sea rippled. In the distance, Artemis stumbled to his knees. The cadaver sack slipped from his hands as he tried to right himself with his staff, though the sack seemed to float across the surface of the Sea rather than sink.

Artemis was less fortunate. The staff plunged into the molten glass and he followed it, arms flailing.

The land seemed to shudder, and the Sea was solid again.

Leos tapped it gingerly with the pommel of his dagger, then stepped onto the reformed surface. The two girls were gone. He saw that the sledge's runners were locked tight in the glass, and cursed.

He tramped carefully across to where Artemis had been, and where now there was only a small bump on the surface of the Sea.

He grinned as he saw Artemis's face, that of the young stranger once again, jutting out from the glass, his head tipped back at an angle. The man's body was a smoky smudge beneath the Sea.

"Played us for fools, eh?" Leos looked over at Agris, who was staring vacantly at the moon and prodding at the wound on his forehead, and coughed. "Well. Played me for a fool, eh? That staff of yours worked a treat. I really thought you were an ancient, dried up old arsehole. Got most of it right, even so."

Leos walked to the sack, which sat undisturbed on the smooth glass. He peered inside to make sure the leathery remains were still there, then slung it over his shoulder and returned to where Artemis's face was grimacing at the night sky.

"Who's the fellow in the sack then? Someone important, I'm guessing." Leos slid a stiletto from his belt and let the point hang over Artemis's eye. "Come on now, you can tell me. I'm all ears."

The trapped man swore, then sighed.

"I don't know his name, or much about him. But he was a king, a great sorcerer who ruled a land thousands of leagues across. Even now, his remains hold tremendous power if used correctly. I need them. I have debts of my own to pay. The kind that can't be paid with coin."

"And you brought us along to shield you from any... protection, was it?"

Artemis groaned and shifted under the glass. "I had to be careful. The people that constructed those towers, who ruled this land... they had great skill. Power beyond belief. How could I know what steps they took to protect their king? I couldn't take the risk myself." He grimaced. "You would have done the same."

"Maybe." Leos looked off across the cold expanse of the Sea, at where the girls had stood not long before. "Did you consider that maybe the Sentinels were there to protect the world from the king, and not the other way round?"

"What difference does that make?" Artemis eyed the blade dangling from Leos's hand. "You don't have to do this, you know. I didn't choose this path. My contacts need the cadaver, and they are important people. We can still travel back to Tanagra, all share in the wealth."

"Nah." Leos waved the dagger. "You want it quick, now? Or you want to wait for tomorrow, and the heat?"

Artemis's throat clicked as he worked his mouth. "Not now. Not now."

Leos nodded. "Fair enough. Well, we're going to dig out the sledge, and then we're going to put this sorcerer-king back where we found him. If you're still breathing when we pass by, we'll have this conversation again."

Back at the camp, Agris was chipping away at the glass around the runners of the sledge with his hatchet. "He wants to burn up in the sun," Leos said. "Seems worse than what I offered, but still."

Agris nodded, then handed Leos the little axe. He slipped his scimitar from its scabbard and looked over at Artemis. His face twitched. "Back, back in a moment."

Leos hacked at the glass, his thoughts on the bailiffs and how he and Agris might pay off their debts, now that Artemis had turned out to be a backstabbing shit.

In the distance, he heard Agris giggle. He was pretty sure what it meant this time.

In the early morning light they placed the shrivelled body in the hole, and piled the chunks of broken glass back on top.

"It'll be easy for someone else to get him out," said Leos quietly. "But not much we can do about that, I suppose."

Agris sucked disconsolately at a waterskin, then slung it onto the sledge. "Not much water... left now. We'll have to be careful on the way back. And lucky, lucky."

"Aye." Leos heaved a sigh. "Another job with nothing to show for it. I don't think our luck is up to much at the moment, 'Gris."

Agris nodded, then wandered to sit in the shade of one of the Sentinels. A few moments later he was snoring roundly.

Leos looked again at the pile of smashed glass atop the hole. "Sorry about that," he said, to no-one in particular.

When he lifted his eyes, one of the pale girls stood on the far side of the grave, a crooked smile on her face. She opened her arms, and from the towers walked three other white girls, striding silently over the Sea. They stood together, facing Leos. They were all alike, but subtly different in hair or eye colour, the shape of their mouths. Sisters, perhaps.

Leos swallowed heavily. "He's best left buried, eh?"

One of the girls knelt on the glass and stretched out her hand to the pile of broken debris. In moments it had gone and the surface of the Sea was intact, the hole vanished.

"Thanks," said Leos a little hopelessly. "Well, I'd best wake my friend over there, or we'll never get off the Sea alive. We'll leave you in peace."

One of the girls held out her hand, then curled her fingers to beckon Leos forward. Not knowing what else to do, he followed. She led him a few steps towards one of the towers, and then crouched. Her hand stroked the surface of the Sea, setting it rippling. The girl motioned for Leos to reach in.

Leos knelt and tentatively pushed his hand into the glass, which was now as cool and wet as a river, and through to the sand beneath. His fingers brushed against something hard.

He grasped it and pulled, slowly dragging it free of the sand and through the watery glass.

A circle of gold, big enough for a child's head.

"Huh."

The pale girl bowed before Leos, grinning widely, and then walked back to her sisters. They turned to regard Leos again, then raised their hands to the sky. Clouds that had not been there before darkened the sun, and moments later a soft rain began to fall, hissing lightly on the Sea. The girls each walked their separate ways, one to each Sentinel, stepping through the stone walls to vanish from sight.

Leos looked at the golden circlet in his hands, drops of rain beading on its glistering surface. He had little experience of handling treasure, to his continual dismay, but he was pretty sure the gold was worth enough to pay their debts with some to spare. Maybe even enough to buy a small plot of land, start a little farm. Smiling, Leos tucked it under his shirt.

Beneath the Sentinel, Agris was still asleep, his mouth open to the rain. Leos made sure the sledge was ready, then crossed to the big man.

"Come on, 'Gris, 'fore you drown."

Agris rumbled awake, then frowned up at the sky.

"Rain? Ain't supposed to rain here, is it?"

"I suppose every dry spell has to end sometime." Leos patted his chest, feeling the gold beneath the cloth. "I reckon ours might be nearing its end, too."

"Well, let's go, go." Agris picked up the rope to drag the sledge. He looked about at the featureless expanse of the Sea, and his brow creased. "I can't tell now the sun's gone. Which way is it?"

Leos turned a full circle, then looked at the flat, grey sky. The wind whipped rain in his face. The Sentinels remained silent. Leos sighed. Every time it seemed that things might improve, the gods emptied their chamber pots over him.

"Why do we bother, Agris? Why?"

Agris ignored him, instead staring at the surface of the Sea with a look of bemusement. "We sure scratched the glass up, dragging... this sledge all the way, all the way. Seems a shame, almost. A shame."

Leos grinned and slapped Agris on the arm, though it was like skinning his fingers on stone.

"Agris, I don't care what everyone else says; to me you're a genius. Come on. We can follow these marks back to the shore." He set off, enjoying the coolness of the rain.

Agris's brow furrowed. "Why, what does everyone else say?"

As he walked, Leos felt the weight of the gold against his chest, and thought of those who had sent Artemis, who sought the power of the dead king. It seemed unlikely that they would just give up when their hireling failed to return. Perhaps, he mused, the circlet wasn't given as a reward, but as a retainer. Payment for services yet to be rendered.

Leos decided that the bailiffs and the farm could wait. He and Agris had a new debt to be paid first.

About the story

I've always loved adventure fantasy since childhood, but as I got older wondered where all those stories about people seeking treasure to improve their lot in life had gone. So I created Leos and Agris to go find some! They always seem to be in debt and never really get any closer to paying the bailiffs, unfortunately, but are perhaps making the world a slightly better place. For this particular outing, I'd been teaching about the Cretaceous–Paleogene mass extinction event (the one that finished off the large dinosaurs) and also reading about the natural formation of glass. The image of a sea of glass, hiding the remains of an ancient civilisation, came along shortly after; and I knew where Leos and Agris were headed to next.

A question for the author

Q: What hero (of any gender) would you name your child after, if we lived in a society with names like that?

A: When I was younger I was determined to name my son Raistlin, after the conflicted character from the *Dragonlance* books by Margaret Weis and Tracy Hickman. Luckily, I haven't, and both my kids have pretty normal names. In another reality, things might well have been different! 'Elric' also has a nice ring to it...

About the author

Rob Francis is an academic ecologist and writer based in London. He spends his days researching urban ecosystems and lecturing students on whatever thoughts happen to arrive in his head during class. On the train to work, he writes fantasy and horror stories.

Rob Francis's story "Beneath the Sea of Glass" was published in *Metaphorosis* on Friday, 13 October 2017.

Lock Rise

Phil Berry

Early on the morning of her seventieth birthday, Magden coiled the rope that moments before had tethered her canal boat to a mooring post, and said, to no-one, "How I *ache!*"

The plan of the day's cruise was clear in her mind, and would start with a right turn at the junction that lay half a kilometre away. She always turned right there. Right, to the periphery; left, to Lock Rise, to the city, to people.

Having straightened her back with caution, she pressed the ignition switch with the thumb to which it was programmed to respond. The engine turned over, spluttered and died.

Magden, who had become a respected pilot on the latticework of waterways since her arrival in the low country many years ago, was not an accomplished engineer. A highly protected upbringing, combined with the pervasiveness of ultra-reliable technology, meant that she had developed no aptitude for mechanical problem-solving. Indeed, her mentor Frank used to laugh as she stared powerlessly at the boat's innards. The engine, assembled from scratch by Frank and powered by polluting hydrocarbons filtered from the purple-black water through fine grilles set in the bow, should have run smoothly for another five centuries; to stop like this was... very unlikely She knew where the engine *was* (under the hatch by the tiller), and she knew what it looked like (a curved hunk of grey metal enlivened by rows of cooler fins), but she had no idea how to mend it. No matter; the canals teemed with experienced pilots who would be happy to assist her — for a fee. Magden tied the boat up again, stepped onto the roof with a hot drink, eyed the pink morning sky, and waited.

While she waited, she reflected on what the birthday meant to her. Very little, actually. The few friends she had on the canal were clueless. Magden, while unfailingly pleasant, considerate, and helpful to those in need, had maintained an opaque exterior. They did not know that on this day, every year, Magden grieved for her younger sister, Elizabeth, whose birthday had fallen just a day after hers. Elizabeth, with whom she had spent so many hours, rushing around the palace, hiding in niches and under chairs, playing games. Killed with all the others, but a death clothed in greater tragedy, somehow.

Images, painful remembrances, pushed themselves to the front of her mind. She knew there were holes. Trauma and grief do not melt over time; they leave vacuums.

Magden's infancy and adolescence had been carefree. Her indulgent father — King Alexus II — had always had time for her. He prioritised her needs, allowed her to select her tutors, and watched her thrive with ill-concealed pride. And then... catastrophe. The Selanuks, a competing family who had amassed a great force beyond the border, had invaded. The coup was swiftly followed by her family's enforced seclusion on a comma-shaped island in the middle of a lake.

Four months passed, during which the maturing Magden observed her father and came to recognise his weakness, his fixed state of denial. This was followed by the inevitable culmination; they were rounded up, they were lined up, and they were executed. The entire family, destroyed in minute. But Magden — known then as Duchess Falona Xenopi — slipped into a cousin's shadow (she was not sure which) and etherealised herself, as she had been taught. Hovering unseen in the air, desperately negotiating the real-world influences on her shapeless form (it had been easier in the palace's specially designed, electromagnetically neutral gymnasium), she watched uniformed chaperones directed by the traitor Rassamunden kick the bodies, turn them onto their backs, and walk away. Stupid men. They did not realise that she had escaped.

Then came the year of wandering, in the company of Frank Linacre, a man who had no interest in politics or palace intrigue. A second father in all but name, he taught her the ways of the water, trained her in navigation and showed her how to survive on the detritus. But after a happy year, when Magden/Falona was still only 24, Frank had been killed in a strike by airborne chaperones. They stormed up the estuary in triangular formation, fifty black crosses moving in rigid rows, a flying graveyard. The pilots, seated at the intersections of the crosses, controlled the holding-beams and granulators that were housed in the limbs.

Frank was crouched on a red buoy at the time, pulling in a pot of estuarine crayfish. He looked up in response to the strengthening hum that reverberated over the flat water. Frank represented no threat to the new regime, but the lead chaperone must have felt frustrated that the sortie from the capital had been uneventful — no enemies to kill in the coastal waters, no dissident camps that might be construed as political gatherings — so he, or she, had released a perpendicular salvo. Frank crumbled, and his fragments slipped into the purple water, the ripples refracting an oily green. There had been no time for him to grant her the boat, but Magden knew his wishes. The boat was her inheritance.

She lingered for weeks near the place of his murder. When she dipped a hand into the polluted water, she imagined that particles of him lay there, in her palm, able to feel her love and regret. She knew that it was possible to live in such a state... possible to re-form, to continue. Magden had done this on the day of the execution; she was one of the very few who could.

Two fathers. One weak, a victim of politics. The other strong, a victim of oppression. They occupied equal niches in her memory.

That had been forty-eight years ago, and Magden had led a quiet life since then. She caused no trouble, and had attracted no attention from the new (not so new, now) regime. Most days were quiet, like this one.

An hour later Simon Parsons, a metal dredger in his late sixties, appeared in the distance. He came from the direction of the great plateau. Magden waved, making it clear that she needed his help. He activated a winch to take his huge magnet up from the canal bed, so as to reduce the drag. What he did for a living was illegal, but he was always careful to hide under the drooping boughs of canal-side trees when he brought the magnet above the surface, turned off the current and picked off the ferrous treasures.

"What's up, Mags?" Only a few metres separated them now.

"Engine failure. First ever."

"Yes, yes, and you are very old. Must be a dammed good engine! I'll take a look. Got tea?"

"Of course."

He prised up the hatch and stepped into the dark space of the hold. His flat-tipped, oil-blackened fingers moved confidently over the pads and switches. Digital readouts scrolled across the upper surface, casting a red glow on Simon's cheek.

"What's this?" he called up, as Magden stooped to deliver a steaming mug.

"What do you mean?"

"The engine, it's giving you a message!"

"How is that possible?"

"The programming... a former owner..."

"It's only had one owner. Frank. He built it."

Simon nodded tactfully. Magden was peering in.

"Has it gone? What did it say?" she asked.

"It's repeating. Look. Read it."

+++ Everything was for a reason - - - go back to Lock Rise +++

Magden felt cold. Frank had not been like this. There had been no shadowed corners in his life. He'd been simple — no, not simple... pure.

Simon asked, quietly, "Will you go?"

"I haven't been back there for years. I hate it. So dirty." At no point during their friendship had she told Simon the truth of her background.

"Ah Magden, it's better now. The water is blue, it's changed..."

Simon stopped abruptly. He had heard the hum. Magden recognised it a moment later. A patrol. Simon leapt from the roof of Magden's boat to his own, flicked a lever near the tiller and sank the magnet back into the water with a splash. Then he slowed down his movements, knowing that he could be observed despite the patrol's estimated distance of five kilometres. He sat next to Magden on a steel storage box in the pilot's well. Both stared nonchalantly over the water, trying to look relaxed. The hum became more insistent with the patrol's approach, then sharpened in tone as the ships slowed before dropping to an altitude of a hundred metres, directly above the seated couple. A scout ship descended, its downward thruster whipping up the water and wetting their faces. The pilot did not notice the chain emerging from the water, or if he did, he did not understand its significance.

"Where is your marina?" boomed a speaker on the ship's underside.

"Oxbow Town, that way!" shouted Simon. Not too respectful, not to humble. Innocent, like.

"Business?"

"Hydrocarbon purification."

The only answer was a dip in the ship's nose, before it accelerated away and covered them with spray. Magden's eyes were wide and unblinking. Her hands held the boat's railing so tightly they were completely white. She stared down into the water. Simon attempted to reassure her with soft words, but they did not get through. When she felt his rough palm on her cheek, a tentative gesture, she at last focused on him, and the tears began to spill.

"Do you want to tell me?" asked Simon.

She shook her head.

"Do you want me to take you? To Lock Rise."

"No Simon. I'll go alone."

Lock Rise separated the central plateau from the low regions. The twenty-nine locks, tall, paired gates enclosing deep columns of water on which boats could rise and fall, allowed pilots to journey onto or away from the plateau. The work involved (opening the gates against fluid resistance, hand-winching the sluices, leaping back onto the roof of the boat after the lock had filled or emptied) tested all but the fittest. When Magden had last taken the flight (part of an ill-advised journey to meet a lover, twenty-five years ago) it had taken two days, and she was so exhausted she promised herself never to do it again. But now the Selanuks had mechanised the run, getting from base level to lock fifteen would only take a couple of hours.

The engine restarted without any further intervention. The message's release had been sufficient to get it going again. The past and the present were connected, through Frank.

Straightforward Frank. What else had eluded her?

The day of the execution — three months after the Selanuk invasion and the deposed royal family's exile to the island. Each member was brought out of the island house (a previous empress's holiday retreat) onto a small, lush field some distance away. Their ages ranged from seven to eighty-four.

The head of the house, King Alexus II, led them out assertively, albeit under the gaze and the guns of the chaperones. He was dressed all in white — jacket, shirt, trousers, shoes, laces too. The air was warm. Foamy water lapped at the rocky shore, portions of which the family could see if they peered over the cliff edge. A launch bearing Selanuk colours drew up at the base of a long stairway cut into the cliff, and two of its crew tied ropes to a rusted, iron loops set into the concrete.

"Why have we been called out?" demanded Alexus II, staring at the most senior chaperone.

"Wait, Sir."

A hint of deference, even then.

Presently, a small group of officials appeared at the top of the steps and walked over the grass towards the King. Two ambassadors in dark blue robes, with five elite, face-guarded chaperones. Their guns were small, but the adults knew they were lethal.

"Who are you?" asked the King.

"Transition party," replied the taller of the Ambassadors.

"Transition? Of what?"

"Leadership. Culture. Destiny."

"You are already in charge. We are your prisoners. What more do you want?"

The second ambassador smiled and turned his head to one of the chaperones. He in turn signalled to his four colleagues.

"Symbolism. That is all." It was not clear which of the two said it, but something in the sentence, an agreed code word, caused the chaperones to open fire. The screams did not leave the mouths of the victims.

Magden etherealised. It began in the extremities, and spread inward quickly. Her clothes dropped to the ground, and she saw an uncle roll, dead, onto them. In the brief phase of expansion, when she was everywhere and nowhere, she saw the scene from multiple angles. The faces of the people she loved. Her mother's pale skin, habitually hidden from the sun to prolong the appearance of youth, divided now by rivulets of blood. There had been no time for shock to transform her expression. The lethal ray must have instantly severed something vital to life. Instead, the expression was... maternal. Her hand was still curled in the shape it had made while cupping the back of a young nephew's head.

Magden looked elsewhere, across the field of carnage. Her father, still stern. Her old nanny, regarded as 'family', whose face portrayed the horror of complete understanding. (Perhaps she knew her imperial history.) And children. All still.

Now the phase of expansion reached an end, and Magden narrowed herself. Invisible still, she slipped over the edge of cliff at its nearest point, like slurry through a waste-weir in the agricultural zone.

Half way down the cliff, with space between her and the carnage above, the emotional impact nearly knocked her out of the state into which she had transformed herself. It took continued concentration to maintain a balance between separation of her elements, and complete, irreversible dispersal. She followed a slim line down to the level of the water and paused in flight, having glimpsed a shape in the shallow water near the cliff. A body? But lifeless, unmoving. They must have jumped to escape the bullets, or perhaps they were thrown back by the ballistic energy. Magden could not linger. She skimmed peripheral canals until sure of her bearings. Then, knowing which direction she must take (away, away from the centre), she followed the trade canals until nightfall. She kept her wide gaze forward, fearful of the dark surface below, fearful that the face of the body would rise, pale and familiar.

As the temperature dropped, she found an unoccupied boat and coalesced in the warmth of its cabin. There she sat on the upholstered, narrow bench. As she began to take in the details of decoration, the tattered books, the dented tech, a hand-painted picture, a light went on and the owner stood before her.

Frank Linacre.

Simon had been right, and the water did begin to clear as Magden ascended Lock Rise to the plateau. The change was very noticeable at lock four, where the water that filled the column ran green rather than black gloss. As she approached lock fifteen, her nerves began to tingle. This was not how she remembered the Rise. When she had ascended it with Frank, the brick walls had dripped with dark green slime; now the brick work was clean. She waited for the sluice to open and for the water level to rise. Then she walked along her boat's roof, scanning the lock sides. Over halfway up Lock Rise now, she expected a sign, a messenger. It was getting dark.

At lock 23 she felt the pressure of another's eyes on her back. She turned quickly, strained to see through the gloaming. A tall man stood on the opposite side of the lock. His hair stood out against a line of dark trees behind, completely white. Long for a man, it turned outwards to rest on his wide, straight shoulders. The face, beneath a deeply ploughed brow, was that of a very, very old man. Yet his stature, his skeleton, was that of a man in healthy middle age. Magden recognised him instantly; it was Rassamunden.

He smiled as he spoke. "Falona Xenopi. I am truly pleased to see you. Welcome back."

Life on the comma-shaped island had not been all bad. The children were schooled and had time to play. Their father studied and worked on his grand project, the development of a military city.

He was a natural soldier, although Magden remembered overhearing conversations between courtiers and civil servants in palace corridors suggesting that he was not an effective general. Nevertheless, his crown, which was hereditary, made him commander-in-chief.

His great military scheme was to establish a great community where soldiers could live with their families and beget more soldiers. Alexus II was not embarrassed about this ambition. The stability of his kingdom depended on a huge and well-motivated army. The first ancestor, plain Rebecca Cranzz, had established her realm on the back of a huge force that changed allegiance during a regional war. She became Sophus I, five-hundred years before Alexus II's ascension. He swore to uphold Sophus's philosophy of rule — maintain the army, honour the army, give the army whatever it wants.

He was happy, at his desk, the sun stretching across his papers and graphic screen as the hours passed. He would spend the morning there while the nannies took the children out to play on the island's limited spaces, and while the older ones, like Duchess Falona Xenopi, attended the classroom. Then they would have a formal lunch together, before Alexus II returned to his project. The other adults smiled indulgently. They, his wife among them, knew the plans would come to nothing. He no longer had power. He lived a delusion.

In happier times, the traitor Rassamunden had entertained them in the palace. He was a musician and poet, elevated to the level of personal advisor by virtue of omnipresence and charisma. Tall and lean, with long hair that was greying at the temples, resulting in a streaked ponytail, his treachery was surprisingly simple in the end — the mere passing of a palm-code to the invading vanguard.

But looking back, there had been hints of disloyalty. In muttered asides, when supervising the children's cultural studies, he would comment on the state of the land, the increasing pollution, the burden of taxes, or the short-sighted nature of universal militarisation. These criticisms were not applied to Alexus II's rule, but to mistakes made by previous societies, or the direction of history. Yet Falona, always sensitive to undercurrents, caught flavours of deep dissatisfaction. Perhaps the king valued a critical voice at court — she hadn't really known. But she was not surprised when, on the island jail, it was revealed that it was Rassamunden who had let the enemy in.

Her father sighed when told, as though he had been taken for a fool. He had, of course.

But wasn't it Rassamunden, at her father's urging, who had urged Falona to become adept at etherealisation? Hadn't she been saved, ultimately, by his careful and insistent tutelage?

Very few were able to do it, though the genetic heritage of the royal line did mean that the Duchess was more likely, statistically, to have the capability than a common child. Even if the talent was there, history had shown that the transformation could be performed only once, perhaps twice, in a lifetime. Half of those who did it twice never reformed. Their elements were still in the atmosphere, or had recirculated into the food chain, or been precipitated onto the land and washed into the ocean.

Etherealisation was a *possible,* for some, but it was not a useful tool.

Nevertheless, Falona took an interest. She read up on famous examples — the criminal libertine who slipped through hangman's noose as it tightened; the child who escaped a land vehicle as it plunged into a chasm; the ninety-year old dowager who undertook interplanetary transfer, seeking immortality — but Falona's comfortable life seemed unlikely to offer such romantic, or dangerous, circumstances.

Her two closest companions studied with her, similarly encouraged by Rassamunden. They were her seven-year old male cousin, Arthuran, and her twelve-year old sister, Elizabeth. . They could be annoying (especially the boy, plump, fair, overtly jealous at times of his position way down the line of succession), but they seemed to worship their older relative and followed her around. Elizabeth modelled herself on Falona; in dress, in manner. Arthuran emulated her attitude — cautious, observant, reserved. And like Falona, both the youngsters immersed themselves in tales of etherealisation. Their eyes grew wide and their imaginations whirred. They were a decade away from having the discipline to do it safely.

Only Falona was close. And Rassamunden knew it. Hence, two days before he let the enemy in, his comment:

"Whatever happens to your family, Falona, remember everything you have learnt. Everything I have taught you."

When it came to the execution, she did exactly that.

In a poorly serviced quarter of the capital, Rassamunden paused in front of an unmarked door, drew the tip of his index finger across it diagonally, and smiled at Magden as it opened with a brief squeak. He sprang up an unlit staircase and knocked at a door on the first floor. A warm-sounding hubbub of conversation and debate within subsided. The door moved an inch, a face flitted across the gap, then it swung fully open. Magden entered, and saw a large group of men and women seated on sofas, wooden chairs or cushions thrown onto the floor. Magden's assessment was instant — revolutionaries. All the way down to the threadbare trousers, leather jerkins, and thin, untrusting faces. The group had a centre; a man in middle age, leaning forward, his hands frozen in mid-gesticulation. Magden recognised his fair hair and nervous eyes immediately; it was Arthuran.

His eyes flicked between the two of them. Three of the group leapt up with guns raised and aimed. Arthuran spread his arms assertively,

"No!"

Magden had not flinched. Rassamunden, standing by her side, beamed, seemingly confident in the advantage he held.

"Arthuran. As promised, I bring you what you have always lacked. Family. Validation."

"I asked you for nothing."

"Come now. With the duchess by your side, you can make your move. The people will love it, to see you together again. It is too good a story."

"Why do this? What do you expect? A baronetcy?"

"I need nothing. By bringing the Duchess to you, I go some way to righting a wrong. I cannot undo what I did of course, but I can—"

Arthuran caught the eye of a comrade and nodded in Rassamunden's direction. The third man walked forward, gun in hand.

"No, Arthuran. You still need me."

"What for?"

"Your father. If you are to avoid the mistakes of the past, you must understand your father better. You must learn the lessons he failed to learn. Only I can show you. Only I was there."

Rassamunden and Magden sat on a bench in a small warehouse near a suburban marina. They could hear the shouts of tradesmen and merchants; the thunder of barrels being rolled across cobbles; the rumble of canal boat motors. The warehouse was locked. A little light came in through spaces between wooden planks that comprised the walls. Outside, two guards dressed to look like canal boat men leaned on the door frame, guns in their belts.

"We have time, before Arthuran returns. Will you talk to me? You must have questions."

Magden had adapted to the disgust he engendered in her. The need to know suppressed the desire to spit, to injure, or ignore.

"How are you... so well? You must be... eighty-nine, ninety...?"

"It's the air! It's the water! Everything is better now, Falona. You've seen it, haven't you? You've tasted it."

"At what price?!" She raised her voice.

"That is the calculation I made, when I let the Selanuks in. The price was your family. I loved you, Falona, I loved all the children, but I could see where your father's policies were taking us. He had no thought for the price of his obsession with the military... his stupid army towns... industrialisation... the armaments. He refused to learn from history on this world or on others... the depletion, the pollution..."

"It was murder. We were children!"

"I was there! I watched. I refused to look away, so I *know exactly* what it was. I counted the bodies, I confirmed their identities. And I *lied,* to keep you and Arthuran safe. I paid off the chaperones. We rewrote history and kept it suppressed to this day. The Selanuks believed you and Arthuran were killed too."

"Where did he go?"

"He was playing dead. You were the only one who could not be found. And Elizabeth of course, for half an hour, before we found her in the lake." Rassamunden shook his head sadly.

Magden was shaken by mention of her sister's name. Rassamunden's expression transformed to one of concern.

"You knew that, didn't you Falona? That Elizabeth fell into the water." The irony of *him* showing concern, pushed Magden into silence for a minute. Rassamunden looked away.

Madgen murmured, pushing images of her sister in the water away, "How *could* you let them in? How could you allow our family to be killed? The children. How could that ever be justifiable?"

"Look at us now. How much better things are. Under Alexus II there were forgotten towns, with forgotten people. He did nothing for the weak, for those whose genetic lines meant they could never make a contribution to his vision. He was interested only in borders, conquests, legacy."

"He was a good father."

"He was dutiful, I will grant you that, Falona. But a bad ruler. You know it."

Magden had no argument. She did not have the strength to challenge this equivalence.

"You say this society is benign..."

"Largely. You cannot rule by kindness alone."

"So why send airborne chaperones along the waterways, into the estuaries, to pick off innocent men?"

"Like Frank?"

"Yes, like Frank."

"Think about it, Falona. How did you find me? The message, in the engine. It was Frank. He was no innocent boatman. He was always a conspirator."

"No. I found him. It was chance."

"It wasn't. Duchess, listen to me. Everything was for a reason."

"Tell me. How was it not chance?"

"Because Frank... was a beacon. After the etherealisation, you were little more than an air-borne current, you were a thread of energy... the path you followed, over the water, was necessary... I know the science, trust me, more than anyone on this planet. I put Frank there to attract you, as a conductor... his boat, that engine, it was a great attractor. In your training, you hadn't been exposed to electromagnetic sources. That was deliberate. I needed you to be influenced, in the etherealised state. By the time you got down to the canals you were in danger of disappearing forever, but he was waiting there for you, and your exhausted body, its particles, rushed to him. It wasn't chance, Falona, it was physics. I'm sorry. You were never going anywhere else."

"I don't..."

"It doesn't matter. It is the truth. Frank trapped you, he picked you out of the air like a fly. And he watched you, for me. He kept you safe. He was your personal guard. Sadly, I could not keep him safe. I am sorry for that. The chaperone squadrons have their own executive structure. The new king ordered that anyone connected with the old line was to be exterminated. A rumour came in through rural intelligence about Frank. Agents tracked him for weeks. I knew nothing of this. I am truly sorry. But you were kept safe. I got a message through to the squadron at the last minute. A great deal of money was required. But you were kept safe, and that at least was something."

Magden's anger was exhausted.

The warehouse door opened. Arthuran stood in the rectangle of sudden light.

"Come on. It's time. Show me."

Rassamunden nodded, and informed the guards of the location.

Magden, Arthuran, and Rassamunden stood in the high-ceilinged examination hall of the capital's military college. On a dais, where invigilators were accustomed to stand and watch the students during the annual ranking tests, were several glass-topped display cabinets. Rassamunden opened one with a key, then propped the glass cover up with a stick on a hinge. There was a slight hiss as the environmental regulator adjusted.

He picked out book as wide as him arm, full of designs for defences and war machines.

"The most sensitive things are always hidden in plain sight."

Beneath the book lay a small, slim folder. Protected from light, its temperature regulated, it looked new. Rassamunden looked up at the royal cousins.

"This is your father's personal notebook. This is where he developed his ideas. Here, handle it. You won't break it."

Madgen put it down on another display cabinet, looked at each page. It was fifty-percent text and fifty-percent design. Arthuran looked over her shoulder.

A city, described in minute detail. A romantic's idea of the ideal community, melded with the autocrat's vision of the self-sustaining military machine. Each building had a label, every street a name. Into the city ran broad supply lines, and from it extended a network of links to the rest of the continent, up to the borders. Magden could place it. She knew where Alexus II had wanted it to be founded. The canals that she knew so well would have been buried beneath new infrastructure.

"Go on," encouraged Rassamunden.

Ten pages in — *Thoughts on the order of battle,* underlined.

The front line, ranks of infantry. Behind them, large ordnance.
coordinated, large scale e.
de-e, behind their lines, then unleash.
e.
e?

She knew.

"Yes, Falona. That was the idea. To train them all in etherealisation."

"But how? You can't train for that. You are born to it. Only the royal line."

"Read on."

A report, pasted onto a page. Written by Alexus II's chief medical officer.

... the genetic penetrance in A, FX, and E is sufficient to be passed to non-carriers...

... After four generations I estimate sufficient numbers to create the first regiment...

... Selection criteria should be based on physical attributes and family history...

... The proposed model pre-supposes multiple partners; this will be more straightforward in the case of the male A...

... A conditioning programme in the cases of FX and E will be presented at the next council meeting...

Magden felt sick. Her hand clawed at the page.

"Don't tear it. It's evidence."

"Get me out of here."

Arthuran eyes were wet, but his jaw was set in a line of pure anger.

To discover one's father was a monster...

Everything that had gone before must be re-evaluated. Every kind touch or gentle word, however sincerely meant in the moment, becomes obscured by the realisation that a hard and ruthless heart lay behind them. The plans he'd had for them, the three who shown early signs of talent...

The nannies; how they must have watched them as infants, looking for signs. The teachers, the tutors, ordered to observe and report on behaviour that seemed to indicate the potential to master etherealisation. So that they, the three who were chosen, could be used... Magden could not bring herself to think it through.

Rassamunden watched her from across the room, a plain kitchen in a second, anonymous safe house. Guards rotated through the rooms. They addressed Magden politely, but were brusque with Rassamunden.

"Can you find it in yourself to understand what I did?" he asked.

"Don't talk to me."

"I must. Because we are at a turning point. Arthuran is initiating a counter-coup as we speak. There is a taste for change, and he may well succeed. Everyone is comfortable on the plateau, but those in the periphery are nervous, the borders are no longer secure. The voice of the hawks is getting louder, and being heard. The lower house is sympathetic to Arthuran's movement. Everyone knows he has been waiting in the wings, but nobody has talked about it publicly. The palace will be overrun, the communications hubs will be controlled, the administrative towns will fall into line. He's probably already in the throne room."

"Why work to reinstate my family when you allowed its destruction? You are just bending in the political wind... again."

"My only concern is the security of this kingdom."

"Were you ever loyal to my father?"

"For many years. Then I recognised what he was planning, and helped to stop it. Now I recognise the passivity of the current regime, and I will help to overturn that. I am loyal to this continent. I am the constant."

"You regard yourself too highly."

"It's immaterial. In the end I am irrelevant, but while I live I will steer things in the way I feel that serves this continent."

"So what do you want of me? Where do I fit? Why did you find me, why lure me to Lock Rise?"

"Be yourself. That's all."

"But you said... Frank said... everything is for a reason. What is my reason?"

"You were always the favourite, Falona. You still are."

Magden's first aerial view of the capital was surprising. The impression she had developed, of black buildings that loomed in harsh silhouette, of imposing facades and fascist architecture, was blown away. There were parks, serpiginous low-rise accommodation blocks designed to encourage sharing of communal spaces, and trees, far more than she remembered as a child. Her view, from half a kilometre up in a commandeered transport, was interrupted by several columns of smoke, where fifth-columnists in fighters (the same black crosses that had stormed the estuary and killed Frank) had taken out strategic targets. There seemed to be no collateral damage.

Magden was accompanied by one of Arthuran's lieutenants.

"Where are we landing?" she asked.

"Palace grounds. Arthuran would like to see you as soon as possible."

"Is it over, the fight?"

"All over. There was no real fighting... only the royal family's personal guard. But their hearts weren't in it."

Magden turned back to the window, felt the transport tip and slow.

"What will happen to them?"

"Exile. Nothing more."

The palace was calm. Magden noticed upturned furniture and elongated scorch marks on the floors or walls. The King's study was destroyed, but the bodies of the personal guard had been removed. There was no blood. Magden and the lieutenant walked through the palace and out the back, into the expanse of the formal gardens which were bisected by a long ceremonial canal. This was a new feature. The banks of the canal were of granite; all straight lines and sharp edges. Half way along, the height of the canal dropped ten metres, and this point was marked by a lock. Beyond the lock was a marina, large enough for fifty boats.

The lieutenant, a long-time supporter of Arthuran, anticipated Magden's question.

"The Selanuks built this. Part of a democratisation strategy... to show they were connected, to the people. On ceremonial days, representatives came in from the towns on their canal boats, moored up and spent the night as guests of the royal family. The Selanuks are, or were, obsessed with honouring the old ways."

Magden had spotted a man several hundred metres away, on the granite side path.

"Is that...?"

"Arthuran. He's waiting for you."

He greeted her with a cold smile. Metal edges on his soles rang on the canal's granite border as he stepped forward.

"We have won, Falona.."

"You have the palace. You don't have the continent."

"One follows the other. So now... what room will you have? Your old one?"

Magden shrugged. She had no intention of living here.

"You know, Falona, I think you may be an imposter."

Magden laughed.

"You are too calm. For someone who saw what you saw, did what you did."

"*What did I do?*"

"Your ability to forget is astounding."

"What are you talking about?"

"Elizabeth. Tell me the truth, and then I will know if you are who you say you are."

Magden looked over his shoulder, to the middle distance. The thinking distance.

"Elizabeth fell into the sea. During the massacre. Rassamunden told me. It makes sense, I saw a body. I did not know it was her."

"You couldn't stop to check, you were in mid-flight. A convenient version, for you."

Magden stared back at him blankly.

"That is not what happened, Falona. I saw! I etherealised, but I was no good at it, could only manage it for a fraction of a second. Then I collapsed back into form, into my own clothes, before they even fell to the ground, and came to lie near the edge of cliff. Rassamunden found me there, touched me with his foot, pronounced me dead... for reasons I still do not understand, But before he arrived, I saw everything. Elizabeth had etherealised first, she must have seen them charge up the guns. But she re-formed too soon, over the shallows at the base of the cliff, and she fell, naked, into the waves. She began to drown in the seconds before you etherealised. As you descended the cliff you left a shadow, or a ripple in the air, I saw it. You skirted the narrow beach, you flew over the water... and you stopped,... but you *did nothing!*" He was shouting now.

Magden looked down, at her feet, at the granite surfaces, at the water.

Yes, she had flown over Elizabeth's body. Yes, she had stopped, re-formed, become tactile.

Yes, she had seen her sister. The shallow waves had refracted the afternoon sun to play unnatural colours over the contours of Elizabeth's face. Her lips had already begun to swell in the brine. Her eyes, half-open, didn't flinch as they should to the sting of it. Yet, there was life there. She was drowned, but not dead. Her lungs were full but her heart was not yet still. Falona could tell. The skin retained a rose hue; there was oxygen in her, enough, perhaps, for life. But Magden could not stop. She must continue, fleeing the chaperones, finding safety, in case she too de-etherealised and dropped into history's lap as the rest of the family had done. She could not stop. So she etherealised again, and Elizabeth had rolled beneath the lake's usually benign waves.

"You killed her, Falona, through your neglect. If she had survived, the three of us, together, might have gathered support, reversed the invasion. The nucleus of the family would have been enough. Even with you gone, one of us could have led the people. Together, as we became adults, we would have turned opinion, not straight away, perhaps, but a few years later. Where was your loyalty? Where was your desire to avenge? *Where where you?*"

Magden had no answer. Arthuran's puce colour faded. He had composed himself.

"So. I say you are an imposter," he spat.

"I cannot be both imposter and murderer, Art."

Arthuran considered. The slim line of the ceremonial canal glowed orange in the low sun, like a crack in the planet that burned beneath. The lock began to empty. Madgen looked around sharply, but saw no one on the sluice handle. An accomplice, hidden at a lever. A dip appeared in the surface of the water, where a whirlpool had been created by the opening of the sluice in the lock gate.

"Imposter. That will do."

"Do for what?"

"For the people. As an explanation... for my first summary judgement."

"Art…"

"After you appeared at our door with Rassamunden, I needed to be sure that you had not established a following, built up a popular movement, despite the humble way in which you present yourself. But my network tells me that I need have no fear… you are truly unknown, living in isolation on that stinking, damp canal boat. Perhaps, once, there would have been a place for you by my side, but not now. Not now Falona. Now you are just a complication.""

He pressed forward, in a rush now, pushing her against the sculptured, thigh-high railing. With the flat of his hands he pressed against her chest.

"Art! NO!" shouted Magden. But he was committed. Unable to resist him, Magden's centre of gravity moved beyond the railing, her fall inevitable. She turned her head, saw the expanding ripples, and became nothing. She disappeared. Arthuran could not halt his own movement. His arms closed on nothing. His waist doubled over the railing, and he fell into the water. He had time to right himself, so that he could kick up and keep his head above the water, but the whirlpool caught him. His outstretched arms rotated like the hands of a crazy clock until the water level fell and his feet became trapped in the hidden sluice. Then it did not take long for the water to lap at his face and fill his mouth.

Magden waited in the foliage of tree, formless still. Her control was perfect. The lock emptied slowly, its drainage partially obstructed. A turncoat chaperone walked past on a routine circuit and noticed some clothing near the lock gate. He looked down closely, and the truth dawned. There were shouts, people running. Rassamunden arrived, his cloak flapping. The gruesome finding did not disturb him. He looked around, and cast a smile at his surroundings, aiming it everywhere, and placed an envelope on the ground. Then he walked away. If he had turned, he would have seen the envelope rise from the grass before being consumed in an unseen cloud.

Simon was preparing his breakfast. It was cold outside, autumn rolling into winter. On a matter of principle, Simon took his breakfast up onto the roof of the boat unless rain, wind, or sub-zero conditions made it unrealistic. With an exaggerated sigh, he settled into the canvas back of a fold-out chair, lifted a mug to his chin, and looked along the canal. Morning mist hugged the breadth of the water's surface and enveloped the tow path. It would probably not clear until after lunch.

A figure emerged from the moist, milky air. Short. Thin. Elderly. Female. Simon waved. The woman waved back. Presently, she joined him on the boat.

"I missed you, Magden. Where's your boat?"

"Just up the towpath. I fancied a walk."

"You found whatever you were looking for?"

She nodded. Simon knew when to push and when to stand off.

"So everything is alright, then?"

"Yes. I think so."

"Good. Come on, let's get you inside. I've enough food here for two. Did you hear the news? New government. Just like that! Some old bureaucrat in charge. Didn't see that coming."

"I need to catch up. Thank-you Simon, I will have some food, if that's OK."

Uncharacteristically, she gave him a huge hug. While she held him, Simon asked, "What did you make of the capital, Magden?"

"Who says I went to the capital?"

"I don't know... you..."

Magden held him, enjoying the musty warmth of his thick top, and wondered... does he know? *Does he care where I come from?*

Later, after dark, Magden opened the envelope under the yellow glow of the bulb in her cabin. It was addressed to her, and was in her father's handwriting. The embossed lilac of the envelope itself had faded to almost white, but the folded letter within had held its colour. But the marks of the paper were uninterpretable. Grey dashes and flecks, grouped in clouds or arcs. If it was an old imperial code, it looked unbreakable, so formless was the data.

Formless.

She held a hand over the paper and concentrated. Her palm and wrist began to etherealise. She controlled it, so that it did not creep up her arm. Looking through the place where her flesh had been, turning the invisible arm so that it refracted the marks in different planes and directions, she began to detect patterns. Words appeared, but they could only be read one at a time. With her other hand, the non-dominant one, she recorded them in the order they were revealed to her. An hour later she had organised them into a paragraph that made sense. Her understanding of her father set the tone, and of course she knew how it would start:

Dearest Fal,

I anticipate your every feeling. I know your anger. That is the price I began to pay even before they took my life.

I know about Rassamunden. Every court has one. What will happen next week is inevitable, history tells us this. If not next week, next year. I cannot save the family.

But I can save you, my best, my brightest. I hope also that Art and El manage to escape. It was my ambition that each of you become skilled enough to fly away when the chaperones arrive. If the three of you survive, our family might come together again. I pray so.

I have made mistakes. I am not a poor leader, just a mediocre one. I did not ask for it.

I will entrust this letter to Rassamunden. If he gives it to you it means he knows that it is time for our family to return. He will help. Use his skill.

Nothing I say can save your memory of me. That is the price I pay.

Father.

Magden's arm solidified. The words broke apart. She hid the letter behind a panel designed to foil searches by passing chaperones, and unfolded a navigation chart on the galley table. At dawn, when the sun began to burn the mist off the water, Magden's boat was gone. The water was calm, the wake of her smooth, reliable engine had subsided. At the junction there were no clues as to which way she had gone; right, to the periphery, or left, towards Lock Rise, the city, and the destiny that she had evaded for half a century. It was impossible to tell.

A question for the author

Can beautiful things be funny?

Rarely. Marilyn Monroe was both; Cameron Diaz and Sandra Bullock have had their moments. Rowan Atkinson is not, by most standards, beautiful, but the laughter and joy he induces in me when I listen to old Not The Nine O'clock News tapes is... beautiful.

About the author

Philip Berry lives and works in London. He began to write short speculative fiction three years ago, having been inspired during his mission to read the sci-fi classics that he overlooked earlier in life. His story 'Sheer' appeared in a 2016 edition of *Metaphorosis*. Others have appeared in Headstuff, Nebula Rift, Liars' League, 365 Tomorrows and Daily Science Fiction. Philip also writes on medical ethics, his day job being a hospital doctor.

www.philberrycreative.wordpress.com, @philaberry

Phil Berry's story "Lock Rise" was published in *Metaphorosis* on Friday, 20 October 2017.

Bluebird

Benjamin Cort

Nelson Towers spent most of his time oiling the feathers. When he had taken the job he had been enticed by the prestige, the travel, and the pay. He quickly came to realize that his work was to be reviled, not celebrated, that everyplace he traveled was more depressing than the last, and that he was mostly paid to oil the feathers. But at least the pay was good.

In the early days he had worked with a small penlight, its thin beam shaking nervously in a sweaty palm. He tried to use it sparingly, but the shape of the wings was foreign to him, and he often found himself flicking it on and marveling at their rough form. He worked when it slept, which was often. He dreaded being in its presence.

Now he worked in total darkness. He knew how it lay as it slept and where to step as he moved around it. It hungrily lapped up oil and soaked it deep into its plumage. For a thing that spent most of its time sleeping in dark, quiet places, it needed to be constantly fed.

He hadn't looked at it in weeks. He had never seen the whole thing at once, nor did he want to. When he worked, it slept. When it worked, he turned away.

Saying that Lexington had let itself go would have been an overstatement. Towers had always considered the town to be a dump. It now just had the outward appearance to reflect that.

He had tracked it here from Harper's Ferry over the course of two long days, and each mile North turned his mood darker. The sky too, darkened with his countenance. Fall this far North was never pleasant, and the road was full of packed cars trundling South. Sleepy children ogled his truck as it drove carelessly over the dotted white lines. His whole side of the highway was barren. It seemed as if the entire North had packed its bags and moved out. Towers was used to this by now. He tried not to take it personally.

When he finally pulled into Lexington Center, it was night. His digital watch read 11:04 in garish green numbers. The buildings hung low with muted colors. The store windows were dark. Some had been smashed in, revealing emptied shelves. This strip was dominated by banks, boutiques, and frozen yogurt stores. Towers slowed his truck down at the intersection. It would be around here somewhere. He switched off the engine and hopped out, leaving the truck in the middle of the road.

In the back, wedged between large drums of oil, his little printer whirred and spat out a sheet of paper. He tore it from the machine. "St. Cuthbert," it read, simply. The smartest, richest, and most powerful people in the entire world had gathered in the City and built an array of satellites that could track both its and his position every second of every day to the meter. He had been given a printer with a radio duct-taped to the side. The City loved to cut costs for people who didn't matter. Towers crumpled up the paper and tossed it into the street.

Leaves crunched under his feet as he plodded over to the sidewalk. Three days ago the square would have been bustling. The restaurants would have rolled out their patios to soak in the last few days of warmth left in the season and the air would have filled been with warm light, idle chatter, and wisps of cigarette smoke. There would be a line out the movie theater door for the eight o'clock showing of whatever was on. Kids would be lounging around the large green lawn in front of the church, waiting for some interesting trouble to spring to their minds.

The church's facade had always made him nervous. But Allison had loved the lawn, so he had pretended to love it too. When they were younger, they would chase each other around it in endless loops. When they were older, they would sit against the trunks of the trees, talking for hours in the shade.

The lawn was filled with leaves now. Towers walked across it, his hands jammed deep into the pockets of his brown jacket. The stained glass face of Mr. Christ stared down at him. Towers lingered outside and met his eyes defiantly. Now it was Towers who had the upper hand. When the bird was done with this town there would be nothing left. He turned off his glowing watch and tried the door. It opened inward to his touch, and he slipped inside quickly, closing it behind him.

The Church of Saint Cuthbert was dark. He could see high above him hints of starry sky through the colored glass. And he could hear it breathing. He hadn't been able to detect its soft, fluttering breaths, at first. He hadn't even thought that it needed to breathe. Now, like it or not, the sound of its breath was the sound of his home.

Towers approached it, ducking under a sharp wing. He moved slowly, feeling his way through the darkness. It had moved the pews aside to fit its bulk into the space just below the pulpit. He sat gingerly on the edge of one of the pews and reached out a soft hand. He stroked the side of its face, feeling its feathers prick him as he did. It was thirsty. He stuck his index finger into his mouth and sucked the blood away. He walked back to his truck, pulled an oil barrel onto his little cart, and wheeled it back to the church. He worked till just before sunrise, then returned to his truck. He smoked a cigarette and threw the butt into the street. It smoldered on the asphalt, the square's single spot of light. He watched it burn out slowly.

Towers slept deeply, and woke at eight as his watch alarm beeped. It was dark. He had a cot in the back of his truck, but he often slept in the front seat, as he had last night. It was probably the hunger that had woken him, or perhaps just the loud rumbling of his stomach. There was a peanut butter and jelly sandwich in his glove compartment, but when he opened it it was all squashed and malformed. He slammed the compartment shut. There was always other food somewhere.

He rolled out onto the street and immediately felt his legs go wobbly. He leaned against the side of his truck and gave himself a moment to fully reenter to world of the waking. His neck was killing him, and he rolled it back and forth a few times. When he was young, he had been told never to do a full rotation, or he'd hurt himself. How or why that would happen had never been explained, but he was still careful.

When his legs were behaving again, he made his creaking way down the strip, past the church, and into the wooded streets of Lexington. He hadn't set out with a specific goal in mind, just that of getting some food from somewhere, but he quickly realized where his legs had begun to take him. He had had a lot of firsts in this town. Why not say one last goodbye to the house of his first love? Besides, they had always fed him well. They might have left something good behind.

He took a break at the top of Weeks Street, perched at the peak of the small hill there. These streets felt the same as they always did. Quiet. He flicked his penlight on. Even back when he lived here, he had needed light to navigate. The streetlights were few and far in between, the streets badly paved and lined with ditches and trees, and when the sun set it did so completely.

He used to sneak out late at night, and scurry across this exact route. There was a tree in Allison's yard he could scurry up to reach her bedroom. Or sometimes she'd meet him in the woods, and they'd spend the night wandering. Of course his starting point had been different, back then, but that house had been knocked down and paved over a long time ago. Time had changed the shape of the route. Trees had fallen and slopes eroded. Feet stamped down new paths. He cut from street to yard to forest and back to street, his feet unsteadily but automatically moving dutifully below him.

He was so carefully looking down that it took him until he stepped from the sidewalk to the short trimmed green grass of the front lawn to notice what was wrong. He could see the grass. How green it was. He looked up in bewilderment. The front windows of the house were awash with light, a latticed shadow scattered across the yard. There was never light. Why would there be light? The electric companies should have turned off the power a long time ago. Mr. Song had always had a backup generator; he was always very proud when the power went out but the house stayed lit. But it couldn't have run for this long without being refueled.

"Who is it!" A voice called out, more accusation than question.

Towers's head pounded. He hadn't heard another voice in so long. He opened his mouth to respond but found his mouth dry and his tongue fuzzy. He coughed, unable to form coherent vocals. He hadn't spoken in longer.

"I warn you, I'm armed," the voice threatened.

Towers stood rooted in place. His cough was really working its way through him now, heaving out big wracking lungfuls of air. He put a hand up in a placating manner, vaguely in the direction of the house's second story.

"I'm coming out!" The voice warned, and Towers heard the front door slamming open. He looked up, but the bright windows were ruining his night vision and all he could make out was a large black shape barreling towards him. The shape skidded to a halt a few yards away, brandishing an implement in a threatening manner. "Jesus, is that you, Nel?"

Towers seemed to have regained some control of his breath and managed to squeeze out a raspy "yes," before beginning to convulse in coughs again. The shape, now clearly a broad shouldered man was a carefully combed over patch of white hair, approached and laid a hand on his shoulder. Towers flinched away, but felt a firm grip of fingers squeeze tight.

"You don't look so good, Nel," the man muttered. "Get inside, I'll get you a drink."

Towers felt himself ushered through the door and into the gleaming house. The front door led directly into the dining room. He had always felt uncomfortable at meals because of this. The looming door implied to him that they were always expecting company. Mr. Song pushed him around the table and into the kitchen beyond, which spilled out into the living room. A staircase wound its way up to the second floor or their left. The back door stood, locked, on their right. Mr. Song laid the rifle on the kitchen table. He opened a cabinet and threw Towers a bottle of water. "There, that should help."

Towers hastily tore the cap off and gulped the water down gratefully. Drinking was such a vital process that he surprised himself with how long he could forget to do it. He crinkled the empty plastic sheepishly, raising it in a half salute. "Thank you," the sound of his own voice was strange, but he liked it. "I guess I needed that."

Mr. Song was looking him up and down with a blank face that Towers couldn't quite read. The man had always made him nervous. He had never felt as if he had earned his trust. "Little Nel," Mr. Song murmured. "Haven't heard from you since you ran off to college."

"It was hard to keep in touch," Towers shrugged. It hadn't been. He didn't know what had stopped him. He suspected that he was a coward. He did know that he hated being called Nel. He hated Nelson more. He had always liked Towers though. Short, strong. Towers and Song. They had fit well together.

A woman appeared in the stairway. Her long red hair had gone straight with age and was held back in a loose bun. She looked tired. And very angry. Mr. Song turned to her. "Look who showed up!" he said, loudly.

Mrs. Song looked into Towers's eyes, and he immediately felt too uncomfortable to meet her gaze. "Nel," she breathed out. "I didn't think we'd ever see you again."

"Neither did I," Towers replied, his heart beginning to pound. "Why are you still here?"

Mr. Song frowned. "Because it's my house." Mrs. Song glowered at him. "Sorry," he corrected himself. "Our house. It's our house! I'm not letting the City take that from us just because that idiot President said they could." He took a few deep breaths. Towers put the empty water bottle down. He very much wished that he had not come here. "But what are you doing here, Nel? Are you looking for Allison?"

Towers shook his head. "No."

"Well, good, she's long gone. Virginia. College too. You would've known that if you had called her, Nel." Towers smiled awkwardly. He glanced at Mrs. Song. Her visage was stone. Mr. Song frowned. "So why are you here?"

Towers paused. No use lying. "I followed the bird," he said. His voice came out low and raspy, almost a whisper.

Mrs. Song didn't move. "Followed the—" Mr. Song repeated, lost. Then his face hardened. "So that's what they taught you at that school. How to sell out your home to the City."

"Actually," Towers found himself correcting, "I work for Drummel. Which is owned by the Hollis Corporation, which is owned by Nanover, which is owned by the Echo Conglomerate. No one works for 'the City.'"

"We're not leaving," Mr. Song stated bluntly. His fingers twitched. Towers took a step back towards the door, pretending to adjust his stance.

"You have to, Mr. Song," Towers said. "All of you." He glanced at Mrs. Song, who had turned her gaze to her husband. "It's pointless. Everyone knows that. Tomorrow morning there won't be anything left."

"We are leaving," Mrs. Song put bluntly. Towers's head jerked towards her. She stood stock still, and her gaze was so caustic he was briefly worried that he might turn to stone himself.

Mr. Song turned away from them, and hunched his shoulders over the kitchen table. His fingers found the rifle's stock. "I will not leave," he said vehemently. Towers couldn't tell if he was addressing Towers, his wife, or himself. "I worked for forty years to buy this house from the bank. It's mine. No one can take it. Not even the City."

"Then don't come," Mrs. Song shrugged. Towers suspected that this was not the first time they had had this discussion. She turned to Towers. "I hear people like us are going West. That there's still something on the coast. Do you know if that's true?"

Towers nodded. "I know some people are going there. So there's something. For now. I don't know what."

"Something is better than nothing. It was nice to see you again, Nel. I'll be upstairs, packing." She climbed the stairs and was gone.

Mr. Song waited until she left, and then picked up the rifle. He turned quickly and aimed it at Towers. His face was impassive. Towers shot his hands up. "Come on, Mr. Song," he pleaded.

"What if I just shoot you right now?" Mr. Song asked.

"They would send someone else. It would take another week, but it would all be gone just the same. And they'd send you to prison for life when they found out what you did."

"Who would send someone?"

"Drummel," Towers replied.

Mr. Song took a step towards Towers. "What if I shoot you now, and then shoot whoever is in charge over at Drummel." Towers moved to speak again, but Mr. Song cut him off. "Maybe not me. But maybe another angry man does. What then?"

"Hollis would promote someone new, and they would send someone else, and Lexington is gone all the same," Towers said.

Mr. Song lowered the rifle. He looked tired. Towers felt a surge of pity for the man. "Why are you doing this, Nel? This is your home too."

Towers shrugged. "It's a job, and someone's going to fill the position. What does it matter if it's me? I might as well be the one getting paid."

"How much, Nel?"

"Enough to live on. You need to get out of here, Mr. Song. It isn't safe."

Mr. Song let the rifle drop back onto the kitchen table. "What's the point, Nel? There's nothing for me in the City. I'm too old. And you'll just catch up to me, eventually."

"You can go West, Mr. Song," Towers felt himself pleading with the man. "There're something for people like us," he cut himself off, and frowned. "Like you out there. There's still work."

Mr. Song was shaking his head. "No, no there isn't. Not for me. I worked in the same library for forty years, Nel. Just down the street. What would I do out there?"

Towers shrugged. "Live." Mr. Song lowered himself heavily into one of the kitchen chairs. Towers took the chair across from him. "I didn't pick this place. I wouldn't have picked this place. But the City did. People like us, Mr. Song? We don't get to make choices anymore. People like me follow the bird. People like you run from her shadow. You're right, there's nothing for you out there like the life you used to have. And if the City had anything for you, you wouldn't be here now. But that's no reason to stay. Go be with your family."

"What do you care what happens to me?" Mr. Song wasn't looking at him, really. He seemed to be focused on the old electric clock on the other end of the kitchen. Towers didn't have to turn to see it. Its black hands floated above a brightly lit blue face.

"I spent more time here than I did in my own home," Towers said. Mr. Song frowned. "You didn't ask for a third child, but you let me know I was always welcome." Towers rose. "Goodbye Mr. Song." On the way out he noticed that the dining room table had been set for four. He shuddered, and left through the front door.

On his way back Towers climbed through the broken window of a gas station and helped himself to some stale power bars from a display in the back. He crossed the street to the old high school. A looming, brick building, it had never laid claim to anything special, neither architecturally nor academically. Towers went around to the side and sat on a wooden bench that overlooked the soccer field. Taking advantage of a rare gap in the tree cover, the moon shone down on the grass. He unwrapped a power bar and bit into it.

"Sit down with me," Towers called out into the night.

A boy joined him on the bench. He hungrily took in Towers's features, from the rough main of stubble to the blackness under his nails to the rings under his eyes.

"Why didn't you come downstairs?" Towers asked.

The boy chewed on his lip. "Mom wouldn't let me." Towers offered him a power bar. The boy waved it down. "I don't want to leave, Nel." Towers flashed him a look. "Sorry, Towers." He rolled his eyes. "She got to call you Nel."

Towers threw away the first wrapper and cracked a second. "Doesn't matter what you want, Sam. I want an office job, with fresh coffee every morning, but I took a test and it told me I wasn't smart enough, so here I am instead."

Sam bore down on his lip in silence. Towers finished his second bar. "How is she?" he asked at last.

"I think she's fine. She's at college. Virginia."

"I came here from Virginia."

"Oh?" Sam asked. Then his face hardened. "Oh." He kicked at the dirt. "Is there anything left?"

"No. Nothing. It's all the City's now. But most people got out." They lapsed into uncomfortable silence for a few minutes before Towers could find any more words. "Did she ever talk about me?" Towers put down the rest of the bars. He had lost his appetite.

"We didn't talk much," Sam said. Towers narrowed his eyes. The goalpost was catching the moonlight and shining a brilliant white in the darkness. "You never called."

"I know."

"Come with us, Nel. We can find her."

Towers shook his head. "I'm not your brother, Sam."

"But," Sam started to say, before Towers cut him off.

"No. I have a job to do."

"What happens when you've been everywhere?"

"Haven't been everywhere yet." Towers moved to his feet. Sam scampered up after him. Towers's eyes had fallen onto the dark shape of the high school. "I'm sorry you never got the chance to go. It was good there. I think I may have peaked there. If happiness is any metric. I don't think it is anymore."

"Can I see it?"

"See what?"

"You know."

Towers started walking. "Sure."

"No lights. Just listen." The church rose up in front of them. He and Samuel Song had been here together many times before. The circumstances weren't too different. Just worship of a different power.

"Can't I just see it for one second? Please?" Sam asked.

"No." Towers said. "No lights on her, not even for a moment."

Sam relented and nodded. Then, his eyebrows knitted together. "Her?"

Towers paused, hand on the wide doors. He shrugged. "I call her Bluebird." Can a machine be alive? He wasn't sure, but he had been alone with her for so long.

"Why?"

"My mother told me that bluebirds steal eggs from other birds. I thought that was very sad when I was little. Still," he pushed the doors open, and lowered his voice to a whisper. "They are beautiful, aren't they? Take my hand."

Towers led Sam into the dark church. The Bluebird shifted as she slept. She was hungry, and she was almost ready. Towers liked to imagine that she could dream. Perhaps she dreamed of a tired man with soft hands. He took Sam to a pew in the back and sat him down. "Don't move, don't make a sound," he whispered.

Her wings had unfurled since the last time he was here. He stepped inside of them and felt their faint heat around him. He ran his hand along their length. His palm bled. She sighed in her sleep. She must be hungry. She always needed so much oil before she worked. Sam fidgeted in the back. Towers sat inside of its wings and leaned against her, waiting out the minutes in silence.

This was wrong. Silently, he moved back to where Sam was sitting, took his hand, and led him from the church. Outside, Sam frowned at the blood and wiped his hand on the door, leaving a red print behind.

Towers folded his arms. "You need to leave."

Sam nodded. But he lingered. "Is it true though, what they say about them?"

"That what?"

"That it was an accident. Discovering them."

Towers smiled. "I used to think that too."

"Used to?"

"Yeah. Used to." He put a finger on the streak of blood on the door, tracing its path down the grain. "I think I wanted to believe that we wouldn't willfully make something so..." he stopped, and took his hand back, wiping it clean on the back of his pants. "Well, anyway, we would. We did. It's a new world, the City. It's better there. But it doesn't care about the old world out here. And it won't stop growing until there's nothing of the old world left." He looked Sam in the eye. The younger boy turned away. "You have to go, Sam."

Sam nodded, mostly to himself. "This is it, then?"

"Yeah."

"I don't know what to say, Nel."

"Me neither."

"Goodbye, I guess." Sam stuck out a hand, and Towers awkwardly took it. Blood squeezed out from between their fingers.

"If you see her," Towers began. But then he stopped. He had no idea where that thought had been headed.

"What?"

"Nothing. Don't tell her about me."

Sam looked away uncomfortably. Then he reached into his pocket and took out a watch. It was battered and cheap, and light in

Towers's palm as Sam handed it to him. "I found it in her room," Sam said, still not meeting the older boy's eyes. "It's yours, isn't it?"

Towers turned away. His eyes were wet, and his cheeks flushed with shame. "Yeah," he muttered. "Thanks."

Sam bounced from one foot to another for a few moments, and then turned to leave. The trees swallowed up his slight frame.

Towers waited outside for a few minutes, and then went back into the church. In the dark he sat, turning the watch over and over in his hand. The morning he left, he had told her how he felt. Then they kissed. Then he got in the car and drove away. "Eight o'clock tonight," he said, before he rolled the window up. "I'll call you." He took off his old watch and gave it to her. "So you know when it's eight," he said with a smile. She swapped it with her own, which was digital and sparkling new. She set an alarm on it for eight, and then gave it to him. "So you don't forget," she smiled back.

For seven years he had kept hers. He had always assumed she had done the same.

He sat there till just before the sun rose. Then he slipped out of the church, oil untouched, and went back to his truck.

Towers lit a cigarette, slid it between his lips, and started the car. He paused, his hands on the wheel, the truck idling loudly underneath him. He drove up Weeks Street and took the long way around to the house. The sun began to peek its head up from the horizon, and thin rays of light filtered through the trees as he stepped out onto the lawn. The house was dark, but he thought he saw a shadow move in one of the second story windows. It looked out across the street at the boy and his truck and then slipped away.

Towers felt a wave of bile rise up in his stomach. What pointless, destructive protest.

He drove a few miles South as the sun rose. He parked his truck on the empty highway and sat on the hood, facing North and leaning back against the windshield.

She woke. Her rising body, propelled by powerful wings, shattered the roof of the church. The steeple fell, its ringing bell cutting through the soft bird calls of the early morning. The church collapsed. The square collapsed. The trees melted. She beat her wings painfully, heavily, each pulse of devastation draining what little oil remained. She was hungry. So hungry. Towers watched. She screamed in frustration. And then she gave up, and flew North.

Towers finished his cigarette and flicked it to the ground. He felt his eyes closing, and let it happen.

He woke at noon, the sun glaring directly down into his red eyes. He licked his dry lips, pressed a hand onto his rumbling stomach, and got back into the truck. It roared to life under his touch. He would have time to take care of himself later.

When he had first taken the job he would always return when it had finished to marvel at its work. He would drive around the perfect, empty circle. No ruins, no signs of life. A clean slate. Weeks later, when he had a rare moment of free time, he would come back to see what had become of the land. Sometimes the City itself would have taken it, its shining glass buildings popping up overnight like weeds. Sometimes it would be a sleekly automated farm, or a rumbling mine, sucking the earth dry to feed the endlessly growing City.

He didn't know what Lexington would look like now. He didn't know if Weeks Street had been far enough from the church. He was too tired to care.

He took the first exit West that he could find. At the bottom of the ramp he found himself blocked by another car. He slowed, and got out of the truck.

Sam Song smiled from his perch on the hood. He turned to his mother. "See? I told you he'd come."

Mrs. Song arched an eyebrow from the front seat. Towers went around to the back of his truck and pulled the fax machine into the street. There was a printed paper in the tray, but he left it there without looking. He smashed his boot into the machine and felt it crumple under his weight. If the City needed to talk to him they could drive West themselves. Then he grabbed his cigarettes and lighter from the dashboard, stuffed them into his pockets, and left the door open and the keys in the ignition. He slid into the passenger seat of the Song's car. Mrs. Song nodded at him. He nodded back. She started the car and they slipped away.

That night, on the road, Towers was woken by his watch alarm. He looked at the bright numbers. Eight o'clock.

About the story

"Bluebird" started as a sci-fi riff on some of the early scenes of Grapes of Wrath. I imagined a cowboy of sorts with a hulking harvester monstrosity talking a family off their dusty farm so that a high tech city could make its way in. The "City" in Bluebird is inspired by another short story I wrote for an American Protest Literature class, which is too long and rambly for publication, but which gave me some fun names for corporations like Nanover and the Echo Conglomerate.

As I thought about writing the story, however, I realized that the farmland imagery isn't quite what it used to be. So I decided to set the story in the suburbs, and have the protagonist be displacing some middle class family that might be more relatable. I also found an anthology about wings I wanted to submit to, so the tractor monster became a bird.

Submission for the anthology closed about ten minutes after I started writing, but the bird stayed with the story anyways.

The actual story, about Towers and Allison, and Towers and his old town, emerged as I was writing, as did most of Towers's character. Little of the original cool cowboy remains, except maybe the cigarettes. I'm a sucker for nostalgia, so I decided the family that stayed behind should be the family of his childhood friend/love. In the original ending there's no watch, the bird destroys the town and Towers heads West in search of an ambiguous "she," which could be the bird or Allison (but it's probably the bird).

Morris Allen of *Metaphorosis* helped me steer towards the more interesting part of the story: Towers's relationship with Allison. Over the course of a few drafts their past became more fleshed out, until the ending changed from ambiguous to happy. Well, happy-ish. Perhaps "not a total bummer" is the best way to put it. I hope for the best for those two, although my hopes aren't too high.

A question for the author

Q: What work of art has been the most inspiring for you?

A: *Eragon* by Christopher Paolini springs to mind. I read it when I was little and fell in love, and am still so incredibly impressed by the fact that he wrote it as a teen fresh out of high school. Part of the inspiration is good old jealousy. I joke a lot to my friends about how far behind him I slip with each passing year of age. But more than that, I think the book goes to show that you can never be too young, too new, or too inexperienced to make something great if you're willing to work hard at it.

About the author

Benjamin Cort hopes to be a doctor sometime before he dies and drinks an unhealthy amount of tea. He spends most of his money on board games and maple cream cookies from CVS. He likes to play guitar, but doesn't do it all that well, and the majority of his musical repertoire consists of Matchbox 20 covers. He often wears a blue knit hat, given to him by a nice old lady on the Appalachian Trail, which he secretly hopes is lucky.

Benjamin Cort's story "Bluebird" was published in *Metaphorosis* on Friday, 27 October 2017.

November

Notes Towards a New Fairytale

Patrick Doerksen

When I was fourteen, my mother sent me off for the summer to my Opa's farm. The idea was to get out of Canada, see a little bit of the world, and learn a bit of German while my brain was yet plastic. "Just think what a head start you'll have on your language requirement," she said, for it had been decided in her mind that I would get a PhD. "It may take you until October to make any real progress, but I've okayed it with the school-board."

I barely knew my Opa; he led a lonely, stubborn life on his farm in the Black Forest, two hours from Freiburg. It was a ridiculous idea. But there I was, on a June evening, watching Opa's twilight silhouette drop its hoe in the garden patch and hustling over to involve me in a skeletal hug.

"*Mein Liebling*," he said. "*Willkommen zum Wichthof!*" Wichthof was what he called the farm.

Inside his cottage, we ate pickles in a kitchen that smelled of pickles. His English was poor and in his throat was an excess of phlegm; it necessitated sharp stops among many consonants, to the effect that his sentences seemed less spoken than whip-tamed.

Opa, I learned, was a folklorist. He showed me his study that first night, and that first night only; after that, he kept it locked. I did not understand what his project was, exactly. He seemed to be gathering local folktales, and I remember him saying something about "correcting the great mistake of the Brothers Grimm." I took a look at the notes on his desk, notes to some essay he was writing, but I did not linger; I did not know I ought to be interested.

The essay will argue that the uncollected folktales of Southern Baden-Württemberg give evidence of a folk-entity distinct from the Fairy of the Irish-English tradition. In the latter, one finds stories of a trivial nature: farmers finding swine tied together by their tails, country folk waking up two hours before dawn, deceived by what sounds like a rooster. This new folk-entity, however, gives us tales of entirely different sort.

I was, I should explain, an avid sketcher. I had begun when I was eight, because of my little sister: she hadn't been born yet and I wanted the first go at her. I spent countless pages getting her eyelashes right, her smile, her bangs—all very pretty of course, prettier even than I thought I was. Then for obscure medical reasons, my mother decided to have an abortion and I never met my little sister.

But the passion lived on. By the time I was fourteen I was declining sleepovers so I might have more time to make pencil studies of the felled oaks in the field behind our house. I read how if one was discerning, one could see a tremendous activity in motionless things; so I tried to become "discerning." I even started preparing to enter a young artists' competition with a big art magazine called *Phenomena*. My future, I was convinced, depended on winning.

Thus it had been with a vast, seething annoyance that I had received the news I would be living on my Opa's farm, far from paint supplies and galleries.

The first morning, before the summer sun had heaved itself like a somnolent cat into squatting position over the property, Opa woke me. The lives of three goats, three sheep, and a dozen chickens depended on us, I was told, not to mention the hundred cabbages in the patch behind the house. All chores were done swiftly as possible, so that noontime borscht could be slurped and Opa could get to his more important work in the study.

There were other expectations for me.

"I give you the old *Gartenanlage*. Is by duck pond," he said, presumably in a gesture of hospitality—for the man could not imagine, the way he zipped pixy-like around his own garden and kitchen, that hands might like to go idle.

The *Gartenanlage* (garden plot) was a great distance from the house, and when I finally found it I wondered why he had called it a duck pond. There wasn't a single duck to grace it with a quack. For three afternoons I worked dully in the plot, finding none of the gardener's satisfaction in the thwunk of a weed's taproot releasing from the soil. Eventually, though, I realized that Opa's mind was truly in his study and he would not be monitoring my progress.

I stopped my weeding. To keep up appearances I would trudge out to the duck pond, carrying my spade and my sketchbook, only to leave the first of these entirely unused. I never planted a thing.

(1) Appearance. In this regard, the folk-entity described by the Grimm stories diverges distinctly from that of Southern Baden-Württemberg. In the former we find diminutive, hominoid and (in one tale) naked entities. In the latter are beings lit from within and as tall as young trees, who appear and disappear on mountain slopes and lake shores. Not uncommonly they are accompanied by servants, often bizarre creatures who serve blindly and know little of the minds of their masters.

There is a place at the edge of every forest where the daylight grows shy; I sat in that garden for hours, trying to get it right. I couldn't. I squatted there, working myself into a fit of self-loathing, until finally—and this demonstrates the extent of my passion, since I was a gentle girl—I threw down my book, stabbed my pencil hilt-deep into the soil and stalked off, leaving them there.

When the rain came, I was peeling potatoes with Opa in the kitchen.

I did not notice right away, not until Opa used an old German expression (Es regnet *Bindfäden,* it's raining strings), and in trying to puzzle out its meaning I also puzzled out the fact. I was out the door before I could drop the peeler. Of course it was too late, but the real blow was that, instead of finding my sketchbook soaked, I couldn't find it at all. I looked until my teeth were chattering, but the wind, like a fussy cleaning lady, had moved it somewhere. It had even taken my pencil.

I was devastated. Four months' worth of studies were in that sketchbook, each of which I'd been sure could win the contest, each of which contained the seed of a whole future of fame and recognition. I catastrophized, lost sleep, tore apart my fingernails. It took me three days to hold my head up again, to improvise a sketchbook out of scrap papers, to return to the garden plot.

That's when I saw it.

The path bent along a copse of poplars which blocked the duck pond from the house, and when I had come to the point in the curve at which my plot became visible, I dropped into a crouch.

I've said that I did not plant a thing. Well, in the center of my weeded garden bed stood a sapling. And beside that sapling was a creature I knew at once was not supposed to exist.

It is very hard not to make something like this sound silly. Maybe it will help if I clarify that this was not one of those mythical creatures, like a gryphon or a unicorn. This was something else. I was so moved by its strangeness that when I was done staring the old habit took over, the habit that governed my response to the beautiful, the weird, the sublime: I took out my pencil and began to sketch.

I still have that drawing among my old work in the attic. If I retrieved it now it would show something like a snake with friendly eyes that had been given a gift of limbs and a thin coat of golden fur. It would show the creature standing about as high as my knees; it would show a tail as long as its body. I do not, however, think it would show the sense of immense patience it exuded. The creature moved so little that its eyes contained the entirety of its activity, and the way it looked around hopefully now and then reminded me of a loyal dog abandoned by its master.

(2) The Name. In the forests around the Schreckensee, people know them as the "Randmenschen" (edge-people), and a Berliner who spent his childhood on a farm two hours from Munich calls them the "geschichtslose Völker" (folk without history). The Grimm brothers call them the "Wichtelmänner." I could use any of these, but I prefer the name my own grandmother used: the Wichteln.

The next few days had me spying on the creature at every spare moment. He did not make an entertaining spectacle, to be sure, for I saw him do nothing other than stand, sit, pace, yawn, and make threatening gestures at incoming birds. But the monotony itself was intriguing, and soon his simple, unflagging diligence began to impress me. Sipping Opa's borscht, I would think: even now he must be standing there, keeping watch. And in bed: even now he's by the duck pond, shivering. Very soon I was pondering how to make my approach.

I was almost sure he did not pose me any threat; I had seen him fall clumsily from the sapling in an attempt to shoo away one of the warblers that came to perch. Moreover, he seemed to grow thinner and more sluggish each day, and his eyes to grow glassy and resigned. Could I bring him a blanket? I wondered. Would he eat sauerkraut?

Finally, it was another night of rain that decided things.

There is something exciting about rain in the country; it turns the land into a great drum-roll, announcing something that never comes. It gave me a jittering kind of courage, and I snuck out the back door with an umbrella and one of Opa's spares.

The creature did not hear me right away. He was slumped miserably against the sapling, flicking his tail listlessly, utterly soaked. I was filled with pity, and, clearing my throat, stepped forward.

Immediately he was on all fours.

Eert eth ave ton yam ou.

What surprised me more than that he could speak was that his voice did not come from his throat. It was an organization of wind and rain and any element it could make use of, which my mind somehow knew how to read. It took me a moment to respond.

"Sorry?" I said.

He looked questioningly at me a moment, then abruptly shook himself. *Ah, that's right. Even speech is forward here.* He appeared chagrined. *I said, You may not have the tree.*

"Oh," I said. "I—I only came to give you an umbrella."

Then I will do you no harm. But, hastening to correct himself, added, *I will do you no good either.*

I was fourteen and not beyond nonchalance in an encounter with the impossible. "That doesn't leave a lot of options," I said. "Other than leaving each other alone."

He seemed intensely curious and ticked his tail against the sapling. *Are there really no others?*

I shrugged. A long silence ensued, of the awkward sort. Because I could see no other way forward, I got back to the point. "So you are... a fairy. Are you a good one or a bad one?"

I don't know how to choose.

I missed the helplessness in his voice. "Then you must be bad," I said lightly.

He hung his head. *Well, if I must be.*

He was, I learned then, a creature of extreme humility, and immediately I was sorry. "Let's start over." I moved closer. "I'm Lizzie. I brought you an umbrella, to keep you dry. Here." I opened it and set it on the grounded next to him.

He let out his tongue into the dry air beneath the umbrella; then, rather clumsily, he seized the handle with his tail and held it above himself. I am certain that at this moment he smiled.

Thank you, Lizzie.

He said no more, but looked about wonderingly, watching the rain fall everywhere but on himself. He seemed to forget about me for a while, and because this time the silence was not the awkward sort, I also said nothing. Eventually the moment became a plurality of moments, and I remembered what patience the creature possessed and began to grow impatient myself.

"You know what's also good for the rain? Warm milk."

Warm milk?

"It'll take a few minutes," I said, and ran back to the house.

(3) Time. The Wichteln have an atypical experience of temporality. This trait, at least, squares with the entities we find in the Grimm brothers' stories—one tale of which describes a servant girl who is invited to hold a child for the Wichtel at a christening. She only spends three days away, but when she returns to her master's house she is accosted by strangers—for she has, in fact, been gone seven years. There are also stories of stolen babies who return again the next day, older than their parents.

It was an easy friendship. He had, it seemed, been sent out in such a great hurry to his task that he had not prepared properly, which gave me the opportunity to act the benefactor. Soon he had a bed of old wool afghans and, when I discovered he did not mind raw potatoes, regular meals pilfered from Opa's cellar. He accepted everything from me, even a name: I called him Wich. It was like *Wichtel,* with the same hiss of the German "*ich*"; I had heard my Opa use the word when speaking about fairies.

The story was, as far as I could gather, that the tree had grown up from the seed of a certain fruit which was not supposed to be there, or anywhere for that matter. To taste it was forbidden.

So Wich was there, guarding it.

"Why don't you just uproot it instead?" I asked, but he appeared so shocked by the suggestion that I apologized. "But how come it's so special?"

It comes from the orchard of the inner courts.

"Where's that? That way?" I pointed to where woods thickened.

No.

Being slow, I pointed another direction.

No.

"Ah," I said finally.

They used to live here, he explained. *Then they discovered the inner courts.*

I pondered that. "And some fruit just fell out, onto Opa's farm? By accident?"

Wich nodded.

"Does this happen... often?"

Not that I know. They are very careful.

Something occurred to me. "Why don't you say 'we'? Aren't they your people?"

Oh no. I am—what is the word? I am just one of their monsters.

At once I protested on his behalf, but he insisted on the word, and indeed seemed offended by any other suggestion. Wich, I've said, was a very humble creature.

I might have told Opa about Wich but for this. Indeed, I had been prepared to, the night I asked him about forbidden fruit. I had received a long talk on Adam and Eve, the Garden of the Hesperides and Ladon its hundred-headed guard-dragon, and various folk ballads like "Thomas the Rhymer"; but all at once he seemed startled by a notion and stared intently at me for a moment. I knew then that to allow those thick-browed German eyes to point that same gaze at Wich —Wich, who liked to be sat with each night when the light left and reassured it would come again—would be wrong.

In deciding this, I decided a certain attitude towards Wich: I would not myself torment him for information about his home.

Quite the opposite happened as a result: I provided him all he wanted to know about mine—and there was a lot. I explained politics and weather patterns and the Gregorian calendar and all sorts of things beyond my competence. Once, hearing my explanation of Opa and his scholarly work, he said, *Ah, then their elders have very different aims than yours.* After that he asked no more questions about Opa.

His curiosity regarding myself, however, was undying, and when I began to show him my drawings he could not get enough. At the end of each day he asked to see my work, and would even make the occasional commissions—a sunset, a mushroom—which he would receive most ceremoniously on presentation. It was not all aesthetic delight, sure, for when I asked him what he liked so much about this or that picture, often his only comment was that it reminded him of home. But he was so enthusiastic that I was glad to oblige his interest.

I will always remember one day in late July when Wich learned, to his astonishment, that not everyone drew, and I found myself in the position of expert explaining what an artist was—a position I did not mind in the least.

"It's very difficult," I said. "And not everyone sees the point. Combine those two, and you get a very unappealing profession."

Is it so difficult, even when you have fingers?

"That's not all it takes. You must have technique. You must find a good teacher and train for years and years."

He shook his head, flabbergasted. *So long... How did you do it?*

"Oh, no—I'm not an artist, not yet. I still have to go through all that. My pictures are very poor when you compare them to the masters, like Cézanne, or Monet."

He appeared very disturbed at this news. "But I'm well on my way," I reassured him. "Already Mr. Irgman, my art teacher, has one of my pictures in his bathroom; he even offered to pay for it, so that he could say he was the first to buy one of my works. I know that I have what it takes. I just have to stick with it."

You really want this.

"More than anything."

How come?

The question brought me up short.

It had always seemed to me that standing in front of a painting was the only place the world made sense. Our lives are lived in a series of images, and their unending succession has always suggested to me an incompleteness: why else would one follow upon another other than to make up for some lack or to improve upon what came before? Taken aesthetically, time is like an artist full of self-doubt and second-thoughts. A painting, however, is not so faithless. It takes a moment from the endless river, holds it up and calls it finished—and if it's a good painting, and if we look hard enough, we can see it's true.

"I want to stop the trees losing their leaves," I said finally, and Wich sighed and shook his head.

I don't think I shall ever understand time.

There had been other hints—like when, on being asked his name that first night, he had begun a series of complex, guttural syllables so long that I never heard the end of it, because thirty seconds in I had to interrupt him: "What's the use of a name so long?"

That doesn't matter back home, he'd said.

I frowned and studied Wich's simple, pleasant countenance for a moment. "Wich," I said. "Isn't there time—where you're from?"

He flicked his tail in a gesture I was learning meant something like an eye roll. *Oh, no. We have something quite different.* Obliging my frown, he continued. *Here, things happen in order; back home, things happen in—in significance.*

"But how would that work?"

He considered. *We don't have to go figuring things out like you do. What should happen next, what to become, I mean. Those things are done for us. We're all too weak for it, even the masters. But then, we have... different problems.*

"But really, it's not so hard," I said, laughing at his gravity.

No? He was looking at his feet, and I could tell there was something on his mind.

"No! I mean, you're in time now, aren't you?"

He looked up then, almost sheepishly. *The thing I can't understand,* he said, *is how you make decisions.*

"Decisions?"

You say that you will paint and sketch every day of your life so that you become a very fine painter. But how do you know you really will?

"Why, you don't *know*. You make it happen."

But how do you know you will make it happen?

"That's what a decision *is*—you say you will! You can't decide on something that's already been decided!" I threw up a stone and caught it, excited by my ability to make sense of the dilemma.

But Wich still did not understand and shook his head in self-chastisement. "You'll get it soon enough," I said encouragingly.

(4) Jägerlust. A common enough story is that of a village scenting an immense feast over the hills, one by one going out in search of it, and one by one getting lost in the woods—for when the Wichteln are at table, they always position themselves upwind. One also finds the idea hidden in the Grimm story, "Brüderchen und Schwesterchen", where we read the curious lines: "When the roebuck heard the hunters outside, he said, 'I cannot bear it, I must go out to them.'" This impulse is the Jägerlust (hunter-desire). It describes the creature who wants to be chased.

I was glad of Wich's company in the following months, for my Opa began to make trips to the surrounding towns, conducting his research, and I was left alone on the property for periods of up to three days (I never told my mother this: Opa and I had an understanding). On these occasions, we would make a small fire and look at the moon and talk about supermarkets, Van Gogh, and all manner of things—especially time.

By mid August, however, the first blossoms appeared on the sapling, which was no longer a sapling but a tree as big as any in Opa's orchard, and when this happened Wich began to behave oddly.

It was like a hormone shift. At first he was only a little more jumpy than usual. But then as more blossoms emerged and the fruit itself began to grow, he began to move around more than he used to. He was like a dog locked in a room, hearing its master crying to it from without. He paced, he looked around at things that weren't there, and he began to watch me from the corner of his eyes.

One night, in the middle of a week-long stretch of insomnia (my sketching was going poorly), I arose, fed up with myself, and I trudged with my blanket down to the duck pond. I wondered if I might catch Wich at rest—for I had never once yet seen him asleep.

As I drew near I saw a glow on the water. It could not have been the moon's reflection, for there was no moon that night. I dropped into a crouch, as I had when I first seen Wich, and approached slowly.

The thing—the being, entity, pick a word—was much taller than me, though when I saw it, it was stooped over Wich, stroking the fur behind his shoulders. It seemed to have candles burning in its chest.

I thought immediately of what Wich had said: I am one of their monsters.

I cannot do better than say it was like an angel, but not from heaven or hell—from some greener, earthier place. I had about five seconds to behold it. Then, responding to nothing I could perceive, it stepped away, and the night seemed to have lost half its stars.

I was stunned by more than what I had seen—I had caught in those fleeting seconds a few wind-borne words, the last bit of their exchange, spoken not by Wich but by the—thing:

It was a sketchbook.

I wondered for a long time at this.

When finally I came out of the brush and sat next to Wich, dropping a few potatoes before him and taking out some leftover sausages for my own midnight snack, it was all without speaking. We ate together. We chucked stones into the duck pond and counted ripples. We watched stars appear. The silence seemed an impossible thing to break.

But then the silence became a different sort when I noticed something on the ground, and reached for it.

It looked very much like an apple, though I knew at once it wasn't. It was too dense; moreover, it was slightly oblong and roughly textured. And, like a living thing, it was warm. I wanted more than anything to take a bite; indeed, I thought of running off with it, bearing it to the privacy of my room where I could sink my teeth into it.

I became aware of Wich's eyes on me.

Please, put it down, he said.

I held the fruit.

Please, Lizze. They— He stopped.

"They were just here, weren't they?" I said. "The ones who eat the fruit."

Wich nodded, nervous.

"What did they want?"

They were only checking on me.

I hesitated. "Do they know about me?"

It was Wich's turn to hesitate. He nodded.

"My sketchbook?"

Wich's silence was like a shrug.

"What would happen, really, if I took a bite?"

He only shook its head, as though the thought was incomprehensible.

"Or if you yourself were to… taste?"

At first I thought he would not answer this either. Then, finally, he said in that same awed, sombre voice, *It's forbidden.*

For many moments I said nothing more, nor did Wich, and I knew the whole time that I held the fruit in my hand, and that Wich was waiting for me to drop it.

I did.

"First windfall," I said. "You'll have to watch out."

He took the fruit immediately with his tail and placed it beneath himself as though it were an egg to incubate. I left him then, trembling all the way back home.

(5) Gifts. It is a commonplace, in stories of Southern Baden-Württemberg, that any pie set to cool on a windowsill will go mysteriously missing, any child left to wander will be stolen, any books left on deckchairs will be gone by morning. Are the Wichteln thieves? Hardly. Among them is the concept of an un-given gift, or rather, a gift that can only be given by first being taken. This is the most counterintuitive aspect of our folk-entity: for it follows that offering such a gift looks a lot like forbidding it, and receiving such a gift looks a lot like stealing it, or at least breaking trust.

It was this night that I was visited, for the first time, by the nightmare. I've had it many times since then.

It goes like this.

I am walking along a country lane towards a church, where I will meet someone. I don't want to keep her waiting, so I hurry along. I feel a kind of reverence, mixed with a sort of youthful eagerness, like on a wedding day. *Mustn't keep her waiting,* I keep thinking. *Mustn't keep her waiting...*

The altar cloth stirs gently as I walk through the doors, and then the place grows very quiet, very still.

From behind the altar a head emerges. It is gaunt, shrunken, the hair is matted, and there is a diseased trembling running up from the spine to the eyes. There's nothing evil about her; she doesn't want to hurt me.

But I am terrified, because I understand what has happened.

It's my unborn sister; I'm sure of it. She is the person I was supposed to meet. She was young once, but I've kept her waiting so long, who knows how long, years, centuries of waiting, and—

Oh, it's horrible. I have made her grow old.

She begins to stand, weakly, supporting herself on the altar, but before she is fully arisen, before I can see her whole figure, I am—mercifully—awake.

The dream came to me almost every following night. Perhaps it was my mounting anxiety: time was passing, and I had sketched nothing that I was especially proud of, nothing I felt sure of submitting to the competition. Like the leaves, one by one the days placidly released their grip. I helped Opa prepare large batches of kraut to trade at the market for winter supplies, I stumbled over German phrases, and I frustrated myself in front of the sketchpad. A second glance at my work revealed lines filled with hesitation, achieving nothing. By the time it was late October and my mother had arranged to pick me up and see the *Pinakothek der Moderne* in Munich before flying me back to Canada, I couldn't believe I had accomplished so little.

I did not mention my leaving to Wich, not until I had but two days on the farm.

Opa was gone that night, so we made ourselves a fire to combat the chill air. Wich had begun to collect the windfalls in a great barrel I had rolled down from Opa's tool-shed, and he sat atop it and flicked his tail listlessly against its side as I explained daylight-savings.

You get a free hour? he said, puzzled. *But where does it come from?*

"We insert it into the day, like this." I lined up a few twigs, then found one more and slipped it in the line-up.

So it comes from outside the day?

"I suppose."

Strange.

I was glad he agreed. I had always loved October daylight-savings—it seemed to me as though all the gratuity of life were upon me in that one free hour, for it was outside scheduling and one could do anything with it: read a book, make cookies, go on a long walk... Of course, for all my excitement, that descending hour always seemed to be meant for something greater than I could give it. That was part of its charm.

"So," I said, "what shall we do with it?" As he considered, I added, "Tomorrow will be my last day with you, so we must use it well."

There is no shortcut through disappointing news. *You're leaving?* he said, immediately rising on all fours and stiffening his tail. I nodded, and he began to pace.

So soon, he said, as though shocked that time could have found another way to bewilder him. *So soon.*

I was touched by the note of distress; in that moment I think I had a keener sense of what I would be leaving than in our goodbye, and a great sadness quivered up into my throat. All around, the twilight redoubled the oranges and reds of the leaves, and watching them fall here and there I felt myself at the center of a great flame burning upside down.

At last Wich ceased his pacing and looked at me. *I know what we should do with the hour.*

(6) The Fruit. This final concept is perhaps the most important—and most ambiguous. It is significant that when the Grimm brothers died with their most ambitious project, a definitive dictionary of the German language, incomplete, the last entry was Frucht (fruit). Most societies—the Greeks, the Peloponnesians, the Jews, the Native Americans, the old Teutons—have story of a forbidden fruit, and yet all differ as to why the fruit is forbidden. In Southern Baden-Württemberg, one hears stories of how the Wichteln live in a place a little closer to heaven than ours, how they grow there a tree with a sacred fruit, how the tree once stood in the first garden at the beginning of the world and was to have been part of humanity's first diet—and how the Wichteln snuck in and claimed it for themselves, so that all our history we have been without our true fruit with God knows what consequences.

I had wondered how Wich would deal with the fruit once the tree was bare. Did he expect to sit atop the barrel until they were all composted in two years' time? He was naive enough to think it possible. To his credit, though, he had a much better idea.

Opa was back, which made things difficult to shuttle the wheelbarrows of firewood to the duck pond secretly. It took many hours. Then, when I had diminished the wood stack as much as possible without alerting his suspicion, I took a hatchet and supplemented our pile with dried bracken. And finally, when the first stars came out, I dropped a match upon it.

It flared, then fizzled, then grew steadily. When it was hot enough, Wich used his tail to fling the fruit into it one by one.

He was in an agreeable mood that night; the anxiety of his duty, after all, diminished in tandem with the pile. Many times he asked, *Is this the free hour, now?* and many times I said, "No, not yet, it comes later." Soon the barrel was empty and the fire was making funny noises, like lips flapping and sucking. We lounged peacefully, studying the flames and the shriveling fruit at their heart. The aroma came up in waves; it was rich and sweet, almost tropical, and made the edges of the nostrils tingle.

Then he looked at me. *So your mother arrives tomorrow? The one who does not ask to look at your sketches?*

"Yeah."

This will be the first goodbye I've ever said.

It was too much. I looked away. "Well I hope it doesn't put you off time or anything."

No. In fact, I've been considering what you said. About time. I think I've figured it out now, and I want to thank you.

"Thank me?" I was surprised, and surprised even more by the curious conviction I saw in him; he stood like something hammered into the ground.

It did seem an impossible thing at first, time. Too difficult for me, perhaps too difficult for anyone. But you've made it seem so simple, and I think I've realized. He paused. *But you already know about decisions.*

I waited for him to explain.

When I first came here, there was an owl that lived in that old hemlock. His voice had become slow, calculated, a stick being forced into the mud. *I used to make sounds at it, and sometimes it would make sounds back. But the crows never let the poor thing alone, and now it's gone somewhere else. It rattled me. Other things too— toadstools growing up out of nothingness one day, eaten by deer the next. And then the leaves started falling, and I thought something terrible had gone wrong. Everything is so full of change here.*

I nodded. The fire gave a crack and gave me an excuse to look away from those intense eyes.

Well, here I was thinking all this change was an awful distraction, something one gets confused by. But really, isn't it all a great hint? A great clue?

"A clue?" I said. "How, Wich?"

Because! You can never be sure what'll last, so everything's simplified for you, you just live, act, decide, how you think you should.

I really did try to understand. But at last the pause became too long and I had to shake my head.

You don't see?

"Doesn't that just bring us back to square one?" I said.

Wich cast his eyes down. *Promise me something,* he said finally.

"What is it?"

When you leave, don't stop sketching. I almost laughed, only he had become so serious that I could not. *Because,* he continued, still looking away from me, *because I really do like them. Because... Because—oh, you don't need reasons, that's just it!*

His words made me blush; I forgot everything and hugged him then, and it was like hugging a rope that flexed in the wind. "I don't need to promise that!" I said. "I won't ever stop."

He looked at me for a long, uncomfortable time, and it gave me the feeling he had been trying to tell me something very different than his words. But then, for some reason, Wich started laughing.

It did not seem incongruous with the mood, his laugh. It was like sticks knocking against each other rapidly, and after a moment I joined in, not knowing why; only once I was laughing did I see. Wich had, according to his alien sense of rhythm and timing, made the mistake said goodbye far in advance of our parting. Now we sat together, feeling parted yet not apart, ghosts in an in-between place.

It was a cold night, for the ghost of winter haunted the air. I took a deep breath, feeling that by it I took a small leap through time into the dark months ahead—and all at once there was too much to look at. I felt unacquainted with the things around me, with the pulsing shadows and the knuckly soil and the colorlessly reflective water of the duck pond, and I kept thinking, I'm real, as though to reassure myself. When Wich began to talk, I followed his words in a trance.

It is strange to burn the fruit like this, he said. When one is used to seeing them at the feasts, on silver platters.

"The feasts?" I said.

They say that at the feasts, they access the sixth, seventh, and twelfth senses. That they see the place where fires go when they are extinguished. That they sit in the place where the stars rest when the day comes, and make images with their laughter.

"I'd like to make an image," I said suddenly.

I took out some paper and began to draw Wich, curled up in himself with his tail by his chin, the fire beside him like a companion. I made every line with a perfect certainty of its meaning and had it finished within ten minutes. Then I promptly forgot about it.

A feeling of euphoria had swelled up in me.

I have long struggled to put the feeling to words, and the best I have is this: it was as though I was aware of the world not through my senses, but through my desire. My whole being had become like a mouth poised in hunger over an apple in the very moment before the down-bite, and life itself was the delicious thing.

"The smoke!" I said suddenly, and stood in a panick. "We're breathing the fruit!"

Wich looked up, confused.

"I have to go!" I yelled again, and I could see by his expression that this time he understood. "I'm not allowed to be here!"

Wich had reared himself up. *But—*

It was all too sudden.

"Goodbye, Wich," I said, hardly looking at him.

Goodbye, Lizze.

The fumes had affected my sense of direction; it took me far longer than it should have to find my bed, and even there I had more finding to do—for though I knew I ought to be proud of myself for resisting the temptation, for responding with such clear-headedness as I did, I also felt that I had left something of myself behind. When at last sleep came, it came with the nightmare: I was walking towards a church where my sister waited for me, growing old.

At some point without my knowing it, the clocked ticked past midnight and the free hour came to an end.

I have summarized six aspects of the folk-entity under analysis. Conveniently, there is a story that combines all of these, told by a woman in Gengenbach. It goes like this: the Wichteln take a fondness to a certain young musician; therefore, they take his lute-guitar. He gives chase and comes to an orchard, where the Wichteln swear they will give back his lute-guitar if he only promises not eat of the fruit. The musician promises, and is allowed to stay with the Wichteln for three days. During this time he sees how, after feasting on the fruit, they are able to make far lovelier music than he has ever heard—so naturally he cannot resist, he eats. When he returns to the world, he is able to play any instrument he likes, and though thirty years have gone by and his family are all dead, this, he knows, is a small price to pay.

And that, more or less, is the end of my story, at least so far as Wich is concerned. That morning, I awoke to the slamming of a car door and ran to the window: my mother was on the porch, emitting great dragon-like puffs of condensation into the October air.

"I wish you'd not look so sad to see me," she said.

"It's not that," I said.

"What is it, then?"

I never answered her, and we began to talk of all the sauerkraut I'd eaten and all the German I'd learned. She was in a hurry; half an hour later I was looking back down the long driveway from her rental car.

I remember that last vision of the farm. It burned with the red fever of autumn, and I thought how the temperature would sink degree by degree when I was gone, how the sun would shorten its visits, how the leaves would continue to fall in staggering numbers. It felt, taken all together, like a great thing giving up.

The months that followed were a strange, unreal time. I wept now and again tears that came out of black nowhere, and more than once I needed to leave class for the privacy of a bathroom stall. My mother told anyone who asked that I was processing their divorce, and perhaps that was it—they had, after all, surprised me with the news on my return to Canada, and I felt like an idiot for thinking the summer away had been about learning German.

But time busied itself with its flattening, polishing work, and these teary episodes subsided. Eventually I stopped thinking about

Wich at all. I might laugh, remembering something odd he'd said; or I might grow sad, thinking of that first night we had met and how there was no one now to bring him an umbrella when it rained (he had never figured out how to open one himself)—but that was the extent of it. Soon college was my whole life. I kept up my German and won all the scholarships that could be had for a student of Art History. I do not even remember thinking of Wich when I was deciding whether or not to continue painting.

It came down to a simple choice, really: did I go on into graduate school, as all my professors, and my mother, thought I should; as I myself wanted? But I knew what that meant for my art.

It took me two weeks to decide. In my heart I would summon the strength for the commitment, for those ten hour days in front of the canvas. But then, as though conviction itself were exhausting, it would fade, I would see just as clearly all the things I'd be giving up— professorship, esteem, contentment—for something uncertain, financially unfeasible, and so alien that I found myself having to defend to my lawyer parents and doctor relatives and politician friends every Christmas dinner, every thanksgiving weekend... And I would think—*But I must! People may talk, my mother may fuss and frown, but all those voice are cant and I would be a fool to listen to them!* And so on.

How can I explain my choice? I had experienced the swell and puncture of certainty enough times that I found myself thinking: *I may this moment understand what my future ought to be—but will I, in that future, understand this moment? Certainty counts for nothing if there is no way to package it for later.*

I entered graduate school. I became a professor. I did my art on weekends, and then not at all.

Not surprisingly, considering the oblique nature of the gift, the above is one of the only instances in which the gift is received properly. More often the strangeness of the Wichteln's cognition makes for a simple comedy of misunderstanding, and we find stories like that told in Dürmentingen, in which a group of Wichteln hope to share their delight in rule-breaking with a certain poor farmer and, accordingly, forbid him to milk his cows (he ceases), forbid him to bake bread (he ceases), forbid him to take a bath (he ceases)—forbid him so many things that he falls ill and dies. So different are the Wichteln from us that they seem almost unable to do us good, though they try—try so dearly to be chased, and to be found.

Then, a few months ago, I received my Opa's notes in the mail.

It was strange timing, for I was at the height of my success: I had just published my second book the year before, received tenure that spring, and that very day had been asked to curate an exhibit of 17th-18th century German oil paintings for a New York gallery. When I arrived home and stood shaking the rain from my coat, I was thinking I might take my daughter out to celebrate. Then I heard her call from her room.

"There was a thing for you in the mail."

It was a manuscript: notes to an essay my Opa never finished, along with a thicker document of even messier handwriting titled, "Thirty-Four Interviews, 1976-81." Inside, the sender (a cousin of mine) had scribbled: "Hey Lizzie, spring cleaning pulled this from storage. I never kept up my German. If you make a translation, send me a copy! And tell me how you've *been!*"

I read the notes. I read the interviews.

Then I read them again.

"What's wrong, Mom?" My daughter had come into the study and stood over me, one strand of hair loose, ticking back and forth. She'd taken out her ear buds.

"Nothing's wrong, love."

"These are my great grandfather's?"

"Yes."

She paused, then, seeing I was weeping, said again: "What's wrong?"

How could I explain what I felt?

Since that day, my nightmare has begun to recur—only, changed slightly. I've begun to stay longer in the dream. The woman I'm walking to meet, the one I'd always thought was my sister—I see her stand fully, see her walk towards me, and see that there is another, far more obvious, reason for our likeness.

"Come," she seems to say (she never speaks). "Let me show you all I've been working on."

And I watch, trembling, as she pulls paintbrush after paintbrush from the back of my own haggard, time-eaten face.

It's happened many times now. I wake, stand against the window pane to look out at the autumn night, and review my life: Have I been unhappy? Have I been discontent? Lonely? Insignificant? No. So why this nightmare? Is it so terrible, giving up one's childhood dream? Millions do it. Millions walk around with the aborted foetus of a different future in their hearts. All have had such desires in their youth as would make them blush now. Why should mine hurt any more than theirs, and why should I feel so accused? And now there's even my daughter—she's begun to get up with me on these restless nights and linger in the moonlit hallway, asking me what's wrong.

"I don't know," I say.

"You know I love you."

"I do."

I can't help smiling at the way she throws the phrase: "So? What's wrong?"

"Nothing's wrong, Laura," I say. "I'm happy. I'm very happy."

And it's true. Yet when she's gone I turn to the window and wonder at the weight of autumn leaves in air, the windfalls of apples and pears upon the ground. Every tree seems to be the Wichteln's tree, and the ground abundant with their fruit—and I can't help thinking how differently I'd live if they were.

About the story

"Notes towards a New Fairtale" was written at a hinge moment in my life. I was trying to decide whether or not to go "all in" with fiction or to let myself keep dabbling and making more career-oriented lifestyle choices. I was discouraged by a number of rejections and feeling quite lost; so I wrote a story about a woman who passes up on her childhood dream to shock myself awake.

The idea came separately: I began to wonder what it would be like to be friends with an entity that guarded a forbidden tree—Ladon, say, the sleepless guardian of the Hesperides. Well, the nature of that relationship would be inherently Tragic, wouldn't it? I set the story in Germany because I was living in Berlin at the time, and because I was interested in German folklore.

A question for the author

Q: What made you start writing?

A: One of the first fictions I wrote was on the back of a church bulletin when I was around ten, because it was more fun that listening to the sermon. So: boredom, first of all.

But though it's true enough, I'm not content with that answer. Looking back, I can see a motive just as important, if less obvious: the urge to communicate what I felt could not, for whatever reason, be contained in face-to-face conversations.

When you look at fiction in the context of human communication in general—gestures, speech, image-making, writing—you can see right away that it gives you something none of the others give. In conversation, you get an idea of the opinions of another person. With fiction, you get an idea of what it is like to be another person. Fiction communicates experience directly through the process of character-reader identification.

Why should we want this? I don't know. When we have an interesting idea, we want to share it. When it's experience, or the qualia of an experience, or the way a bunch of experiences are strung together, why shouldn't we want to share that too? And all the more sense it makes to crave sharing what it is like to be ourselves—what it's like for me to be me, or for you to be you.

So I guess I started writing because I wanted that, and fiction was the most practical way of going about it. I suspect that a lot of writers are people who are dissatisfied with their ability to communicate and so turn to a medium that allows revision, demands sustained attention, and can be ignored but not interrupted. I think a person senses all that when they begin writing, and it's exciting. No one is telling you the rules. It's just you and the words, and you can take as much time as you need to figure out how to say what you want to say.

About the author

Patrick Doerksen lives in Vancouver, British Columbia. He wishes that his carbon footprint were smaller and his repertoire of long German compound words were bigger. He is glad a bookish lifestyle furthers both goals.

Patrick Doerksen's story "Notes Towards a New Fairytale" was published in *Metaphorosis* on Friday, 3 November 2017.

The Number of the Tribe

Gerald Warfield

Gurn levered himself up from his bed of furs, hoping he hadn't cried out. A few embers glowed in the fire pit, casting warm light on the roof of skins. Around him, he heard only gentle breathing and the snoring of his mother. No one else was awake. No one's pulse raced but his.

He could never sleep after a visit from the white figure, and so he rose, naked, and quietly skirted the fire pit to reach the entrance of the lodge. When he pulled back the flap, cool air brushed his body, and he took a deep breath to cleanse his head of the vision. But he could not help a darting glance among the other huts. She was not there, of course.

One of the dogs raised his head, black eyes glittering in the starlight. Gurn walked a pace and knelt to scratch the dog's head. Looking up, he could see the shaman's mountain, dark above the ovals of the other lodges. He knew where the white figure came from, and who had sent her.

When he abandoned Shomar, prematurely ending his apprenticeship, he had feared the old man's wrath. But he, Gurn, would become a hunter. He would provide for his village. An old man's curse could not change that. And he did not want to live alone in a cave. He drew comfort from the closeness of his clan. He had heard stories of villages that had vanished over the winter. They had starved or died from coughing sickness. But his tribe was strong. The hunters would provide for all, and the shaman would....

The shaman. Shomar.

Gurn's leave-taking had hurt the old man. And it had hurt him as well. He should go back; he should reconcile with his former master, convince him of the wisdom of the choice he had made.

With a final stroke of the dog's shaggy head, he stood. Glowing dimly above the mountain he saw the tail of the bear that ever circled in the night sky. The last thing that Shomar had said to him was that his future, both their futures, lay among the stars, but then Shomar often spoke in riddles.

Gurn climbed the barren mountainside, worry of the encounter to come adding weight to every step. The last time he had sought the cave of his former master, the path had been covered with ice. But now, the stones were only cool against his feet, the sun having yet to clear the mountains behind him.

In one hand, he carried his spear thrower, though uncertain why he brought it. Perhaps to prove his new status to Shomar?

In the other hand, he hefted a reed basket with his savory offering wrapped in leaves. It was good for the tribe to honor their elders, and by now, the old shaman might have reconciled to Gurn's decision.

Reaching a broad outcrop of rock, he turned to look back at the lodges clustered at the river's edge. Wisps of pale smoke rose from holes at the top of their mounded roofs.

Almost, he started back to the village, but turning again to the path, he came at last to the dark opening of the cave. The cracked skull of an aurochs rested on a narrow ledge above the entrance, its horns spread wide. He remembered, as a child, being frightened by the skeletal head.

Taking a deep breath, he leaned forward and called out. "Honored one. May I enter?"

His words reverberated from within the cave.

Motionless, he waited. Shomar had become thin and frail since the last snows, and it occurred to him that he might be too late to present his offering to the aged shaman.

Gurn pressed his lips into a thin line and crept to the narrow entry between the cold fire pits. Bending, he stepped from sunlight into shadows. Before his eyes could adjust, the smell of Shomar enveloped him, bringing to mind the mornings of his boyhood when he crept reverently into the damp cave, eager to learn the mysteries of spells, and of herbs, and of the reading of bones.

A rustling came from one side of the cavern, and he saw Shomar, his back turned, his skeletal shoulders topped by a tangle of white hair. Gurn quietly backed out into the sunlight.

"You may enter," came a frail voice from the darkness.

Inside once more, Gurn was troubled to see that Shomar sat on his rock of judgment, his hyena skin hanging from his shoulders, his necklace of lion's teeth resting on his sunken chest. In his hand, he held the horsehair switch that Gurn had made for him. Grunting, the old man gestured with the switch, indicating the stone where Gurn should sit.

Seeing that Shomar was already seated, Gurn walked stooped at the waist to show respect. In his childhood, he had crawled into Shomar's presence.

"Yesterday's hunt was successful," he said kneeling before Shomar and placing the basket before him. "I killed a spotted horse and have brought you a shank." He had brought one of the rear shanks, smoked overnight, and usually reserved for the chief. He watched to see if the old man would accept.

Shomar pulled the basket to him and lifted one of the broad leaves in which the shank was wrapped. He bent closer to sniff and then raised his eyebrows. "The spotted horse is fast and wary."

Gurn nodded, gratified the old man appreciated both the skill that it took to bring down such an animal and the generosity of his gift. He had decided that morning, after the sleepless remainder of his night, to bring the shank as tribute and to persuade Shomar that he had, indeed, become a hunter, and a hunter he would remain.

It had been three long moons ago that he walked from Shomar's cave, leaving his younger brother to train as the tribe's next shaman. Since that day he had thrilled to the hunt. He had learned hand signals for stalking and excelled at the flaking of stone.

"I practice long and hard with my atlatl." He raised his spear thrower. "The cup is made according to a new image in my mind."

Shomar glanced at him before reaching out and taking the smooth wooden rod. He nodded as he rolled his thumb in the bowl at the end of the shaft. "This is a fine thrower."

Gurn took back the rod and nodded again, pleased at the old man's praise.

"You do not visit me as often as you used to."

The smile left Gurn's face and he shifted on the stone. "It is the hunt, honored one, and the making of my weapons. They take all my time."

"Do the other children still call you Shomar's boy?"

Gurn's shoulders tensed. "No, honored one. My brother Cullen is now Shomar's boy."

"Ah, do they call him that?"

"Not yet, but he has only apprenticed with you three faces of the moon." When Shomar did not respond he added. "I hope he learns his lessons."

"He is not attentive."

"Then I shall strike his ears. He will learn to be an honored shaman one day, like you."

Shomar waved his hair switch as if to dismiss Gurn's response. "Nevermind. We shall celebrate your hunt. The baskets in back," he said, inclining his head to a shelf at the rear of the cave, "fetch me— the sixth one."

Gurn raised himself, and again bending at the waist, crept farther into the shadows where the air was laden with dampness and the odor of mold. On a shelf, which he, himself, had gouged into the wall, he could barely see a line of small baskets.

He counted to the sixth and reached for it, but stopped. Shomar could be devious. Gurn would not be manipulated by the old man, although he could not be certain what Shomar intended, if anything. He picked up the fifth.

Returning, he knelt and placed the small basket before Shomar. It contained dried berries.

The old man rocked forward and back. "Ah, you remember 'six' like I taught you."

Gurn frowned and lowered himself onto the sitting stone again. "I am afraid most of the numbers no longer remain in my head."

"Yes, memory is fleeting like the forest bison. There," he pointed with the switch. "Take some. They are the berries of contentment."

Gurn raised his eyebrows and looked at the old man for reassurance. Berries of contentment were rare, greatly sought after and hardly ever used outside the ancestor rites. Shomar nodded, and so Gurn took a handful and put some of them in his mouth. A bitter flavor rolled on his tongue as he began to chew. He had never actually tasted them before, but he knew that a pleasant feeling would come. Shomar had responded with a gift worthy of his own. The meeting was going better than he had hoped.

Meanwhile, the old man had taken out a shell that contained white powder, spat onto it and stirred with his finger. He made a vertical mark on his forehead ending at the bridge of his nose, and then began to draw horizontal marks on his wrinkled cheeks.

"You will hear the wisdom of my words."

Gurn bowed his head to signal his acceptance and to hide his dismay. He had hoped to be gone from the cave by now, escaping while Shomar was still in a good mood, yet reverence forbad his departure until he was dismissed. While the old man was occupied, Gurn reached for more berries. At the least he would feel contentment the rest of the day.

Shomar wiped the remaining pigment from his finger onto his loin cloth, and then reached behind him to bring out a handful of bones.

"Do you know how many there are?" he said, throwing them on the ground between them.

Now, there was no doubt that Shomar was testing him. He counted nine, but suspecting what Shomar intended, he said "seven."

"Ah," Shomar's voice fell. "You do not know your numbers as well as I thought."

"As I said, honored one, I am a hunter now. The numbers you taught me have vanished with my childhood. I am not fit to be a great shaman like you."

"But you counted the baskets correctly. All but the sixth contained berries of death."

Gurn's eyes widened, and he looked at the remaining berries in the basket and then at those in his hands. His gaze returned to Shomar in time to see the faintest curl of his lips.

"Ah," he drew out the sound again. "It seems that I'm all out of death berries today. Perhaps you would like to count the bones again?"

Cold crept into Gurn's gut. The meeting was not going as well as he thought. He moistened his lips. "There are nine."

"And do you know what they are?"

"As any hunter would know, they are leg bones of the baboon."

Shomar spat. "Look again. Look beyond the eyes of a hunter."

Gurn remembered his lessons as a child, when Shomar struck his ears if he gave the wrong answer. Scowling, he saw that each bone had been crossed with a series of horizontal scores.

"There are marks upon the bones," he said.

"And how many on the one that is pointing toward you?"

Gurn picked it up. Clearly, the old man had sawed each mark with a cutter. Furrowing his brow, Gurn began to count. After several moments he said, "More than twice two hands."

"Two hands twice and seven."

Gurn thought for a moment. "Yes, I can see that."

"It is the number of our tribe."

Gurn looked up.

"You must learn to count, boy."

"I am a hunter, Shomar. I do not play with bones."

Quick as a snake the old man's hand shot forward, striking Gurn across the mouth. Gurn cried out. The blow was not heavy, but his heart thumped in his chest as if he had been struck by a much greater force.

"Do not prattle about what you will not do!" The old man's voice trembled with rage. "If the goddess speaks, you will listen." And then he snatched something from his lap, raised it and struck the ground. When he removed his hand the pale image of the goddess faced Gurn. Pure white, carved from the tooth of the great mammoth, the small figure stood erect, its pointed feet stuck into the earth between them. "Tell *her* that you will not be a shaman."

Chills traveled up Gurn's spine, tingling into his scalp. It was the image from his dreams. The carving itself he had seen but twice before, and again he was overwhelmed by the ample breasts and bountiful hips. No woman in the tribe was her equal. Shomar's hand closed over the tiny statue, and it was removed from his sight.

Trying to hold at bay the fear that had swept over him, Gurn spoke quietly. "My deepest regrets, honored one. All tremble before the goddess, but you know that the hunt calls to me, and I despair at so much to learn. It is Cullen, my brother, who dreams of being shaman."

"Cullen dreams of wearing this," Shomar clutched the lion tooth necklace, causing it to rattle. "He does not understand that," and he pointed to the bones.

Gurn ground his teeth, determined to resist the old man, even the goddess if he must. "This is only the leg of a baboon," he said, shaking his head and lifting the bone before the face of Shomar. "You offer the tribe bones, while I offer meat. Our children will not cry for food in the dead of winter, because our hunters will provide. I will not be an old man sitting alone in a cave, dependent on others to bring me food."

"And that is exactly what your brother would be, but you are not like your brother. I have seen behind your eyes the working of your thoughts. It is within your grasp to understand."

"What is there to understand?"

Shomar grinned, ignoring the disrespect and leaned forward. "If you can count a thing, you can rule it."

Gurn looked down at the bone again. They were only marks, yet marks could be numbers and numbers could be things. Shomar had taught him that, like six for the basket of berries he had just fetched—or was it five? His thoughts had become clouded. Perhaps he had eaten too many of the berries.

The old man bent closer. "You are the next shaman. I shall teach you to enter the eye of the falcon, to possess the dreaded cave lion, and to understand—the magic within numbers." The old man traced a spiral sign in the air above his head and then reached out, extending a gnarled finger, and touched Gurn on the chest.

The touch caused Gurn's breath to leave him, and he began to tremble. More potent even than the slap, it drove thoughts from his head. He could not speak.

Shomar's white eyes floated in the shadows. "I have discovered that there are numbers big enough to count all things, and thus all things can be ruled."

Gurn gasped, trying to resist the spell. "How is that possible?"

"The goddess gave me a vision. She did not give it to my teacher, Bargwa, or to Sundar, his teacher, she gave it to me alone, and yet..." he spread his hands and closed his eyes, "it is not for me to fulfill that vision."

"But your knowledge is vast, honored one. Surely, more numbers are known to you than any other shaman."

"You do not realize how great the task." Shomar raised his hand, his first finger extended. "Hear now the vision that the goddess gave to me: One night in the far future a great shaman will step forth from his cave and look into the night sky. He will raise his hands and see far, very far. And then he will count the stars, and he will rule over them.

"Alas, it will not be me to fulfill this vision, or even you, but you will learn the symbols for many numbers, so many numbers that they could fill this cave with bones."

"You condemn me to sit in a cave marking bones while others hunt the forest bison and the tusked pig. It is *they* who provide for the future of the tribe."

"There are many hunters, and they provide but for the following day. The shaman, there is but one, and he provides for generations to come. There is a long future, Gurn, longer than you can imagine. I cannot master so many symbols before I die, but if I teach you... "

"No!" Gurn rose to his knees, his breath coming in gasps, his heart pounding. "You know I do not want to be shaman. Why do you do this to me?"

"Because I do not want to die."

Gurn stared at the old man, withered, bent and frail, yet defiant. A soft light gleamed from his white eyes. Gurn said quietly, "I do not want to die either, but... "

"It may be a very long time before the vision of the goddess is fulfilled. My own eyes no longer reach the stars, but in my youth, when I began counting, I learned that there are far more stars than I thought. And stranger still, there may be even *more* numbers, for although the stars will end, I do not think the numbers will. But with the symbols I teach you, you will count farther than I, and you will hand down the numbers to your apprentice, and he to his, so that when the time comes, and the great shaman steps forth, he will count the stars, and they will be his. And on the night that happens... " His eyes grew watery, and he struggled to speak. "At that moment I, Shomar, will live, as will you, and all the shamans that come after us."

Gurn raised his head but closed his eyes.

"I am asking," the old shaman said, "to live forever. You have the power to give me that gift. And one day, you in turn will ask another that you, too, will live, and the line not be broken."

Desperate, Gurn staggered to his feet and backed away. "I cannot," he stammered. He willed his legs to move, to carry him to the mouth of the cave. But at the entrance a white figure blazed before him, radiant with sunlight. He gasped and raised his hands against her brilliance. Turning his head away, he saw the light stream past him and strike a flat stone embedded in the back wall of the cave.

Chipped into the stone were symbols, scattered on the smooth surface. They had not been there his last visit to Shomar's cave, but he knew at once what they were.

The glare from the White Figure behind him faded. It was simply sunlight. He had withstood the spell, had resisted Shomar. But the symbols drew him. Mesmerized, he crept forward, reaching out to touch the stone as if to assure himself that it was real.

"Ah, you have discovered my symbols." The old man hobbled to his side. Both their shadows overlay the stone.

"What does this one mean?" Gurn pointed to one of the figures.

"That one is 'five.' You can recognize it by the cross stroke."

"Then that one must be ten?" He pointed to another.

"How quickly you grasp their meanings. It is a rare gift. It is from the goddess."

Gurn turned and looked at the old man, but said nothing.

Somar looked down and shrugged.

"What about this one?" Gurn pointed to one near the edge of the rock a lone symbol, different from the others. It was a bone scored with cross cuts.

A wrinkled smile spread across Shomar's face, "I will let you ponder upon that one."

Gurn nodded. It was Shomar's sign, of course. Gurn knew already what he would chose for himself. It would be a spear thrower.

When Gurn left the cave, he looked up into the night sky and wondered about counting the stars. There were so many.

His brother, Cullen, would not take the news well, that Gurn would be the next shaman. He sighed. He'd give Cullen his spear thrower; his brother was easily distracted. And Shomar was right, Cullen would never understand the numbers.

And he wondered about dying and about what it was like not to die. No one else in the tribe would understand that, either, but if, one day, the great shaman *were* to count the stars, he would need the patterns that Shomar had shown him. Gurn would learn them all and pass them on to the shaman who would come after him, and he to the next, and to the next. That pleased him. He pictured the line of his successors stretching to the edge of the valley and on to the horizon, and he wondered how long it would be before the great shaman came to count the stars.

Author's note: In Ishango, near the headwaters of the Nile, a baboon bone was discovered in 1960 with sequenced notches dating from the upper Paleolithic. According to *The Math Book* (Sterling Publishers), by Clifford Picking, the notches were arranged to show a knowledge of doubles, odd and prime numbers. Older sticks have since been found, in Swaziland a 37,000-year-old stick and in Czechoslovakia a 32,000-year-old tibia that displays notches in groups of five. The makers of these artifacts were surely the pioneers of mathematics.

About the story

I love to speculate on the origin of things, how one concept is built on another, is built on another, all the way back to—when? Mathematics should be traceable to a time when someone realized that it was useful to have more numbers than one had fingers. But the specifics of those earliest events will remain forever shrouded in the proverbial mists. I like to think they were "secrets" guarded by shamans and passed down through a lineage of magicians, priests, and witches. How tenuous such knowledge must have been, conceived perhaps many times before entering the mainstream of what was then civilized thought.

A question for the author

Q: What's a typical writing day like for you?

A: I work late, very late. Somehow, my life gets going in the course of the day, and I don't usually start writing until the afternoon. It may be something to do with being old. A day is like a reflection of my life. I seem to be most productive at the end.

About the author

Most of his adult life Gerald Warfield lived in New York City, on the upper west side and in Chelsea. His first job was at the Library and Museum of the Performing Arts at Lincoln Center. He marched in the first Gay Pride Parade in 1970. After leaving music, he supported himself writing how-to books in finance, and textbooks in music; his formal education was in music theory and composition (UNT and Princeton). He's an old man now and lives in a small Texas town where he's very out of place. He was accepted into and survived the Odyssey Writers' Workshop in 2010. That's where he really learned to write.

www.geralwarfield.com

Gerald Warfield's story "The Number of the Tribe" was published in *Metaphorosis* on Friday, 10 November 2017.

My Book Report on Starlight

Joachim Heijndermans

It's strange. The school isn't like I imaged it would be at all. I figured it would look more like in the movies, with long hallways of lockers and posters that say things like: 'reading is fun' or have quotes by famous people I've never heard of. But it's nothing like that. The hallways aren't even hallways, when you get down to it. This place looks more like the dome at a spaceport, but with even whiter walls and a giant glass ceiling that gives you a great view of the outside. And there aren't any posters of any kind. Instead, there are these blue metal spheres that float by, projecting little holo-clips of people talking and playing sports, but it's all in Carillian, so I don't understand any of it. It's a beautiful school. And I don't like it.

"You nervous?" Mom asks. I shake my head, even though I'm lying. To be honest, I'm terrified. Every step I take makes my backpack feel even heavier, like an anchor keeping me away from my new class longer and longer. A part of me wants to grab Mom's hand, but I'm not going to. I'm not a kid. I can do this on my own. But I'm still glad she came with me.

We hear this pinging sound coming from above. A tube of blue light appears in front of us, like if someone were shining a spotlight down at the floor. A man zooms down through the tube. When he reaches the ground, the light vanishes, leaving only a blue circle to indicate where the tube once stood. He's from Caril, but he's dressed in Earth clothes, with a tie and pocket protector and everything. It's too bad, since I actually like the clothes they usually wear on this planet, with all those frills and color patterns that look like cherry blossoms in a garden. These clothes makes him look like every other teacher I've ever had, aside from his bluish skin, four green eyes and a flat nose. He smiles his sharp looking teeth and introduces himself to Mom in Carillian, then turns to me and shakes my hand.

"Hello, Graze. How do you are? I am prinzeepal Solalaron," he says in a thick accent. It's the first time I've heard someone from Caril speak an Earth language. I'm actually glad to meet someone I can understand, even if it is another adult. I doubt I'll actually talk to him all that much. Adults never seem to really talk with you, just at you.

"I'm fine. And it's Grace, like 'place'."

"Ah, of course, yes. Apologizing," he says. He then turns to Mom and goes back to talking to her in Carillian, gesturing with his hands and clicking his teeth rapidly, while Mom does her best to keep up with him. While she can understand him for the most part, I can tell from her face she's wishing he'd slow down just a little. I just wish I understood what he's saying at all. Right now I'm guessing he's bragging about the school and what the students do all day. It'd be nice if he actually told *me* any of this, but I guess he's leaving that for Mom to translate.

"Grace, you liking the sports?" he asks.

I nod. "Gymnastics," I say. I could tell him about the championships I won back home, and how my team managed to make it to the nationals, but I don't. I just clam up and look away, peeking at the school grounds outside of the glass dome. The principal just nods and smiles, then says something to Mom in Carillian.

Mom turns to me. "Sweetie, you're going to your class now. But since most teachers and students aren't fluent in English or Spanish, and their English teacher won't be here until next month, you're going to be assigned a helper who is."

"A helper? What does that mean?" I ask.

"It means that a student from a different grade is going to sit in with you every now and then and help you along with assignments and translating whatever you don't understand. He'll be your '*study-buddy*', so to speak."

"Ok," I mutter. While I don't know what to expect with this 'helper' (I'm not calling him a '*study-buddy*'), I'm just glad that I'll be talking to someone that I hope is going to be around my age. Though I am curious what kind of student it'll be, since Dad once told me the people of Caril don't know many languages outside of their own. "Does my 'helper' really speak English?"

"Yes, he doing the speaking very well," the Principal says. "Better than me," he laughs. "Top student. Good grade very."

"Well, doesn't that sound great, Grace?" Mom says, trying to be uplifting.

"I guess," I mutter back.

The principal says something to one of the metal spheres, which causes it to zoom away. While we wait, the principal starts showing Mom some artwork that the students made, as I look through the massive window at the Carillian landscape outside.

The purple grass on the school grounds has been cut very short and into weird shapes. I have no idea what they're supposed to be. They look like boneless animals that are falling in on themselves. There's a groundskeeper robot who's pushing its lawnmower around.

The sky has an orange tint, while off in the distance, above the azure mountains that mark the border of the valley, I can see Bron Wyverns flying. This planet really is beautiful. I hate how much I like looking at it.

Mom calls out to me. "Grace, your study-buddy is coming."

I groan, loud enough for her to hear me. While I don't mind the company, I wish she'd refer to him as anything other than 'study-buddy'. She is the reigning champion when it comes to making me feel like I'm eight again. I'd regret asking her come with me on my first day here if I wasn't so terrified of going alone.

She points to the end of the hall, and I nearly jump up three feet in shock when I see him. Here I'm expecting a skinny Carillian kid, one with glasses and a lisp like they always give to geeks on TV. Instead, a nine foot, four-armed, pale-skinned, one-eyed creature comes toward us, his feet never touching the ground as he glides through the air. With his single half-blue, half-green eye, he looks at me. I've never seen anything like him.

The principal introduces him to Mom, who then introduced him to me. "Honey, this is Bowie-san-Gath. He's another immigrant student, like you, but from the Zig system. He speaks over eighteen languages-,"

"Nineteen," a voice echoes in my head. Mom heard it too, as she looks just as frazzled as me. It's his voice, though he doesn't move his mouth when he talks. I don't know if he even has a mouth, or a nose, or ears. It's like his head is just there for that one big eye of his.

"Oh, sorry. Nineteen," Mom corrects herself. "And, as you probably guessed, he speaks English. He'll be helping you with anything that you have trouble with. At least until you feel comfortable enough to study on your own."

He holds out his hand to me, but with his six fingers upward, showing me his palm. "Pleasure to meet you, Grace. I am Bowie-san-Gath, from Zig-Gimma-Tjon."

"Ehm, hi—," I mutter. I place my hand on his, which I'm hoping is what he wanted me to do. He doesn't seem to get angry, so I'm taking that as a yes.

"How are you liking the school?" he asks. It's weird to keep hearing his voice in my head. How does he even do that?

"It's fine, I guess."

"Trust me, it will grow on you in time, as it did for me."

"How long have you been here?"

"Nearly a *qiollicath*. That is roughly a 'year' on your planet."

"Oh," I say, which is the dumbest response I could think of, and yet I said it anyway.

"Would you like me to escort you to your class?" he asks. I find myself looking at Mom, needing assurance that it's okay, feeling even more like an eight-year-old. Why not ask her to hold my hand as we walk to it? Urgh! Stupid!

"Yeah. Cool," I say, trying to sound self-assured. I have no idea who I'm trying to impress here.

"Right this way," says Bowie-san-Gath. "It's on the eighth floor, right above auditorium *Demma*. All you need to do is step on the lift-stream."

"The what?" I ask.

He points to the blue circle thing on the floor. "The blue circle thing, if you wish," he says.

"Huh? That's funny."

"What is?" he asks.

"It's like—," I say, but I stop. "Never mind," I chuckle. For a second there, I thought he read my mind or something.

"I did read your mind," he says. "Low-level telepathy. It is not deliberate, so I must apologize."

"Hey! You stay out of my head, you hear me!" I snap.

"I will try," he says.

I find myself looking back at Mom. She gives me a nod, telling me it's OK and I'll be fine without saying it aloud. That doesn't make it any less scary to follow this giant pale alien guy onto glowy light. When I step on the blue circle, we're suddenly zipped several floors up. It feels like I'm pushed up by an invisible disk, though there's nothing beneath us. When we finally stop, Bowie-san-Gath motions for me to follow him.

We enter another hallway, walking past the classrooms. I catch a few glimpses of what's going on inside (mostly students staring at the teacher in the front), but I don't want to be left behind by my — *ugh* — "study-buddy", who walks very fast for someone whose feet don't touch the ground. He then stops in front of a classroom with a blue door.

"This will be your class. Your teacher is Ms. Gorarawin. I will make introductions between you two."

"Okay. And then what?"

"I will sit in with you for the remainder of the morning, but then I must return to my own classes and studies afterward. I hope that is all right with you."

My first instinct is to say: *no, please don't leave me here all alone with no-one to talk to*. But I tell myself I can do this. I'm alright. I'm fourteen, aren't I? I steel my face and strike an *'I'm cool'* pose, and say; "Yeah, that's fine. Whatever."

"There is nothing to be scared of," he says.

"Who's scared?" I say. He looks at me for a bit, which I think might be a comment, then opens the door without actually touching it. We walk in.

The whole class, all Carillian students, turn to look at us. Even though one of us is tall, six-armed, pale-skinned and has only one eye, I know it's me who catches the most attention. Some girls whisper. A few guys give each other looks, the *'what's up with her?'* look. The teacher, an older lady with silver hair braided into three rows, walks toward us. She shakes my hand and greets me in the only three Carillian words I know (which are *hello, how,* and *you*) before she goes on and loses me with these long drawn out sentences.

"Ms. Gorarawin welcomes you to her class. You are to sit over there in seat *Hwo-ax,* which means B-12. She is currently covering level-two mathematics. However, since you have not mastered Carillian yet, she will allow you to perform extracurricular activities."

"What does that mean?" I ask.

"You may do other things, as long as she deems them productive and befitting of your school time. You came prepared for this, did you not?"

"Are you reading my mind again?"

"No. I just assumed it's the reason why your backpack is so full."

He's right. Since I didn't get any of my new schoolbooks yet, my backpack if filled with some old school books from back home, a few journals, Mom's old Carillian dictionary, and a copy of a novel I never got around to read. I look at the teacher, who's giving me this expecting look, so I put my backpack down, open it, pull out the novel and hand it to her. "Is this okay?" I ask.

She looks at it, inspecting the cover and the back. I think it might be the first time she's seen a book printed on paper. Once she sees the picture of K'un Di, the author, on the back, she smiles and hands it back to me, saying something in Carillian to Bowie-san-Gath. He doesn't answer her, but she talks like he has. I wonder if you can only hear him if he wants you to?

"The book is fine. You may read during class, although I would suggest you try and see what the other students are studying. Do not be afraid to ask me to translate anything for you," Bowie-san-Gath says in a tone that I think is supposed to be inviting, but sounds more like a lecture. He doesn't really talk like a student or a teacher. More like a hallway monitor, or someone who really digs school to a weird degree. I nod and take my seat, opening the book to page one, while my alien 'helper' sits beside me.

It takes nearly ten minutes for me to actually read a word, as I use the book to hide my face more than anything. It takes another ten before I start to remember what I just read. I keep peeking around to see whether the students are still staring at me, which they're not. They're just doing their school work, listening to the teacher and passing notes to each other. Perfectly normal schoolkids in a perfectly normal school, on the other side of the universe. I've never wanted to go home so badly. Actual home. Not this planet. I'm doing my best not to cry, and even that I'm blowing, as tears roll down my cheeks.

The first week went by really quick. It's Friday (or *sjo'zath* as it's called here), and while everyone has been nice to me (for the most part), I still feel like an outsider.

For example: yesterday, right before lunch, these two girls came up to me and asked me something. Bowie-san-gath wasn't here, so I had absolutely no idea what they wanted. I smiled and shrugged, after which they laughed and walked away. Another girl, Urasuwa I think her name is, snapped at them. After that, no-one has bothered or laughed at me. I wish I could stand up for myself like that. But I just don't know what to say and I feel super awkward when they all laugh. I know it's probably a joke amongst themselves, but I just can't shake that feeling like they're laughing at me. Whether it's in my head or not, it awful being on edge like this.

Ms. Gorarawin checks in on me from time to time, always asking the same thing each time. "You…okay, are yes?", followed by "Gud jop," when I nod to her. She mostly lets me read my book, which is fine, I guess. It beats doing homework for now, though I don't know what I'll do once she realizes I finished the book already. Twice, in fact. It's much better than I thought it would be. It's got action, some cute romance parts and plenty of space travel. Good stuff, and it keeps my mind occupied from other things, like how no-one understands a word I say.

I know it's been only a week since I started, but the language issue is really kicking me down. Mom is helping me out after school with her old books on Carillian, but she can only do so much considering her busy schedule, and her old study material crashes repeatedly whenever I boot it up on my tablet. Bowie-san-Gath is not much help either, as he retreats into himself most of the time. I know a lot more words than before, but it's the sentence structure and the speed at which native Carillian speakers talk that's really kicking my butt. It's like everyone is running laps around the running track, while I'm on my hands and knees trying to keep up. And now they have students coming up to the front of the class, each doing some kind of speech about something, I'm left staring at them, in the dark to what they are talking about. I just wish I knew what was going on, even for just a little bit.

It's lunch, and I'm sitting by myself again. I'd sit with my class, but not saying anything for thirty minutes straight while I chow down is much worse when you're with others. No one ever told me you could even be lonely in a crowd.

"Hello," says a voice in my head. I flinch, knowing exactly who it is without looking up.

"Hi, Bowie," I say.

"Bowie-san-Gath, if you please," he says, sounding somewhat annoyed. "May I join you?"

"Sure," I sigh. It's been a few days since I've seen him when he sat in with me last Friday. He's transfers me translated copies of homework assignments from his old classes every now and then, but he hasn't shown up in person till now. It's the first time he's met up with me for lunch.

"Enjoying your meal, Grace?" he says, crouching down so he doesn't tower over me.

"Meh."

"Is the food not to your liking? The cafeteria staff can show you visual options if you have trouble reading the menu."

So that's why they kept showing me pictures. To be honest, on my first day I didn't know what to think of it. I've never had a lunch of mostly beans, fruit and beets. Imagine my surprise when I looked up these rambutans they gave out for dessert on the MAYNE-Frame, only to find out they're actually from Earth.

"It's not the food. It's just..."

"Just what?"

"Nothing," I sigh. He sits down beside me, and while I'm happy he does, I don't show it. I don't know why he annoys me so much. He hasn't done anything to get on my bad side. If it were up to me, he'd be in my class all the time. Maybe it's the fact that he makes me feel like a side-project. I'm just something to deal with when class isn't in session, or if he's got all his homework finished. I might as well be the class pet in a glass cage, an aquarium without water.

"Terrarium," he says.

"What?"

"A waterless glass containment unit for non-marine animals. Terrarium."

I stand up, fighting the urge to slap him across his white domed head. "Stop reading my mind!"

"I don't mean—," he says, backing away as I shake my finger at him.

"Yeah, you told me, you don't control it. But it's still really creepy. Now stop it!"

It's then I notice people are looking at me. I can feel my face turn red when all the other kids start mumbling among themselves, throwing glances my way. I don't know why, but I drop back down, grab my book and hide behind it. I hope that they'll either ignore me or that the ground will swallow me up. Either sounds good enough.

"Are you enjoying *'Protovech Ghan'*?" Bowie-san-Gath suddenly asks, pointing to the book.

"Proto-what?"

"*'Protovech Ghan'*. The novel you're reading. It's the first part of the *'Odakkar'* saga by K'un Di, isn't it?"

I hold it up, pointing at the title. "Yeah, it's by K'un Di, but it's called *'Starlight'*."

"Ah, yes, I see. I've only read it in its original Zon. *'Starlight'*, was it?"

"Yeah."

"Amusing. That is not a correct translation of the title at all."

"Why? What does 'Protovech Ghan' mean in English?"

"The Sun Queen's Laser Spear."

I chuckle. "No offense, but I like *'Starlight'* better as a title."

"None taken," he says. "You've been reading it non-stop since you started school. I take it you enjoy it?"

"It beats doing nothing or getting homework I can't read," I say, trying to sound cool and aloof. I don't think he buys it, because I get the feeling he can tell from my voice that I'm about to re-read my favorite chapter.

"Are you at the part where Solea meets the Harbinger yet?" he asks.

"Just about. I—," I say, stopping when I know I just gave myself away.

"Second read through?" he asks.

"Third by now," I mutter. To my surprise, I hear him laughing. It's a pleasant laugh, one that is understanding. I laugh too, which I realize might be the first time I've done that in front of him.

"I'm sorry I snapped at you," I say.

"I'm sorry I read your thoughts."

"Start again?" I ask.

"What do you mean?"

"I think we got off on the wrong foot," I say. "Tell me more about yourself. Why'd you come to Caril for schooling?"

He locks his hands together. "After some...issues on my home world, my previous diploma's and degrees have been rendered invalid. I had to retake my classes on Caril so I can have the appropriate grades and certifications for this part of the galaxy."

"Oh. But you like it here, right?" I ask.

"It is pleasant enough. But like you, being the only one of my kind here with no-one to speak my native tongue with was intimidating."

"Yeah, I bet. But I only know English and Spanish. You know a dozen more languages than I do," I say, chuckling. "Did it take you long to learn Caril?"

"It's not so difficult one you practice it. I mastered it in a *tymwull* — a month."

"Jeez. All I know you could fit on a single page. It'll take me more than just a month," I sigh. He looks at me, without saying anything. I break the silence; "So what about friends? You seem to be popular here."

"I do not have any friends. Not in the way you define it."

"Why not? You're easygoing, as far as I know."

"I suppose I am not in the habit of making friends. Even for lunch, I sit alone."

"Really?"

"Yes. My studies keep me preoccupied. It seems friendships are simply one of those things that I am unfit for," he says, sounding actually kind of sad. "How about you? Are you fitting in?" he asks. "Made any friends yet?"

I laugh, but it's not a happy laugh. "I haven't. And I'm not fitting in either. Either I avoid people, or they avoid me."

"How come?" he asks.

"Because I have no idea what to say to anyone, and I don't have a clue to what's going on in class. I sometimes feel I might as well be on the moon."

"Which one?" he asks, looking up at the ceiling as two of the large moons pass over us, the blue one being much bigger than the rainbow colored one. The third one should be on the other side of the planet at this point.

"Good one," I chuckle.

"Humor is not as alien to my kind as it may seem. You will find my culture is quite versed in the art of comedic timing."

"Yeah? Know any good Zig knock-knock jokes?"

"No, but our Xenxnex cabaret is similar to the Owarai comedy from your planet. Are you familiar with it?"

"Not really."

"It's a Japanese style of comedy. It is very popular on some of the outer colonies, like the Brbrrrb satellite near Tensemt and Colo, where the Technarcy have embraced it."

Wow, those are a lot of names I'm probably not going to remember. "You've been all over the universe, haven't you?"

"I have moved around quite a lot."

"Do you miss your home planet?"

"Not really. But you do, don't you?" he says.

"It's obvious, isn't it?" I groan.

"It is all right to be homesick. But-," he starts.

"Yeah, I've heard that. From my mom, my dad, even people I've e-mailed back home. But that's not what's bothering me."

"Then what?" he asks.

"Can I be honest?"

"Of course," he says, moving closer to me. His one eye changes color to a deep brown. I'm not sure if that means something.

"I'm actually really bored here."

"Bored? Does Ms. Gorarawin not assign enough homework?"

"I think she does, but I get the feeling she doesn't give me all of it. Just mini math assignments. Outside of that, she just lets me sit there and read."

Bowie-san-Gath chuckled. "I know several students who would prefer that to actual homework."

"Yeah, I get that. But how am I supposed to fit in when I get pushed aside all the time? I can't add anything to a conversation. I can't give answers to a question. I'm the Earth girl in the back, who no-one can talk to. I just feel like a whole bit of nothing. Like I'm just wasting my time until class ends, and then I have to do the whole thing again the next day. Like today, when one of the kids — Horth, I think his name is — went up to the front of the class and talked about something with all these pictures to back him up. And while everyone else is commenting and asking questions, I'm just sitting there, gawking at them. I feel so stupid, like I should be in the remedial class or something. I mean, what was he even doing? What are any of them doing?"

Bowie-san-Gath presses two of his long fingers against what I think is supposed to be his chin, and sat there, lost in thought. I figured he drifted off somewhere, bored by my story, when he suddenly sits up and pulls out his schedule planner.

"Your grade seems to be in the midst of their *Yurngahli-do*."

"Oh, okay," I say. "And what's that?"

"Basically, it's an assignment where the students hold a presentation about any literature of their choice."

"A presentation? Like a book report?"

"Yes, exactly like that."

"Any book?"

"Yes, any book, as long as the presentation conveys the content in proper terms."

"What does that mean?"

He rubs his head for a bit, trying to find the words. "You need to be able to retell the story under a set time limit, and it is encouraged to explain what it is about the book that spoke to you the most. Like I said, it's a small assignment."

"Oh, okay. And does everyone in my class have to do this?"

"Yes. Everyone except you, of course."

"Yeah. Right. Of course."

We sit there for a minute or two without saying anything. Me, chomping down om my PB&J, him absorbing water spheres through his chest. I try to think of a new topic, but I just can't seem to get my mind off of book reports. I'm glad I don't have to do one, but at the same time, I'm not. I mean, I have been reading the same book for nearly two weeks straight. I could do a report on it. It'd be better than sitting around and doing nothing. But I couldn't go out there and talk in front of the class. I barely speak a word of Carillian. It's insane. It's impossible. It's—

"Are you thinking of participating in the Yurngahli-do?" Bowie-san-Gath asks.

"Are you reading my mind again?" I ask.

"I didn't have to," he says. "Your face speaks more to me than a mild mind probe ever could."

I feel myself blushing. "Forget it. It's just a stupid idea. It's not like I even have to do it."

"No, that's correct. You are not obligated to."

"Right. I mean, I'm not sure I even can do it."

"True," he says in the most deadpan tone ever. "Your Carillian is poor, so what would even be the point to go up in front of the class and speak about a book you don't even like?"

"Excuse me, but I happen to like '*Starlight*'. Just because I don't speak Carillian, doesn't mean I can't do a book report on it. I could do just as well as anyone else."

He turns to me. I see my reflection on his face as he quietly stares at me. Then it dawns on me what he's trying to get me to realize. Sneaky alien kid.

"Look, just because I can do it, doesn't mean it will be good. I wouldn't even know where to start."

He quietly hands me a small driver. "Place that in your tablet. It should help."

"What is it?"

"My old Carillian/English dictionary. It also has a phrase generator and can adjust poorly formatted sentences. It should still have all my notes."

"Wow, thanks. Did you get this when you first enrolled in school?"

"No. It was a gift from a Carillian peacekeeper."

Peacekeeper? I'm afraid to ask, but I've heard Dad talk about the Caril government sending soldiers to wars in the past.

"I don't know about this. I don't—," I begin, but Bowie-san-Gath calls one of those blue spheres over. He mention Ms. Gorarawin's name, after which the ball zooms off. A minute later it returns along Ms. Gorarawin, smiling broadly. Bowie-san-Gath talks to her, pointing to me, the book, and the blue sphere that shows some clips from today's class. I catch a few words here and there, realizing what he's setting up for me. I actually getting excited about it.

"Ms. Gorarawin has agreed to allow you to participate. You will have twenty minutes to present your speech on '*Starlight*' in front of the class in any matter you deem fit."

"Great! So will you help me with the—"

"I'm sorry, but I cannot assist you with a book report. I have not the time to help you on this."

"What? But it was your idea!"

"No, it was yours. I simply helped you along with making the first step."

"But...can't you just help?"

"Are you asking me to put own schoolwork in jeopardy to help you on an assignment?"

I don't say anything. I feel like such a jerk now. He's right. That's exactly what I'm asking him to do. "But there's no way I can do this on my own," I stutter.

"I beg to differ," says Bowie-san-Gath. "Besides, you were the one who said you were bored, right?"

"Yeah..."

"I believe this book report is what you need to break the barrier. A way to share who you are with your class."

"But why can't—"

"—I help you? Because I have six exams that hour that I need to complete to pass my classes."

"That hour? Don't you mean that day?" I ask.

"No," he says. From his tone, I can tell he's neither kidding or lying.

"But...but—," I stammer, wanting to finish with 'I can't'.

"Yes, you can," he says. "I feel that you doing this on your own is the push you need to overcome your shyness and fears. Call it a baptism of fire, to quote your planet's writers."

It's ridiculous. On the one hand, I don't think I can do this. But on the other, I can't just sit around doing nothing forever. I live here on Caril now. This is my home and my this is my school. He's right, even though I don't like it. If I can do this alone, I show the class who I am and what I'm like. I have a voice, and I want to be heard. "All right. I'll do it. I'll do my book report on 'Starlight'."

"Excellent," Bowie-san-Gath says.

"One thing," I say.

"Yes?"

"What's 'Starlight' called in Caril?"

He laughs. " 'Tyun-fo', as in 'The Light of The Sun Queen'."

That's actually not half bad, but it still can't beat 'Starlight' when it comes to titles. I repeat the title to Ms. Gorarawin, who smiles and nods, then pulls out her tablet and begins writing something down. She slowly talks to me while showing the schedule. She marks the last box with a 'G', which I think stands for 'Grace'. "Toleallir?" she asks me.

"Uhm, yeah. Sure. Fine," I say, turning to Bowie-san-Gath. "What did she say?"

"She said you will be doing your report on toleallir. Thursday."

"Ah, ok," I say. "Which Thursday?"

"This upcoming one," he replies, before hovering off to the lift-stream. "Good luck," he says, waving at me, while I stand there, speechless and frozen with panic. I have five days to prepare. Right now I'm glad that Bowie-san-Gath is the only one who can hear me screaming in my head.

I'm stuck. Trying to read is a chore. Not that I didn't understand the material. I got the book just fine. But trying to retell it in a language I barely grasp is impossible. The English/Carillian dictionary is lying there by my feet, waiting to be used, but I just can't make any sense of the sentence structures.

I'm pacing back and forth, biting my nails, trying to figure out some way I can pull this off. I stop when someone knocks at my door.

"Grace? Honey? You coming down for dinner?" Mom asks.

"In a little bit."

"Dad found a place that makes pizza and brought some home."

"Pepperoni?"

"No, sorry. They don't make sausages out here. Are peppers and tuna all right?"

"That's fine," I sigh. She opens the door and peeks in, instantly seeing my frustration the second our eyes meet. "What's wrong?" she asks.

No point in hiding it. Not from her. "I agreed to do a book report in front of the class this Thursday."

"That's great," she says.

"No. That's not great. I'm going to look stupid, standing there with nothing to say."

"Didn't you read the book?" she asks.

"I read it four times. I know the story front to back. I can dream it. But I can't talk about it because no-one will know what I'm saying."

"Oh, I see. Can't...what's his name? Your 'study buddy'? Ziggy-zen...?"

"Bowie-san-Gath. And no, he can't help. He's doing six exams that hour."

"You mean that day, sweetie," she laughs.

"No, I don't."

"Oh," she says. "Do you need me to help you? I can help you write out what you want to say after dinner."

"That would help. Or you could come to school with me and translate?"

"Sorry, honey. I can't. You know I would if I could, but I have to meet the housing representative and—"

I stop her. "I know. I'm not serious," I say, although part of me is a little bit. "But even if know what to say, how do I know I say it right?"

"Well, how about you eat first? I'm sure you'll think of something once you've got some food in you."

We walk downstairs to the kitchen. Dad and Danny are already chowing down, with Danny holding his pizza in one hand and a red robot toy in the other. "Rrr! Gigator-7 has come to save the pizza planet."

"Don't play with your food, Danny," Dad mutters.

"Gigator-7 needs to eat too, Dad. He's been fighting the Omni-armies all day."

"Oh, and how did that go?" Mom asks, playing along.

I envy Danny. He doesn't have as a hard time fitting in. He already made a few friends and picked up some Carillian, even watching that robot show on TV without any problem. I watch him play for a while as Mom cuts me up some pizza, listening to him recreate today's episode of Gigator-7. He uses his toy to show Mom and Dad all the moves that Gigator used to beat up Tarno-saur. Left kick. Right punch. Barrel roll slam. He makes it sound so real. Like it actually happened.

Then it hits me. An idea. I know how I'm going to do my book report on 'Starlight'.

"Danny, can I borrow some of your toys for school this Thursday?"

I watch the clock ticking down. It's almost hour 70, two-thirty in Earth hours. I'm holding onto the box of book report stuff like it's a treasure chest. I hope I'm not making the biggest mistake of my life. For all I know, I'm gonna go down as the girl who played with toys in front of her class. I'll get a zero-minus on my record for the rest of the year. They'll put me in some sort of remedial class, where I have to carry Bowie-san-Gath's books until he graduates.

No. I'm being silly. I'll just go up, do my thing, and get it over with. It's time I stop being the wallflower from Earth in the back of the classroom.

"Graze?" Ms. Gorarawin says, motioning for me to come on up. I feel like I'm on autopilot, as I want to stay seated and curl up into a ball and vanish, but instead, I get on up and walk down the steps, passing by the other students, with the box in my arms.

"You begin, yes?"

"Yes. Thank you - so-fath," I say. I take a quick look around the class. Most of the students throw each other looks. A few of the girls laugh. Ms. Gorarawin gives me two thumbs down, but I think that is meant as encouragement, as she's smiling and nodding. I take out my copy of 'Starlight', and hold it up for everyone to see. I'm really doing this. Here goes nothing.

"This is my book report — mae Yurngahli-do — on 'Starlight' - 'Tyun-fo'. It's a novel — tiullitan — about Solea, the Queen of the Starlight," I begin, opening the box and pulling out my old Malibu Amy doll, which I've put in a yellow dress and taped a fork to her hand. Some of the students laugh. My heart skips a beat. For a second I think about bolting out of the classroom while I still can, but I keep going. "She's the creator and the ruler of all the suns — ila zonea. She's a good queen. But she's at war — brokarr — with an awful enemy: the Dark," I say, pulling out Terror-man, the scariest toy from Danny's collection, and I begin my report.

One by one I take the dolls and toys out from the box and place them on the desk, while I roll off the names of the cast. Once I've given every toy their name, I talk about the first part of the book, where the Sun Queen comes out from hiding after the destruction of the green sun of Torra. I pause every now and then to translate a few things with the Carillian dictionary, or I just use props from my box to gesture it (the green sun of Torra is played by an orange). I get stuck a few times, but Ms. Gorarawin jumps in to translate. After a while I talk without any hiccups for so long, I don't even worry about looking at the class anymore. All my nerves are gone, as I move onto the last part, where Solea is attacked in her castle by the Darkling army, loses all her servants and has to fight by herself, which I play out by slapping Danny's old Terror-man toy with my Malibu Amy, although the battle ends with her being thrown from her tower, played by the teacher's desk. She falls into the inky sea of ebony, ending the story on a bleak note. But then, when everything seems lost, her sun spear suddenly comes floating out of the inky blackness. To be continued.

"So I really liked this book. I didn't think I would, at first. I mean, I kept putting it off, never giving it a chance. But it didn't turn out as bad, and I'm glad I finally did give it a go" I say, not sure if I'm still talking about the book or not. I look over the class, seeing everyone intently listening. "Well, that's the end — dexfini — of my book report — mae Yurngahli-do — on 'Starlight' — 'Tyun-fo'. Thank you — so fath — for listening."

I stand there, holding Malibu Amy and Terror-man in my hands. The rest of the class is looking at me. My heart stops. Then, one of the boys in the front row, Horth, begins to clap. The students sitting next to him join in. Urasuwa, the girl two seat in front of me, yelps out. Soon, the whole class, Ms. Gorarawin included, are clapping. No one is laughing. Not one of them made fun of me. I feel so ridiculous, for even thinking they would. Then, I hear a voice in my head. "Well done."

I look around, seeing the tall figure of Bowie-san-Gath in the back of the class, throwing me a wave. The lunch chime blares from the blue spheres, causing the classroom to empty out. I walk to my desk with my box of props, where Bowie-san-Gath is waiting for me.

"Hey," I say. "You watched it?"

"Yes. It would have been regrettable had I missed it," he says.

"You skipped your exams for me?"

"Of course not. My instructor still thinks I'm there. Small mind trick I learned long ago. But I wanted to be here and see how you did. And I believe it was a success. You should be pleased."

"I am. Thanks for your help."

"What help?" he says, making a strange sound that I think is a laugh. "You did all this on your own."

"Well. You still helped by being a friend."

He looks at me. His single eye shines a new color, with dashes of orange added in. Is he blushing? "We are friends?" he asks.

"Yeah. I figured we are."

"Hmm," he mutters.

A finger taps me on the shoulder. It's Urasuwa, who has hair braided into six tails and a pencil-thin visor on her nose. "Graze… goud worke," she says, before saying something, which I think meant either "seeing book" or "watching wood".

"She asked if she can see your book. She has never read it and your presentation has piqued her interest," Bowie-san-Gath says.

"Oh. Of course," I say, handing '*Starlight*' to her. "So-fath," I say.

She looks at the cover and flashes me a smile. I smile back. When I turn around, I see Bowie-san-Gath heading out of the classroom. He waves at me before the door closes behind him.

I've been in school for a tymwull — a month. Things have gotten a lot easier now, especially since I became part of Urasuwa's group. One of the students in the fyio-gi class lend me a Carillian copy of '*Starlight*' for on my tablet so I can learn some words and phrases, and Urasuwa has been helping me whenever I get stuck. Also with the arrival of Mr. Subra, the English teacher, I now attend his class on Carillian for English speaking students (I'm the first to attend any such class on the entirety of Caril, so I'm top of the class).

I've also joined the school gymnastics team. Mr. Frunadnar, the keileion (that's like a coach) doesn't need to do much talking when barking orders at us. He's all right though, and he let me know through Ms. Gorarawin that if I keep up with my studies and practice, I might be able to make the school team next year.

I don't see Bowie-san-Gath as often. He's still around, throwing me a wave when we pass each other or leaving me a book that helps me practice my Carillian. So I'm surprised he showed up right before class today.

"How are things?" he asks.

"Things are good," I say, before trying it in Carillian. "Ginn to finwa si garr."

"Hinn, not ginn," he says. "But not bad."

"And you? How'd your exams go?"

"They went well. Very well indeed. In fact, I am to be transferred to the more advanced levels in the school's southern campus."

"Really? Where's that?"

"A few days travel from here."

"Oh, but that means—," I mutter.

"Yes. I'm sorry to say, but it does," he says. His eye turns dark, a near black. "That is why I wanted to give you this before I leave." He hands me something wrapped in brown paper. It feels lighter than it looks.

"Thanks. But this isn't goodbye, you know? I've had my fill of goodbyes."

"Then we shall meet again. And when we do, I hope you'll have finished my gift. So until then, see you soon, Grace."

"Later, alligator," I say.

"What?"

I turn red. Great. Way to go, Grace. But I think he knows how embarrassed I am, as his eye turns a greenish color. He waves and floats off.

"Grace, quero da hui ki forre?" asks Urasuwa, which means 'what did he give you?'. I shrug and begin peeling the paper off the gift. It's a small file driver, which I quickly load onto my tablet. A picture of Solea, queen of the sun, pops up on screen. I read the title.

"'*Solarmax: part 2 of the Starlight saga*', by K'un-di, with annotations in Carillian and Zon," I read aloud. There's a message encoded with it, popping up as I load the first page.

"Dearest Grace. I hope this next installment will illuminate your life on Caril. Signed; Bowie-san-Gath. Your friend."

About the story

My family moved from the Netherlands to the USA in 1998, when I was about 8 years old. I did not speak a work of English and was terrified of the prospect of attending a school where I couldn't talk to anyone. By a pure stroke of luck, the school I attended had another student who also spoke Dutch. She guided me along for the first month, up until I got the hang of the language. Not long after, she returned to the Netherlands. I'm not sure what happened to her, or what her name was, but her help with easing me into this new place gave me the confidence to master the language.

A question for the author

Q: What's your favorite type of pie?

A: My favorite would be 'appel taart', or apple pie. While we don't really call it a pie in Dutch ('taart' can also apply to cake, and while 'vlaai' is closer to a pie, this certainly doesn't fall under is), I am very fond of our apple pie. Though don't confuse it with 'Dutch Apple Pie', because trust me, it is nothing like that.

About the author

Joachim Heijndermans writes, draws, and paints nearly every waking hour. Originally from the Netherlands, he's been all over the world, boring people by spouting random trivia about long-extinct animals and comic books no-one remembers.

www.joachimheijndermans.com, @jheijndermans

Joachim Heijndermans's story "My Book Report on Starlight" was published in *Metaphorosis* on Friday, 17 November 2017.

The Wife of Fabian Vitalik

Mariah Montoya

The day that Fabian Vitalik's wife left, rain masked the roar of the sea just beyond their rock garden. Fabian ended fishing early because of the storm, and came home to find his wife dozing on the sofa by the window, unfazed by the sharp *pat pat pat* of rain fingers on glass.

He found her enthralling when she was still and senseless like this, so he sat down and watched her breathe, the pearl necklace that rested on her chest rising and falling like waves. Their handmade string of seashells hanging from the ceiling tinkled above her head.

"I love you," Fabian whispered to her sleeping figure, rubbing fish grease on his pants. He thought his wife was most beautiful when she was human.

Of course, she was famous for her shape-shifting. When he'd first seen her high up on the stage, twirling and morphing into other things, the audience had gone wild for the black sleekness of her cat's fur, the shine of her teapot porcelain surface, the perfume that wafted from her petals when she mutated into a lilac bush. Oh yes, he remembered the hoots and howls of men when she danced her way across the stage as only a dress, the movement of shimmering fabric emphasizing the curves of the woman that would be underneath.

He had stared up at her in that crowd, marking the flashes of skin when she would have to, for a moment, be herself again before transforming into something she was not.

Now her overalls were fraying, her hair graying at the roots, the creases of fake smiles ebbing over her face. But so beautiful. Perhaps that was why she had married him, a simple fisherman living in Camber who'd tracked her down when the rain started pouring and the audience dispersed with newspapers over their heads. Nobody had glanced her way after she converted back into a woman, rain-soaked and delicate and normal. Nobody but him. And thirty years later, Fabian could not stop staring.

It was only when the rain stopped that she tensed and shifted her body on the sofa, as if the lack of pattering on the window was an alarm. The seashells clinked to a still. Her eyelids fluttered open.

"How did you sleep, love?" Fabian asked from his armchair, drinking in her presence.

She blinked at him, flexed her fingers as if amazed that she had fingers at all. Far off, they could finally hear the ocean again, roaring and crashing onto the beach. She looked back up at him. "What have you been doing this whole time?"

"Reading," Fabian said, although his book lay unopened on the other end of the coffee table.

"How'd fishing go? I assume the rain ruined things."

"Caught some, but not much. Had to come back early."

"Hmm." His wife glanced out the windowpane, where the rainstorm had leaked into a gray drizzle. The stones in their garden glistened with the residue of the storm. "You know," she said, "I have always wanted to shift into wind. Or fire. An element of some sort, but I don't know how. Which muscle do I reach for? Which thought do I think? Which color do I let fill me up?"

Fabian did not answer, only stared at the curve of her mouth, thinking about love and fishing and the sea. How many times had he woken from a night of lovemaking to find something else on his wife's pillow — a dusty book, a glass doll, a starfish? When she was transforming, she was so much like the sea, wild and unpredictable. But when she was human, she moved like a butterfly, gently, gracefully...

"— simply rise and plummet where I please."

Fabian nodded, not knowing what she had just said. He remembered his wife giving birth to their three children, who were all grown and traveling now — Josiah had come out covered in fur, his shape-shifting abilities stuck between some kind of animal and the baby he was. The doctors had panicked until the little guy had given a sharp, sputtering cry and shifted back into baby skin.

None of their other children could shape-shift, and Josiah never did again. The curse, the blessing, of having an ordinary father.

"— hear me, Fabian? Does it not faze you, what I just said?"

"What?" Fabian jolted out of his visions, refocusing on the woman before him.

"I don't want to stay here anymore. With you, with this dratted, God-forsaken house." His wife stared at him with the haltingness of a sand crab caught by a seagull eye. "I want to simply rise and plummet where I please. You, Fabian, do not appreciate my needs to escape confinement, and —"

The crash of the ocean. Fabian's ears roared with the sound. He did not know whether his wife meant confinement in his house, or in her body, or both. She was touching the pearls on her neck, the pearls he had plucked from shored oysters himself.

"— and my love has crumpled inside me, Fabian. I feel like a rock when I am with you. You never admire me when I'm a cricket singing you songs at night, or when I'm a vase of flowers in our kitchen, or when I'm a wardrobe holding our clothes." Angry blotches were rising on her cheekbones now. "I feel like a rock," she said again. "I have since I met you. I want to feel like — I don't know, *something* lighter, something more free and beautiful and untamed than I am now."

Fabian stared at her. He wanted to say he didn't *need* a cricket to sing him songs, her human heartbeat was enough at night. He didn't *want* a vase of flowers to make their kitchen pretty, his wife cooking was enough. He didn't need another wardrobe to hold his clothes. He wanted to hold *her.* That was all he'd ever wanted. Why couldn't she appreciate it, the boundless depth of his love?

But the words curled inside him, drowned by hers. *I want to feel like — something lighter, something more free and beautiful and untamed than I am now.* Flashes of soft butterfly wings fluttered behind his eyelids.

"Do you understand, Fabian?"

He blinked. Those seashells above her head turned on their strings, but did not touch each other, and so were silent. "I understand," he said. "I want you to feel like a b- to feel beautiful too, darling."

She did not reply, only rose from her seat and wafted toward the kitchen, wispy like wind. He could hear her clanging in their cupboards and fridge, bringing out wrapped tuna and a knife. He could hear the metal of the knife slicing through scales and skin, the smell of innards floating into the living room. Fabian only stared down at his fishing calluses.

I feel like a rock. Did she really think all his fishing and hard work and love only amounted to rocks? Was she really so cold to his efforts?

Long after the knives quit chopping, he heard the sudden disappearance of his wife and the padded prowling of some creature that took her place. But for all his curiosity, he did not look back to see what his wife, in her disguised grief, had transformed into this time. He only knew that no butterfly was about to flutter over to him and rest gently, silently on his shoulder.

Fabian lugged his empty fishing bag through Camber, past the barber shop and post office and butcher's, all vacant in the grayish night. His footsteps splashed in cobblestone mud. He didn't know why he was making his usual daytime trek through town in the dead of night, especially when he'd spent the last few weeks simply staring at the sea, not brave enough to face fishing with his wife disappeared. But he'd heard the fishermen talk of her performing again and wanted to know, wanted to *see* her one more time....

Up ahead, lights and shouts from Patty's Tavern grew with every step. Music, clapping, hollering, a man stumbling onto cobble with his boots on his hands. Fabian slunk to the open front door and peered inside, where an audience was roaring and hooting, circled around a spectacle in the center of the bar.

She danced and twirled and morphed. She was a spinning wheel, polished, rotating, churning out strands that a few men reached forward to touch... Fabian felt a sharp prick of jealousy... and then the thread was gone. The men staggered forward, fell on their knees to the roar of audience laughter, and there was a split moment when Fabian saw his wife again, her glowing face and upturned smile and brief mien of concentration, the pearl necklace he'd made for her still dangling around her neck.

Then she was a violin playing itself, a bluebird that screeched and spiraled into a waterfall of buttons, which exploded and clattered to the rotted floorboards. A single button rolled to the doorway. Fabian bent to pick it up, but just as he touched the button's smooth, rounded edge, it disappeared between his fingers, and in the center of the bar there was suddenly a fishing boat, rocking as if on a boiling sea.

She knew he was there. Knew his touch.

The empty fishing sack slipped through Fabian's fingers. He left it there, left it at the open doorway where his wife was performing, and staggered around like a drunk, away from the tavern, back toward his home. The world spun around him. Shapes bloomed in the darkness — buttons, birds, spinning wheels, flowers, teapots. Even the eyes of some nighttime cat seemed to glow green in the darkness between two run-down houses. Fabian yelled at them. The eyes blinked and vanished, but other shapes continued to blossom in the darkness, haunting Fabian until he made it to his doorway. He reeled inside and ran to his bed, where, for a moment, he thought he saw his wife's sleeping figure breathing on the bedsheets.

But no, she was long gone, entertaining other men, transmuting into other things.

Fabian stumbled to their closet and rummaged through shoes, coats, dresses, anything that his wife might like to turn into, anything that he could pretend was her until morning. He knew she would never morph into anything simple; his fingers clasped something cold, and he pulled out an old candlestick she had used to hold candles during winter storms. With its twisted, ornate silver twining around the hilt, the candlestick was intricate enough that it would do. Fabian brought it to his bedside and gently placed it on his wife's pillow.

Then he crawled into bed. The coldness pressed in all around him, but he looked at the candlestick where his wife should be, and its shape comforted him.

"Goodnight, my love," he said to the candlestick. It did not reply, but he placed his fingers on its silver and soon found himself sinking into dreams, dreams where his wife was not betraying him in the tavern; instead, she drifted back home to lie by his side once more.

He awoke to her meow.

He mumbled, reached out across his pillow, found the cold hilt of the candlestick. Something wet touched his hand. He opened his eyes to see a cat staring at him on its haunches — his wife, *his wife was finally back*. Fabian's chest leapt with a burst of adrenaline. He wiped his eyes and sat up to look at the cat better.

But his wife was always a sleek, black cat when she morphed, not this dirty tabby nudging his hand, its ears crooked and nose scarred.

"What...?" Fabian asked. The cat jumped off his bed, knocking the candlestick to the floor.

Perhaps she had aged so much that her cat form had aged too. Fabian tried to think back to the last time his wife had become a cat and couldn't recall. Suddenly he wished very much that he had turned around to see what she had become in the kitchen the day she'd left.

The cat yowled, racing into the living room and out his front door, which Fabian must have left wide open last night. He staggered after it, every step making his stomach plummet as he realized that the cat was not his wife, and the candlestick was not his wife, and all the chairs and windows and outside trees were not his wife. When he saw the tabby waiting for him in his rock garden, he could have kicked it away.

But then he noticed what was resting at the tabby's feet in the rocks, like a mouse that the cat had dragged to his doorstep as a prize: his wife's pearl necklace.

"What did you do to her?" Fabian said slowly, bending to pick up the necklace. The cat meowed again. Fury tumbled inside him. "*Where is she?*" he said. "*Where the hell is my wife?*"

The cat turned and streaked down his yard toward Camber.

Fabian ran after it, past all his neighbors' houses and onto the main street of the town, through the daytime vendors who shoved flower seeds and shish kebabs and painted seashells in his face.

The cat weaved through the crowd, past the dry and emptied Patty's Tavern, shooting down a shabbier, muddier avenue, where hedges lined the yards of run-down hovels. Fabian followed it to the furthest hut, where the cat slipped inside the open doorway and meowed a greeting to whoever was stirring inside.

"Fabian Vitalik?" somebody called.

"Who...?"

A man from beyond the open doorway shifted, then emerged onto his front steps with a wan smile. Fabian recognized, with a jolt, the town herbalist, whom he'd only ever met once at a neighborhood funeral.

"Come in, Fabian Vitalik," the herbalist said with a beckoning hand. "Your wife — she is here."

Fabian did not hesitate as he ran into the depths of the house after the man. Soil caked the floor, moss was growing on the molding, and sunlight surged through a vast open window toward the back of the house. Sitting on an earthy rug below this window, surrounded by an array of plants in clay pots, was his wife. She was human.

She was also swaying, as if to music that Fabian couldn't hear.

"Darling," Fabian said, but the herbalist put a hand on his shoulder. The cat was twisting itself around his wife's rocking body, meowing.

"We found her in an alleyway last night, Fabian Vitalik, soaking wet and unable to speak. My little helper here —" He nodded at the cat. "— is adept at sniffing out illnesses, and brought me to her. I believe she has suffered some kind of stroke from excessive shifting."

Fabian clutched the pearl necklace tighter. The herbalist moved toward a rounded table, where he swept a hand across bowls of powder and jars of dark green liquid. "I have given her turmeric stewed at midnight, but she still won't speak. Ashwaganda ground in halibut. Thyme and flax seeds. Her condition has not changed. She has the mind of a three-year-old, and I fear —"

"— Darling," Fabian said again, crouching low, not wishing to hear the rest of the herbalist's prediction. His wife looked up at him. Docile eyes. A sweet expression that softened her wrinkles. She would not stop swaying.

"She needs someone to take care of her, Fabian Vitalik. I fear she will not get better." The herbalist crouched beside him and peered into her face. "She certainly cannot shift anymore, and if she attempted to it would be catastrophic. She needs fed, bathed, dressed, put to bed —"

"She's not my wife anymore," Fabian said for the first time. "She left me. Somebody else has to take care of her." He felt the coldness rush up his spine at these words, desire and anger clashing like crests against a boat. His wife smiled sweetly at him, and he felt bile in his throat. If he had just stayed at Patty's Tavern last night and stopped her from continuing to perform... of course she would have hated him for it, but she *already* hated him.

The herbalist was watching him steadily. His wife swayed like waves.

"There is no one else to take care of her, Fabian. No one else that cares for her when she is stuck in this form."

"She left me," Fabian said again, the pearl necklace in his hand slipping in sweat. He did not want this to be so valid an excuse that she couldn't stay with him, but he wanted an apology, a sad sheen of understanding in her eyes, some subtle sign that she was sorry, and that even if she had not gotten sick, she would be returning to him.

But vacancy stayed spewed across her face.

"She is the mother of your children," the herbalist said gently.

And at this, Fabian felt himself break down. Of course. Of course he would take her in. He would slave over her until she got better, because she *had* to get better. And then he would let her go, for surely, even if she couldn't shift, she would want to leave him again when she healed.

"Fabian," the herbalist said, as if in reply to his thoughts. The tabby meowed. "She *mustn't* try to shift. I doubt she would be able to, but if she *did* manage it... she would be stuck. Stuck in another form forever."

"There'd be no way of bringing her back?" Fabian asked, finally standing up. He tried to imagine his wife stuck in her cat form, or worse — some kind of inanimate object. A decoration, or a candlestick.

The herbalist bowed his head. "If she shifted, there would be no way of bringing her back, no."

A cloud must have passed over the sun, because in that moment, the room was cloaked in eerie, greenish shadows. Fabian bent, strung the pearl necklace around his wife's neck once more, and heaved her into his arms. She allowed this as if she were little more than a rag doll. Fabian started toward the door, then hesitated.

"Isn't there anything that can be *done*? She — she hates her human body." His wife seemed to feel the tremor that ran through him, because although she did not stop smiling, a flicker of unease ran across that strangely vacant face.

"As far as concoctions go, none that I know of. Just love her, Fabian Vitalik."

Fabian nodded, turned away from the herbalist and the cat, and stepped back into broad daylight. His wife's dead weight threatened to bring him to his knees, but he did not stop carrying her, not when he made it to Camber's main street again, not when pedestrians stopped their market trading to stare. He hauled his wife all the way to their house at the shore, sweat beading on his forehead. When he finally made it through their rock garden and set her down underneath their string of seashells, she began swaying again.

His wife was back.

Yet Fabian wanted her to be capable of talking. Of shifting. Of leaving him again. Because only if she was capable of leaving would her staying mean she loved him back.

Shouts, music, and the clanking of glasses washed over him in a buzzing void, but Fabian, sitting at the bar in Patty's Tavern, concentrated on one sound. A pepper-haired man was giggling as he and some comrades danced around an empty plastic pail by the smoke pit, chanting, "Shape-shifter, shape-shifter, alter faster! Quicker! Swifter!" They hooted, hollered, whistled like they had that first night Fabian had peeked into the bar, and eventually a guitarist began strumming his instrument in tune to the mantra. Soon, so many men turned on their stools that half the bar was singing to the plastic pail, slopping beer down their shirts, believing the pail to be Fabian's wife.

"You know what I think?"

A woman slid onto the stool next to him. Tall, long legs. Her jacket swelled where it buttoned up over her breasts, and oh, she smelled good, like lilacs and shellfish and wine. His wife used to smell like that, whenever Fabian would come home exhausted and lay his head down on her lap and listen to her hum songs.

"Well, if you're not going to answer," the woman said, fingering her shot glass, and now, at last, Fabian was zeroed in on something other than those wretched men fawning over a plastic pail. "The name's Zoey. And that bucket was being used to catch a leak in the roof long before those assholes came in. If you ask me, the shape-shifter's anywhere but here. After that one fiasco last month? I'd say she's out of the continent."

Fabian grunted, took a swill out of his mug as he pictured the shape-shifter lying on his bed half a mile away, taking her daytime nap, very much in the continent. A word surfaced to his brain.

"Fiasco?" he repeated.

"Yeah, I was there." The woman brought her glass to her lips and drained it in one gulp. She wiped her lips. "The girl — well, she's more an old lady now — she was performing, you know? And she was turning into all kinds of things, vines and animals and all that drat. She said to get ready for her grand finale, that she was going to turn into wind — and then she just... exploded. Into all these butterflies"

"Exploded into butterflies," Fabian said. In his mind, he heard, *I want to feel like a butterfly again,* although he wasn't sure if his wife had actually said it or if he had simply fabricated those words in his mind.

"Yes, and the butterflies began twirling like a tornado. Almost wind, but not quite. Only, the tornado was screaming. God, it hurt my ears. Then the whole thing just disappear — hey! Where are you going?"

Fabian had fished into his pocket, smacked some coins on the counter, and started toward the door, leaving the woman and her long legs behind. Once out on the street, he targeted the peddler's cart that sold flower seeds, and asked the vendor which flowers attracted butterflies.

For the past few weeks, he had been trying to get his wife to talk. Shifting would be, as the herbalist put it, catastrophic, but *talking*? Fabian had thought she'd find her voice again if he read to her, but maybe she needed a reminder of what was beautiful before she found herself again. Maybe she needed butterflies in their garden instead of rocks.

Once the vendor had sold him a packet of daylily seeds, Fabian hurried to the house, where his wife would be waking up from her nap. He left the seeds on the kitchen table and rushed into the bedroom, where his wife was sitting up in bed, swaying, smiling pleasantly.

"Hello, beautiful," Fabian said, opening the window blinds to let sunlight through. "Are you hungry? I've finally gone fishing again, and I found some mussels with nice, hearty meat in them. You love mussels, remember? And I have a surprise for you, too. It might take a while — they need to grow first, but you're going to love it."

His wife just smiled.

Fabian began his usual routine of setting his wife near the sofa where he slept at night, cooking, cleaning, talking to her as if he expected a reply. Occasionally, when he had the spare money, he would buy some paper and finger paints and place them on the floor in front of her. These were the only times she would finally quit swaying, dip her fingers into the paints, and create.

The pictures were crude, to say the least, as if a toddler had painted them. But Fabian had still been able to decipher wind, fire, earth. Today, as he popped open the mussels and set them over a small kitchen fire to sizzle, she was drawing a distorted ocean. Sun glaring down on miniature whitecaps, seashells as big as ships, curling, spiraling waves.

It happened after feeding her supper and taking the trash out. Fabian came back inside to find his wife's pictures abandoned on the floor. For one jolting moment, he thought she was gone.

Then he saw her swaying in the kitchen. She was sitting neatly in their tarnished tin tub that he bathed her in at nights. Her clothes were in a pile on the floor, so that only her pearl necklace gleamed on her bare chest.

"It's not bath time yet, darling," Fabian said, shaken. He started forward to pick up her clothes and dress her when a change flashed over her face. A frown. Then that soft, sweet smile again. But for a brief moment, he had seen the crunch of her eyebrows, that concentration she wore when she was trying to shift.

"How about we just have bath time now, then?" Fabian said slowly. But even as he walked toward the faucet, he saw that flash of concentration again, heard the small whimper escape her mouth. They stared at each other. His wife's smile was still etched on her face, but the corners of her mouth were quivering. And suddenly, Fabian knew that he needed to plant those seeds *now*.

"I'll be right back," he whispered, backing away. "*Right* back. Please don't go anywhere."

He grabbed the packet of seeds from the table and in a flash, leaving his wife in the tub, was on his knees in the rock garden. The sky overhead was churning and the sea's high tide was a sharp crash in his ears, but Fabian dug rock after rock out of the dirt and threw them to the side. He felt the sharp plop of water on the back of his neck, but he welcomed the rain that splashed onto the soil beneath his fingers.

"Butterflies," he murmured, ripping open the packet and pouring beetle-black seeds onto his palm. He dug into the dirt, feeling the prickle of time pepper his head, as if he could only save his wife by planting fast enough. He dropped the seeds into those little cavities in the earth, covered them back up, and stood, panting.

His front door was still ajar.

Fabian crept back into the doorway and peered inside, where the shadowed sky cloaked their living room and kitchen in dim shades. His wife's picture was flapping in a sudden wind that swooped past Fabian, into the house. Her clothes still lay discarded on the floor.

But the tarnished tub was empty.

"Hello? Where — where are you, darling?" Fabian called. The paper flapped, moving across the floor. The sea still sounded in his ears, but otherwise there was no sound.

Fabian moved further inside and called his wife's name. He went into the bedroom, but she was not there either. And now his heart was crashing in his chest, and he began racing to every corner of the house, calling for her, trying to find her again, and the sound of the sea was slapping against the shore, slapping against tin...

Against tin?

Fabian halted. He turned, looked at the tub still sitting in the kitchen. The slapping sound was coming from the tub's direction, so Fabian took a step toward it, then another. When he was finally hovering over it, he looked down and saw that the tub was not, as he had thought, empty.

Water was sloshing inside, sloshing as if desperate to free itself. His wife's pearl necklace bobbed on the uneasy surface, tossed back and forth by miniature waves.

Fabian fell with a thud to his knees. He clutched the edge of the tub and moaned into it. The water shuddered, rippled, whirled like the sky and sea outside.

If she shifted, there would be no way of bringing her back, the herbalist had said. When Fabian had thought of all the things she might turn into, he had pictured animals, objects... things he could continue to protect and serve if need be. He had never imagined *water,* wild and ancient, something he could not contain even if he wanted to.

But deep within himself, he had known she would never be satisfied in her human form. Not when the whole world waited for her.

Love her, the herbalist had said.

So Fabian grabbed hold of the edge of the tub, dragging it across his living room and over the threshold of his front door. The cleared circle of soil in their garden was soaking up the rain, but his wife would never see it. Never see it, unless —

The tub flinched forward in his hands, her water centimeters from slopping over the edge and splashing onto the soil.

He could water the flowers with her, and when the first buds poked through the earth, when the first petals uncurled themselves, stretching toward the sun, they would *be* her. The butterflies that came to rest gently, silently among the flowers would be her, too, and when he drank coffee on his morning porch he might feel their weightless presence rest upon his shoulder, as if his wife was touching a delicate hand on him once more...

Love her, the herbalist had said.

He just wanted to *be* with her, but she wanted to be a butterfly, or something like a butterfly, free, beautiful, untamed, always stationed in his garden, always with him...

The realization bubbled up inside Fabian just as he was tipping the tub to pour it over his seeds. She did not want to be a butterfly captive in a garden. She never had. She had morphed into an element for a reason.

Love her, love her, love her.

Fabian looked down into the contents of the tub, saw her water drinking up the rain. He had always loved her how he wanted to love her, not how she wished to be loved.

With a sudden surge of will, he put both hands on either side of the tub and lifted the whole thing. It was heavier than his wife's human weight, but he blundered toward the roiling shore, the tub pressed up against his chest, the sound of her waves mingling with the sea's. Pebbles turned to sand. Water lapped up to his boots. Sea foam sprayed his cheeks like tears.

Fabian collapsed. The tub overturned on its side, and he watched as the water within gushed out, joining with the sea he loved.

The pearl necklace caught on the tub's handle, and for a moment, Fabian had an urge to snatch it, to keep that last remnant of his wife.

But he found his fingers untangling it, feeding it to the sea. The waves dragged it underwater and out of sight, and then she was truly gone, freed as she had always desired. He exhaled, touched his lips to the surface of the water to give her a last kiss.

Then he retreated, leaving the tub lying by the shoreline, using the last of his strength to get to his feet and limp back to the house alone. Once inside, he eased the door shut and looked past the string of seashells out the window. In that garden, flowers would still grow. Butterflies would come to rest among them, although they would only be fluttering reminders of what he had wanted his wife to be.

But past the garden, Fabian would always be able to see his wife in her true form: a dazzling ocean, swaying, untamed, free — constantly ebbing to kiss the shoreline where he'd stand.

About the story

I first started writing "The Wife of Fabian Vitalik" after hearing a few real-life stories about husbands or wives who left their spouse after several years of marriage (these were situations where the split seemed entirely one-sided). I wanted to explore the concept of separation – what makes someone leave? What makes someone stay? Of course, Fabian's wife had to be a shape-shifter, to emphasize how some people are constantly changing while others never change at all.

A question for the author

Q: Do you read more fantasy or SF (hard or soft)?

A: While SF is something I'd love to delve into, I definitely read more fantasy. My high school math teacher once told the class that he loves calculus because you can find real answers by using non-real numbers. Well, I think fantasy is like that too: we find truths within non-truths, and reality within magic.

About the author

Mariah Montoya is a contemporary and fantasy writer from Idaho. When not reading or writing, she currently spends her days trooping to college classes, eating oatmeal, and rambling to friends and family about weird ideas.

You can find her on Instagram at @mariah_author.

Mariah Montoya's story "The Wife of Fabian Vitalik" was published in *Metaphorosis* on Friday, 24 November 2017.

December

The Cure for Cancer

Ryan Fitzpatrick

The cure for cancer exists. It can be found in the Mato Grosso region of Brazil, an intertropical convergence zone in the heart of the country. Due to the minerals and nutrients blown in from both the North and the South Sea, the area is covered in a thick blanket of rainforest, making the region rich in a biodiversity that extends not only to flora and fauna, but to other, harder to classify biota.

The cure for cancer grows, when the conditions are right, in the cell membrane of a rare and specialised fungus, belonging to the class of Basidiomycota known as Polypores. The conditions for the fungus to reach maturity are extraordinarily singular, and contribute to its sparse numbers. For example, because the fungus is saprotrophic and seeks its nutrients from decaying matter, the fallen tree on which it grows must meet the following criteria; dry yet near water; sheltered from rain, but unobstructed from the suns rays for eleven of the twelve hours it gives in this part of the world; and outside of the borders of any Capuchin or Tamarin tribes, both of which have evolved to find the hymenium of the polypore to be something of a delicacy.

However, in a cruel twist of biological fate, the polypore cannot survive the journey through the intestinal tract of either of these species. The fungus has also not evolved to feature basidiospores, and as such, its spore dispersal is limited and localised.

Due to these facts, the entire colony of the unnamed polypore can only be found in a thirty centimetre circle on the bark of a fallen rosewood, sheltered by a tilted rock and tucked into a bend of one of the Rio Negro's many unmarked tributaries.

To extract the cure, the plant must be harvested approximately one week before it reaches maturity. The husk-like casing of the ruptured volva must then be picked, peeled, and dried, preferably under laboratory conditions to avoid contamination. However, open air drying would work too if necessity demanded it. Either way, this initial stage of the process can take between twelve and fifteen days, and visual indicators (a browning of the volva and a curling of the stem) will indicate when the fungi are ready for the next step.

When fully dried, the husks of the fungi should be removed and the remains discarded. The collected husks should then be crushed or blended into a fine dust and soaked in an aqueous solution of methylecgonidine. After three days (stored at room temperature in a dark space), the liquid should be passed through a neutral paper filter cloth to leave a dark, tea coloured liquid. It should be viscous in consistency.

The remaining mixture should be boiled at 95°C in sterilized equipment and the condensate collected and refrigerated. The mixture can then be administered intravenously in diminishing doses until the cancer is in remission. The remaining liquid can be ingested orally (either in pill or liquid form) or via transdermal patch. Long term use will complete the treatment, and the patient will be cancer free.

This is a relatively simple extraction process for medication, and although the conditions of the fungi's growth are rare in the wild, they are easily recreated in the lab. What's more, with only a few generations of selective breeding, the fungus could be made to be more potent and faster acting, making it a cheap and reliable source of continued good health for the 8.8 million sufferers of cancer per year.

But no man has yet discovered this, and it is possible that no man will.

A low rumbling sounds out across the landscape and birds scatter. It is the sound of gasoline combusting inside an engine.

A three-toed sloth moves sluggishly in the opposite direction, crossing the forest floor in a calculated but rare moment of risk. Her elongated claws, mottled as they were with patches of moss, lightly caress the group of fungi, knocking a few from the fallen trunk and into the mud. A few moments later and the sloth is gone, seeking refuge in the comparative safety of the tree tops.

If the sloth were sentient enough to be poetic, she might see the tree on which she now drowses as the mast of a sinking ship, the lookout for an ever diminishing life boat. In the distance – although not as distant as yesterday – the harvesters and forwarders continue their purge of the rainforest, pushing deeper, leaving behind them a wake of palm oil production.

The sloth closes her eyes, the buzzing of the far away machines lulling her into easy sleep. Beneath, predators and prey alike continue to cling to the lifeboat, battling for space as the walls close in around them. In the centre of it all, the Rio Grande, sometimes fast, sometimes slow, continues its unending journey. The cure for cancer awaits its fate.

A question for the author

Q: What would your animal totem be?

A: Totem (noun): a natural object or animal believed by a particular society to have spiritual significance and adopted by it as an emblem.
(Thanks, the Oxford English Dictionary Online!)

I'm not sure about spiritual significance, but I can tell you that I have a bit of a thing about sloths. Three-toed or two-toed, brown-throated or pale-throated, I love 'em all, and if you've read my short piece The Cure for Cancer, you'll notice that the slow-moving, moss-covered bradypodidae makes an appearance right there amongst the foliage, brushing up against the eponymous mushroom itself.

A couple of years ago, when I released my first few solo pieces of music into the world (spoiler: I'm not very good), I chose a cartoon picture of a sloth as the tracks 'album art'. When I should be writing but I begin to doodle instead, it's a sloth I draw. And, when I worked in Peru, for a few short minutes I was elated to finally see one in the flesh; a disappointingly shapeless brown blob at the top of a distant tree.

Oh well.

I don't know what it is about them. I love animals in general, and can barely fall asleep without the soothing tones of a nature documentary somewhere in the background. Learning about the natural world is bad ass, and I suppose I could have chosen any animal to rub up against the cure for cancer in my story. But I didn't.

I chose a sloth. And maybe that's enough to make it my totem.

About the author

Ryan Fitzpatrick lives and writes in the UK. His work has previously been published by *Every Day Fiction, Hinnom Magazine,* and *Nthanda Review.*

Ryan Fitzpatrick's story "The Cure for Cancer" was published in
Metaphorosis on Friday, 1 December 2017.

Sharpington Coffers – Current Score: 49.8

Erik Goldsmith

A perfunctory stare hovers above the counter of Sharpington Coffers, a small antique store on the south side of Picadilly Circus. The owner of the stare, one Mr. Bartholomew Sharpington, watches his entrance with the patience of the rat catcher, waiting outside a hole for his prey, his customer, who will be walking through those doors… any… second… now. *Ching. Ching.*

A tall man in a black hat steps into the store and shakes his wet jacket onto the floor without so much as an apology. Sharpington, used to the rudeness of Londoners, pulls his cheeks up into a smile as if…

I can't seem to finish the analogy here. He smiles as if… what?

Some Notes for Future Revision:
- Get rid of the words "perfunctory," "of the store," and "rat catcher" (instead say, "… with the patience of a cat." Or "a cat's patience." Pick one.)
- Get rid of "without so much as an apology." Unnecessary.
- Do you need the *Ching Ching?*
- Don't forget, the Insta-Karma people said that when you remove his visor, make sure the red light is off, even if his identity doesn't take, otherwise the degeneration might accelerate. DON'T FORGET.

A stare hovers above the counter of Sharpington Coffers, a small antique store on the south side of Picadilly Circus. The owner, one Mr. Bartholomew Sharpington, watches his entrance with the patience of a cat waiting outside a hole for its prey, for his customer, who will be walking through those doors… any… second… now.

A tall man in a black hat steps into the store and shakes his wet jacket onto the wooden floor. Sharpington, used to the rudeness of Londoners, pulls up his cheeks into a smile as if editing this story might take your mind off it... Why are you still trying to fix it anyway? It's just that... *Sharpington Coffers* isn't going to be published... The 30 polite, but canned rejection letters seemed to be saying as much... not quite what they're looking for, they said... *Not quite,* as if my story just slipped their version of acceptable by a thin margin, as if a human being had actually read it, as if they hadn't just noticed it's 49.8, and chunked it in the fucking garbage... I spent an hour on that last sentence... Flawless.

I don't know if you know this, but the qualifying score to be considered a creative person is a fucking 50.00; if your story scans below that, well... We all keep the Creativity Aggregator a secret from the public, but every publication uses the machine to scan the new writers... It works better than an intern, but something is definitely lost without the human touch... At the office, we set the bar at 50, but I had hoped, I guess... I had just hoped, for my own sake, that a CA score of 50 wasn't the industry standard... It's hard not to take the score personally. Some writers can score above a 60 *consistently...* even without having editorial access to a CA... But I do have access, and it took four different re-writes and a bunch of antiquated words just to get *Sharpington Coffers* up from a 49.7... And honestly, I don't even know if it's better for the effort, over-edited doesn't seem like the right word... I've stranged it... combed out every redundancy, every derivation... every similarity to anything in the Library of Congress's database, syntax, flights of language, algorithms of style and word frequency... I know how the machine works, I just can't seem to game it...

When he was still him, Dad told me that the creativity aggregator might make people forget the value of simplicity... I think he meant it as encouragement, but I took it poorly... My story's not simple, I said. None of my stories are simple, I said. But he merely shrugged and told me it wasn't a bad thing... I didn't get what he was saying until it was too late for me to say so... At the time, I just couldn't bring myself to... turn my head towards the right way of looking at it or... I don't know, it's hard to say, and maybe that's my fucking problem. Maybe, you're just not good at this shit... or at least not good enough to write a 9,486 word murder mystery set in Victorian fucking London... The cannibal twist isn't interesting, Sharpington's character is dead on arrival, and no one even remembers what a bicycle is, let alone a torture device made out of one... I can't even remember the story's original score.

A good writer should be able to sense when the creative winds are strong enough to spin the blades of the mill and when they are nothing but a capricious breeze trembling the sails. A good writer would know the difference and a better writer would know when to quit. They'd be able to sense their own lack of subtlety; their inability to penetrate a psychology other than their own... Can a good writer ignore the distortion of self-appreciation? A great writer would be able to feel their entire mechanism faltering under the strain of the task, and just... A non sequitur: Why is it so hard to get published? It seems an odd question to intrude among pretentious speculation, like it jumped the queue, or was the pretentious speculation merely a disguise to hide insecurity... I can fucking hear him... through the wall, I can hear him moaning something about wolves... it sounds so fucking awful, he can't sleep... the visor must be hurting him...

Hector told me he got one for his mom... He said her dementia was gone in the first 6 hours. Now, he says, she walks around the house griping at him about laundry and his ex-wife, which are both totally legitimate concerns as far as Hector goes... He says it's given him a fresh take on annoyance... But, he was lucky... The Insta-Karma people told us we'd know if the visor works within the first 48 hours... It's been 36. After the first 48, the window closes... some identities, they said, for *whatever reason,* can't be re-read once they've slipped away... I'm gonna try to sleep.

I can't sleep... **11 hours**.

I've been staring at the words above my cursor for a while now, and I think I like them better than the 9,500 below it... That's not a good sign... I've been trying to think of something more to say, rubbing my forehead... I don't know why I might need to find some coherence in all this... Fuck, isn't that what that group counselor told you, that you need to externalize... I can't even finish the sentence...

"You're a writer, why don't you try writing it down?" she said. Make something coherent out of what's going on with your life. It'll give you a context for all this, and maybe it'll provide you with a sense of control... She didn't say that last part actually, I just wish she had, but she didn't, because it's probably not true... I need some coffee... I'm going to get coffee...

I'm back... Let's pretend me needing coffee and rubbing my head's enough context for all this... sitting here, drinking coffee... talking to myself... listening to him moan about wolves... pretending this is all a fucking story... Wolves... Is he remembering?

He showed it to me a long time ago, one of the few stories he let me see... What was it? ... A man playing in the snow at night and a wolf. The man was making snow angels with his son, looking up at the stars, and then suddenly a white wolf is standing over both of them. The man rolls on top of the boy, crushing him into the snow, and starts yelling at the wolf to go away. The boy is crying underneath him and tries to push him off, but the dad is too heavy... Stop Moving... I remember Dad stretched the scene out way too long, and made it seem like the boy was suffocating, but he kept using words like "almost" and "just about" for pages. And then with a single sentence the wolf leaves and that's it. "Suddenly, the white wolf padded away and didn't look back." No fireworks, no climax, the wolf just runs away. Or something like that, it's here somewhere... Then they just walk home and the man apologizes to the son and then it ends... I told him it read like a pastoral tone poem, hiding my derision with college. He told me I didn't get it... It's on this computer somewhere.

They scanned it and every other hard drive we had in the house, all our photos, his buying habits, where we've lived, all his unpublished stories, all of it, right before strapping him into a brain scanner... fuck they made me talk to him about mom, while he writhed around, confused... 4 MRI's... We even had to sit across from that young asshole in VR goggles, pantomiming around my father's entire life from the inside, just in case he had a question for us... Did we really need to be there for that?... I suppose digital information can only contain so much information... Is that funny?

By the end of it, the technician printed out an approximate neural map of what my Dad's brain looked like before it deteriorated. I remember staring at it, offended by its visibility. When I asked my Dad if he still wanted to go through with it, to try and remember, he said he did. They fitted him for the Identity Keeper visor, downloaded the map into it, took all my money, and sent us home with a box full of foam packaging.

Some of it spilled on our rug when I pulled the visor out... I remember he took it from my hands, set it in his lap, and intentionally, I know he did, refused to acknowledge it. I remember him turning his head... toward nothing, an open doorway maybe, and interlocking his fingers across his stomach, a familiar posture in the house. Maybe, he remembered sitting with the technician; I wasn't sure, but I let him hold for a few moments. Then I took it back... and put it on his head, and the man. fucking. winced... I saw it. He winced. I couldn't believe it... He didn't tell that fucking technician the visor was hurting him, he told him it felt fine. "Really?" the boy asked. "Usually we have to adjust it..." He let us go home with it after almost no alterations. It's probably still hurting him. I tried to adjust it myself and he made this fucking noise... I've been listening to it all day, this noise, letting it feed me a steady drip of stress at the office... Obviously it wasn't just physical discomfort, because he was smiling too when he made it, but... Imagine you understand the perversity of this situation without knowing the context, or our relationship, which I don't have the skill to adequately express. He moaned because he thought I'd find it funny and he was in pain and he couldn't remember what was going on, but he remembered just enough to be stressed the fuck out. All of it... What time is it? He's got 10 hours... I'll have to call in to work soon, tell them I'm not coming in... They won't need me tomorrow anyway... The whole thing's formatted already. After our editor's meeting, I spent most of today locked in the VR server, updating our author's databases, sending out teaser blurbs about the 8 stories, going over the check list, watching to see if that girl got any branches... **10 hours**...

We got lucky this month. Three giant authors, all-frequencies no less, reached out to our publication in the same week and we snatched them up without reading them. Tremendously well written stories by today's top authors:

1. Johnny Grab - The You in the Light Switch – 4,300 words. - *"A subtle elegy on the various ways one might see death differently... not positively, differently."* (64.8)
2. Obri Okafor - Images of Neo-Glasnost – 8,000 words. - *"Gorgeously worded barbs of deceit and intrigue wrapped around a post-modern essay on contemporary politics."* (59.9)
3. Mia Paladucci - A Tremor Nearer – 2,400 words. - *"Too often short fiction allows us a reprieve from our present day problems without easing us back into the real world, but Paladucci's prose provides us both an escape and return passage back to our own lives, better for the trip."* (60.3)

"The first two are fine, but the Paladucci blurb needs to be re-written. I'm surprised you didn't catch it, Frank." The head editor says this to me in front of the other editors.

"What's wrong with it?" I ask.

"It's just generic, son." he says. "Not incisive." he says. "Keep the alliteration." he says. "Lose the shittiness." he says.

I immediately start re-writing it while he discusses a formatting issue with the Johnny Grab story. I realize my editor sounds like a shitty character; would be a shitty character if it were fiction, and I wonder if it's because I don't understand him; wouldn't bother trying, though. Maybe I'm a good writer after all.

3. Mia Paladucci - A Tremor Nearer – 2,400 words. *"Too often short fiction leaves the reader feeling short changed, but Paladucci's*

prose packs the same punch as a trilogy of novels... simply incredible."

"Better." He admits. "Okay, we've got 5 slots left... and 9 options. I'm assuming we've all read the picks."

There were almost 400 submissions, maybe 500, I could look up the exact number, but a small town sent us their stories ... unimaginable time and effort... And from those, the creativity aggregator decided just 9 were creative enough. It's a big time saver, designed to weed out stories that we shouldn't bother reading. Needless to say, the device cannot truly measure the worth of a good story, but I'd say a good 90% of the time, it's an accurate measure of shit... I usually read one or two of the stories that score below a 50. I've only found 3 that weren't absolute garbage... I don't know what that says about me.

Anyway.

After ditching *them,* the remaining choice is between five stories from semi-established authors with more than 100 pre-downloads and four back-ups with 0 – in other words, newbies. The newbies don't have much of a chance, since our readers customize their subscriptions. Some authors have 100 pre-downloads, some have more than 10,000 (the all frequencies), others have none. The honest truth is that most authors, as in most people, have no pre-downloads, so people, like readers and editors, overlook them. 5 stories. 5 slots. The End. The decision is a foregone conclusion, but it's our dramatic policy to vote on every story, and it's a good thing we do.

We unanimously vote for four of the five established authors without discussion, but the fifth draws debate. It is a woman with just 124 pre-downloads, hundreds less than the other 4 authors. I vote against it like the other editors do, and listen to their complaints. They found it boring. It lacked action, no real hook. They say its themes were heavy handed and the characters didn't seem realistic. One of them says, "Caricatures of archetypes... Lifeless. What is her problem?" I know what her problem is; she's in free-fall. The woman has only been published twice in 6 years, but the memory of being accepted, that sweet dopamine rush, addicted her to this gambling. She couldn't stop trying to get published, even when she began to realize those two stories were flukes. She can't stop. She's not good enough. The hurt claws from her story like a zombie, implying pain between her clumsy syntax and the many skipped words that might as well have been intentional. I say nothing and we dump it like an unread suicide note... **9 hours**.

Which leaves the newbies.

"Any of the other 4 even slightly published?" Asks our lead editor, flipping through the pages. Hector's in charge of our newbie slush pile. He shakes his head.

We look at their titles and the names of the authors. None of us have heard of any of them:

1. "The Trapeze Parallax Quandary." - Temple Ritter
2. "Shotgun Party" - Polita Valdez
3. "A Chance to Remember" - Athena Moonglow
4. "There Won't Be Much Left" - Gretchen Pull

I have no illusions about this process. The reality is that we are deciding which invisible stranger will be dancing around their kitchen in their underwear re-evaluating their own self-worth and which invisible strangers will simply sigh and remind themselves they knew it'd never happen anyway.

"Well, which story should we pick?"

None of my father's stories were ever published. Sometimes, he'd try to hint that I should publish them at my prestigious job, but I didn't bother. My reputation was tenuous as it was, considering that of the 6 editors, I am the only writer without pre-downloads of my own, so I couldn't get published there either... In fact, very few times have I been published at all. Only once at a semi-professional publication early on, a now-defunct paper magazine. It was about a cat that gets run over on a highway. It was a stupid story... When I ran it later, the creativity aggregator only gave it a 52.4, but it was mine and it was published, which is more than I can say of any of my dad's stories... **8 hours**.

"It hurts my ears."

When I tried adjusting it for him, he asked, "What is this thing, Frankie?"

"It's the Insta-Karma Identity Keeper. You wanted it, remember?"

He shrugged as if none of it mattered and looked away, cool and disaffected beneath my hands.

I remember I finished messing with it and asked, "That still hurt?" but he said nothing and interlocked his fingers.

"Hey Pops." I asked. "You said it hurt your ears... does it still hurt?"

"My ears don't hurt." He told me innocently.

Then he told me "all that" foam packaging would need to get cleaned up before I went home. I couldn't believe he said it. It wasn't the nerve of him telling me what to do, but that he thought I was leaving, that I could leave... What did he think home was? How far back did he have to go to believe I was only there for a visit? He pointed to the mess on the floor and smiled like that was the joke. To be honest, this was all his idea, he just can't remember, and this cowardly smile must be so fucking deep within him if he's still doing it by rote. The little disguise of kindness he makes when he imposes on others... My mother once told me that his kindness was never a disguise, after I delivered that line to her in the kitchen. "It's irritating how he disguises imposition with kindness." I said proudly, publishing myself in the air between us, but she overlooked the sentence's deft syntax and literary merit and just told me I didn't know shit about my father. I already knew that.

"I'll clean it up." I said.

"You made a mess."

"I know I did, Pops. s'okay."

He smiled. "It's not that big."

He winked when he said it, and I just seem to... I don't know what I was going to say there. I read over what I wrote, and I'm afraid he's coming off like a sad bastard, and I know that's a cardinal rule for writers: show, not tell, but he's not a sad bastard. He's amazing, and in person his patience still gets translated through him despite his failing mind, but somehow I can't even show it with a few fucking words... I'd have to use flashbacks from other times, of... other things in our lives that penetrated memory, experiences that might show the other side of the coin for you, make it shine underwater. My writer's impulse, another limp breeze, would like to show another flashback, a tender moment between my father and my mother, but I don't want to. I can't think of one... **7 hours**.

A good writer could... and a better writer would have realized there's no more story to tell long before and gone to sleep... They would've quit mid-way through the second paragraph and decided to move on to something else, something easier, something within their framework of experience without simply wallowing in the distortion of self-appreciation or pity, whatever that means... a better writer would make the shit with my father and my stupid job interweave, use them to make sense of the other. Do they offer contextual counterpoint? Do they amplify each other like a goddamn helix because nothing's fucking happening... When Dad finally put it on his head, the red light blinked, and so did Dad. Nothing, but something was supposed to be fucking happening, so, I looked at the instructions again, very aware of his agitation and stress. I had to yell at him not to take it off. He didn't know why he couldn't take it off. I wish he'd forget about anxiety altogether, but that never seems to leave. He's not that far gone... but it's encroaching on us, I can tell. Some secret whisper, some inside joke he's hearing out of context... In fact, Jesus, that's what it's all about, isn't it? The slow slip from context. Fragments. Dropping dishes. Staring at something uninteresting too long. I don't know. The way he starts doing some things and not doing others. Improvising... Trying to clean the food off his plate, scraping it into the sink even though he's still hungry...

It's supposed to have been cured by now. They've been telling him this his whole fucking life... Advancement after god damn advancement, just a few more years and they'd have it. The future will save you... "With VR imagery we can analyze the micro-biology of neural pathways to best determine how to restrict degeneration and possibly... " He's getting up. He's using the bathroom... At least, we're not there yet... He's got **6 hours** left and she still hasn't gotten any branches... Since, I run the publication's servers, I can monitor the database from home, but there's only so much I can do with my Dad's desktop... I had planned on buying a VR hook up so I could actually work on the server from home, but instead I bought an expensive hat... I might be able to get a cheaper one later this year, but it won't be one with the same visualization...

Interweave.

Imagine a giant globe; not outside of one, but rather inside... you're inside this giant 1,000 foot VR globe. It's filled with blinking lights all around. Thousands and thousands of different colored lights fold across your horizon. Every light is one of our subscribers, and the light's variegated color is actually code for that particular subscriber's location, among other things, like credit card information blah blah blah. But you're inside of it and it is massive. You'll have to look up because the interface doesn't let you fly around or anything, just kind of situates you at the base of the sphere in front a 1,000 foot translucent column of light that stretches all the way to the top of the globe. This simple visual is actually the... you know, just imagine I said some inscrutable techno-nonsense like most sci-fi writers do and pretend I know what I'm talking about... The file, some story we're publishing, waits beside me like a giant firefly winking soft purple and gray plush and when I pull it into the beam, it floats up the column of light towards the very center of globe. It is very beautiful, because... it's just beautiful, and as it ascends, the story stops in the globe's center, gently hovering in the air. Then, it explodes. Branches of white light burst from the author's story towards pre-downloaded subscribers, growing into a giant tree of pure light. Each branch a memory. In real life, the story is simply being uploaded into the public access servers, but in the VR space, it appears like it is being raptured up to heaven, not a joke... barely figurative. Potentially thousands of people might access it, converting it to memory, immortalizing it. It's as good a rapture as any.

I sit inside the VR globe sometimes, pretending to work, and watch the process as a little known author's story finds its readers. Unlike the automatic pre-downloads, the voluntary downloads grow, not from the story outward, but from the reader, reaching inward, like a hand. I always see it like that, like a hand, from the reader to the story. The dim beam emerges from the subscriber, a single point of color and slowly extends into the center beam, so that column and branch become one. Then they read it. Every sentence that passes through a reader's processors, makes the branch become brighter and brighter and brighter... Some readers quit midway, and after a week the beam spreads the accumulated glitter across its length, gradating the dim inwards... saving memory. Let's say I described that well enough... But, if the reader finishes the story, the beam turns into a solid white light, fully downloaded into the reader's memory banks. Once this happens, famous author or not, there is no way to tell which branches were pre-downloaded and which were voluntary. They all look alike. By the end of the month, most of our stories look like luminous pixelated trees, a shimmering digital core floating within it like a sleeping princess waiting to be kissed. Then, we flush it, waive our rights, and start again... **5 hours**.

Uploading an all-frequency is not as beautiful as uploading a story with only 500 pre-downloads, because there's no nuance to the form, no subtlety, no anticipation... just an immediate transference. They do not look like trees with branches in various states of glow, they look like fucking sunbursts. These people are so famous, that every one of our readers has digitally said, "I want any story by this author downloaded directly into my brain. No questions asked." Sometimes, I wonder if the other editors even bother reading them. I wouldn't blame them if they didn't. What would be the point? They float up and then, boom, sun. And, maybe this is the jealousy talking, but I'd bet that stories who get their branches from subscriber to story voluntarily are often better... Truth be told, I've found a few stories by all-frequencies that scored below a 50. We don't run all-frequencies through the aggregator, but I do, just to see... just like I sneak in and run my own stories... Flawless segue.

"What are the newbies' scores?"

"77.8, 58.2, 57.1, and 60.6."

"Is the 77.8 the parallax one?"

Hector nods.

"Did it gets its score for the reasons I think it did?"

He nods again.

"Well then, don't include it next time... The 60, which one's that?"

"It's called "A Chance to Remember" by Athena Moonglow?" The newbie editor's voice rises like it's a question, "It's good."

"Shitty title... Shitty fake name... Fine. We'll load it up. Does it need any work?"

"Some, but—"

"Anybody else read it?" he asks.

I did. She speaks with the voice of someone who has known real loss, her words shaped around the outlines of... absences, ghosts, things that weren't there, presences, and not just implications. She's got it... but I take too long to say so.

"No one? Well, let's upload it anyway. We're already set this month." He shrugs at the newbie editor. "Hopefully someone'll read it besides you."

Not an idle threat... I've seen a few stories go the full month without getting a single branch. They just hang there in our server for 30 days like a ghostly tree trunk, uncommitted to memory. Athena Moonglow...

I am in the doorway when Hector tells Athena Moonglow her story has been accepted. She screams so loud the display glitches and he has to call her back. She claps and agrees to everything he asks. We're addicting her to gambling, just like the woman with 124 pre-downloads. I have to leave the room. For some reason, we treat her like a professional writer and give her online access to her own download stats, so she can sit there and watch how many people read her story... or don't read her story... all month. I'm worried for her... My father was so cavalier about his own rejections. It wasn't that the editors didn't get it, he'd say, it was that they couldn't... He's moving around again, I can hear the mattress creaking... Maybe it's hurting his ears again, maybe it got roughed by the pillow when he came from the bathroom. I tried tilting it before he went to bed so that the diodes weren't rubbing against his temple, but then he started telling me a story about something he and mom did a few years ago... Then, he looked around and asked me about her... wondered where she was. I started to make something up, then I just said I didn't know, which was the truth, and let him go... **4 hours**.

Let's say I manage to tie these two narratives together into a satisfying conclusion. If I were a better writer though, I'd just stop now, instead of sitting here at 5 AM waiting for my dad to wake up and watching the stats for *A Chance to Remember*. It's a stupid fucking title. It's been in the public server all day and nothing. Not a single download... Athena Moonglow... A non sequitur: Why would anyone label themselves that on purpose? The name shrieks insecurity. It begs the game of Jungian shadows, right? We have to assume that Ms. Matthews, or whatever her real name is, I didn't check, would be sifting through her own potential memories, an avid reader herself, and a new name would pop across her perception, why, it's an author she's never heard of before. Athena Moonglow... 'What a name!?!' She'd think. 'This fellow goddess cloaks herself in the diction of mystery and power; therefore, her narratives must be weighted with the grace evoked from a supreme feminine majesty... just. like. me!' And then, Ms. Matthews would instantly download the new author's story simply because of the name, Athena Moonglow... The name surely echoes when you say it out loud. This young girl, watching her screen, refreshing the page again and again... The worst part was the sight of her stupid novelty glasses bobbing around her excited face; the frames were MOON SHAPED! Imagine that. Whoever she meets, she knows the moment her fancy pseudonym drops, the mystery will begin to unravel. They'll make the connection... 'Their eyes seem to be focused on *something*,' she'd think to herself... but she knows where they're looking; what they're thinking. They are assigning her, Ms. Matthews, depth; a depth that is not suggested by her common name and her common face. Name. Glasses. Name. Glasses. She wouldn't dare draw attention to it, but she'll let them figure it out for themselves like a good author. And because she's afraid she isn't what she wants to be, she uses her glasses, just like her name, as a not-so-subtle instruction for others to know how they should see her, how colorful she is, how quirky. It's a verifiable fact, look at my fucking glasses. 'Here's a girl that has the creative spark bubbling beneath those unique rims.' She'd think they think... and we must assume that Ms. Matthews believes the rest of the world operates using that exact same inanity, opening their mouths, stretching out their sanitized tongues, waiting for the right words to trigger their

It's six in the morning. I'm holding the visor. He walked in and made me take it off him. He's back in bed now... I've put it on my own head. Don't worry, I made sure the red light was off. That'd be strange, wouldn't it? De-limited to only think and feel like my dad... used to. I could access his memories... but only the way he used to perceive them. Strange. I'm not even sure it works like that, but it sounds like an interesting story... Best to leave it for a better writer. I'm too good for it.

The thing finally uploaded his identity at 6:12 in the A.M. **Almost 45 hours later**. It worked. He woke up, himself again, and the first thing he remembered was her. My Dad, fully my Dad, made me take it off him. I tried to make my Dad keep it on, talk to my Dad, reason with my Dad, but he didn't want it and he handed it back to me, cognizant of what it meant. I couldn't help but tell him I love him, and watch him, sentient, process the words before he faded from me again... smiling all the way down. He knew it was an imposition on me.

His tree, the map of his identity... they gave me a copy of it. Oh my God, that, *A Chance to Remember,* I swear I'm not doing it on purpose like those fucking glasses... Anyway, I had the thought, at the time, that the file's programming appeared as text, or could be translated into it at least. I said so to the technician and he told me "sure." It's not farfetched. The text appears linear, from top to bottom, or rather inside-out. From core motivations outward to convictions, beliefs, contradictions toward quirk, minutiae, preference. Beginning, Middle, and End. Trunk, branch, leaf. Parts 1, 2, and 3. Each particular is punctuated with a quantized memory, the one most idiosyncratically aligned with the neural shape to serve as an example of the programming's... what... veracity? A flashback, I guess. The whole thing comes to around 6,500 words, a short story. Of course, it occurred to me to upload it.

I'd watch my father's identity, rise into the air, and witness reader after reader reach out to his story and dedicate it to their memory. The branches of light, a multiplicity, plenary apotheosis, a sycamore of pure energy goading forever to chuckle at the seed of his former limitation, until it finally became the sun itself... Or... all the more likely, no one would read it and it'll just sit there in the upload beam for a month ghosting, and then I'd get fired. It probably wouldn't get above a 50 on the aggregator anyway. That's not to say it's bad, just not original... But, I wouldn't fucking know. I'm not reading it.

Athena still has no downloads. I want to anonymously tell her that when we publish even one all-frequency, let alone three, chances are, people will venture out less. Usually, people only read one story a month. Space is a commodity... It doesn't mean her story is bad. It's just that everything unfamiliar is an unread magazine beside a mental toilet. Choice is hard. If a subscriber didn't pre-download it, they'd have to manually click on it and brave the potential for boredom without spraying pre-nostalgia all over their experience like pesticide. They'd have to decide to read something new without any memories, commercials of familiarity, providing a cozy context for the story's consumption... I'm not going to do it.

I thought about buying a subscription under my dad's name and pre-downloading Athena Moonglow, subscribing to her. She'd see it, know someone read her story, but so would the other editors. They know my name, my Dad's name, Sr. I'm not going to do it.

You know, when I first started editing *Sharpington Coffers* two years ago, I was so egotistical as to imagine that each tiny change was so profound, would be so appreciated, that I actually... I actually imagined releasing it as a book, from first draft to final draft, each re-iteration a chapter... I wonder if good writers aggrandize their own thoughts into narration, the way shitty writers do... Maybe good writers know the difference between what is story and what is simply themselves.

The visor is heavier than it looks and it's hurting my ears... I take it off and set it on some of Dad's legal junk. He's not going to wear it. I should've known. He'll never wear it... and it was so damn expensive, too. The thought makes me laugh... I'm going to bed.

Some Notes for Future Revision:
- Write an epilogue. Explain how you randomly found this file a week ago, and when you ran it through the creativity aggregator without the vestigial 9,500... IT GOT A 54.7! Talk about how you're thinking about publishing it, as is...
- Try to fix it so you don't come across like an asshole...
- Delete extraneous ellipses and the sentence fragments.
- Re-write VR process imagery without the self-conscious nonsense.
- Tie up Athena Moonglow thing. Find out how many reads she got last month, like 100 or something. Talk about how that's not bad for a new writer. (Change her name and that embarrassing title... maybe, pretend the whole thing is fiction... like you wrote it all on purpose.)
- Mention how the woman with 124 pre-downloads still hasn't published anything... Why would you do that?
- Re-iterate how you know you'll have to re-write the whole thing - Tie into the ending somehow. Should you bookend the thing by finishing the paragraph you started at the beginning?
- Pick a tense.
- Pick a point of view.
- Re-write descriptions of Dad's personality. They're not right and sound incomplete. Include a flashback with Mom, and write a better summary for his wolf story. You could do better.
- In epilogue of story, include how you've tried putting the visor on him again, but each time, 45 hours later, he makes you take it off. Talk about how you knew he would, but you do it anyway just to see him in that moment. I've done it 8 times... Don't include that. Maybe write some poetic nonsense... a happy ending?

- *"My dad was the perfect reader for his own story, but in the end, even he didn't want to read it. It didn't let him escape, but instead brought him back to reality... 4 out 5 stars."* (Revise.)
- Since it's fiction now, what is the overall task the narrator cannot seem to accomplish? His writing, some anger he can't express... Does the narrator worry whether his father knows he loves him? Can he adequately express it? (Revise thematic questions.)
- And since it's fiction now, tie the happy ending into the speculation about writing from the beginning... Is there a sense of authorship that accompanies a memory, something that brings it to life? Is that good? Tie this question of the authorship of memories throughout, and for the final paragraph, write a gentle meditation about revision, hinting at the parallel with real life... don't make it obvious.
- And since it's fiction, make it seem like the narrator got a higher score on the aggregator... 64.9 or higher... and change the title to "Wolves." It'll sound cooler.

About the story

I wanted to write something about an unknown author (like myself) and how frustrating the publishing world can be. I don't know about other people, but sometimes I get this gnawing feeling. rejection after rejection, that I'm not creative enough to published, objectively speaking; that it's not the story's fault, but my own lack of ingenuity and the editors can sense it... It's not a good feeling, but It did make me ask the question, what if publications could calculate an author's creativty? What if they could objectively measure how good one author was from another? However, as I developed this idea, I also began to realize the pettiness of it all compared to real life, and that's when it all came together. Why do we need other people's eyes to validate our thoughts, feelings, and stories; our lives? What drives this insecurity to be seen? So, I wrapped it within a story about someone losing their memories to put the need for appreciation in perspective. How different is life from a story and why do some people mix up the two? Ironically, the biggest issue I had with the story was why these words were being written at all. I think this is something that every author, famous or not, has to contend with if they write in the first person: Why is my character writing this? And consequently, why am I? Who am I talking to?

A question for the author

Q: How do pets/children/significant others help/hinder your process?

A: It's a routine. I'll be in the middle of writing, they bother me with love, I huff, then feel guilty for feeling bothered, analyze my own priorities in life, stop writing and give them my attention anyway. This process, as I get older, while still there, is becoming less and less verbalized in my house. It's healthy. And honestly, without them, I don't think my life experiences would be rich enough to create anything worthwhile at all

About the author

Erik Goldsmith is a high school English teacher in Houston. He lives with his wife and son.

Erik Goldsmith's story "Sharpington's Coffers - Current Score 49.8" was published in *Metaphorosis* on Friday, 8 December 2017.

Wytchen Wood

Lori J. Fitzgerald

A decade of shavings covered the floor of Lewys's carpentry shop. He didn't bother sweeping any more, although he probably should — wood without magic produces a drab dust that desiccates the throat, shrivels the lungs. He coughed and gulped from his flask, stepping back from his work. Carving the finishing scrollwork on yet another hope chest for the latest bride-to-be in town did nothing to fill his own hollowness.

"Wait for me," she had whispered in the wytchen grove so many years ago, her berry-scented breath caressing his cheek, "I will come back to you." She'd taken magic with her, in the wytchen dust glinting in her sunlit hair as she waved goodbye from the newly-carved wagon. She took his heart as well, but left hope in its place.

Over the years, hope had drained into loneliness, empty and aching, present in the sound of his saw's jagged edge, the taste of his own cough-strained, stale breath, the starkness of his bedroom above the shop. No chance of a bride now, for him, in this small town where he had spurned all coy glances sent his way, waiting for his true love to return.

He wished he hadn't waited.

Still coughing, Lewys threw open the window shutters. He gulped fresh air. Delighted cries of children entered with the breeze.

A pageant wagon creaked into the town square outside his shop, horseless, shedding curls of magic onto the cobblestones from its warped wytchen beams. Children dropped coins into a box attached to the wagon's carriage and scrambled for seats. Eyes widening in shock, Lewys unconsciously dug his fingernails into the windowsill. The wagon's wood was peeling, its stage floor crooked, but it was still the same one. The only one.

As the threadbare curtain opened, more wood peels and sparkling dust showered the stage from the covered wagon's rafters, a natural emission of the enchanted wood, once cut and carved. A princess puppet slumped against a painted forest backdrop. She wore a gown the deep blush of sunset, the falling wytchen dust creating a net of crystals in her golden hair. With the clack of wooden joints, she began a light, graceful dance. A troll, lumbering in from stage right, tore a gasp from the children.

Lewys saw what the audience did not know to look for: The shadow of the puppet master's hands weaving along the stage floor. These puppets had no strings. The wytchen wood itself conjured the play, the magic within the wagon and the carved puppets animating them, their movements directed from above by the puppet master's hands.

After the princess outsmarted the troll, she befriended a dragon, its velvet tongue unfurling like a panting dog. Adults and children alike cheered when she saved a village from a witch.

The curtain closed; the crowd dispersed.

Lewys grabbed his jerkin and dashed outside.

The wagon's damage looked even worse up close. Red rope secured the corners, but it was a temporary bandage for the cracked joints which exposed the wood's inner pith.

The old puppet master emerged from behind the curtain. "Master Lewys, look how well your craft weathered the years. Although, I must admit, some repairs are needed."

"Master Rhodri, you take me for my father," Lewys replied. "He is gone these last ten years. I have his carpentry business as well as his name now."

Hobbling towards him on gnarled joints as the stage boards shifted and groaned, the old man squinted at Lewys. "Aye, I remember you," Rhodri said, beckoning the carpenter to follow him into the narrow living space behind the stage backdrop.

"Is your daughter here?" His lips were dry; his heart constricted with a bare remembrance of hope.

A slow smile deepened the lines on the old man's face. "You remember Roselyn?"

The first time Lewys had seen Roselyn, she was sitting on a stump in the wytchen grove, her hair a curtain over her face and lap. He was passing through on his way further into the forest, hatchet slung over his shoulder. "My lady?" he said, approaching carefully, as he would a hare in a thicket, "Are you well?"

She looked up then, and instead of a face smudged with tears as he expected, he saw one smudged with ink from the parchment and quill in her hands. Her eyes were startled, as blue as an open sky. The sun blinked through the branches and transformed her hair into spun gold.

Lewys caught his breath.

"Indeed, I am very well," she replied. "Do you like stories?"

"What? Uh...yes. Doesn't everyone?" he stammered.

"Good!" She jumped off the stump and pocketed an inkwell that had been lying in the grass. "This one is finished. You can be our practice audience." She grabbed Lewys by the wrist and he let go of his hatchet in surprise, dropping it behind him. He spluttered a weak protest — he was supposed to meet his father for work — but the girl tugged him away, into the stand of birch trees that bordered the road into town.

"Audience for what? You don't even know me!"

"Of course I do. Father!" She shouted as they came upon an old wagon pulled into the grass on the side of the road. "The carpenter's son has agreed to see the new play!"

Lewys recognized the man sitting in the grass in front of a small fire, stirring the contents of a pot hanging from a tripod. He was an itinerant toymaker; every girl in the village had at least one of his wood and cloth dolls. Lewys himself had a painted jester on a stand, cleverly rigged to somersault when a button was pressed. It was still on a shelf above his bed, even though he was too old to play with it now.

Master Rhodri looked from his daughter to Lewys and back again. "Roselyn, are you sure..."

She pulled her father to his feet and thrust the parchment into his hands. "Look, I finished! It's the perfect story for the new puppets! Oh, be careful, it's still wet."

"All right, then," Rhodri said, pulling a handkerchief out of his vest pocket to wipe his fingers, "but only if the young man does not mind."

Lewys did not. Roselyn showed him where to sit in the grass beneath a tree, the gentle push of her hand through his shirt sending thrills along his skin. She was a flurry of activity, her bright hair and patched dress swinging to and fro as she fetched the puppets and whispered to her father as he studied the parchment. The puppets were exquisitely carved, like all the dolls Rhodri made, but these had moveable joints and strings, each attached to a cross of wood. Their hair was tangled yarn and their clothes multi-colored swatches of fabric.

Roselyn and her father climbed into the wagon and lowered the puppets into the grass below. The wooden figures clacked as they began to move, and within minutes Lewys forgot about the strings connected to the pair in the wagon above, their hands moving the crosses gracefully. A curtain lifted in his mind.

The story unfolded, wordless but spoken through the puppets' movements. Within Lewys's eyes, the wagon turned to mountain ranges, the grass to a river ford, so real that he could feel the cold wind in the high cliffs and hear the rush of the river. He was immersed in the hardships the brothers faced as they searched for each other. His heart leapt at their final happy reunion. When the puppets bowed, the story's spell over Lewys's mind broke, and he returned with a jolt to his seat in the grass, cooled by the shade of the tree. Roselyn's pleased face smiled down at him from the wagon. He broke into spontaneous applause.

"That was well done," a voice called from further back in the trees. Lewys turned and sprang to his feet. His father approached with his two apprentices. "No wonder my son has shirked his duty for the day." He held out the hatchet. Lewys took it as his father said more quietly, "I was afraid something happened to you, lad." Lewys's face reddened.

"It's my fault," Roselyn said, as she gathered the puppets up. "I did not give him much choice. Please do not be angry with him."

Rhodri came down from the wagon. The carpenter shook his hand, then looked up at the girl, his eyes squinting against the high sun. "Well," the Master Carpenter said, then turned sharply to Lewys, whose color deepened to scarlet. "I can see the appeal of such a play." The apprentices, a few years older than Lewys, grinned and elbowed each other.

"The puppets," he turned back to the toymaker, "are they a new crafting?"

"Yes. My first two. My daughter has great plans for me to make others. She wants a dragon and a witch in particular. And a girl puppet, of course."

The elder Lewys rubbed his chin, dark with beard. "There was something about that play, something quite powerful. I forgot where I was for a while. And I realize that I am long overdue for letters to my own siblings."

"My daughter wrote the story," Rhodri said proudly. "First I had the puppets in mind as another toy, but it was Roselyn's idea to perform plays with them. Do you truly think others will enjoy such entertainment?"

"Truly, but you need a proper stage — a pageant wagon, perhaps, so you can still travel as you do." The carpenter hesitated, glancing at his apprentices, then looked up at Roselyn again. He seemed to make up his mind, and continued, "There is a special wood that I use only for certain projects. I would like to build a pageant wagon for you with this wood. I never take payment for wytchen," he added quickly, when Rhodri blanched. "As I said, it is only for special creations. And I believe this project, and your work, is worthy of it."

Lewys looked at his father in shock. He vaguely remembered the wizened man, passing through town, who had shown his father how to cut wood from the strange trees that no axe could fell before, how to craft an object — for him, it was a staff — with tools and words.

His father had used the wytchen only one other time, as far as Lewys knew, to build a cradle for their neighbor's infant born two months too soon. It was a gift that his father carved in haste, neither eating nor sleeping, in order to finish it by dawn the day after the birth. Within hours after a peaceful nap in the cradle, the child stopped struggling to nurse, and thrived thereafter.

"Come with your daughter to my workshop tomorrow," the master carpenter continued, waving away Rhodri's stammering gratitude. "I'll draw up the plans and we can talk about them over supper." He gestured to Lewys as he turned, a slight smile on his lips. "Let's go. Enough stories for today. Back to chopping wood, lad."

The aged puppet master did not answer Lewys's question, but he did not have to. There was no sign of his daughter among the clutter of tools, wood, parchment, and ink pots on the table. Clothes spilled out of a trunk, child's dresses with snippets removed. A torn blanket lay rumpled on the floor. Lewys's heart sank.

How foolish he had been to wait.

The puppet princess was sitting upright in a cabinet with the troll, dragon, and witch on a shelf beneath her. A pile of bedraggled puppets lay at the bottom.

"I'd like to commission you for repairs."

Lewys looked at the rafters and walls, sunlight spearing through the gaps. Rhodri added, "I have the coin to pay you, whatever the cost."

"It's not that, sir." He tried to control his tone, but anger still sharpened his words even after all these years. "There are no wytchen trees left." One of the apprentices, addled with mead in the tavern, had broken his oath and spilled the secret of the grove; news that the master carpenter could release the trees' magic had spread like fire afterwards. The townspeople turned on his father when he refused their foolish requests for wedding rings, pendants, furniture, even an entire house made from wytchen. But the final demand, a flagship, had come from the duke himself in his manor on the coast, delivered with a subtle threat on the carpenter's son's life.

The entire grove was consumed. His father had fallen ill during the ship's crafting and died soon after it was completed.

"But surely you can repair the existing wood?"

Lewys regarded the puppet master, with his bent back and knotted bones, and said kindly, "All due respect, Master Rhodri, but perhaps a warm hearth in a home without wheels would serve you better now."

The old man nodded. "It probably would. But," he gestured to the puppets in the cabinet, "I must continue to tell her stories."

The puppet princess was as finely crafted as porcelain, the warm scent of beeswax polish lingering on her milk-white skin of peeled wytchen wood. Lewys slipped his fingers along the gold cascade of her hair, a silken balm over his callused skin. He had touched Roselyn's hair this way, shyly, so many years ago in the wytchen grove, as his father cut and shaped the wood for the pageant wagon. The elder Lewys murmured words under his breath as he worked, words that he whispered in Rhodri's ear when he handed him small blocks of wytchen.

Coaxed by his daughter, Master Rhodri had fashioned them both toy swords out of plain oak. Lewys and Roselyn pretended they were heroes, fighting trolls and witches, befriending dragons, crafting their own fairy tales from shadows at the forest's edge. Lewys was awkward and reluctant at first, feeling as if he were too old for this play, but Roselyn's earnest imagination captivated him. And it was worth the teases of the other apprentices just to sit close to Roselyn afterwards, their heads touching, as she penned their play into stories for the puppets.

Her lips were always stained blush from the wytchen berries they were not supposed to eat, the red berries marked with stars that she hid in her dress pocket. When the pageant wagon was completed, oiled and shining like the moon, Lewys watched as it rolled away from the grove without need of a horse, Roselyn blowing kisses as she peeked out from behind the curtain. When it was gone, he ate the berry she had slipped into his hand with a whispered promise.

It had flooded his mouth with bitterness, the taste surprising him after a her sweetly-scented breath.

Lewys finally asked the question he had been dreading. "Roselyn is happily married, then?" He tried not to sound bitter, but her name was no longer sweet in his mouth either.

"No. She is not. I wish…" Rhodri took a deep, shaky breath. "Her heart just…stopped." The words were a hammer blow to Lewys, leaving him cold and numb, his mouth drier than bone. His fingers, still caressing the puppet's hair, froze. "One minute she was reading aloud her new story and the next…. It was soon after we left the grove. I don't know what happened."

The old man paused, wiping his eyes with a grimy handkerchief from his pocket. "My wife had died when Roselyn was an infant. My daughter was all I had. My heart lies in that grave with her. To keep living, to keep going…." His voice cracked, and he cleared his throat. "I wanted to save her, to bring her back to life. Impossible I know, but a father will do anything for his child…at least, like this, she can live on in her stories. The stories that she loved, that she lived to write. Her legacy." He reached out and touched the puppet's hair also. "Roselyn and her mother had the same color hair. It is beautiful, isn't it?"

Lewys snapped his hand away, stumbling over the puppet detritus spilling out from the cabinet's bottom.

"You must understand — I could not let her go! But she grew so cold...her hair was the only thing unchanged. It was the only thing still her." The old man twisted his hands, choking back a sob. "Everything I did, all my carving, was for my daughter. *She* was the meaning behind my life's work. She still is. And I have to give her what life I can."

Master Rhodri's struggle to contain his grief echoed in Lewys's own hollow chest. After a moment, he said, "I do understand."

Slowly Lewys collected the puppets from the floor, a mess of small swords and fractured oak limbs. All princes. "Can I fix these for you?" he asked.

Composing himself, shaking his head, the puppet master replied, "They were my gifts, to commemorate her birthdays." He cleared his throat again. "She never got the chance to create a story of true love. I thought perhaps I could write one for her. But the words never came, and the princes never worked right. And I'd find them damaged the next day. If they were made of wytchen, perhaps it would be different, but I used all the blocks your father gave me. Nevertheless, I keep trying, every year."

Lewys was silent for a while, his hands cradling the broken princes. Wytchen dust drifted down from the wagon's ceiling, glittering bright as a promise that had not been broken after all.

I will come back to you.

"I will do something for you, Master Rhodri. And for her."

Back in his room he packed a satchel with a flask of water and food from his meager pantry, then secured a hatchet to his belt. Walking through the bare patch that had once been the grove, he glanced behind him, making sure he was alone before entering the thick forest beyond. He had released the apprentices after the flagship was completed; his destination was a secret only he knew, now.

After an hour, the woodland sloped upwards as the pine trees thinned. He came to a ledge where a single tree grew, slanted trunk and low, leafy branches thriving against the crisp sky: The wytchen sapling that Lewys and his dying father had transplanted here, hidden from human greed. It was larger now, although not as thick and full as the ancient ones in the grove had been. Another sapling, perhaps a year or two old, grew in a sunny spot near its parent. Lewys swallowed the sudden lump in his throat.

He poured water on the roots as an offering, giving some to the sapling as well, and tied a red ribbon around a thick branch as he had seen his father do. Then he sat, the trunk pressing into his jerkin, thinking of what could have been, while the sun painted the sky the color of the princess's gown, of Roselyn's lips, which had never touched his. As the sun descended into the dark forest below him, he hefted his hatchet and spoke his request to the tree.

He hoped he was worthy.

When Lewys came back to the wagon Rhodri was snoring in a corner, blanket wrapped around him and tucked under his grizzled chin. He used the old man's tools, peeling and smoothing the small branch the wytchen had granted him, carving a face, body, and limbs, whispering his father's words to the wood for the first and last time. Rummaging through the trunk, he found the remnants of a white shawl which he cut with a pair of silver scissors to make a doll-size tunic and pants, needle and red thread moving as deftly as when he sewed patches into his own clothing. He painted the eyes and mouth.

Lewys took the puppet princess down from her shelf, arranging her carefully on the work table next to the newly carved prince, staring at her for a long time. He touched her hair again. Leaning close, his lips almost touching her cheek, he breathed deeply. As his lungs filled with her wytchen wood scent, his heart returned, brimming with magic and love as when they had been younger. "Roselyn," he murmured, "I kept my promise too. I waited."

With the scissors he cut his own hair off, and stitched the dark locks to a small felt cap. Uncorking a bottle of pine resin, he brushed the thick glue on the cap and attached it to the puppet prince's head.

Wooden hands twitched, clacked against each other.

Lewys's joints buckled and he flopped to the floor.

His name, whispered against his cheek. A whiff of familiar berry.

Lewys opened his eyes. He was sitting in the old wytchen grove under one of the trees, crisscrossing branches spread out above him, and for one disorienting moment he thought the branches were the rafters of the pageant wagon.

Someone was sitting next to him. He turned, and Roselyn's smiling face filled his vision. Reaching out, tentatively, to touch her cheek, he whispered, "Are you real?" His fingers felt strange, stiff.

She laughed. "As real as you," she replied, standing. A pile of berries cascaded from her billowing silk skirts. She pulled him to his feet, and his joints cracked loudly. Lewys pushed the aches in his body aside — Roselyn was here, in front of him, alive and looking more beautiful in a sunset-colored gown than he had ever beheld. Her hair was a curtain of golden strands over her shoulders, a net of crystals holding the strands away from her perfect face.

"I am glad you are finally here, with me, my love," Roselyn whispered, standing so close to him, her eyes sparkling. Lewys folded her into his arms, his heart overflowing, seeking out her lips with his own.

"Not yet," she said, placing her fingers over his mouth. A loud roar sounded from the depths of the forest. Roselyn broke from his grasp. "Father wrote us a story. I don't know all the details, but I know it has a happy ending. We have to work to get there, of course." She gestured to the sword buckled at his hip and, when he stared at it dumbfounded, unsheathed it for him and put it in his hand. The blade was etched with runes. "You're a prince, Lewys."

She pulled a matching sword from a concealed fold in her gown. "I found this one hidden in a wytchen trunk before you came."

Another roar, closer this time, shook the leaves of the trees. Both sword blades began to glow.

"An enchantment! But do you know why?" Prince Lewys asked.

"No," Princess Roselyn said excitedly. "I suppose we will have to figure it out! Remember that friendly dragon? Things aren't always what they seem. We must be clever as well as brave." She smiled up at Lewys, and he had never known such happiness, such excitement.

"We have a new life ahead of us, my love," Roselyn said, and Lewys ached to kiss her. "Are you ready for adventure?"

Magic fell in curls and crystals from the wytchen wood above them. Strange shadows began to move beneath their feet. Lewys took his true love's hand, and together they turned to face the beginning of their story.

A question for the author

What tools do you write with?

My workspace is half of our basement, with my giant teacher's desk where I used to write lesson plans and mark essays, and a long wall lined with bookshelves. I married a fellow English major and of course both our children are bookworms, so as you can imagine, our bookshelves runneth over. Usually our little black dog is either curled up next to me or trying to get on the desk because she needs to know what is more important than playing fetch with her. Once we are settled in, I conjure ideas from the imagination realm with my yew root wand. Then I capture them with a mechanical pencil and a beautiful notebook. Moleskine has the creamiest paper, but I have others with more decorative, inspiring covers too. There is a different magic in writing longhand, so the first draft is always in my own handwriting. I move onto my computer for revisions in Scrivener, which I love and highly recommend because you can easily have more than one document on the screen at once, and finally I export to Word. I am always amazed by the organic growth of a story from idea to the final manuscript, and it's a wonderful (albeit frightening) feeling to send a story off from my old desk with the hope it will speak to a reader's soul.

About the author

Lori J. Fitzgerald lives in Queens, NY with her husband, two children, and a small black rescued dog. She was a junior high school English teacher for over a decade and was well-known for her dramatic readings of The Princess Bride. Medieval Arthurian literature is her specialty and she loves a good joust. She writes mythic fantasy from her book-filled basement.

www.whiteravenwriting.blogspot.com, @MedievalLit

Lori J. Fitzgerald's story "Wytchen Wood" was published in *Metaphorosis* on Friday, 15 December 2017.

Dekker's Miracle

Frank Oreto

Charlie "Bull" Dekker drove his cruiser down the East Valley Road and thought about a woman who wasn't his wife. Donna Swanger, the woman in question, had recently made her interests in Charlie fairly obvious. And for the first time in his twelve years of marriage he found himself tempted. Donna was a fine looking woman with the kind of long red hair that Charlie had always been partial to, but it wasn't her looks that pulled on him. It was how she talked. Specifically, how she talked about leaving Hope's Rest, Tennessee.

"It's a big world, Bull. We could find someplace better than this."

Charlie loved his wife, Lisa, and she him, but Lisa would never leave Hope's Rest. She had deep roots in this town. So did he. But while Lisa's roots anchored her, Charlie's only seemed to tie him down. And on days when the low mountains surrounding his home town seemed more like prison walls than a pretty view, Charlie thought losing his marriage and his reputation might be worth it if it gave him a chance to escape.

Movement on the road shoulder jerked him out of his reverie. He pulled over and watched a man with a backpack walking toward him. Charlie had seen a few hippies come through town. In this "Summer of Love", as the reporters called it, half the kids in America seemed to have hit the road.

As the man drew closer, Charlie saw that this was no longhaired kid. He looked to be pushing seventy. Hippy or not, the Hopes Rest Sheriff's Department had a standard procedure when it came to strangers with little means. You struck up a friendly conversation and offered them a ride to the county line. Not very neighborly, but it helped avoid problems, and problem avoidance was Charlie's stock and trade.

Charlie hauled his six-and-a-half-foot, two hundred and eighty-pound frame out of the squad car and walked toward the stranger. "Howdy. Hot day for a stroll."

The man unclipped a metal canteen from his belt and took a long sip. "It's not so bad where the trees cover the road."

Charlie nodded. "Thing is, there's nothing but baked gravel for the next few miles. I could give you a lift. Take you as far as Grundy County." As Charlie gave his prepared speech, he looked the hiker over. The man was no vagrant. He wore expensive L.L. Bean camp wear, dusty but not worn.

"Listen, officer…"

"It's Sheriff. Sheriff Charlie Dekker. Some folks call me Bull."

"I imagine they do. Well, Sheriff Dekker, is there something wrong?"

"Oh no," said Charlie. "I guess you could say I'm sort of the welcome wagon."

"Fine, I get it." The man reached into a pocket and pulled out a card. "Here's my driver's license. My name's William Kearns. I'm a retired science teacher from Pittsburgh, Pennsylvania."

Charlie took the card and looked it over.

"My family tree springs from around here. I thought I'd like to see the town, maybe do a little genealogy research. I may not have a car, but as far as I know hiking across our lovely country isn't a crime."

"Hold on, Mr. Kearns," Charlie said. "No reason to get riled." He handed back the I.D. "You got to admit it's a bit strange, a man your age traveling rough."

"No law against being strange either," Kearns said, but the anger had left his voice. In fact, he sounded like someone who had just won an argument, and Charlie supposed he had.

"It really is a scorcher of a walk into town. I'd be happy to give you a lift."

"I believe I'd rather not arrive in a police car."

"Suit yourself," said Charlie. "There's a place name of Dottie's on Walcott Avenue right off the town square. They make good iced tea. If I run into you later, maybe I could buy you a glass."

"Maybe," said Kearns and surprised Charlie by extending a hand to shake. "Nice meeting you, Sheriff."

Charlie watched William Kearns lug his backpack down the gravel road, the image going wavy with heat. He scratched his sweaty brow. Somewhere, during the "official friendly conversation," Charlie had lost the upper hand.

He had expected a hobo and instead gotten a pillar of the community, but pillar or not, there was something off about the man. A cop develops a sort of radar after a few years. Charlie's radar told him Mr. Kearns had something on his mind he did not want to share with the local authorities.

"Hell, if he robs the Savings and Loan, he'll be the only senior citizen hiking out of town with a backpack full of cash." Charlie tried to muster a chuckle, but it wouldn't come. The I.D. had looked authentic at least. Charlie could place a few calls. He walked back toward the car, eager to get on the radio.

A few hours later, Charlie took the last smooth sip from his glass of sweet tea at Dottie's. Kearns had not taken him up on his offer of a drink, but he wasn't far off. Charlie could see him through the plate glass window. He stood only a few yards away, staring up at an oak tree with what looked like amazement.

Checking the license had turned up some information. Mr. William Everett Kearns, a seventy-four-year-old widower, was indeed from the Steel City. According to Sherriff Hancock over in Dawesville, he had until recently, also been the proud owner of a seven-year-old white Cadillac, which he'd sold for two thousand dollars and a ride over Walker Mountain to the Collier County line. *No law against selling your car is there, Mr. Kearns?* Charlie thought. *No law against staring at trees way longer than normal, either.*

Kearns had finished his tree examination and now walked toward the town library. It was a good choice on a hot day. The library was an architectural beast built in the mid-1800s in a fit of robber-baron philanthropy. Even without air conditioning, its high ceilings kept the building cool in the summer. As Kearns disappeared through the doors, Charlie stood and laid a dollar bill on the table.

Eight years on the job and I'm on my first stake out, Charlie thought and laughed. He wondered why he even bothered, but the answer was the same as always. Nothing much else to do.

Charlie crossed the town square to a long green bench in front of the courthouse. It was filled by old men with dried-apple-faces wearing overalls and flannel shirts despite the heat. They sat there most days, weather permitting, whittling and telling stories. Teenagers called it the dead pecker bench. But if Hope's Rest had a council of wise men, these were the guys.

Charlie nodded at the gruff chorus of "Hey there, Bull." He stood at the end of the bench where he could watch the Library doors and still hear the old timers' mix of gossip and tall tales.

He was listening to how in '47 the Reverend Horace Snapp had walked into a cornfield after church and never came out, when William Kearns stumbled from the Library.

Charlie cut across the square to where Kearns sat on the steps at the building's entrance. The old man's complexion had gone as grey as the stone pillar he leaned against.

"You all right, Mr. Kearns?" Charlie asked. As he spoke, he took the canteen from Kearns' belt. "Take a sip of this."

"There was a fire," Kearns said his voice tinged with hysteria. "I don't think it could have reached..." He looked back to the library.

Charlie glanced through the building's peaked windows. Inside, people sat at tables calmly reading.

"Where, Mr. Kearns? If there's a fire, I can get help. Do you remember who I am?"

"I have to get to them," Kearns said. "Tell them what's happened. I have to get them out."

"Listen to me, Mr. Kearns. If there are people in danger, you have to tell me."

Charlie's words finally seemed to seize Kearns' attention. He stared at the Sheriff for a long moment and laughed. Just one bark, loud and high. Then he took the canteen and drank. Recognition and a little color filled the old man's face.

"Sheriff Dekker," Kearns said in a still tremulous voice. "I suppose we ran into each other after all. Perhaps we could have that glass of ice tea. I think I have a favor to ask you."

"What about the people you need to get to?" asked Charlie.

"There's still time," Kearns said. "More than enough."

Charlie led Kearns back to the same booth at Dottie's he'd only recently vacated. He ordered tea and a couple of hamburger platters.

Kearns stared at the library across the square and Charlie waited. When the food arrived, the old man surprised Charlie by plowing through the big meal like a teenager.

"Listen," said Charlie, as Kearns finished off his last steak fry. "If you have a favor to ask, ask it, or at least tell me why you're here. You drive all the way from Pittsburgh, sell your car, and walk into Hope's Rest. It may be legal, but it isn't normal."

Kearns stared into his empty plate. When he looked up, his eyes were hard, as if he had made a painful decision.

"There's a room in the library. I need to get into it."

"Okay," said Charlie. "And...?"

"It's a secret room. I know how to get in. At least, I used to. But the building's changed."

"Back up. What's in the room?"

"I told you, I'm a bit of a genealogist. My great-great uncle and two other men were at the library's dedication. They disappeared that night and no one ever saw them again."

"Wait, you're talking about, um, Cranwell and Mercer. That's one of the stories they tell on the dead-peck... the bench where the old-timers sit. I've heard it—wealthy families, one of them designed the building?"

"Yes, Cranwell. He secretly built a hidden room in your library. He and Mercer are inside that room. I thought I could just walk in and find it."

"But?"

"But there was a fire and now there are complications. Complications I think you could help with."

"If this is true, we'll go to the Mayor and tell him. They'll find this room of yours and exhume the men. Hell, the historical society will go nuts. Probably put in a mini-museum."

"No, it has to be just you and me."

"But why?"

Kearns leaned forward, his face grown red. "Because Cranwell and Mercer are not dead."

Charlie said nothing for a long moment. "What do you mean?"

Kearns ignored the question. "There was a fire. The building's changed. I can't get to them. At least, not without your help."

"This is crazy. How am I supposed to help? Hell, why would I?"

"Kearns shook his head." I noticed you watching me today, Sheriff. Following me around for hours like I was public enemy number one."

"Doing my job."

"Job, my ass. I think you're bored out of your ever-loving mind."

Charlie didn't like being read so easily, but he was too honest to deny the charge.

Kearns licked his lips, looking to Charlie like a man playing his last card. "You help me, Sheriff Dekker, and I'll show you the damnedest thing you've ever seen."

Charlie's radar was up again. Something odd, even mysterious was occurring here. In his experience, things like this did not happen in Hope's Rest. It was irresistible.

Charlie left Dottie's and headed to Hales' barbershop, hoping to catch Deputy Dan Carter shooting the shit. Sure enough, there he stood, leaning against the wall under the mounted form of a big mouth bass. The resemblance was striking.

"Let's take a walk," said Charlie.

The two men left the barbershop and walked towards Charlie's squad car. "How'd you like me to work your shift tonight?" Charlie asked.

"What? Give up patrolling until three in the goddamned morning." Dan laughed. "Seeing it's you, Sheriff, I guess I could make the sacrifice."

"Great," Charlie said. "But you got to do me a favor. Call my wife and ask to talk to me. Sound sick."

Dan nodded. An obnoxiously wide grin filled his thin face.

"What?" Charlie asked.

"Well, it's none of my business, but I think this might be the night Bull Dekker finally gets himself a little strange."

Charlie shot Dan a glare that knocked the grin off his deputy's face.

"Sorry, Sheriff. None of my business. I'll make the call."

Charlie watched the slump-shouldered deputy head back to the barbershop. *The night I get a little strange,* he thought and chuckled. Dan was wrong, but only about the details. Charlie had been seduced, sure enough. Not by Donna Swanger though. He'd been seduced by the story of an old man who was either crazy or a damned good liar. *I'm not cheating on Lisa, Dan. I'm cheating on Hope's Rest and my whole same-shit-different-day life.* And damned if it wasn't kind of exciting.

Lisa accepted Charlie's double shift with the stoic grace common to the spouses of law enforcement. She sent him into the night with a kiss and a meatloaf sandwich.

Hope's Rest tucked in early. By the time the First National's big digital clock neared midnight, it was lights out, except for LJ's Gas and Gulp. Charlie did one more loop around the main drag, gazing at the same storefronts he had ridden past as an eight-year-old on a Schwinn. At the library, he parked and walked to the big building's back door. After a minute of fishing through his official key chain, Charlie stepped inside.

He had his flashlight on in case of stools and book stacks. He didn't want any extra attention, but if anyone saw the light, Charlie was who they would call. He made his way up a flight of stairs to the seldom-used second-floor bathroom and knocked. "It's me."

William Kearns stepped out, squinting at the flashlight.

"Any problems?" Charlie asked.

"No. No one even came up to check for stragglers."

"Where now?"

"The basement," Kearns said stepping toward the stairs. Charlie followed behind, shining the flashlight and watching the older man's body language.

Kearns seemed nervous. Nowhere near the shell-shocked man who had left the library earlier, but Charlie could tell he was not looking forward to what lay ahead.

Soon, the two men stood in a small basement room dominated by a huge boiler. Charlie turned on the overhead fluorescents; not worried about lights in this small windowless space. Mr. Kearns pointed at the floor. "Underneath here there's a small room, a sort of sub-basement. The tiles seem solid, but if you know where to look, there's a seam. As he spoke, the old man knelt down and brushed dust away with his hand. Charlie's eyes scanned the floor where Kearns worked. Sure enough, he spotted two seams running parallel to each other about three feet apart.

"See the spot where it looks like one of the tiles got chipped?" asked Kearns pointing. "You just push your thumb in there and with a little leverage the trapdoor lifts right up"

Charlie stared blankly for a couple of seconds, then it jumped out at him like seeing Christ's face on a tortilla. A moment later, he saw the complication. Resting on the top right corner of the trapdoor sat the impressive bulk of the Library's boiler.

"The fire was in 1955," Kearns said. "They have pictures of the damage hanging in the lobby. Evidently, they put in a new boiler as part of the repairs. It just needs to be shifted a little."

Charlie stared at the boiler's glowering bulk. "You're joking," he said. "If you'd told your story to the Volunteer Firemen's Association and they came down with the Women's Auxiliary and a forklift maybe they could have moved that thing. I mean, I know I'm a big guy..."

Kearns said nothing. He didn't have to. Charlie had come too far not to try and they both knew it.

Charlie examined the boiler. At least they hadn't bolted it to the floor. Probably assumed sheer weight would keep it from moving. Charlie thought this was a pretty fair assumption. There was some wiggle room. A good two feet in back and on either side of the behemoth. What worried him was the network of pipes branching off the boiler. Each one connected to a radiator somewhere upstairs. It would be like moving an upside down stump. Except this stump's root system was a few hundred feet of copper pipe. And instead of a tractor to do the work, there was Charlie.

He squatted down and felt around the base for a grip. On the boilers side, raised letters six inches high spelled out the word DUNKIRK. The damned thing even sounded heavy.

Charlie stood and gave the boiler a good hard shove. He thought the thing might have shaken a bit, but he knew immediately this would be a lift and push job.

He squatted again and found his handholds. People claimed Bull Dekker was the strongest man in three counties, maybe the state. Now he would see if he deserved the title. Kearns knelt down by the tile with the chip in it and pressed his thumb into the right spot.

Charlie started counting to himself. One, two...

"You're not standing on the trap, are you?" Kearns asked in a whisper.

"No" Charlie hissed out, "now shut up."

Again, he started his mental count. *One, two...*

"Don't forget to lift with your legs."

Three.

A roaring in Charlie's mind drowned out Kearns' last interruption as he poured himself into lifting. For an eternal moment, the world went away. The cold metal pressing against his face, the bite of the handholds into his palms, his heartbeat pounding in his ears, none of it reached him. Lifting and pushing were all there was. Then a burning pain blossomed into his consciousness like a light through dark water and he knew he was finished.

Charlie fell back into a sitting position. He slowly opened his hands gazing dumbly at the angry red welts across his palms.

"Sheriff Dekker," said a distant voice. Charlie moved his hands to his lower back kneading the knot of pain that pulsed there. He tentatively flexed his spine, bending from one side to another. It hurt, but not in the way that laid a man on his back for six weeks.

"Sheriff Dekker."

This time Charlie recognized the voice and looked over. William Kearns stood by a gaping square hole in the floor.

Charlie patted the Dunkirk and pushed himself up. His back twinged again, but he could stand. The boiler row sat approximately three inches from where it had. Charlie was glad he wouldn't be the one starting up the radiators come winter. He stepped over to the edge of the trapdoor. Lights from the fluorescents filled the exposed subbasement, revealing an iron ladder bolted to the wall. On the wall opposite the ladder hung two overcoats, and at the narrow end of the small room was a closed door.

Kearns went down first. Charlie followed, pausing on each rung of the ladder as new and interesting pains shot through his throbbing back. He hoped whatever came next wouldn't require another feat of strength.

Kearns looked from Charlie to the door and back again. The old man was sweating even though Charlie had done all the work.

"Mr. Kearns, would you mind if I called you Bill?" Charlie asked.

A smile flickered over Kearns' face as he answered. "My friends used to call me William."

"All right, William. Why don't you tell me what's really behind that door."

Kearns ran a hand through his thinning hair and nodded. "Behind that door, you'll find the bodies of Elliott Mercer and Randolph Cranwell. What you won't find are the bones of two men long dead."

"Randolph is probably taking the first draw on one of those god-awful cheroots he used to smoke. Elliot will be setting up three empty glasses for a toast. There should be a third man William Kearns."

"Your great uncle."

The old man shook his head and went on. "William was a chemist. A damned fine one. He made a discovery. One so miraculous he convinced Randolph and Elliot to back him in its development. A mixture of chemicals—some rare, some common—that, combined correctly with the right amount of heat, produced a kind of stabilizer. It looked like a glowing blue light. You could fill a closed area with that light and drastically limit change of any sort." Kearns' face twisted into a mixture of shame and pride. "Time itself would slow down.

"William should be in that room with them, but he isn't. Do you want to know why?" Kearns didn't wait for Charlie to answer.

"Young William forgot the brandy. That was the plan, you see. He would prepare the chemicals and light the brazier. He'd measured it out. Just enough so the time it took them to have a drink and smoke a cigar would be a month to their worried friends and families. Then they would walk out and show the world their miracle. He'd performed countless experiments. Had the whole process down to, well, a science. No danger at all, really.

"But you can't have a toast if you leave the brandy in your coat hanging in the other room. So out stepped William Kearns. He knew immediately something was wrong. The air in the tiny subbasement was stale as an Egyptian crypt. He climbed the ladder to the library; told himself he would just check on how the joke was going over, but William was careful to make sure he closed the trapdoor behind him.

"Turns out, in the few moments William had spent in that small room, there had been a war. Hell, there'd been several, and the Japanese had just started another. It was all in the library's racks of newspapers. Ninety Years in a few minutes time. Some joke, huh?"

"I don't believe you," Charlie said. "There's no goddamned way you're some time traveler from the eighteen-hundreds."

"You don't have to believe. It doesn't make things any less true. Can I tell you the rest? Before I show you." He motioned toward the closed door.

Charlie nodded. "Why not?"

"I ran," William said. "I think I went a little crazy at first. Crazy with loss and fear. It wasn't my world anymore. In the end though, it boiled down to cowardice. Easier to face down machine guns on some island in the pacific then to face Elliot and Randolph. To say to them: Sorry, I think I must have measured something wrong and now everyone we know and love is gone."

"You came back, though."

"Nothing noble about it. I lived a life while they've been in there. Worked, married, grew old. If I hadn't outlived my wife and son, you never would have met me. Sometimes, I almost convinced myself it wasn't true. That I had gone a different kind of crazy that night in the library."

Charlie thought about that different kind of crazy. He wasn't angry at Kearns for wasting his time, he was sad. Suddenly, he wanted to climb right back up that ladder. He had started out the night thinking he'd get a funny story. Something to share with the old timers on the dead pecker bench. But not now. Now, he wanted—no, he needed—more. He needed those men frozen in time. Needed William Kearns to be not just crazy, but a man cast adrift, making his way through a world made bizarre by the passage of so many years. *He's going to open that door and show me some old empty broom closet,* Charlie thought. *And god damn if it's not going to break my heart.*

William stepped forward and took hold of the doorknob.

"Don't." Charlie said. "Just don't."

Kearns looked back over his shoulder. "I'm not crazy, Sheriff," he said and pulled open the door.

Inside was a miracle.

Charlie didn't realize he was backing up until he felt the wall behind him. Looking through the door, he could have been staring at an old-fashioned photograph if it hadn't been for the scene's depth and the fact that a pale blue light suffused everything. The men were there. One sat at a small table with three glasses in front of him. Another, no doubt Randolph, stood with a long thin cigar clamped between his teeth. A motionless flame crowned the match in his hand.

Kearns was sobbing and smiling in equal measure. He wiped tears from his cheek and gazed at his liver-spotted hand. "I guess I don't have to worry about proof," he said. The two men looked at one another, neither finding words that fit the moment.

"Thank you," Kearns said finally and stepped through the doorway.

He did not just walk into the room. For a moment, the strangely viscous light bowed inward with Kearns' weight, refusing to be breached. On his third step, the light, with no discernible movement, suddenly surrounded the old man. There he stopped, in frozen union with the friends he had abandoned so long ago.

Afterward, Charlie made a list. All the things he would want to take if he decided to step into that room and step out again into some strange far-flung future. It read like something from the Road Warrior movies. Over the years, he narrowed it, bit by high-caliber bit, until he had it down to a cold six-pack and an extra-large Gondola's sausage-and-bacon pizza. Gondola's put the cheese on top like God intended.

Charlie squatted and slipped his thumb into what looked like a chipped spot on a tile. He didn't have anything as formal as a schedule, but he came here often. The need to once again witness the unbelievable tugging at him until he gave in and made his way through the darkened library to the boiler room. His back twinged as he shifted his weight and opened the trap door. Even if he had left that first night some twenty odd years ago and never come again, his back would have kept him from ever forgetting the experience. That and the way the library's radiators hissed and banged each time they fired up.

Charlie grasped the iron ladder and climbed down. He'd put a chair in the room. Nothing fancy, just a metal folding job with one of those seat pillows with ties at the corners. Charlie lowered himself on to it and gazed into the blue room. He had the scene pretty much memorized. The distinctive tread of William's too-modern hiking boot, the signet ring on Randolph's finger. But it still filled him with awe. Charlie had always thought of himself as a big fish in a little pond. He needed that awe to remind him that Hope's Rest was a lot bigger and more mysterious a pond than he'd realized.

"So why didn't you go?" Charlie asked himself. No messy divorce. No one asking why. It would be so easy. *Maybe I will,* he thought. But he doubted it. Charlie didn't necessarily think he'd grown wiser over the years. No need for the old timers to make room for him on the bench yet. He guessed it was more like perspective. Knowing he could leave gave him the chance to appreciate what he had, let him feel like his life was a choice.

He looked at William's back. Imagined the man turning, beckoning Charlie to come join him. And he felt the urge. Not now, but someday, maybe when his age matched William's and life felt like it was wrapping things up. But not tonight.

Tonight, Charlie had a town he'd chosen to protect, and a wife he wanted to go home to. He took his thermos of coffee from his jacket and lifted it in a toast.

"Here's to you, William. Thanks for the miracle."

A question for the author

If you could talk to your novice-writer self, what bit of advice would you give? Write more. And remember there's more than one good way to tell a story.

About the author

Frank Oreto was born in the hills of Tennessee and after a few decades, finally settled in the slightly less rural hills of Pittsburgh, Pennsylvania. The view was oddly similar regardless of his location as he spent his life surrounded by bookshelves. He haunted libraries and bookshops until old enough to find work at them. And when the shelves didn't hold a story he wanted to read, he wrote his own.

@FrankOreto

Frank Oreto's story "Dekker's Miracle" was published in *Metaphorosis* on Friday, 22 December 2017.

Rowboats - a cautionary tale of linguistics

Filip Wiltgren

"Rowboats?"

"Rowboats, sire."

"Perhaps the Oracle is wrong."

"The Oracle is never wrong, sire."

"Yes, but... Rowboats? She may have meant navy."

" 'He who has the best rowboats shall rule the land.' The Oracle's exact words, sire."

"We could put oars on our ships-of-the-line. A 118-gun first rate would make one mighty rowboat."

" 'Best rowboats', sire. A man-o-war would make a very poor rowboat, indeed."

"And Napoleon has heard of the prophecy?"

"He has, sire. The French are building rowboats for their army even as we speak."

"Good rowboats?"

"Adequate. The French are skilled shipwrights."

"But lousy sailors. Very well, notify the Board of the Admiralty to use the proceeds from selling apples to initiate their rowboat program. By order of his majesty, et cetera, et cetera. And put my Privy Seal on it."

"At once, sire."

"And Neville..."

"Yes, sire?"

"Make sure that our rowboats carry weapons of glass destruction."

"Of course, sire."

www.wiltgren.com, @FilipWiltgren

Filip Wiltgren's story "Rowboats - a cautionary tale of linguistics" was published in *Metaphorosis* on Monday, 25 December 2017.

Emeralds or Amethysts

Alexandra Grunberg

If Lucy could cry, she would, but she is frozen in stillness by her unnatural sleep. She can feel the soft embrace of silk sheets, she can taste the salty dryness of her tongue, and she can hear the sounds of another man who has come to try to save her, but she cannot cry any more than she can speak, or eat, or wake.

Lucy has been sleeping for so long, she does not know if she could speak, even if given the chance. Her voice may be as dusty and dry as the roof of her mouth. She does not know if she can see, even if she opens her eyes. Perhaps they are empty holes, perhaps they are crawling with maggots, or perhaps they have petrified into emeralds or amethysts. She cannot remember the color of her eyes.

There is the sound of a great door crashing, wood splintering, and the groans of a man at work.

Perhaps he is a prince, and he has come to make her his princess. She will wear gowns as soft as her silk sheets, and pile her loose hair on the top of her head, and eat sweets all day and dance at balls all night. She will walk through towns to be admired by the villagers, and they will gape at her beauty, and crave her wealth, and hate her for her luck. If only they had been cursed and locked in a tower! If only they had been fortunate enough to be pursued by a prince! One night the ball will be disrupted by the sound of shattering glass as the villagers invade their palace, and she will be dragged into the town, and the rough dirt roads will tear her silk dress to tatters. They will cut off her long hair – Golden hair? Black hair? She cannot remember – and they will rest her neck on the guillotine. Or else, she will live happily ever after.

There is the sound of footsteps on the stairs, leaping to avoid cunning traps hidden in the stone, and Lucy can hear each gasp and exhalation.

Perhaps he is a fearless explorer, an adventurer only interested in the chase and the promise of treasure. He will take her on trips around the world, to places never touched by the feet of men, and they will see creatures only described in fairytales, with large wings and horns and teeth. He will kill them all and dress her in their furs and feathers, and make her a necklace out of their teeth and claws, and they will create a kingdom for themselves through their travels. As they cross wild oceans, their ship will be overtaken by pirates, and she will watch as they make him walk the plank, and she will hear his screams as he is eaten by sharks. They will taunt her and torture her until they have had their full, and then they will throw her fractured body into the sea to join him. Or else, she will become a pirate queen.

There is the sound of roaring and the clashing of metal as a man fights the ogre guarding her door.

Perhaps he is a poor boy, desperate for a challenge that will make him feel like a man, and against all odds he has made it to her bedroom. He will take her home to cows and chickens and ducks, and she will keep the fire warm and the house clean. She will love him, and she will grow with a child that is all she has ever wanted and needed to feel truly awake and alive. She will feel pain and blood as the midwife tries to keep her calm, she will suffer from a fever and delusions, and the world will rush away in the sound of her own wailing. Or else, she will be fulfilled.

Lucy hears the door creak open, and she knows the sound, though it has never happened before. She hears short breaths of exertion and anticipation. She feels the brushing of lips against hers, and if she wants to, she can open her eyes.

She could be murdered, or happy. She could be tormented, or exhilarated. She could be broken, or revived. All possibilities are real, all of them are true, all of them are happening to her at once and forever, as long as she does not open her eyes, and now she can cry, and though her eyes are still closed, she does. She will need to open them soon, but she keeps her eyes closed for just a second longer.

When Lucy opens her eyes, she still does not know what color they are. But his eyes are blue.

About the story

I was reading *The Great Encyclopedia of Faeries* by Pierre Dubois, and came across a section on Lucia, and her various incarnations as the "Sleeping Beauty." Though the faeries/princesses of these myths tended to wake up to charmed lives, I was disturbed by the thought of the less-than-noble princes who took advantage of these sleeping beauties, and wondered if some victims of this curse might prefer to remain sleeping.

A question for the author

Q: Do you generally start with mood, title, character, concept, ...?

A: I start my writing process with concept; a myth that fascinates me, a song or phrase that gets stuck in my head, or the discovery of a new mythological monster. However, once I introduce the characters, they take control of the concept. Sometimes they let me write the story I set out to write, and sometimes they take the story to unexpected conclusions. I usually don't know what lesson I'm going to learn, if the story will be funny or scary, or whether the ending will be happy or sad, until my characters make those decisions for themselves. For example, I started "Emeralds or Amethysts" sure that my princess would not open her eyes, but Lucy ended up being much braver than me.

About the author

Alexandra Grunberg is an author, actress, and screenwriter. In the fall of 2017, she will be pursuing her Masters Degree in Creative Writing at the University of Glasgow. She enjoys reading Stephen King novels by day and binge watching Netflix by night.

Alexandra Grunberg's story "Emeralds or Amethysts" was published in *Metaphorosis* on Friday, 29 December 2017.

Copyright

Metaphorosis Publishing

Metaphorosis offers beautifully written science fiction and fantasy. Our imprints include:

Metaphorosis Magazine

plant based press

Metaphorosis Books

Driftwyrd

Vestige

Help keep Metaphorosis running at
Patreon.com/metaphorosis

See more about some of our books on the following pages.

Metaphorosis
a magazine of speculative fiction

Metaphorosis is an online speculative fiction magazine dedicated to quality writing. We publish an original story every week, along with author bios, interviews, and notes on story origins. Come and see us online at magazine.Metaphorosis.com

Keep Metaphorosis running! Support us at
Patreon.com/metaphorosis

You can also find us at:
Twitter: @MetaphorosisMag, @MetaphorosisRev, @Metaphorosis
Facebook: www.facebook.com/metaphorosis

We publish monthly print and e-book issues, as well as yearly Best of and Complete anthologies.

Metaphorosis:
Best of 2018

The best science fiction and fantasy stories from *Metaphorosis* magazine's third year.

Metaphorosis 2018

All the stories from *Metaphorosis* magazine's third year. Fifty-two great SFF stories.

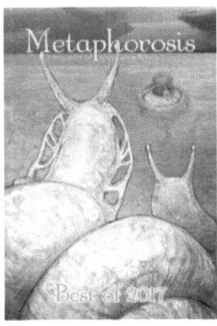

Metaphorosis:
Best of 2017

The best science fiction and fantasy stories from *Metaphorosis* magazine's *second* year.

Metaphorosis 2017

All the stories from *Metaphorosis* magazine's second year. Fifty-three great SFF stories.

Metaphorosis:
Best of 2016

The best science fiction and fantasy stories from *Metaphorosis* magazine's first year.

Metaphorosis 2016

Almost all the stories from *Metaphorosis* magazine's first year.

Vegan-friendly science fiction and fantasy, including an annual anthology of the year's best SFF stories.

Best Vegan SFF of 2018

The best vegan science fiction and fantasy stories of 2018!

Best Vegan SFF of 2017

The best vegan science fiction and fantasy stories of 2017!

Best Vegan SFF
of 2016

The best vegan science fiction
and fantasy stories of 2016!

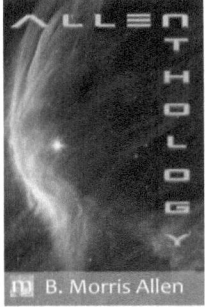

Susurrus

A darkly romantic story of
magic, love, and suffering.

Allenthology:
Volume I

A quarter century of SFF,
including the full contents of
the collections *Tocsin, Start
with Stones,* and *Metaphorosis.*

Science fiction and fantasy books for writers – full of great stories, but with an additional focus on the craft of speculative fiction writing.

Score

an SFF symphony

What if stories were written like music? *Score* is an anthology of varied stories arranged to follow an emotional score from the heights of joy to the depths of despair – but always with a little hope shining through.

Reading 5X5

Five stories, five times

Twenty-five SFF authors, five base stories, five versions of each – see how different writers take on the same material, with stories in contemporary and high fantasy, soft and hard SF, and a mysterious 'other' category.

Reading 5X5

Writers' Edition

All the stories from the regular, readers' edition, plus two extra stories, the story seed, and authors' notes on writing. Over 100 pages of additional material specifically aimed at writers.

www.ingramcontent.com/pod-product-compliance
Lightning Source LLC
Chambersburg PA
CBHW030919020726
47498CB00001B/30